JEN WILLIAMS lives in London with her partner and her cat. She started writing about pirates and dragons as a yo̶u̶n̶g̶ girl and has never stopped. Her short stories have featured i̶n̶ numerous anthologies. This is the blistering seq̶u̶el to her d̶e̶b̶u̶t̶ novel, *The Copper Promise*. Keep an eye out f̶o̶r̶ *The Sil̶v̶e̶r̶ T̶i̶d̶e̶,* coming in February 2016.

Praise for *The Iron Ghost*:

'Williams has thrown out the rulebook and injected a fun tone into epic fantasy without lightening or watering down the excitement and adventure. . . Highly recommended'   *Independent*

'The second outing is as entertaining as the first, being absolutely stuffed with ghoulish action. There is never a dull page' *SciFiNow*

'Just as magical, just as action packed, just as clever and just as much fun as its predecessor. . . You'll find a great deal to enjoy here'   fantasy-faction.com

'Atmospheric and vivid . . . with a rich history and mythology and colourful, well-written and complex characters, that all combine to suck you in to the world and keep you enchanted up until the very last page'   realitysabore.blogspot.co.uk

'Everything you need for a great fantasy read is right here'
                                                    lizlovesbooks.com

Praise for *The Copper Promise*:

'*The Copper Promise* is dark, often bloody, frequently frightening, but there's also bucket loads of camaraderie, sarcasm, and an unashamed love of fantasy and the fantastic'
      Den Patrick, author of *The Boy with the Porcelain Blade*

'*The Copper Promise* is an exce̶l̶l̶e̶n̶t̶ ̶.̶.̶.̶ ̶t̶h̶e̶ ingredients of sword and sorcery ̶.̶.̶.̶ ̶i̶t̶'s a shamelessly good old-fashioned̶ ̶.̶.̶.̶ ̶ ̶c̶ fantasy the way it's meant to be̶ ̶.̶.̶.̶
                              Joan̶

'The characterisation is second to none, and there are some great new innovations and interesting reworkings of old tropes. . . This book may have been based on the promise of copper but it delivers gold'   Quicksilver on *Goodreads*

'It is a *killer* of a fantasy novel that is indicative of how the classic genre of sword and sorcery is not only still very much alive, but also still the best the genre has to offer'
                                        leocristea.wordpress.com

'If there was one word I'd use to describe *The Copper Promise*, it would be "joyful"'   graemesff.blogspot.co.uk

'Fast-paced and wonderfully-realised, Jen Williams' first novel is a delight. The reader will encounter pirates, dragons, zombies, gods and demons, to name but a few, on their journey through this exciting new world'   readerdad.co.uk

'Each page is a wild ride into the unknown and follows a cast of characters that you will root for from start to finish'
sleeplessmusingsofawellgroomedmoustachedman.wordpress.com

'A wonderful sword and sorcery novel with some very memorable characters and a dragon to boot. If you enjoy full-throttle action, awesome monsters, and fun, snarky dialogues then *The Copper Promise* is definitely a story you won't want to miss'
                                        afantasticallibrarian.com

By Jen Williams and available from Headline

The Copper Promise
The Iron Ghost

THE IRON GHOST

JEN WILLIAMS

headline

First published in 2015 by
HEADLINE PUBLISHING GROUP

First published in paperback in 2015 by
HEADLINE PUBLISHING GROUP

1

Cataloguing in Publication Data is available from the British Library

ISBN 978 1 4722 1114 9

Typeset in Sabon LT Std by Palimpsest Book Production Limited,
Falkirk, Stirlingshire

Printed and bound in Great Britain by
Clays Ltd, St Ives plc

Headline's policy is to use papers that are natural, renewable and recyclable
products and made from wood grown in sustainable forests. The logging and
manufacturing processes are expected to conform to the environmental
regulations of the country of origin.

MIX
Paper from
responsible sources
FSC
www.fsc.org FSC® C104740

HEADLINE PUBLISHING GROUP
An Hachette UK Company
Carmelite House
50 Victoria Embankment
EC4Y 0DZ

www.headline.co.uk
www.hachette.co.uk

For Marty, with love.

PART ONE
Heart of Stone

1

It was Siano's turn to walk the sky-chain.

She touched the tips of her fingers to the pitted rock of the cliff face behind her, taking satisfaction in its familiar solidity. Below her the tiny province of Apua crowded within its crevasse, the stacked red bricks of the monasteries fighting for space, and on the far side, the twin to the cliff she now perched on sat like a thick bank of storm cloud. Between the two cliffs hung the greatest of the sky-chains; the sky-chain for the Walk of Accuracy.

The chain itself was a wonder, each link a foot wide, and made of gold. Or at least, that was what Father Tallow said, although personally, Siano suspected the gold was only a covering and, underneath, the chain was made of something a little more reassuring. It stretched away from her and dwindled to a fine golden line high above even the tallest of the monasteries, until it met the far wall. Beneath it, Apua was teeming with people going about their daily lives, but you could be sure that there would always be a few pairs of eyes looking up, because you never knew when someone might attempt to walk a sky-chain. You never knew when someone might fall.

Siano had walked all three chains more times than she could count.

She stepped out from the small platform built into the rock and placed her foot on the first great link, testing its strength, feeling the soft thrum as the wind pushed against it, and the slower, more gentle rocking underneath that. She had taken her boots off and her bare foot looked warm and brown against the sun-bright gold.

'Are you going to take all day, Siano?' came a voice from behind her. She glanced back to see Leena grinning at her, nervous energy making her step from foot to foot. She was another of Father Tallow's pupils, but she had yet to walk a single sky-chain or take a single life. Siano pitied her.

'Please.' Siano stepped fully onto the chain, the drop yawning away beneath her feet, and sketched a brief bow. 'If you have finally gathered your courage, you are more than welcome to go first.'

She watched a grimace spasm across Leena's face.

'Just get on with it.'

Siano smiled and turned back to the chain in front of her. To either side the other sky-chains stretched into the distance: black iron for the Walk of Silence, blistered lead for the Walk of Secrecy. Taking a deep breath, she let herself feel the weight of her own body and its place in the universe. She let herself feel the texture of the link under her feet, warm and rough and solid. And then she walked.

I'm the best there is. Leena knows it, and Father Tallow knows it. She held her hands out to either side, feeling the wind beginning to push at her now she was out from under the shelter of the cliff face. *I will be a weapon to turn the fate of the world.*

There were shouts from below, although whether they came from observers of her walk or just people going about their general noisy lives, she couldn't tell. Her eyes wandered to the tall segmented building that lay on the far side of the chain, directly under its path; the House of Patience, its broad, red bricks painted with rich images of dragons, birds and women. Some people believed that places such as the House of Patience should be hidden from view, that they should be disguised as more wholesome establishments, but Apua was famous for the profession. Why hide it? For a little while, she forgot entirely about the golden links and the deadly drop inches from her feet. In there, right now, Father Tallow would be teaching his children all the ways of Patience, and none of them would be quite as skilled as Siano.

The wind picked up a little, blowing her hair across her eyes.

4

Most people would tie it back before attempting to walk across a sky-chain, but Siano had barely thought about it.

She was over three quarters of the way across and enjoying the thin sliver of sunlight warming her back when the bells began to toll, over and over. Siano paused, the wind pulling playfully at her jacket. When the children of the House of Patience were small, they were given a song of their very own. Each one was subtly different, and they all learned their own by heart. It was their second name, their signature. Siano listened, and after a few moments, smiled. They were calling her name.

Siano spread her arms and ran the rest of the way across the chain.

'Siano, my child, come with me.'

The monks in their scarlet robes had ushered her up to the top floor of the House of Patience, ignoring all of her frantically whispered questions, and now Father Tallow himself was here to greet her. He was a tall, painfully thin man with a fringe of grey beard on his chin, the hair on his head oiled back into a long braid. His hands were long and delicate, a woman's hands, save for the thick yellow fingernails. He grasped Siano's shoulder with one of those hands now, and the girl was reminded of the strength hidden in them.

'What is it, Father?'

'Keep a civil tongue in your head, and speak only when spoken to.' Father Tallow led her through the opulent Receiving Room, where clients were served iced wine and tiny honeyed cakes – the cakes and wine were usually left untouched, since their clients were, by necessity, uncommonly paranoid – before being plied with reassurances and relieved of their money. Next to this was an anteroom that Siano had never been in, and this was where Father Tallow led her now. Before going in, he squeezed Siano's shoulder again, apparently responding to the girl's questioning look. 'An important client, Siano. It is a great honour.'

Inside, the room was dark and stuffy. Small red lamps lined the walls and there were richly decorated screens to all sides. Siano's training immediately provided her with a hundred places to hide, and a hundred places to expect danger. There were thick rugs on the floor and small clay pots burning incense that smelt of scorpion oil and lilies, and in the middle of the room was a low table. In the centre sat a large black lacquered box.

The room was crowded, small, dark – perfect for a job – but there was no one else present. Even behind the screens, Siano sensed there was no one. Perhaps the client would be brought to her?

'Here, Siano, you will kneel.' Father Tallow indicated the space in front of the table. Siano went to her knees in the waiting posture, her palms lying face-up on her thighs, showing no weapons: a gesture of respect. 'Good. I have taught you much, Siano. As much as anyone learns at the House of Patience before plying their trade out in the world, perhaps. I ask you now particularly to remember the lessons of secrecy and stillness.' Siano glanced up, trying to read her old teacher's face. She felt her own stomach clench. 'Are you listening, Siano?'

'Yes, Father.'

Father Tallow nodded, and then walked forward and knocked three times on the lacquered box. There was a curious change in the atmosphere of the room; rather than stuffy, it now felt cold. The darkness was no longer a useful tool, it was threatening. Siano shivered.

'I am here.'

The voice came from the box.

Siano let out a low cry of surprise, quickly silenced by Father Tallow's warning look. Her teacher reached forward and opened the box, revealing a bloody severed head sitting upon a plump cushion. The head was either not particularly fresh or had experienced a rough journey, as much of the skin was missing, and the eyeballs had been gouged out. Strange angular shapes had been carved into the small pieces of flesh that had been left intact.

'Good, good. This is the one, is it? She looks an eager sort.' The voice was old, and cultured. It sounded relaxed, and faintly smug. 'Your best, you say?'

Siano swallowed hard. She was untroubled by the sight of the severed head – she would not have lasted long at the House of Patience if such things worried her – but the voice was something else.

6

'Siano has trained in all the methods of Patience, my lord, and excelled at them all.' Father Tallow's voice was steady, to his credit. 'We feel she has a natural talent for the business.'

'Ah, good. A child of mine, then. Yes, this will be perfect.' The severed head did not move inside the box, but that was where the voice was coming from. 'You have the names?'

'Yes, my lord. We have the list, and information on all the families mentioned. It will not be a problem.'

'Excellent. Blood and names, it always comes down to that, in the end. Siano, is it? Look at me, girl.'

Siano raised her head respectfully, gazing on the bloody holes where the thing's eyes should be.

'Magic has returned to the world, do you know that?'

Siano nodded, and, at a glance from Father Tallow, cleared her throat. 'Yes, my lord. There was a dragon in Creos, and griffins were seen to fly across Ynnsmouth.'

'Heh, *griffins*.' The voice sounded both amused and sour. 'Ede is thick with magic once more. Places and creatures that have been dormant, shall rise. And so it is time for a friend of mine to return, for old debts to be repaid. And you are going to help me with that, young Siano. You will be my instrument.'

'Yes,' murmured Siano.

'I have given your master a list of names,' continued the voice. 'Many years ago I hid the seeds of a spell in the blood of three men.'

Siano frowned slightly at the mention of a spell, but she kept her silence. The voice coming from the severed head continued.

'These men were servants of mine, and they agreed to carry the seed in their blood for the granting of certain . . . privileges. I do find it quite fascinating, my young friend, how much a person will agree to when it is not them who will pay the price.' Siano kept very still. She had no idea what the voice was talking about, but she assumed that either Father Tallow knew or it would be explained to her in time. 'The descendants of these men have carried the seed in their blood, a quiet little passenger through the centuries, and it is time for this blood to be spilled, and the spell set in motion. There are three families on this list, Siano, and you will kill them all, and you will collect vials of their blood.

7

Do you understand? You must be fast and deadly and quiet, a dark hawk on the wing.'

'Yes, my lord.' Siano realised that she could smell the head now, even over the heady scents of scorpion oil and the warm echo of polished wood. The head smelt like the back entrance of a butcher's on a hot day, when the floors were washed and waves of pink water came down over the step.

'The House of Patience can do this.' Father Tallow came and stood behind Siano and briefly rested his fingers on the back of her neck in a gesture of support. 'It is my belief that Siano was brought to us for this very purpose. To be your weapon, lord.'

The voice chuckled.

'That is most fine. I am fond of my weapons. Siano, there will be women and children on these lists. The blood lines must be severed. Do you have any objection to this?'

Siano sensed the danger in the question and was seized with a sudden, morbid curiosity. What would happen if she did object? What would be her fate if she said no? It was like looking into a glass tank at a deadly viper, and contemplating putting your hand inside.

It hardly mattered. Siano was made for such a task.

'I have no objections, my lord.'

'Good.' The mineral stench of the severed head increased, and as Siano watched the partially scabbed wounds began to bleed again. 'Then you will kill in my name.'

2

Wydrin leaned against the guardrail and watched as dark, solid shapes passed them by slowly, the river making soft, insistent noises against their hull. It was late evening in this strange, cold country and the last light of the day turned the featureless grass-lands grey and milky violet, but it did little to illuminate the sentinels on the banks. Their own lamps cast the faintest glow over the surface of the nearest one and she could make out a rough stone face, contorted with rage, or pain, and then it was gone again, lost in the dark.

'What do you suppose they are?' she asked Sebastian.

The big knight had been staring off to the north where the shadows of the distant mountains haunted the horizon. He turned back to her, shaking his head slightly as if to clear it. 'I don't know. Statues of local gods? It is difficult to make them out.'

'Oh good, *gods*,' said Wydrin. 'We haven't had enough of that lately, after all.'

They were sailing up the river known as the Comet's Tail, heading towards Skaldshollow, a city in a land so distant that Wydrin had never heard of it before the letter had arrived; the latest plea for their services, another generous promise of coin. Their work was certainly taking them to some strange places these days.

She glanced up towards the stern of the boat. The crew of the *Molly Sings* were moving with purpose, black shapes in the dusk, but one figure was still, his narrow shoulders and the white shock of his hair covered in a dark hooded cloak. She knew the shape of him and the way he stood, and that in itself was an annoyance.

Sebastian caught her looking, and she cursed inwardly.

'Give him time,' he said. 'Frith is stubborn, but he's no fool.'

'That's what worries me.' Wydrin shivered and pulled her own furred hood over her head. The wind that filled their sails was icy. 'Here, there's that boy again. I think he likes you.'

Sebastian glanced up and a young sailor briefly caught their eyes before heading rapidly past. The youngest son of the captain, he had been sniffing around them since they came on board. Wydrin had started to think that he must have heard of them, that their fame had reached this tiny river tribe, until Sebastian had been caught in a sudden downpour about a week into their journey upriver; the rains here ended as quickly as they came, soon to be replaced with a freezing, driving wind. Sebastian had stripped off his soaking shirt below decks, and the young sailor had dropped an entire tray of dirty dishes.

'Do you think so?'

'Are you kidding? If you jumped in the river right now he'd jump straight in after you.'

Sebastian looked away. 'He's just a boy.'

Wydrin snorted.

'What? He's my age, at least. Don't you think he's cute? I think he's cute. A bit wet-looking maybe, like he'd sit at your feet and fetch your slippers, but—'

'You prefer the complete bastards, of course.'

Wydrin ignored this. 'How long's it been, Seb? Are you really going to let those Ynnsmouth fools ruin everything?'

Sebastian shook his head, and the look he shot her was edging towards angry. 'It's not that. Everything that's happened, with the demon, and then with the brood sisters . . .' His voice trailed off. The wind was coming on fiercely again, bringing with it the chill of the mountains they were gradually snaking towards. In the morning they would see them clearly again, a grey fracture against the sky.

'What do you need?' Wydrin eyed her friend warily. There were deep lines at the corners of his eyes – lines that hadn't been there a year ago. 'Do you want to talk about what happened?'

Sebastian smiled. 'I just need time, and distractions. And you've always been good at those.'

'Yes, well. This promises to be a good one.'

Crammed into his tiny cabin Sebastian slept deeply, although there was no rest in it. He dreamed of the demon again, of Ip's small pale face, as clean and innocent as the moon, and of her feet, red to the ankles with blood. The demon's disguise had been so perfect he had never suspected what travelled within the girl; at least not until the Ynnsmouth knights were dying and a deal with the creature that called itself Bezcavar had felt like his only hope. In the dream he saw his sword turn the brittle colour of ash again, felt the enchanted armour settle against him like a second skin. And then in that way that dreams have, Ip's face turned into that of another girl, the one with the scarlet hood dotted with pearls. She had screamed at the edge of the lake and the brood sisters had turned to him with blood on their claws, and he knew it was his fault.

The brood sisters. The daughters of the dragon-god Y'Ruen, and somehow his too, a connection via his blood that he still did not quite understand; a fever born of death. In his dreams he saw them on the battlefield of Baneswatch again, their faces green and beautiful, their silvered hair streaked with blood. Ephemeral standing knee deep in the bodies of his brothers, reaching out and calling him 'Father'.

And then in the midst of these fever-bright dreams there came a different voice, and it was like a cold hand on his brow. He moved towards it, desperate to feel cold, to be able to shiver.

. . . *and he stood once more before Isu, a boy again. There was the great dark chasm from his dreams, and the mountain was a heavy presence in his heart, a relentless pressure now weighted by guilt and a need for redemption. He could feel snow under his bare feet and in his hands he carried a goblet, filled to the top with something red. The mountain was speaking, in its voice as slow as ice ages.*

'Where must I go?' he asked, unsurprised that his voice was now a boy's voice. 'I don't understand what you want.'

The mountain gave him nothing more, save for the image of

a tiny green plant miraculously untouched by dragon-fire, and a man with ice in his veins . . .

And then the voice was gone and Sebastian woke in the darkness, his arms thick with gooseflesh.

In the daylight they could see the statues clearly, and they were no more reassuring. Made of some sort of dark granite, they depicted a full range of hideous monsters: women with snakes for hair and holes where their eyes should be, huge hulking shapes with twisted, ruined faces, men with many arms, their clawed hands holding severed heads. At the bottom of each was a small pile of food, or coins, or swatches of brightly coloured silks, all covered in a thin layer of frost.

'Offerings,' said Sebastian. They were back on the deck in the cold dawn light. Wydrin was eating a lump of salted pork wrapped in yellowish bread. 'Offerings to what though?'

'I don't know,' said Wydrin around a mouthful of pork. 'But I don't like how they're all facing the river.'

Frith came up onto the deck then, his brown face as narrow as a knife blade within his fur-lined hood. After a few moments a great black bird flew down from the morning skies and settled on his shoulder. He caught sight of them and came over reluctantly.

'The captain says we will be within sight of Skaldshollow by the evening. We can travel on foot from there.'

'It's been a long journey,' said Sebastian, keeping his voice neutral. Wydrin was picking pieces of crust from her bread and flicking them over the side.

'Too long,' said Frith. 'I only hope that the journey halfway across Ede is worth the coin.'

'Your castle will still be there when you get back, you know,' said Wydrin. She held out a piece of the crust to the bird on Frith's shoulder. It tipped its head to one side before snapping up the offering with its clever beak.

'Unlike some people, I have responsibilities.' The young lord looked away, his grey eyes stony. 'It will not be far now.'

In the early afternoon, the boat stopped to pick up a new passenger. A short, rotund woman called Jayne hauled herself up and over the side, her full pack clanking and rattling as she came. She wore the rags and bags of a travelling tinker, and had a belt studded with hipflasks, which Wydrin soon discovered were filled with several varieties of rum. They quickly became friends.

'So, what are these all about?' Wydrin gestured at the statues as they shared a tipple that tasted like the bottom of a stove. The featureless grasslands had given away now to hills, the river weaving between them, but the grim river watchers were still there.

Jayne made a complicated gesture with her fingers, which Sebastian took to be a sign of protection.

'Old things are rising,' she said. Her voice was a croak, pickled by a long association with strong drink. 'You must have heard the rumours, the stories?'

'I'm a bit tired of rumours at the moment,' said Wydrin.

'There was a dragon, crawled out from under the stones in Creos.' Her bushy grey eyebrows disappeared up into the mop of her hair. 'And there was an army of green monsters.'

'Ah, we might have heard those particular rumours.' Sebastian cleared his throat.

'Aye, well, the dragon might be gone now – I saw it go myself, falling into a hole in the sky – but it ain't the only thing. I've heard tell of old stories coming to life all over. Dormant places that haven't stirred in hundreds of years. The Singing Catacombs in Creos are filling the moonless nights with their music again, and the plains of Pathania are said to be haunted by strange lights.' Jayne coughed a little, worn out by her own poetry. 'These are strange times.'

'You could say that,' said Wydrin. Sebastian stifled a smile. 'But what does that have to do with the statues?'

'People are afraid.' Jayne took her hipflask back and swallowed down a large gulp. 'If the old gods are returning, maybe it's time to bring back the old ways of worship.' She lowered her voice. 'It's not so bad here. Here it's flowers and grain and wholesome things. Out in the wilds of Briskenteeth and Tsold I've heard that the sacrifices are . . . fresher.'

'That seems a little extreme.' The hills were covered in trees now, and they passed tall pines and oaks on either side. It made

13

everything a little darker, and in this cold land the light was already draining from the sky. It occurred to Sebastian that thieves could easily hide in those trees, and take a passing river boat with barely any fuss at all. He shifted, feeling the weight of his broadsword at his back. 'What do they believe is coming for them?'

Jayne shrugged. 'This land is full of magic, deep magic that goes right down into its bones. My ma used to say that the stones was haunted. That it was a natural place for ghosts. Some places are more magical than others, you know that?'

Sebastian nodded, thinking of what O'rin, the god of lies, had told them about magic. Edenier, the magic of the will, used by the mages and lately by one Lord Aaron Frith; and Edeian, the magic that was inherent in the soil and air of Ede. He had felt it too, down in the tunnels under Pinehold and in the Citadel itself, where the dragon had waited for them.

'Strange places, yeah, there's loads of them,' said Wydrin.

'And it's been getting worse, too.' Jayne fixed them with an ominous look. Sebastian suspected she used the same look when trying to shift a few bottles of ointment or a dubious good luck charm. 'Ever since the dragon, the strange places have been getting stranger. And it's like I said: this is a haunted land.'

It was dusk before the river took them out of the hills and the landscape opened up again, revealing the mountains, now impossibly close. Nestled at the bottom of the closest one was the city of Skaldshollow. The full moon hung over it like a wart, bloated and strange.

'There it is,' said Frith. He had stalked out onto deck as the sun set, apparently eager to see their destination. 'A long journey, on a few words and a promise of gold.'

'That's how adventurers work, Frith.' Wydrin smiled a little. 'The copper promise. The fun is in finding the adventure as you go.' Her smile faded. 'Not that you'll need to worry about that much longer.'

Sebastian cleared his throat and pointed. 'It looks to be carved right into the bottom of the mountain. It must be a cold place.'

It was too dark to make out much, but Sebastian could see

14

clusters of stone buildings and steep roads like scars leading up out of the settlement towards the mountain peak.

'This entire land is too cold,' said Wydrin. 'Who would want to live in a place where it's always winter?'

There were lights too, lights everywhere; red, orange, white and green. And a lot of them appeared to be moving. Lights, and the darker spaces behind them. Sebastian frowned.

'Is it me,' he asked, 'or are parts of the mountain walking around?'

Next to him, Wydrin sighed. 'But of course. We wouldn't journey to any old *normal* city in the middle of nowhere. I wonder what weird crap is waiting for us this time?'

Sebastian shook his head. Looking at it made him think of his last journey with the brood sisters – a different mountain, not so long ago. The dangers there had been obvious, but he had been a fool. He turned away from the view.

'We'd best get ready. We've a long journey ahead of us.'

3

A different mountain, not so long ago . . .

There were many secret paths through the god-peaks known only by the Order; sacred paths Sebastian had been shown as a novice, the act of walking each an expression of worship for their gods. He thought of them often as they travelled through the lakelands of Ynnsmouth: himself and forty-eight members of the brood army, all of them confused, frightened, and battle-weary, heading towards the sacred mountains. The daughters of the dragon were cautious, quiet, their strikingly beautiful faces turned to the ground as they walked. He could feel their disquiet in his own blood, and when he looked back at them he saw their yellow eyes narrowed against the last light of the day. It must be strange for them, he mused, to not have the vast shape of Y'Ruen flying above them, keeping watch. Now they had only him.

Once he had promised Gallo that he would show him the abandoned temple of Isu; now it seemed that he would walk the secret paths again after all, and with company he could never have imagined. If he earned the wrath of Isu and the other mountain gods, then he would deal with it as best he could.

'We travel alone, Father?'

He turned to see Ephemeral at his elbow. She had scavenged a hooded cloak from somewhere so that her face was thrown into shadow, and in the failing light her green skin looked grey. Around them many of the remaining brood sisters wore similar garb, their golden armour and shining white hair hidden away

16

as best they could. Beyond them, he could see the still mirror surface of Lake Cataloun, reflecting the mauve sky of twilight.

'Who did you expect to come with us?'

She frowned slightly at his question. 'Your sister-in-arms. The woman with red hair.'

Sebastian had to smile slightly at that. 'Wydrin will visit us when we're settled.' He took a slow breath, wondering what 'settled' could possibly mean in circumstances like these. 'She wants to catch up with her brother. She has a few debts to pay in that direction, I think.'

'And the mage?' Ephemeral's voice was uncertain now. 'He who . . . took our mother from us. Who banished Y'Ruen.'

'I keep telling you, Ephemeral, we were all responsible for that.'

Ephemeral sniffed. 'I do not like mages.'

'I am not surprised.' Sebastian stopped. Around them the brood sisters moved on, heading towards the mountains in the distance. They had been walking all day and not a single one showed any sign of tiring. 'Ephemeral, in time you will come to know other humans, and eventually you will . . .' he paused, struggling for the right words. Make friends? Forge relationships? 'Eventually you will be able to interact with human beings every day, but right now we must keep ourselves separate.'

'This is why we do not travel by the roads and paths that other people use,' said Ephemeral, nodding slightly. 'This is why we did not go into the city of Baneswatch.'

'Yes,' said Sebastian. 'Visiting Baneswatch would have been a mistake.'

There was a flurry of noise from up ahead as two or three brood sisters suddenly ran off into the trees. Immediately Sebastian's hand went to his sword.

'What are they doing?'

Ephemeral blinked, watching them vanish into the shadows. 'They are hunting, Father.'

'Yes, but hunting what?' Sebastian took a few steps forward, his heart beating thickly in his chest, but Ephemeral laid a clawed hand on his arm.

'Deer, Father. They hunt deer. There are so many in this forest, can you not smell them?'

17

Sebastian let out a breath he didn't know he'd been holding, and shook his head. 'No, I – No, I don't smell them.'

When the light had vanished completely from the sky they made camp where the trees were thickest. The brood sisters who had gone hunting returned with two young deer, four fat rabbits, and a portly looking snow grouse, its white feathers now stained scarlet. Crocus, one of the hunters, threw her deer down by their small fire, a look of extreme satisfaction on her face.

'It ran, but I was too fast for it.'

Her sisters nodded approvingly, and two of them moved forward, claws ready to disembowel the animal. Sebastian, remembering all too clearly the gore and mess of their previous meals, stepped in to intercept them.

'Indulge me for a moment,' he said, pulling the skinning knife from his belt. 'How about we cook our meat first this time?'

There were a few faces pulled over that, and Crocus crossed her arms over her chest, her brow furrowed.

'The meat will be ruined.'

One of the other brood sisters stepped forward. She was shorter than Crocus by perhaps an inch, her white hair hanging loose against her cheeks. In the days since Baneswatch, Sebastian had done his best to learn each of the brood sisters' newly chosen names, but this one still referred to herself as the Second.

'We cannot eat the flesh while it is alive. Now we cannot eat the flesh without burning it first?'

'Mother would often burn it,' pointed out Ephemeral in a reasonable tone of voice. 'We have all eaten burnt flesh.'

Sebastian held up the hand not holding the knife. 'Not burnt, merely cooked. You might like it. And, you see, we can use this animal's skin for clothes, its fats for ointments. If we tear it all to bits, then you will only get this one thing from it. Using all the parts of what you hunt – this is one of the things I will teach you. In the mountains.'

The one called the Second frowned. 'When you make us your Ynnsmouth knights?'

'No,' said Sebastian. He took a slow breath, thinking of the globe of blue glass in his pocket. 'But I will show you what is useful to know.'

18

This hunger was new to them. They had eaten before, of course – Sebastian didn't like to dwell too long on what they had eaten before – but from what Ephemeral had told him, Y'Ruen had sustained them simply by being there. The flesh and blood they had eaten, torn often from victims who were still alive, had been for enjoyment only. They could have marched for months with nothing in their bellies, surviving on the nurturing presence of Y'Ruen alone. Now that she was gone they were experiencing real hunger for the first time, and like children, it was something that troubled them incessantly.

'This will take too long,' said Crocus. She stood over Sebastian as he quickly skinned the deer carcass. 'I am hungry now.'

'I am also hungry now.' This was Toast, a brood sister who looked curiously younger than the others. Ephemeral had told him that she had been the Eight Hundred and Forty Second, back in the birthing pits. 'I am so hungry it hurts.'

'Patience will be something else I will teach you about in the mountains.' It wasn't easy in the light from their small fire, but Sebastian deftly separated flesh from pelt, and spitted the animal quickly. There was some blood, and for a strange moment he found he could not quite look away from the red smears on his hands. *It is the remnants of the demon*, he told himself firmly. *A demon that I have long since left behind.*

'Here.' He lay the carcass across the fire, and rubbed his hands on his cloak. 'Soon it will be cooked, and you will be able to smell it.'

'How soon?' said Toast, her wide yellow eyes riveted to the bloody meat.

'Soon enough. Here, turn this.' Sebastian gave her the end of the stick. 'Keep turning it over, but slowly, so that it cooks on all sides.'

'It is a waste of meat,' said the Second, already eyeing up the deer and rabbits still to be skinned. 'I could be full by now. We could all be full by now.'

'Trust me,' said Sebastian. He met her eyes steadily. 'A lot of what I show you will not make sense to begin with, but I can help you to live in this world. As a part of this world.'

'Trust you,' said the Second. It wasn't quite a question, but

19

when the meat was ready she would not taste it, and Sebastian gave up the second deer carcass to those who still wanted their meat raw. They took it away from the fire at least, and then fell on it like wolves. Sebastian sat with his back to the fire, listening to the sounds of flesh being torn.

'Give them time.' Ephemeral came and sat beside him. She pulled her long hair out of its braid and began to drag a comb through it – some small souvenir stolen from a town or village they had sacked under Y'Ruen's instruction.

'Time. That I can give them.' Sebastian toyed with the meat he'd served up himself. It did not taste how he imagined it would – it was flat, and stringy. He longed for some salt. 'Time, and a place to be away from the world for a while. The sum of my own experience.' He laughed a little at that. 'I don't know if it will be enough, Ephemeral. I don't know what could be.'

'It is something,' said Ephemeral firmly. She found a knot in her hair and yanked the comb firmly through it. 'It is a start.'

'Did you enjoy the cooked meat?'

Ephemeral nodded enthusiastically. 'When Mother cooked it, it was mainly black and crusty. This is better.'

Putting his dinner aside, Sebastian reached into his pocket and pulled out the blue globe Crowleo had given him. The Secret Keeper's apprentice had meant it as a way for Sebastian to remember who he was, he understood that now – a great gift indeed. Sebastian was fairly sure he didn't deserve it.

The flames from their fire danced green within the glass and he could see the god-peak again, distant and alone. Should he have let the soldiers of Baneswatch slaughter the brood sisters, as they had wanted to? What did it mean, to save murderers from murder?

'It is very beautiful,' said Ephemeral. She had put her comb away now and was staring at the glass ball. 'When you look at it your face becomes calm.'

For a long moment Sebastian didn't say anything at all. 'A good friend made this for me,' he said finally. 'When I look at it, I am reminded of him.'

He noticed then that his fingers were still smeared with blood, so he put the globe away. On the far side of the fire the brood

20

sisters who had eaten their dinner raw were returning, with the Second at the forefront. The ends of her long white hair were stained red.

'Soon,' he told Ephemeral, 'we will have to leave this forest and travel down through the lakelands themselves. There it will be harder to hide, and we shall have to be especially careful. Those of you who have hooded cloaks should be sure to wear them. Those who don't will travel in the middle of our company.'

'There are many people down there?' asked Ephemeral. She was braiding her hair again, her fingers deftly portioning her hair into three pieces before weaving them together. 'Many human places?'

'Many human places,' agreed Sebastian. 'And it may not be safe.'

Not safe for us, he thought, *and not safe for them.*

4

'Tamlyn? Tamlyn Nox is coming here?'

Barlow took her furred hat off and turned it round in her hands before thinking better of it and wedging it back on her head. The bitter cold was a slap round the face.

'Gamlin saw her hisself, with his lenses.' Yun shrugged unhappily. 'She's coming up the Bone Road on her own war-werken.' He paused, and scratched his patchy beard. 'I'd quite like to see that up close, actually. They say it's the fastest one she's built, and sleek, too.'

'You'll get to see it up close, all right,' said Barlow, scowling. 'I might well ask her if she can get it to eat you, then you'll see it real close. This is all I bloody need, a visit from Tamlyn in the middle of an excavation. I've got charges about to go off all over the place.'

'She could be coming to do a blessing,' pointed out Yun mildly. 'She knows the mountain like no one else, and since we lost the Heart-Stone—'

'Lost it? We didn't lose it, Yun, you idiot.' Barlow glanced behind her into the quarry, the very heart of Skaldshollow. Men and women, looking like ants at this distance, scurried across the brown and grey rock, the earth-werkens themselves moving slowly, huge dark shapes of rock against the flesh of the mountain. They were too far away for her to see the intricate patterns carved into their stone hides, but she knew them as well as the ever increasing lines at the corners of her eyes. Ever since the Heart-Stone had

22

vanished, her workers had been skittish, and why shouldn't they be? Without it, their work would eventually become pointless. And now Tamlyn Nox was coming, with her sharp eyes, her sharp tongue, and her witch's ways. The best werken-crafter of them all, of course, Barlow was never going to argue with that, but she was hardly a reassuring presence. 'How soon?'

'About now, I'd reckon.'

Barlow whipped round and, sure enough, a giant shape was cresting the top of the Bone Road. It was a clear day on the mountain, and she could see the thick veins of Edeian that riddled Tamlyn's war-werken, which was, as Yun had promised, a sleek four-footed model shaped rather like a giant cat with a long pointed face. Its eyes glowed green. She could also see Tamlyn herself, riding between the creature's enormous shoulders. Her dark hair was pinned into a careful gathering on top of her head, but the wind was making short work of that.

'An unexpected pleasure, Mistress Crafter!' Barlow scurried forward, plastering a smile on her face. 'I wasn't aware you were visiting us today, but obviously—'

'I'm not here to catch you out, Barlow.' Tamlyn dismounted, climbing down the steps chiselled directly into the werken's stone flank.

Barlow's awkward smile froze into place. 'Oh, of course not, no . . .'

'You misunderstand me.' Tamlyn marched over to them, glancing around at the sturdy buildings that marked the hub of Skaldshollow's mining operation, and the dormant earth-werkens that squatted here and there. She wore only a padded coat, no hat or furs. Her skin, the warm colour of clay bricks, carried a flush of red on the tops of her cheeks, the only sign that it was freezing on the mountain. As ever, Barlow found it difficult to look away from her face, with its broad nose and narrow, black eyes. It was a face that could have been carved from a mountain itself, every bit as cold and beautiful.

'Mistress?'

'There has been a sighting.' Tamlyn nodded at Yun, who was doing his best to vanish into the background. 'You. Yun, isn't it? Are there lookouts in place?'

23

The scrawny man looked horrified to have been addressed directly. His eyes jumped from Tamlyn to her werken and back again. *Perhaps he thinks she really is going to feed him to it,* thought Barlow.

'Yes, mistress!' squeaked Yun. 'I mean, the usual, the usual lookouts. No one has reported anything, mistress.'

Knowing that nothing had happened but needing to check anyway, Barlow glanced at the distant beacons ringing the pit. All were unlit, as expected.

Tamlyn cocked her head slightly, as though listening to something they couldn't hear.

'The usual lookouts?'

Barlow winced and opened her mouth to answer but Tamlyn spoke over her.

'Our greatest treasure is stolen, from right under our noses, and you see no need to watch the skies more closely?'

For the briefest moment Barlow's traitorous mouth wanted to ask how the great Mistress Crafter of Skaldshollow had failed to protect the Heart-Stone, but she bit down on her cheek until the urge passed.

'There should be more war-werkens up here, I've said that before.' Barlow paused as Tamlyn's eyes narrowed at her. 'If we should find another—'

'There will be no other,' snapped Tamlyn. 'The Heart-Stone is unique, and it is ours.' She touched a red-beaded necklace at her throat. 'We will take back what is ours, and the Narhl will bleed for what they've taken.'

'Yes, mistress.' Barlow felt a faint swell of pride, and corresponding anger. The bloody Narhl, with their cold hearts and flying lizards. They had no right. 'You know we'll always do our best for you, you only have to ask.' She heard Yun cough slightly as he held in a snigger, and she made a note to confiscate his rum ration later.

Tamlyn looked closely at them both, a twitch of uncertainty at the corner of her lips. 'See that you do,' she said, turning back to look at her werken, which was crouched obediently in a thin covering of powdery snow. 'The quality of the rock – it is the same?'

24

Barlow nodded, glad to be back on familiar ground. 'Yes, mistress. If anything, the Edeian is getting stronger the deeper we go. The werkens constructed from these rocks will be the best we've ever made. Er, the best you've ever made.' *Although now we've no Heart-Stone to waken them*, she added silently.

Tamlyn nodded. 'Good. It is time we surprised the Narhl. On the advice of the Prophet, I have—'

There was a shout from across the pit – Barlow heard it clearly on the frigid air – followed by the soft *wumph* of a beacon being lit. As one, they turned to see the first of several warning beacons flaring into life on the other side of the mine, and above that, in the crisp blue sky, the wriggling shapes of a Narhl attack formation.

'Fuck me sideways,' muttered Yun.

Tamlyn was already running for her werken, shouting commands as she went. Men and women were moving in all directions; some making for safety, others looking for weapons. Barlow stood frozen for a moment, torn between looking like a coward in front of Mistress Nox and being caught out in the open during a Narhl attack. And then Yun was running, waving at the men and women in the pit to get down, so she followed him, her eyes flickering from the rocky ground in front of her to the shapes in the sky, now much closer than they were just a few seconds ago. The Narhl were fast.

Together they made it to one of the supply huts, but men and women in armour were streaming in and out of it, fetching range weapons and the portable catapults, so they crouched by the wall.

'Can you see them?' asked Yun, his teeth chattering. Barlow couldn't understand how he could be cold; she was suddenly sweating.

She peered around the hut and there they were, seven pale blue wyverns, rippling across the sky like eels in a stream, their short bat-like wings held out stiffly to cither side. On their backs she could just make out the gaunt forms of the Narhl riders, their mottled faces stark and strangely angular. They wore glass goggles over their eyes, and each carried a clutch of ice-spears on their backs – she couldn't actually see those, but she'd seen their work often enough.

25

'Just a small force,' she whispered, and then wondered why she was whispering. 'They won't hang about.' *If we're lucky*, she added silently.

There was a tremendous crack followed by a chorus of screams as the first of the Narhls' ice-spears fell, directly into the mine itself. Barlow winced, pulling her hat down over her ears as far as it would go. The men and women in armour were now on their own werkens, and all around them huge lumbering shapes of black and brown and grey rock were stirring into life, but the problem was the same as it ever was: the Narhl attacked from the sky, and the werkens could not reach them. Even so, some were fitted with giant catapults and as they watched, huge balls of granite were flung into the sky, scattering the sky-lizards. Flurries of fire arrows followed them up.

'Tamlyn knew they were coming,' hissed Yun. 'That's why she bloody came up here, she is a witch just like they say.'

An ice-spear fell and struck the ground no more than twenty feet from where they were crouched. There was a crack as the air instantly froze and three unlucky men stood frozen in their tracks. One of them fell and shattered into pieces.

Barlow scrambled to her feet. 'Come on, we have to get inside somewhere.'

They edged round the corner of the squat building, listening fearfully to the chorus of screams and shouts that now filled the pit. *We were lucky we weren't down there*, thought Barlow. *A few more minutes and I would have been, if Tamlyn hadn't dropped in like that.* As if summoning her, they saw Tamlyn on the far ridge, seated on the shoulders of her cat-like war-werken. She was impossible to miss with her black hair now streaming behind her like a banner, and the four-legged werken was as fast as Yun promised. It tore across the rocky ridge, chasing the distant sky-lizards. More ice-spears fell like deadly hail.

'We should get down the Bone Road,' said Yun. 'Get under a sturdy roof.' But he wasn't moving. Like Barlow, he was watching with wide eyes as the soldiers under Tamlyn's command urged their werkens to climb on top of each other, forming a rough pyramid of rock and glowing Edeian. Tamlyn turned her own werken and urged it on, running towards the formation at full pelt.

'Is she . . .?' Barlow cleared her throat. 'She's not . . .?'

The werken scrambled up its brothers and leapt clear into the sky. A sky-lizard wriggled sharply away but didn't move fast enough. The werken collided heavily with the creature and down it came, squealing and thrashing. Tamlyn and the werken landed beyond the ridge, throwing up rocks and snow in all directions. The Narhl rider was trapped, held in place by his own straps and belts, and with a sharp stamp from the werken's heavy foot his mount was dead. The remaining Narhl troops threw the last of their ice-spears and left, heading back to the mountains of the north-west, the centre of their own territory.

'She brought one down!' crowed Yun. He hopped from foot to foot. 'She bloody well brought one of the bastards off his stupid bastard flying lizard! I told you that werken was the tops, I *told* you.'

'Come on,' Barlow reached up and wiped away a palm full of sweat from her forehead before it could ice over, 'I want to go and see it.'

By the time they got there, the Narhl was already tied up, and already dying. He sat in the snow with his goggles slightly askew where someone had pulled them up. He had apparently fallen badly when his sky-lizard fell, as there were bones sticking from his bare chest and dark blood pooling in his lap. Tamlyn was standing over him, a short sword in one hand and a small circle of soldiers surrounding her.

'When is the next attack? Where is our Heart-Stone?'

The Narhl looked up at her with little apparent interest. Barlow felt her breath catch in her throat at the sight of him; up close, the Narhls were a tall, well-built people with wide shoulders and narrow waists, and their skins were mottled white, black, grey and brown – the colour of a pebble-bottomed mountain stream. This man's eyes were pale blue and his black hair was crusted here and there with what looked like green lichen.

'There is little to say to mountain-killers,' he said. His voice was soft. 'Did you enjoy our brief visit?'

Tamlyn said nothing for a moment, and then reached down with her gloveless hand and touched his face. He hissed between his teeth and tried to pull away, but the two soldiers behind him stepped up to hold the Narhl soldier in place.

'Uncomfortable, isn't it?' she said. 'You are all so weak.'

The Narhl scowled. 'We are part of the mountain, and part of the cold. It is our honour to live as—'

'Shut up.' Tamlyn gestured to her men. 'Take him down to the Hollow and we will question him as much as we can before he dies.'

They dragged the man to his feet and towards a waiting werken, and at this he began to shout, features contorted with rage.

'These creatures are the heart of the mountain!' he screamed, looking around wildly at the men and women gathered there. His eyes caught Barlow's briefly, and she shivered. 'They are sacred, and you use them as carthorses! Animals!'

Tamlyn turned back to them as the man was dragged away. 'They are laughing at us,' she said, her voice as bitter as ashes. 'They have the Heart-Stone and yet still they attack.'

Barlow shifted from foot to foot, uncomfortable at being brought into Tamlyn's confidence in this way. 'What does the Prophet say?' she asked, her voice sounding too young to her own ears. 'Does she not have any advice?'

Tamlyn Nox sheathed her sword. 'The Prophet advises,' she agreed. 'And I have listened. There is help on the way, and with any luck it will be the ruin of the Narhl. Their king will grovel at my feet, eventually.' Tamlyn smiled, a cold tensing of flesh. 'And we will have the Heart-Stone back.'

With that she left, mounting her war-werken and moving off down the Bone Road, following her prisoner. Barlow watched her go with a mixture of feelings; relief that she had been here when the Narhl attacked, and deep unease at her words. No one saw the Prophet but Nox, and there were those who whispered that it was all a fabrication, an extension of her growing madness. Such whispers were dangerous, of course.

'What do you think of that, then?' said Yun. Now that they

were out of danger some colour had returned to his sallow cheeks. 'The Prophet knows how to get the Heart-Stone back, it seems.'

'She better had,' snapped Barlow, glancing back down into the pit where her workers were tending to the dead and injured. 'Or all this will be a bloody waste of time.'

5

Wydrin crouched low over the warm neck of her sturdy pony, trusting it to follow the others without her guidance. As they travelled out of the riverlands and on towards the mountains, the world grew colder, and now it was snowing, a soft, silent fall that covered her hood and crusted her gloves.

'I didn't bring enough mead,' she muttered, watching as her breath turned into puffs of white vapour. 'Although I doubt there is enough mead in the world for this arse-hole end of Ede.'

'Look, there it is,' called Sebastian. 'That must be the southernmost wall.'

Reluctantly, Wydrin looked up into the snow. The foot of the mountain rose before them like an ominous storm cloud, and rising from its centre was a great wound filled with lights and stone and smoke – the city of Skaldshollow. In front of it was a huge stone wall, at least two hundred feet tall and carved from huge pieces of grey rock. There were fires along the top, spaced out like sentinels, although she could see no men. And that wasn't all she couldn't see.

'If that's the wall, where's the bloody gate?' There was no portcullis, no obvious entrance. 'I don't think my pony is up to climbing that.'

'I can fly over on Gwiddion,' suggested Frith, from the back of his own pony. His griffin, in its bird form, was perched on the top of his saddlebag. 'Although I'm not sure he could take all three of us.'

Sebastian frowned. 'It must be further along. We shall have to follow it around.'

There was a rumble and the snow in front of the gate suddenly rose up, revealing a shifting, mountainous mass of moving rock. Wydrin cried out, automatically unsheathing Glassheart, while Frith held up his bandaged hands, the soft yellow glow of the Edenier forming instantly between his palms.

'By the Graces, what is that?' Wydrin's pony took a few hurried steps backwards and she patted it behind its ears in an attempt to reassure it. The stone creature shook itself fully out of the snow it had been hiding in and turned towards them, its great blocky head and snout almost bear-shaped. Its eyes glowed green, and it was covered all over in intricate carved patterns, dark against the paler stone, almost like tattoos. There was another rumble and the snow next to the creature fell away, revealing its twin. In front of her, Sebastian unsheathed his broadsword.

'They are unlikely to respond to ice spells, no doubt being monsters native to this land, so I shall use my flames . . .' Frith was raising his hands when a section of the stone wall rumbled away to reveal a previously hidden door, and a young man came running out, waving his arms over his head.

'Sorry, sorry! Do not be afraid. These are just our gate guardians.'

Wydrin glanced back at the stone monsters. They were enormous, each over ten feet tall, but now that the young man had appeared they were still, apparently as attentive as dogs.

'They're your what?' She waved a sword at them. 'Can't you just have a fat old man in leather armour like everyone else?'

The man laughed as he jogged over to them. He had black hair tied back into a small knot on the back of his head, and he had warm copper skin and narrow, dark eyes. He wore thick furs and moved easily in them, as though he wore them every day of his life. As he got closer he waved again, looking from face to face.

'You are the Black Feather Three, yes?' He stopped, and Wydrin saw that he wore special wide boots, the better for running on the snow. 'Lord Frith, Sir Sebastian, and the Copper Cat of Crosshaven?'

'That's us all right,' said Wydrin. She put Glassheart away, feeling faintly foolish. 'But what are those?'

The young man turned back to the wall and waved, ignoring her question, and at once the thick granite walls split down the middle and began to draw away from each other, rumbling back to reveal the settlement beyond.

'Please, follow me,' he said, as the stone monsters settled back onto their haunches. 'My aunt is very anxious to meet with you.'

Inside the walls, Skaldshollow was a bustling warren of stone and smoke. Buildings of black, white and grey granite crowded everywhere, and in the distance Frith could see dwellings that had been carved directly into the flesh of the mountain itself. The men and women of Skaldshollow wore thick furs, much like the man who had brought them inside, as well as jewellery carved from glittery quartz and animal bone. The stone creatures were here too; slightly smaller than the enormous guardians on the gate, moving along the crowded streets like fat beetles in a nest of ants. When they were still, they were utterly still, seeming to merge into the landscape, and then, at a word or a gesture from one of the locals, they would lumber suddenly into life, green eyes flashing in the washed-out daylight. Frith flexed his fingers, feeling the Edenier churning within. What was this place, where the stones walked?

'You say they're called werkens?' asked Wydrin.

The young man who had greeted them at the gate had introduced himself as Bors Nox before arranging for their small mountain ponies to be stabled. Now he led them through winding streets, heading into the centre of the settlement.

'These are earth-werkens,' Bors replied, holding up a hand to halt their progress as a giant stone creature thundered past, dragging a cart full of hessian sacks behind it. 'We make them from the rock in the heart of the mountain. As you can see, they make fine carthorses, guardians, even war mounts.'

'Are they alive?' asked Sebastian.

'Oh no,' Bors led them across the street. 'They have a semblance of life, of course, because of the Edeian in the rock and their connection to us but they are no more alive than a fungus.'

'You know about Edeian?' Frith couldn't quite keep the surprise from his voice.

Bors shrugged. 'Of course. Our lands are riddled with the old magic.'

'And we are here because you have experienced a theft?' Frith prompted. There were too many mysteries in this place, too many questions. *We could be stuck here forever trying to unravel it,* thought Frith, and with that came an image of Blackwood Keep and its small graveyard, the earth damp and dark. His home would be full of people again by now, the floors scrubbed clean of blood. Just waiting for him to come back and take up his father's empty throne.

'Yes,' agreed Bors. 'Our means to waken the werkens has been taken from us. But my aunt will tell you more about that.'

'How do you control them?' asked Wydrin. She was watching as a huge, strangely lithe-looking werken pounded down the street opposite, a woman dressed in furs riding between its shoulders. It was as sleek as a cat. 'I mean, how do they know what you want them to do?'

'Werken riders are all joined.' Bors took off his glove and turned his palm to face her. In the middle there was a chip of green stone about the size of a penny sunken directly into his flesh. 'There is a corresponding piece of the Heart-Stone in my own werken.' Catching her look, he grinned. 'Don't worry, it doesn't hurt. Not too much, anyway.'

'Do we have much further to travel?' Frith broke in. 'Our time is limited.'

'And expensive,' added Wydrin.

'Not at all. We are here, in fact. Welcome to the Tower of Waking.'

The Tower of Waking, as Bors called it, rose from the centre of Skaldshollow like a giant splintered bone. It was clearly a part of the mountain they'd left intact, building their homes and streets around it, and what was left was a flinty, sharp-edged protrusion of grey and black rock. It was shaped a little like an arrow head, and here and there narrow windows like scars flickered with guttering flames. Two werkens stood by the entrance, strange winnowed creatures with long, jagged heads and what appeared to be huge iron swords by their sides. Two human guards stood next to them, nodding briefly to Bors as they passed.

Inside they were immediately met by a great sweeping staircase that led up to a cavernous hall. Shadowy chambers branched off to all sides, lit with smoking oil lamps. Frith found himself looking everywhere at once, very aware that numerous werkens could be hiding in this dark, stony place. On his shoulder Gwiddion squawked quietly into his ear.

'Quite a place you have here,' said Wydrin, and her voice sounded strange and small in the huge space. In the middle of the hall the floor rose up to form a great empty plinth, and in front of it stood a woman with red-brown skin and long black hair loose over her shoulders. She wore a mixture of leather and furs, a red-beaded necklace at her throat, and she watched them carefully as they approached. Her mouth was a thin slash below her nose and the corners turned down just before she greeted them.

'Thank you, Bors,' she said. Her voice was low and clipped at the edges. 'You may go.'

Bors didn't move immediately. He was looking around at the chambers above them. 'Is my sister here?'

'Nuava is assisting me.' As if answering a summons, a young woman appeared from one of the shadowy tunnels to their left. She shared the same warm skin as her brother and aunt, but her hair was a mass of unruly dark curls, tamed beneath a pale blue scarf. She had an armful of heavy books and she eyed the newcomers warily.

'She is shut up in here with you all the time,' said Bors. He shifted from foot to foot, as though he wasn't as sure of himself as his words suggested. 'It's not healthy. I want her to come out with me, just for a few hours. The snows are clearing and . . .'

'Nuava is *assisting* me,' repeated Tamlyn Nox.

'Nuava is becoming you, you mean,' Bors took a step forward, not looking at his sister. 'Teaching her your witch-ways, keeping her in the dark until—'

'I'm sorry, but can you have your family disagreements another time?' said Frith. His voice rang out in the empty hall. 'I believe you have a job for us?'

34

Tamlyn Nox shot Bors a look and the young man retreated, walking back down the steps without a single glance back. Nuava put the heavy books she was carrying down onto the plinth, the tops of her cheeks flushed faintly pink.

'Indeed.' Tamlyn nodded to them. 'Lord Frith, your companions. I wish to employ you to retrieve an item that was stolen from us.'

'That sounds straightforward enough,' said Wydrin. She padded over to the plinth and ran a hand over the smooth top. 'First, what is it? And second, do you know who took it?' She cleared her throat. 'And third, how much are we getting paid?'

Tamlyn Nox frowned. 'The item that was stolen was the Heart-Stone, Skaldshollow's most precious artefact. It was kept here, on that very plinth you are currently rubbing your greasy fingers over.'

'Big plinth for a stone,' said Wydrin, taking her hand away.

'It was a big stone,' said Nuava, speaking for the first time. She picked up one of the books and turned to a page that showed a drawing of the room they stood in. The illustration showed the plinth in great detail, and on it stood a huge green crystal, squarish and half as tall as a man. 'The Heart-Stone is actually smaller than this drawing suggests.' Her voice was quiet, scholarly. She did not meet their eyes as she spoke. 'This illustration was made over fifty years ago, and since then the stone has dwindled.'

'By the Graces, though, that's still a big damn lump of rock,' said Wydrin. 'Your thieves just walked out of here with it stuffed up their jerkins?'

Tamlyn Nox glowered at her. 'It was stolen by the Narhl, a tribe of –' her face twisted as though tasting something bitter – 'a tribe of people from beyond the northern mountain pass. We have long been enemies.'

'Why would they take it?' asked Sebastian. The big knight had been strangely quiet, watching the proceedings without comment.

'Why?' Tamlyn snapped. 'The Heart-Stone is the centre of Skaldshollow, the foundation of our lives, of our every success. You have seen the werkens? The Heart-Stone wakens them for us, and Skaldshollow prospers. Without it, we are crippled, limited to the werkens we have already constructed. To see us fail . . .' She touched the beaded necklace at her throat. For the first time, Frith noticed that, like Bors, she had a piece of green rock embedded into the palm of each hand, and two more pieces set into the lobes of her ears. 'To see us fail is the only goal of the Narhl.'

Nuava pulled another book from the plinth and flicked through the pages. Almost absently she added, 'The Narhl believe the mountains to be sacred, and that the Heart-Stone is truly the physical heart of a great mountain spirit. They object to us chipping bits of it off.'

'Superstitious nonsense,' snapped Tamlyn. She shot Nuava a dark look. 'The Heart-Stone is pure Edeian, that is all.'

But Sebastian's long face was stern now. 'How do you know it is not the heart of the mountain? How do you know you are not doing harm?'

Tamlyn scowled. 'When I employed the Black Feather Three, I did not expect superstitious objections. I expected action.'

'And you'll get plenty of that, don't you worry,' said Wydrin hurriedly. She fingered the pages of one of Nuava's books. 'These Narhl – you believe they've taken this Heart-Stone back to their own settlement?'

Nuava passed her a map. 'They live beyond the treacherous mountain pass known as the Crippler, in a fortress called the Frozen Steps. This is where they have taken the stone.'

'Why do you not retrieve it yourselves?' asked Frith. He saw Wydrin glare at him from out the corner of his eye and ignored it. 'These werkens of yours seem formidable. Can you not take a force of these creatures and storm the fortress?'

Tamlyn Nox snorted. 'Do you not think we would have done that if we could?'

Nuava cleared her throat. She briefly met their eyes before looking back down at her books. 'The pass is called the Crippler for a reason. It is so narrow that men and women must walk it single-file, and therefore much too narrow for a force of werkens. The Frozen Steps itself is made of sheer ice, impossible for a werken to scale. The Narhl have an interesting relationship with ice.'

'But you three,' Tamlyn came over to them, her dark eyes narrowed, 'if the stories are true, you will have the talents necessary to get past their defences.'

36

Frith nodded, thinking of the boiling flames that were only a moment's thought from his fingers. 'That shouldn't be a problem.'

'Good. Then we have an agreement.' Tamlyn nodded shortly. 'How soon can you leave?'

'We'll need to rest up after the journey we've just made,' said Wydrin. 'We'll want to prepare, and get some supplies together as well.'

'Very well.' Tamlyn gestured to her niece. 'We have rooms prepared for you. Bors will show you where they are.' With that she left, marching across the enormous hall without looking back. Nuava gathered up the books and hurried to one of the chambers, casting a curious last look at them before she vanished from sight.

Tamlyn moved through the dark corridors of the Tower of Waking with her eyes on the polished floor, letting her familiarity with its stones guide her to her destination. She was troubled.

First, she did not know what to make of the Black Feather Three. If the stories were true, then they had done the impossible and defeated one of the old gods, and the retrieval of one simple rock should present no serious difficulty. But bringing strangers here to solve their own problems felt like a misstep, whatever the Prophet said. Worse than that, it felt like cowardice.

And then there was the Prophet herself, of course.

She was working her way gradually upwards now, following flights of dark uneven steps, lit here and there with guttering candles. The Prophet had insisted on being ensconced in the highest room in the tower, so that she might look out across the mountains.

Thinking of the Prophet, Tamlyn felt a thick rope of worry twist in her stomach, and she swallowed it down. Whatever the Prophet was, she'd been right about everything so far. Whatever she was, she had great wisdom, beyond even that of an Edeian Crafter.

Tamlyn paused outside the room, taking a few steadying breaths. For some reason she had rushed the last part of the way and now she almost felt giddy. She put her hand up to knock when a soft, young voice called from within.

'Come in, Tamlyn dear.'

Inside, the room was cosy, or as cosy as any room in the Tower of Waking ever got. The floor was covered in thick, colourful rugs, and huge tapestries covered the bare rock walls. Braziers were dotted here and there, and oil lamps covered several small tables; the Prophet came from a land of endless sun and warm breezes, and they had endeavoured to make the room as comfortable as possible for her. In the middle of the room was an enormous four-poster bed, draped in several layers of thick, white gauze. Tamlyn could just make out the slim figure of the Prophet beyond the curtains, a ghostly shape sitting cross-legged on the bed.

'They're here, then.'

Tamlyn cleared her throat and held her hands clasped behind her back. She never felt comfortable in the Prophet's room. It was probably the heat.

'Yes. They are just as you described. The woman seems eager enough. The lord is cautious, and the knight is downright reluctant.'

The shadowy figure rocked back and forth slightly, chuckling. 'Of course, of course. The Black Feather Three, indeed. They are exactly who you need, Tamlyn Nox, Mistress Crafter.'

Tamlyn shifted her weight, feeling the first trickle of sweat run down her back. Had there been a hint of derision in the Prophet's voice?

'I hope you are right. Without the Heart-Stone—'

'Yes, yes, without your precious stone your world will end; it is all very tragic. Tell me, do they look well?'

Tamlyn blinked. 'I . . . they look well enough to me.'

'And the knight?'

Tamlyn shrugged, unsure if the Prophet could see such a movement through her curtains. 'He had a scar on his face and he looks tired, but they have journeyed from far Crosshaven, they are bound to be weary.' She bit down on her own impatience. 'Either way, he looks as strong as an ox.'

'Or a werken, would you say?' asked the Prophet, a playful note in her voice.

'I suppose I would say that,' said Tamlyn. 'They will be leaving once they have their supplies gathered, and Nuava has made copies of all the maps for them. I must go and check their supplies over myself.'

'Oh, just one thing, Tamlyn, my dear.'

Tamlyn paused, half turned towards the door. 'What is it?'

'Show them the tomb, won't you? Before they go.' The Prophet scooted over, bringing her face closer to the curtains. It was possible now to make out the round shape of her head, the darker shadows where her mouth and eyes were. 'Take them down there, give them a tour.'

Tamlyn scowled and touched the beads at her throat. 'Why should I do that? I mean, why would you have me do that?'

The Prophet made a gesture, lost behind the curtain. 'Oh, I think they'll enjoy it. This lord is a mage himself, after all, and I think he'll be curious to see such a thing, don't you? Really, Tamlyn, you must learn how to be properly hospitable to your guests.'

Tamlyn glanced around at the lavish room. The smell of smoke from the braziers was tickling the back of her throat. 'As you wish.'

6

Siano watched the man come into the room, all shuffling and
unaware. He paused, the light from the dingy oil lamp painting
a yellow circle on his bald head.

He can smell it somehow, thought Siano, suddenly certain. *He
can smell the death in the room.*

But the older man simply took a ragged bundle from the table
– wax and string, curls of treated paper for messages – and left,
never coming over to the dark corner where Siano crouched, her
fingers still pressed deeply into the throat of the man's son.

I am too jumpy, mused Siano. She turned the head gently in
her hands, listening to the little crunching noises that signified a
broken neck. *I'm looking for difficulties where there are none.
But it is best to be cautious.*

Caution was an essential lesson at the House of Patience.

Silently she laid the body of the younger man down on the
floor, making sure it lay deep in the shadows, and quickly opened
a vein with her smallest knife, filling the slim glass vial in seconds.
When she was done, she put out the oil lamp before moving over
to the open door. It was late in the morning, the sky a pale blue,
and most of this family were already dead. She had killed the
aunt on her way up the hill, a sturdy woman with bird shit on
her shawl and a face crinkled from years of living in this sun-
soaked tower. The old woman had caught sight of the flicker of
shadow as Siano danced out behind her but had turned too late,
and the long, thin knife had threaded up through her back, piercing

her heart. The bags of potatoes and leeks she'd been carrying home for that night's dinner had slipped from her fingers, and Siano had caught her and dragged her off the road, the only sound the scrape of her boot heels on the stones.

She listened at the doorway. She could hear the birds cooing and chirping in their chamber at the top of the spindly tower, and the soft music of the flute-shaped weather vanes that sprouted all over like strange bronze plants. She could also hear the old man's footsteps as he made his way up the spiralling outer staircase, no doubt on his way to attach a message to one of the birds and send it on its way. Siano reached within her belt and removed a shining silver wire suspended between two pegs and, holding it comfortably in both hands, made her way swiftly up the steps behind him.

Only two more to go, and it was hardly midday. Siano allowed herself a moment of pride. The client had asked that the entire family be killed quickly and without fuss, and Siano was performing as expected: perfectly, in other words.

Still, the thought of that severed head and, more specifically, the voice that came from it, made her uneasy, so she pushed it from her mind and refocussed. No distractions, no speculation. Only patience.

The aviary at the top of the tower came in sight so Siano slowed, watching the entrance. She moved up to the top step, her soft boots making no sound at all on the worn wood, and watched as the father of the family moved unconcernedly around the elaborate clay coops, muttering to himself. It was colder up here, and the wind was erratic, so Siano kept especially still, aware that a sound at the wrong moment could easily reach the man on the changeable air. She touched her hand to her belt where the vials were securely attached, each wrapped in its own slip of velvet to stop it clinking against its neighbour.

The old man bent to one of the coops and came up with a bird in his hands. Siano was watching him attach a message to its leg when a pair of birds returned to the aviary, causing a flurry of squawking and feathers.

Siano took half a step backwards, more from the sudden waft of bird shit stench than any real alarm, and the old man saw her.

41

'Who are you?' The old man let go of the bird and it flapped to his feet. Siano pursed her lips. She hadn't been trained to talk to the victims.

'I come from the House of Patience.' She cleared her throat. 'You—'

'If you want to send a message, you need to pay up below like everyone else. You don't come traipsing up here, disturbing my birds.' The man nodded, a dismissive gesture. 'My boy is below, he'll take your coin.'

Your boy is dead and boneless in the dirt, thought Siano. Something in her face or her stance must have given her away, because suddenly the old man looked worried, his skin turning grey almost as Siano watched. Or perhaps he'd seen the wire in Siano's hands.

'Here, who are you?' He backed off, scattering birds. 'You can't just come up here.'

The wire was really a weapon of surprise, a lethal knot round the neck when the victim was looking elsewhere. Siano didn't want to grapple with the old man; there was bird shit on his shirt, and it would ruin her fine black velvet. She tucked the wire away, making sure the old man saw her do it.

'Many apologies, sir. I come from the House of Patience, and it is my honour to attend you today.'

'House of Patience? Never 'eard of it.' The old man pursed his lips, but the look of fright on his grey face had been replaced with confusion. 'What are you talking about?'

Inside her jacket pocket Siano's fingers closed around the handle of her throwing knife, and this time the old man really did sense something because suddenly he was off, running for the archway on the far side of the aviary. Siano's arm moved of its own accord and the knife followed him, a deadly silver streak that caught the old man dead in the centre of his wrinkled neck just as he made it to the stairwell. Siano saw the blood fly from his throat in a red shout, so bright against the blue sky, and then the old man was tipping over the side. A brief scramble against the stone and he was gone.

Messier than I would have liked, thought Siano. *And now I will have to go and collect my knife.*

She walked through the aviary, feeling the half-mad gaze of a hundred birds settle on her back. She had just reached the balcony and was peering over the side to see where the old bastard had landed when someone started shrieking from below. It was a young woman, arms held stiffly to her sides, her mouth wide with shock. She'd obviously just seen the man fall, may even have seen the blood in the air when the knife took him, and she was clearly his daughter; the last name on this particular list.

'One more to go,' muttered Siano. She took a serrated disc of metal from an inner pocket and curled her wrist. 'It's almost too easy.'

7

'I thought, somehow, that they'd put us up in that big tower. I mean, aren't we visiting dignitaries or something?' Wydrin poured a shot from the dark bottle on the table. The scent of alcohol rising from the glass was enough to make her blink rapidly. 'Not that I mind too much. That place looked draughtier than a whore's best knickers.'

Sebastian snorted with laughter. 'Tell me again when we've actually spent a night in these rooms. I think there was ice in my fireplace.'

The inn was at the far north of the settlement and at the top of a winding, stair-pocked hill, all carved directly from the mountain. It was called, somewhat ominously, The Last Breath Inn, although Bors had assured them that this was in reference to how this unsheltered corner of Skaldshollow caught the winds on certain nights. Cold as death itself, he'd said, and as darkness fell it was living up to its name

'The princeling won't be pleased,' said Wydrin archly. 'He's probably back at the tower now, demanding a better suite of rooms for his griffin.'

Sebastian clinked his cup against hers. 'That's hardly fair, Wyd. We've stayed in worse places in the last few months and Frith has not made a single complaint.'

As if the words had summoned him, Lord Frith came in through the back door, weaving around the tables, a powdering of snow across the shoulders of his black cloak. His limp was very slight now, but Wydrin could still see how carefully he moved.

Sebastian cleared his throat and stood up. 'I'm going to go get the fire started in that room. It's going to be a while before it warms up.'

'If it's not warm enough by the time I make it up there, I'm setting fire to the whole place.'

Frith seated himself next to her as Sebastian left. There were a few moments of icy silence which Wydrin used to down another shot of the fiery drink.

'They call it grut,' she said eventually, gesturing at the bottle. 'I think that probably describes the flavour and its effect on your insides afterwards. It warms you up some, though.'

Frith nodded. He poured himself a glass and took a sip. When he'd finished coughing, Wydrin gestured to the barkeep for another bottle.

'What do you reckon to this job, then?' She pulled the cork from the new bottle and tried not to wince when the fumes hit her. 'I'm not sure I trust this Tamlyn Nox. Too sour by half, and we've hardly had time to upset her yet.'

'She is holding something back,' said Frith. 'This may turn out to be a complicated job, as you call it.'

'And you are keen for it to be over.'

For a few moments the young lord didn't say anything at all. Wydrin concentrated on pouring another pair of shots for them both.

'The three of us have had some extraordinary adventures since Baneswatch,' he said eventually. 'We've achieved much.'

'We've caused some trouble, even done some good,' agreed Wydrin, not looking at him. 'The Black Feather Three are the most infamous swords for hire across Crosshaven and the Horns.' She waved a hand vaguely at him. 'Or magic for hire, whatever. People are falling over themselves to give us work. You know, we have a letter from the Empress of Leonnosis, offering us as much gold as we can carry away just to go and talk to her. She wants to hear the stories first-hand, you see. We're at the very height of our game, Frith.' She swallowed, the grut burning in her throat like a hot coal.

'This is a great opportunity for the Blackwood, one I have to consider. It was what my father wanted, and I have certain responsibilities.'

45

'Responsibilities? What about your responsibility to us?'

'You and Sebastian will be fine. And when the brood army are ready, there will be none to match you. The Black Feather Three will still be infamous.'

'What is left of the brood army.' Wydrin shook her head. 'You know what happened as well as I do.' She chucked back another shot, and struck the glass on the tabletop. 'The whole thing is a bloody mess. Besides which, people won't call us the Black Feather Three any more, will they? There'll only be two of us, for a start, and you'll be taking Gwiddion with you.'

She looked up at him then, and saw that those grey eyes – eyes that she had seen brighten over the months as they'd adventured their way around Ede – were cold again.

'I have a place in this life,' he said. 'And I have left it empty too long. I cannot spend for ever gallivanting around with you and Sebastian. I have to be responsible. Of course, I shouldn't have expected you to understand that.'

'That wasn't even your first mistake.' Wydrin downed the last shot and stood up, gathering her furred cloak.

'Where are you going?' Frith glared up at her, his jaw clenched.

'Bors promised to show me some of these werkens, the ones that haven't been joined to anyone yet. I've a mind to ride one myself.'

'What for?'

'Because I'm curious. Because it looks like fun.' Wydrin pulled her hood low over her face. 'Neither of which is very responsible, obviously, but I suspect you've come to know that about me by now.'

By the time Wydrin had stomped her way over to the Tower of Waking the hot fury that had been keeping her warm had petered out, and instead she felt tired and, worse, completely sober. A bitter wind gusted against her all the way, pushing stinging handfuls of ice crystals into her face, so that when finally she stood beneath the flinty edifice, she almost didn't see Bors, who loped towards her out of the dark.

'There you are! Thought you'd decided to stay in the warmth of the inn.'

'Ah, it wasn't that cosy, really.' Wydrin pulled her cloak closer over her shoulders. 'Please tell me these werkens are inside somewhere?'

Bors grinned. 'Follow me.'

They circled around the back of the Tower of Waking until they came to another pair of giant werkens, these two mounted with riders, standing in the middle of a wide, paved area. Bors hailed them and, as one, the enormous stone giants leaned down with huge granite fists and pulled on a pair of iron handles set directly into the ground. In the dark and the snow Wydrin hadn't seen the door at all, and now there was a set of wide stone steps leading down, apparently directly underneath the Tower of Waking itself. Inside, the staircase was lit with tall thin oil lamps, throwing jagged shadows across the rough walls. Bors led her down, Wydrin casting an uneasy look back over her shoulder.

'Those doors can only be opened by a werken,' said Bors. 'Too heavy for anything else to lift, you see. What we keep down here is very valuable indeed.'

The stairs eventually levelled out into a long, low room. The floor was strewn with tools – hammers, chisels, other instruments Wydrin couldn't name – and the sides of the room were divided into deep alcoves, with each alcove housing an inert werken.

Wydrin paused by the first one. It stood on two legs, and was roughly human in shape although its arms were much too long. There was space on its shoulders for two riders to sit, and ripples of Edeian like green crystal covered it as though it wore its veins on the outside. It had no face as such, save for two faintly glowing pits that served as eyes, and it was covered all over with intricate spiral patterns. These carvings were at their thickest at the joints, the places where rock met rock.

'And this thing is awake now?'

'Well, they're not awake, as such, but yes.' Bors stood by her side. 'You see how the eyes glow? This one has already had its piece of Heart-Stone inserted into the head cavity. Now the corresponding piece waits for a rider to take it, to become joined to this werken. We keep the pieces of Heart-Stone that await riders in a strongbox. Tamlyn has the only key.'

Wydrin frowned. She was sure she could feel the thing watching her. 'And what does it do until then? It just stands here, waiting? Not doing anything?'

Bors chuckled. 'Of course. As I said before, the werkens have a semblance of life, but it is not real. Without their riders, the werkens are still pieces of rock. Pieces of rock with potential.'

'It's beautiful,' she said. 'Strange, but beautiful.'

They walked on down the row. In the next partition was a werken shaped like an enormous bear, its bulky head low to the ground. On its back was a tree trunk, sharpened to a point.

'It took Tamlyn a while to give up on her plan to assault the Narhl directly,' he explained. 'It was thought we could carry battering rams, or even cauldrons full of boiling oil, but the logistics of it were a nightmare.' He cleared his throat. 'I put forward a few designs myself, but Tamlyn rejected them all.'

'Does she make all of them?' Wydrin paused in front of another stone creature, looking into its glowing green eyes.

'She has a small team that assist her with the construction, but the designs are all hers. It is a gift, to be able to craft the Edeian so. I fear I do not have it.' He shrugged, looking slightly bashful. 'When I was younger I thought that if I studied hard enough I would eventually be able to use the Edeian in the rock the way she does. My sister has more of an understanding.'

'I had a friend who could do that,' said Wydrin suddenly, thinking of Holley's careworn face and her callused fingers. When Bors raised his eyebrows she continued. 'She made magical glass, from the Edeian in the ground. The glass could show you secrets, and other things.' Unbidden she remembered the Children of the Fog, dancing towards her with their identical grins, bathed in blue light.

'She would have been a crafter, like Tamlyn, then. There are some people who can feel the Edeian better than others, and can shape it. Here, though, is one of Tamlyn's very few mistakes.'

They had stopped in front of the last chamber on the left-hand side. Inside it was a much smaller werken, wolf-shaped and about the size of a pony. Its long, lupine head was bowed to the ground, its snout brushing the floor. Green eyes glared balefully in the shadows. Around each leg were thick iron cuffs, each chained to the stone wall. Carvings swirled along its long flanks in a series of waves.

'What's wrong with it?' Wydrin knelt in front of it and slid a hand over its smooth snout. It was cold to the touch.

'Even Tamlyn isn't sure, but it moves without a rider. Not all the time, but every now and then it will shudder, jerk around. It does not stand and wait silently like the rest of the werkens.' He shrugged. 'A flaw in the Edeian, perhaps, something not quite right in the design. It is unlikely it will ever be joined to a rider now, though, even when these few we have left have been assigned. Eventually, we will break it down into its component pieces again so that it can be used for something else.'

'Is it dangerous?'

'Not as such, although you do not want one of these blundering about unsupervised.' He grinned at her. 'You wouldn't believe how many broken feet we have to deal with, and that's just from riders in training. No, not dangerous as such, just useless.'

Wydrin straightened up. 'Give him to me, then.'

Bors looked at her. 'What?'

'If he's useless, and he'll never be part of your war-werken army, then give him to me.'

Bors shook his head, although more in confusion than denial. 'No one outside of Skaldshollow has ever been joined. And even in pieces, it is valuable.'

'Then consider it my payment for this job.' She smiled at him and laid a hand on his arm. 'I have some sympathy for broken outsiders, and I want to ride a werken. It seems a shame to leave him here, chained up in the dark.'

Bors sighed, but she kept her hand on his arm and she could see him considering it.

'I'll talk to my aunt in the morning,' he said eventually. 'But I doubt she will be happy about this.'

8

At first Sebastian brushed it off as exhaustion, or his body's own adjustments to the thinner air, but the further out of Skaldshollow they travelled, the more uneasy he felt.

He and Frith followed the diminutive figure of Nuava, her wild curls hidden under a grey rabbit-fur hat. They were walking one of the many paths out of the city that led up the towering mountain behind it, and they had passed the enormous quarry some time back, gaping off to their right like a wound. Sebastian had caught sight of the stony forms of the werkens, reflecting the bright morning sun; they looked like the bones of the mountain come to life. It was a clear day, the sky so blue that it was almost too bright to look at. Normally Sebastian would have been comforted by the resemblance to his home in Ynnsmouth, but there was no longer any comfort to be found in that memory.

'I'm not sure this couldn't have waited until after we retrieve the Heart-Stone,' he said, hating the slightly petulant tone in his own voice.

Frith shook his head. The young lord had thrown back his hood and in the strong sunshine his hair blazed as white as the snows.

'To visit the tomb of a mage? I could hardly pass up such an opportunity. Besides which, Wydrin isn't ready to leave.' His mouth turned down at the corners. 'She has been off with that Bors all morning.'

Ahead of them, Nuava glanced hesitantly over her shoulder.

50

'My brother seems to think she is interested in becoming joined to a werken.'

'Joined to one?' Frith scowled. 'By all the gods, why would she want to do that?'

Sebastian laughed shortly. 'I don't know, that sounds rather like Wydrin to me. You wouldn't believe the number of tattoos I've talked her out of. How much further do we have to go, Nuava?'

'Not much further.'

To one side the path branched off to a small plateau, sheltered by a clutch of thick pine trees, bristling with dark green needles. The tops were dusted with snow. Nuava led them between the trees.

'This seems a strange place for a tomb,' said Sebastian. As they moved through the trees a cold hand walked its way up his spine. 'A strange, lonely place.'

'The story of Joah Cirrus is a strange one,' answered Nuava. 'You do not know it?'

'I recognise the name,' broke in Frith quickly. 'From the histories of the mage wars. An important name, I remember, but I must confess I know no more.'

'An important name . . .' mused Nuava. 'He was born with the name Joah Cirrus, later to be known as Joah Lightbringer, and eventually, Joah Demonsworn. According to the books I have studied, he was widely considered to be the greatest mage of them all, able to command the mages' powers with greater skill than anyone who came before him, and he was able to craft the Edeian too, a rare skill in a mage. A rare skill in a man, in fact.'

Sebastian caught Frith's eyes and he shrugged ever so slightly. They'd passed through the trees now. In front of them was a small clearing fringed with pine trees, and at its heart was a pool of water, as deep a blue as the sky. Dried pine needles danced on its surface.

'Should that not be frozen?'

'It must be a natural hot spring,' said Frith dismissively. 'Unusual but not unknown.'

'The final resting place of Joah Demonsworn shall never know cold,' answered Nuava, as though she were quoting from something.

Now that Sebastian looked, there were no snows around the pool; in fact, he could see grass around its edge, thick and green as if they stood in a summer's valley.

'The Joah I am thinking of,' said Frith as they neared the pool, 'was not thought of fondly.'

'No,' agreed Nuava, pulling her hat down to hang around her neck by its ties. It did feel a little warmer by the pool. 'Not thought of fondly at all. Great is not always the same as good, I suppose.' She coughed into her hand. Sebastian suspected she did not often spend so long talking to other people. 'Joah was the greatest mage Ede had ever known, but he quickly grew tired of the language and knowledge of the gods. Instead he turned to other, less savoury sources.'

Sebastian's throat grew tight. They were almost at the edge of the pool now, and for some reason he was afraid to look on its surface. He fought the urge to hang back.

'Other sources?'

'A demon,' said Nuava shortly.

And there it was below them, the final resting place of Joah Cirrus, Joah Lightbringer, Joah Demonsworn, greatest of all mages. The pool was as clear as glass, and Sebastian could see right down to the shadowy bottom. Rock had been torn from the mountain by some unknowable force, leaving huge grooves in the bedrock, and in the centre was an elaborate sarcophagus carved from what looked like black marble. There were words scored in silver on the lid, words in the language of the mages now known only by the Regnisse Concordance of Relios, and Lord Frith himself. In the very centre was carved a great snarling face with fangs and mad rolling eyes, like a monstrous rabid dog.

'It is extraordinary,' said Frith. The young lord crouched down and peered closely at the clear water, no doubt trying to read the words written on the coffin. 'This must be a thousand years old at least. How is it still here? Surely it would have been looted a long time ago.'

Nuava gestured to the pool. 'You can try putting your hand in the water if you wish, Lord Frith.'

He glanced up at her, wary, before dipping the very ends of his fingers into the pool.

Instantly, the water erupted into a boiling fury, churning white and steaming. Frith snatched his hand away and stood up.

'We believe there are other spells on the tomb,' said Nuava quietly. The waters were already settling down. 'But that one has always sufficed.'

'What do you know about it? This demon?' asked Sebastian. He couldn't drag his eyes from the snarling dog face on the black lid. 'What happened to Joah?'

Nuava glanced up at him. She was enjoying this chance to talk about her studies, he realised.

'Anyone in Skaldshollow could tell you, it is a famous story here. Joah and the demon conspired together for many years and created many terrible works. Terrible, and extraordinary. Joah crafted new words and new spells, singlehandedly increasing the knowledge of the mages tenfold. They say that he and the demon . . . consorted with each other.' Nuava cleared her throat, blushing slightly. 'He grew too powerful, the costs too high.' She stood up abruptly. 'He was killed by the mage Xinian the Battleborn, and buried here.'

Sebastian took a few steps back. He wanted to leave this place. Frith, however, seemed eager to explore. He prowled the edge of the pool, careful not to disturb the water again.

'But why? They have gone to a great deal of effort here – the tomb, the spells – when by all accounts he was a villain, an ally of demons. Surely his body would have been discarded or burnt. And yet they have given him a lavish resting place.'

Nuava looked concerned, as though that part didn't make sense to her either. 'He may have been terrible, but he was still one of their own. From some of the accounts I have read, it seems that many of the mages blamed the demon more than Joah. He was a genius, but he was fragile. The demon overwhelmed him, flowed in through the cracks.' She brightened. 'I have several texts about it in the Waking library, if you would like to see them?'

Frith nodded. 'That would be most kind. It is extraordinary to see such evidence of the mages. Even in Whittenfarne, there was . . .' He paused. 'There was nothing of interest in Whittenfarne. Perhaps I could—'

'Is there anything else to see here?' asked Sebastian. He saw

Frith glance at him in surprise, but he kept his eyes on Nuava. Her words were echoing around his head: *The demon over-whelmed him, flowed in through the cracks.* 'I think we have wasted enough of the morning.'

Nuava pulled her hat back onto her head. 'Of course. If we don't get the Heart-Stone back soon my aunt will do something extreme.'

'And speaking of which,' Frith straightened up, looking away from the pool, 'we should probably check on our mutual colleague.'

Wydrin looked uneasily at the contraption as Bors fiddled with the inner workings; tightening a bolt here, loosening a cog there. He seemed anxious that this should go well – Wydrin wasn't sure if that was reassuring or unnerving.

If I'm making a list of rash things I've done in my life, she thought, flexing the fingers of her left hand, *whereabouts does this come? It's got to be in the top five, at least. Somewhere between jumping off the top of the Queen's Tower with Frith, and claiming I could dive for pearls off the Bararian coast.*

They were in the courtyard of the Tower of Waking. Tamlyn Nox herself stood off to one side, her arms crossed over her chest and her expression unimpressed. Wydrin and Bors were standing on a wide stone dais, next to a steel confusion of clockwork and globs of black oil. There was what looked like a giant steel glove on the top, and this was what Bors was motioning her to put her hand into.

'So I stick my hand in there,' Wydrin asked, still not quite doing it; her palms were itching, 'and that big spiky thing comes down?'

There was a prong stationed above the glove, taut like a scorpion's tail, and on its point was a shard of bright green crystal. It had been sharpened until it glittered under the sunlight. The steel glove, lying palm-up, had a hole in the centre about the size of a large coin.

'That's right,' said Bors. The werken, the wolf-shaped one that had been chained beneath the Tower of Waking, had been brought out to sit on the cobbles next to him. 'Don't worry, it's not actually as painful as it looks. The Edeian has special qualities, you see.

There will be a moment of, uh, discomfort, but the rock wants to be a part of something else. It will want to bond with you.'

Wydrin cleared her throat. 'And you clean this thing regularly, do you?'

'Honestly, Wydrin, it will be fine. I've done it twice.' He grinned at her, and she smiled back. 'Just put your hand into the gauntlet and I'll do the final measurements.'

'Are you sure you wish to go through with this, Wydrin Threefellows?' said Tamlyn, her voice coldly amused. 'Not everyone can handle the joining. And you are no Skald.'

Wydrin forced herself to look away from the contraption and meet Tamlyn's gaze. 'Oh, it looks fairly straightforward. Are you sure you want an outsider playing with your toys?'

Tamlyn Nox shrugged one shoulder. 'No Skald will lower themselves to be joined to a defective werken, so you are welcome to it, particularly if it saves me the coin you were promised. Once you are joined, though, you will go outside the city walls to practise.' The corner of her mouth twitched a bitter smile. 'We do not want you blundering around with our experienced riders.'

'Fair enough. Can't be worse than riding a horse, can it?' Wydrin turned back to Bors, and whispered, 'I'm actually terrible at riding horses.'

He grinned at her. 'You'll be fine. Are you ready?'

She nodded once and, taking a deep breath, pushed her left hand inside the metal gauntlet, splaying out her fingers to fit into the steel tubes. Her palm was turned up, and she could see the small circle of her own pale skin through the aperture. What if this damaged her hand permanently? She needed both hands in her line of work. She opened her mouth to ask Bors about this, when a familiar voice shouted from the edge of the courtyard.

'This is worse than that piercing you wanted to get in Traguard. That at least didn't have such large accessories!'

She turned awkwardly to see Sebastian and Frith walking towards her. She waved at them with her free hand. 'Seb, you were just jealous because the guy said you didn't have the ears for it. Where have you two been?'

Frith said nothing, and Sebastian looked uncomfortable.

'Just exploring the local history. Are you really going to go through with this?'

'Sure, why not?' Wydrin turned back to Bors, hoping that they couldn't see the thin sheen of sweat on her forehead. 'It'll be fun. Frith will have his griffin, I'll have my . . . stone beast. Seb, we can get you some sort of big horse, one with wild eyes and an untameable spirit, like a knight should have, that kind of thing.'

'I'm going to check on our supplies,' said Frith, already turning away. 'Come and find me when you're finished with this foolishness.'

Wydrin watched him go, narrowing her eyes at his back. Sebastian came over to the dais, an expression of worry on his face she'd seen many times before. Again she thought of the pearl-diving incident.

'Really, Wydrin,' he said in a low voice. 'Are you certain this is a good idea? No one will think any less of you if you back out.'

'No,' she said, more firmly now. 'I want to know what it's like. Besides which, I'm hardly the first to be joined to a werken. Are you ready yet, Bors?'

The young man nodded, wiping oily fingers on his coat. 'The mechanism is loaded.'

'Let's do it,' she replied, bracing herself.

Bors checked the shard of Edeian once more, and wrapped his hands around a big metal lever. 'You may feel some dizziness at first,' he said, and he yanked the lever down.

The prong pounced, the whole contraption wobbling with the violence of it, and the shard of Edeian stabbed into Wydrin's unprotected palm. She yelped – the pain was brilliant, ice-white like a snapping bone – and instinctively yanked her hand out of the steel glove, grazing her fingers on the metal edges. She curled her hand into her chest, feeling the pain throb down through her wrist to her arm. Was there blood? There must be blood.

'Hurts like a pissing bastard!' she gasped.

And then the pain softened. The jagged shape of the crystal shard in her palm seemed to melt somehow, and instead her hand felt very cold, like she was resting it in a mound of snow. She felt a hand on her shoulder and knew it was Sebastian, so she leaned against it and closed her eyes, following the feeling of the cold down into the dark. There was a sense of her awareness leaking away, a sense of part of herself being briefly severed. She opened her eyes and looked into the glowing green eyes of the werken. 'Ye gods and little fishes,' she whispered.

'Wydrin, are you all right?'

Sebastian was standing over her; at some point in the last few minutes she had dropped to her knees, and he had hold of her shoulders, shaking her slightly.

'She will recover in a moment or two,' said Bors. 'It's bound to be disorientating the first time.'

'I'm fine, I'm fine.' *Help me get up, you big idiot*, she thought, and suddenly a cold snout nosed under her arm, pushing her up. It was the werken. She glanced down at the shard of crystal in her hand; there was no blood, not a drop, and it glowed a faint green – the exact same shade as the eyes of the creature now pushing her to her feet. 'Whoa, good boy, good boy.'

'The connection appears to be solid,' said Bors hurriedly. 'People react to the joining in different ways.'

Wydrin patted the werken on its solid stone flank. There were shallow handholds cut into its side, so you could easily climb onto its back, and there were white scratches around its legs where the iron cuffs had been chipped off. She looked closely at the joins, trying to see how the thing was put together, but everything was smooth and unknowable. It was like looking at a house hanging in the sky; both utterly impossible and yet obviously heavy with reality. The carvings that swirled all over it, the spirals and the loops, made her think of the sea.

Can you hear me? The werken stood next to her, unmoving. *If you can hear me, lower your head.* The long lupine head moved downwards smoothly. Wydrin laughed.

'Are you making it do that?' asked Sebastian. He was looking at the werken like it might bite him. Which was ridiculous; the thing didn't even have a mouth.

Tamlyn Nox came over then, her dark eyes coldly amused. 'The first outsider to ride a werken. I hope you realise how greatly we are honouring you, Wydrin of Crosshaven.'

'You should sell these things, you know. You'd make a fortune at the Marrow Market.' In her head Wydrin told the werken to take a step backwards and it did, startling Sebastian. 'He needs a name. What do you reckon?'

Bors glanced uneasily at his aunt.

'It is not done for the werkens to be named,' said Tamlyn. Her lips were drawn into a thin line now, and she no longer looked amused.

'If he doesn't have a name, how will he know when I call him?'

'It is an *it*,' answered Tamlyn, biting down sharply on each word. 'Not a he. And it will come to you because you are joined to it.'

Wydrin slapped the creature's flank again. 'Rocky? Pebbles? Old Stone Face? Or,' she grinned, 'Cliff?'

Sebastian took her arm then, steering her away from Tamlyn and her nephew. 'This thing has a stable it can wait in, I imagine?' When Bors nodded, he spoke in a lower tone directly into Wydrin's ear. 'I think we're done winding up the locals now. Let's go and get a drink.'

9

Minh's favourite time of the day was the very early morning. As he made his way down to the spider enclosure in dawn's first light, the forest would be just waking up, and the relentless sun had yet to turn the air between the trees into a humid fog. He would listen to the birds and the shriller calls of the bats, a great invisible world beyond the leaves that he only caught the occasional glimpse of, and for a little while he would feel at peace. Later, Tunhi and Balje would be jabbering in his ear again, fretting over the price of silk and how much stock they would have for that day's market. They would pick over what he had collected and tut at it, running their fingers over the silvery strands and shaking their heads, regardless of the actual quality of the silk. Minh would stand and wait patiently for it to be over so he could retire to the dye shed and spend the rest of the day mixing powders and ignoring them.

Sisters. Who'd have them?

The webs were also at their most beautiful in the early morning light; dew sparkled on each strand like a string of diamonds.

'Ah, you have been doing fine work, my friends!'

The enclosure itself was a loosely constructed circular fence that surrounded seven tall trees. The spiders had industriously covered the entire area in huge, glistening webs. Minh stood for a moment admiring them, until a flurry of movement in the undergrowth caught his eye.

'Up early today, my friend?'

The spider was roughly the size of a dog, its abdomen covered in thick brown fur. Muscular purple legs churned up the grass as it came, and behind it were three more spiders, almost identical.

'You just want to see what's in my bag, don't you?'

Minh dropped his pack and pulled out a small hessian sack. Ignoring the smell, he reached inside and drew out a handful of dead baby rats, which he threw up into the collection of webs. Some missed entirely, but most hit the thick sticky strands and stuck there, sending vibrations into the trees. The spiders scurried back to their webs, and for a while Minh just stood and watched them work; maybe this was his favourite part of the morning after all. There was something oddly soothing about watching his spiders package up their food.

When they were done, he walked into the centre of the enclosure, taking care not to disturb the webs. Reaching into his pack again he took out a fat paper bundle shaped like an onion, and using his pocket flint, he lit the top and set it down on the ground. Once he was sure that the bundle was producing enough of the thick black smoke, he stepped hurriedly away and waited outside the fence until he heard the soft thump of spiders falling from their perches.

The smoke bomb burnt itself out soon after that and Minh ventured back in, the spider-spindle in one hand.

'Harvest time, my friends. Let's have your best, shall we? It would be good to see my sisters without sour faces for once.'

The first spider he came to lay on its back with all eight legs in the air. It was still alive, and if he looked closely he could see the shiny black eyes quivering, but for him to collect the silk, the spiders needed to be asleep. With the ease born of long practice, he pressed the spider-spindle to the spider's spiked rear end and caught the first glob of pearly web. Once that was caught it was simply a case of turning the spindle, and within a few moments there was a thick ribbon of silk shining on the wooden slats. He turned it sharply to one side, cutting the thread, and began to pick his way through the undergrowth, looking for more spiders. They weren't difficult to find.

Dimly, Minh was aware that some people might have been unnerved by his job. He had once visited friends in the distant city of Relios, a beautiful place of red brick and holy temples, and whilst staying in a friend's house he had watched with polite shock as the children shrieked over a tiny spider in their washbasin. It had been a minuscule, baby thing, no longer than his smallest finger, and Minh had picked it up with his hands and taken it outside. That night he had been jokingly declared the hero of the house and they'd drunk several glasses of wine in his honour.

Imagine if they found you in their washbasin, he thought as he rubbed one spider's furry belly. *They could not wash you into the gutter.*

When he was done he had six full spindles, and a quick glance told him that this was a fine harvest that should fetch them a great deal of coin. *Perhaps,* he reasoned, *if my sisters did something about their sour faces at market, we would make more money.*

He emerged from the trees so deep in thought that he almost didn't notice the solemn young woman standing there; she was a patch of shadows hidden amongst the tall trunks.

'Can I help you, miss?'

Minh was not alarmed, only curious. It wasn't unusual to come across travellers in the Silk Woods, although most foreigners were unnerved by the giant spiders and moths that made their homes here.

'This is most fascinating.' The young woman came out of the shadows, barely making a noise as she stepped through the undergrowth. 'These are your spiders?'

'Yes, miss.' Minh slipped the spindles back into his pack. 'My family have worked this part of the Silk Wood for seven generations.'

'And they do not wander off? Make webs elsewhere?' The young woman was by his side now, staring up into the trees where the spiders were beginning to climb back to their webs, still slightly sluggish.

'Oh no, we feed them well. Every other morning I come down here and I stock up their webs for them. They could, of course, survive elsewhere in the forest, but why would they move when their stomachs are always heavy with food? Besides, they know me, and I know them.'

'You said your family work this patch. What do the rest of the family do?'

Minh pressed his lips together, considering his next words. He did not wish to speak ill of his sisters to a complete stranger, but it was rather fine to stand here while the forest warmed up, chatting idly for once. Tunhi and Balje had no time for idle banter.

'I have two sisters, miss, and once we have woven the silks and dyed them, it is their job to take them to market. Mostly, I believe, they gossip while they are there and do very little selling, and then they have the cheek to blame our poverty on our spiders' silk.' He paused, and cleared his throat. 'If you would like to buy a sample of our wares – a silk scarf perhaps – then go to the market and ask around for Tunhi Ariani. She will give you a good deal, no doubt.' *Certainly she will*, thought Minh, *when she sees your face. You will be the prettiest woman at the market, and Tunhi can hardly resist that.*

'Thank you, I shall do that.'

For a moment Minh thought he was suffering a heart-storm, like that which had taken their father from them, but when he looked down he saw a short bone handle protruding from his chest. He was sure the young woman hadn't moved, and yet there it was. His hand fluttered up to it and he felt his own blood flooding through his vest, obscenely hot.

'Why?' He looked up into the young woman's face – there was no anger there, no murderous intent, only the same polite curiosity. 'I would have given . . . given you the silk, only . . .'

'Do not worry yourself.' The young woman put a hand on Minh's shoulder and gently pushed him to the ground. 'I am just an unexpected mishap. The predator in the woods.'

Minh sank to the floor, the smell of the earth and his own blood mingling in his nostrils. It was warm now, and would only grow warmer. He did not want to die in the heat.

Siano stood and watched the man bleed out into the dirt, before leaning down to force some of the blood into one of her vials.

'Your sisters next, then,' she said to the corpse. 'They should be easy enough to find. Thank you.'

There was a chittering from the trees ahead of her, and as she watched several of the huge fat spiders slid down from the webs on long rope-like threads. Their mandibles were flexing excitedly, and belatedly Siano wondered if they could smell the blood, and what they made of it. She took a few hurried steps backwards and drew a thin-bladed short sword from the concealed sheath on her back; a last resort weapon this, for when all hope of secrecy and striking in the dark were lost.

The first of the spiders reached the fence and skittered over it, perching on the top and watching Siano with glistening black eyes. It raised its front legs slowly, an unmistakably hostile gesture, and three of its fat brothers followed suit. Siano tensed, considering running for it rather than taking on four dog-sized spiders with one slim sword, but the idea of having these creatures at her back was even more unnerving.

There was a long, slow moment. Siano could hear birds in the trees, and there was sweat on her brow.

And then the first spider crawled down the fence and over to the body, where it began to tear long strips of flesh from the dead man's face. After a moment or so, the creature's brothers joined it and began to do the same.

Siano watched them for a moment, fascinated by the industrious flexing of legs and mandibles, and then she put her sword away and walked back through the forest.

10

Looking back on his journey through Ynnsmouth with the brood sisters, Sebastian would come to decide that the girl had been a bad omen. He should have known from that moment that only grief and disaster awaited them in the mountains, that the only sensible option would have been to turn and flee, but there is nothing as stubborn as a man whose self-righteousness is born of guilt.

They had been moving down through the lake-duchies of Ynnsmouth, skirting those places at the very edge of the lakes where settlements tended to grow like mould, and staying as far out of sight as they could. Sebastian walked at the head of their group, his own hood thrown back so that anyone approaching could see his face, while the rest of the brood sisters kept theirs hidden. He had refused any requests to send scouts forward, wanting to keep everyone where he could see them – perhaps, he'd reasoned, people would see their travelling group from a distance and assume they were a company of unknown mercenaries on the move, and therefore best not approached.

It was a cold, bright day, sunlight covering the lakes in a film of gold. The girl came running down the rocky path to their right, arms pin-wheeling to keep her balance, and for a few seconds Sebastian was too shocked to react – seeing her was like a memory suddenly come to life.

She wore the traditional scarlet-hooded cloak of girls training to be lake-singers, the hem dotted with creamy white pearls, the back stitched with the leaping shape of a trout. It was a lake-singer's job to sing the men out on their boats every morning, and sing them safely back in again in the evening, and when Sebastian had been small, three or four of the girls in his village had taken up the vocation. He remembered so clearly the scarlet blaze of their hoods, and how they had become so mysterious to him then; they had joined some exclusive club that was closed off to boys and men, and when he saw them, their heads would be bent together in whispers. They had to embroider the fish on the cloak themselves, Sebastian remembered, but their mothers sewed the pearls. That was how it had always been.

Stumbling onto the grass in front of them, she looked up and caught Sebastian's eye. The sight of the girl, red hood flapping and a simple wooden flute clutched in her right hand – it was, he remembered, the first instrument the lake-singers learned to master – surprised a grin out of him, and any trepidation the girl might have had at the sight of this rag-tag bunch immediately vanished. She grinned back at him.

'If you see my da, don't tell him I came this way,' she said, looking over her shoulder. Turning back to Sebastian, she adjusted the line of her scarlet cloak. Underneath the hood her hair was a mass of dark brown curls that hadn't seen a brush for some time. 'I'll go back in a little while, I just wanna practise by myself.' She held up the flute as if that were explanation enough.

Behind him, Sebastian could feel the brood sisters grow still, waiting for him to make the first move. The girl hadn't taken any notice of the figures behind him just yet, but that could all change in a moment.

Keeping his face as open and friendly as possible, Sebastian bent his knees, resting his arms on his thighs so that she could see his hands were empty. It seemed important to do that.

'You have a testing soon, lake-singer?'

Her face brightened at the use of the title she had yet to earn. 'This evening, when the boats come in,' she said, her gaze not moving from his face. 'Da wants me to go back and have an early bath,' she rolled her eyes at this, 'and brush my hair out and all that, but I just want to go through my songs one last time without Ma giving me the eyeball.'

Sebastian smiled and nodded. Behind him he heard one of the brood sisters moving from foot to foot. He could feel their anxiety like a tremor in his blood. They wanted to know why they did not just move on.

'Lake-singers must always have clean faces, I remember that much,' he said. The girl looked pained at this, so he winked at her. 'Tell you what. Play the boatmen a verse of "Kaylee Catch Me Calling" this afternoon, and I won't tell your father a word.'

She smiled again, and nodded. 'I know that one, it's easy,' she said. She turned to go, her eyes already set on the silvery lake that spread beneath them, lazing in the summer light. 'I'll be back in plenty of time to wash—'

There was a shout from above them and a thickset man with a dark beard and a bald head appeared over the top of the low hill. His cheeks and ears were red with exertion.

'Denia, what do you think you're playing at?' he bellowed, chugging down the slope in a slow jog. Belatedly, he spotted the group beyond his daughter, and that was where it all went wrong.

'Good sir,' Sebastian straightened up and immediately approached the man, hoping that his open face, so stamped with the lines and tones of Ynnsmouth, would put him at his ease, 'many apologies for waylaying your daughter on her way back to you, but it has been many years since I heard a lake-singer practise her craft, and—'

It was too late. Sebastian watched as the man's eyes flickered from him to the figures standing behind him. The man took a stumbling step backwards, almost falling straight back down onto his rear end.

'What are you?'

Sebastian held his hands out, palms up. 'Just travellers, passing through. We mean no harm.'

'Denia, you come back here right now.'

The girl looked back up to her father with an expression of deepest puzzlement and slight affront.

'I just want an extra practice, Da, and you know I like to do it down by the lake.'

'Denia!' The man bellowed her name, his red cheeks now showing spots of white at the tops. 'Get away from them RIGHT NOW.'

The girl blinked, glancing up at the shifting crowd behind Sebastian, and he saw her eyes grow wide. In a second she was screaming, apparently rooted to the spot. Her small wooden flute fell into the grass.

'Denia! Denia!'

The portly man came down the hill rapidly, still keeping his eye on Sebastian and the brood, and then from behind him another figure appeared; he was much younger, perhaps eighteen and broad across the shoulders. He had dark curls too and Sebastian would have put money on this being Denia's older brother. *Gods be cursed.*

On hearing his sister's screams, the young man came pelting down the slope at them, already brandishing what looked like a rusty sword.

'Hold fast!' Sebastian turned to the brood, trying to look all of them in the face at once. 'Do nothing, do you hear me?'

If the boy had come brandishing nothing more than his fists, they wouldn't have reacted – or at least that was what Sebastian told himself. Two of the brood sisters leapt forward, their hoods falling back; the first to reach him knocked the sword from his hand, the other grabbed him as though to kiss him, and sunk her teeth into his neck instead.

'Stand down!' Sebastian drew his own sword, despair thick at the back of his throat. 'I swear by the god-peak if you do not—'

The young man's blood fell on the grass in a hot shower. Sebastian grabbed the shoulder of the brood sister and yanked her back; her eyes, when they turned to him, were wide and yellow, the pupils shrunk down to narrow slits – *Tidal,* he thought belatedly, *that's her name* – but now the girl was running. As one, he felt the attention of the brood sisters latch on to her fleeing shape.

'Stop! Don't run!'

The father was standing, his mouth hanging open as his son's blood ran into the dirt. The girl was already some distance down the slope, her scarlet hood flapping wildly. The brood sister who had disarmed the young man had already joined the chase, her white hair streaming behind her.

'Damn you all!'

Sebastian set off after them, pounding down the grass with his heart in his throat, but another shape quickly overtook him. At first he thought it was another brood sister joining the hunt, but then he saw the familiar swinging shape of Ephemeral's braid. Within seconds she had caught up with her sister, who, thankfully, had yet to catch the girl, and tackled her forcefully to the ground. There was a chorus of hissing and Sebastian arrived just as Ephemeral was threatening to tear her sister's throat out. Denia was still running to the lake – so quickly, that Sebastian feared she would run straight into it.

'I hope you are happy.' Sebastian took a deep breath, and shook his head. 'You may well have doomed us all.' The brood sister on her back looked up at him and bared her teeth. He wasn't very surprised to see it was the Second.

'The human ran,' she said. She was breathing hard. 'It is prey.'

'Not any more it's not. Get up.'

Ephemeral eased her weight off and the Second scrambled to her feet, shooting her sister a poisonous look. Sebastian glanced up to where the rest of the brood army waited. The father still stood there, amazingly, looking punch drunk. He was swaying gently on his feet.

'Isu be cursed,' muttered Sebastian. He could feel a rage building inside him, a hot slither like a snake in the dark. 'Any hope we had of travelling through this land without attracting attention has gone. And that boy –' he turned to the Second, his hands grasping the pommel of his sword, too tight – 'he could never have harmed you. Any of you.'

'Father, what will we do?' Ephemeral was watching the girl, who had made it to the shore of the lake and had fallen to her knees. 'The humans will sound the alarm.'

'We must kill them,' said the Second. There was no hunger in her face now, no need for the hunt. Just a simple pragmatism. Sebastian wasn't sure which he hated more. 'The girl and her father, or we forfeit our own lives.'

'No.'

Sebastian could feel Ephemeral looking at him. 'No,' he said again, 'we've spilt more than enough blood today.'

With a heavy heart, he walked back up the slope. The bearded

68

man had fallen at his son's side now, cradling the boy's head in his arms. He was shaking all over.

'Get away from him,' Sebastian snapped at the brood sisters, who were standing and watching the man's grief with blank faces. He knelt by him and placed a hand on his shoulder, but the man just shook his head. His eyes were dry, and when he turned his face, Sebastian saw that it had lost all of its previous ruddy colour.

'You must go to your daughter,' he said in a low voice. 'She is frightened. Take her home, and—' He stopped, thinking of young Denia's first lake-singing test. She wouldn't take it now, of course. How many lives had they ruined just by walking this path? 'Take her home. There is nothing I can say to repair what has been taken from you. But if I can help you one day, I will.' The man looked at him, uncomprehending. 'I am sorry.'

Sebastian stood up. Tidal, the brood sister who had torn out the young man's throat, was standing at the very edge of the group. Her mouth and neck were red with rapidly drying blood, and she looked almost as lost as the man kneeling on the ground.

'Move,' he said, gesturing brusquely down the slope. 'Quickly now. We'll likely have a mob after us before the sun goes down.'

Much later, when the brood sisters were safely hidden away in a thicket of dark forest, Ephemeral came and stood with Sebastian while he kept watch at the edge of their camp. He had forbidden any fires, and she was little more than a light patch of gloom in the forest, her hair the brightest thing he could see.

'Will we be safe?'

Sebastian laughed a little, although he had no humour in him. 'Oh, we're safe. It's everyone else who's not.'

Ephemeral nodded, as though she had expected this answer. 'When one of us disobeyed Y'Ruen, she would kill us. There was never any question. But you have let Tidal live.'

Far off in the dark forest, an owl fluted its evening call. A moment later, another owl answered.

'If I had killed Tidal, if I became her executioner, then I would be no better than Y'Ruen. I will not say I did not want to. For a moment I could have killed her, and the Second too, and I may not even have regretted it.' Sebastian sighed. It was a freezing

69

night, and he could feel his fingers growing numb through his gloves. The brood sisters did not like the cold, and many had complained about the lack of a fire on the coldest night they'd seen so far. 'Ephemeral, I am responsible for you. That boy's blood is as much on my hands as it is on Tidal's. I can only try to stop it happening again.'

'I did not like to see it,' said Ephemeral. When he looked at her, she shrugged. 'The boy dying. The screams of the girl. It was . . . unjust. There was no joy in it.'

Looking back into the darkness between the trees, Sebastian wondered if the alarm had been raised yet. The man would have eventually taken his daughter home, or perhaps more family members would have come out to find them. It might take some time to get any sense out of Denia or her father, but the words would come in the end, and then they would remember the stories of the army of monstrous green women who had marched across Creos and Relios, right up to the city of Baneswatch. The rumours that some had survived that terrible battle would be confirmed.

'Why did they come with me, Ephemeral?' he said, still looking into the darkness. 'Why did these ones follow me? Plenty of your sisters wouldn't.'

'And they all died at Baneswatch,' said Ephemeral. He looked at her, trying to gauge if her comment was as sardonic as it sounded, but it was impossible to make out her expression in the gloom. 'My sisters are confused, and as alone as they have ever been. You are the only thing that makes sense to them, the only link their blood has left. The Second laid down her sword when she saw Mother torn through the sky, and the way forward has been lost to her.'

Sebastian shook his head. 'If they cannot see a running human without thinking they must kill them, then we will never make it to the mountains.'

'They will listen to you,' said Ephemeral. 'Mother's voice has gone from their hearts and they are looking for a new one. You must give it to them.'

The next morning, Sebastian gathered them together in the weak grey light of dawn. Tidal was sitting on her haunches, still looking as though she expected a blow to fall any moment, while the Second stood at the back of the group with her arms crossed over her chest.

'I will only say this to you once, and I hope that you will listen,' said Sebastian. 'If you want to continue living in this world, you must not take another human life. You must *not*.' He looked around at them all; he saw fear there, and reluctance, and confusion, just as Ephemeral had said. 'You must swear it to me. I can help you to learn about the world, and I can help you to live in it, but I must have this promise from you.'

There was a murmur of assent.

'If you break this oath, I will not kill you.' He looked down at Tidal, who was staring at the ground. 'But I will cast you out, which will be as good as death. You are strong, yes, frighteningly strong, but alone you will be lost, and without your sisters at your side the humans you meet will bring you down eventually. They might need a mob to do it, but they will. If you can keep this oath, then we will make it to the sacred mountains and there we will have space and time to learn what you need to.' He paused. Off to his left he saw Ephemeral, standing utterly still. 'Do you swear it?'

After a few moments' silence there was a chorus of assent. Some sounded more enthusiastic than others, but Sebastian was glad to note that every one of them took the oath, even the Second, who nodded once when he met her eyes. When it was done, he slung his pack over his back and ran a hand over his chin. He would need to shave again soon.

'Good. And I swear to you that I will do what I can to give you a life here. I swear it by the god-peak.'

71

11

'How does it feel?'

Wydrin came to a stop, shifting her legs around, trying to get comfortable. Beneath her the werken stood utterly still, its legs half buried in the sun-bright snow. She had tied a leather seat around its waist, which did something to cushion her behind, but even so, her rear end was already complaining. Ahead of her Bors sat astride his own mount, a werken shaped rather like an enormous bear, its shoulders broad and rounded.

'It feels like my arse has gone to sleep for ever.'

Bors laughed. 'You'll get used to that. In Skaldshollow, most of us are riding werkens as soon as we can walk.' He smiled. 'My father used to take Nuava and me out on his werken and do circuits of the city wall. It was safer back then.'

'What a fine collection of rock-hard bottoms you all must have.' She caught up with Bors and they stood still for a moment, looking out over the snowy landscape. They were to the east of the quarry that split the ground above Skaldshollow, following a rarely used path that headed deep into the mountains. Below them, Wydrin could see men and women and werkens working in the pit. She could hear their voices on the cold air, the chilly chink of hammers on rock, and every now and then the soft *crump* of an explosion as they delved deeper into the mountain. 'Safer?'

'The Narhl attacks weren't so frequent then.' Bors tugged at his knot of hair, not quite looking at her. 'My mother and father were both murdered by the Narhl just after Nuava's fifth birthday.

They used to be Edeian trackers. It was their job to look for new veins of Edeian out in the northern territories.'

'I am sorry to hear that.' Wydrin thought of her own brother lying in his cabin, half his body covered in burns after their deadly encounter with the dragon. Thanks to Frith's magic, Jarath had survived, and that wasn't something she'd forget in a hurry. 'You and your sister are close, then?'

He nodded. 'We lived with Tamlyn after that, and Nuava has flourished under her tutelage,' he said reluctantly. 'She will be a fine crafter one day.' He paused, and shook himself. 'Anyway, I meant how does it feel to be riding the werken?' He smiled at her, his honest face lighting up. Wydrin smiled back. 'I imagine it is quite strange for you.'

'Well, you know,' Wydrin leaned forward and urged her werken beyond Bors and his mount, dragging stone legs through powdery snow, 'I was always quite useless with horses. Big, flighty creatures, altogether too nervous. They can tell when you've had a drink, did you know that? I was brought up on an island, you see, not much call for them. I spent more time on boats than on horseback. This, though,' she patted the werken on the space between its arrow-like stone ears, 'this is easier. It's an extension of myself, like the dagger in my hand. I think about doing something, and the werken does it.'

Bors looked pleased. 'I think you are a natural. You must have the mountains in your blood somewhere.'

'Nah, that's Sebastian.' She looked down at the chip of green crystal nestled in her palm. It no longer hurt at all. 'Although I suppose with this, now I do, in a way.'

They moved on further, following a rough trail almost lost under fresh drifts of snow, until the quarry was out of sight and in front of them was a shallow dip in the terrain. Dark trees lined the far side of it, and above them rose the face of the mountain proper.

'Are you feeling up to a race?' Bors' bear-shaped werken rose up briefly on its hind legs, displaying stony paws, before thumping back into the snow. 'First one down to the treeline buys a round of drinks.'

'Ho, that's hardly fair!' crowed Wydrin, although she moved her werken to the edge of the ridge, and curled a hand around the leather strap attached to the saddle. 'You've been doing this all your life, and I've only just started. I would need at least a week to get used to how this stone beast handles and even then – GO!'

She focussed all her thoughts into that single command and the werken leapt, surging forward with a burst of speed she had barely guessed at. Screaming with delight, she held on for dear life as the werken sped down the steep incline, sending snow flying in all directions. She could hear Bors shouting something – she couldn't make out the words but his surprised amusement was clear – and then there was a startling thunder as his bear-shaped mount came after her, now struggling to keep up.

'This bastard can move!'

All at once the dark treeline was looming very close, and Wydrin yanked back on the leather strap, in her panic resorting to the little experience she had with horses, but the werken was suddenly turning, skidding into a stop with its back legs stretched out. Snow flew up in a wave, pelting the tree trunks with a wet splatter. Such was the violence of their sudden stop that some of the snow hit the back of Wydrin's cloak, and she cried out in mingled delight and disgust as some of it slipped down the back of her collar. A handful of seconds later Bors joined her, although much slower; the bear-shaped werken thumped over to the trees at an amiable pace, having clearly given up the race.

Wydrin grinned and leaned forward, patting the werken between the ears again.

'You know, I think he likes going fast. He may not be as quick as yours over deep snow, but give him space to run and he'll make the most of it.' She laughed. 'Mine's a mead, by the way, none of this grut nonsense. And a bowl of stew while you're at it, I'm starving.'

Bors smiled, although he seemed to have lost some of his earlier humour. 'They don't *like* anything, Wydrin, they can't. Your werken is a sleeker model, and it moves fast over short distances. Saying it likes going fast is like saying . . . like saying a table enjoys having food on it.'

Wydrin wriggled in the saddle. The snow had melted and was now trickling down her back. 'How can you know that for certain?'

Bors and his mount moved closer. The edge of the blue sky was tainted with heavy clouds, promising a storm later. His hair, smoothed back into its tight knot, looked very black against his grey furs.

'My friend, I have been down in the quarry myself, I have chipped the rock from the mountain. It is solid, inert, as you would expect. And I have seen it carved into functional shapes by my aunt, crafted into forms that will move. It is the magic of the mountain that gives it a semblance of life – it is that, that causes the werkens to follow our actions. They are a mirror, that is all.'

'This one moved without a rider. You said it was defective, but what if it was something else?'

Bors smiled again, his expression tight. 'You're an outsider here, so it's not surprising you don't understand. But listen, don't go talking like that around my aunt, all right? The Narhl believe that the werkens are feeling creatures, and that belief fuels this war between us. Tamlyn – Tamlyn wouldn't care to hear such views from guests, particularly guests she is giving large amounts of coin to.'

Wydrin shrugged. Just for a moment, she tried to reach out with her mind to the werken – instead of issuing a command, she left her mind open. *Are you there? Can you hear me?* There was nothing, only the cold presence beneath her, and a potential for movement. 'If you say so.' She leaned forward in the saddle and wrapped her hands around the leather strap again. The werken had almost been as swift as the griffin, and she wanted to see how fast it could go. 'How about another race, then? Back down to Skaldshollow, last one back buys the bottle.'

12

Tamlyn and Bors Nox came to see them off. Frith thought that the older woman looked unsure of herself, her wide brow furrowed into lines. She kept touching the beads at her throat, and whenever her nephew spoke to her she snapped at him, until the younger man hung back, not making eye contact with any of them. Not for the first time Frith wondered whether or not hiring them had, in fact, been Tamlyn's idea.

'We have given you all the tactical information we have on the Narhl,' she said, when they were loaded up and ready to go. They stood on one of the winding paths that led up out of Skaldshollow; they would follow it out of mountain and into Narhl territory. 'You must remember that they are savages, and that they care more for the dead stone of the mountain than they do about human life.'

Sebastian, adjusting the way his broadsword hung over his back, frowned at this. 'We shall see.'

It was a five-day journey to the outskirts of the Frozen Steps, across cold, inhospitable hills and around winding paths that, half the time, Frith couldn't see until they were right on top of them. Wydrin's werken came along after them. Frith had protested at first, complaining that the creature would slow them down or make the narrower paths impassable, but Wydrin had insisted, pointing out that it could carry all their supplies and gear, leaving them able to move freely. And so far, its slim, narrow shape had caused no significant problems, although Frith often found it unnerving to glance back the way they'd come to see two points of eerie green light staring back at him. His own steed, Gwiddion, flew above them in its bird form, sometimes perching on rocky outcrops and waiting for them to catch up.

Looking at the bird made him think of O'rin; his old teacher had never been far from a pack of squawking birds on Whittenfarne. Since Y'Ruen had been cast out of Ede, tumbling through a hole in the sky – a result of O'rin's own long-planned spell – the god of lies had made himself scarce, preferring to stay at his Rookery, away from the world and its problems. He had paid Frith a few brief visits, usually when he was alone, walking in the Blackwood or in his own bare suite of rooms in the castle. The old god would appear in a flurry of feathers, full of questions and pointed comments about the welfare of his griffin, his great curved beak nodding rapidly. He would pretend that these visits were a result of his naturally curious nature, but Frith suspected that the old god was keeping an eye on him. That, or he was lonely. It seemed ludicrous that such a powerful being could want company, but he was the last of his kind now. And Frith had some idea what that felt like.

They came to the Crippler on the evening of the third day. The path was every bit as hair-raising as Tamlyn had hinted; it curved around the sheer western side of the mountain in erratic fashion, sometimes so narrow that they had to walk single file, leaning heavily against the solid rock to their right, and sometimes so full of rocks and snow that Frith was convinced that they had lost track of it completely. Dizzying drops loomed off to one side, so that more than once he considered calling Gwiddion to his griffin form so that he could fly off ahead, but his pride kept him from doing so. Here it looked likely that they might lose the werken – in several places the path did not look solid enough to support its weight – but it came steadily on, and Frith had to admit he was glad not to be carrying a heavy pack when he needed all his concentration just to stay on the path.

Eventually, the chilly afterthought that passed as daylight in these lands gave way to a dark, freezing night and they agreed to stop and rest. The Crippler had widened enough in this section for them to be able to make a small camp and Frith set about making a fire for the night; a pile of dry sticks from Wydrin's pack, and the word for Fire inked onto a bandage in his fist. Within seconds he had a merry blaze going and Wydrin and Sebastian drew close to it, holding out their hands for warmth.

'We are not far now,' he said, trying to find a comfortable place to sit amongst the rocks and snow. The werken stood behind them as if it were a guard dog, or a statue of one. 'When the sun comes up we should be able to see the Frozen Steps.' Gwiddion fluttered down from the shadowy spaces above their heads and perched on top of the werken's head. The werken did not move.

'We'll have a better idea of how we're getting in there then,' said Wydrin. She was busily unpacking a small bag; salted meat wrapped in greasy paper, hard black bread, a small cask of beer. She took a knife from her belt and began slicing the meat. 'And how we're getting the bloody thing back out. Still, at least we've got Mendrick here to carry it for us.' She slapped the werken companionably on one big stone paw.

'You've named it Mendrick?' asked Sebastian. He took the cask from Wydrin and began filling their tin cups. 'I thought the Skald were set against naming their beasts of burden.'

'It's after a man I met in the Horns. He was part of a travelling magic show.' She waved a hand at Frith. 'None of your blowing things up or freezing your companions to death or any of that. This was more card tricks and silk scarves. He used to juggle with radishes.' She looked wistful for a moment. 'That's the thing with stage magicians, good with their hands.'

Frith coughed and took a sip of beer. Beyond the path and their small circle of fire the night loomed, star-lit and streaked with ragged clouds. He thought of their final journey with Y'Ruen, the dragon nipping at their heels as they danced just out of reach. How the sky had opened up and revealed a darkness beyond that made this pitch-black night look like an early morning sunrise. The thought was not a reassuring one.

Sebastian took first watch and Frith turned over to sleep, pulling his hood down over his face as far as it would go. When he woke again, it was for the final watch, and he sat and waited for the sun to come up. Cold yellow light seeped in from the east, turning the snows and ice briefly golden and too bright to look at. The sky crept from silvery-violet to pale, pitiless blue, while on the horizon darker clouds lurked, promising heavy snows later. Frith turned his hand to the embers that were left of their fire and it burst back into life.

Wydrin sat up, rubbing a gloved hand over her face.

'Well,' she said, 'I am pleased we haven't fallen off the cliff while we slept.'

'I have passed more comfortable nights.'

She stood up, stretching her arms over her head until the bones in her shoulders popped before reaching over to gently kick Sebastian in the rear end.

'Up you get, Seb, we've got sacred stones to steal, and the fewer nights spent on my back in this mountain the better.' She turned back to Frith, and then stopped, her eyes caught by something on the horizon. 'Speaking of which –'

Frith looked where she pointed. From this vantage point, with the early morning light seeping across the land like honey, the Narhl territories were a wild and jagged confusion; white snow and deep purple shadows, grey rock tearing at the sky like serrated daggers, layered with the deep lethal blue of glacial ice. The mountain of Skaldshollow was small and timid in comparison to these ancient giants. Nothing moved on that landscape, save for the occasional swirl of mist, and Frith found himself thinking that Sebastian's religion, where the mountains were feared and pandered to, was suddenly not so difficult to understand. Below the path they clung to was a snow-clogged valley, and at the far end of that was a great looming structure of what looked like broken glass. *No, it's ice,* he corrected himself. *The Narhl have built the outer wall of their fortress from ice.* It was shaped roughly like a series of arrow heads, the tops glittering with points that looked sharp and deadly. As he watched, the sun caught it and sent a shimmering parade of golden lights across the valley floor.

'Have you ever seen such a place?' His voice was instinctively hushed. There were shapes moving on the top of the wall, men and women with spears. A long sinuous shape alighted briefly there, a blue-skinned creature with a long, narrow head. These would be the wyverns that Nuava's books had warned them about. After a second or so the wyvern leapt off the wall and up into the sky, wriggling like an eel. It was most disconcerting. Gwiddion alighted next to him and *cawed* once, as if he, too, were alarmed by these dragon-like animals.

'That doesn't look like it's going to be easy to get into,' said Sebastian, his voice still groggy from sleep. Frith had to agree. Beyond the ice wall it was just about possible to make out the hazy shapes of what looked like buildings, and in the distance four white towers stood shining above everything else; somewhere in there, assuming they could get through the wall, they would have to locate the Heart-Stone.

'If Tamlyn Nox and her army of werkens could not break it . . .' Frith flexed his fingers. He had already prepared a number of silk strips with spells that he hoped would be appropriate. 'And even if we manage, somehow, to breach the Frozen Steps, how are we to get to the Heart-Stone with a hostile population between us and it?'

'You have forgotten, princeling, that we are the Black Feather Three,' said Wydrin, stepping over the fire to join him at the edge of the path. She passed him a flask of sour-smelling wine. 'We defeated a dragon. We can do anything.'

Frith smiled a little despite himself. Her hood had fallen back and in the sunlight her hair was an impossible colour. *Like the heart of a fire*, he thought, and then pushed the thought aside.

'I take it you have a plan, then? Something that can get us over that wall and to Tamlyn's stone and out again?'

'Of course I do,' she said, patting the dagger at her hip. 'It involves sneaking about, the cover of night, and good old-fashioned beating people up. And we're going *through* the wall, not over it.'

13

Siano stood outside the doors to the great dining room, listening. It was early evening, and normally the busiest time in the household, but all the servants were absent. She'd given them the night off, so to speak.

From inside the dining room came the soft familiar sounds of people eating dinner; murmured conversations between bites, the clink of cutlery – always the right cutlery for the right course, obviously – and the gentle glug of wines being poured. Gradually, the sounds changed, and now Siano leaned her head against the grain of the wood, drinking it in. Conversations became stilted, the words that were spoken shrill and confused. The clatter of cutlery became more violent as people threw down knives and forks, or dropped their spoons onto the stone floor. There was, gloriously, the unmistakable sound of someone vomiting violently, followed by the screech of chairs being pushed back from the table. Siano heard a muffled shout, someone calling for servants that were never coming, and there was even the brief stumble of someone attempting to make it to the door. After a moment there was a thump as whoever it was hit the floor like a sack of rocks.

And then, eventually, silence.

Siano opened the door. Inside, the room was as opulent as she expected: a great fresco painted directly onto smoothly plastered walls, golden candlesticks dripping from every surface, pewter plates polished to a brilliant shine, and in the centre of the table a great stuffed bird surrounded by fruit.

It was spoiled somewhat by the guests themselves. Siano stepped carefully over the man who'd almost made it to the door – portly, bearded, the father of the family – and worked her way down the table, admiring her handiwork. A woman of middle-age sat slumped at the head of the table, her yellow silk dress smeared with thick gobbets of vomit and her mouth wide open, revealing a fat purple tongue. The tiny capillaries in her eyes had burst and in her last moments she'd smeared blood across her face.

Next to her was a young man, perhaps no older than Siano herself. He had fallen face down into what looked like a bowl of stew, although Siano was no longer sure where the stew had ended and the vomit began. The young woman next to him, who had probably been very beautiful before the poison did its work, had scratched bloody lines into her own throat as she suffocated.

Twenty diners, all wiped out before the dessert course. Not all of them were members of the family she'd been instructed to kill; she'd checked the guest list in the footman's papers and there were seven men and women here who were merely friends and associates. But it hardly mattered. The client had said nothing about avoiding the deaths of innocents, and somehow Siano doubted that the severed head would mind. She drew the slim knife from her belt, preparing to draw blood from the corpses, when she stopped. There was one chair empty. The plates that sat before it were clean and untouched.

'What is this?'

Unnerved, Siano counted them again, checking numbers against the list she had memorised. There should be twenty guests: seven who didn't matter, and thirteen family members. Except one was missing.

She put the knife away and went to the offending chair. There were pillows on it, two fat pillows, as though the person who normally sat there was too short to reach the table. The plates were smaller too, and there was a thick round cup instead of a tankard.

'The youngest child, then,' she murmured, reaching out to touch her fingers to the clean plate. 'A child who has not come down for dinner. Sent to bed early for some misdemeanour, or perhaps he is ill.'

She glanced down the table, her gaze passing over faces bloated and smeared with blood and vomit. The poison she had used was odourless, tasteless, and absolutely lethal. It also cost a small fortune, as it was made from the powdered bones of a tiny lizard that lived in a small patch of jungle in Onwai, but her client was hardly going to quibble over her expenses. And it had been too tempting; a family dinner, all of her victims gathered in one place. So simple to slip into the kitchens, so easy to find the correct dishes. She'd used more than one vial just to be sure – she didn't want to miss someone, for example, just because they didn't fancy fish soup that evening. And then once the food had been delivered, a razor-sharp knife in the shadows of the corridor waited for those servants still left alive.

Perhaps someone had taken the child some food up to its room – a parent, or, more likely, a kindly servant – and perhaps the child was already dead, purple-faced and twisted around the bed covers. But she would have to check.

Siano left the dining room at a pace, still moving silently out of habit, even though she was reasonably certain everyone in the house was dead. Everyone save for this one child, the last link in the family chain.

She moved up the staircase, feeling the cold solidity of the wooden banister through the fine silk of her gloves. Once she was on the upper landing, she stopped, holding her breath with her mouth slightly open, allowing herself to hear the full silence of the house. A creak down the corridor, wooden floorboards settling, the distant susurrus of the wind through the trees outside, birds singing somewhere. And there: the slight huffing snort of a child at rest, or perhaps just waking up. It was coming from up ahead, from one of the rooms on the right-hand side of the corridor.

Siano moved into the shadows but the child was already up and moving; she heard its heavy footfalls stomping across the room and then it appeared, hair mussed from sleep. Siano stood as still as possible, unable to tell yet if the child – a boy with a swirl of blond hair like corn silk and an overly doughy face – had seen her.

The child stood for a moment in the hallway, rubbing small

fists across his eyes, before he glanced up and looked straight at Siano. The assassin didn't move. She felt suddenly very aware of what she must look like to this child; a tall slim stranger, dressed in black, gloves on her hands and her hair swept back from her head with a thin black cord.

The boy blinked at her sleepily. 'I'm hungry now,' he said. 'I know Mama said no food, but I'm hungry now. Are they done with dinner downstairs? I don't want to eat with them.'

'They are done with dinner, yes,' answered Siano. People were so good at fooling themselves sometimes it astounded her. If you were in their house, then surely you must be allowed to be there. Anything else would be unthinkable. 'Would you like some pudding now?'

The boy's eyes lit up. 'Is there lemon cake? Cook said there would be, but that was before Mama got all angry.'

Siano took the boy down to the kitchens, being careful to take him via a route that avoided the slumped forms of servants, their throats gaping and red. The boy seemed oblivious to the unnatural silence of the house, and even appeared unworried that the kitchen was entirely empty of staff. Instead he went and sat himself at the big, scarred wooden table, waiting to be served.

'I know Mama said no dinner,' he said again. 'But she doesn't really mean it. Pudding is better, anyway.'

Siano nodded. There was indeed lemon cake, a huge pan of the stuff, still softly steaming and smelling pleasantly of hot summer days. Siano cut a portion and slid it onto a plate before dousing it liberally with the poison from the last of the vials.

'Here,' she plonked the plate in front of the boy. 'Your favourite, no?'

The boy peered at her. For the first time he seemed to be questioning the appearance of this strange woman in his house.

'Can I have a spoon, then?' he said eventually.

Siano nodded graciously. 'Of course.'

She fetched one from a huge tureen of washed cutlery and set it next to the boy's plate, but still the child didn't touch his pudding. Instead he looked up at her, his brow beginning to furrow in a way that either meant stomach trouble or an oncoming tantrum. The boy opened his mouth to speak, perhaps to ask where everyone was, and Siano smoothly spoke over him.

'You were in trouble, then? Sent to bed with no dinner?' She forced a smile, attempting to look like the sort of shadowy stranger dressed in black that you might confide in.

The child shrugged, looking slightly more cheerful. 'I was teasing the puppies again. Ned, the groundskeeper, one of his dogs has just had puppies, and I wanted to play with them, but Meela the kitchen girl caught me and Mama said I wasn't to play with them like that.' The boy took a breath and picked up his spoon, but he only pushed the cake around his plate.

'How were you playing with them?' Siano stood to one side. In the back of her mind she was still listening to the sounds of the big house, just in case someone unexpected should choose to visit. The boy began to mash the cake with his spoon, chopping it into honeyed lumps.

'I was only teasing them,' he said, tucking his chin into his chest as he spoke. Siano suspected that he probably did the same thing when talking to his mama, perhaps imagining it made him more appealing. It did not. 'There were hot coals in the farrier's shed, and I was only *playing*. They weren't really hurt. They just make a lot of noise and Meela got upset.'

'Yes,' agreed Siano, 'puppies make a lot of noise. When I was younger than you, my family also had dogs, lots of them, and there were always so many puppies. My parents did not notice when one or two went missing, or even three or four. I took their little ears, and sometimes their eyes. Your mistake, child, is that you were playing where other people could hear.'

The boy was looking at her with wide eyes now, the lemon cake completely forgotten. He looked, in fact, like he might never feel like eating cake again.

'Didn't you get in trouble?' he asked, a slight tremor to his voice. *He is noticing*, thought Siano, *that I did not call him by his name, and he is beginning to realise I shouldn't be here.* 'Didn't your mama and papa get mad?'

'They did, yes, when they found out. And they found out about lots of things, eventually, although I believe they had been pretending not to know about it all for a long time. Parents are good at that. But then they sent me away, and what I am was put to good use.'

'Where is my mama?' the boy said, and now his voice was thick and close to tears. 'I want to see my mama now.'

'Aren't you going to eat your cake?' asked Siano, taking a step closer. She wasn't concerned – there was no chance of this child outrunning her – but she was starting to get bored. 'It's very good. And it's your favourite, no?'

The boy stared at her, the spoon trembling slightly in his podgy fingers.

'No,' he said, and he threw the spoon down onto the table. 'It's not my favourite and you don't know anything!'

Siano sighed and slipped a dagger from within her jacket.

'Very well. But you would have enjoyed the cake more.'

14

Frith crouched in the snow. He could feel it soaking into his cloak and through his trousers, icy cold, and soon, he supposed, he would be thoroughly wet and miserable. The night was cloudy, with very little light from the stars and the moon, and that in itself was an enormous stroke of luck, because there was no way this godsforsaken plan had a chance of succeeding otherwise.

Next to him Wydrin shifted, peering over the pile of rocks that was in fact Mendrick, half covered in snow so that the faint glow of the Edeian wouldn't give them away. Around fifty feet away the jagged ice wall of the Frozen Steps rose in front of them, grey and ghostly in the dark, and there were two guards that he could see: one standing in front of the wall, a slim shape holding a long spear, and another on top of the wall, only visible as a patch of lighter darkness against the sky. They both had strange lamps next to them, glowing with a bluish light. There were more guards further down, at regular intervals, but as Wydrin had pointed out, they only needed one section of the wall to themselves.

She crouched down next to him, her face a mosaic of grey shadows. 'Are you ready?' she whispered. 'This is as good a time as any.'

Frith glanced up at the sky, wondering where Sebastian was. 'Are you sure we're close enough?' The constant wind picked up a little, and Frith paused, making sure it wasn't travelling in a direction that would reveal their presence to the guards. When he was happy it wasn't, he spoke again. 'You will have to move quickly over this ground.'

'It's fine,' she said. 'I am known for being fast and quiet. Just make sure he doesn't get the word out.'

Frith nodded and shifted round so that he had a clear view over Mendrick's shoulders. The word for Stillness was already painted on the bandage around his hand and the Edenier was churning within his chest. All he needed to do was reach for the word, see it clearly in his mind's eye, and then focus. The ancient mage magic surged into life, focussed through the words painted on the silk.

The guard by the wall, who had been shifting restlessly from foot to foot, suddenly stood rigidly to attention. Frith tightened his concentration down, focussing the bulk of the spell on the man's head. *If he sounds the alarm, this will all be over very quickly.* Wydrin was already up and moving, scurrying across the snowy ground silently. She had drawn her dagger.

'Hold still,' murmured Frith. It occurred to him, slightly too late, that such a focussed use of this spell might actually stop the man from breathing. *He can hold his breath*, he told himself. *For a while at least.*

Wydrin was next to the guard now. She reached up and removed the man's helmet before neatly smacking him around the back of his head with the pommel of her dagger and kicking snow over the small lamp. She waited a moment, and then waved to Frith. He let go of the word in his mind and the guard slumped, sliding down the wall into the snow. They now had this section of the wall to themselves.

He came out from behind the rocks and moved as quickly as he could over to where Wydrin stood. 'Is he out?'

'Cold.' Wydrin nudged the guard with her foot. 'Have you seen his face? I've never seen anything like it.'

Frith peered down. It was difficult to make out in what little light there was, but the man's head was narrow and sharply angled, his skin mottled with different colours. He looked grey to Frith's eyes, but then everything did in these shadows. He shook his head; it was hardly important.

'Here comes part two of the plan,' said Wydrin, pointing upwards.

Out of the cloudy night sky Sebastian and Gwiddion fell like a stone, sweeping towards the top of the wall impossibly fast. There was a muffled '*Oof!*' from somewhere above them and suddenly that part of the Frozen Steps was empty too.

'Quickly now,' Wydrin whispered. 'We won't have long before someone notices they're gone.'

Frith turned to the wall behind them. Up close it was solid and grey, a chunk of rock-hard ice that had clearly been there for hundreds of years. He summoned the word for Fire and focussed it down to a tiny dot between his palms; a fireball, as satisfying as that would no doubt be, would also be spotted much too quickly. Instead, he sank the fiercely burning point of heat into the ice and immediately part of the wall fell away in a cloud of steam.

'Whoa,' said Wydrin, her voice hushed. 'Careful with that, princeling. We don't want to bring the whole thing down on our heads.'

'Let's move quickly, then.' He pressed forward, melting a hole in the ice big enough for them to walk through. It was easy really, just a question of focussing the word down to this tiny point – all of the power of the fire spell, but almost all of it converted to heat rather than flames and light. He remembered doing the same to Fane's helm, and he smiled in the dark.

'What are you grinning at?' asked Wydrin. She was standing close to him in the newly forged tunnel, her sword already drawn, and although she stood ready to fight, she was smiling too. All at once it was too easy to remember why he enjoyed doing this.

'Keep close to me and watch our backs,' was all he said. 'I'm not sure how far we have to go.'

Leaving his squadron to their dice game, Prince Dallen, first and only son of King Aristees of the Frozen Steps, made his way to the very top of the war tower. It had been a long day of patrols and exercises, and he felt curiously heavy; a side effect of spending all day in the sky. Now the men and women of his unit were opening their first bottles of grut, and already he could hear the bone rattle of the dice in their cups. He half smiled to himself; they would regret that, come the morning – as the king's son, he was expected to lead the dawn patrols, regardless of how busy a day they'd had – but he didn't have the heart to order them to their bunks. Instead he found his habitual seat by the window, and looked out across the Frozen Steps, the pack they'd found that day held loosely in his hands.

It was a quiet night, the winds having died down, the skies thick with cloud. Cold-lights shone across his home, blue and white like stars, and everything was still. And familiar. Dallen shifted in his chair. How was it possible to love a place so much, and yet to feel like you'd be glad to see the back of it at the same time?

Wanting to distract himself from these long thoughts, he opened the pack. They'd found it on their eastern patrol, next to the frozen body of some luckless traveller. From the condition of the corpse the man had simply lost his way and succumbed to the cold, before being partially eaten by a host of Arichok. At least, Dallen hoped that the man had died first.

Fiddling with the drawstrings, he emptied the contents out onto the wide stone sill. A greasy paper package full of salted meat, a leather roll of dried tobacco – this he held up to his nose, fascinated by the scratchy, spicy scent – a set of tin plates, dented and crusted with the tinker's last meal, a thick tangle of silver charm bracelets, all turning slightly green; and, joyously, three maps curled into tight rolls and sealed with waxed bands. One was of the Frozen Steps and the surrounding territories, unsurprisingly, but the other two were of lands Dallen had never seen, and had heard of only in tales; Onwai, the vast country to the far east, and Pathania, a place of plagues and gold.

For some time he sat with the maps spread across his knees, following the unfamiliar shapes with his finger, murmuring the names of places he would likely never see. The man who had been travelling through the Frozen Steps had written notes here and there on the maps, the ink smeared in places. Dallen read them out loud to himself.

'Do not go back to The Star Pocked Axe, Annie will not forget tonight in a hurry. The old Steaming Baths have closed, now run by a right rum sort. The bridge over the Falling Fate river has space underneath to sleep, take blankets, do not remove shoes.'

Dallen looked at it a moment longer, trying to imagine these distant places, with their wide streets and warm houses. There must be so many people, so many voices.

He looked out the window again, trying to find some solace in the beauty of the Frozen Steps. In the tower next to him, he told himself, his wyvern and the wyverns of his squad were resting, their noble faces curled against their scaled hides. No other people in the world, as far as he knew, flew on the backs of wyverns – it was a gift that belonged only to his people. In the morning, he would lead the squadron, and there was no one faster in the sky than he, and no better captain – despite what his father might have to say. There was glory here, and pride, in the Frozen Steps.

Yes, he thought to himself, *they're certainly frozen. Frozen and unchanging.*

He half turned from the window, deciding that he would take a drink with his squad after all, when the wall caught his eye again. It took him a few seconds to notice what was different, but when he did, he felt a trickle of unease move down his back: one of the cold-lights on top of the wall had gone out.

'They've probably dropped it,' he told himself. 'Kicked it off when they weren't looking.'

As he watched, a part of the night sky seemed to come to life; a black shape moving impossibly fast darting across the clouds. He saw it rise sharply and then drop down, briefly outlined against the ghostly grey of the ice wall. Whatever it was, it was huge, and it had wings.

Prince Dallen ran, grabbing the small pile of tin plates as he did so, already hollering for his squad. When he reached their barracks room, he threw the tin plates right into the middle of their dice game, scattering dice and cups.

'Move,' he told their surprised faces. 'We're under attack.'

Leaving them, knowing that the grut would slow them down and his own head was as clear as spring water, he turned sharply and ran down the branching corridor that led up to the wyvern aviary. The bridge was open to the night air and the cold hit him, awaking the ice in his veins. He looked over to the wall as he ran – the missing light was an ominous patch of darkness now – and there it was again, the alien creature in their airspace.

He stumbled into the aviary, having only a few seconds to get his bearings. Half the animals had been put in their stables, the wyvern-keepers clearly thinking they had all night now the main patrol was back. Nile, the head keeper, was so surprised to see his prince that he dropped the tack he was cleaning.

'A-a night ride, your highness?'

'Is Rillion still up?'

'Y-yes, you know how she won't rest until the whole team are down. Should I . . .?'

'We're under attack. Get them all ready. The rest of the company are coming.'

Dallen grabbed a discarded harness from a corner and hurriedly strapped it across his chest, before filling the long pouch on the back with a clutch of ice-spears. He moved from there to her enclosure, and her long head came out to meet him, narrow nostrils flaring.

'Did you smell me coming, Rillion?' He rubbed her nose fondly. 'How do you feel about some night-time flying?'

Rillion was the largest of their team of wyverns, and therefore their leader. She was twelve feet long from nose to tail, and the pale blue of an early morning sky. Her sleek body rippled with muscles as Dallen adjusted the saddle, and she tore crystal claws across the flagstones, already impatient to be off.

'Hold on, girl, we're nearly there.' He climbed into the saddle, and pulled the last straps home. Behind him he could hear the other members of his squad stumbling into the aviary, shouting at Nile and generally causing chaos. 'And, hup!'

Rillion crouched, coiling like a spring, and then they were in the air, flying upwards into the night sky. Her short, bat-like wings extended with a sound like a whip being cracked, and her powerful tail, rigid with fins, propelled them forward. Dallen shifted in his saddle, crouching over her neck and watching the sky. There it was.

'You see it, don't you girl? Go!'

They shot upwards, turning so rapidly that Dallen's field of vision was suddenly filled with the ground rather than the sky, and then they righted, and the creature was right in front of them.

'What *is* that?'

It looked like a huge black bird, except that it had four legs and a thickly muscled body. There was a man riding on the back of it, and, for a brief second, Dallen caught sight of his face – handsome, clean shaven, and apparently just as surprised as Dallen. The creature gave a harsh cry, almost like that of a mountain eagle, and then it was speeding away, its enormous wings kicking up a formidable backwind. Dallen pressed his knees to Rillion's sides and they shot off in pursuit.

The bird and its rider led them a merry dance, soaring up towards the clouds and then plummeting down, corkscrewing through turns and moving unnaturally fast the whole time. He kept getting glimpses of the rider, his broad shoulders hunched, clinging on to his mount for dear life. *He's not Narhl,* thought Dallen, his heart beating rapidly in his chest, *and he's not a Skald either. What is going on?*

There were distant ululating screams, indicating that the rest of his squad were out of the aviary and in the air, but Dallen only had eyes for his prey now. The creature made a mistake, turned right when it should have turned left, and suddenly he was close enough. Dallen snatched a spear from his back and threw it, but the rider and his mount dropped like a stone, and his spear sailed harmlessly past.

Swearing under his breath Dallen tugged hard on the reins and sent Rillion into a swirling dive, her enormous tail rippling, her wings folded to her side, and they caught up with them again. Taking the chance that his wyvern would be heavier than the strange giant bird, he drove Rillion directly into the creature. There was a moment of friction, a flurry of black feathers, and the interloper slipped away again, but not before Dallen noticed something else: the rider, despite being attacked from above, had been looking down at the ground. And he looked worried.

Dallen pulled up and forced himself to look away from the man and his strange mount, and below them, on the snow-covered streets of his home, he spotted two more interlopers. They were moving in the shadows, slowly and quietly, and yet they had made it so far into the Frozen Steps that they were only a short run from the Hall of Ancestors, the place where his father was keeping the sacred heart of the mountain. Dallen brought Rillion a little

93

lower and noticed something else: there was a heavier shape in the shadows moving alongside them. A werken. They would dare to bring a werken here, of all places?

Filled with a sudden fury that made the blood run cold in his veins, Prince Dallen yanked up on Rillion's reins, ignoring her squawk of outrage. There was only one way to finish this quickly.

He caught up with the other rider and his monster easily enough; he saw now that he had been trying to distract him all along, to keep him from noticing the rest of his men on the ground. Dallen held out one hand towards the man and called it to him – that which never left them, the soul of this frozen land: the cold. The ice in his veins sang, and the temperature surrounding them dropped. He saw the other rider shout in surprise as the wings of his animal were suddenly fringed with frost, and then his rising panic as the air around them became too cold for him to breathe. *Too cold for a warmling to breathe, anyway*, thought Dallen, smiling slightly.

The winged creature struggled for a moment, and the rider even drew the short sword at his waist, as if a weapon could be any use against the cold. And then they both fell from the sky.

15

Frith had to admit, the werken certainly could move quietly. They were edging their way along the streets as quickly as they could without making any noise, keeping to the shadows thrown by the strange, ice-covered buildings. The whole place looked as though it had been flash-frozen; he could see houses built of stone, but they were all encased in thick sculptures of clear ice. Some were simple, squarish hovels, others were more elaborate, with icy waves and spikes clustered on roofs and over doors. The street they walked along was cobbled beneath the snow.

'Are you sure this is the way?' whispered Wydrin. She was leading, her hood drawn over her head. Frith looked around uneasily but there was no one to hear her; it was the small hours of the morning now, and the Narhl streets were quiet. Even so, he still had the word for Stillness wound around his hand, and he was ready to use it should they see anyone.

'Of course,' he whispered back. He had spent many hours of their journey studying the maps given to them by Nuava. All the information they had collected indicated that the securest part of the Narhl stronghold was the Hall of Ancestors. It was also their most sacred place, according to the young scholar; considering the importance they attached to the Heart-Stone, it was very likely to be hidden there. 'It's just up here. Once we have the stone we'll have to move fast. Will Sebastian be ready to cover us?'

Wydrin glanced up. 'Don't worry, he—' She stopped, and he saw her straighten up abruptly. 'Sebastian?'

Frith looked up to the sky just in time to see Sebastian on the back of Gwiddion, lurching off to one side as what looked like a huge blue snake collided with them. It was one of the Narhl wyvern riders – Nuava had given them notes on them, too – and now Frith could see the man on its back.

'Shit!' Wydrin pointed beyond Sebastian to a set of four white towers in the distance. More of the flying blue snakes were coming from that direction, all heading towards Sebastian on the back of the griffin. 'We have to get out of here.'

Before they could do anything, the wyvern already attacking Sebastian seemed to draw off. Frith saw the man on its back hold out one arm, and suddenly it grew much colder, so much colder that Frith saw the feathers on Gwiddion's huge black wings grow white, and then the griffin was falling, with Sebastian holding on for dear life.

Wydrin screamed wordlessly and the werken shot forward, racing for the spot where Sebastian would land.

'Wydrin!'

It was too late. The other wyverns had spotted them now and were headed straight for them. Frith ran after her, summoning the word for Stillness in his head as he did so, before flinging up his right arm, the Edenier warming his cold fingers. It was close, but he felt the spell catch hold of Sebastian and the griffin and although he could not quite keep them in the air – *concentrate, concentrate* – it was enough to slow them down, just enough.

The lizards were on them. Frith saw Wydrin, Glassheart drawn and a snarl on her lips, running around the front of Mendrick, and then he was knocked bodily from his feet, landing in the snow some feet away. He lifted his head with some difficulty, summoning the word for Fire in his head, but darkness was closing in at the edge of his vision. He managed to remain conscious long enough to see one of the wyverns land next to him, its long reptile face filling his vision, and then he slipped away.

Frith awoke to the familiar sound of Wydrin arguing with someone.

'I want to know what has happened to my friend! What have you done with him?'

He turned over, wincing as several parts of his body started complaining at once. They appeared to be in a small stone cell, and Wydrin was standing over by the door, talking to a tall Narhl woman. She was solidly built, with the same mottled black and grey skin they'd seen on the guard Wydrin had knocked unconscious, and she wore tough grey leather trimmed with fur. She looked unimpressed by Wydrin's ranting and held a short spear to one side.

'The prisoner is with our prince,' she said, in the tones of someone who has already said this several times before. 'He is being questioned. And then King Aristees will decide his fate. As he will decide all your fates.' She glanced over to Frith then, and instinctively he raised his hands, but the strips of silk with all of his carefully inscribed words were gone. He looked down, holding his arms out in front of him dumbly.

'Oh yes, we took those from you while you were asleep,' said the Narhl woman. She was smiling slightly now. 'We have some knowledge of mages here, although I admit I don't think anyone ever expected to see a living one.' She stepped back to the door, lowering her spear to waist level in case either of them were thinking of making a run for it. 'Even so, don't try anything. You will notice that you are inside a small box. It is very easy to kill things that are kept in small boxes.'

She left, sliding several locks into place as she went.

'They know enough about mages to take my spells away. That's reassuring.' Frith shifted on the cold floor, gasping as another bruise made itself known. 'Did I get hit by a landslide?'

Wydrin came and stood over him, her hands on her hips. They had also taken her dagger and her sword, he noticed, which went some way to explaining the look of thunder on her face.

'Almost. You were hit by a wyvern.' Her face creased with distaste. 'You know, I have had more than enough of flying bloody lizards. The one that hit Sebastian was being ridden by the prince of this grotty little iceberg, one Prince Dallen. That,' she gestured towards the door, 'was his second in command, Olborn.'

'Well,' Frith struggled to his feet and looked around their cell. It looked solid enough. Even if he'd still been armed with the words, he doubted he'd have been able to punch a way out. 'So much for your plan.'

'You know, I'm always ready to hear suggestions from you two.' Wydrin paced back and forth briefly, before standing still and crossing her arms over her chest.

'This Olborn woman. Did she say anything about what happened to Gwiddion? Or to your werken?'

Wydrin shook her head, before sighing and abruptly sitting down.

'Unsurprisingly, they're being very tight-lipped about that.'

'What do you think will happen to us?'

'Well, they've caught us breaking into their city with the intent of stealing something they consider sacred, we burnt a hole through their wall, and got into a fight with their prince.' She shrugged. 'I would guess, something messy involving knives.'

Frith nodded slowly. 'I've always enjoyed your optimism.'

'We tried to capture your steed, but it . . . it turned into a bird and flew away.'

The young man doing the talking had barely stood still since he entered the cell. He paced back and forth, shooting looks at Sebastian with eyes that were a paler blue than even his own. Every now and then he would remember that he was supposed to be questioning a prisoner, but he couldn't quite keep the excitement out of his voice.

'Yes, it does that,' said Sebastian. He was starting to feel warmer now. They had piled blankets on top of him when they'd dragged him in from outside, and the terrible cold that had seized him before had faded gradually, although his fingers and toes ached fiercely with it. 'It is a griffin, my lord, and it belongs to my associate.'

The man the other soldiers called Prince Dallen paused. He wore faded leather armour, patched here and there with fur and other scraps. His skin was mottled black, white and grey like a handful of pebbles, and his brown hair was untidy and shoulder length, while his beard had been cropped close to his jaw. There were also patches of what looked like grey lichen: on his armour, on his skin – there was even some in his hair. *They look to be a part of the landscape itself.*

'A griffin?' said the prince. 'Surely that is a creature from a child's story.'

Sebastian smiled. 'Where I am from, my lord, flying lizards only live in tales. Well, most of the time.'

'You will refer to Prince Dallen as your highness,' cut in the woman standing in the corner of the cell. She was icily beautiful, her dark grey skin contrasting strikingly with hair that was so blond it was almost white. The woman had come in with the prince, and hadn't taken her eyes from Sebastian once, a short spear held at her waist. Prince Dallen shot her an impatient look.

'That hardly matters right now, Olborn,' he said before turning back to Sebastian. 'You came for the Heart-Stone, yes? You have a werken with you, so you must have come from Skaldshollow, but none of you have the look of a Skald. Tamlyn Nox has employed you then, has paid for you to come here and take the heart of the mountain back?'

Sebastian shifted under the blankets, impressed by the young prince. The feeling was coming back to his feet, and with it a rush of pins and needles.

'Yes, your highness.' There seemed little point in denying it now. 'We were told that your people had stolen it from them, and as I understand it, the Heart-Stone is the key to their livelihoods.'

The prince snorted, and for the first time Sebastian saw real anger on his face.

'Ah, yes, the werkens. We have yours, by the way, in our war tower with the wyverns. It is being cared for. Do you know, truly, what a werken is, Sir Sebastian?'

Sebastian thought of the great stone monsters outside the gates of Skaldshollow, and of Bors Nox telling them they were only a 'semblance of life'. He dearly wanted to stand up now, to get some blood back into his legs, but Olborn was watching him closely, and was already too eager to use her spear.

'I must confess, your highness, that I do not.'

'What the Skalds call the Heart-Stone, that piece of glowing rock they have been mutilating –' The prince paused, rubbing one finger along the line of his jaw. 'It is the soul of a mountain, Sir Sebastian. They have ripped it from the living earth, digging deep into its flesh with their quarries, and now they take bits of it to create their werkens. A sacred spirit, split into a thousand pieces

99

and then forced to do their manual labour.' The prince's voice was brittle with disgust, and as he talked, Olborn's mouth turned down at the corners. 'It is obscene. We have taken the stone back, Sir Sebastian, to save what is left of the mountain's soul.'

Despite the heavy blankets piled over his shoulders and legs, Sebastian felt a shiver work its way down his spine. He was thinking of the dream he'd had aboard the *Molly Sings* – the voice of Isu, so cold in his head.

'All we knew, your highness, was that we were retrieving stolen property. We are adventurers, sell-swords. We have no interest in becoming involved in a spiritual war.'

Prince Dallen sighed, all the anger seeming to leave him in one breath. 'There is that. I was not in favour of the methods we used, but when the information came through it was too good not to use.' He paused, and seemed to brighten. 'They tell me you have also burnt a hole through our ice wall. Impressive, for sell-swords.'

Olborn cleared her throat. Sebastian could see that this conversation wasn't taking the violent direction she had been hoping for. 'Your highness, the king will want to speak to them soon. It might be best if we—'

Dallen waved a hand at her dismissively.

'He hardly needs to know about this small matter. Let him stick to his feasting and drinking.'

Olborn looked pained. 'He already knows, your highness.'

Dallen turned back to her and now he did look angry. 'You told him?'

Olborn nodded once. 'It seemed appropriate, your highness.'

Dallen frowned, and ran a finger across his chin again. 'I'm sure it did. Leave us, please.'

'But—'

'Now.'

The woman looked briefly furious, but she bowed once and left, pulling the door shut with a sonorous clang. Prince Dallen let his breath out slowly. It occurred to Sebastian that he was now alone in a cell with the man who had taken him prisoner, a man who was a good head shorter than him. Sebastian would certainly have the upper hand in any fight. But that didn't quite take everything into account, did it?

'I nearly froze to death,' he said quietly. 'May I ask how you did that, your highness? Are you a mage, like my colleague?'

Prince Dallen smiled, and of all things, Sebastian felt his face grow warm. It was the smile of an intelligent man, a man who was shrewd but not unkind. Sebastian found it rather appealing.

'It's a talent that runs in the family, you could say. The Narhl are a part of the mountains. We truly *live* here, in a way that you do not. It's the magic, you see, so thick in this part of the world. If you live here for long enough it becomes a part of you. The *landscape* becomes a part of you. I can summon the cold, as can my father, and my aunts and uncles. The Narhl royal family are truly a part of the ice and snow.' He smiled again, and yet he looked sad. 'It ties us here in ways you cannot imagine.'

From beyond the cell door came the sound of someone shouting, along with the slightly quieter sounds of other people trying desperately to slow them down. Prince Dallen winced.

'Speaking of which, it sounds as though I can delay your meeting my father no longer.'

16

The Narhl were taking no chances. They bundled Frith and Wydrin from the cell, quickly tying Frith's arms behind his back with a stern warning not to even attempt to use the Edenier, and then they were marched from the low stone building onto an outside path. Frith got a brief impression of snow and cobbles, elaborate dwellings of stone and ice looming to either side, but he wasn't given much opportunity to observe. Next to him, Wydrin kept up a string of pointed questions dotted here and there with lively obscenities, which the guards took no notice of whatsoever. They were quickly joined by Sebastian, who looked dishevelled but still alive at least.

'Where have you been?' asked Wydrin. 'Do you know what's going on?'

Before he could answer they were brought up short in front of a long, low building. It was built entirely from black ice, as smooth as marble, with enormous golden doors set into the front. These were carved with images of wolves and walruses, and as they were pushed up the steps, Frith realised that this had been their destination all along: the Hall of Ancestors. There was a flurry of shouts and the doors swung open, revealing a long room with a wood-timbered roof, the planks dark and polished to a shine. Points of blue and white light hung in the rafters, and to either side stood enormous blocks of clear ice. At first, Frith couldn't make out what the slim dark shapes at their centres were, and then it clicked into place.

'Oh, this is cheery,' said Wydrin, her voice tight. 'Is that what happens to your prisoners? A set of antlers on the wall are usually decoration enough for most people.'

'These are our honoured ancestors,' said a woman to their right, and Frith saw that Olborn had joined them. Her lips were thin and bloodless. 'They stay within the hall for ever, advising our king.'

They were marched up the hall, past the icy coffins with their shrivelled contents, and at the far end came to an enormous throne made of more ice. It was occupied by a huge, bearded man in his late middle-years; rather than robes and finery he wore leather armour that looked like it saw a lot of use, and there was a great axe propped at his feet like a faithful dog. His beard and hair were salt-and-pepper grey, his skin white and brown and crusted with greenish lichen, and he watched them come towards him with eyes as bright as chips of onyx. He shifted in his seat as they came, either eager to see them or eager to be elsewhere.

Next to the throne and a few diplomatic steps behind, stood a young man with a short brown beard and untidy brown hair. He also wore armour, and a silver circlet on his forehead; this, Frith guessed, was the Prince Dallen Wydrin had mentioned. Beyond the prince were more Narhl men and women, some dressed in lavish furs, others grasping spears and swords. There was undisguised anger and disgust on every face.

Frith saw the prince murmur something to the king, and the big bearded man twitched with irritation.

'Warmlings, the lot of them.' His son had been softly spoken, but King Aristees had no such qualms about projecting his voice. His words boomed around the hall. 'Trailing their stink through our city, bringing their filth and disease! Melting a hole in our wall!'

Prince Dallen cleared his throat, but Aristees got to his feet, lifting his enormous axe as easily as a broom handle. Thick muscles bunched at his neck.

'Come to steal from us, have you?'

Sebastian took a step forward, the guards still flanking him.

'Your majesty, I am Sebastian Carverson. This is Wydrin Threefellows of Crosshaven, and Lord Aaron Frith of the Blackwood. We were employed by the people of Skaldshollow—'

'To come around thieving, that's what you were employed for!' bellowed Aristees. 'To steal the very heart of the mountain!'

'Well, we were given to understand it was more a case of us stealing it *back*,' said Wydrin. 'Since you stole it from them first.'

'Stole it?' Aristees stomped down from the dais towards her, his axe held out in front of him as if he meant to chop their heads off right in the middle of his own throne room. 'We gave it freedom! Skald scum have been tearing the soul out of the mountain for generations, and we finally said, enough!' He punctuated this last by letting the axe head fall to the stone floor with a crash. Frith tensed, feeling the Edenier churning in his gut. He did not have the words to channel it and his hands were tied, but perhaps, if he focussed hard enough . . .

'Clearly, we weren't privy to all the facts,' said Sebastian. 'Perhaps it would be best for all if we—'

'What would be best,' King Aristees thumped his chest with one giant fist, 'would be if you stinking warmlings never came here at all. Sweating and pink, like pigs in filth.'

'Hold on,' said Wydrin. 'I've had at least two baths this year.'

'You!' Aristees poked a thick finger into her face. 'You people are a disease!' There was a murmuring of agreement from the Narhl gathered in the hall. 'You sicken my people, and you destroy the mountain spirits!'

'Please,' tried Sebastian again. 'This has all been a misunderstanding.'

Abruptly Aristees turned his back on them, pounding his way back to the throne.

'Cut off their heads, Dallen,' he said, in a bored tone of voice. 'Spill their warmling blood into the snow and let them grow cold, as all things should be.' He sat back down in his chair, letting the axe fall to the floor again. 'Do it at sunrise, on the eastern cliff. Aye. We'll give their small bodies to the mountain, so she will know we mean to heal her.'

Wydrin and Sebastian both began talking at once, but Frith shouldered his way between them. *Let the Edenier move as it used to*, he thought, *when I had no control. I will burn them all . . .*

The magic poured out of him, lighting him up like a taper

– violet, churning light. He saw the men and women at the back of the room gasp, and scramble away.

'Let me show you what I think of your threats!'

The light grew brighter, the beginnings of orange flames licking at the edge of the aura. *Fire,* he thought, *burn them all . . .*

And suddenly the prince was there, holding out his arms towards him, and the temperature in the room dropped like a stone. Frith gasped, and the air he dragged down into his lungs was so cold it was like swallowing glass. The violet flames vanished as quickly as they'd appeared and Frith dropped to his knees.

'Please,' said Prince Dallen, his tone sorrowful. 'I'm sorry, but it will do you no good at all.'

'What are you doing?' Frith could hear Wydrin's voice next to him, but his vision was growing dark. It would be easier to lie down and sleep than to face this cold. He gasped again, and his mouth felt coated with ice.

'Stop it!'

There was a scuffle as Wydrin struggled with the guards, and then abruptly the cold was gone. Frith shuddered violently, his limbs tingling.

'Take them to the pens with the rest of the beasts,' said Prince Dallen. 'They will die in the morning, as the king commands.'

The 'pens' turned out to be a godsforsaken caged enclosure in the shadow of the great ice wall, made of what looked like the giant bones of a whale, sealed and fortified with glittering rivets of ice. The three of them were thrown inside, next to a cage full of animals; a fat mother goat, which smelt as though she was currently suffering from a chronic illness of some sort, eyed them without curiosity. Wydrin immediately went to the bars of their cell, running her gloved hands over the bones. It was very cold, with little shelter from the winds and the mists, and the watery sun was already setting. A small crowd of guards stood off to one side, sharing jokes and a bottle of something.

'Well, the room in that draughty inn looks a lot better now,' she said, eyeing a goat hungrily. 'Do you think they'll feed us before they give us to their mountain?'

Sebastian sighed.

'Wydrin . . .'

'What are we going to do?' snapped Frith. They had untied his hands at least, but the Edenier had retreated inside him, as if it were afraid of the terrible cold the prince had summoned. 'We need to come up with some sort of plan before sunrise.'

'I suspect that if we can talk to the prince again, we may be able to come to an agreement of some kind,' said Sebastian. He sat down on the rocky ground with a grunt. 'He seemed more reasonable than his father.'

'More reasonable?' Frith shook his head in disbelief. 'This prince of yours almost froze me to death, and knocked you out of the sky.'

'Frith is right,' said Wydrin, turning away from the bones. 'As unlikely as that sounds. We need to come out of here fighting. Is there anything we can use as a weapon? If we can take the initial flurry of guards, we're actually quite close to the wall. The princeling can burn our way back out again . . .'

Sebastian was frowning.

'Take them all, without our weapons? We're deep in enemy territory, Wyd, and they are hardly short of reinforcements. No, our best chance will be diplomacy.'

They argued over their meagre options for hours, not coming any closer to a decision. Eventually, Frith came to realise that it was just a way to pass the time, a way to distract themselves from the inevitable, grisly end that faced them at sun-up. The thought only made him feel worse. Sebastian leaned back against the wall with his arms crossed over his chest and went to sleep. Frith went and sat with Wydrin.

'This is an unfortunate ending to your last adventure,' she said, reaching for the flask on her belt that was no longer there. She swore under her breath.

'You could say that.' He cleared his throat, uncertain of what to say next. Outside the night sky was clear, and they could see stars like diamonds, almost unnervingly bright in this cold air. 'It has certainly been interesting, though. I mean, all of this. Since the Citadel.'

'Any regrets?' Wydrin caught the look on his face and smiled lopsidedly. 'Apart from the obvious.'

'No,' he said softly. 'So much of my life has been about death and vengeance. Or at least, it's felt that way. The last year or so wasn't about that, and that was good.'

Silence pooled between them, filled with the mournful wailing of the wind over the jagged walls, and Sebastian's relaxed breathing. It was freezing in the enclosure, but they were sitting close enough that Frith could feel the small amount of warmth coming from Wydrin. He realised, with sudden clarity, that it would make him very happy to take her hand at that moment. He also knew, with the same painful clarity, that he could not do it.

At some point in the small hours of the night he fell asleep. He awoke with his head on Wydrin's shoulder, his back agonisingly stiff. Someone was whispering at them urgently, and Wydrin jumped to her feet, letting Frith slump awkwardly to the ground.

'What are you talking about?' she demanded.

Frith blinked the sleep from his eyes to see Prince Dallen standing in their enclosure. It was still dark, and he could no longer see any guards stationed outside. Sebastian was already on his feet.

'Please, keep your voice down. You must come with me,' said the prince, his voice hushed. 'You must be quick, and you must come now. I cannot answer your questions yet.'

'Why should we trust you?' asked Frith. 'You weren't so keen on us escaping before. I still have the frostbite to prove it.'

The prince turned to him, frustration evident on his mottled face.

'If I had let you burn down the long hall, as you so clearly wanted to do, my father would have had you executed then and there. I needed you moved somewhere that I could get to without being observed. And now we must move – there's always a chance one of the guards will mention my sudden visit to the wrong person, and we'll all be for it.'

'I say we take the chance,' said Sebastian. 'It beats staying here with the goats.'

'Here.' Prince Dallen turned back to a large sack at his feet, and began pulling out thickly furred cloaks, patched here and there with grey leather. They all had deep hoods. 'Put these on.

107

It's still dark enough out there, and with your faces hidden I should be able to get you out of the Shambles Gate without alerting any suspicion. Come on.'

They dressed quickly, and Dallen led them away from the enclosure, moving swiftly towards the towering wall of ice. Three shadowy figures joined them as they walked, and Frith recognised one of them as Olborn, Dallen's second in command. It was difficult to make out her face in the poor light, but her stance was tense.

The Shambles Gate was an iron door set directly into the ice. Prince Dallen spoke briefly to the two guards stationed there, and they were waved through without a word.

'It seems our prince often makes nightly visits beyond the wall,' muttered Wydrin. 'I'll bet his father doesn't know about that.'

Beyond the iron door was a long corridor carved directly into the ice. The walls were sheer and pale blue, the cold radiating off them like a fever. Once they reached the far end, another set of guards opened the far door onto a sweeping black and white world of snow and jagged mountains.

17

Siano pulled the pieces of sacking away from the head – despite her attempts to be as clean as possible, they were all soaked through – and with a wet cloth began to clean away some of the blood from the face. It had gathered in the crevices at the corners of the man's mouth, in the weathered pockets of lines by his eyes. Some had plugged the nose, and this she brusquely wiped away, grimacing slightly. When she was satisfied that she could see clearly enough to work, she put the head back down on the sawdust, removed her best knife from her belt, and looked again at the instructions.

The pattern was intricate, but not impossible to follow. She cut quickly and with a steady hand, and now that the man had been dead for some time the blood was thick, settling in his cuts like black jam. When she was done she propped the head up on a wooden box and cut her own finger. With this drop of her own blood she smeared a rough shape onto the forehead – it looked a little like a letter B – and shuffled back to kneel before it.

The effect was immediate.

'You have done well, Siano.' The voice was the same as it had been in the House of Patience: old, self-satisfied. 'You are talented indeed.'

Siano inclined her head.

'My lord, I trust the job has been done to your satisfaction?'

'Oh yes, although we are far from done yet, my child. That

109

doesn't concern you, does it? You haven't lost your taste for this sort of work?'

Siano shook her head, then remembered that she didn't know if the owner of the voice could see her or not.

'It doesn't concern me, Lord. I was made for this.'

'Yes, yes. You are indeed one of my creatures. Good. Now, we have a few more steps to complete before I can welcome my friend back to the world. Technically, this last part should involve patricide.'

Siano blinked. Deep inside, something very small was calling out a warning, but she pushed it to one side easily enough. She hadn't listened to that voice in years.

'My father is dead, my lord. He passed away some years ago.'

'No matter,' said the voice, cheerily enough. 'This is my game, and I make the rules. Blood isn't the only chain that binds you.'

Father Tallow became aware of two things at once. First, that he was terribly, painfully cold. It was a cold that sat on his chest and squeezed at his heart. And second, that he wasn't alone in his bedchamber.

'Who's there?' He didn't like how his voice sounded. It was the voice of a frightened old man. He cleared his throat and tried again. 'Is there someone here?'

'It is only me, Father.' The old lamp on his bedside table flared into life, revealing a tall, slim figure by his bed. The girl's face looked longer, more serious, and she held herself differently. *The girl has become a woman*, thought Father Tallow. *Has she really been gone so long?*

'You are back already?' Tallow tried to raise himself from the pillow but found he was too weak to do so. *I must have been in a very deep sleep*, he thought.

Siano nodded. 'I don't think I'll come back again, though,' she said. 'I think it's time for me to make my own way in the world, Father. I wanted to wake you up before you went, to tell you that, and because, well, I thought you would want to be awake. At the end.'

Father Tallow tried to move again, his head swimming. He was thinking of all the locks on his windows, the traps by the door, the

110

plates in the floor that triggered alarms all over the building. There were the men who patrolled the corridor beyond his bedchamber. What had happened to them? It wasn't hard to guess.

'Why?' he asked, knowing it was a ridiculous question to ask a child of the House of Patience. It was always the same answer: because the client willed it. Because the client paid for it.

'It will be soon now, Father.' Siano came forward and touched his bare arm, and for the first time Father Tallow saw the glass tube there, filled with his own blood. How long had it been there, siphoning away his life? Quite a while, if he were judging by his own weakened state. Siano would have numbed his arm first, possibly with some ice or, more likely, with a particular type of unguent the pupils were taught to make in their very first year. Father Tallow allowed himself to feel proud, just for a moment.

'Good, that is good.' In the end, wasn't it better to go this way? Rather than coughing his last into a bloody hanky, too weak and old to be of any use to anyone, he would die by the hand of his most talented pupil – a final demonstration of Father Tallow's life's work. He tried to focus on this thought, but still he was afraid. Siano's face in the lamplight – so solemn, so absent – was not a reassuring sight.

'Your heart is beating quicker, Father.' Siano bent to examine the tube. 'Your blood is rushing to leave you. You are not afraid, are you?'

Father Tallow shivered. Did it have to be so cold? The cold was the worst of it.

'Please, Siano.' His voice was little more than a whisper now. The room was growing darker all the time. 'Pull the blankets over me. I am so cold. I don't want to die feeling this cold.'

Siano did not move.

'There is no point. And I did not think you would be afraid.'

Father Tallow opened his mouth to ask again, to plead, but there was nothing left to push the words out. The light faded, and his last sight was of Siano's face, her eyes watchful and empty.

When it was done, Siano removed the old man's head, carving the sigils faster this time, barely thinking about it. She'd always had a good memory. As she worked, she imagined what her brothers

111

and sisters would think when they found Tallow decapitated in his own bed, the silk sheets and thick carpet soaked in blood. She hoped it would put the wind up them.

'Yes, good, very good.' The voice came through even clearer this time, almost as though she could hear it in her head. 'This was very fine indeed. He was afraid of you at the end, did you know that? I can still taste it in the room. A very fine type of suffering.'

'I did it well,' said Siano. 'He was afraid, but he was also proud.'

The voice chuckled. 'I'm sure that was of *great* comfort to him as he bled all over his own bedcovers.'

Siano shifted. The room stank of blood now, a thick mineral smell like copper pennies. Surely someone else in the House of Patience would smell it soon, and she would have to be gone before then.

'What is our next move, my lord?'

'Oh, you must come and find me next, Siano. Come and find me in Skaldshollow. We're going to have such fun.'

112

18

Nuava walked down the corridor hurriedly, one hand on her pocket. Tamlyn had given her the knife, muttering something about it being the right tool for the job, but she hadn't met Nuava's eyes, and had turned away when she asked more questions. Now the knife was a weight in her pocket, and it was heavier than she'd been expecting, in more ways than one.

'He is already dead,' she told herself again. She kept her eyes forward, concentrating on getting this task done without delay. 'It won't matter to him either way.'

Nuava nodded to the guard on the door. 'I am here on the Prophet's business.'

His eyes widened slightly at that. *And he doesn't even know about the knife*, she thought.

Inside the cell the body of the Narhl prisoner slumped on a narrow straw bed, a lifeless sack. *A sack of bones*, she thought grimly. Her brother was standing over him, scratching words onto a length of parchment. He looked up and saw her, his brow creasing in immediate worry.

'Nuava? What are you doing here?' He shifted slightly so that he blocked her view of the body, although she'd already seen the various burn marks streaked like sooty trails across the man's grey and white flesh. 'This isn't something you want to see.'

She lifted her chin, holding her face still and composed.

'Tamlyn sent me. I have a task to perform for her.' She stepped neatly around him, peering down at the body. 'Did he die from – what we did to him?'

Bors sighed and put the parchment on a small blood-stained table.

'No. I think it was the heat, in the end. I keep telling them, it's too warm down here, with all the lamps.' He looked away from her, his lips pursed. 'The Narhl can't cope with it, not when they're already injured.'

Nuava bent down and pressed her fingers to the man's arm. This one had been a lone rider, scouting around the edges of Skaldshollow on the back of a wyvern. One of the war-werkens had been lucky with a shot from a catapult, and they'd brought him back to the Hollow before he'd regained consciousness. His skin was smooth, and still quite warm. She blinked. Of course, a healthy Narhl would be cold, she told herself.

'What are you doing down here, Nuava?' Bors came over to her. 'I need to make an inventory, a report to the werken council. Everything Tamlyn needs to know will be in that.'

Nuava straightened up. 'Tamlyn wishes me to remove his fingers. His finger bones. I'm to bring them, cleaned, to the Prophet.'

There was a moment's silence. She didn't quite dare look at her brother's face.

'You're doing *what*?'

She cleared her throat. 'You heard me, Bors. Just leave me alone, all right? I can do this.'

'What could the Prophet possibly need those for?'

'It is all part of the training.' She reached into her pocket and drew out the knife. 'What does it matter, anyway? It's just his fingers, and he's dead now.'

Bors laid a hand on her arm. He looked bewildered. 'How can this be part of the training, Nuava? How can this have anything to do with crafting the Edeian?'

'And you know about that, do you?' she snapped, shaking his hand off. 'You are not her pupil, as much as you would like to be.' He frowned at that, and looked down at his feet for a moment; a classic sign that her brother was struggling to control his temper. 'Bors, these are the ways of the Edeian. They are not for everyone, and it is not my place to question our aunt. *She* is Mistress Crafter.'

114

'You know this is wrong.' He made her meet his eyes. His broad face was tense, his eyes pleading. 'No one hates the Narhl more than I. They've terrorised us, taken the Heart-Stone, killed our people. Our mother and father, Nuava. But desecrating their corpses? We call them savages, worse than animals, but what are we if we carve their bodies into pieces? Nuava, the Prophet –' he lowered his voice, glancing uneasily at the door – 'I'm not sure we should be following everything she says. We don't even know where she came from.'

'Shall I tell her you said that?' Nuava immediately regretted the words; such a thing was an open threat, and to her own brother. But she had a task to do, and his discomfort was less painful than Tamlyn's fury should she fail. 'I'm sure people have asked before where the Prophet came from, and why we should listen to her. Do you know where they are now, Bors?'

For a long moment he said nothing. Nuava found herself wanting to look at the corpse again, anything to avoid the pain in her brother's eyes. *This is my path*, she told herself. *If I must walk it alone, then that is what I will do.*

'Tamlyn is no longer in control,' he said. 'You know that, I know that. We are trusting our lives, and the lives of all the people of Skaldshollow to . . . to that thing that calls itself the Prophet.'

Nuava drew in a sharp breath. Instinctively, she glanced at the door to see if the guard was still there but he had gone.

'Bors, you can't—'

'It hurts me to say it, but our aunt has lost her way. This –' he gestured to the dead Narhl – 'has nothing to do with crafting the Edeian, and everything to do with whatever sick game the Prophet is playing. You are too clever, Nuava, not to know this. Don't be so proud that you ignore it.'

She opened her mouth, not at all certain what she was going to say, but without another word he walked past her into the corridor and was gone, leaving her alone with the dead man.

Nuava looked down at the knife. She'd been gripping it so tightly that her knuckles had turned white.

'It is a simple enough task,' she told herself. Her voice sounded very small to her own ears. 'Once I have done this, Tamlyn

115

will know I am serious about being a crafter. And it's not like he'll be using them again.'

She stood for a moment, taking a number of deep, steadying breaths, and then she bent to the task.

After wrapping the severed fingers in a piece of cloth, she took them to the small home she shared with Bors, and shut herself in the kitchen. Luckily, he wasn't home, and she set about stripping the flesh with one of her own paring knives. While she did this she pictured the werken she would someday build: tall and mighty, greater than anything Tamlyn had created. Next she boiled up some water in their small black cauldron and threw the fingers in. While they tossed in the heated water she washed her hands repeatedly, wearing their small block of soap down to a nub.

When eventually the bones were clean of flesh, she took them from the cauldron and lay them on a blue cloth she'd found to wrap them in. She looked at them: innocuous white sticks, she told herself, or the bones of a chicken carcass. Nothing more.

However, when she folded up the cloth and put them in her pocket, she briefly had the impression of holding someone's hand, and the wave of nausea that moved through her was so powerful that she staggered and had to lean on the sink for some time. Her mouth filled with saliva and her eyes watered, but she did not vomit.

The urge to get them out of her pocket was enormous. She had to concentrate on not running to the Tower of Waking, instead forcing herself to walk sedately, her chin up, as befitted the heir to the Mistress Crafter. The bones in her pocket were not as heavy as the knife had been, but she felt them there all the same.

On her way into the tower she met Tamlyn just coming out. The older woman looked distracted, her thick padded jacket half undone. She looked at Nuava for some moments, as if she couldn't quite remember who she was.

'I've done it,' she said, trying to sound full of flinty resolve and wincing inwardly as her voice came out in a wheezy squeak. 'Shall I take them up to her?'

'What?' Tamlyn scowled.

'The bones, I – I've brought them, as you asked.'

'Oh. Yes, of course. Take them up.' Tamlyn looked past her. They stood at the foot of the great staircase and the front doors looked out onto an afternoon that was growing darker by the minute. 'There has been no news,' she said. 'They should have been there by now, and they should be on their way back, but our furthest patrols have reported nothing so far.'

Nuava blinked rapidly, realising that her aunt was talking about the mercenaries who had left to retrieve the Heart-Stone. It was difficult to think about anything else while the bones were in her pocket.

'They could have been delayed on the Crippler,' she said, not really caring either way. She thought of the paring knife, sliding smoothly through flesh as grey as slate, as grey as werken-rock, and she felt her stomach clench uncomfortably. 'If the weather has been bad, they could be late by days.'

'Yes,' said Tamlyn. She narrowed her eyes at her niece. 'Or they could have been caught by the Narhl and killed, and we are still without our Heart-Stone. Go on, then, get up to the room. It is best not to keep the Prophet waiting.'

Nuava opened her mouth, suddenly close to asking so many questions. Why would the Prophet want the finger bones of a Narhl warrior? Who was she, anyway? Why were they listening to her advice? But Tamlyn swept past her, and the moment was gone. Nuava watched her walk to the door, and then sprinted up the steps, across the hall, and up the many spiral staircases that led to the Prophet's suite. When she stood outside the door she stopped, leaning against the raw rock wall. Her head was spinning.

My werkens, she told herself, *will be magnificent. They will be greater than anything Tamlyn has created, and I will be Mistress Crafter.*

A soft voice called from within. 'Don't stand out there, wheezing at the door, Nuava, dear. It's most unseemly.'

Nuava entered the chamber. As ever, it was much too warm; a sweat broke out on her back immediately, and she wished she'd thought to leave her furs indoors. The Prophet was on the huge four-poster bed, hidden by the thick canopy of gauze curtains. Nuava had never seen her face.

'I've brought what you wanted,' she said, forcing her voice to be calm. Soon she would be free of the bones, and she could forget all about it. 'The bones. I have them here for you.'

'Oh good! Come over here, child.'

Nuava did as she was told, blanching slightly at 'child'.

A slim white hand slipped through the curtains, small and unblemished. The fingernails were slightly over-long.

'Put them in my hand, dear.'

Suddenly, the nausea was back. It was that voice, paired with that small, slim hand. It made no sense at all, and the wrongness of everything the Prophet was hit her. Bors was right, of course he was.

'Are you quite well, child?' Nuava could see the shadowed form of the Prophet beyond the curtain, and although the face was nothing more than a dark shape, she could hear the smile in the voice.

'Yes, of course. Here.' She shoved her hand in her pocket and placed the bundle of fabric on the Prophet's hand. It didn't move.

'That doesn't feel like bones, Nuava.'

'They're in there,' she said. 'They're in the cloth.'

'I asked you to put the bones in my hand, Nuava.'

Nuava took the bundle back and opened it. Trying not to notice how smooth they were, how slightly warm from her own body heat, she gathered the bones and quickly passed them to the Prophet's hand. The small, tapered fingers closed around them and passed back through the curtain. The Prophet made a small noise of delight.

'Oh, very good. Yes, very good.'

Nuava bowed rapidly, already backing away towards the door. She wanted to wash her hands again.

'Wait one moment!'

Nuava stopped, holding her breath.

'Tamlyn tells me that you are quite the little scholar.' There was laughter in the voice now. 'That you study all hours. That you wish to be a crafter of the Edeian, as she is.'

'Yes,' said Nuava. From beyond the curtain came the soft clatter of bones being moved against each other. 'I want to make my own werkens one day.'

'It is a rare thing, to be able to craft the Edeian,' said the Prophet in a conversational tone. 'I have known a few who could, and they were . . . special. Tell me, Nuava, what do you know of Joah Demonsworn?'

'I know he was a great mage that lived and died not far from here. I visited his tomb just recently, with the mercenaries.'

The Prophet chuckled. 'Yes, I'm sure they enjoyed that. But that is what everyone knows, Nuava Nox. What do you know from your *extensive studies*?'

Nuava coughed. The smoke from the braziers was making her chest tight. 'He made a pact with a demon, and through that made his greatest and his most terrible works. He crafted the Edeian, as well as wielding the powers of a mage. But one day he asked to see the true form of the demon, for he had grown fond of it. When he saw its real face, he went insane.'

The shape of the Prophet was very still now, and the clacking of the bones had stopped. Nuava swallowed hard, wondering if she should keep talking. 'It was terrifying, they said, and ugly beyond anything mortal. They said that if he were a normal man, he would have been struck blind as well. They said—'

'That is quite enough, Nuava.' All the good humour had vanished from the Prophet's voice. 'You can leave now.'

Nuava, her nerve finally broken, turned and ran out into the corridor.

19

Glaciers rose high above them, impossibly blue and shining with bright mirrored light. They were travelling through a narrow canyon, the sides sliced sheer by the passage of ancient mountains. The ground underfoot was made of brittle sheets of snow. Every now and then Sebastian would glance up to see one of the wyverns flying overhead, their long bodies wriggling like eels in a stream. Looking at them, he felt a strange sense of wonder, a tightness in his chest; their skins were a pale shimmering blue, touched here and there with white fur, and their long snouts were narrow and lined with small, peg-like teeth. Their short wings stretched out to either side of their bodies, as taut as sails, and he realised that these creatures felt alive to him in a way he didn't quite understand. He thought of Ephemeral and her snakes. *Was this blood calling to blood, as she claimed?*

Once or twice he'd seen a black bird too, flying high above them. Gwiddion was following along at a distance, it seemed, and that thought cheered him a little.

'Where are you taking us?' asked Wydrin. According to the prince her werken was waiting for them at their destination, so she walked by the sturdy little ponies that carried their kit. Dallen walked with her, an ice-spear at his side.

'It's a place between our territories,' said Prince Dallen. He gestured ahead, where the ground in front of them sloped gradually upwards again. 'Once we are out of this canyon we will be close.'

'If it is between your territories, then who does the land belong to?' asked Frith. With him they were still openly cautious; his hands were firmly bound once more, and he had been forced to ride one of the ponies, much to his obvious discomfort.

'It is neither Skald nor Narhl,' said Prince Dallen. 'The place where I am taking you is just on the edge of our home, a thin strip of land that lies between us and the very outer reaches of where the Skalds dare to travel. It is neutral territory, and therefore the best place that I know of for peace talks.'

Frith snorted derisively; the young lord was very sceptical about Prince Dallen's apparently earnest talk of peace, but Sebastian was inclined to give him the benefit of the doubt. When they met up with the rest of Prince Dallen's squad, still moving furtively under the cover of night, they had been shocked to find the Heart-Stone waiting for them there, also smuggled out of the settlement without King Aristees' knowledge. Sebastian had caught sight of its eerie, green light, painting the surrounding snows with a colour like seawater, before someone had hastily thrown a blanket over it.

When Sebastian had asked him about it, the prince had actually grinned ruefully, looking mildly embarrassed.

'You were entirely right, Sir Sebastian. The stone is, technically, stolen property. It should not be ours, no more than it should be the Skalds'. If I take it to a neutral place, then perhaps we can begin to sort things out.'

Sebastian surprised himself by laughing bitterly. 'Your father was ready to cut our heads off for the sake of that stone. You yourself told me that the Skalds are defiling a sacred spirit. Now you talk of diplomacy?'

'We are not savages, Sir Sebastian, whatever the Skalds would have you believe,' said Prince Dallen. And then in a lower tone of voice, 'my father's throne room is no place for the Heart-Stone either.'

Sebastian had asked him what his father would think of his plan, and Prince Dallen had looked uneasily over his shoulder, as if expecting an army to sweep down on them at any moment.

'If we don't move quickly, we may find out,' was all he'd said.

* * *

Now Sebastian glanced over at the prince, who was chatting easily to Wydrin, remembering that look of rueful cheer. *He wants to change things,* he thought, *and somehow we've given him an opportunity to try.*

'So this place we're going to,' Wydrin was saying now. 'Why isn't it part of your territory? Why have neither of you claimed it?'

'That's because it's haunted,' said Dallen mildly. 'A cursed place.'

'Oh, good,' said Wydrin dryly. 'I haven't been to a cursed place for ages.'

'This land is full of magic, Wydrin Threefellows,' continued Dallen. 'And certain places are more sensitive to it. No one knows why this particular piece of land is haunted, but everyone feels it who ventures there. Even the stone-headed Skalds. Now it is inhabited only by animals, who live even closer to the Edeian than we do.'

Eventually they came out of the canyon, as Dallen had promised, and were faced with another lonely snowscape. Here and there were soft peaks, like sand dunes, with the black teeth of rocks poking through. Sebastian was surprised to see movement in this place; a herd of distant animals, their shaggy white hides standing out in stark contrast against the black mountains that circled them. He paused, trying to make out what they were. There was something about their shapes that looked wrong to him.

Dallen saw him looking, and smiled.

'A colony of arachnos,' he said. 'There are many such gatherings in the wilder parts of Narhl territory.'

'What are they?' asked Sebastian. He noticed that the prince wore a tuft of white wyvern fur on a cord around his throat, next to a tooth that looked like it had belonged to a bear once. There was a lot he was noticing about the prince. 'Are they dangerous?'

For a time Dallen kept looking at the distant beasts, until Sebastian thought he wasn't going to answer.

'They are not dangerous, no, not unless provoked. We are heading towards them, Sir Sebastian, so you'll get a closer look soon enough.'

Dallen was right. Another hour of walking, the wyverns flying above them like unlikely standards, and the strange herd of animals swerved across their path. They were enormous, twice as tall as a man, with broad furry bodies supported by four long, tapering legs. Their fur was white and grey, and their heads, which nestled close to their powerful shoulders, were dotted with four glassy red eyes. Underneath these apparently lidless organs was a pair of black mandibles, half hidden in the long fur. The overall effect was that of a giant, white-furred spider with four legs, and they moved with slow grace over the brittle snow. The herd that moved past them had around thirty members, the biggest twice as tall as Sebastian, with the smallest the size of a large cow.

Next to Sebastian, Wydrin shook her head. 'Please tell me those things eat grass.'

'They do eat flesh, but instances of them attacking humans are very rare,' said Prince Dallen. He had ordered the group to a standstill while the arachnos passed. 'And accidental, mostly. You see, they can form the ice like we do, and use it to build traps under the snow. A thin layer of ice over a deep hole. Unfortunate men and women have been lost this way, but an actual attack from an arachnos? I have never heard of it happening. They are peaceful animals.'

Wydrin had gone slightly paler under her hood.

'As if falling into a hole in this place wouldn't be bad enough, without a giant snow spider showing up to eat you afterwards.'

Dallen chuckled. 'I fear I have accidentally portrayed the arachnos in a poor light. When we get to our destination, I will be able to show you a different side.'

They reached the unclaimed lands under a sky ragged with black clouds and moonlight. The land had been gradually sloping downwards again, until they came to a sudden drop and, beyond that short cliff, was a wide, shallow bowl filled with snow.

'What are those, then?' asked Wydrin. Dallen's squad led them down the cliff, along a rough path carved directly into the rock, and she found her eyes turning again and again to the strange objects nestled in the snow.

'This is where the arachnos lay their eggs,' said Dallen. Frith had been turfed off the mountain pony, and was walking with his arms held awkwardly behind his back, while Sebastian brought up the rear. 'Aren't they beautiful?'

'They are that,' agreed Wydrin. The wide expanse of powdery snow was covered in round hemispheres of ice, all clustered together like bubbles floating on the top of a puddle. They glittered in the moonlight, as though they had been sprinkled with diamonds. As they got closer, Wydrin could see that they all had a small hole where the ice met the ground – small for the arachnos, anyway; a human could walk in and out without much trouble. 'Very beautiful. Are you really telling me you've brought us to where those things *nest*?'

Dallen gestured with his ice-spear. 'This nesting site is long since abandoned. They never lay their eggs in the same place twice, and certainly wouldn't reuse their ice-warrens. Look.' They had reached the first cluster now, and Dallen's squad were swiftly unpacking their goods from the small mountain ponies, while the wyverns and their riders landed some distance away. 'They lay their eggs and then cover them in a protective shell of ice. When the young arachnos hatch, they claw their way out with their mandibles.'

'This is all fascinating,' said Frith from behind them. 'Perhaps one day I shall return and write a book about it.' Wydrin shot him a look, amused; she could tell from his tone that he was close to losing his temper. 'However, if I do not get to sit near a fire soon I shall be forced to set myself on fire.'

Dallen glanced over to him. 'Of course. I have had your belongings brought here ahead of us.' At his word, five more men and women appeared from within one of the arachnos' nests, and they were carrying their packs.

'You intend to give them back to us?' asked Sebastian.

'Perhaps not immediately.' Prince Dallen smiled slightly. 'Which I'm sure you can understand. Wydrin, your werken is also here, although I wish to talk to you about that before we go any further. I want to talk to you all about what I intend to do here.'

'Sure.' Wydrin glanced at Frith and Sebastian. Neither of them objected. 'I don't suppose you've got something to drink while we have this chat? My insides feel like I'll never be warm again.'

124

'We have plenty of grut,' he said, gesturing to one of his men. 'I hesitate to recommend it, though, on my honour as a prince.'

'That'll do,' she said. 'I've had worse.'

'I must demand that my hands are untied,' said Frith as soon as he was seated. His hood had fallen back from his face and his brown skin was the warmest thing Wydrin had seen in days. She looked away. 'I am the Lord of the Blackwood, and I refuse to suffer this indignity any longer.'

They were sitting inside one of the ice nests, with a cold-lamp wedged in the snow between them. Inside the nest the ice was cloudy and white, with fine swirling lines traced all over the surface like giant fingerprints.

'You may as well untie him,' Wydrin said. 'You won't get a word of sense out of him until you do.'

Prince Dallen nodded reluctantly before leaning over and cutting Frith's bonds with a knife. The young lord made a great show of rubbing his wrists.

'I imagine you're wondering what I have planned, taking you away from the Frozen Steps in the middle of the night.' He sat forward slightly, the leather armour gaping open around his neck. He seemed utterly unconcerned by the cold.

'It has crossed my mind,' said Sebastian. He was watching the prince closely. Wydrin thought she saw more than mild curiosity in that look. *So he is not dead below the waist after all.*

Dallen chuckled dryly.

'We have been in conflict with the Skalds for as long as anyone can remember. My father is a very traditional man. As you may have noticed.'

'He's very keen on his axe,' said Wydrin. 'I noticed that.'

'The king wants us to stay behind the walls of the Frozen Steps, to carry on with the way of life we've had for thousands of years. Everything must stay the same.' He tugged at his small beard with his thumb and forefinger. 'And I cannot really blame him. The Narhl are a part of this land, and our way of life has served us well. Our relationship with the land is unique, and perhaps it is necessary that our contact with outsiders is so strictly controlled. But I fear it is unsustainable. One day, I will be king, and I do not want to lead my people into a future of constant war. Of continual solitude. I believe,' he shifted on the ground, speaking slightly faster now, 'I really do believe that we can benefit from learning more about the outside world. That it can lead to better lives for my people. There is so much we don't know, hidden away behind those walls, and we will never know any of it if we must be continually at war with the Skalds. On the other hand, their practices are a direct insult. An attack on the Narhl soul.' The prince paused, looking up to meet their eyes. 'It is not a jest when we say that they are destroying the mountain spirits. We all feel it, in here.' He tapped his chest. 'They cannot continue to treat the Heart-Stone in this way, chipping pieces of it off to make their slaves.' He glanced down at his own hands, as if to keep his temper in check. 'Werkens, as they call them, are pieces of the soul of the mountain. They are sentient, thinking, feeling creatures, as capable of thought and emotion as you and I.'

'From what I have seen, the Skalds will not give them up on your say-so,' said Sebastian softly. 'The werkens are how they build their homes, how they defend their city. Werkens are at the heart of Skaldshollow.'

Prince Dallen nodded.

'Oh yes, I am quite aware of that. Even so, I want to build a peace between our peoples. I want to start building it now, while there is still a chance for the mountain spirits. I want the leaders of Skaldshollow to come here, to meet with me, and we will talk. Properly. As we haven't for generations.'

'They will not come,' said Frith. 'You give them no reason to. You have stolen their property, killed their people. Now you propose they give up that which they hold to be the very centre of their civilisation.'

'That is why I want you to take them a message. Wydrin, can you feel the werken in your mind?'

Wydrin shrugged, and reached out for Mendrick. She could feel it close by, a chilly extension of herself, just waiting in the dark.

'Tell me about the werken,' he said. 'How does it feel in your head?'

Wydrin shrugged. 'It doesn't feel like anything much. It's a cold feeling, like a little part of me is somewhere else.'

'You do not feel its mind? There is no sense of another being?'

'Not really, no,' she smiled crookedly, realising that she was actually a little sorry to disappoint Prince Dallen.

'There is a link between you,' said Dallen, 'but it is very faint. I can open that link, deepen it, and show you that the werken you are ordering around is a thinking, feeling being. When I have done that, you can take that message back to Skaldshollow. Perhaps then they will listen.'

'Hold on a moment,' said Frith. 'The joining seemed violent enough, and quite frankly, it was a foolish thing to do in the first place. How do we know that this isn't going to hurt Wydrin?'

'Foolish?' Wydrin shot him a dark look. 'Foolish would be chucking yourself into a lake full of mage magic, surely? Or getting cold-cocked by a bird-headed god.'

'The procedure is not without its risks,' said Dallen. He met Wydrin's eyes, and she saw the desperation there. 'And you have to be willing for it to work. There is no way any Skald would agree to this. Don't you see? This is the perfect opportunity, the perfect chance to heal things while it's still possible. You will know, and then you can tell them.'

'I don't know.' Sebastian shook his head. 'I appreciate what you're saying, your highness, but we came to do a simple job, not to broker a peace. In all honesty, we're probably the last people you should approach for that.'

Wydrin thought of Mendrick, how the werken had moved before it was joined, its cold green eyes glowing in the dark. If she was imposing her will onto another thinking, feeling being, wouldn't she want to know about it?

'Is it reversible?' she asked. 'Once you've deepened this link between us, can we ever go back?'

Dallen nodded. 'You would need to remove the piece of Heart-Stone from your hand, that is all.'

She took another gulp of the grut, welcoming the heat it brought to her stomach. She could feel Frith and Sebastian looking at her. 'Let's do it then,' she said. 'I've always said I'll try anything once.'

20

Wydrin had visited Sebastian in Ynnsmouth a month or so after the incident with the lake-singer. It was a bright, cold day, the sun turning the snows to a silver glitter that made your eyes water.

The brood sisters on duty that morning, Nettle and Umbellifer, reported her approach a good hour before she arrived; Sebastian had posted lookouts along the path from the moment they'd arrived, and there wasn't a second when the way to the temple wasn't watched. He had taught Wydrin the directions to the secret path years ago, reasoning that the abandoned temple might make a handy bolt-hole should any of their more morally dubious jobs blow up in their faces – after all, the last place anyone would think to look for an exiled knight would be in Ynnsmouth.

She came up the wide stone steps, an expression of wry amusement on her face. She wore her habitual travelling leathers and a furred leather cap on her head, and long gloves and boots. Her pack looked both heavy and well-used, as though she'd been travelling for some time.

'Hello, stranger,' she said, breaking into a grin. 'I hope that ugly pile of bricks has a big bastard fireplace.'

Sebastian folded her into a hug, laughing. The temple stood alone on its hill, sheltered within the shadow of Isu, the grass overgrown, the roof blistered and leaking. He and the brood sisters were already working on fixing it, and most of the debris of so many untended winters had been swept away.

'It certainly has,' he said, after planting a kiss on the top of

Wydrin's head. 'The brood sisters are not fond of the cold at all, and they keep it roaring at all times.'

At that Wydrin's grin faltered, and she looked down the training slopes. He watched her taking in the sights. Below them a row of ten brood sisters were moving in slow, considered formation, wooden swords clasped in their green hands, while across the snow another group of ten were at the tanning racks, repairing clothes and armour with expressions of intense concentration.

'It's quite the set-up you have here, Seb,' she said carefully. 'Have you got them doing your old exercises?'

'They've taken to it all quite naturally. Here, come into the temple and I'll get you some tea.'

Sebastian led her up the steps and through the lacquered doors. Inside the cold daylight painted brittle squares on the flagstones, while huge oil lamps burnt in all four corners. The fireplace was at the far end, tended by Ephemeral. In the roof there was a great square skylight, filled with clear glass and miraculously intact after years of abandonment. Through it, it was possible to see the distant peaks of Isu, white and deadly against the blue.

'Ephemeral, is there a brew on?'

The brood sister turned away from the fire at the sound of his voice, and then broke into a smile at the sight of Wydrin.

'Wydrin Threefellows, I am very glad you could come and visit with us,' and then to Sebastian, 'the pot is still full, Father.'

'Thank you, Ephemeral. Crocus wanted your help with a bit of darning she was struggling over.'

Ephemeral looked reluctant to go, her eyes roaming over Wydrin with a hunger Sebastian couldn't name, but after another nod that was almost a bow, she left. Sebastian dragged a pair of wooden chairs over to the fire, and fetched the clay cups from a tray on a table.

'Now when you say tea, Sebastian, I'm assuming you actually mean brandy or something, because I've been walking for days and every bit of me is frozen. I wouldn't be surprised if I take my clothes off later and find out that bits of me have dropped off.'

'I will put some brandy in your tea.' He poured her a cup, adding to it from a silver flask at his own belt, and poured himself a measure too. They sat for a few moments in companionable

129

silence. It was good to see Wydrin's face, and strange also – for the past two weeks he had seen no one who did not have yellow eyes and pointed teeth.

'So,' she said eventually, when she'd downed her first cup of laced tea and refilled it with rather more brandy. 'How is this all going?' She gestured round at the temple. It still smelled of the incense the Order had burnt for their rites, so many years ago. 'Any problems yet? Anyone eaten anyone else?'

Sebastian looked down at his tea. 'It hasn't been entirely plain sailing.'

Very quickly he told her of the lake-singing girl and her family, watching as her normally cheery face grew more troubled. When he'd finished, she reached across and took the brandy flask from him, drinking directly from the bottle.

'Ye gods and little fishes, Seb. And no one caught you after that?'

'We were very careful. We travelled mainly by night from then on. Once or twice we found a hiding place and stayed there for days, while I went on ahead to find the safest route. I saw hunting parties several times, but I made sure we left as little track behind as we could. We crossed back and forth over rivers, covered our scent with mud.' He half laughed. 'All that stuff I learned as a novice actually came in handy.'

'Even so, that's bloody risky. And you've had no trouble since?'

He shook his head. 'I don't think they believed that we'd go into the sacred mountains. And we don't even know if they'd have taken the father's report seriously. Besides which,' he poured himself another cup of tea, mainly to warm his hands up, 'hardly anyone knew about this place. Once, it was a secret temple, known only by knights who had reached a certain level in the Order. And then the path that led to it was lost in an avalanche, and it was forgotten.'

Wydrin tipped her head to one side. 'Can you be absolutely certain of that, Seb?'

He shifted in his chair. For the first time he felt faintly irritated. There were always so many questions with Wydrin.

'You forget, I saw the vast majority of the Ynnsmouth knights die under Y'Ruen's flames. And most of those that were left will have died at Baneswatch. Besides which, this particular temple had been abandoned for decades before I was even a novice.'

'Why even come here, Seb?' She was looking at him with her head tipped to one side. 'Ynnsmouth, of all places?'

'We could hardly go back to Relios, could we? This was the closest *safe* place I could think of. And we won't be here for ever. We just need time to . . . get things straight.'

Wydrin nodded and kept her silence, a sure sign she wasn't convinced. He decided to change the subject.

'I half thought you would arrive with company.'

She raised an eyebrow at that. 'Well, I could have brought a fleet of pirates with me if you'd only mentioned it. They would have drunk you out of brandy though.'

'You know who I'm talking about. Where is Frith now? I had the brood sisters looking out for a griffin.'

To his surprise, it was Wydrin's turn to look uncomfortable. 'He is at his castle, of course. We visited there on our way to see my brother.' She paused. 'While we were there, Frith received a message of some sort, and suddenly it was like talking to a lump of stone. He spent hours in his study, he wouldn't see me. You know he's always been a moody sod, but this was different. It was like he was frightened to talk to me.'

Sebastian frowned. 'Did you find out what the message was?'

'Of course. I bribed one of his servants to peek at the letter for me.' She fell silent then, staring into the fire.

'Well?'

'It was nothing. Just a message from some Lady something or other, a fancy sort who owns land on the other side of Litvania. An invitation to meet up.' She shrugged. 'You know what these lords and ladies are like, they have to write everything down on gilded parchment in case they forget who they're supposed to be having tea with. When I eventually got him to talk to me, he said that he had to arrange a few more things in the castle, that he had responsibilities that needed his attention, and he wouldn't be coming with me to Crosshaven.' She took a deep breath. 'We have word of a job at Stingingmoon Bay, an island to the north of the Horns, so when I'm done here I will meet him there. With you, if you're able to come.'

131

'We'll have to see about that.' He looked up at her, examining the way she sat on the edge of the chair, the way she fiddled with the ties on her leather belt. 'Did you two . . .? *Are* you two . . .?'

'Did we what? Wrestle bears? Go tree climbing?'

'Wydrin, forgive me, but you've never exactly been coy about the men you wanted. There have been times, in fact, when I would have sacrificed a leg of my own to the god-peak *not* to hear about your conquests, and yet, with Frith, you dance around the subject. You dance around each other.'

She looked up at him, her green eyes both annoyed and amused.

'Well, if that's what you're asking, we are *not*. He is . . .' She threw up the hand not holding the cup. 'Infuriating. Exasperating. Fascinating. Half the time I want to stab him, and half the time I want to eat things off his body.' She sighed heavily, and then laughed at the look Sebastian was giving her. 'He's a mess. I'm not sure I've got the patience to wait for him to stop tying himself in knots over everything.'

'Maybe it's not a choice you get to make.'

'Oh give over. You know me, Seb. I don't take these things too seriously.'

Sebastian smiled, pouring more tea, but, watching his friend's face, he wasn't entirely sure he believed her.

'I'm more concerned about the situation here,' said Wydrin. 'They are still calling you Father, I notice. How do you feel about that?'

Sebastian shrugged. 'They don't all call me that. Some of them do. It seems to make all this easier for them to understand.' Wydrin was suddenly conspicuously quiet so he kicked her boot. 'What?'

'I don't know, Seb. This all seems very risky. You could be found up here by someone, or they could turn on you. I don't like you being alone with them.'

'They wouldn't harm me.'

'See, I think that's something else you can't be sure of. I saw what these soldiers can do first-hand.'

'Then what was I supposed to do? Just leave them to their fate at Baneswatch?' He put down his cup of tea, too agitated to hold it. 'For better or for worse, my blood awoke them at the Citadel, and now we are linked by that blood. I can still hear them sometimes, in my head, like whispering at a distance.' He shook his head at Wydrin's look of concern. 'It's under control. The brood sisters that are left are my responsibility.'

'Oh, the dragon was your responsibility, and now her daughters are your responsibility? Sebastian, not everything is your problem to solve.'

'And not everything can be run away from.'

Wydrin raised an eyebrow. 'I don't know what you think you mean by that, but—'

Someone cleared their throat behind them, and Sebastian looked up to see the Second standing a short distance away. Her hair was still loose over her shoulders, tangled and dirty, and she was breathing hard. In her left hand she clutched what looked to be the remains of a mountain rabbit, ragged and bloody.

'What is it?'

'The beast has returned.'

The Second led them back outside, down the temple steps and along a narrow path that cut easterly across the long grass. Sebastian and Wydrin followed slightly behind.

'And what is this about?' asked Wydrin.

The path turned abruptly, and below them the ground fell away to reveal a shallow valley far below, thick with trees. There was a wide river running through it, splitting into three tributaries. They shone like an elaborate diamond necklace.

'We set up traps around the perimeter of the temple for rabbits, goats, other small animals. About a week ago we realised that something big was stealing what we'd trapped, and, more often than not, tearing it to shreds on the spot.' The Second glanced back at them, apparently to make sure they were still following, and led them along a section where the path was little more than a suggestion. 'I've seen this before. It's a meadow wolf.'

'Oh, that sounds rather pleasant,' said Wydrin. 'Does it frolic in the grass and make daisy chains?'

'Hardly.'

Ahead of them, the Second stopped. They had come to a small

clearing shadowed by young pine trees. On the ground, half hidden in the tall grass, was a broken wire snare. There was blood all around it, standing out against the green like rubies.

'It came from the valley,' said the Second. She crouched by the broken snare and pressed her fingers to the ground there. They came away bloody. 'I have tracked it back that far.'

Sebastian frowned. 'You went scouting by yourself?'

'I tracked it,' she said again. Out of the corner of his eye Sebastian saw Wydrin cross her arms over her chest.

'You know that we have to be very careful about how far we travel from the temple.'

'You are afraid to hunt the beast? Is that what it is?'

Wydrin laughed. 'Sebastian has hunted much bigger prey than your little wolf, Snake-eyes. Remember what happened to your mother?'

The Second glowered, her clawed hand going to the belt where her dagger hung. Sebastian held up his hands.

'The wolf will be dealt with, but first—'

'We go there now. Together,' said the Second. Her hair hung over her forehead in tangled mess. 'All three of us. We will hunt the wolf, and kill it, and leave its carcass on the path so that other beasts know not to come this way.'

Sebastian sighed and shifted his weight. 'Fine,' he said. 'We hunt and we kill the wolf. But let's move quickly now. The valley is not unknown to visitors.'

The trees were alive with the sounds of water and birds; the continual drip of melting snow, the trilling cries of small feathered things. Sebastian moved slowly, half in a crouch, relishing how quietly he could move when he really tried. Wydrin was nowhere to be seen, circling around to his left, and the Second was a green shape in front, moving with steady confidence. They had been tracking the wolf for some hours now, and they were close, very close.

Sebastian touched his left fingers to the badge of Isu he still wore at his breast. He mouthed a silent prayer to the god-peak, remembering how this token had turned Gallo's blade from its killing stroke. *The mountain watches*, he thought.

In front, the Second suddenly crouched, and made a quick gesture over her shoulder. Their prey was in sight.

Sebastian moved forward and saw it, a lithe brown shape standing at the foot of a tree, its snout down, scenting the earth. Its shoulders were thick with fur and muscle, its dark snout wrinkling back to reveal curved yellow teeth in black gums.

Ahead of him the Second slid a long throwing knife from her belt, keeping her palm over the blade so that the light wouldn't catch it and forewarn the wolf. It was a long dagger, and fearsomely sharp. As he watched, the Second lifted it carefully over her shoulder, her arm tensing while the rest of her body was still.

A flex of muscle and the blade was flying through the air. Sebastian saw it strike the animal across the back, splitting the fur and flesh there like it was butter. In an instant the wolf was away, fleeing through the trees.

Without thinking about it, Sebastian followed, his heart in his throat. The thought of it getting away suddenly seemed untenable, and the simple movement of it – the sudden fleetness, the wounded panic in its gait – was like a fire in his blood. He pounded after it, dimly aware that the Second was running too, that she was moving alongside him, her pointed teeth bared in a grin. In front, the brown shape of the wolf flickered between the trees like a ghost and Sebastian forced himself to run faster. It was suddenly glorious to be here, out in the green earth-stinking world, his prey fleeing ahead of him and its sudden death weighing heavily on his short sword. Soon, he would spill its blood.

Wydrin appeared in front of them, startling the wolf and throwing it off course. It was enough for Sebastian to close the gap between them and he struck out with his short sword, paring the wolf open along its belly. Moments later the Second fell upon it, her short blades flashing, first silver and then red. Sebastian brought his sword down again, nearly severing the animal's head from its neck, and then he stopped. The thunder in his blood had abruptly left him. He felt cold, disappointed. The Second looked up at him, grinning. Her teeth were already stained crimson.

'You can feel it,' she said. 'The joy of the hunt. It runs from our blood to yours, and I can see it in your eyes.'

Wydrin appeared at that moment, tramping noisily through

the undergrowth now that there was no need for stealth. 'Nice job,' she said, grimacing at the wolf's bloody corpse. 'Although it might have been useful to keep that pelt intact.'

Feeling faintly ill, Sebastian put his own short sword back in its scabbard.

'We did what we came to do.' He caught Wydrin's curious look and ignored it. 'Let's head back.'

136

21

The scarf Siano had tied around the lower half of her face was damp and starting to ice over, so she paused in her ascent to unwind it. Away to the west, dusted with erratic moonlight on this cloud-streaked night, were the stones and lights of Skaldshollow. She watched them for a moment, noting how some of the lights were moving. A strange place, this distant neighbour of Apua, and one rarely mentioned in the House of Patience – not once in its long history had a client ever requested an assassination there – but she remembered what little she had been taught. The land and the mountains that scarred it were soaked in magic; it was a place of unforgiving weather, of curses, and of ghosts. Perhaps that was why the House of Patience had seen no business there – who wanted to take the chance that the man whose death you ordered might hang around to haunt you afterwards?

Siano snorted at such superstitions. She was approaching the settlement at an extreme curve, not wanting to get too close to the enormous granite walls. Instead, she intended to skirt close enough to be able to watch the city, and then follow one of the paths up to Joah Demonsworn's tomb, unobserved and in secret.

Settling herself under the low branches of a clutch of pine trees, she pulled the rabbit she'd caught earlier from her pack and deftly began skinning it, before building a small fire. She was still far enough away from Skaldshollow to not worry too greatly about being seen, and the Narhl territories were far to the west, beyond the mountains that loomed all around her.

Once the rabbit was skinned she went to slip the knife away, but instead she sat with it still held between her fingers, staring away into the night. After a moment she began to cut again, digging deep into the flesh of the animal this time, gouging a rough pattern. She did it unthinking, her hands seeming to move of their own accord. She remembered the puppies in her father's woodshed; so many small warm bodies, half blind and helpless. Flesh and skin and blood, the yielding and the gristle . . .

When the voice spoke she jumped violently, almost cutting one of her own fingers off.

'You are so close, young Siano. You have the blood ready?'

Siano looked down at the rabbit. The remains of its raw face were still, but the voice was issuing from its narrow throat.

'That is my dinner you are speaking through.'

The voice laughed hard at that, and despite herself Siano shivered.

'Many apologies, but I wanted to check everything was going smoothly.'

'You made me cut the rabbit,' said Siano. There was that quiet voice inside her again, warning her to be careful, but she had to know. 'You just pushed my mind to one side.'

'Just a little push, young Siano. Your mind is accustomed to my presence. And what a mind it is. So cold and empty, with so little to grasp on to. I had thought – well, it hardly matters. A shame, though. If you were just a touch more human on the inside, you would have been perfect. Human minds are so much more comfortable.'

Siano shook herself. Once again, she had no idea what the voice was talking about, and it made her uneasy.

'I've brought the blood,' she said, trying to recover. 'Vials from every family member you asked me to kill. It made for quite a heavy pack in the end.'

'I'm sure it did!' The voice sounded amused again. 'And you will need every last drop. I will be with you again, before the end.'

And then the voice was gone. Siano sat for some time, looking

138

at the bloody mess of the rabbit, before spearing the remains with a long stick and propping it over the fire. After a few minutes, the fat began to spit.

The Prophet knelt on the bedclothes, playing with the Narhl finger bones Tamlyn's niece had brought. Into each it had carved a sigil, an ancient sign known only to one other.

'The girl would have been a good host. Stronger, faster than this one.' It held out a hand, looking critically at the long, delicate fingers. This body was growing, that was true, and at this time of the girl's life it would be very fast now. Already she was much taller than she had been, her long legs coltish and awkward, and the Prophet found it was very comfortable in this mind – it was so easy to use this voice, to move this face into the right shapes. So easy to push the girl's own personality to one side. Now that the Prophet had such a firm hold in this body, there was no need to let her speak any more, and in time there could be lots of advantages to this body, that was true. The Prophet longed for an adult body, one that had been trained to kill and maim with precision, but sadly Siano's mind was all wrong – it was cold and featureless, with none of the useful emotions and anxieties it used as a way to anchor itself to a body. And she was not willing. A host had to offer themselves, and although there could be no doubt that Siano was one of the Prophet's creatures, she was much too closed off. The revulsion she'd felt when she'd realised she'd not been entirely in control of the knife had been very clear. 'I am stuck here for now, it seems.' It ran the girl's fingers over the bones, listening to their soft rattle. 'And there are worse places to be.'

There was movement at the door. Tamlyn Nox was there, the shape of her mind hot and feverish.

'Do you have a moment?' Her words were polite but her tone was clipped and precise.

This one won't be strung along much longer. 'Of course. Do come in, Tamlyn dear. Close the door behind you though, there's a terrible draught.'

There was a soft click as the door shut, and Tamlyn came over to the bed, a dark shape beyond the curtains. The Prophet could see that her hair was loose across her shoulders, and as it watched the Mistress Crafter paced back and forth in front of the bed, her hands clasped behind her back.

'The first part of the plan has failed,' she said eventually. 'The mercenaries you recommended have let us down. No doubt they have been captured by now, and executed, and the Heart-Stone remains in Narhl territory.'

'This is unfortunate.'

'Unfortunate?' The anger Tamlyn thought she was so good at hiding briefly rose to the surface. Behind the curtains, the Prophet grinned. 'Unfortunate? That stone is the lifeblood of Skaldshollow. Without it we are crippled.'

'It is not so important. You place so much significance on it, Tamlyn dear.'

'I can craft nothing of use! We can make more werkens, but we cannot awaken them.' She came over to the bed and knelt in front of it. After a moment, she put her hand on the curtain. When she spoke again her voice was little more than a whisper. 'What you have told me about your friend – it is all true?'

'Tamlyn, when he comes again, you will learn so much. More than you could imagine. These trifling, stumbling creatures you make now will be the least of it. You and he will create wonders.'

'But before . . . all of our histories tell us—'

'Propaganda,' said the Prophet dismissively. 'The truth was twisted, and that is always the way of history. Believe me. My friend was the greatest crafter of the Edeian that ever lived. Imagine what you can learn from him, Mistress Crafter.'

Tamlyn's hand clutched at the gauze. 'But the price . . .'

The Prophet reached out with the girl's own small hand and took hold of Tamlyn's fingers through the curtain. It gripped hard, letting the fingernails dig into the older woman's skin.

'Do you not wish to see the Narhl wiped from this world? To cleanse the mountain of their savagery? Never again will you see the blue streak of their wyverns in the air, and hear the screams of your people as the ice rains down on them. You will bring a war to them they can't possibly hope to win. Forget about the Heart-Stone, Tamlyn Nox. I bring you a much greater gift.'

For a few moments there was only silence on the other side

of the curtain, save for Tamlyn's ragged breathing. When she spoke again her voice sounded very young.

'When?'

The Prophet let go of Tamlyn's hand. 'Very soon now, actually. Very soon.'

22

'This procedure. What does it involve, exactly?'

Sebastian had managed to catch Dallen alone for a moment as Olborn supervised his soldiers; they were moving furs and blankets into one of the icy egg sacs, creating a small, comfortable space for the prince to work. Wydrin was standing over by the ponies, drinking steadily from a flask.

'I must use the cold-summons to take her deep into a trance, to try and connect her to this land as we are connected.' Dallen looked him straight in the eye. 'I won't lie to you, Sir Sebastian. Warmlings, uh, that is to say, people who are not Narhl, tend to find this quite uncomfortable. But your friend is strong.'

'And stubborn. It's not in Wydrin to say no to something like this, but she doesn't always have her best interests at heart.' Sebastian absently touched the scar on his cheek. 'It is normally down to me to keep her from getting herself killed, your highness, and I am not happy about this.'

'I mean her no harm, and I will be as careful as I can be.'

'We could just tell the Skalds,' said Sebastian. He had suggested this already, more than once. 'I, for one, would be glad to carry your message. My own people believe mountains to be sacred.'

Dallen shook his head. Behind them, his soldiers were decking the ice dwelling with cold-lamps, so that the little dome shone like a piece of daylight, lost.

'It's not enough. I don't doubt your conviction, but the Skalds don't *want* to hear the message. This is our best chance.'

'Wydrin is dear to me. If you should harm her –' He paused. 'Actually, if anything goes wrong, it may well be Frith you have to worry about first. He is no stranger to vengeance.'

Lord Frith was lurking by the entrance, his face hidden within his hood. He hadn't spoken to anyone since the plan had been agreed.

'They are close, then? They make a strange couple.'

Sebastian smiled, amused by the genuine bemusement in the prince's voice.

'Not a couple, not as such. A mess, is how I'd describe it.'

'I have found that relationships often end that way.' Prince Dallen looked away, apparently having said too much. He took a deep breath before speaking again. 'Your people worship the mountains as gods, then?'

Sebastian nodded.

'In Ynnsmouth we live under the four god-peaks, Ynn, Ryn, Isu and Isri. As a knight I swore to abide by their codes, and as a child I dreamed of the mountain's voice.' He cleared his throat. That had all ended so well, after all.

Dallen looked at him, and there was that shrewd glitter to his gaze again.

'You should have been born Narhl, I think – although we do not name the mountain spirits; they are too unknowable for that. Look,' he nodded towards the mound of hollow ice, where Olborn was standing to attention, 'it appears we are ready.'

Wydrin lay back on the blankets, suddenly feeling rather self-conscious. Prince Dallen knelt next to her, his face carefully composed, while Sebastian and Frith lurked at the entrance, neither looking particularly happy.

'Is there anything I need to know?' she asked. She had brought Mendrick into the ice cave and the werken was now crouched at the edge of the blankets.

'You'll be cold,' said Prince Dallen evenly. 'You may find it difficult to breathe. You may see things. I can't tell you what you'll see, or experience. It could be unnerving.'

Wydrin grinned at him. 'Your bedside manner isn't reassuring, your highness. What if I backed out now? Decided I didn't want this deeper link after all?'

143

Prince Dallen's face grew more serious. 'You are still my prisoners. The future of my people depends on your taking this message to the Skalds.'

'Right. Well. Hold on a moment.' She slipped a flask from her belt and took several large gulps. 'That should keep my insides warm at least.'

Dallen leaned over her and held out his hands, palms down. She glanced up at his pale eyes, his mottled face. After a few moments she felt the temperature around her drop, slowly at first and then sharply. She gasped and saw her breath cloud in front of her.

'This is unwise.' It was Frith's voice from the entrance. From the corner of her eye she saw him try to elbow his way over to her, but Olborn held him back with the tip of her spear. 'Your prince nearly killed me with this power of his.'

'I did nothing of the sort,' said Dallen shortly, never taking his eyes from Wydrin. 'I merely incapacitated you briefly. Now please, be quiet.'

Wydrin began to shiver violently, her teeth chattering. She wrapped her arms around herself, trying to sink further back into her thickly furred cloak, but it did little good.

'Accept the cold, do not hide from it,' said Dallen. 'This will be easier for you if you don't fight.'

Wydrin tried to nod, but she was shaking too violently. She gasped a breath inwards, trying to speak, but the air was so cold it bit at her throat, and the air that slipped into her lungs was as freezing and deadly as icicles. There was a pain in her chest now, and the world seemed to be going dark.

What a stupid way to die, she thought.

Prince Dallen's face filled her vision. His beard was fringed with frost, and his hair looked as white as Frith's. She remembered standing in the Blackwood with Frith, how his healing magic had been so warm, the complete opposite of this cold death. It was difficult to remember what warmth felt like.

There is no deeper link here, she thought, no longer able to move even her fingers. *There is only the cold and lifeless mountain.*

The pain in her chest grew so enormous there was nothing else, and even Prince Dallen's face disappeared behind the tide of black. There was a sensation of sinking, like drowning in the deepest part of the ocean . . . and a star woke in the darkness. A single point of light, followed by another, and then a sprinkling of lights, and suddenly the darkness was thick with stars, pregnant with them; glowing swirls of blue, red and purple stars, some too bright to look at.

The stars are dying, she thought, and somehow it was possible to feel the violence of their passing, even as the silence pressed in on all sides.

Wydrin looked down from the night sky to find that she was standing alone in a wide grey landscape, featureless save for some piles of rocks scattered across the ground. The land was entirely flat, and went on for ever, fading at the horizon to become a soft reddish blur. She also realised, with a start, that she was no longer cold.

'Hello? Any mountain spirits about at all?'

She turned in a slow circle. Above her the sky was heavy and unknown; she'd had years of using the heavens to navigate all over Ede and she'd never seen stars like these.

'This is either the very beginning of the world, or the very end.' She didn't know where this knowledge came from, but she knew it was true. What would Ede have looked like before the mountains came? What would it look like at the end of time?

Wydrin walked a short distance, kicking up small clouds of dust as she went. The landscape didn't change, but a low rumble started beneath her feet. The small rocks and pebbles on the ground began to jump and tremble, and all at once there was a dark figure ahead of her; impossibly tall, an enormous shadow against the grey land. It was difficult to tell how big it truly was. One moment it looked as tall as one of her father's three-masted ships, and the next, it was mountain-sized and looming. She could make out no features – just a shape with arms and legs, and even that she sensed was a rough pretence so that she might fit this – whatever it was – into her mind.

'Hello,' she said. Her voice was a constricted whisper, so she hurriedly cleared her throat. 'I take it you're who I'm looking for?'

The rumble beneath her feet increased in volume, and she stumbled awkwardly, trying to stay upright. Her hand instinctively went to her dagger, but when she looked there was only the ghost of Frostling, a glittering shape nestled inside its scabbard. She shook her head at that and turned back to the giant figure.

'You're supposed to give me a deeper link to the land. To this werken I have. One of your people, Prince Dallen, needs this to happen.' She took a deep breath. At least her chest didn't hurt any more. 'An answer either way would be good, before my real body freezes to death.'

Now the rumble was a roaring, the sound of the land being torn asunder. It was the voice of the mountain, she realised. It did not love her. It did not love any of the warm creatures that had appeared on the skin of the world like a rash in these recent years. Wydrin fell, cracking her knees painfully on the stony ground, and the dark figure reached out for her. Its shadowy hand, bigger than a house, bigger than Y'Ruen, bigger than the world, closed over her head and she knew darkness again . . .

. . . And in the darkness, there was a bright thread of green light. Wydrin followed it instinctively, not worrying too much about where she was, not yet anyway, and it pulsed away in front of her, drawing her on through the pitch-black. She could sense a huge weight above her, as though they were far underground.

'Where am I?' she asked the light.

'You are in your own mind. You are in my mind. You are in the space where they join.' The voice of the light was mild and faintly male.

'It's a bit dark. I'd have thought my mind would have more lights. You know, maybe even a fireplace, somewhere to sit.'

'We have only just started,' said the voice, and another streak of light appeared, branching off from the first one like the delicate veins in a leaf. 'In time, this space will be brighter.' As it spoke, more veins of light branched off the first one, creating a softly glowing net. Wydrin reached out to touch them, filled with wonder. There was a truth to this, she knew it, a truth that was deep inside everyone, but which was so deeply hidden it remained unknown. Her hand passed straight through.

146

'Who are you?' she asked, belatedly realising this should have been her first question.

'I am the being you call Mendrick.' Now the veins of light were a brightly shining web, stretching off into the distance. Wydrin thought she'd never seen anything so beautiful.

'Then you can speak?'

'Only on this very deep level. Our minds are touching.'

'Bloody hell.'

'Previously, you have thought of me as an extension of yourself, yes? A tool to be used?'

'Yes,' Wydrin frowned slightly. 'I didn't know. I didn't know what you were. I don't think any of them do. Bors is a good man, he wouldn't allow this if he knew.' She thought of Tamlyn Nox and realised she couldn't say the same of her. 'They think you're less than animals, just stones and rocks that can walk if you're pushed. But if you're not that, what *are* you?'

'I will show you,' the voice said simply. The green light pulsed once, blinding her, and Wydrin suddenly knew what it was to not be alone in her head: She could feel the mountain, so enormous and old, looming above her like the sky – *so much bigger than we imagine*, she thought, *because we don't think about the roots of it*. And she could feel a smaller part of it next to her, a part that had been shaped to move, and it was regarding her now, watching her from its place on the ground. She knew that mind, could feel it nestling next to her own. She could feel the weary patience that came from eons of life, and a certain amount of curiosity too – she knew that Mendrick was examining her own mind, no doubt as equally alien to it. Him.

'Why do you do it, then?' she asked. 'Why obey them at all?'

There was silence from the mountain-spirit for some time. She could sense Mendrick trying to understand the question.

'It is my purpose to be silent,' he said eventually, a note of uncertainty in his voice. 'It is unnatural to communicate like this. And it is all so distant. The magic in our flesh moves us, when touching a human mind. It is impossible to convey our wishes.'

'That's because they don't speak mountain,' said Wydrin. She could feel Mendrick's discomfort like sandpaper against her own skin. Even talking to a human on this level was exhausting to

147

him. 'But you would rather this didn't happen? That the Skalds would leave you alone?'

There was silence for a moment. 'It is disruptive,' he said finally. 'A discordance in my rock, in my mind.'

'I can tell them for you,' she said. 'Stay with me, and I will show the Skalds that they have to stop, and then you can go back to your silence.'

'I will agree to this.' There was a flicker in the green light. 'I will stay with you for now.'

Wydrin opened her eyes to Sebastian and Frith staring anxiously down at her.

'She's awake.' Sebastian turned away to talk to someone she couldn't see. 'Quickly now, we'll need that fire, and I want something to warm some food in.'

'Wydrin,' Frith took hold of her shoulder, 'are you all right?'

She opened her mouth to tell him that she was perfectly fine, and could he stop fussing like an old baggage, when the pain hit her. It was like being thrown against a brick wall, every part of her crying out at once.

'Fuck!' she gasped, curling up into a ball. 'By the graces, that hurts.'

Prince Dallen appeared, shouldering Frith out of the way to throw another blanket over her. 'Help me now,' he said to Frith. 'There is a fire outside, and we'd best get her to it quickly.'

They half dragged, half carried Wydrin from the cave, depositing her in front of a small fire some distance from the main camp. Prince Dallen retreated swiftly, not coming too close to the flames, while Sebastian was already stirring a black pot. Frith wrapped her in several more blankets, until she started to wonder if he was trying to suffocate her. Her arms and legs were tingling painfully as the feeling returned to her limbs, and Sebastian had to hold a cup to her lips. It was bark tea, bitter but hot.

'Where's Mendrick?' she croaked, when she could speak again.

Frith raised his eyebrows. 'The werken? It's still in the arachnos' nest.'

Wydrin reached out to that newly revealed presence, and a dark shape loped out of the darkness towards them, green eyes shining like moons. Wydrin looked into its cold, wolf-like face and remembered the tendrils of light that linked her mind to his. A pretty neat trick, that.

'Good, that's good. Once I've eaten the rest of that stew and my arse has melted, we'd better get a move on. Because I have one hell of a message for bloody Tamlyn Nox.'

23

23

'I have the linen and the ink you asked for.'

The Prophet smiled to itself behind the curtains. Magic grew ever more sophisticated, but there were some basics you could never quite get away from. It parted the curtains and Tamlyn passed over a bundle of ink pots, brushes and clean white cloth.

'Can I ask what this is for?'

The woman's voice was tense all the time now, full of unspoken questions.

'Just for my own amusement, Tamlyn dear. Leave me now, please.'

The Mistress Crafter of Skaldshollow stood there for a moment longer, apparently wrestling with her own need to know what was going on, and then she was gone. The Prophet began to tear the linen into long strips, and then, using the poor selection of horse-hair brushes Tamlyn had provided, began to paint the words. It had been years since it had written the words of the mages, yet it came easily. Once learned, they weren't easily forgotten. Some of the ink spilled onto the bed sheets, but it hardly mattered. They wouldn't need them for much longer.

'He was made for so much more than the witterings of paltry gods,' the Prophet mused as the girl's delicate fingers danced the brush across the material. 'But it is only right that I present him with some of his old tools. He will appreciate that.'

When that was done the Prophet slipped out of the huge four-poster bed, and swiftly dressed in woollen leggings and jerkin, thick fur coat and gloves. The white shift the girl habitually wore was bundled up and casually thrown into one of the braziers, where it vanished in a curl of orange flame.

The strips of linen were shoved into a pack which the Prophet slung over one shoulder, before pausing to tie the girl's long brown hair back into a rough braid. Glancing in the mirror, it was briefly annoyed to see that face looking back at her – still so young, so small.

'You've served me well, Ip, truly you have. But I do wish you would grow a little faster.'

The Prophet left at a pace, paying no heed to the guards assigned to the corridor outside the room. If it wished, the Prophet could of course pay a visit to the tomb without actually leaving the Tower of Waking, but there were some matters that really required your physical presence. And Bezcavar – prince of wounds, master of broken things – wasn't missing this for the world.

Siano crouched just under the trees, where the grass was damp and the air was heavy with the scent of pine needles. In front of her the pool that sheltered the tomb of Joah Demonsworn was utterly still, a silver mirror to the overcast sky, and the vials of blood sat in a bag next to her. It was unnaturally silent in this place – no birds sang, and even the wind was quiet. It was unnerving, but she had been waiting for some hours now, and was prepared to wait for hours more; unsurprisingly, patience was the first lesson of the House of Patience.

Eventually though, she heard light footsteps approaching through the trees. She retreated back into the shadows, although judging from the weight of the step, this was just a child. She felt a flicker of annoyance at this further distraction, then swallowed it down.

A girl walked into the clearing. She looked no more than twelve or thirteen years old, tall for her age and yet to grow out of her awkwardness. For a moment she just stood, looking at the water, and then she turned towards the trees and looked straight at Siano.

She stumbled backwards, pressing herself up against the tree trunk. She was certain the girl couldn't have seen her, yet it was as if she hadn't needed to search; she'd *known* where to find her.

151

'Come on out, Siano,' she said, not raising her voice. 'I still have some work for you to do.'

Siano froze. Her first instinct was to pluck a throwing dagger from her chest belt, but her curiosity stopped her. Instead she came out from between the trees, moving slowly.

'Who are you?'

The girl grinned at her, and even Siano, who had long since cast off anything that might have been considered warm or human, felt a real moment of crawling terror. Her smile was madness and fever.

'Are you saying you don't know me, Siano? Because I think you do.'

'You are . . . the client.'

'I speak through a severed head, a dead rabbit, a girl child. What difference does it make?' Her voice changed then, became cultured and sly and old. 'Does this help convince you?'

Siano swallowed hard. 'Forgive me my caution, master.'

'Do you have the blood?'

Siano retrieved the bag containing the vials and held them out to the girl, but she shook her head. Instead, she pointed to the pool.

'Do you see the tomb, Siano? The history books say that the mages, in their sorrow, built a tomb for Joah Demonsworn and covered it in protective spells. It's interesting what you can make people believe when you are old enough to tamper with the histories while they are being written. It was I who honoured Joah, who gave him the burial he deserved, and these are my spells – cast to protect his bones, so that the end might not truly be the end. Now, the blood you've collected for me contains another spell.' She grinned up at Siano. 'Can you guess what it does?' Turning away, she plucked up a rock from the ground, and threw it into the pool. Immediately the water churned as if it were boiling. 'You will have to go down into the water and retrieve his body, Siano.'

'I will never make it. It will take my skin off before I get halfway there, master.'

'I want you to drink half the blood in those vials. Half from each vial, and mind that you don't drink more than that. If you

152

do, I will pull your entrails out through your throat. Do you understand me?' The girl turned to Siano, and her eyes were full of blood, from lid to lid. 'This magic, this spell that has been hidden in generation after generation, I only have one chance to use it. If you cause it to fail in some way, you will wish your parents had killed you as they originally planned to, Siano. Drink the blood, and you will pass safely through the water.'

Siano did as she was bid, grimacing slightly at the thick, metallic taste of the partially congealed blood.

'Good,' the girl said when she'd finished. 'Now get in the water. You will have to open the coffin while you are down there and bring his body out. The sarcophagus will be far too heavy to move by itself.'

Gingerly Siano stepped into the water, but it remained calm, and she shivered a little as it quickly soaked into her velvet trousers and tunic. She walked in until the water came up to her chest, and then she took a deep breath and pushed herself fully under. Siano didn't particularly enjoy swimming – for one thing, the water that filled her ears and pushed at her eyes dulled her senses, always a dangerous state for an assassin – but she had been trained to proficiency at the House of Patience. The pool wasn't especially deep, and in a short time she had her fingers wrapped around the coffin lid, her feet braced against the rocky bottom. This close she could see the intricacy of the runes and sigils etched into the lid with silver, and the snarling dog face loomed at her, jagged teeth bared. It made her distinctly uncomfortable to be that close to it.

The coffin lid was tremendously heavy, but with an enormous shove she pushed it away and it sank to the ground, throwing up a gritty cloud of sediment. When it was clear, Siano was greeted with the unpleasant sight of a grinning corpse; she had a brief impression of yellowed teeth, greenish strips of flesh sprouting like tufts of grass, and then her chest was burning with the need to breathe again, so she bit down her revulsion and pulled the figure from the coffin and swam for the surface, the corpse slung over her back.

The child was waiting for her on the bank. She watched as Siano dragged the rotten skeleton out onto the grass, her eyes bright with some emotion she couldn't place. Siano stood up, soaking wet and already starting to shiver.

'He's looking about as well as can be expected, I suppose,' the girl said.

Siano glanced down at the corpse. It was little more than a yellowed skeleton now, furred here and there with mouldy tatters of flesh. It had been dressed in fine robes when it had been buried, but these were now brownish rags, streaked with bright gold thread. She wondered how long the body had been in the pool.

The wind picked up then, cutting through Siano like a knife. For the first time, she began to wonder when this job would ever be over.

'Will there be anything else?' She forced the words out through icy lips.

The girl turned her blood-filled gaze on her, incredulous.

'Well, he's not going to drink the blood himself, is he?'

Siano nodded shortly. She collected the vials, all still half full, and knelt next to the skeleton, cradling its skull in her lap. Getting its jaws open was no easy task, and for one, uncertain moment, Siano thought she had pushed a finger through the spongy bone, but it was only a piece of rotten flesh. One by one she poured the contents of the vials between its teeth, until there was just the final vial to go. She glanced up at the girl, who was watching her fiercely, her small hands curled into tight fists.

'Yes, do it,' she said, in her strangely old voice. 'It's time Ede saw what a true mage can do, and he has waited long enough.'

The last of the blood trickled between the cadaver's teeth. Dimly, Siano was aware that most of it was actually soaking into her trousers.

'That's it,' she said, sitting back on her haunches. She cast the last vial into the grass. 'I am uncertain what other rites you wish me to perform, but I feel I must state that my contract is for lives taken, and I'm not sure this constitutes—'

The skeleton suddenly convulsed in her lap, the blood-streaked jaws clapping open and shut.

'What . . .?'

The skeleton's hand, thin bones and rotten flesh, snaked up

and grabbed Siano around the wrist, so tightly she cried out – that grip was strong enough to break her arm. She went to stand up, to attempt to shake the thing off her, but the other arm looped up around her neck, pulling her back down like an over-amorous lover wanting one more kiss. Those bony jaws clapped shut again, and this time they caught at Siano's cheek, tearing a lump of flesh from her face. Blood spattered like rain over the skull's forehead.

'I am sorry, Siano.' She could just about hear the girl's voice over her own screaming. 'It pains me to lose you, it really does.'

The skull lunged again, hungrily now, like a dog who's discovered that this old sack contains something tasty after all, and although Siano pushed with all her might she couldn't break that vice grip. With a lurch of horror she realised that it was *chewing*, that the skull was chewing pieces of her *face*, and as she watched she saw that the flesh was growing back across the yellowed bone. For every piece of Siano it ate, the corpse was regaining what it had lost.

'No,' she gasped, 'no no no,' and that was when the skeleton dragged her down into a deeper embrace and bit off her tongue. Siano felt the hot gush of blood, the insistent gnawing of the skull's teeth against her lips, and the skittering of finger bones in her hair.

'It'll be the eyeballs next,' said the girl in a matter-of-fact tone. 'He'll want to see what he's doing.'

Beneath her, Siano heard the skull laughing with her own tongue.

PART TWO
The Riven Soul

24

Nuava ran across the practice yard, her heart hammering in her chest. She spotted the familiar form of Bors over by the repairs pit – he was working on a werken with a cracked foot – and she gasped in sudden relief. *Everything is fine,* she told herself firmly. *You are jumping at shadows like a child.*

He looked up and, seeing her, waved cheerily enough, although his face took on the familiar creases of worry as she got closer. 'What is it, Nuava? Are you all right?'

She nodded rapidly, suddenly feeling foolish. There were a few men and women here on this overcast afternoon, repairing their werkens or just putting them through their paces. 'Yes, I mean, no, I'm not sure. It's just—'

Bors put a hand on her shoulder and squeezed, just as he had when she was a little girl who'd hurt herself playing on the ice. She took a deep breath. 'A few moments ago, there was this tremor in the Edeian. I could feel it all around me, like the whole world shifted. Did you notice anything?'

Bors frowned and shook his head. 'You know I can't sense the Edeian as you do, Nuava. I've noticed nothing unusual.' He gestured at the yard. 'And the werkens are all functioning well. Have you felt anything like this before?'

'No, that's what worries me. Have you seen Tamlyn?'

'Not since this morning.'

There was a commotion at the gate. Nuava turned to see a tall man dressed in long, old-fashioned robes walking rapidly towards

159

them. Next to him was a young girl of about twelve or thirteen and – Nuava blinked rapidly. She knew who it was. It was the Prophet, out from behind the curtains of her bed, walking with her head uncovered and her small moon-like face turned up to the sky. She was grinning, and Nuava felt bile pushing at the back of her throat. *Something is very wrong.*

'Who is that?' asked Bors. He put down the chisel he'd been holding in his free hand and wiped his fingers on his jerkin. 'Another mercenary?'

'I don't know. I don't think he's one of them. I don't think he's one of them at all.'

The man had shoulder-length brown hair, thick and shining with health, and a neat brown beard that framed an open, handsome face. As he drew nearer she saw that he had large brown eyes, and his brows were creased into an amiable expression of slightly bemused good cheer. He was smiling gently, looking around at everything as though he'd never seen such a place before. The robes he wore were dark green silk, and fringed with gold – very beautiful, and extremely inappropriate for the weather. Already the bottom of his robe was heavy with melted snow. There were lengths of linen tied around his hands, linen painted with intricate shapes, and that sent a cold shiver down the back of Nuava's neck.

There's only one mage left in the world, she thought, *and we've met him. So who is this?*

'Hello,' called Bors, already approaching the stranger. Nuava grasped at him, but he brushed her off. 'Can I help at all?'

'Why, yes.' The man's voice was warm, educated. Reassuring. His smile broadened as he reached them, and he took Bors's hand and clasped it briefly. 'I've been away for such a long time, and I've so much to catch up on.'

Bors smiled, the puzzlement clear on his broad features.

'You're from around here?'

'Oh you could say that,' said the man. 'A very long time ago, of course. But you've been so busy! These creatures you've crafted with the Edeian are quite extraordinary.'

Nuava saw her brother relax slightly, and she twisted her fingers into the fabric of her coat.

160

'Well, our Mistress-Crafter, Tamlyn Nox, does most of the actual crafting – she's my aunt – but thank you. We've all worked very hard and I think—'

The man reached out, quite casually, and laid the tips of his fingers against Bors's chest. Bors glanced down, confused, and then he jumped backwards a foot, arms flailing. For a few seconds Nuava couldn't connect the sudden wet warmth on her face with the bright, arterial splash now painting the cobbles, but then her brother fell over backwards and she saw the hole in his chest.

'Oh, so sorry about that,' continued the man, an expression of slightly abashed chagrin on his face. 'But it has been *ever* such a long time.'

Distantly, Nuava could hear screaming. She knew that some of it was coming from her. The man turned to the child standing beside him.

'My first gift to you, Bezcavar. The first of many.'

They turned away then, and Nuava fell to her knees.

Tamlyn staggered in the street. The man she'd collided with turned towards her with angry words on his lips, but, seeing who it was, he swallowed them down. Instead he nodded hurriedly, backing away.

'Many apologies, Crafter Nox.'

She frowned at him, not even seeing his face. The tremor in the Edeian was still reverberating inside her, and the chips of Heart-Stone in the palms of her hands and her ear lobes were burning and itching. In all her years of crafting the Edeian she'd never felt anything like it, and she had no idea what it meant. Moving away down the street she glanced up to the north of the settlement, to see the warning beacons still unlit. Not an attack, then, or at least not from the Narhl.

It was late afternoon, and Skaldshollow was thick with people going about their daily chores. From where she stood she could see four werkens hauling goods, and one war-werken stationed at the corner of the Tower of Waking. Her own werken, sleek and terrible, was squatting next to it, ready for her planned journey back up to the quarry. Just a normal day, she told herself. Whatever it was, she'd imagined it.

As if to mock her, a terrible scream rent the air. The crowd ahead of her parted, the people falling back in confusion, and a tall man walked towards her, a young girl at his side. He was talking quite calmly to the girl, his hands clasped loosely behind his back, but the bottom of his green robe was stained dark, and where he walked he left a smeared trail of blood.

'The Prophet,' muttered Tamlyn through numb lips. 'And him. It's him. She really did bring him back.'

'There you are!' The Prophet's voice was clear as a bell across the milling crowds. 'Tamlyn dear, I would like to introduce you.'

'I know who that is.' There was a crunch and the thunder of stone steps as her werken trotted towards her back. Just as instinctively, her hand hovered above the short sword at her waist. 'What have you done?'

The Prophet shrugged. 'Nothing you didn't know about, Nox. Just think of everything you can learn now.'

A slim figure forced its way through the crowd. Nuava's face was streaked with tears and blood, the skin beneath her eyes purple with shock.

'They killed Bors!' She stumbled forward. 'Just killed him, for no reason, in the street.'

'I have brought him to you,' said the Prophet, talking easily over Nuava. 'Joah Cirrus, Joah Lightbringer, Joah Demonsworn. Just as I said I would.'

The crowd began to mutter more loudly now. The man – and it *was* Joah, every line of him having stepped living and breathing from a history book – looked vaguely disgruntled.

'What have you done?' Tamlyn asked again. She had thought this would be simple, that they could contain it somehow, but there was the blood . . .

'He killed Bors.' Nuava ran forward and grabbed Tamlyn by her sleeves, her eyes wide. 'He just tore the heart out of him. My brother.'

'Bors?'

'He's dead!' Nuava was screaming again, her fists curled into the fabric of Tamlyn's clothes. 'I h-had to leave him, to find you, to warn y-you.'

Tamlyn looked back to the Prophet. The child who wasn't a child.

162

'Why?'

'These werken creatures are quite extraordinary.' Joah was peering closely at Tamlyn's own mount, which now stood to her left. He showed no fear of it, even though its head was some distance above his own. 'You have put them together yourself, and then activated them with the Edeian?'

Tamlyn shook Nuava off with some difficulty and took a few stiff steps towards the Prophet.

'Why? Why murder a member of my family? You said nothing of this to me.'

The Prophet shrugged. 'I'm sure I mentioned that he could be unpredictable. Think not of what you have lost, Tamlyn, and really that is so little – another soldier, his only advantage that he shared your blood. Think of what you will gain. You can learn so much from Joah, and your werken army will be unstoppable.'

Tamlyn glanced at the mage. He was running his fingers over the stone of the werken now, muttering under his breath.

'He cannot go around slaughtering where he will. I have my people to protect.'

'You knew about this?' It was Nuava again, her face slack. The girl's skin had gone so pale she looked grey, and Tamlyn guessed she was a few moments away from passing out. 'This was the Prophet's plan all along, and you knew about it?'

Tamlyn shook her head irritably. 'No. I wanted to retrieve the Heart-Stone first, to try and fix this by ourselves. That's what the mercenaries were about. This was a last resort. Listen to me, Nuava. With Joah's knowledge we can build an army that Ede has never seen. He will teach us, you and I, all the secrets of the Edeian.'

'I'm sorry,' Joah stepped back from the werken, his handsome face creased into a mildly apologetic expression, 'but I shan't be doing that. Look at you, you're not even a mage. Playing with the Edeian, bashing rocks together like primitives.' He waved a hand at the werken and it floated up into the air, as if it weighed nothing at all. The crowd around them gasped, and a few, the wiser ones, began backing away. The werken spun softly, and although Tamlyn summoned it fiercely inside her own head, it would not move.

'It's all the same as it ever was,' continued Joah. The Prophet was grinning now, revealing neat white teeth that looked too sharp for a human face. 'Humans grubbing around in the dirt, grasping to create even the most basic toys. Why would I stoop to teach you anything?' He smiled again, almost kindly. 'I'm sure you'll understand. You are not my people.'

He pitched his arm around, as though casting something away, and the werken flew over Tamlyn's head and crashed into the crowd. People, cobblestones, even half a building; pieces flew in all directions. Within seconds the street was filled with screaming, with people trying desperately to get away, but Joah Demonsworn would not let them leave. Those that made it to the end of the street found themselves crashing against an invisible barrier, before being dragged back by the same unknowable force.

'It has been ever such a long time,' he murmured.

'Kill them for me, my Joah,' said the Prophet. Tamlyn heard each word like a strike against her heart. 'Kill them in my name, as you used to.'

The man called Joah grinned and spread his fingers, and a wave of bright fire appeared from nowhere, rolling up the street to smother the men and women trapped there. The screaming became inhuman howls, and Tamlyn pressed her hands to her ears.

'Stop it!' she cried. She could smell scorched flesh, and the fires were already blazing out of control. 'You cannot do this!'

The mage was already summoning more spells; war-werkens that arrived, thundering up the street to try and stop him or at least put out the fires, were tossed into the air, smashing into buildings and sending avalanches of rock and mortar down onto the cobbles. Tamlyn saw people crushed under the collapsed buildings, saw their blood smeared on the rocks. And in the centre of it all Joah Demonsworn stood content and untouchable with the Prophet at his side. He was sending fireballs after the people still left alive, their hair, their furs, roaring into life like beacons, and the scent of burning meat was everywhere. She could hear Nuava screaming still, and the thunder of more war-werkens approaching, but none of it seemed very important. Joah turned to the sound of more troops arriving, an eager smile still on his face and his hands held up to meet them.

Amongst the devastation the Prophet appeared, to lay one cold hand on Tamlyn's.

'It's beautiful, isn't it? All of that suffering, and in my name.' When Tamlyn didn't answer, she squeezed, hard enough to be painful. 'He always was so wilful, though.'

25

Nuava moved quickly past the rubble, trying to keep out of sight. She passed several dead bodies – one a man with his face boiled away, another lost within a partially formed chunk of ice – before she rounded the edge of the building. Here there were three or four broken werkens, in so many pieces that it was difficult to tell where one began and another ended, and beyond them she could see the mage and the Prophet, talking animatedly. As quietly as possible, she crept up to the wreckage of the werkens and waited, straining to hear what they were saying.

It hadn't taken long for Joah Demonsworn to throw Skaldshollow into a confused state of terror. When Tamlyn had recovered herself enough to speak again, she'd summoned a further force of war-werkens, which Joah had seemed to treat like some sort of challenge – he'd picked each one up and thrown them into the crowds, or simply through buildings, with tremendous force. When the soldiers had come at him with short swords and crossbows, he'd actually laughed.

Nuava squeezed her eyes shut, remembering.

There had been the wave of freezing ice, picking up men and women and solidifying around them. Nuava had seen their eyes as they'd suffocated one by one. There had been the fire, a wall of it that moved down the street leaving twisted, blackened corpses behind. And there had been the look on the man's face: simple, honest joy as he'd torn men and women apart.

166

'I am asking you just to wait for a moment, Joah, my dear one.'

The wind had changed, bringing their conversation to Nuava's hiding place. She tensed, trembling all over. In her fist she clutched the knife Tamlyn had given her to cut the fingers from the Narhl soldier. It wasn't much, but it might be enough.

'I'm busy.' The man's voice was slightly dismissive – the tone of a man who had far too much to do and too little time in which to do it. 'So many spells still to test, and then I should travel to the Citadel. I must have so much to catch up on, and I'm sure all that business will have blown over by now.'

'They're all gone, Joah.'

Behind the pile of rock that had been a werken, Nuava frowned. The Prophet's voice sounded almost *tender*.

'What?'

'The mages. They are all gone. You are the last true mage, now that you have returned to us.'

Joah shook his head, bewildered. 'How can they be gone?'

'Time, Joah, took them all. They did away with the gods, and then the Edenier faded from this world. They scrambled around as best they could, of course, clung on to their tiny magics in their desperate need for survival, but in the end they all died, ancient and decrepit. Which was all that they deserved, after how they treated you.'

'How long? How long have I been gone?'

'A thousand years, give or take a few centuries.'

'That cannot be. Such a loss is unthinkable.'

As Nuava watched, Joah Demonsworn looked down at the ground, his long hair swinging forward like a curtain. Whatever expression was on his face now, it displeased the Prophet. The girl tipped her head to one side, an oddly childish gesture, and now there was petulance in her voice.

'The age of the mages has long since passed. Don't you remember what they did to you? You do not need them, you never did.'

The mage turned away, shaking his head irritably. 'They might have hated me. Feared me, even. But they were the only family I had. And now I am alone?'

'You have me,' said the Prophet. 'We can be together again.'

'I have unfinished work.' His voice was so quiet now that Nuava could barely hear him. 'I shall go to the hills.'

'Wait.' There was a tone of command from the Prophet that made the hairs on the back of Nuava's neck stand on end. 'I need you to do something for me first, Joah. Now that you've had your fun here.'

'Yes?'

Nuava shifted around, moving closer to the edge of the rubble, the knife still held tightly in one hand. The mage was distracted, and perhaps if she got close enough she could end this. All she needed was one chance, a moment to slip the knife between his ribs, and maybe that would be enough. He'd killed her brother, so she had to at least try.

'There are some enemies of mine near here,' continued the Prophet. 'A knight called Sebastian, a woman sell-sword, and a lord. They are travelling through a strip of land on the edge of Skald territory. Go there, kill them for me. I have grown weary of them, so kill them quickly. And then you are free to continue your work.'

Joah nodded, once. 'Fine. It will be a pleasure.' The mage bowed low, and Nuava forced herself into a run, knife flashing. The Prophet turned towards her, slowly, uncaring, and then Nuava was barrelling into Joah himself, stabbing wildly with the knife and striking nothing. She could smell rot, deep in the folds of his cloak, and the sound of her own screams echoing in her head.

He laughed once, and his arms tightened around her.

'Coming along with me, little one?'

And the world around her twisted away into nothing.

'How are you feeling?'

Sebastian passed Wydrin a fresh cup of tea. The three of them were huddled closely around the small fire the Narhl had allowed them, although it was starting to snow again, and Sebastian thought it wouldn't last much longer. The last light of the day was now a distant dirty smudge on the low-hanging clouds to the west.

'Fine, I'm fine.' Wydrin took a slurp of the tea and waved his concerns away. 'I just ache a little, that's all.'

'I honestly doubt that,' said Frith. The young lord was poking their fire with a stick, with more violence than was strictly necessary. *He hates to be disarmed,* thought Sebastian, *and I can hardly blame him.* 'The cold this Prince Dallen cast down on me was an agony. I wouldn't be surprised if we both suffer for this later on.'

'I guess I'm just tougher than you, princeling.'

Frith shook his head at that and turned to Sebastian. 'What is our next move?'

'We do as Dallen says and go back to Skaldshollow,' said Wydrin. 'I tell them that the werkens are sentient beings and what they were doing is essentially slavery. Then we leave, and they can argue about the Heart-Stone all they want. We go somewhere very warm where I can lie on a beach and drink rum all day.'

'Are you mad?' hissed Frith. 'We are still prisoners here, and you want us to obey this prince? We shall be caught in the middle of a war.'

'Prince Dallen wants peace,' said Sebastian. He glanced over to the Narhl camp, where he could see the shape of Dallen standing with his second in command. They were near the supplies, and the bulky shape of the Heart-Stone. All their weapons were there too. 'I think we can trust him.'

Frith snorted in disgust. 'Trust? How much do you suppose they trust us? Have they returned your weapons, Sebastian? They asked Wydrin to risk death today, and yet they don't even return her dagger. And they still watch me, constantly, waiting . . .'

There was a flash of blinding blue light, illuminating the space around them as if it were midday, and for a moment Sebastian thought Frith had decided to punctuate his argument with a demonstration of the unbridled mage powers, but when his eyes recovered he saw a stranger standing between them and the Narhl camp. He wore long green robes, and his loose brown hair swirled about his shoulders.

'Who the hell is that?' gasped Wydrin, spitting half her tea back into the cup.

Sebastian stood. He could see now that there was a girl with the man, crouched down by his feet and half hidden by the robes.

'Is that Nuava Nox?'

The Narhl soldiers were shouting commands to each other, quickly fanning out into a circle around the man. Sebastian could see Dallen approaching, his eyes wide with shock.

'Look at him,' whispered Frith urgently. He was standing now too, and was helping Wydrin to her feet. 'Look at his arms.'

The man had spirals of white linen around his arms and hands, and all of them were inked with strange, looping patterns. Sebastian had seen Frith at work often enough to recognise what they were. All at once he missed his broadsword more than ever.

'Who are you?' shouted Prince Dallen. He pushed to the front of his soldiers, clutching an ice-spear in one hand. 'What do you mean by coming here?' Sebastian could hear the confusion in Dallen's voice, barely overridden by caution.

'This is quite the place,' said the man. He sounded relaxed. The girl who had been crouching at his feet suddenly ran, skittering towards their small campfire and running to Wydrin, who grabbed the girl to her. The man watched the girl go, and then paused to brush some snow from his shoulders. It was coming thicker now. 'I came here once, a long time ago. It is as haunted as it ever was.'

Olborn stepped forward, her spear jutting upwards, aimed at the man's throat.

'You will answer our prince or you will die.'

The man glanced at her, seeming mildly surprised by her existence. 'Oh, I am here for them,' he gestured over to their fire carelessly, and Sebastian automatically took a step backwards. Was this a rescue? Somehow, he thought not. The girl, who was indeed Nuava Nox, gave a low moan in the back of her throat. 'But I would just like to try something.'

Olborn charged forward, throwing her ice-spear at the man's unarmed chest. The man held out one hand and the spear froze in mid-air, hanging like an unlikely toothpick, and then he threw out his other hand, and the snow on the ground around them began to churn.

'He's a mage,' spat Frith. 'Where has he come from?'

'Not any mage,' said Nuava, and her voice was low with dread. 'That is Joah Demonsworn, Joah the Mad. H-he killed my brother.'

170

'Bors? Bors is dead?' Wydrin was supporting her now. The front of the girl's tunic was crusted with dried blood.

'The animals that make their nests here also bury their dead here. Did you know that?' continued the rogue mage. He flicked one hand, almost distractedly, and the ice-spear flew off into the dark. He was looking at the ground with great interest. 'Not all of their young make it to term, you see. It's quite fascinating, because they don't discard or eat the bodies like most animals do. They bury them, and with great reverence.'

The ground at Joah's feet burst open, and a pair of pale bundles rose into the air. It took Sebastian a moment to realise what they were, and then one of the bundles turned slowly, a single skeletal leg peeling free.

'I fear it has been very, very cold for them, all these years,' said Joah. 'But I think, with the right push, I might be able to wake them up.'

Wydrin blinked rapidly, fighting a wave of dizziness. The girl, Nuava, was leaning on her heavily.

'What's happening, Nuava?'

'The Prophet brought him back from the dead somehow. He attacked the city, killed hundreds of people . . .' She sucked in an agonised breath. 'The Prophet ordered him to find you and kill you.'

The rogue mage knelt down and traced something in the snow with his finger. Wydrin couldn't make out the pattern, but when he stood up, the snow all around them began to churn violently.

'What is he doing?'

'That was a mage's word he wrote into the snow,' said Frith, his voice low and urgent. 'One I don't recognise.'

The two dead arachnos young hanging in the air began to twitch, and then as Wydrin watched, their long skeletal legs unfolded. Their bodies were like hollow baskets made of bone so thin it was almost see-through, covered in dark downy fluff that would eventually have become thick white fur, but the ends of those skeletal legs ended in cruel-looking pincers, and these started to flex ominously.

'We have to get to our weapons,' said Wydrin, taking a few shaky steps forward, but now the ground all around them was

171

erupting, and the dead arachnos young were tearing their way out of their graves. Sebastian leapt back as one scrambled at his boot.

'Stop!' shouted Dallen. 'Stand down or we will kill you! Send these creatures back.'

'Stand down?' The rogue mage sounded genuinely amused. 'Don't you want to see what these things do?'

The ground was alive with the spider-like creatures now, each one about the size of a dog, each one flexing razor-sharp pincers. There was a moment when they seemed confused, their long legs tangled with each other in the snow, then at a gesture from Joah Demonsworn, they surged forward, all towards Dallen's soldiers.

'Ice-spears!' bellowed the young prince. 'Now!'

There were several deafening cracks as the spears fell among the writhing creatures, but although a few were caught in the freezing traps, most surged on and over, and in seconds they had overwhelmed Dallen and his men. Wydrin had a moment to see Olborn trying to wrestle one off her leg as its flexing pincers sheared her flesh away from its bone, and then the woman fell, immediately vanishing under the swarm of animals.

Mendrick?

The werken stood from its crouched position in the snow and came over to her. The screams of Dallen's soldiers were growing frantic.

You called?

Shaking off Nuava, Wydrin ran to the werken's side. 'You're talking to me now?'

The link has been deepened. Our minds are meshed.

Wydrin scrambled up onto his back, and waved to the others. 'Follow me,' she said. 'I'll clear a path.'

She pictured what she wanted, no longer sure how this would work, and then she felt Mendrick's agreement in her head. They surged forward, crashing over the churning spider-creatures. In the snow and the confused dark she spotted Joah, standing with his arms crossed and watching the fighting as though this were some faintly entertaining spectator sport. Above them, the wyverns descended, summoned by the Narhl soldiers. They came, jaws wide and snapping, but Joah lifted a hand and as one they burst

172

into flames, becoming brightly burning comets. Wydrin cried out as they crashed to the ground some distance away, their screams abruptly silenced.

'To him then.' She leaned forward. 'Let's see if we can't take this bastard down before we see any more of his tricks.'

Immediately, Mendrick leapt to the right, skidding slightly on the icy ground, and they pounded straight for Joah's back. There was a high-pitched scream of warning, probably from Nuava, and suddenly Joah turned to look straight at them, robes flying.

'Oh, don't think I've forgotten about you.'

He gestured towards them and Wydrin gasped as the ground dropped away. She flung her arms around Mendrick's neck, watching with horror as they floated higher and higher. She could see Sebastian below them, now at their packs and frantically searching for their weapons. Frith was near him, his face turned up to her. From up here the battle looked already lost – the dead arachnos young had swarmed over Dallen's soldiers, and she could see bodies on the ice, their blood a dark smear against the grey.

'I don't suppose you can fly?' she whispered in Mendrick's pointed stone ear.

I am a mountain.

'How's the view?' called up Joah, his voice full of laughter. 'These stone monsters of yours are extremely clever, but I have noticed they are quite *heavy*. In fact, I rather tire of holding you up there.'

Wydrin tightened her grip round Mendrick's neck, and they dropped like a stone.

'No!'

Frith watched her fall with his heart in his throat – unbidden, he remembered their flight across Ede, Wydrin falling from her griffin over the Horns – and a great pulse of light issued from his chest. As it had in the Queen's Tower, the Edenier reached out and held everything still, including Wydrin and her werken. The power churned deep inside him, desperate, and he staggered. Everything else lurched back into motion, but Wydrin and her mount came down slowly, landing in the snow with a soft crunch. Next to him, Sebastian had retrieved his broadsword and Wydrin's sword belt.

'Quick, give this to her.'

Frith snatched it up and ran to the dark form where Wydrin had landed. She took it gratefully, pausing to lay a hand on his arm.

'Nice catch, Frith.'

He nodded, still amazed that the Edenier had acted by itself again, when they all became aware of an eerie silence. The arachnos had all stopped moving, their skeletal forms falling away as the false life Joah had imbued them with vanished. Wydrin saw Dallen still standing, blood running from a number of wounds, a short sword clutched in his hands – the rest of his squad were bloody mounds on the ground.

Joah Demonsworn was standing in the midst of the arachnos corpses, staring back at their small group. Even in the poor light and the whirling snow, it was possible to see the surprise on his face.

'What', he muttered, 'was that?'

Wydrin was hurriedly tying her sword belt back on. Sebastian appeared at her side, his hands full of long silk strips.

'They didn't throw them away,' he said, handing them to Frith. 'They were in the pack with all our stuff.'

'*What was that?*' Joah repeated.

'Looks like we've upset the lunatic.' Wydrin took a silk strip at random and tied it around Frith's arm. 'Let's get armed up.'

There was no time. Joah turned on them and the night was lit with balls of fire, streaking towards them like yellow suns. One hit the pack horses and exploded, and everything was fire and screaming and the scent of burning horse flesh. The arachnos-corpses too were moving again, lurching out of the shadowed dark, hungry pincers clutching blindly. Wydrin's sword, Glassheart, whirled back and forth, shattering the delicate forms where she could, while Sebastian swept his broadsword from side to side, trying to reach the prince.

Frith glanced down at the spells he'd managed to tie around his arms. The words for Fire, Ever, Guidance and Cold. It would have to do.

He broke cover, moving to get a clear shot at the man calling himself Joah, and he threw up a wall of ice. It struck the man low, freezing the lower half of his body. He saw the man turn, incredulous, before melting the ice away with a sweep of his hand. He looked up at Frith and their eyes locked.

'You,' said Joah, strangely clear amongst the carnage. 'Where did you come from?'

'I might ask you the same question,' muttered Frith, before pushing his hands out in front of him and summoning the words for Ever and Fire. A stream of blood-red flames gushed out of his fingers, sending up clouds of steam from the icy ground below, but again Joah turned this away as though it were nothing. Instead, he began to walk towards Frith, sending no counter spells himself. The look on his face was one of intense concentration.

'Bezcavar told me they were all gone,' he said. His voice was soft now, but Frith could still hear it. 'And yet it is true the demon lies, sometimes.'

'Get back!' Frith tried another stream of extreme cold, briefly turning the other mage's robes pure white, but his spells didn't seem to be able to grip him. 'I'm warning you . . .'

Part of the night fell down from the sky in a thunderbolt of black feathers; Gwiddion, enormous and powerful in his griffin form, flew at Joah, razor-sharp beak snapping dangerously. The rogue mage fell back, shouting in surprise, and the griffin flew on past, missing Joah but tearing a long strip from his robes. As Frith watched, Gwiddion banked sharply in the air, coming in for another attack, and Frith felt a moment of fierce joy – who else could command griffins? – and then Joah threw his arms up and Gwiddion was no longer there. Instead, something soft and half broken landed at Frith's feet. Back in his bird form, Gwiddion lay stunned, small beak opening and closing.

'No.'

Taking no notice of Joah, who was now moving swiftly towards him, Frith bent down and gathered up the small body of Gwiddion, hiding him within his furred cloak. He could feel him there, small and warm next to his chest. Not dead, he told himself. Not dead yet.

'So many surprises.' Joah was an arm's length away now, and once more he looked relaxed and happy. He was smiling at Frith as though he'd just found something extraordinary. Without turning away, he reached out with his right arm and a bulky shape rose from the piles of their supplies; it spun gently, and part of the covering slipped away to reveal a bright chink of green crystal. The Heart-Stone. It floated swiftly through the air towards them and hung just behind the man called Joah. *To have such control, to be doing all this at once*, thought Frith. *I have only just begun to scratch the surface of what a mage can do.*

He glanced over to where the others were, surrounded by the spidery dead and still fighting. He caught Wydrin's eye briefly, and saw her look of alarm as she realised how close he was to the rogue mage. He saw her mouth open, saw her shouting to him, and then Joah's hand was on his shoulder, and he was embracing him like an old friend.

'There is no need to fight,' whispered Joah into his ear. 'You are with me again, brother.'

The world around them began to twist and warp strangely, and just before he vanished, Frith distinctly heard Wydrin calling his name.

26

The two men appeared from nowhere in a blinding flash of light. Grondel, who had been preparing that night's fire, staggered back from it and hurriedly kicked snow over the glowing embers, but a second's observation showed him that neither man was Narhl, and they had not spotted him within his ring of rocks.

Crouching low, Grondel peered closely at the two men. They were deep in the heart of night by now, but the skies were clear this side of the Adrean pass and the bottom of the hill was filled with moonlight. One man wore strange, scholarly robes, while the other was thin, his hair a shock of unruly white. As he watched, the man in the robes took hold of the other man, who had fallen to his knees. He could just about hear a voice, but could make out none of the words.

Grondel relaxed slightly. Whoever they were and whatever strange magics had caused them to drop down out of the sky, they weren't Narhl, so they wouldn't be interested in him and his fire. He would wait for them to leave, and if they didn't, well, his seeing-charms would have to wait for another night.

Now the slimmer man was struggling, staggering back from the other as if he dearly wanted to get away. There was another flare of light, yellow this time, and it was as if the white-haired man had shot a comet from his hands. It missed the man in the robes, arching up into the night and fading.

'Such magic,' muttered Grondel, forgetting himself. 'To be able to summon fire. I could conjure all the seeing-charms I wished.'

There was a fierce argument ongoing between the men. Grondel saw more crackles of light, crawling across the snow like the spirit lights that sometimes hung in the sky to the north. Inside his chest Grondel's heart quickened; he was a shaman and an outcast, a Narhl who suffered the torments of the fire for the visions it sometimes accorded. He wondered what visions he would see with such magical fire. He half stood, dangerously silhouetted against the snow. *Perhaps,* he thought, *perhaps if I ask them they would lend me such light.*

The argument below seemed to reach some sort of crescendo, and the white-haired man flew backwards, knocked off his feet by some unseen force. He lay unmoving in the snow, while the robed man stood stock still, apparently uncertain of his next move.

Grondel crouched again. Now that silence had come back to the hills, he no longer wished to be so exposed. There was an uncanny quality to the man now standing, looking at his fallen opponent. Grondel's hands went to the prayer bones at his throat and he counted through them, fingers trembling. *The fires never showed me this, no matter all the burns I took for them.*

Abruptly, the figure turned away, looking up towards the low hills that rolled away behind him, and with a gesture, the ground began to shake violently. Grondel let out a low cry as he stumbled to his knees, striking his shin painfully on a rock. When he looked up again, the hill directly in front of the figure had seemingly split down the middle, revealing a rocky crevasse lit with flickering cold-lights. The man paused to fetch his unconscious companion, slinging his inert body over his shoulder, and then he disappeared into the hill.

Grondel stood there for some time, waiting to see if the opening into the hill would close up, or if either of the men would come back out again. There appeared to be nothing stopping him from climbing down to the crevasse and following them both in. Perhaps he would find kindred spirits there, men who understood that to truly see you must suffer the purity of the flames, and perhaps they would teach him the secrets of the fire they summoned from their own hands.

But as he stood there with the night growing colder, he found himself thinking of the way the man had stood in silence, waiting and listening, and he knew that to follow him into the hill would be to rush to his own death. This place had a dark history, and in the past that had been useful – he could commune with the fire here safe in the knowledge that he was alone – but a new curse had come to the Wailing Hills. Grasping his prayer bones in a hand that was still shaking, Grondel made his way into the night.

27

'All of them. Dead.'

Prince Dallen stood staring at the bodies, swaying slightly on his feet. He looked like a scarecrow, ragged and bleeding from numerous wounds where the dead arachnos had snipped at him with their pincers. Sebastian kept as close as he dared, ready to grab him if he should fall. He didn't look strong enough to be standing.

'Your highness – I am sorry.'

Dallen shook his head. His eyes were deeply shadowed. 'They never attack like that,' he said, still not looking at Sebastian. 'The arachnos can be dangerous, yes, but if you give them space and don't provoke them . . .' His voice trailed off. 'I've never known anything like it.'

'It was dark magic,' said Sebastian. Blood trickled down the prince's fingers and dripped onto the packed, white snow. 'The mage who attacked us caused them to act that way. There was nothing you could have done.'

'I've flown with these men and women for all of my adult life, Sebastian. They looked to me as their prince, yes, but I was also their squad leader. And the wyverns –' They had found the bodies of the wyverns by following the sooty smears they made as they landed. Charred and smoking, they were unrecognisable as the extraordinary creatures they had been. 'I raised Rillion from a yearling.'

Now Prince Dallen did stumble, the strength seeming to drop

away from his legs, and Sebastian took hold of his arm quickly. The prince leaned on him briefly, gratefully, and then stepped away.

'Your highness, we must do something about your injuries. I have bandages and salve in my pack, if you will let me—'

'You cannot touch me,' said Dallen. Seeing the look on Sebastian's face, he gave him a watery smile. 'I do not mean to be rude. But the touch of a warmling can be very uncomfortable for us.'

'Your highness . . .' Sebastian bit his lip, wondering if he was overstepping his boundaries here, 'it would be easy to give in to grief. I have been where you are now, and I urge you not to.'

For a long moment Dallen didn't say anything at all.

'I should like to do what I can for the bodies, first,' he said eventually. 'I can do that much for them at least.'

They began to gather the men and women of Dallen's squad together on the ice. Their injuries were extreme, and more than once Dallen had to stop, the back of his hand pressed to his mouth. Wydrin came over to lend assistance, but Sebastian sent her back to the small fire they had made, telling her to rest up. She looked as though she might argue with him at first, but she was still pale and exhausted from her experience with the werken – he could tell from the careful way she moved – and eventually she relented, joining Nuava by the fire. Watching her go, Sebastian felt a familiar heat in his chest. The urge to find this mage, to hunt him down, was enormous. He could feel it as a restlessness in his blood, the same as when he hunted with the brood sisters. The wyverns had burnt like tapers, screaming in the night; someone would pay for this.

When the bodies were lined up together, Dallen asked for some privacy. Sebastian moved back to the fire, and then watched as the young prince summoned the cold with his own strange magic. Within seconds the corpses were covered in a thin layer of glittering ice, beautiful under the moonlight. Dallen raised his hands, trembling with the effort, and a long, sinuous shape formed on top of the ice; a simple wyvern, its long head bristling with icicles. The ice wyvern lay across all of them, binding them together.

'I will take those bandages now, if you have them,' said Dallen afterwards. 'I will bind my wounds myself.'

Sebastian nodded, not questioning. He retrieved his pack from its place by the fire, and passed Dallen what supplies he had.

'That is extraordinary,' he said. 'What you did with the ice. And beautiful.'

'The cold-summons isn't just about disabling enemies,' said Dallen. 'It is also how we build. The talent runs strongest in the royal family.' He paused, his bruised face tense with pain. Sebastian thought it likely he was thinking of his father again. 'I will take these some distance from your fire. It is difficult for me to heal so close to a heat source.'

Sebastian let him go, and then headed back to their small circle of light. Wydrin was standing now, her arms crossed over her chest.

'So you're saying this mage has been dead for centuries, and now he's back?' Her lips were pressed into a thin line and there were two points of colour, high on her cheeks.

'Joah Demonsworn. It was him. She even called him by the name.' Nuava was still trembling slightly all over, like a cornered rabbit. Wydrin had brewed her a hot cup of tea heavily laced with grut, but she was just holding it in her hands.

'This is the same mage whose tomb you took Sebastian and Frith to see, isn't it? So why is he suddenly so bloody lively?'

Nuava shook her head, spilling a little of the tea over her hand. It must have been scalding, but she didn't appear to notice.

'It was the Prophet. All along. She wasn't who she said she was. We should have known, I should have known, but Tamlyn was so adamant we listen.' She took a shaky breath. 'There was something wrong about her from the beginning. That voice, the way she spoke. It wasn't right for a child.'

Sebastian felt his stomach drop a few inches. It was probably nothing, he told himself. There were many strange things in Ede, and they were thousands of leagues from Relios.

'What do you mean?' continued Wydrin. 'Who is this Prophet?'

'She came to us some months back. Tamlyn was at her wits' end by then. Skaldshollow was under near continual attack from the Narhl, and then the Heart-Stone was taken.' She glanced over to Prince Dallen, but he was turned away from them, far from the fire and their conversation. 'The Prophet promised that she could solve the Narhl problem for us, and she told us lots of things that seemed very wise.' She sniffed. 'They *seemed* wise at the time. There were other incidents. She healed one of our soldiers, closing up his wound and banishing his fever. She seemed to know so much, for someone so young. My aunt was convinced, Bors less so.' She paused then, and Sebastian saw tears slipping silently down her cheeks. He reached over and squeezed her shoulder.

'What did this Prophet tell you to do?'

'She told us that help would come from outside Skaldshollow, and that she'd had a vision. Of three black griffins.' Nuava swallowed hard. 'That's how we knew to hire you.'

Wydrin caught Sebastian's eye, and he saw the knowledge there as cold and certain as the moon. He cleared his throat.

'Nuava,' he said, 'what did the Prophet look like? You say she was a child?'

'No more than twelve or thirteen years old, I'd have said. She had long brown hair and wore it in a braid, and she had blue eyes. But when she spoke, she didn't have a croaky voice, like an old woman, but she sounded *old*, like she'd lived for so much longer than anyone you'd ever known. Like everything was a joke and we had yet to understand it.'

'The girl the demon inhabited would look around twelve now,' said Wydrin, still looking at Sebastian. The spots of colour had vanished from her cheeks. 'And this sounds like her. Like Bezcavar.'

Sebastian winced at the name.

'The demon would have reason to lure us out here,' he admitted. 'This Joah did say he was here for us. Bezcavar was looking for revenge.'

'Except that Bezcavar's man scarpered, taking Frith with him.' Wydrin stood up abruptly, and Sebastian recognised from the way she was stepping from one foot to the other that she was looking for a fight. 'You have to summon it, Seb. Get the demon here so we can question it.'

Nuava was looking at each of them, turning back and forth. Her eyes were wide and wet.

'And how do you propose I do that?' said Sebastian, trying to keep his own temper under control. 'Wydrin, I cast off my oath to Bezcavar. We destroyed the armour that summoned the Cursed Company. I have no ties to that creature any more.'

Wydrin shook her head. 'I don't really believe that. Do you? You swore an oath in blood. I think if you tried, if you really tried, you could get that snivelling demon bastard to show its face.' One hand was resting on the pommel of Glassheart now. Sebastian thought it likely that she didn't know she was doing it. 'We need to find out where he's taken Frith. We need to know what this Joah's intentions are.'

Sebastian touched the scar on his face, remembering the sharp sting as he'd pressed the blade of his own sword to his cheek: the moment he'd forsaken his own gods in a desperate ploy to save the lives of men and women who had already exiled him in disgrace. 'We can try,' he conceded finally. Nuava started, spilling more of her tea.

'You are going to summon her here? You are bringing the Prophet here?' The fear in her voice was clear.

'It will be all right, Nuava. The being you call the Prophet may not even come.'

Feeling faintly foolish, he took off his gloves and slipped a dirk from his belt. He pressed the blade against the palm of his hand, feeling the pain. *Letting* himself feel the pain, because that's what Bezcavar craved, of course. The Prince of Wounds.

'I spill this blood in the name of Bezcavar.' The blood welled up and he cupped it in his hand. 'I know you're there, demon. I know you're listening, so why don't you come and play?'

For a long moment, nothing happened. Wydrin paced by the fire, one hand on her sword, while Nuava seemed to be trying to make herself as small as possible. Dallen had approached the fire again, his arms and legs now partly bandaged.

Sebastian opened his hand, letting the blood drip onto the snow.

'I spill this blood in the name of Bezcavar. Come on, demon. I know you must hunger after all paltry offerings, desperate little creature that you are.'

'And your offering certainly is paltry, good Sir Sebastian.'

They turned as one at the sound of that voice, and Sebastian

184

felt his blood grow cold. There she was, standing in the dark, lit in shades of grey and orange by the moon and their dying fire; a girl, taller than he remembered, wearing leathers and furs, her long brown hair brushed back from her face and secured into a braid. Her eyes were filled with blood, and her hands were red to the wrists. *When we first met it was her feet that were covered in blood*, he thought distantly. He squeezed his hand into a fist, sending a spike of pain up his arm, and Ip smiled in corresponding pleasure.

'It is you,' he said. 'Do you have nothing better to do than to pursue us, Bezcavar?'

'But Sir Sebastian, we never said a proper goodbye.' The demon in the shape of a girl came a few steps closer, and he could see how her face had changed too; the roundness of a child's features were growing sharper, more angular. *When she is older, she will be quite beautiful*, thought Sebastian. 'When you rudely threw my sword to the ground and dismissed me, did you think our pact was over?'

Wydrin stepped between them. Her dagger was out of its scabbard.

'Where is he? Where have you had him taken?'

For the first time there was a flicker of unease from Ip. She looked away from Wydrin towards the fire, and smiled.

'Ah, Nuava, it is good to see you again.'

The girl shrank back, saying nothing. Ip shrugged.

'For what it's worth, your brother hardly suffered at all. A great personal disappointment to me, you must understand.' She turned to the Narhl prince. 'Your people have been most entertaining. I felt each of them die, and it was glorious. Joah always was so good at causing the maximum amount of pain to many people at once. It has been quite the tonic, this little battle.'

'Enough,' said Wydrin. 'You will answer my question, demon, or I will open your throat.'

Ip rolled her scarlet eyes at that.

'I am not *here*, tavern-brat. My physical body is still safe in Skaldshollow, warming itself on the many fires that are now destroying the city. And besides which, could you really do it? Kill a child in cold blood? Ip is still in here with me, you know, and she would die too.'

'Is she, though?' asked Sebastian. 'Perhaps Ip is long gone, or perhaps she longs to be set free from your tyranny. Do you even let her speak any more?'

Bezcavar laughed at that. 'Dear Sebastian, you are as ignorant as the rest of your ridiculous order. I am here by Ip's choice. She accepted me into her head, and has no qualms about the agreement. Indeed, I can only be here by invitation.' She grinned then. 'Would that make it easier for you to kill her? You came very close at my temple in Relios, Sir Sebastian.'

'Tell me where this Joah has gone,' said Wydrin again. 'Tell me where he has taken Frith, or I swear on my claws you will suffer for it, demon.'

And there it was. Just for the briefest moment, Sebastian saw the confusion on Ip's face. She recovered her habitual sneer quickly, but it was enough.

'It will be you that suffers, sell-sword,' said Bezcavar through Ip. 'I will feed on all your deaths.'

With that she vanished. Wydrin let out a growl of frustration, stalking back to the fire with her shoulders rigid.

'By the graces, I will cut that demon's head off myself,' she spat. 'What are we going to do now? We have no idea where they could have gone, and if he's used the same spell that Frith used to spirit us away from the Citadel, it could be anywhere.'

'We don't know where they've gone,' said Sebastian, 'but the good news is, neither does Bezcavar. Did you see Ip's face when you mentioned Frith? The demon was expecting us to be dead, Wydrin. Whatever this Joah has done, it wasn't according to Bezcavar's plan.'

Nuava cleared her throat. 'I've been thinking,' she said, her voice strained. 'Joah lived and died in these mountains. His stories are written everywhere, in this land. Before he took me away from Skaldshollow, he was talking to the Prophet about carrying on his work.' She looked up at them, and for the first time since she'd appeared with the mage there was a glint of something like defiance in her eyes. 'We don't know where he is, but we might be able to guess.'

186

28

28

'What on Ede does he think he's playing at?'

Bezcavar came back to Ip's body with a sudden jerk, shivering violently at the transition. The girl was hiding underneath a discarded cart, its load of barrels scattered all over the road. All around her Skaldshollow was in chaos; Joah's rampage had left hundreds dead and many more injured, and now she was stuck here by herself. Tamlyn Nox, no doubt, was out for her blood.

This was not how events were supposed to pan out. Joah had always been Bezcavar's most loyal servant – impetuous perhaps, and occasionally hot-headed, but he had done what the demon asked, most of the time. The demon had tried looking for him, searching for the familiar shape of the mage's mind, but Joah had always been powerful enough to hide if he wanted to. It was one of the things that made him interesting, when they had worked together so long ago.

And, back then, Bezcavar had inhabited an adult woman, a famous warrior from a forgotten land. The demon remembered that body with fondness – strong, beautiful, fast. It was a shame that it had come to bones and muck, as all human bodies did eventually.

Ip shuffled forward to peer beyond the wheels of the cart. Men and women were still shouting to each other, but the panic was starting to fade as it became clear that the man responsible for the destruction had vanished. The magical fires he had set had proved to be quite difficult to extinguish, even in this frigid part of the world, but they were starting to get them under control.

'Where is he? And why has he not returned?'

The mercenaries were still alive, and bold enough to summon the demon. Worse still, Joah had taken the upstart mage somewhere, and something about that caused a slow trickle of fear in what passed for Bezcavar's heart. He should have been glad that the mages, his old enemies, were gone, and yet there was that look on his face. Almost like grief.

A woman fell against the cart, sobbing loudly. The bottom of her furred skirts were blood-stained. A man came and put an arm around her shoulder, leading her away. Ip shuffled back into the shadows again.

If only the girl were older. If only this were the body of a warrior, a man or a woman with brute strength behind their sword hand. In a different body Bezcavar might have been able to clear a path towards the great stone gate, but Ip was hardly big enough to lift a sword, let alone wield it successfully, and every guard would be on the lookout for her now. It was just a matter of time before she was found and brought before Tamlyn Nox.

In the dark under the cart, Bezcavar twisted Ip's face into a grim smile.

'I am not out of tricks just yet.'

Ip took a dagger from her belt and began to chop at her hair, now mostly loose from its braid. It came away in clumps, until her hair was cut closely to her scalp and she could feel the bitter cold around her ears. Once this was done to her satisfaction she picked up a handful of the dirtier snow and let it melt into her hands, before rubbing the muck over her face. Finally, she stripped off the warm fur overcoat, and rubbed some more dirt into her linen shirt. Not much of a disguise by anyone's standards, but she had only ever been seen clean and well-dressed, and she had spent most of her time behind the thick gauze curtains of her bedchamber.

Ip scrambled out from under the cart and began to walk slowly down the street, not making eye contact with anyone. It was important not to run, not to appear guilty. If she looked like she belonged in Skaldshollow – just another lost child, reeling from the unexpected attack – then no one would look too closely, or wonder who she was. And she might be able to survive a few days, by which time Joah would almost certainly have returned from his unexpected trip.

A pair of soldiers walked past her, their werkens following. The men looked at her but she turned her head away, her gaze focussed down the street as if she'd spotted someone she knew. Ip moved away easily, still not running, still not running.

Frith awoke and looked up into a clutch of glowing ruby eyes.

Blinking rapidly, he scrambled to his feet, almost colliding with a low stone table directly behind him. He was in a cavernous patchwork room with a domed ceiling, the air stinking of ancient dust. The walls were constructed from a confusion of stone and dark pitted lumps of metal, layered over the top of each other like scales. The eyes he had seen were red lamps in the ceiling, casting a ruddy light down over the jumbled contents of the room. Someone, presumably Joah Demonsworn, had lit an oil lamp and left it on a stone bench.

Frith held on to the table for support. His head was swimming, and his vision was dark at the edges. There were tables everywhere, all of them covered in tools that looked like they'd seen better days, the dust on them nearly half an inch thick, and there were other items that Frith was less than pleased to see: a tray of knives of various sizes, like those Yellow-Eyed Rin had once used, along with rusted hacksaws and an ornamental dagger covered in dark stains. One of the walls was made of black iron plates, daubed here and there in strange dark writing that Frith didn't recognise. There were steps on either side of this wall, leading up to a flat platform at the top that Frith couldn't see properly, although, set directly below it, was a chamber with a wide glass section, like a window on to nothing. The glass looked very fine indeed, even better than the glass the Secret Keeper had made, and the chamber shone with a strange pale light. Underneath that was another smaller aperture with no glass, and it was empty. Looking at the metal wall, with its glass prison and its ragged black writing, Frith felt a fresh stab of fear. What was this place?

'Ah, you're awake.'

The mage who Nuava had named as Joah Demonsworn

appeared from behind him, wiping his hands on an oily rag. There were several doors leading out of the room, although Frith found he couldn't have said which one the mage had come through. It was difficult to think.

'Good to see you up and about,' he continued. His voice was calm, even slightly distracted. 'I was beginning to think I'd hit you too hard.'

Frith glanced quickly down at his hands. His last bandage was the one for Force – all the rest had vanished into dust by now. He flung his arm up, planning to throw the rogue mage against the iron wall with enough violence to disable him, but Joah merely waved at him and Frith collapsed back onto the floor, suddenly unable to breathe. It felt as though there was a steel band around his chest, slowly contracting.

'No . . .' he gasped.

'No indeed,' agreed Joah mildly. 'Can't be having any more of that, my friend. It's all very well, a bit of a scrap when we're getting to know each other, but we have work to do now.' He bent over Frith and quickly untied the remaining silk strip, tucking it away inside his robes. 'I'm going to let you up, but please bear in mind that I can remove your ability to breathe at any time.'

The steel band vanished, and Frith hurriedly sucked in some air.

'There's a good man.' Joah turned away from him, looking around the room. 'It is much as I left it. Somewhat musty, of course, but that can't be helped. All the important parts are still operational.' He slapped one of the stone tables fondly.

'Who are you?' said Frith eventually. His head was still throbbing, and deep inside he was starting to panic. This mage was alarmingly powerful, and obviously much more at home with the Edenier than Frith was. Save for the glass chamber, there was nothing resembling a window in the strange room, and the sense of claustrophobia was overwhelming. 'What do you want?'

'I am Joah. Here,' he came over to Frith and carefully pulled him to his feet. He even paused to brush some dirt from Frith's clothes. 'You must forgive me, brother, for bringing you out here without even a chance to fetch your belongings, but as I'm sure you can see, the situation is not ideal.'

'I am not your brother.' Frith shook his head. 'Where have you taken me?'

'You *are* my brother, of course you are.' Joah took his shoulder and squeezed it. 'The only one left, if Bezcavar was not lying to me about that too. How glad I am to find that I am not entirely alone.' He smiled then, and it was the friendly smile of someone who was slightly nervous and eager to please. Frith had to remind himself that this was the same man who had appeared out of nowhere and killed so many of Dallen's soldiers.

'I didn't . . . I thought there were no other mages,' said Frith, hating himself for the confusion in his voice. 'All dead, for centuries.'

Joah nodded, full of sympathy. 'Yes, you would have been quite alone. Luckily, Bezcavar, wily creature, made it possible for me to join you in this new age.' He grinned. 'And now, instead of labouring by myself, I will have you to help me.'

'I will not help you do anything,' said Frith flatly. 'You have taken me against my will.'

Joah's grin faded and he shook his head, as if Frith were a child refusing to eat his vegetables at dinner time. 'It's quite all right, Aaron. I understand completely. You're bound to be disorientated.' He chuckled a little. 'I am rather disorientated myself. The world is so different now, and so much has changed. Still,' he clapped his hands together, 'we have all the time we could need. We'll come to terms with this together, Aaron.'

'Do not call me that.' Frith felt a wave of dizziness move through him. The last people to call him Aaron with such easy familiarity had been his brothers. 'How do you even know that's my name?'

'Ah, well,' Joah wagged a finger at him, 'just one more little trick you'll come to learn in time, my friend. A most useful one, one that will make things much easier for us here.'

Frith leaned heavily against the table. There was a weak fluttering against his chest, and belatedly he remembered pushing the small bird-body of Gwiddion inside his cloak. He rested his fingers on the feathered warmth hidden there, hoping it would bring the griffin some comfort. He realised he had no idea if Joah Demonsworn knew he'd taken Gwiddion with him.

'What is this place? Are we underground?'

Joah beamed, pleased to be answering civil questions.

'This place? It is my secret workshop, and now, I suppose, it is the heart of my greatest project. I did much of my best work here, you know, Aaron. I used to call it the Forge.' He cleared his throat. 'You know, obviously, that there are two types of magic in Ede? Edenier and Edeian? Of course you know, you are a mage.'

Frith nodded cautiously. 'Well, the old mages were so obsessed with the Edenier that they were uninterested in the possibilities of any other magic.' He went over to one of the stone tables and began fiddling about with pieces of what looked like broken plate armour. 'They didn't understand what you could do if you combined both of them, you see.'

'From what I heard, you were more interested in the powers granted you by a deal with a demon,' said Frith, staring at the armour. He knew it was unwise to antagonise the man, but he felt strangely reckless. 'And deals with demons cost lives.'

Joah shook his head irritably. 'You're missing the point. You're missing the point just like they did.' Joah's hand tightened around a piece of plate until his knuckles turned white. 'Don't . . . don't be like them. It will make things difficult.' He forced a smile. 'Please. Listen. The demon, Bezcavar, was another tool, another way of using magic. Through what it knew, we could move away from relying on the language of the gods. We could become independent! I made some extraordinary things, blurring the Edenier and the Edeian together, through the lens of that demon's knowledge.'

'You made the armour,' said Frith. He couldn't believe it had only just occurred to him. 'The armour that Sebastian wore at the battle of Baneswatch, the one that summoned the Cursed Company.'

'That's right!' said Joah. 'And a fine piece of work that was too, if I do say so myself. It's one thing, of course, to create enchanted armour, but to make armour that still has magical properties – different magical properties – when the pieces are separated . . . I was rather proud of that one.' He took a slow breath and nodded before turning back to one of the low tables.

There was a thick squarish package there, wrapped in cloth and furs. He began unwrapping it. 'That is nothing, of course, in comparison to what I can do now that you are with me, brother, and now that I have this.'

The fabric fell away to reveal the Heart-Stone, its green crystal light subdued under the red lamps.

'And what do you intend to do with that?' asked Frith. He wondered if he could ever get close enough to use a conventional weapon; there were plenty in the Forge, after all.

Joah raised an eyebrow at him, as though Frith were teasing him somehow. 'That will all become clear, Aaron, I promise you, but I do not wish to overwhelm you at this stage. You've had quite a shock, after all.' Joah held out a hand to the Heart-Stone and it gently lifted off the table to hover in mid-air. 'I have never seen such a pure source of Edeian. This is a remarkable find. All the plans I had, all those years ago, will be possible now with this.' He grinned, and gestured at the stone so that it moved smoothly through the air towards the smaller aperture in the iron wall, and it was into this dark crevice that he gently flew the Heart-Stone. It settled with a hollow clang, and the soft green light of the stone immediately turned a darker shade, painting the rag-tag walls in eldritch hues. Looking at that light, Frith felt ill again, and he clutched at his stomach. It was difficult to think, with that light.

'Can you feel that?' cried Joah jubilantly. 'It's already having an effect. Soon, my Rivener will be working again, and better than it ever did.'

'Rivener?' asked Frith. 'What's that?' But the words were clogging his throat, and his head was swimming. He pressed his fingers to his forehead, trying to concentrate.

'You are wearing yourself out.' Joah went to him and put an arm around his shoulders, guiding him away from the work benches. 'Aaron, I am sorry, I have put you through so much, and then thrown all this information at you. I am such an inconsiderate host. Here.' He took Frith to a door and opened it to reveal a small cavity with bunks built directly into the walls. The blankets looked musty and ancient, but when Joah sat him down on the nearest one, Frith found that he could barely keep his eyes open.

193

'That's it, rest for now, my brother. We have plenty of work to do yet, and I need you at your best.'

Frith opened his mouth to protest, and even that small action was too much. Instead he lay down on the elderly blankets. *I must leave*, he thought over the tide of sleep now approaching. *This place is demon-tainted. Evil.*

Just before unconsciousness took him, he thought he saw a face in the darkness watching him – not Joah, but a woman with dark skin and a shaved head. She watched him with eyes that were fierce and full of anger, and somehow he knew that Joah did not know she was there. He tried to speak to her, to ask who she was, but she turned back into shadows and left him. Frith slept.

29

'Tell us everything you know.'

It was the next morning, and the sky was a pure, thankless blue. The sunlight had revealed the full extent of the previous night's terrors – dark blood on the snow, the twisted forms of the arachnos young, their skeletal legs stained red – so they had moved away from the nesting site to a rocky bluff that sheltered them from the wind. Wydrin had spent some time looting the Narhl packs and was now doing what she could to prepare a breakfast for them all. Nuava sat with her, taking the food that was offered with her eyes downcast. When she looked up at Sebastian again, he saw that the defiance he had heard in her voice the previous night had turned into a fragile sort of reserve.

'I am afraid I can't tell you much beyond what was written in our history books, but it may still be of some use.' She took a savage bite from the black bread Wydrin had handed her and chewed for some moments before continuing. 'When Joah came to the northern lands, he built himself a great workshop in which to perform his terrible deeds.' Her mouth twitched with some sour amusement then, and Sebastian guessed that this was a line she'd read often in a textbook, never expecting to experience Joah's 'terrible deeds' herself. 'He called it the Forge – a twisting labyrinth of rooms hidden somewhere in the snowy territories of the north. There were rooms, they said, where he would commune with his demon, and rooms where he would make terrible objects dedicated to its name. And there were rooms where he would keep the men and women he stole. Children too, sometimes.' She swallowed hard. 'His own sacrifices weren't enough to feed the demon, you see. Sometimes he would sacrifice other people to its appetites.'

Wydrin scowled. Sebastian knew she was thinking of Frith now, and their own history with this particular demon.

'He was making something within the Forge, something enormous, they say,' continued Nuava, 'but he was killed by the mage Xinian the Battleborn before he could complete it. The Forge was hidden within the Wailing Hills, a huge stretch of treacherous land, some miles from the edge of Skald territory, and no one ever knew where it was exactly. It was said that he moved it around, that it was never in the same place twice. I don't know if that's true, but there's nothing in any of our ancient texts that indicates where it was.' Nuava chewed on another piece of the black bread. 'But if he's gone anywhere, and if he's not with the Prophet – I mean, the demon – then I bet he has gone back to the Wailing Hills.'

'Of course he has,' commented Wydrin dryly. 'All his demon-encrusted crap is there.'

'Then we need to find it,' said Sebastian. 'A giant forge can't be that difficult to spot—'

But Nuava was shaking her head. 'You don't understand. It was hidden deep inside the hills themselves, and that stretch of land . . . it's huge. It would take us a month to walk it end to end, and it was not marked. Joah may have been mad, but he was by no means stupid.'

'This Xinian the Battleborn, the mage who killed him the first time round.' Sebastian glanced again at Prince Dallen, but the young prince was sitting some feet away from them, taking no notice of their conversation. 'How did they find Joah, then?'

'I don't know, not exactly,' said Nuava, shaking her head. 'The mages would have had methods to find him, and in any case, he did not die at the Forge. She killed him in the lost city of Temerayne.'

Wydrin shook her head abruptly, and touched a hand to her temple. She looked as though she'd come down with a sudden headache.

196

'Wait. Mendrick may have something here. He says there is a way, if we could—'

There was a sound, like a number of giant flags flapping in a gale, and it was coming from above them. Sebastian glanced up in time to see seven enormous wyverns swimming through the sky towards them at a tremendous speed, the bright sunlight glinting off their gold-chased bridles. He stumbled to his feet, instinctively reaching for his sword.

For the first time in hours, Prince Dallen spoke, his voice low and hopeless. 'It seems that my father has caught up with us.'

The wyverns came straight at them and turned sharply in the air. Sebastian caught sight of King Aristees himself, his muscled arms bared to the cold. They landed with a crash, throwing up sheets of snow to either side. Next to him, Wydrin was on her feet, Glassheart held loosely in one hand. She had clearly not forgotten that their last meeting with King Aristees had ended with him ordering their execution.

When the king dismounted, however, he ignored both of them and strode straight over to his son, who was still sitting cross-legged on the ground. Aristees had already pulled his great battle axe from the strap on his back and had it gripped in both hands. He stopped in front of his son, and kicked a shower of snow and dirt into his face.

'You!' he bellowed. 'Betrayer! Worm! What have you got to say for yourself?'

Prince Dallen shook his head slightly, letting the small clods of dirt fall back to the ground.

'Father—'

'Father? Father! I have been cursed. For letting the Skalds poison the land I have been poisoned myself. With you, my weakling, scheming son. My prisoners freed, the Heart-Stone taken, and all by my own cursed flesh and blood.'

Dallen opened his mouth to speak again, but his father's voice became quieter, and somehow more deadly. 'And have I not just passed the graves of your squad? Led to their deaths out in this godsforsaken place.'

Behind him, the king's wyvern, a huge beast with long furred eyebrows sprouting from its horned head, hissed and spat at them in apparent reaction to the king's anger. Sebastian's hands tightened around his sword. Looking at the wyvern gave him a tight feeling in his chest, and it was hard to drag his gaze from it. The rest of the king's guard had stayed mounted, each of them with an ice-spear in his or her hand. Their faces were as cold as the landscape.

'Father, please.' Sebastian watched as Prince Dallen struggled to his feet, roused to action by mention of his lost soldiers. In the bright sunshine he was a sorry sight, bedraggled and blood-stained. 'I was only doing what I thought was right, for all our people.'

King Aristees sneered. 'What you thought was right? You disobeyed your king! And where is the Heart-Stone now? Tell me you at least have that, Dallen, or gods help me, I shall part your sorry head from your sorrier body right now, in the middle of this cursed place.'

Sebastian stepped towards him, ignoring Wydrin's murmured words of warning.

'Your majesty, the Heart-Stone was taken from us by a man long thought dead.' King Aristees turned to him, his lichen-crusted eyebrows raised in surprise. 'Your son and his followers fought valiantly to keep it from enemy hands, but there was very little they could do. Very little any of us could do, in truth.'

'Fought valiantly?' Aristees boomed. Sebastian felt a fine spray of spittle settle on his face, and fought the urge to wipe it away. 'What would a vile little warmling like you know about fighting valiantly? Your head has been on your shoulders for much longer than I wish it to be, warmling, and it's time I corrected that.'

Aristees took a step towards Sebastian, brandishing the axe, and Dallen stepped in front of him, pushing Sebastian back with a light touch to his arm.

'The prisoners are still mine, Father. You will not harm them.'

Aristees' face grew rigid, darkening with rage. Sebastian saw him staring at his arm where Dallen's hand now rested, and he realised at once that they only knew the barest part of this conflict. *This is an old wound between them*, he thought, *and I have only made it worse.*

198

'It's like that, is it?' Aristees bared his teeth at them both, and his eyes were bright with hate now. And something else, Sebastian thought – relief. *He's been waiting years for an excuse like this.* 'And who took the Heart-Stone from you so easily?'

'It was a mage,' said Dallen. 'A mage so powerful—'

'A mage,' spat King Aristees. 'Are we suffering a plague of them now? Warmling nonsense.'

'Father—'

King Aristees hefted his axe, but he just used the flat head of it to push his son in the chest, hard. Dallen stumbled backwards, one wary hand going to the pommel of his sword.

'I cast you out!' spat Aristees through gritted teeth. 'I cast you out from the Frozen Steps, from all Narhl territories!'

'No!'

'You will no longer be my son, and your name will not be spoken again in the Hall of the Ancestors. I cast you out of the Frozen Lands, and you can die with your warmling friends, in their hot, stinking *civilisation*.'

King Aristees turned and headed back to his mount, which lowered its shaggy head at his approach. The soldiers still mounted looked unmoved by the king's rage, and Sebastian wondered how often they witnessed such outbursts, and exactly how long this day had been in coming. He glanced back to Wydrin, who was standing next to Nuava. She gave the tiniest of shrugs.

Dallen seemed to come back to himself then, and he ran a few steps after his father. All at once he looked much younger.

'Wait,' he said, and all the shrewd diplomacy was gone from his voice. 'Wait, Father. You can't do that. I'm the heir to the throne, the only one you have! What will you do?'

King Aristees had settled himself back into the saddle, his great battle axe once more slung comfortably across his shoulders. His face could have been carved from stone.

'What will I do? I am young yet, whatever you may think, boy. I will take another queen, and hope that her flesh does not produce another warmling snake like you.'

He flicked the reins once, and the wyvern turned on them all, long tail sweeping out towards them. Sebastian staggered back, convinced for a moment that it would knock them all to the

199

ground, and then it was off, pouncing up into the air and away. After a moment, the rest of the king's soldiers followed, and in seconds they were a clutch of blue snakes, wriggling away from them.

There was silence in their small, sorry camp. Wydrin cleared her throat and sat back down, continuing to sort through the Narhl baggage, while Nuava looked up at them all, her own woes temporarily forgotten.

'Your highness,' started Sebastian, and then immediately regretted it. 'Dallen, I . . .'

Prince Dallen turned to look at him, and his smile was very bleak indeed. 'This day has been coming for a long time, Sir Sebastian. I had hoped that I could turn it from its path somehow, stall it, but in the end I only hurried it along. I just – I wish it hadn't cost the lives of my soldiers. They were good men and women. The best, in fact.' His voice broke a little on the last word.

'What will you do now?'

Prince Dallen touched his hand to the furred pendant that hung around his neck. 'The only thing I can do. My father will never have me back, that much is certain, but I can at least restore some small portion of my honour.' He met Sebastian's eyes, and his gaze was cold and clear. 'I shall help you find your friend, and I shall restore the Heart-Stone. I can help the mountain-spirit, if nothing else.'

Sebastian smiled. 'We would be glad of your help, Prince Dallen.'

'Please, just Dallen now. I could do without being reminded of that just at the moment.'

'One less princeling, that's what I like to hear,' said Wydrin. 'Come and have a drink, Dallen, and we'll figure out how we're getting our other one back.'

30

It had seemed important to Sebastian that the brood sisters have some sort of routine, a framework to structure each day. He took to training them as he'd been trained, and as the weeks passed, he saw them settle to it as if they'd been born to such a life.

He stood in the thick grass, watching them work through their exercises as a strengthening breeze pushed at his back. They were near perfect now, their movements swift and confident. A number of them had proven so adept at the old routines that he had singled them out for a kind of promotion; Crocus, Skylark, and Becoming had taken over his role as master-at-arms, and now they walked up and down the rows, adjusting posture and administering praise. They were becoming a genuine unit – whereas before they had thrown themselves into battle with wild abandon, now they moved with surety, with strategy. With their own natural skills and the powerful bond they felt with each other, they would eventually become an unbeatable army. A small one, no doubt, but absolutely formidable.

The day was overcast, and turning colder. The clouds to the south had a yellow tinge to them, a sure sign that snow was coming. Sebastian reached into his pocket and closed his fingers over the blue glass globe in there. Above him, Isu was a looming presence.

'You are pleased with our progress, Father?'

Ephemeral appeared at his elbow. She was dressed in thick furs

– the brood sisters all felt the cold keenly – and she had a fat book under one arm.

'Very much so, Ephemeral. You certainly learn faster than I did, or any of the novices. I wouldn't like to meet your sisters in battle.'

Ephemeral was quiet for a moment. Normally, she was a cauldron bubbling with questions, and Sebastian felt a tremor of unease for the first time that afternoon.

'What is it?'

The brood sister tipped her head to one side, considering. Idly she stroked the cover of her book with one clawed hand.

'You train us for war, Father, and yet we have taken an oath not to take another human life. I do not understand.'

Sebastian took a slow, deep breath, thinking of his own training on similar slopes. Had he thought then about the lives he would take? It was difficult to remember.

'There is more to this than the ability to swiftly injure, or to kill,' he said. He scratched at the scar on his cheek, caught himself doing it, and quickly took his hand away. 'The training teaches discipline, calm thinking in the face of conflict. It teaches you how to defend yourselves. It makes you stronger. I learned all of this when I was a boy, and it gave me structure.'

'Then you do not intend us to fight?'

'I . . . no, Ephemeral. I just want you to be able to live in this world peacefully, and I want to give you –' He paused, uncertain of what to say next. 'I am teaching you what I know, for better or for worse, I suppose.'

'And once we have learned this discipline, we will be able to explore the world?' Ephemeral peered up at him, her eyes narrowed. 'I am eager to go, Father. I want to see the other places, the places that Wydrin spoke of when she was here. I want to see the Marrow Market at Crosshaven, or the Seven Waterfalls at Burning Rock. Or the jungles of Onwai. There is so much to see.' She broke into a grin. 'I will see all of it, and it will be whole and unburnt.'

Sebastian bit his lip. 'Shall we take a walk?'

Ephemeral nodded. They left Skylark shouting commands at the brood sisters to walk around the back of the temple. At the rear of the red brick building there was a long narrow garden. In the distant past it had been planted with hardy vegetables and medicinal plants, but now it was a confusion of overgrown shrubs and weeds. The outer bed had been planted with elder thorn bushes, which the knights had ground down to make numbing salves. These had now overtaken much of the garden, their ruddy thorns wickedly sharp.

'There is a great deal more to being a knight than simply learning to fight,' said Sebastian. He pushed through the bushes, unmindful of the thorns as they scraped against his leathers. 'There is learning, and meditation too.'

'Oh yes,' said Ephemeral eagerly, stepping alongside him. 'I have read all the books you were able to bring us. In one of them I found a great list of other libraries, enormous ones where you could read and read for years and never finish all the books. I will visit those one day too.'

'Yes,' said Sebastian, although his heart sank a little. 'One day, you will travel with us.'

'One day soon, Father?'

Sebastian nodded reluctantly. 'It may be necessary, at first, for you to travel quietly. As we did on the journey up from Baneswatch. People will be wary of you. They may be frightened.'

'We have taken an oath,' said Ephemeral, stepping around another bush. 'We will do no harm to another human being.' She hesitated. 'I am sad, for the lives I have already taken.'

Sebastian looked at her, remembering the battlefield in Relios. The screaming brood horde, so alien and strange in their golden armour, with their crystal swords. She looked so human to him now, with her braided hair and the smudge of book dust on her cheek. Would they look so human to anyone else?

'You know, Ephemeral, that you were not truly responsible for that.' He spoke in a low voice. 'Y'Ruen commanded you then. When your commander is evil,' he struggled to find the right words, 'when the person who commands you is evil, you may find yourself doing evil deeds.' Part of him recoiled at that, knowing it was a terrible simplification, but the anxiety in the set of her mouth was too clear.

'It is more than that though, isn't it?' Ephemeral looked down

203

at her feet. 'Our blood is the blood of the dragon. The god of destruction birthed us beneath the ground, and death and destruction runs in our blood.'

Sebastian put a hand on her shoulder, making her meet his eyes.

'But you have a choice, Ephemeral. And it's what you choose to do now that matters. I truly believe that.'

There was a rustling hiss from behind them. Sebastian turned just in time to catch sight of a scaly tail disappearing from sight.

'A thorn adder,' he said. 'They often make their homes under these bushes. We shall have to cut all this back and replant, I think. It would be a good project for us.'

Ephemeral was already pushing past him, following the snake. 'Are they poisonous, Father?'

'No,' Sebastian went after her, smiling faintly. 'A bite would be no worse than a bee sting, although I wouldn't recommend it.'

They tracked it to the very back of the garden, where a low stone wall marked the boundary. Here the elder thorn was particularly thick. Ephemeral bent down and pushed the bushes back, revealing a swirling, hissing nest of snakes.

Sebastian took an involuntary step backwards. 'Careful,' he said. 'It looks like they're riled up.'

There had to be at least twenty snakes curled up in the natural hollow between the bushes. Their brown and teal scales were dull and dusty, but their eyes were chips of gold, glinting in the overcast daylight. Sebastian had seen many such snakes in his boyhood, but something about this nest caused a fierce knot of tension in his stomach – it was the way they were moving, he told himself, twisting and slithering agitatedly, as though the nest were being poked with a stick.

'They can feel my sisters,' said Ephemeral in a matter-of-fact tone. 'They can sense the dragon blood all around, and it confuses them.'

'What do you mean?' Sebastian found his hand straying to the pommel of his dagger. It might be best to deal with this nest as they had dealt with the wolf. 'How can they feel you?'

'Blood calls to blood,' Ephemeral crouched, peering closely at the snakes. 'Once these creatures were cousins to the dragon, when the world was young and full of magic.'

'How can you know that?'

Ephemeral shrugged. 'It is one of the things I just know. I can feel them, as they feel me. Look.' She reached out a hand to the snakes, and they all stopped moving as one. Not a single tail twitched. No tongues nipped out to taste the air. 'They are so small, and easily swayed.'

'How?' Sebastian swallowed hard, staring at the unnaturally still snakes. 'How are you doing that?'

'It is the connection that flows through our dragon blood.' She looked up at him, almost shyly. 'You feel that connection too. That connection to us. Can you feel the snakes?'

Sebastian took a step backwards, frowning. 'No, of course not. They are just snakes.'

Ephemeral stood up, and the nest of snakes began writhing again.

'Just try it. Reach out for them. In your head they will feel a little like we do.'

Sebastian stared at her. The tension in his stomach had spread to his chest, and he felt a rising note of panic there.

'They can feel you too,' she said. 'Trust me. Just try it.'

Hardly knowing what he was doing, Sebastian looked back down at the snakes. They were all watching him as they writhed, eyes like molten gold. And there was something, a cold tickle in the back of his mind. Was that his imagination? Did his link to the brood sisters give him a link to such low creatures?

'I don't—'

As one, the snakes began moving faster, their glistening sinuous bodies slithering against each other in a frenzy, as though they were being heated over a fire. One, then two, then five of the snakes turned their arrow-shaped heads up to Sebastian and hissed, revealing swollen throats and fangs dripping with poison.

Sebastian stumbled away.

'You did it,' said Ephemeral, cheerily enough. 'You found the connection. Do you still feel it?'

He did – a cold thread in his chest, a silvery chill that was somehow appealing. To be so single-minded, so pure of purpose.

He touched a hand to his forehead, and found that he was sweating.

'Let's go,' he said, already turning away. 'Tomorrow we will burn all these bushes back.'

31

Frith woke to a surge of bile in the back of his throat. He sat up rapidly, swinging his legs over the side of the small bunk and concentrating fiercely on not being sick. The cramped bunk room was still dark and damp smelling, and he could see a thin line of bruise-coloured light under the door. There were noises beyond it, the sounds of someone moving about briskly, occupied with some important task.

After a few moments the nausea passed, and Frith looked cautiously around the room. There was no sign of the woman he thought he'd glimpsed before he'd surrendered to sleep, and it now seemed likely she'd been an hallucination, brought on by shock and the effects of Joah's strange magic.

'I must leave here soon,' he muttered to himself. 'Or I shall become every bit the lunatic Joah Demonsworn is.'

At the sound of his voice, low as it was, there was a scuffling from inside his cloak. He reached within and retrieved the warm bird-body of Gwiddion, who peered up at him with bright, intelligent eyes.

'You are still with me, then.' Despite himself, Frith smiled. He turned the bird over carefully in his hands, gently pressing here and there for injuries. As far as he could tell, nothing was obviously broken, but Gwiddion squawked indignantly as his hands passed over his left wing. Sitting alone in the dark, Frith attempted to summon the healing magic as he had done for Wydrin and her brother, but without the words to channel it, the Edenier stayed silent.

'I'm afraid you may have to wait awhile, Gwiddion.' Frith bundled together a number of the foul-smelling blankets into a sort of nest on his bunk, and placed the bird inside. Gwiddion opened and closed his beak, swaddled now like a small child. Frith took a step back, suddenly feeling vaguely foolish. He was strangely glad that Wydrin was not here to witness this. 'Stay there,' he said in a low voice. 'Don't make any noise.'

Cautiously, Frith stepped through the door and back into the Forge room, being sure to pull the door closed behind him. Joah was there, carrying a pile of stained rags towards a crate that already looked half filled with rubbish. The Heart-Stone, still caught within the aperture in the wall, was glowing and flickering oddly, spilling out its sickening, greenish light. The stone itself looked darker than it had, as though it were cast into permanent shadow.

'Aaron, you're awake!' Joah dropped the rags into the crate, grinning broadly. 'I've just been tidying up. I did what I could, of course, to keep this place held in the same moment of time, but even my spells have struggled with over a thousand years passing. I should be glad that any of it has survived at all, I suppose.' He paused to slap a thick stack of leather books, which sent a cloud of dust up into his face. He coughed, waving a hand in front of his face. 'I do apologise, dear Aaron. It's really quite filthy.'

Frith looked around the room, desperately searching for something he'd missed on his initial visit, but the place was as confusing as ever; a great, round room, with myriad iron doors leading off to who knew what, the red lights in the ceiling glowing like dying stars.

'I was wondering if –' He took a deep breath. His stomach was roiling unpleasantly, and the light from the Heart-Stone was giving him a headache. 'I was wondering if you wouldn't mind showing me around this Forge of yours.' He found himself slipping into the formal courtesies he'd once been so familiar with, back in his life at Blackwood Keep, before Fane and his followers had destroyed his life. *You are visiting another lord's home,* he told himself, *and you must be polite. Feign interest. See what you can find out.* 'It all looks very interesting.' He forced a smile, and watched as Joah lit up. This was exactly what he'd wanted to hear.

'But of course!' Joah immediately abandoned the box of junk and came over to take hold of Frith's shoulder, steering him towards one of the iron doors. 'It's much bigger than people realise. Here, let me show you.'

It was a labyrinth of horrors.

The door opened onto a corridor, made from the same riveted iron plates Frith had seen before. It immediately turned sharply left, seeming to curve around the central Forge room, and on the opposite wall were more doors with narrow horizontal windows. They reminded Frith uneasily of jail cells, until he realised that's exactly what they were, more or less.

Joah paused by the nearest one, his expression suddenly uneasy. 'What you must understand, Aaron, is that Bezcavar is a creature with certain appetites. In order to grow powerful, and therefore grant power, it requires the suffering of living beings. It appears to feed off it.'

'I am aware of that,' said Frith, remembering the cauldron of blood in the great hall, and the men and women in chains. The Edenier was a dull heat inside his chest, and he curled his hands into fists. 'Very aware, in fact.'

'Of course,' said Joah, not quite looking at him. 'At first I was quite happy to provide such sacrifices myself. After all, what is some pain in the pursuit of knowledge? The things I was learning, Aaron, were extraordinary, far beyond anything the mages could have taught me. But in the end that became inconvenient, and the demon, as it grew stronger, was demanding more and more suffering in its name. I could only provide so much, alone.' He paused, and pulled open the door. Inside, the cell was narrow and dark, the floor stained and pitted. Joah gestured once, and two enormous iron plates facing on opposite walls began to move slowly towards each other, reducing the space in the room until it would have been impossible to move around. Eventually, they were so close that anyone caught in there would have been crushed between the plates.

'You put people in here? You . . . killed them with this contraption?'

'A simple idea,' said Joah, 'but I think you see its application.'

Frith found he couldn't say anything at all, so they moved on to the next room. In here the floor was covered with long iron strips, which Joah heated with the Edenier. Within seconds they were glowing a baleful red, and Frith could feel the heat against his face. There was also a distinct aroma of cooking meat, as the heat caused some old stains to grow warm again.

Joah cleared his throat. 'Of course, when you have the Edenier at your disposal,' he said, 'you have a great many more tools. You can wreak a great amount of destruction with the mages' magic, as I'm sure you know.'

Frith remembered storming his way through Blackwood Keep, crushing a man's bones with a mere thought.

'The people you brought here. Were they your enemies?'

Joah looked at him strangely. 'Enemies? Why, no. They were simply whoever happened to be closest. Whoever was most convenient.' He paused, and his voice took on a more serious tone. 'I would not consider myself to have enemies, Aaron, save for those mages who could not understand what it was I was doing here. Bringing them to this place and interring them in these rooms would not have been so straightforward, of course.'

'No, because they could have fought back,' said Frith, but Joah did not seem to notice his bitter tone. Instead, he led Frith around the curving corridor, showing him room after room of horrors. In one the floor was funnel-shaped with a hole in the centre covered with a grill, and Joah explained how he had slowly flooded the room with an acidic liquid that did not kill immediately, but instead gradually caused skin to separate from flesh. A few doors down from that was a room filled with a complex web of what looked like wire, although when Frith reached out to touch it, he realised it was razor sharp; a thin line of blood appeared across his finger before he was even aware he'd made contact.

'Made with the knowledge Bezcavar gave me,' said Joah, a hint of pride in his voice. 'No blacksmith could forge anything so thin or so sharp.'

The final room was a simple box, with nothing in it at all. When Frith looked at him questioningly, Joah shrugged.

'In here I would starve people. Perhaps it is not as impressive as the other rooms, but hunger can lead to extraordinary levels of suffering.'

All at once, Frith felt the slim barrier of politeness he'd erected shatter. The Edenier swarmed in his chest like something alive. He rounded on Joah.

'You are a monster,' he said simply. 'No better than a demon, and worse even than the man who took my castle from me. He did it for personal greed at least, but this? Pretending this is in the pursuit of knowledge?'

He gestured at the room and a flicker of violet flames appeared at the ends of his fingers. Joah's reaction was immediate. Frith felt the full force of the blow in the centre of his chest moments before he collided with the solid iron wall behind him. It was enough to knock all the air from his lungs and cast him to his knees, while Joah stood over him.

'No,' he said, his voice tight. 'You're not listening, Aaron. I need you to understand.' He ran a hand through his hair, his hand trembling slightly. 'You are the only one left, so you *cannot* be against me.'

Frith looked up at him, trying to ignore the pain in his back. He did not trust himself to speak.

'The rest of them have gone,' said Joah. He seemed to be trying to convince himself of something. 'They are gone, and now there is only you and I.'

After prissily brushing himself down, Joah helped Frith to his feet again. Frith staggered, leaning heavily on the rogue mage before pushing himself away abruptly, repulsed by his touch. It would be so easy to die here, without seeing daylight again. And knowing that he was afraid only made him angrier, of course.

'Didn't you feel *anything*?' he said quietly. 'Do you have no sympathy for your fellow human beings?'

Joah chuckled indulgently. His outburst of anger appeared to have vanished as quickly as it manifested.

'But Aaron, you and I are no mere humans. We are god-touched, and demon-taught, if we so wish it, and we have great things to accomplish. Such worries and moral questions are for other people. Here, I have one last thing to show you.'

211

At the end of the curving corridor was a set of metal steps. Joah led them down into another wide circular room, supposedly the twin of the Forge just above. Rather than work tables and instruments, this room was full of smooth black iron discs – some as big as cartwheels, a few as small as plates. They hung together in a strange network, some supported by other discs, others just hanging in mid-air. It looked hellishly complicated, and every single one was engraved with a complex covering of symbols – Frith recognised a few mages' words here and there, but mostly he saw the black shiny writing he'd seen elsewhere in the Forge. It was like looking at the heart of some great, unknowable animal.

'Isn't it magnificent?' said Joah. He walked over to one of the discs and touched it with his finger. Immediately it spun into life, the mage word carved into its surface glowing with a faint pearly light. 'This took me years to build, and now, with the Heart-Stone, it may finally work.'

'What is it?' asked Frith. He was looking for meaning in the discs, but could see nothing. Now that one plate was moving, another next to it had started spinning too, the black writing on it appearing to run together.

'It is the heart of my greatest project,' said Joah fondly. 'Each disc contains a web of spells, and when they are connected and moving, a mesh is created.' He interlocked his fingers, and then laughed at Frith's perplexed expression. 'Well, you will see soon enough, Aaron. Oh, would you look at that?'

One of the plates was spinning in a wobbly fashion, falling off its axis. With a gesture from Joah it stopped moving, and he slipped it from its place easily enough. It was the size of a large platter, and the outer edge of it was dented, part of the demonic writing scraped away.

'It all requires so much maintenance.' Joah rolled up his sleeves. For the first time, Frith noticed that both his arms were laced with tattoos, all of them mages' words.

'Does that work, then?' he asked despite himself. 'Having the words written directly on your skin? The Edenier still channels through them?'

'Oh yes,' said Joah. He slapped his right forearm and smiled up at Frith ruefully. 'I don't have all of them, of course, there are

212

just too many and I only have the two arms. It works just as well as having the words written on cloth, but it is *extremely painful*. You know, of course that the words eventually destroy themselves and the cloth is burnt away? They still try to burn themselves off your skin. I have to have them inked back on, every couple of years or so, but it has always been worth it.' Joah leaned forward and, holding his hands over the bent plate, produced a soft red ball of light, which he then sank directly into the metal. After a few moments, the iron itself grew to a rosy red colour, and with his other hand, he pushed with the Force spell and began to bend it back into place.

He is using both at once again, thought Frith, *and with great precision.*

When the plate was straight once more, Joah extinguished the heat and began to murmur under his breath. As Frith watched, words began to appear on the plate in the same sticky-looking black substance he'd seen all over this strange place, seeming to sweat their way out of the metal. When the plate was covered in words, Joah stopped, and simply slotted it back into place.

Frith thought of the enchanted armour Sebastian had worn at the battle of Baneswatch. There was clearly much more to using the Edenier than simple brute force, and he would need every possible advantage if he were to have any chance of escape. Trying to put what he'd seen in Joah's rooms from his mind, he forced an expression of polite interest onto his face.

'Can you teach me?' he said. 'Can you teach me how to do that?'

Joah grinned, wiping his hands on the front of his robes. 'I thought you'd never ask.'

213

32

Away from the spawning grounds of the arachnos, the Northern lands grew flatter and stranger. Mendrick led them now, not quite moving of his own accord but remaining present in Wydrin's mind, pushing her to go first directly north, and then gradually east. Eventually, they came to a low cliff looking out over a great stretch of clear ice covered here and there with snow. Enormous black monoliths poked through the ice, their tops curving and narrowing to lethal points like the sharp beaks of ravens. Initially she thought they were some sort of strange natural formation, but when she nudged Mendrick with this question the reply that came back was abrupt and disinterested.

Not our doing, was all he said.

'Are we to travel across that?' asked Sebastian. 'Will the ice take our weight?'

Wydrin nodded, but Dallen spoke before she could. 'That ice was thick before you were born, Sir Sebastian. It could hold an army.'

Carefully, they made their way down a narrow path, faces turned away from the biting wind. Nuava sat atop Mendrick, bundled in her thick coat and a blanket donated by Wydrin from the Narhls' ransacked packs. Her ruddy face was still and expressionless, and she had said very little since Wydrin had revealed Mendrick's idea to the rest of the group. She seemed shaken by it in a way that Wydrin couldn't quite understand.

Sebastian appeared next to her. The young prince was walking

214

off in front, and she noticed how her friend's eyes lingered on his narrow back.

'Wydrin, if this turns out to be some sort of long-winded joke of yours, I will throw you to the wyverns myself. The werken is really telling you where to go?'

Wydrin half smiled. 'It's the strangest sensation, Seb, having another presence in your head. I wish I could describe it to you.' She sighed, flexing her fingers inside her gloves. 'Mendrick is fairly certain it will work. And as far as I can tell we don't have many other ideas at the moment. Aren't you the one who's always talking about listening to the mountain? This should be right up your alley.'

Sebastian frowned. The big knight had thrown back his own hood and the tops of his cheeks had grown pink with the cold.

'I do not know these mountains,' was all he said.

Eventually, they reached the bottom of the low cliff and walked out onto the thick ice. To Wydrin's surprise it was as clear as glass, and below her furred boots she could see deep blue shadows, and the soft curves of ancient ice formations. There were shapes moving in the depths, too, shoals of what looked like bulky, armoured fish. She wondered what could survive down there, and what might be feeding on those rapidly moving shadows.

'This is a dangerous place,' said Dallen, coming over to where they stood. He travelled light now, with a pouch of ice-spears strapped to his back and a short sword at his belt. Wydrin felt cold just looking at his light armour, but the prince seemed entirely comfortable – save for the haunted look of grief that shadowed his eyes. 'We should not stand too long in one place, in case we attract the attention of something below.'

Wydrin grimaced as an unwelcome wave of vertigo moved through her. 'You said this ice was too thick for us to fall through,' she said, trying to sound casual.

'Yes,' said the prince, 'but there are things much bigger than us in the frozen lakes.'

They moved on quickly. Presently they came to one of the huge black monoliths they'd spotted from the cliff edge. Up close, they could see that it was carved with thousands of tiny scratches and jagged shapes, pale grey against the black stone. The wind moaned around the winnowed shape, giving the cold a voice.

'Did the Narhl put these here?' asked Sebastian. They had paused in front of it, and Wydrin found it difficult to look away. It drew the eye, like a warning beacon in darkness, or the blackened remains of a tree struck by lightning. She shook her head abruptly.

'It wasn't us,' said Dallen. 'These structures belong to a much more ancient people, ones who recognised this land as cursed and sought to warn others away.'

They walked on, boots crunching on the topmost layer of ice. Wydrin watched Mendrick moving in front; she could still feel him as a cold place in her head, a strange intelligence nestled next to her own. If she wanted to, she could reach out to that presence, but her mind shied away from it; it was too large, and too alien.

I can find the place you seek, he'd said, in that endlessly patient tone, *if we can get down deep enough.*

The daylight began to seep from the sky and the clouds above them shaded from white to bruised-grey. A flurry of heavier snow came, gusting across the flat ice and showering them in a fanfare of icy flakes. Wydrin felt them against her face like a thousand cold needles and, once again, she wished for a warm hearth in Crosshaven and a place to take her boots off.

'This is a sorry state to be in,' she said to Sebastian, casting her voice low as they stumbled along together. 'One of our number lost, and babysitting these two.'

Sebastian smiled wanly. 'They've been through a lot, the pair of them.' He nodded to Prince Dallen walking in front with his head down. 'I wouldn't expect them to be the cheeriest of travelling companions.'

'Huh,' sniffed Wydrin, 'can I just remind you, before you spend too long crying over Good Prince Dallen and his current poor fortunes, that he knocked you off our griffin and nearly froze you to death?'

'A prince protecting his people,' said Sebastian, pulling a flask from his belt and taking a quick sip before passing it to Wydrin. Below them the clear ice yawned away into a blue darkness. Wydrin couldn't help thinking of the invisible bridge they had walked from the Secret Keeper's house. 'You can hardly blame him for that. And he let us go afterwards, when his father would have opened our throats to the sky.'

216

'Oh yes,' said Wydrin. She took a long swig from the flask, savouring the heat of the rum.. 'Because that ended so well.'

'I think he's a good man,' said Sebastian, and the desperately concealed note of caution in his voice made Wydrin grin. She punched him lightly on the arm.

'Oho,' she said. 'Well, he's certainly striking to look at. And he seems to know what to do with that spear of his.'

Sebastian choked back laughter. 'This ice may be thick, Wydrin, but I still think I could cut a copper cat-sized hole in it just for you.'

Wydrin passed back the flask. 'Just you bloody try it, Carverson.'

Sebastian slipped the flask back into his belt. Ahead of them, Nuava, Mendrick and Dallen had reached another of the black monoliths, and were preparing to make camp for the night. It would, Mendrick had informed her in his chilly, precise manner, take another half-day of walking to reach the place they needed to get to.

'You seem to have cheered up, anyway,' said Sebastian as they caught up with the others. 'You know, Frith will be fine. He can look after himself.'

'He certainly can do that,' replied Wydrin dryly. 'He has always had a particular talent for it, if I remember correctly.' She touched her fingers to the hilt of Glassheart, wondering where the lord of the Blackwood was now, and if he was even still alive. 'I'm sure he's out there somewhere, annoying the living shit out of this Joah character.'

Beneath the great slab of black stone they ate a cold meal hunched around the light from Dallen's lamp. Wydrin passed around portions of the broth she'd made earlier, now largely turned greasy and congealed. Nuava took it gratefully anyway, and Wydrin was glad to see it; if she were hungry, then perhaps she was beginning to get over her shock.

'You know a lot about these lands, don't you?' said Wydrin, catching the girl's eye. 'Do you know what these bloody great big rocks are about?'

For a moment Nuava looked confused, as though she'd forgotten there were other people present. Wydrin nodded in what she hoped was an encouraging manner.

'The ancient peoples . . .' Nuava began hesitantly. 'They erected

217

these tablets as guardians. They are all over the northernmost places, but particularly here. For reasons lost to history they considered this place in need of a great deal of watching over. They believed there were monsters under the ground.' Her voice had started to take on the slightly scholarly tone Wydrin recognised from the Tower of Waking. 'And perhaps they were right. Joah Demonsworn was said to haunt this land.'

'And hopefully we will find him soon,' added Sebastian. 'Wydrin –' he glanced at the werken, who was crouched off to one side, green eyes staring forward like twin moons – 'does Mendrick truly know the way?'

Wydrin nodded. It was very clear when Mendrick explained it in her head, but less easy to convey in words to the others.

'He says there is a place, some distance beneath the crust of the world, where the flesh of the earth is linked by the Edeian. He thinks of it as the nexus. If he can get there, he can send his mind out through this nexus and look for the place where Joah is hiding. He needs to be with the nexus to be able to do it.' She shook her head abruptly. 'I don't pretend to understand it, Seb, but he's very certain. We just need to get down to this place where everything is connected, and there are paths leading down to it near here.'

In this haunted place, echoed Mendrick in her head.

'You will want to post a watch,' said Dallen suddenly. He was still a ragged sight in the dying light, his face gaunter than it had been. 'A watch through the night, and I would strongly suggest vigilance during the daylight hours too. There are creatures here that would consider us a healthy meal.' He shifted, casting his face into deeper shadow. 'I would be glad to take the first watch. Sleep seems far from me at the moment.'

Wydrin glanced up at Sebastian, and saw him give the tiniest shrug. They would trust the prince this far, then.

'Fair enough, your highness,' she said. 'Mendrick will find our path tomorrow. If you can keep any animals from chewing on our flesh until then, I'd be very grateful.'

Sebastian woke in the middle of the night to a cold hand on his arm. He looked up into the pale eyes of Prince Dallen, who shook him once more and stood back.

'It is your watch,' he said. 'But come quietly, I want to show you something.'

Sebastian stepped over the sleeping forms of Wydrin and Nuava; the girl was curled in on herself, barely visible amongst her blankets, whereas Wydrin slept as she always did, limbs flung in various directions. Dallen led him beyond their small circle to the pile of rocks where he'd been sitting. Beyond it the world was a collection of blacks and greys, gently touched with starlight. The wind picked up then, gusting across the ice and swirling loose snow around their ankles. Sebastian gritted his teeth, wondering if he would ever be warm again.

'Do you never feel the need to get warm?' asked Sebastian in a low voice.

'The Narhl don't cope well in warm temperatures,' said Dallen. 'The heat from a fire, if I sat next to it for any length of time, would cause me to sicken and, eventually, to die. It is also rather uncomfortable. We are tied to our lands, Sebastian; in this and many other ways.'

'That must be difficult,' said Sebastian, wishing he hadn't brought it up. To be so inextricably linked to a place, and then exiled from it. Reluctantly, Sebastian remembered leaving Ynnsmouth, disgrace heavy on his shoulders. 'What was it you wanted to show me?'

'Here, look out towards that rock.' Dallen pointed, and Sebastian peered into the dark. There was another monolith close by, smaller than the one they were camped next to – at some point in the past the top half had broken off, and chunks of black rock were scattered at its base. He looked at the debris, and the area around it, but he could see nothing unexpected. In the far distance he could just make out the grey haze of more mountains. 'What am I looking for?'

'Follow the left-hand side of the slab downwards, and then look for the biggest rock. You should see two small points of light.'

Sebastian did as he was told and after a few moments, he saw them. Two small milky white circles, hovering just in front of the rock, where the darkness was thickest. He frowned. It was like suddenly discovering you were being watched by a blind cat.

219

'What is that?'

In answer, Dallen took the cold-light from his pack and, turning a small dial on the casing, cast a circle of silvery blue light ahead of them. Sebastian saw a bulky shape briefly illuminated before it skittered sideways and behind the monolith; he got a brief impression of white fur, arched chitinous legs, and serrated claws opening and closing rapidly.

'By Isu, what was that?' Whatever it had been, it was a lot larger than the glimpse of its milky white eyes had indicated. Despite himself, Sebastian took a hurried step backwards, and he caught an amused glance from Dallen. It was the first sign of cheer he'd seen from the prince since his soldiers had been killed, and Sebastian was glad to see it, no matter how small or whether it was at his own expense.

'A snow crab. Our old Narhl word for it is Arichok. A smaller cousin of the arachnos –' His words dried up and he cleared his throat. 'A smaller cousin of the creatures that attacked us. Some Narhl actually farm these creatures, and make a very tasty soup from their flesh.' Dallen glanced at him. 'A cold soup. Wild Arichoks are much bigger, much more dangerous. Did you see the great claw?'

Sebastian nodded. 'I could hardly miss it.'

'Also, their mouths have many sharp moving parts, and these they use to tear . . .' He stopped again. 'You see my point.'

'Yes,' said Sebastian, thinking of the skeletal arachnos young, and how quickly they had killed Dallen's squad.

'They tend to hunt in packs. Where this one was, there will be others. And they can move alarmingly fast when they want to.' Dallen paused. 'I just thought I should tell you that. Before you took over.'

'Thank you,' said Sebastian, wondering why the atmosphere between them was suddenly tense. 'I shall certainly keep an eye out. A glimpse of that monster was enough to wake me up fully, at least.'

Dallen nodded once. 'I will leave you my cold-light,' he said, and again there was that sense that he wanted to say more but couldn't force the words past his lips.

'Is there something wrong, your highness?'

The prince's eyes grew wide, just for a moment, and then he shook his head.

'No. I am as well as can be expected. I shall go and see if I can get some sleep before we move off in the morning.'

He left, not looking back, and Sebastian settled himself on the snow, looking out into the silvery night. He was remembering how King Aristees had glared at him when Dallen had grasped his arm; of the disgust and fear that had been in that glance. He'd seen that look often enough, and he wondered if Prince Dallen had grown up seeing it on his father's face, and on the faces of the men and women of the court. And now he didn't even have them.

Sebastian pulled his cloak closer around his neck and looked out into the night, watching for the milky eyes of the Arichok.

33

Gwiddion sat in Frith's lap, still wrapped in a blanket, opening and closing his beak while Frith tried to drop small morsels of meat down the bird's narrow throat.

'Be still, Gwiddion, and this will be a lot easier.'

Frith had smuggled the scraps of food back into the bunk room inside his cloak. He had no idea whether Joah knew about the bird, or cared, but instinctively he felt it was safer to hide the creature, particularly as Gwiddion still seemed unable to turn back into his griffin form. Food had eventually been provided by Joah after Frith had complained about feeling hungry, and the mage had fetched a quite random dinner from who knew where: a large chunk of cold lamb, the fat turned wobbly and white, a handful of heavily spiced bread rolls, and some small, tough yellow fruits that tasted under-ripe. Joah had seemed distracted, barely interested in the food at all, and Frith suspected that if he hadn't mentioned it, the rogue mage would have carried on working until he dropped down with hunger. When he wasn't looking, Frith shredded small pieces of the lamb between his fingers and hid them away.

Gwiddion finished up the last of the meat, snapping his beak in what Frith decided to take as a sign of appreciation. From the central chamber there came a sudden low roar, followed by the sound of Joah laughing. Frith hid Gwiddion back on the bunk and went back through the door. The Heart-Stone was now glowing fiercely, almost too bright to look at, while Joah crouched in front of it.

'What is happening?' asked Frith. The light coming from the stone flickered, and he had to close his eyes for a moment.

Joah turned round. In the greenish light his face looked skeletal. 'Oh, Aaron, there you are. I wondered where you'd got to.' He stood up, wiping his hands on his robes. 'I wanted you to see this. The Heart-Stone was the final piece of the puzzle, and I would never have found it if I hadn't been brought back to this place, at this time. I think it was meant to be.'

Frith approached cautiously. The colour of the stone was changing, the eldritch green draining away to become a mottled, bruised colour.

'Do not look so alarmed, Aaron,' said Joah. 'It is quite safe.'

'What is it?' Frith asked. The glass tank above the aperture that housed the Heart-Stone was still glowing faintly with its own light.

'This is the Rivener, my friend, our path to an unlimited source of Edenier.'

'The Rivener.' Frith shook his head. The pain was like hot needles being driven into his head, and already his stomach was rolling again. 'What does it do?'

'Here, sit. There are a few things I should explain first for you to appreciate it fully.' Joah pulled a pair of chairs over to a low stone table. There was a bottle of wine there, and Joah poured them both a glass. The liquid looked black in the sickly light. 'Do you know, Aaron, where Edenier comes from? Where it originated?'

'I – no. It is the magic of will. That is what I was told.'

Joah nodded and took a sip from his wine, briefly pulling a face. 'It is, in a way. It is the magic of will, of spirit, quite separate from the magic that suffuses Ede, in places like these hills and mountains.'

Frith sniffed the wine. It smelt better than it looked. 'I understand that, yes.'

Joah smiled. 'Of course you do. What you might not have heard is how mages came to have this power in the first place. You see –' he cleared his throat and glanced back at the Heart-Stone, 'before the old gods, there was the First God. A being we called Ede, just as we called our world. She was so old that her existence was

223

linked with the world itself. She was a creature of pure will, of spirit alone, and it was said that she was all powerful, and benevolent.'

'I have heard the name before,' said Frith. 'Linked to a goddess, yes. Beyond ancient.'

'She was, my dear Aaron, and she was pure Edenier. Spirit unencumbered by the physical form, by human needs and vices. Back then the peoples of the world were divided into tribes, and the strongest of these tribes grew wily and clever. They saw the power of Ede, and wanted it for themselves. They took up arms, and with their clever new weapons they slew Ede.' Joah frowned. 'The histories, such as they are, are rather vague on this point. And when they killed her, they ate her and claimed the Edenier for their own. That tribe were the very first mages, Aaron.'

Frith nodded, taking this in. He turned the glass around on the table, still not drinking it. 'I see. Forgive me, but this sounds like the sort of story that my nursemaid would tell me when I was small.'

Joah chucked the rest of the wine down his throat, and then pointed a finger at Frith. 'You are quite right. I do not know how much of this is true. But the idea that Edenier is soul-magic is absolutely correct. Did you know, Aaron, that every living thing contains a sliver of the divine?'

'I don't follow.'

'All of us, even non-mages, have a certain degree of Edenier in our souls. Impossible to access and use for almost everyone, of course – mages carry it inside us like a passenger, whereas, for most people, it's like a shadow. Intangible. Except that I have found a process that allows us to remove it.' He waved up at the Heart-Stone. 'The Rivener takes living things and removes the useful Edenier, storing it for me to use later. It discards the useless husk.'

Frith took his hand from the glass. 'Husk?'

But Joah was already up and moving again, pointing to the glass section in the iron wall.

'The Rivener is much bigger than this room, Aaron, much bigger than the Forge. I will show you that, one day soon, but the point is we have an endless source of Edenier. You and I, Aaron, will be the most powerful mages ever to have lived.'

Frith swallowed hard. The idea of Joah gaining any more power than he had already was alarming.

'I'm afraid I still don't understand.'

'Here, I shall demonstrate for you.'

Joah left through one of the doors and when he returned a few moments later, he had company: a short, scrawny man dressed in rags and furs. From his mottled face he was Narhl, and he had both hands tied behind his back. Joah dragged him into the room with relative ease, the smaller man's eyes round with shock.

Frith stood up, knocking over his wine glass in his haste. 'What are you doing?'

'Here, watch.' Joah marched the smaller man over to the steps that led to the platform above the glass tank. Belatedly his prisoner began to struggle, trying to wriggle away from Joah's iron grip.

'Forgive me, masters!' gasped the man. 'I was only curious, please! I have never seen fire like it, and I had to know its secret, but I see that I was wrong now.'

'Joah, what do you intend to do to this man?' Frith came forward, holding out his hands. 'Please, let him go.'

'Don't be a fool, Aaron. How will you understand the Rivener if I do not show you?'

Without another word he half dragged, half carried the protesting man up the metal steps, and when they reached the top, threw him into a hole Frith couldn't see. A moment later the scrawny man landed behind the glass of the tank. He turned his face towards Frith, his mouth wide open.

'Now,' said Joah, coming back down the steps, wiping his hands absently on his robe. 'You will get to see the Rivener in action.'

The man in the tank was panicking now, beating his fists against the glass. Frith could hear him yelling, but his voice was muffled.

'Please, Joah, there is no need.' Frith looked from the tank to the rogue mage. 'I believe you. Let the man go.'

Joah smiled at him, shaking his head slightly. Instead he crossed to the Heart-Stone and, muttering under his breath, began to trace a shape on the surface of the crystal. After a few seconds, the

225

stone seemed to bleed, and a shining black shape appeared; jagged and somehow unsettling, it was a twin to the writing Frith had seen elsewhere. *Demon writing.*

There was a soft *wumph* and the bruise-coloured light, now a murky violet, seemed to both brighten and darken at the same time. At that moment Frith felt a violent twisting in his gut, and he staggered backwards. For a few seconds the light turned a vivid, virulent purple, and the man inside the tank began to scream, twisting around on himself as though he were trying to crawl out of his own skin.

'Stop it!' cried Frith. He went over to the glass and placed his hand on it, but the man inside was shuddering, not looking at him.

'Wait, Aaron, just a moment.'

The man stopped moving, his body suddenly rigid, and a slim flicker of something curled up from the body. It looked like some cousin of both light and smoke, a swirling shape that was somehow alive, and then it dissipated. Joah came over and stood with Frith at the front of the tank. The man lay on his back staring at nothing, his eyes dull, as though they had gained a covering of dust in a few brief seconds. He moved weakly, his mouth opening and closing but forming no words.

'The shape that you saw was the Edenier,' said Joah. 'Extracted directly from his soul. Not very much, but the process certainly works. And now he is empty.'

The floor inside the tank fell away, dropping the body of the man into the dark recesses beneath the Forge. Frith stood very still.

'Is he still alive?'

Joah shrugged. 'Not for much longer. Without the spark moving it, the *spirit*, the body will eventually give up on the idea of breathing.'

Frith swallowed hard. 'Why do this?' He couldn't quite keep the horror from his voice, but Joah didn't appear to notice. 'What is the point of it all?'

'It's all about gathering resources, Aaron.' Joah rubbed absently at his beard. 'It has always seemed to me to be the most efficient approach. Yes, we can achieve much with the mage powers we have, but how much more can we do if we use *everything*? The Edeian naturally present in the world, the knowledge of demons, and the Edenier harvested from living things – all of this together, Aaron, and we shall be the greatest mages that ever lived.'

There was nothing but bright enthusiasm in his brown eyes.

'You will be, at least,' Frith replied, forcing some jollity into his words. 'I am afraid that I will never be able to handle the Edenier with the skill that you do. All of this is new to me, and I suspect I will likely never catch up.'

Joah took hold of his arm, squeezing tightly. 'You mustn't believe that, Aaron my friend. By all the gods, you can hardly be blamed for being slightly behind. You have been alone, all this time, with no other mages to guide you, to pass on their knowledge!'

'From what I've heard, Joah,' inwardly Frith winced at the familiar use of the name, 'you were much more than an average mage. I spoke to the girl Nuava about you when we visited your tomb. You were a genius, they said. A prodigy.'

For several long moments Joah just stared at him. His eyes were wide and slightly unfocussed, as if he were looking at something only he could see. Eventually, he shook himself and turned away.

'Yes, genius. Prodigy. That wasn't all they called me. Listen, Aaron, there is a very quick way I can pass on some of my knowledge to you, but it will require a degree of trust between us. Do you think you can trust me?'

Frith stared at him. He could taste bile at the back of his throat. *Everything is wrong here,* he thought, *and I have no advantages. Perhaps if I know what he knows, I will find something to improve my position.* He thought of Wydrin and Sebastian. If they were looking for him now, he would need to be ready to act if they arrived. He needed to be stronger.

'I trust you,' he said. 'Please show me.'

34

Joah took him out of the Forge and down a metal corridor he hadn't seen before. At the end of it was a heavy iron door, covered in rivets painted with the black sticky writing. Joah muttered something, tracing a complicated shape on the surface of the door. There was a sound of metal scraping against metal, and the door swung open, revealing high walls of ragged earth to either side. Frith was startled to discover that it was late in the afternoon, with the sun glaring down through the narrow strip of sky overhead. Inside the Forge it felt as though he were trapped in a perpetual night.

Joah led them out of the Forge and up a nearby slope, where a circle of grey stones stood. Frith looked around wildly, trying to take in their location, and whether that held any advantages for him, but there was nothing; only the hills and the snow, and the painfully bright sky.

'It's best if we do this outside,' said Joah. 'With the daylight on our faces. The crossing can be an uncomfortable experience.'

'The crossing?'

Joah nodded, kicking some of the snow away and sitting down next to one of the standing stones. After a moment, Frith joined him. *If I ran, he would strike me down in moments*, he reminded himself.

'It is a method, given to me by Bezcavar, of joining two minds together for a brief time. The crossing of memories, sensations, and therefore knowledge, becomes possible.'

'You did this with the demon?'

Joah glanced up at him, his brown eyes momentarily sad. 'I did, indeed. Here, give me your hand.'

After only a moment's hesitation, Frith held out his hand, palm up. Joah reached inside his cloak and retrieved a small metal ball about the size of a walnut. It was covered in tiny thorns, with wickedly sharp points.

'In a moment I shall grasp your hand,' he said, holding up the ball so that Frith could see it. 'There will be a moment of intense pain, and I want you to concentrate on it. That moment will open your mind to me, and I shall use that as my way in. Are you ready?'

Frith looked at the ball, trying not to think about the torture rooms inside the Forge. 'Go on then,' he said. 'I must learn what I can.'

Still holding the ball in the cup of his hand, Joah leaned over and took Frith's hand as if to shake it. He squeezed, pressing the thorn-covered ball into the soft skin of his palm. Despite himself, Frith yelped with pain and made to pull away, but to his horror the needle-like thorns had buried themselves deep, and it was not so easy to escape.

'Relax now, Aaron,' said Joah. 'I need you to relax.'

He reached up with his other hand and took hold of Frith's head, pressing the length of his thumb against the side of his nose, digging his fingers behind his ear. Frith gasped, feeling the hot trickle of blood running between his fingers, and then something else; it was like a long, thin blade, as hot as glowing coals, slipping through his forehead.

'You can feel it now I think,' said Joah. 'That is my mind meshing with your own. Hold still, just a moment, and let me show you.'

Frith blinked and then Joah and the snowy hills seemed to twist away from him, falling down a deep hole. In their place was a small, lavishly furnished room with no windows; the carpets on the floor were golden, and the walls were covered in mosaics, all created from tiny glittering gems. In front of him stood a tall elderly woman with deep brown skin and carefully plaited white hair. She wore a sleeveless robe of pale aquamarine and her arms

229

were bound with silk strips, all painted with the mage's words. She was staring at Frith with an expression of weary patience.

'I've seen you do this exercise a thousand times,' she said. Her accent was from Relios, all clipped tones and smoky vowels. 'Do you jest with me, boy?'

'I-I don't,' Frith stuttered, looking around the room. He could see enormous clay jars, very similar to the ones they'd seen in the depths of the Citadel, and a long table covered in pots of ink. Just in front of him, between him and the tall woman, was a low marble table with a piece of warped metal on it. He glanced down at his hands, and was alarmed to see that they were not his own – the skin was pale, and the fingers longer.

I am in his memories, he thought. *I am seeing his past.*

And then his hands were moving of their own accord, and as he watched the piece of metal in front of him rose several inches from the table, spinning slightly, and he could see the word for Hold in his own mind. A few moments later and the word for Heat joined it, and the piece of metal began to glow a rosy red.

'That's more like it,' said the tall woman, raising a single perfect eyebrow. 'Let's see the rest.'

More words joined Hold and Heat in his mind – Force, focussed down into a blunt weapon, and Push, and then all of them at once. Frith marvelled at the control of it all, but he could also see how it was possible; Joah was stacking the words on top of one another, a careful mental balancing act. Another word, this one for Change, and as he watched it began to appear in the metal itself, forced there with the strength of Joah's mind.

'Very good, Joah,' said the woman. 'You have achieved so much in your time here with us.'

'I am not Joah,' Frith started to say, but the room shivered and vanished, to be replaced with a lush green field, the grass coming up to his waist. Another woman stood next to him, and this one was short with waves of dark blond hair caught in a silvery net. She wore some sort of elaborate armour – all black leather and silver spikes – and her eyes were red from lid to lid. She was grinning at him and brandishing a knife.

'I will teach you some letters the gods have never dreamed of,'

230

she said, and her voice was old and strange. 'And with those you will do terrible things in my name. Won't that be marvellous?'

'Bezcavar,' said Frith, trying to back away. This was the creature who had driven Fane and the Children of the Fog, its eyes filled with blood just as Sebastian had described. The demon carried on as if he hadn't spoken.

'Come here, then,' she said, waving at him impatiently. 'I know you remember how I teach you things.' She held up the knife. 'Come and lie down with me.'

A flicker, and the vision was gone, but the knowledge was not – he felt the burning of a hundred alien letters on his skin, and deep inside he knew, he *knew* how he could use them. Next there was a young boy sitting on a great boulder in a forest, naked save for a series of leather belts around his waist and upper arms. He was counting out a number of small grey stones in front of him, and after a moment they began to jump by themselves. Then he was gone too, and Frith had a glimpse of a fierce old man with a thick beard and a bare chest, his shoulders covered in what looked like a bearskin. His hands were thick with blood and gore, and he was telling Frith something, and although he did not understand the words, the knowledge slid into his mind, chilly and alien – how to make the mages' words clearer in your head, how to make the passage of the Edenier more efficient. With growing excitement, Frith felt his mastery of the Edenier expanding rapidly. So much that had been a mystery to him was becoming clear. The man with the bearskin faded away, to be replaced with the blond-haired woman with Bezcavar's eyes again. This time they were in a tent, and through the gap in the silks Frith could see endless sands the colour of autumn leaves. The demon woman was cradling something in her lap, a globe constructed from shining black metal – just looking at it, Frith knew it was incomplete, and she was shaking her head slowly.

'It is a fine idea, Joah,' she said in the demon's voice, 'but it is a waste. Destroying the Edenier of your enemies is one thing, but imagine if you could take it and keep it for yourself.' She set the globe down on the woven mat between them. She was wearing a loose silk wrap instead of the jagged armour, and her bare skin was brushed here and there with sand. 'I have a much better idea . . .'

Then the woman and the tent twisted away to be replaced with a flickering myriad of images: a forest in high summer, a vaulted marble hall with great glass windows in the ceiling, the view from a ship's mast, the clouds blackened and storm-laden. Soon the images were moving so fast that he felt like he was falling, catching glimpses of things that meant nothing to him – a pair of hands cupped around bright blue beads, a man with a golden crown sobbing into a bloody rag, a waterfall parting to show a hidden cave beyond, the red eyes of the demon, crinkled at the edges with pleasure. And along with the memories came the knowledge, bright and unending and *right*; new mages' words, the demon's knowledge, the latent power of the Edeian, and how they could be combined. Towards the end of it he caught sight of something else: the woman he'd seen in the Forge with the brown skin and the shaved head. She was crouching, one arm thrown out behind her for balance and the other striking forward, holding a sword that shone oddly. Frith could see sorrow in her face, and triumph, and then it was gone and Joah was shaking him gently by the shoulders.

'Aaron, are you well? Are you back with me?'

Frith blinked at him owlishly. The ball of thorns was still sticking out of his hand. Gingerly he took hold of it with two fingers and pulled it free with a gasp.

'I am here,' he said. 'At least, I believe I am.'

Joah sat back on his haunches. He was sweating slightly. 'Forgive me, Aaron. That went much deeper than I intended, but I was so fascinated by what I saw.'

Frith flexed his hand, wincing. He ran Joah's words back through his head. 'What . . . you saw?'

Joah nodded. 'It is an exchange, remember. While you experienced visions of my past, I saw some of your own.' He stood up, and helped Frith to his feet. It had grown dark while they had been sitting there, although to Frith it felt as though only minutes had passed. 'We should get indoors. It is not wise to be out here after dark.'

They went back inside the Forge, Frith stumbling slightly as they made their way down the narrow passage. He was trying to process what he'd seen. There was too much of it, far too much, and yet most of the information had stayed with him. He could feel the knowledge crowding in his head, making clear much that had been confusing. Was this what it was like, to be a trained mage?

Once inside Frith began to feel unwell again, and he staggered into a chair, sitting down with his fingers pressed to his lips. Joah didn't seem to notice, and was bustling back and forth in front of the Rivener, bathed in the violet light.

'I think I need something to eat,' said Frith eventually. 'Perhaps it's the effects of this crossing, as you called it, but I am feeling quite ill.'

Joah looked up, distraction evident in every line on his face. He stared at Frith as though he'd forgotten he was there. 'Oh, but of course. I shall fetch us dinner.'

He vanished back through one of the doors for a few moments while Frith sat and looked at the Rivener. He remembered how the man had shrieked and thrashed as the Heart-Stone's light grew in intensity, and how the pain in Frith's head had tripled along with it.

Joah returned with two deep bowls full of steaming stew, setting one before Frith carelessly so that some of the brownish soup slopped over the sides.

'I think it worked, you know,' said Frith when it became clear that Joah wasn't going to talk. 'The crossing. I saw images of your past – a lot of which I won't pretend to understand – and the knowledge seems to have stayed with me. Some of it, anyway.'

Joah looked up, an expression of genuine pleasure briefly lighting his handsome face. 'Good, that is good, Aaron. I'm glad it has helped to bring you some small part of your mage inheritance.' He paused, twirling the spoon through his stew. Lumps of what Frith hoped were meat rose and sank again. 'I saw some strange things in your mind, Aaron. I should like to ask you about them.'

Frith took a sip of his stew. It was salty, but not altogether bad. 'Of course,' he said.

Joah nodded, looking down at his bowl. When he looked up again his eyes were filled with a feverish interest that immediately put Frith on his guard.

'I saw a man with a bird's head,' said Joah. 'I saw him flying in a great cloud of birds.'

Frith felt a shiver move down his spine. It was so quiet in the Forge, with only the gentle creaks of the corridor settling, or the shifting sounds of the earth around them. He knew, somehow, that it would be a very bad idea to reveal anything of O'rin to Joah, although he couldn't have said how he knew that. He pushed his face into a frown.

'Well, I'm sure I don't know what that could be. A man in a festival costume, perhaps? We had many such festivals, back in my home in the Blackwood.'

Joah shook his head. 'No, no, I know what a man in a mask looks like, and this was very different. I wonder . . .' he sat forward slightly, actually reaching one hand out to Frith's face. 'I wonder if I might take another look, just to satisfy my curiosity.'

Frith flinched away from him, leaning back in his chair. 'I am sorry, Joah, but I'm feeling somewhat fatigued. I fear that this demonstration of yours has quite exhausted me.'

Joah put his hand down slowly, looking abashed.

'Of course, of course,' he murmured. 'We have all the time, after all. All the time we could wish for.'

After Frith had retired to his bunk room and fed Gwiddion what scraps he had managed to save from dinner (he had no idea where Joah slept, and did not wish to know), he lay on his back in the dark, wondering if his new-found knowledge would aid him in any way. Certainly he felt as though his mastery of the Edenier had increased enormously, but he had no ink, no strips of silk, and, for all Joah's apparent distractions, he was still scrupulously careful about keeping such things away from his guest, even refusing to bandage Frith's wounded hand. The Edenier remained an unreachable force inside him. Eventually, he grew drowsy, and only when he turned on his side did he see the strange collection of shadows in the corner that formed the shape of the shaven-headed woman. She was watching him in the dark, her eyes like small wet stones.

'You do see me, then,' she said. She did not move. 'If you can see me, boy, then things aren't looking too good for you.'

Frith sat up slowly, hardly daring to breathe. 'Who are you? What are you doing in this place?'

At first the woman didn't answer. She continued staring at him in the dark. 'I am trapped here, like you are trapped here,' she said eventually. 'Although I am not Joah Demonsworn's toy.'

Frith shook his head at that. 'I saw you,' he said. 'When Joah showed me his memories, I saw your face, towards the end. But everything he showed me happened over a thousand years ago, which means . . .'

'Which means I am long dead,' answered the woman. Her voice was husky and low, and jagged with bitter humour. 'What are you, little man? I see the Edenier burning within you, but this land has been without the mages for the longest time.'

She shifted, moving further into what little light there was, and Frith could see that she was dressed in a ragged collection of furs and leathers, and her left arm ended in a smooth stump. Now that he could see more of her, he could also see that her shaven head was tattooed with the mage-word for Forbearance. It was one of the words he had learned since leaving Whittenfarne, one that had not been forbidden by the Regnisse of Relios.

'How can you be here? You look too solid to be a—' He bit down on the word.

The woman smiled. 'A ghost? This is a place of Edeian, and it is not so easy to escape, even when we are dead. Unfortunately for you, little man, you are moving closer and closer to that state every day, which is exactly why you can see me so clearly.'

'Don't call me that,' snapped Frith, raising his voice slightly. Immediately there was a scuffling from outside the bunk door.

'Are you well, Aaron? I can hear you calling out in your sleep.'

Frith swore under his breath, glancing towards the door, but when he looked back to the woman she was gone; the collection of shadows was just that again, empty and dark.

'I'm fine,' he answered, flexing his injured hand. 'Better than ever, obviously.'

35

'Well, this is ominous.'

They stood at the entrance to the cave, which, to Wydrin, looked more like a jagged hole in the ground. She could see the rock-strewn path within sloping steeply down into the darkness. At the very lip of the cave were five small, furry bodies – two lean rabbits, and three mangy foxes with pale, yellowed fur. Their blood had long since dried to a brown stain on the rocks.

'Are they offerings?' said Sebastian. 'Is this a holy place?'

'Perhaps they're offerings to whatever lives in this cave,' said Wydrin, pulling a face. 'Maybe if you leave it dinner it doesn't come out looking for you.'

'I don't like it,' said Sebastian. 'Are you sure about this, Wydrin?'

Wydrin sighed. Mendrick was already speaking in her head, that cold, dispassionate voice like a handful of pebbles down her back.

This is the place, he said. *This is where I can reach the nexus.*

'I don't like the look of it much either, Seb, but old stony face here is insisting. Nuava, you will stay up here with Prince Dallen while Sebastian and I—'

'I want to go with you,' cut in the girl. She crossed her arms over her chest, not looking directly at the Narhl prince. 'I want to see it. This nexus. It could be the key to – it could teach me so much about the Edeian, and how to craft it.'

Dallen looked up sharply at that, but said nothing.

'We can't leave the prince on his own,' said Sebastian. 'He is wounded and we don't know how long this could take.'

236

'I will be fine on my own,' said Dallen, in a slightly affronted tone. 'I am more at home in this place than any of you.'

'I want to go,' said Nuava again. For the first time in days her face was creased with something other than grief, and she was standing a little straighter. 'I have lost many things, but I am still a crafter in training. I wish to see this nexus, if it exists.'

Wydrin could see from the flinty look in the girl's eye that she was not convinced that Wydrin could hear Mendrick's voice at all; perhaps she thought it was an elaborate joke at her expense. Taking a deep breath, Wydrin lifted and dropped her arms dramatically.

'Fine. If Nuava fancies falling about in the dark with me and a giant pile of moving rocks, then let's do it. Sebastian, you can stay up here and make sure the prince doesn't get too bored.' Catching the look on his face, she waved a hand at him. 'I'd really rather there were someone up here watching our backs. I don't want anything hungrier than me following us down here. We'll be in and out before you know it, I swear on my claws.'

Sebastian watched them disappear into the tunnel with a feeling of dread thick in his throat. Wydrin had given Nuava the small light-globe originally gifted to them by Crowleo, back at the Secret Keeper's house, and she had drawn her dagger ready. When she'd seen his worried look, she'd tipped him a wink.

'I'm just exploring some mysterious tunnels. What's the worst that could happen?'

Mendrick followed in after them, the strange wolf shape that was so much a part of the landscape moving smoothly and with barely any noise. After a few moments they were lost to sight.

'Hurry up,' Sebastian murmured. 'Do what you need to do and get out of there.'

He and Dallen settled in to wait at the cave entrance. The tunnel Mendrick had led them to sat at the bottom of a shallow bowl in the rock, and they were surrounded by snow and ice, all weathered into strange shifting shapes by the wind. They had left the frozen lakes with the armoured fish and the monoliths behind, although Sebastian still felt that they were travelling through a cursed land, deemed as wicked by an ancient people.

And underneath that was another feeling: a cold joy in the lack of humanity here, and a connection to this place that he couldn't begin to understand. He wondered what Ephemeral would make of that.

The prince removed a long, glass bottle with square sides from his pack and took a sip. The liquid inside looked thick and brownish-yellow.

'I would offer you some,' he said apologetically, catching Sebastian's look, 'but this is a drink we call Old Father. It's made from whale fat and goat's milk, and left in vats for months. When we have traded with warmlings in the past, none of you would touch it.'

Sebastian smiled. 'I'm not surprised. Thank you anyway, but Wydrin has left me with half her rum supply, which is a surprisingly large amount of rum.' He pulled a flask from his own belt. 'Although if I drink too much, I'll be for it.'

'Here, look at that.' Dallen pointed up to the low clouds just in time for Sebastian to catch a tremor of movement up there. 'Keep watching, they will come down again in a moment.'

Frowning slightly, Sebastian narrowed his eyes, wondering what he was looking out for, when three long eel-like shapes slipped down out of the clouds, wriggling frantically. Their shining blue skins looked like banners the colour of a summer's sky, and Sebastian could just make out the twisted white forms of their horns. The three wyverns slipped along together, like porpoises in the sea, before vanishing back up into the cloud. Sebastian smiled; their shapes pleased him in a way he could not name.

'Wild wyverns,' said Dallen. There was both pride and sadness in his voice. 'There are nests not far from here. Every few generations we come to the nesting grounds and collect a few eggs for ourselves, and then we hatch them in the war-towers.' A look of pain moved across his face. 'It does the wyverns good to have new blood in the squadrons every now and then. Rillion's mother was from a new egg. She loved to fly higher than the others, and my father always said it was because she was closer to her wild cousins.'

'Has anyone from outside – has anyone who wasn't a Narhl ever ridden one?' Sebastian asked, not quite sure why he needed to know.

Dallen looked at him in surprise. 'Never. The wyverns dislike warmlings even more than my father does, as difficult as that may be to believe.'

'You are close to them,' said Sebastian after a few moments. He was thinking of the nest of snakes under the thorn bushes, and how Ephemeral had stilled them with a look. 'There is a connection between you?'

Dallen nodded. 'I felt the death of each wyvern as keenly as I felt the death of Olborn, of Krestin, of all of them. To lose all of them at once . . . such grief will never leave me.'

They lapsed into silence, and the sky grew gradually darker. Light flurries of snow began to fall and Sebastian pulled up his hood.

He thought of Wydrin and Nuava, somewhere beneath the ground now, looking for this mysterious nexus. *She'll be fine*, he told himself. Wydrin had faced down a dragon, not to mention half the tavern owners in Crosshaven. She could take care of herself.

'Tell me about your order,' said the prince into the silence. 'Your order of Ynnsmouth knights.'

Sebastian shrugged. 'There is not much to tell. I thought it was where I belonged, but I was wrong. I paid for that mistake, and, in the end, so did they.'

'I like to hear about these things, you see,' said Dallen softly. The snow was dusting the top of his head, and as Sebastian watched, a few errant flakes landed in his beard and on his eyebrows. They did not melt. 'I've only ever known this place, all my life. My soldiers used to laugh at me for it, but I collected all sorts of items from outside the Frozen Steps. Maps, books, even cooking utensils, scavenged from travellers coming through these northern lands. Anything I could get that reminded me that there was a world outside this cold place.'

Sebastian nodded. He could feel his own beard growing rigid with ice, but he felt strangely comfortable even so. Soon he would have to move away from the prince and build a fire, but just for the moment it felt good to sit here looking out across the broken rocks with this strange man at his side.

'We were a celibate order,' he said, ignoring the heat suddenly

239

suffusing his cheeks. 'And I fell in love with a man in my company, a man who looked up to me as a leader. It did not end well.'

Dallen nodded carefully, not quite looking at him. 'The Order of the Ynnsmouth Knights . . . they did not tolerate . . . such things?'

'No. There are places that do,' said Sebastian, turning towards the prince. Suddenly it seemed quite important to say this. 'Out in the world beyond the Frozen Steps, and beyond Skaldshollow. Where Wydrin comes from, for example, a place called Crosshaven, such things hardly merit a raised eyebrow. There are better places, out in the world. But Ynnsmouth was not one of them. I was exiled, cast out from my order and banished from the land of my birth.'

'This is most interesting,' said Prince Dallen. His voice had taken on a carefully speculative note. 'My father, and indeed most Narhl, would not look kindly on such things. It may have,' he took a deep breath, 'it may have made life difficult for me, over the last few years.'

For a little while they sat in silence. The snow grew heavier, sending swirls of white flakes dancing around the broken rocks and shadows, making them look like they were almost moving themselves; a great waltz of ghosts and stone.

It didn't take long for it to become clear that this was a cave unlike any Wydrin had been in before. The tunnel walls were curiously rounded, as though something had bored its way through the earth, and the deeper they went the smoother it became. After a time, they started to see small patches of odd creatures that Wydrin could only guess were some sort of cross between a fungus and a living animal; she paused by one with her dagger out, and gestured to Nuava to bring the light closer.

'Here, look at this.'

It looked rather like a swollen bunch of grapes, except that each small sac was pale and translucent, and gathered in the very centre were a number of tiny appendages, like rubbery fingers. When Wydrin placed the point of her dagger on one of the swollen sacs, the entire thing seemed to thrum with anger and the ends of the small appendages lit up with a pearly green light. There were hundreds of the things, on the floor and the walls and the ceiling, some growing in patches as large as a man.

Nuava peered at it closely. 'I've never seen such a thing,' she said. Without seeming to think about it, her hand drifted towards the notebook on her belt. 'But that light. It looks to be Edeian-generated. Perhaps the creatures here, living in such close proximity to the rock, are affected by it. I should very much like to make some drawings, take a few notes.'

Wydrin snorted. 'We don't have time for that I'm afraid, Nuava. While we're in here messing about with weird plants our murderous mage could be up to anything.'

Nuava stepped away a little unsteadily. 'Let's keep moving, then.'

They walked on down the tunnel, the familiar heavy tread of Mendrick coming on behind them. He was silent in Wydrin's head, but she could feel him there clearly. It was strange, she realised, to know that someone was there with you but to have no idea of their mood. There were no expressions on his stony face to interpret, and his voice was a disembodied echo inside her own mind.

As they moved deeper under the ground, the bulbous plants grew thicker, so that they brushed against them continually and, consequently, the tunnel was soon lit with enough green light for them to barely need the light-globe.

Do you know what these things are?

For a moment there was no reply from Mendrick, only the echoing silence. *They are lights for someone*, he said eventually. *And now lights for you.*

That's not exactly helpful, she replied. *Are we going the right way?*

Yes, he replied, *although we have a way to go yet.*

They walked on, Wydrin still with Frostling in her fist. They started to pass other tunnels, ones that bisected their own and passed on into the dark. All of them were smooth and round. Wydrin glanced at Nuava. The girl was looking at their surroundings with wide eyes, as though she could somehow drink in the knowledge by seeing everything at once.

'For what it's worth, I am sorry about your brother.'

Nuava looked up, her eyes filled with pain again, and inwardly Wydrin winced.

'I mean, he was very kind to me. I'm sure that doesn't help at all, but he seemed like the sort who was always helping people when he could, and those are the best sort of people. Rare people, often.'

Nuava sniffed and nodded. 'I – I can't believe he's gone,' she said. 'We argued a lot, because we both wanted to craft the Edeian, but I was the only one naturally inclined that way. He would study Tamlyn's designs for hours, and it never really helped.' She paused, then shook her head. 'That's a lie actually. About the arguing, I mean. *I* would argue, and he would just listen, patiently, and then try to make me understand. It was infuriating.'

Wydrin smiled, thinking of Sebastian. 'I know the sort.' The girl was walking with her head down now, looking at her boots. 'Some people will tell you it gets better,' she said, 'but that's not really true, and I won't tell you that. There's a piece missing from you now, and you never get it back, but you do learn how to exist alongside that missing piece. It gets easier to navigate, over time. It's terrible, really, that you can learn to live with such a thing, but you do. People are horribly resilient in that way.'

Nuava sniffed again, and quickly wiped a gloved hand across her face. Wydrin pretended not to see.

'You've lost someone, then?'

Wydrin nodded shortly. The tunnel ahead of them branched off into two separate entrances, and after a moment she heard Mendrick in her head again. *To the left*, he said, so she led them on. The glass globe cast its sunny light over walls thick with the strange, vibrating creatures, and somewhere she could hear water running.

'My father –' she began as they made their way through the left-hand side passage. This way was narrower, and she and Nuava had to walk much closer, their arms brushing together periodically. 'He was a merchant, and sometimes a pirate. He went looking for something impossible over the horizon, and never came back.'

'He could still be alive, then,' said Nuava hesitantly. Wydrin heard the hope in her voice, the irrational hope that the dead could somehow be returned to them, and felt a sliver of pain in her own heart. *No*, she thought bitterly, *it doesn't work that way. We must live for the living.* 'He could just be lost, or stranded somewhere. I've read about that, in stories. Men and women in shipwrecks, getting washed up on deserted islands.'

'It's a nice thought,' said Wydrin, desperately trying to hide the sour note in her voice. 'But it's been years now. My father was no fool – at least, he wasn't a fool in that sense – and he would have found a way to get a message to us by now. My mother and my half-brother have both looked for him, up and down a hundred coastlines.' She sighed, suddenly annoyed that she was thinking about this at all. 'If he ever did turn up at my door again, I'd probably knock him straight back into the sea for making us worry so much.'

Nuava half laughed, a tiny, nervous noise that echoed strangely off the walls.

'The last time I saw him, he'd won a cargo boat full of oranges off some idiot in a card game.' Wydrin smiled at the memory. 'He was trying to figure out what he was going to do with them all, but I said to him—'

The ground beneath their feet trembled, causing Nuava to stagger to one side. Wydrin drew Glassheart in her free hand and looked around, but there was nothing to be seen.

'What was that?'

Nuava shook her head. They had reached another of the inter-sections, and she stood where the tunnels met, looking back the way they'd come.

'I don't know. Perhaps the rocks are shifting?'

Something lurched out of the dark from her right, knocking her forward and then gathering her up in one movement. Wydrin had time to see a huge, segmented creature that half-filled the tunnel that passed through theirs, its body covered in shiny brown blisters like earthenware plates, before it had snatched up Nuava with a set of writhing mandibles, and then she was faced with its backside, disappearing off down the tunnel. The thing had scurrying, insectile legs, hundreds of them, and it was moving alarmingly fast.

Nuava screamed, once, and then already she was out of sight.

'Ye gods and little fishes!' Wydrin sheathed her dagger and scrambled up onto Mendrick's back. 'Follow that centipede!'

Mendrick pounded down the tunnel, sending up showers of stone and grit. The strange plants shimmered and shone, lighting their way down the passage. Ahead of them, Wydrin could just make out the barbed read-end of the monster that had stolen Nuava; the creature was twisting and turning, seemingly at random, and for long moments they would lose sight of it altogether, before Mendrick would put on an extra burst of speed.

'The lights,' she gasped as she clung to the leather strap around the werken's neck. 'You said they were someone's lights. You could have mentioned that that someone was a giant carnivorous centipede!'

It is not carnivorous, said Mendrick. *Not as such.*

'Not as such?'

They tore around another corner, and now they were very close. Wydrin could see that the long, horn-like barbs on the centipede's rear end were flexing at them aggressively, and there was some sort of dark fluid oozing from the pointed ends.

'Of course it would be poisonous,' she muttered. 'Bastard thing that ugly would have to be.'

From ahead they heard Nuava shouting again, and Wydrin leaned forward over Mendrick's neck.

'Go for it, Mendrick,' she urged. 'I know you can catch this thing.'

Mendrick leapt forward, attempting to land on the creature's rear end and crush it, but the centipede vanished from view, and then suddenly they were falling, catapulting down into the black. Wydrin heard Nuava screaming, and then realised she was screaming too. There was a confusion of lights – the light-globe, somehow still with Nuava, the weird shimmering lights of the wall fungus, and the twin green lamps of Mendrick's eyes – and in it Wydrin caught sight of what looked like a whirlpool directly beneath them.

'Shit!'

Clinging to Mendrick's neck she closed her eyes and braced for the splash, but instead they landed with a messy crunch, quickly followed by a deafening chorus of chittering and clicking.

'What the—?'

Wydrin opened her eyes. They had landed in a swirling mass of giant centipedes, all squirming together on the floor of a giant chamber. She and Mendrick had apparently fallen directly onto the back of one of them, causing its stringy yellow guts to explode messily all over its neighbours. Glancing to the head of the creature, she saw it raise its head weakly and wave lightly furred antennae, before keeling over.

We're here, said Mendrick in her head.

'We're *what*?'

'Wydrin? Wydrin, are you there?'

Nuava appeared out of the gloom, clambering over the back of one of the writhing creatures, stumbling slightly as she came. Her clothes had been torn and she was spattered with centipede gore, but otherwise she looked unharmed. Wydrin waved at her.

'It just dropped me,' she said. Her voice was trembling. 'It brought me all the way down here and just dropped me.'

'Perhaps it was giving you a lift.'

Now that they were down in the chamber, the centipedes did indeed seem to be ignoring them. Wydrin urged Mendrick towards the girl, and the werken moved awkwardly against the whirling tide. The centipedes were all moving together, circling a stone edifice in the middle of the cavern which Wydrin couldn't see clearly.

'I could do without help like that,' said Nuava. They reached her and Wydrin pulled her up onto the back of the werken. 'I think I threw up a little.'

'Entirely understandable,' said Wydrin. 'I think I need to throw up a little myself.'

Next to them, a centipede moved past with something stiff and furry in its mandibles. It took Wydrin a moment to figure out that it was a dead fox like the ones outside the cave, now hanging from the monster's jaws, its legs limp.

'Where's it going with that?' she said, to no one in particular. 'Do they just enjoy carrying things around?'

I imagine, she heard Mendrick within her head, *that it's taking it to feed her.*

'What do you mean, "her"?' asked Wydrin, but already her

stomach was trying to crawl out of her throat. Looking closer at the stone edifice, she realised that it wasn't entirely made of stone at all but of grainy grey flesh and strange, bulbous sacs. She saw a great pulsating maw in the middle, fleshy and pink, and a set of nine black eyes set in a circle around it, all vibrating slightly. There were skeletal appendages sprouting from behind the jaws, and as Wydrin watched, one of the centipedes approached the creature, with what looked like a dead goat in its mandibles. The centipede reared up, launching the front half of its body into the air, and the skeletal arms of the vast creature reached down and plucked the offering from it. There was a brief moment of consideration as it turned the goat around in its claws, before the animal was popped whole into the gaping throat.

'Oh, shit.'

I did say that the centipedes were not themselves carnivorous, said Mendrick in his polite, distant tone. *The nexus is beneath her, by the way. She is resting her egg sacs upon it.*

'Oh *shit.*'

36

'Did you hear that?'

Prince Dallen was up on his feet, ice-spear in hand. Sebastian blinked rapidly – he'd been dozing off, thinking of Ephemeral and her sisters, wondering what they were doing now – and looked around. Evening had been settling over them in this strange land with its short days, and now the snow and rocks were soaked in a deepening indigo light.

'Hear what?' He stood up, trying to shake some life back into his limbs.

'There was a rumble, far below.' Dallen lifted up his cold-light, turning it on the dark, and then back onto the cave entrance. There was nothing. 'More than likely it was just the earth shifting far below, but I might take a quick look around.'

Dallen made to walk away, but slipped on a loose patch of stones. His wounded leg gave out on him, dropping him towards the ground but Sebastian was faster. He grabbed the young prince by the upper arm, and held him steady.

'Hold on, Dallen, take it easy. That leg of yours hasn't quite caught up with the rest of you yet.'

Dallen laughed, a rueful expression on his face.

'At least I got you to call me Dallen. And it only took me falling over like a newly born calf.'

Sebastian smiled back. 'I could never resist a prince in distress. Uh, that's to say—'

Suddenly Dallen had slipped an arm around his neck and was

kissing him, his lips cold against Sebastian's own. Startled, Sebastian took an involuntary step backwards, before thinking better of it and wrapping his arms around the smaller man's waist. The prince tasted of snow and strong alcohol, and a deeper mineral taste Sebastian couldn't place. After a few moments in which Sebastian completely forgot how cold he was, and how dangerous their situation, Dallen pulled away from him, staggering slightly. His blue eyes were wild.

'I'm sorry,' he stammered, shaking his head, 'I don't . . . I'm sorry.'

Sebastian cleared his throat. He could still taste the prince, so cold and strange and completely welcome. He ran a hand through his hair, his heart racing. He hadn't kissed anyone since Gallo, and he'd forgotten what that heady rush was like. *How terrible, to forget such a thing*, he thought.

'Nothing to be sorry about. Nothing at all. Really.' The prince was leaning over slightly, one hand on his chest. 'Are you unwell, Dallen?'

The prince laughed slightly, shaking his head. 'It's just that you're so warm. I've never . . . not with a warmling. Being near you is exhausting.'

That surprised a laugh out of Sebastian. 'I'm not sure whether to take that as a compliment or not.'

Dallen looked up at him, grinning.

'It's pleasure and pain at the same time. To be near such a source of warmth.' He shook his head. 'It was an exhilarating experience, but I suspect too much could kill me.'

'Well,' Sebastian took a step towards him, 'I'm not sure I've said this for a number of years, but . . . we could take it slowly?'

'We'll have to be fast.'

They'd found a small alcove at the outer edge of the chamber. Wydrin and Nuava had scrunched up inside it, peering out at the centipedes over the barrier of Mendrick's still form. Now they were out of the way the centipedes paid them no attention at all, but that wasn't making Wydrin feel any safer. The sound of thousands of chitinous legs scratching against the stone was deafening, and there was a rank, alien smell to the place, like the wet underside of a forgotten rock. The giant creature at the centre of this mass adoration was continuing to accept its offerings, happily pushing each new corpse deep into its cavernous throat. The thing didn't look to be getting full up any time soon.

'Are you insane?' hissed Nuava. 'You're seriously going to go over to that thing? They were going to feed me to it!'

'That's where the nexus is, so that's where we're going.' She glanced at Nuava's stricken expression. 'Yes, I said we. Unless you'd like to stay here and study these creepy-crawly bastards? Just in case they hold the key to your mastering the Edeian and becoming an all-powerful pain in the arse like your aunt?'

Nuava scowled. 'We won't get more than ten feet.'

Wydrin shifted so that she was leaning on one elbow and pointed with her free hand.

'You see that hideous wobbly yellow sac thing that's draped over the lower half of the rock?'

Nuava nodded.

'Mendrick says there's an entrance under there, a gap that leads directly to the net of Edeian that connects all of these mountains together. It's the only way through. Now, I doubt that Mummy Centipede is going to move for us, even if we ask nicely.' Wydrin wriggled a little further out of their hiding place, trying to see better. It actually looked like the giant sprawling monster couldn't move, or at least couldn't move much; Wydrin could see large patches of the strange glowing foliage growing over both the creature's egg sacs and the rocks below it. The thing probably hadn't moved in years. 'So what we'll need to do is distract it.' Reaching to her belt she pulled Frostling out of its scabbard and passed it to Nuava, who took it with a look of horror on her face. 'Whatever you do, don't lose that. I'll feed you to Mummy Centipede myself if you do.'

'What am I going to need this for?' Nuava was still looking at the dagger like Wydrin had handed her a freshly toasted weasel.

'You're going to need it, Nuava, to cut through that thing's egg sac.' Wydrin pulled herself out of the hole entirely, and, still crouching, drew Glassheart from its scabbard. 'I'd do a quick job of it, if I were you.'

'What?'

'Don't worry, I'm going to keep its attention elsewhere. Just get that egg sac out of the way for me, and be ready to run.'

'But I can't . . .'

'Of course you can. You've got my lucky dagger, haven't you?'

Nuava watched, speechless, as the sell-sword woman, sword in hand, scrambled up on top of the werken and crashed off into the crowd of centipedes. There was an immediate uproar as Mendrick stamped over several segmented bodies, and Nuava saw centipedes leaning back on their rear legs, mandibles slashing at the air as Wydrin and the werken passed by, heading for the centre of the cavern.

'By all the gods, what is she doing?'

Wydrin was shouting now, waving her sword at any centipede that got too close. Her blade connected with the side of one's head, slicing clear through its wetly shining eyes and splattering Wydrin's leather armour with black ichor. The enormous creature with the egg sacs stopped its relentless feeding session and turned to watch, its gore-smeared mouth hanging open.

With a lurch, Nuava realised that this was her moment. She shuffled out of the hole, both hands wrapped awkwardly around Frostling's hilt, and then stopped. The centipedes were still churning by, still ignoring her, but she would have to go past them to reach the egg sac. She would have to go through them.

'I can't do this,' she muttered. 'I just can't!'

Across the cavern, Wydrin had reached the stone outcrop where the giant creature sat, and was now leading Mendrick in tight circles, jabbing her sword at the rolls of shiny, grey flesh. Horrifyingly, she looked as though she were enjoying herself. Nuava shook her head to try and clear it.

'I can't do this,' she said again, all too aware that there was no one there to hear her excuses. 'I've never even held a proper weapon before. I've barely even been outside the walls of Skaldshollow!'

Except that wasn't entirely true, she reminded herself. She remembered the knife Tamlyn had given her, that she had used to cut the fingers from a Narhl corpse, and then later failed to use on the resurrected Joah Demonsworn. In the uncertain greenish light and the alien-smelling dark, Nuava's face flushed with shame and guilt.

'I did that demon's bidding,' she muttered bitterly. 'And I failed to avenge my brother. If nothing else, I can do this. I can try to do this.'

Without pausing to think about it further, Nuava got to her feet and ran. Immediately she was met by the scurrying form of a centipede, its narrow legs scrabbling in the dust, so she used her momentum to clamber up over it. The creature's back was smooth and slippery, and it wriggled in outrage, almost causing her to lose her balance and fall straight back to the floor, but she jumped, landing on the back of another. This one writhed, rippling its back to throw her off and, without thinking, Nuava plunged Frostling down between one of its segments. The blade bit deep and she held on for dear life as the insect bucked like an untamed horse.

Nuava glanced over to where Wydrin was. The sell-sword was still shouting, her sword a flickering sliver of silver in the poor light, but there were more centipedes around her than there had been before. It seemed they had finally perceived her as a threat to their queen, and Nuava suspected Wydrin had only a few minutes before she was overwhelmed by insectile bodies.

Pulling the blade free with a yell, Nuava threw herself from the back of one centipede to the next, keeping her eyes on the distant egg sac that was her goal.

They can't stop me, she told herself, *nothing can stop me.*

Twice she fell, hitting the rock floor on her side, briefly lost in a terrifying world of translucent orange legs, needle-like and unrelenting, and once the head of a centipede hit her flat on the stomach, its furred mandibles churning against her vest, its antennae slapping wetly against her neck. Nuava slashed out with Frostling, screamingly wordlessly, and fled before she could see what damage she had done.

And suddenly she was there. The rock rose in front of her, dotted here and there with the weird glowing plant. Nuava shoved Frostling through her belt and scrambled up until she saw the fat yellow bulge of the egg sac. She glanced up. The centipede queen rose above her like a quivering monolith, strange skeletal arms striking out at something Nuava couldn't see. At the moment, it was paying her no attention.

That'll soon change, thought Nuava grimly.

She focussed back on the egg sac. It was enormous, almost as long as she was tall, and it thickened towards the bottom like a great teardrop. The skin of it was tight and faintly see-through; in the intermittent light she could see the shadows of tiny, many-legged things, curled and waiting within the sac. And somewhere beyond it was the opening that led to the nexus.

Nuava drew Frostling from her belt, preparing to start slashing at the sac, and then paused again.

'If I just start stabbing wildly, that thing will turn on me,' she muttered under her breath. Her mind immediately provided an image of her being speared by one of those skeletal arms, and dangled over the queen centipede's hungry mouth. 'I need to do this quickly, and in the least number of cuts.'

She took a deep breath, forcing herself to look again, more slowly this time. *Look at how it fits together, Nuava.* She could almost hear Tamlyn's voice in her head, her stern face devoid of sympathy. One of the key principles of crafting a werken was looking at how an object's component parts fitted together. *Except apparently they're not objects*, she thought, and then pushed the thought away.

The sac was attached to the main body of the creature only at the very top, where it hung from a number of waxy-looking pustules. Nuava pulled herself up further onto the rock, until she was lying alongside the sac, and with one quick movement drew the edge of Frostling across it, just under the pustules.

Several things happened at once. First of all, the centipede mother screamed, a noise so loud and piercing that Nuava very nearly fell straight off the rock and back into the press of centipedes. The sac itself dropped like a stone and hit the ground below in an enormous splash, scattering white fluid and half-formed baby centipedes everywhere. The centipedes on the ground stopped their endless circling and began to writhe, driven into some sort of madness by the contents of the egg sac. Nuava was so busy watching this that she was very nearly impaled by the flailing skeletal arm that swung down from above her. She glanced up to look into the shivering, nine-eyed gaze of the centipede queen.

'Ah,' she said. 'I wouldn't have thought such a face could convey anger so accurately. Fascinating.'

'Watch out!' Wydrin came careering around the corner on the back of Mendrick, sword outstretched. As she passed she leaned out and scored a long tear in the queen's gut, spilling more foul-smelling blood. 'Get in the bloody hole, you idiot!'

Nuava didn't need to be told twice. Dropping to her hands and knees she crawled into the hole as rapidly as she could, scraping and tearing her trousers on the jagged rocks. Inside it was pitch-black and she couldn't see an inch in front of her face – no wobbling light plants in here – but it was still preferable to the screaming horror in the chamber. She heard Wydrin climb in behind her, followed by the solid stone footsteps of Mendrick, who promptly sat in the entrance to the tunnel, blocking off all light and any overly attentive centipedes. Despite herself, Nuava gasped as a strong hand grabbed her upper arm. She could hear the grin in Wydrin's voice.

'I'd say that went pretty well, wouldn't you?'

37

It was a mistake to be here.

Sebastian knew it even as he passed the low stone walls that marked the boundary of the village. His father had hewn those stones, and had built part of that wall. He had spent many of his later years repairing it, often while young Sebastian watched, dangling his legs off the side, munching on the handful of nuts his mother had given him that morning.

It was a mistake, but the brood sisters needed things that couldn't be grown or scavenged from their hiding place – rope, oil, soaps, salt – and this was the closest place.

There are other villages, he told himself even as he walked past the wooden smoking huts that marked the boundary of Ragnaton, the scent of the yellow fish thick in the air. *Another day's walk and you would find yourself in a village where you did not grow up. And you swore you would never come back here.*

'It seems I never made an oath I wouldn't break,' Sebastian muttered under his breath.

It had been many years since he'd walked this dirt track, but everything looked much as it had done. The stone markers that led the way to the village square – again, most of them carved and put down by his father, Samuel Carverson – were still there, pitted and colourful with moss, yellow and green. He passed the shrine to Isu, which had at least seen a coat of paint since he'd left, shining blue and red in the sun. Idols carved from mountain rock twirled at the end of their ropes, the copper bells clattering their childish music to the air. Sebastian paused, as he had always done before, mouthing a brief prayer to the mountain god before moving on.

The centre of the village was the same square of mud and stalls, although someone had taken the time to install wooden planters at the edges, full of the wildflowers that could be found in the valleys all around Ynnsmouth – pink Glasswort and red pasque flower, buttercups and creeping thistle. He wondered if that was his mother's touch, but told himself that he was simply looking for signs of her.

It was busy in the square. He kept his hood up so that his face was cast into shadow, and he hadn't shaved for some weeks in preparation so that his beard was thick and dark. He was careful not to make eye contact with anyone, giving the men and women that passed only the barest of glances. It had been years, of course, and he knew from his own mirror that he was no longer the fresh-faced knight who had been exiled from these lands, but he had grown up here. Anyone he cared to bump into might have played with him as a child, or sold him apples, or even looked after him while his mother was ill.

Why come here? When so much was at stake? It was not a question he could answer. He made a quick circuit of the stalls, picking up the supplies they needed, keeping all conversations short. To his surprise, he recognised no one, or at least not well enough to name them, and soon enough he stood back at the edge of the market with a heavier pack and an emptier purse.

'Time to go, then,' he said quietly. 'Just turn around and leave this place once more.'

Except he couldn't quite do that. Instead, he walked down a certain street, his head bowed as though he were weary or deep in thought. Here, the wooden and thatch dwellings slumped next to each other, the smell of wood fires and peat thick in his nostrils. A group of children ran past him, several of them clutching wooden swords, and then they were gone. On the corner between two houses, three teenage girls stood. Two of them wore the scarlet hoods of the lake-singers, and one of them lifted her face to look at him as he came up the road. Sebastian hurriedly turned away.

The road seemed shorter now. Sooner than he'd expected he found himself standing outside a house built of stone rather than wood, a pair of short stone knights flanking the doorway. One of them, he noticed, had fallen and broken through the middle. No one had repaired it.

He looked at the windows, his heart beating so heavily in his chest that it was difficult to breathe. He half expected to see her there, her pale face framed in the bright daylight – where else would she be? This was where he pictured her, when he thought of her at all. But there was only a dark space, and no smoke came from the chimney.

'She could be dead,' he murmured to himself. 'I would never know.'

He stood for some time, staring at the wooden door, uncomfortably aware of how suspicious he must look but, even so, unable to move. If he knocked on the door, would she answer? Would she even speak to him? Or would her mouth turn down at the corners, as it had done on the last day he saw her, her eyes filling with pain before she summoned the guards?

Looking back to the broken stone knight, he felt a small knot of anger in his chest. His father would not have approved of that. Stonework was to be cared for, repaired and cherished. He had been so proud when he'd made those; full of the quiet, faintly disappointed happiness of a man who had expected his son to follow him into the family business, only for him to take another, greater path. Not for the first time Sebastian felt a surge of gratitude that his father hadn't been alive to see how it had all ended.

Abruptly, he turned away from the stone house and walked up the street. There was a small ramshackle tavern there called The Running Fox. On a whim he stepped through the open door, peering around the gloomy interior – a single drink, a toast to his father perhaps, and then he would leave. A handful of men and women sat at tables nursing tankards of ale, and the bar at the back was empty but clean. Conversation was lively, and he caught snatches of it as he stepped up to the bar.

'She left him in the end, did you hear that? Just took the girl and left. My sister knows the lake-singer mistress there, and that's what she said.'

Sebastian turned slightly. There were two women sitting at the nearest table, one round and matronly, her hair pulled back with a kerchief, the other thin and wiry, and clad in riding leathers. The slimmer woman took a mouthful from her pint and gave the other woman a significant look.

'Well, I think that's terrible,' said the other woman. 'With him losing his boy, and then she takes the girl away as well. That's just heartless. Does she not believe him?'

The wiry woman shrugged. 'There was a time when Rollo was known for his drinking, wasn't there? He'd pulled himself together lately, but I think she was just waiting for him to slip back. Maybe she thinks his head is addled.'

'But the bite marks,' insisted the other woman. At the bar, Sebastian stood up a little straighter and turned his face away from them. 'My cousin's Junie saw the body, and she said the throat was all torn out.'

'Could have been a meadow wolf.' The woman wearing leathers didn't look like she actually believed that. 'Perhaps he was scared and left the boy to his fate, and now he's making up stories of these dragon women to make himself look better.'

'A meadow wolf down here, on the lakes?' The woman with the kerchief pulled a face. 'Methinks you've been at the drink yourself, Gertha. Besides which, the girl saw them too.'

'She could be lying for her da. She could be scared out of her wits. If there were a troop of green dragon women in Ynnsmouth, do you not think we'd have seen them?'

'What happened in Relios was real,' said the other woman, her voice low now. 'The battle at Baneswatch was real. My Willem was there, and he saw them.' She paused, and Sebastian saw her mutter a prayer to Isu. 'Thank the god-peak he got out of there when he did. You mark my words, Gertha, there are monsters walking Ede these days, and we are living in dark times.'

'Can I help you?'

Sebastian started, nearly dropping his pack. The tavern keeper was leaning over the bar next to him, thick dark brows lowered over a gaze that already looked suspicious.

'I'm sorry?'

'A drink? That's what people normally comes in here for. If

you've come in here merely to rest yourself against my bar, well, then I'm afraid I may have to charge you rent.'

'No, thank you. I thought I did – I thought I was meeting someone here, but I've come to the wrong place.'

The tavern keeper opened his mouth to say something else, but Sebastian was already heading for the door.

He did see her in the end, just as he was leaving the boundary of the village.

A tall figure swathed in a long grey cloak left one of the smoking huts and passed him on the right-hand side. She wore a cloth over the lower half of her face – tending the fish in the smoking huts was difficult on the lungs, she had always told him that – but he knew it was her from the way that she walked, from the slight stoop of a woman who had always been taller than her friends. Her black hair was mostly grey now, white in places, and she did not even glance at him as they passed, so close that Sebastian could have reached out and touched her arm.

A few seconds was all he had in the end, to take note of the new lines around her blue eyes, to drink in the sight of her. A few seconds and he was past her and beyond the stone markers. He walked on, feeling as though he might never breathe again. *So foolish*, he told himself, his heart racing in his chest. *If anyone would know me on sight, it would be her. Isu must truly be looking out for me today.*

He stopped and turned back, not quite able to resist, and saw her standing there looking back at him. A solemn figure in grey, a basket of smoked fish on one arm, her face covered. He knew then that she had seen him, that she had known him even in that brief second; that there was no way she could not.

After a moment or two, she turned away and walked further into the village, and although he watched her until she was out of sight, she never looked back at her son.

258

38

Frith awoke in the middle of the night to a series of painful cramps in his stomach. He just about managed to roll out of the bunk – eliciting an angry squawk from Gwiddion – before the bile surged up the back of his throat and he vomited awkwardly onto the metal floor. When it was over he knelt for a moment in the dark, feeling the room spin around him, and he imagined he was being carried in the belly of a great, terrible machine. Laughing weakly, he wiped his mouth on one of the filthy blankets and climbed shakily to his feet. Throwing up had not relieved his nausea. If anything, he felt even worse.

'If you think that's just the bad food, little man, you are a fool.'

Frith looked up sharply. The woman was there again, standing at the back of the narrow room. She was little more than a shape in the darkness now, but he knew she was there.

'Who are you?'

The woman said nothing. Frith shook his head in frustration.

'Damn you,' he spat. 'If you're not going to help me, you could at least let me be ill in peace.'

The woman sighed, a small noise of amusement. Frith clenched his fists.

'I am Xinian the Battleborn,' she said eventually. 'My presence here is . . . limited. The world fades in and out. It is difficult to describe.'

Frith ran a hand through his hair, grimacing at the old sweat he could feel there. It was so difficult to think.

'I know that name.'

'Of course you do, mage-child, but that man's bastardised magic is unmaking you. Can't you feel it? Can't you feel it in your blood?'

Frith swallowed, his throat sour. The bunk room smelt of sickness and dying, and he needed suddenly to be elsewhere, ghosts or no ghosts. He stumbled out of the room, pushing the door closed firmly behind him. The central forge room was empty, the light of the corrupted Heart-Stone playing over empty tables and chairs. Glancing at it warily, Frith made for a door to the far side, where he could hear the steady tread of someone walking backwards and forwards.

'Joah? Are you in there? I need to speak to you.'

He walked into the room, and stopped. Joah was standing in the middle, while all around him objects hung in the air, suspended by magic. Frith saw open books, their pages frozen in the moment of turning, knives twirling around each other like errant dance partners, and lengths of silk, fluttering as though caught in a breeze. Joah stood amongst them, his face drawn and pensive. It seemed to take him a few moments to notice that Frith had entered the room.

'Ah Aaron, I thought you were asleep.' He blinked, and the objects settled gently back down onto the floor. The room itself was otherwise bare, save for the scrawled sigils in black paint on the walls. 'I was just thinking some things over.'

'I saw a woman,' said Frith, no patience left to dance around the matter, 'in your memories. Just before I woke up. She was fierce, and had brown skin and a bald head. She was missing her left hand, and in her other she carried a strange sword. I should like to know who she was.'

Joah stood very still for a moment, before smiling tightly. 'Shall we return to the main room, Aaron? We have much to talk about, it seems.'

They returned to the centre of the Forge, and although being back in that violet light made his head throb painfully, Frith sat where Joah bid. The rogue mage sat down opposite him, the easy smile back on his face.

'I propose an exchange of information,' he said, reaching up to push an errant lock of hair back behind his ear. 'I will tell you what I know of Xinian the Battleborn, and you will tell me what you can of that bird-headed man I saw in your own head. Yes?'

'Yes,' agreed Frith. He looked down at his own hands and saw that they were shaking, so he balled them into fists. 'I will agree to that.'

'Good. Xinian the Battleborn was a mage from my time, Aaron, and a very powerful one at that. Back then, some mages chose to take a more martial approach to the use of the Edenier, and Xinian was a famed warrior and general. She led the Howling Battalion against the Eight Hosts of the Yellow Night, and single-handedly fought the demon Brugula to a standstill.' Joah waved a hand dismissively, half laughing. 'All ancient history now, of course. I'm sure you've never even heard of such events. She was an extraordinary fighter, combining offensive magic and a keen strategic mind. She was also the mage they sent to kill me.'

Frith raised his eyebrows. Joah's tone was mild, as though they were discussing what to have for dinner, but his previous outbursts were still fresh in his memory.

'To kill you?'

'Yes. In the end the ruling mages of the time considered what I was doing to be too dangerous. Too risky. They sent envoys to me, men and women with silver tongues, desperate to talk me away from the path, but they just didn't understand, Aaron. Not like you do.'

Frith pressed his lips together. *Why does he believe that I am on his side?*

'The envoys didn't succeed, and, well, Bezcavar took exception to their attitude.' Joah leaned back in the chair, looking at a point over Frith's left shoulder. 'It was all quite messy. And so eventually they sent Xinian and her remarkable sword.' He seemed to come back to himself then, and he gestured at his own chest. 'She succeeded in taking me from the path, but not permanently, as it turns out.'

'What was so remarkable about her sword?' asked Frith, but Joah was already shaking his head.

'All ancient history, Aaron, but I hope I have sated your curiosity at least. Now, to the bird-headed man I saw in your memories. What of him?'

261

'Ah, yes.' Frith cleared his throat, his mind racing. 'I have been thinking on this, since you expressed an interest, and I believe I may have figured out where the memory came from. It would have been one of my earliest, in fact, when my mother was still alive. She took me and my brother Tristan, who was a babe in arms at the time, to a travelling market run by the Cheoria.' Frith paused, trying to think of details that would make his story more plausible. 'My brother Leon was already at that age where he felt that such things – particularly things that involved being escorted by our mother – were beneath him.'

'Ah, yes, your brothers,' said Joah in a musing tone. Again he wasn't quite looking at Frith; instead he was looking down at his own hands. 'And you lost both of them. How sad.'

'Yes,' agreed Frith. 'It was. At the travelling market there were a group of mummers, performing several plays. One of them was a series of skits on the earliest days of Ede, and one of the actors wore the most outlandish headdress.' Frith forced a laugh. 'When I was a child, I remember it scared me quite badly, so that I demanded to leave the play, much to my mother's exasperation. I had nightmares about it for months after, would you believe? It is strange the things that affect us as small children.' When Joah didn't answer immediately, Frith continued falteringly, 'There were lots of strange masks of course – wolves too, for the twin gods, and another of a woman's face with long green hair streaming from the back of it – but it was the bird mask that scared me. I can only imagine that's why—'

Joah leapt from his chair, reaching for Frith's throat. Giving a startled yelp, Frith threw himself backwards, almost toppling to the floor, but Joah caught him, one strong hand at his neck and the other pushing a tiny knife into the bony part of his shoulder.

'Remember,' muttered Joah directly into his ear, his breath hot and feverish, 'concentrate on the pain.'

Frith threw a punch at Joah's midriff, only for it to be deflected with a wave of force that took all the feeling from his fingers. In response, he felt the Edenier rising in his chest once more, fuelled by pain and fury and ready to spill out in any means possible, but then there came a fiercely hot pain in the centre of his forehead; Joah was forcing a 'crossing' on him again, and he felt the rogue mage's mind slip into his own like a heated blade. He screamed, unable to stop himself – the intrusion of it, the terrible sense of tearing – and then he was lost in a tumult of images, although these ones were all too familiar.

His brother Tristan playing with a toy horse on the rug of the great hall, their father a distant blur on his chair; falling beaten and half naked onto the ice-covered stones of the courtyard and glancing up to see their bodies hanging, black and purple, from the battlements; holding a folded piece of torn cloak to the wound in Sebastian's chest, feeling his life's blood slipping through his fingers; the waters of the Mages' Lake, glittering with a thousand points of light; Wydrin's face, creased into her usual smirk, a length of linen curled between her clever fingers; an island of black rock and steaming pools –

At this image Frith tried to draw back, knowing that these memories would contain information that Joah should not see, but the rogue mage was relentless, pushing aside his resistance as though it were made of wet paper.

Jolnir hobbling towards him out of the mist, enormous bird mask nodding alarmingly; sleeping in a conical hut made of grass, lying and listening to the lonely sound of the wind and feeling lost; sending fireballs into a nest of flying lizards and watching as they fell, blackened and crispy; Jolnir removing the headdress and revealing his own terrible face, the face of an old god; O'rin the trickster god taking his powers with one touch, and letting him fall to the ground, senseless . . .

Here the onslaught stopped. Frith had a brief impression, as Joah withdrew his mind, of the woman Xinian the Battleborn, and then it was gone. Back in his chair in the Forge, he slumped awkwardly half to the floor, gasping for breath. Joah was standing over him, his face pale and his eyes wild.

'The lost god?' He was shouting, but Frith suspected he had no idea of the volume of his voice. 'O'rin the trickster god lives?'

Frith pressed his hand to his forehead, once more attempting not to be sick. Darkness was crowding in at the edge of his vision.

'What did you do to me?' he murmured. 'What have you done?'

'Don't you understand, Aaron? Don't you know what this means? One of the old gods lives! I had always assumed that that

263

particular source of power was forever lost to me, but here it is, and you have brought it to me.'

Frith groaned, his stomach roiling. *It's the Rivener*, he thought, *I can barely be in the same room as it.* He glanced up to the aperture that housed the Heart-Stone, and saw that it was now a ghoulish grey, and almost black on one corner.

'Oh do stop making a fuss, Aaron, I just needed to retrieve the information you were hiding from me.' Joah bent down and lifted Frith up with one arm. 'And I shan't pretend to understand why you would do that, but it hardly matters. Do you see what we can do now? Do you see?'

Frith pushed away from the rogue mage, supporting himself with one of the stone tables.

'What?' he spat, no longer able to keep up his pretence of manners. 'What is it I'm supposed to see?'

'A god! A source of pure Edenier, of pure spirit.' Joah grinned. 'We shall eat his flesh, Aaron, and be mighty.'

39

The tunnel was narrow and low-ceilinged, so that Wydrin and Nuava had to crouch awkwardly as they made their way down deeper into the earth. There had been an unhappy few minutes where Nuava had guarded the entrance to the tunnel while Mendrick and Wydrin shoved some larger stones and boulders in front of it, but the centipedes seemed to have forgotten about them already, and Wydrin only saw a few segmented bodies rushing past in their haste to service their queen. Nuava had been shaking when she'd reached her, hands and vest covered in sticky translucent fluid and blood, but now she was holding the light-globe steadily and her face was set into a stern frown. *The kid is learning.*

'I really hope there's another way out of here, Mendrick,' Wydrin said aloud, 'as I don't particularly fancy our chances with what's left of Mummy Centipede if we have to go back through her dining room.'

There are other ways, replied Mendrick in her head. *Once we have found the nexus, all shall be clear to me.*

Nuava glanced up at her warily. 'Did it . . . did it reply?'

'He did,' said Wydrin. 'We'll be back under the blessed sky soon enough, thank the Graces.'

'It really speaks, then? In your mind?' Nuava was gazing at the werken with a mixture of disbelief and religious awe.

Wydrin nodded. 'He's not the best conversationalist, to be honest. He's a bit dry. As you'd expect, for a big chunk of living rock. I don't imagine he knows many jokes.'

'All these years,' said Nuava, 'and we never had the smallest clue that such a thing was even possible.'

'Really?' said Wydrin, looking at her side-on. 'They can walk around, and obey your commands. Someone at some point must have considered the possibility.'

They made their way in silence for a few moments more. The sound of thousands of centipedes writhing together had faded the further down they travelled, and now there was only the sound of their own footsteps and the distant drip of ice melting somewhere. *Is this how it sounds in Mendrick's head? A great waiting silence, for ever.*

'Someone probably did,' Nuava eventually admitted, biting her lower lip. 'Long before I trained to be a crafter, one of my ancestors must have looked into it. Perhaps they didn't look very hard.' Nuava brushed angrily at her furs, dislodging some imagined piece of dirt. 'No doubt it was easier to carry on with what we were doing than to stop.'

'Do you think your aunt knew?'

Nuava's shoulders stiffened. 'She knew about the Prophet, and her plan to resurrect Joah Demonsworn. After that, I'm not sure anything could surprise me.'

'What will you do?' asked Wydrin quietly. 'Once all this is over?'

'I honestly do not know. All of this is very difficult for me to take in. My whole life, I have been taught to treat the werkens like objects. Beasts of burden that did not require feeding, or care. Just *things* that existed to do our will.' Her mouth twisted. 'It is not so easy to brush all that away on the word of a sell-sword and the prince of our enemy.'

Wydrin raised her eyebrows at that, but before she could answer, Mendrick spoke in her head again.

The nexus is in the chamber ahead. I can feel it.

The tunnel widened out, allowing them to stand and move more easily. The ground under their feet changed abruptly from rough stone to a surface that was almost as smooth as glass. Nuava lowered the light-globe, and it showed them a black glossy surface, almost mirror-like. In the centre of the chamber the smooth surface was broken by what looked like a gathering of

266

roots stretching from the ceiling to the floor, but made of bright green crystal.

'It is just like the Heart-Stone!' cried Nuava, automatically moving to run to it, but Wydrin laid a hand on her upper arm.

'Easy now, kid,' she said, not unkindly. 'I don't hold with such things myself, but I suspect this is a place that would be sacred to Mendrick, so perhaps we shouldn't immediately go trampling all over with our big ugly boots.'

Nuava looked briefly annoyed before nodding shortly. 'Right. Fine.'

Indeed, Mendrick's green eyes were like lamps, and they seemed to grow brighter as they approached the knot of crystals.

It is the nexus, he said, and for the first time Wydrin detected the slightest hint of an emotion in his voice: excitement. *From here I will be able to see everywhere.*

'All right, Mendrick, you do what you've got to do and then let's get moving.'

The werken reached the nexus and lowered his stone snout until it touched the crystal. The effect was immediate; the crystal glowed with sudden blinding brilliance, and all across the glassy floor beneath them bright green fractures like fingers of lightning appeared, shooting out from the nexus to hit the far walls. As Wydrin watched, they flared again and again, a living heartbeat of the mountain.

'This is like when we joined minds,' she said to Nuava, pleased to see such a wondrous sight again. 'All green flashing lights like getting hit really hard in the head. I was—'

And then Mendrick was in her mind, pushing all other thoughts aside. Absently, she dropped to her knees, and Nuava's voice was very distant.

See this with me, said Mendrick. *See where they have taken your friend.*

It was like flying through the heart of the rock; darkness and silence and the unending pressure of a thousand years. Then she saw snow, places where the heart of the mountain broke through the surface like the back of a great, black whale, before she was thrown past a series of small, bleak hills. She saw a circle of standing stones, and a place where the hill was broken. No, worse:

267

it was diseased. Whoever had come here had poisoned the land, and was doing it with its own flesh. Instinctively, she recoiled – it was like looking down at your hand to see that it had been replaced with something dead and rotten – and she felt Mendrick's horror inside her head too.

He has tainted it, he said. Now the emotion in his voice was anger, and that wasn't hard to spot at all. *The human man has twisted us, broken us.*

Wydrin reached out, wanting to see more. There was an image of a place heavy with iron and drowning in a sickly violet light; it was riddled throughout the hill like the tendrils of an infection. She saw Frith curled up in a foul-looking bunk and even from the brief glance she got she could see that he was very ill; his normally warm brown skin was almost grey, and there were dark circles around his eyes. He fretted in his sleep, murmuring something over and over. There was sweat on his brow.

Mendrick broke the connection, and Wydrin came back to herself with a gasp. Nuava was standing over her, her brown eyes full of worry.

'Are you all right? You looked like you were barely breathing.'

'I'm fine,' said Wydrin, struggling back to her feet. 'But I think my friend needs our help urgently.'

40

Frith awoke with a start to find Joah kneeling over him, one hand resting on his forehead. He'd been dreaming about his time at Whittenfarne, and the many long conversations he'd had with O'rin, the god of lies. He pulled himself back towards the wall away from Joah's touch, all the while mindful of Gwiddion, concealed in the blankets at the foot of the bed.

'What are you doing?' He felt ill again, and shakier even than when he'd fallen sleep.

'Just looking,' said Joah. He didn't seem perturbed by the way Frith was scowling at him. 'Searching through the rest of your memories. It really is quite fascinating.'

'You performed a crossing? But I felt nothing!'

'It gets easier,' said Joah dismissively. 'The more often I do it, the wider the path. And you were very deeply asleep. I saw a woman in your memories, Aaron. A woman with red hair and a dagger at her hip. She seems to have been in your thoughts a great deal.'

'A sell-sword,' said Frith. 'A woman I have travelled with recently. I paid her to help me retrieve the information I needed from the Citadel in Krete.'

'Aaron, it is clear that she is more than that to you,' Joah said softly, 'and it does us no good to become attached to people such as her. She will be nothing to what we will eventually achieve. What we will eventually *be*. Such attachments are a distraction and I will not tolerate them.'

'Tolerate?' Frith clenched his fists. 'How dare you . . .'

Joah held up a hand, and Frith felt his entire body freeze solid, as though he were suddenly stuck in amber.

'And there is another woman. This woman . . . she has long dark hair, and wears silks and satin, and elaborate fancies of gold and diamonds. I see her in a great castle surrounded by tall trees. Another distraction?'

Frith hissed through his teeth. The hold spell was so strong that it was difficult to breathe.

'There was a marriage proposal. A contract to bring our lands together. Her name is Lady Clareon. Her lands are as ancient as the Friths', and she thought it would be mutually beneficial for us to marry. Since my family were wiped out . . . It would mean security for the bloodlines, and for our lands.' He gasped more air into his lungs. 'I was considering it.'

Joah nodded thoughtfully, and all at once the pressure holding Frith in place was gone.

'You are concerned that if you do not enter into an agreement with this woman you will lose everything that your family once meant. That this is what your father would have wanted you to do. But there is a great conflict in your heart, and you cannot commit to either path.'

Frith stared at him.

'I can feel your mind, Aaron. I'm beginning to know how you think.' He looked at him, his brown eyes completely sincere. 'I know that you miss your family. I am sorry.'

Frith looked away. 'That is none of your concern.'

'That is where you are wrong.' Joah stood up. 'You are my brother now, Aaron, and your concerns are my concerns. Your pains are mine, and I shall suffer them with you.'

Frith slid his legs out of bed, ignoring the way it made his head spin.

'That is gratifying, Joah, but really not necessary.'

'Yes. You must put these human concerns from your mind, Aaron, because we have a lot of work to do. The Rivener must be in full working order as soon as possible.'

Frith squeezed his eyes open and shut, trying to keep up. 'Why, exactly?'

'In order to capture O'rin, of course!' Joah spread his arms wide. 'Once we have him where we want him, we shall eat his flesh like the mages of old, and we shall become all powerful.'

Frith laughed despite himself. 'You think this god an idiot? He will come nowhere near you. O'rin, remember, hid on an island for centuries, pretending to be a mad old priest. I have never met a being so full of cunning and caution. What are you going to do? Ask him nicely to dinner?'

Joah grinned and wagged a finger at him, as though Frith had made a particularly groan-worthy joke.

'Oh yes, I am very aware of his tricks. We thought that we had captured him in the Citadel with his siblings, after all. But I have searched through your memories, Aaron. You must remember how it was that O'rin first came to you?'

Frith frowned. 'He didn't come to me, I came to him. I travelled through the Nowhere Isles to Whittenfarne in search of the mages' words.'

'Think again. When you arrived on the island, after you had been abandoned by your ridiculous guide, what happened then?'

Frith glared at Joah. He seemed to be enjoying the conversation, as though they were in a tavern sharing tankards of ale.

'I walked across Whittenfarne. It was an awful place, covered in pools and mists.' He paused, remembering. 'I fell into one of the pools, actually. And something bit me.'

'And?'

'And the Edenier flared up, covering me briefly in fire and boiling the pool. O'rin found me after that.' Frith blinked, the truth finally hitting home. 'He felt it, or sensed it somehow. The magic. That was why he suddenly appeared, and that was why he agreed to teach me. Because he knew all along what I was.'

Joah nodded happily. 'And so it will be again, Aaron. We will create a blast of Edenier so powerful that your old teacher will not be able to resist it, wherever on Ede he happens to be now.'

'He won't be that stupid,' said Frith. 'And even if that were the case, he'll just assume it is me. Before you made your unexpected appearance, as far as anyone knew I was the only mage on Ede.'

'Not with the magical explosion I'm planning, Aaron. No one

271

man would be able to generate such levels of Edenier, and I don't think O'rin – lying, curious, interfering god – will be able to resist.'

Frith stood up, shaking himself brusquely. *The stone has made me sick*, he thought, *but it has only made him more insane.*

'How then? Are even you capable of such a feat?'

Joah laughed. 'You are forgetting, Aaron. We have the Rivener! With that we have a potentially unlimited amount of Edenier at our disposal, providing we can find a large enough supply of viable subjects.'

Frith paused. 'Viable subjects?'

'Yes. There is a small town nearby to begin with. We will need a larger population to get the sort of effect I'm looking for, so we'll start there, and move east across—'

'No!' Frith found himself close to shouting, and Joah took a startled step backwards in response. 'You would tear the souls from hundreds of people? It's monstrous! You are mad, completely insane, and I will not—'

Joah lunged for him physically this time, throwing him hard against the bunk. Frith fell awkwardly to the floor, wincing at the sound of Gwiddion's outraged squawks.

'Don't call me that!' howled Joah. The colour had dropped from his face, leaving him paper-white, and his brown eyes looked black. 'Don't you dare speak to me that way!'

'You are mad,' said Frith again, in a softer tone now. He put a hand to his mouth; there was blood on his lips where Joah had struck him. 'Somewhere underneath it all, you must see that. It's the demon, and the Heart-Stone. They've twisted you into something less than human.' He took a deep breath. 'These terrible things, they have changed you. But it's possible to come back from that. You have a choice.'

Joah stalked past him and began casting the blankets off the bed until Gwiddion was exposed. Frith scrambled to his feet, sick with the realisation that Joah had known about the bird all along.

He saw Gwiddion's tiny black eyes regarding him, intelligent and confused, before Joah picked the griffin up in his bird form and snapped his neck in one quick movement. The sound it made was pitifully small.

272

'Stop distracting me, Aaron,' said Joah. He threw the small feathered body at Frith, who caught it awkwardly in his arms. 'We'll never get anywhere if you keep distracting me.'

Wydrin, Nuava and Mendrick made it back to the surface just as the sun was creeping up over the horizon, lining the snow and the black rocks with a golden glow. They came out to the south of the original cave entrance and had to circle round to find their camp. Nuava had given Frostling and the light-globe back to Wydrin with a relieved expression and now sat atop Mendrick with her hood pulled up over her head. She was exhausted, but she no longer looked quite as lost, which Wydrin took to be an improvement.

When the small camp came in sight they saw Sebastian first of all, on his feet and tending a battered cooking pot he'd managed to suspend over a small fire. Dallen was some distance away, lying on his back. As they approached, Sebastian waved at them.

'How do you fancy some crab stew?' he said, gesturing with a spoon at the contents of the pot. Unidentifiable lumps floated in a thick, pinkish soup. 'Arichok stew, technically, but Dallen, that is, Prince Dallen, says it's perfectly fine to eat the flesh, although, of course, they usually eat it cold in the Frozen Steps and the variety they hunt there is significantly smaller than the beasts that you get this far north.' He pointed to a bloody carcass lying off to one side; segmented, furred legs pointed up to the sky. 'I've tasted a bit and it's not bad, better than endless cold meat anyway.' He paused for breath, during which Wydrin gave him her most withering raised eyebrow. 'Did you find what you were looking for?'

'I'll have some stew,' said Nuava. Sebastian passed her a cup, but Wydrin wasn't so easily deflected.

'What's the matter with him?' she said, nodding over to where Prince Dallen was lying, pointedly ignoring them all.

'Him? Just heat exhaustion. He'll be all right in a little while,' Sebastian pressed a cup of hot crab stew into Wydrin's hands, an expression of calculated innocence on his face that rang about as true as a fish with legs. 'We had a swarm of these Arichok attack all at once. Got quite frantic for a while there.'

'I bet it did,' said Wydrin, fighting not to smirk. 'I'd like to say we had an equally diverting time but I'm afraid we just spent the night fighting giant centipedes.'

'Giant . . .?'

'Giant centipedes.'

'Really, really ugly ones,' added Nuava.

'The good news is we found the nexus and Mendrick was able to locate Joah's base,' continued Wydrin. 'Even better news than that, it's not that far from here – no more than a day's hike.' She took a slurp of her crab stew, pausing to chew on a fatty lump. 'This *is* pretty good, actually.'

'I'm getting the impression', said Sebastian, 'that you're about to follow up these observations with bad news. Significantly bad news.'

Wydrin sighed. 'The bad news is that this Joah is madder than a box of cats in a storm, and although Frith is alive, he doesn't look like he'll be alive for much longer.'

'We should go, then,' said Dallen. He stood up and came over to them, pushing his hair back behind his ears. There were specks of what looked like sweat on his grey and brown forehead, and he looked unsteady on his feet. 'If we wish to save your friend and retrieve the Heart-Stone, we must move quickly.'

'How?' said Nuava. She had finished her stew and was in the middle of spooning more into her cup, but she stopped to look up at them. 'You saw how powerful he is, and what he's capable of. How can we hope to break into his stronghold?'

'Oh, we'll think of something on the way,' said Wydrin. 'That's what the Black Feather Three specialise in, you see – impossible tasks, snatching forbidden items from cursed temples, generally defying death for a modest fee. Well, Black Feather Two, I suppose.' She waved a hand at their small group. 'Black Feather Four, then. Or five. Whatever. We'll think of something. Sebastian, did you drink all my rum?'

41

'Wake up, little man, you must wake up!'

Frith groaned, trying to sink back down into featureless sleep, but the voice was insistent and loud. He opened his eyes and had a moment of extreme dislocation; he wasn't in the bunk room at all, but lying awkwardly on a steel-plated floor in one of the Forge's many red-lit corridors. He was still cradling Gwiddion's small body in one arm.

'What?'

Memories started to come back. The Edenier had burst into flickering life, covering his hands and arms in bright green flames, but Joah had laughed, had actually *laughed* at him, before a simple gesture had thrown Frith to the ground once more. After that he'd run, and Joah had made no attempt to come after him, apparently happy in the knowledge that Frith would never be able to force his way out of the Forge. Frith had sprinted down corridor after corridor, trying to summon the pink healing light for Gwiddion and failing, still failing. Eventually, his vision had grown dark at the edges and his legs had given way underneath him. And now he was here.

'It's you,' he said, although he could not see her. 'I know who you are.'

The darkness immediately to his left shifted and grew solid, and Xinian the Battleborn glared down at him. She was vivid but colourless, a person built of cold greys and blacks. Her ragged leathers and furs hung on her like spoiled flags.

'And you know what I did?'

'You killed him,' said Frith weakly. It was difficult to care about anything at the moment and the stern look on the woman's face exhausted him. 'Although, apparently, you didn't do a very thorough job.'

'Now it is your turn, shadow-mage. You have to stop him.'

Frith laughed softly, trying and failing to get to his feet. 'He killed Gwiddion, you know. I can't bring him back. He was my griffin.'

'Even now Joah Demonsworn is readying his spells and bringing them to life again. He is waking the Rivener and soon it will move.' Xinian's mouth turned down at the corners. 'He will kill thousands, as he has killed thousands before, and, poor excuse for a mage that you are, you are all that stands between him and the power he seeks.'

Frith braced his legs against the floor and pushed, sliding himself up the wall. Gwiddion's body began to fall out of his cloak so he carefully tucked it back into his wide inner pocket.

'It is impossible. Joah, although far from sane, is significantly more powerful than me.'

'So you will just give up?' said the woman. 'Fall down and let him do as he wishes?'

'No, I will not give up,' said Frith, feeling some of the old anger rekindle in his chest. 'And I'll thank you not to speak to me that way. And what do you mean, the Rivener will soon move?'

Xinian Battleborn crossed her arms over her chest and stepped back into the darkness, becoming nothing once more.

'If you do not hurry, I suspect you will find out exactly what I mean, shadow-mage.'

Frith stumbled down the corridor. There was a blinding pain behind his eyes now, and his stomach churned constantly. He wasn't sure exactly where he was, but he could hear a distant thrumming noise that also seemed to be vibrating up through his feet. Every now and then it went up in pitch, as though growing more urgent, so he headed towards it, figuring that he'd find Joah wherever the noise was coming from.

Eventually he came to the stairs that led downwards, and found Joah in the large room filled with iron plates. All of them were spinning now, the sigils on some of them glowing with pearly light. Joah moved between them, touching one to still it before pressing his fingers to another so that the sigils grew brighter. They doused his face in light as cold as the moon. At the sound of Frith's footsteps he glanced around before turning back to his work.

'Oh there you are, Aaron. I wondered where you'd got to. We are almost ready to go.'

Frith swallowed hard. 'To leave this place?'

Joah laughed. 'No, no, not at all. We could hardly do that.' Joah's hands flew over the sigils, lighting and extinguishing them, over and over. The thrumming grew louder. 'All those years ago, Aaron, when they took against me and they sent their assassins, they had a great deal of trouble finding me. And do you know why?'

He shot Frith a look over his shoulder, the look of a child with a scandalous secret.

'Because I would move the Forge. The whole thing. Just up and take it somewhere else. The spells involved are impossibly complicated, of course, the whole thing a fine mesh of Edenier and Edeian and demon magic, but it was a sight to see. And now the Rivener is so much more powerful than it was.'

Frith shook his head. 'Let's say I believe whatever it is you're raving on about.' He was too tired and too sick to be tactful now. 'Where are you taking it?'

'I'm glad you asked that, Aaron.' Joah reached into his robe and removed a piece of yellowed parchment, which he glanced at briefly before dropping it on the floor. 'A small settlement nearby, just to try the old girl out, and then I have a whole list of places where humans have gathered over the years. Should be more than we need.'

Frith took a deep breath, gathering his strength. If he was going to do anything he would have to do it now, before whatever it was that Joah was setting into motion truly got under way. He tried to summon the Edenier within him, to bend it to his will without the conduit of the mages' words. His fingers itched.

'Joah, please stop to think about this.' He came a few steps forward, forcing a smile on his face. 'I was hoping that we could have more time together, that I could learn more from you before we do anything rash. I feel so behind.'

Joah flapped a hand at Frith impatiently. The sigils on the plates were staying lit now, glowing with a brilliance like starlight.

'Don't be silly, Aaron. Once we have O'rin where we want him, neither of us shall have to struggle to know anything ever again. We will be gods ourselves.'

'I just want more time to think, to plan,' said Frith, edging closer. *If I can just get within reaching distance,* he told himself, *I will put my hands around his neck and pull forth all the Edenier I can. Perhaps if I surprise him, I will have some sort of chance.* 'I want to help you, Joah, I really do, but I want to be prepared.'

'You are afraid, Aaron, and that is understandable.' The plates were now spinning at a tremendous rate. 'After everything you've been through, my friend, I wouldn't expect anything less.'

At that moment there came a great clanging sound from down the corridor. Joah looked up, startled. 'What was that?'

The sound came again, a great metallic crash, and then again.

'I couldn't say for sure,' said Frith, feeling faint, 'but it sounds rather like someone is knocking on your door.'

Without looking at him, Joah ran from the room, robes flying, and Frith followed, struggling to keep up. They pounded up the darkened stairs and emerged once more in the central Forge room, the violet light of the Rivener seeming to stab at Frith's eyes. In here, the sound was much louder, as though someone were banging on the roof above them.

'What could that be?' said Joah, looking up at the red lights in the ceiling. For the first time he looked truly uncertain. 'There shouldn't be – there couldn't be anything up there.'

Frith looked around and spotted a knife lying on a nearby bench. He walked over to it and picked it up, keeping his movements slow and casual.

'An animal, perhaps?' he suggested in a normal tone of voice. He rolled up his sleeve and began to cut directly into his arm, willing himself to remember the shapes accurately enough. A curve here, a straight line there. Blood ran down his arm and soaked into his shirt, but he kept the blade moving, and his face blank. Joah still wasn't looking at him. 'You do seem to get some strange wildlife here.'

'But we are protected!' cried Joah. The noise came again. Clang, clang, clang. Flecks of rust floated down from the ceiling. 'The Forge is hidden.'

Frith cut the last part of the word, and immediately the Edenier surged within him, eager to be free after having been imprisoned for so long.

'Perhaps you are not as protected as you think.' He lifted his arm and summoned the word for Fire, throwing a fireball directly at Joah's head. The magic burst forth, burning a bright agony along every carved line in his flesh, and in close quarters, Joah was caught entirely unawares. The blast threw him across the room and into the wall, setting his robe and part of his hair on fire. Frith laughed and staggered, barely able to believe he'd managed it.

'How does that feel, you mad bastard?' He held up his arm, ready to throw another wall of flame, but Joah was already on his feet and Frith was frozen again, one hand held out in front of him. As he watched, unable to move, Joah extinguished the small fires on his robes, and patted his hair down absently. One side of his face was lividly pink, and his right hand was bleeding. His eyes were alarmingly blank.

'Oh,' he said. 'Oh, Aaron.'

Frith strained against the spell holding him in place, feeling the cuts on his arm burn fiercely. Nothing happened. Joah came over to him slowly, almost dragging his feet.

'We're brothers, you and I,' said Joah in that strange, empty voice. 'My only brother. You lost yours, and I thought I could be a replacement. Someone to make up for what happened to Tristan and Leon.'

Frith tried to force a scream up through his throat. *How dare you?* he wanted to scream. *How dare you think you could replace them?* The clanging noise from above continued, an unceasing rhythm.

Joah stood in front of him. Up close, Frith could see that the fire had done more damage than he'd initially thought. If Joah had been a normal man, he would have been in serious trouble.

Quick as a snake, Joah grabbed Frith by the throat and dragged him, helpless, over towards the corrupted form of the Heart-Stone, burning with its evil light. It was almost entirely black now, a crusted lump run through with veins of glowing amethyst. Frith could feel the poison coming off it in waves, like a fever, and tried with all his strength to pull away.

'You probably think I haven't noticed', said Joah absently, 'that the Heart-Stone has had a debilitating effect on you. It is a shame, that to use it so causes such a poison to leak into the air. How is it looking now, Aaron?'

Joah shoved him forward, pushing so that Frith's head was halfway into the aperture and his vision was filled with the stone. The pain behind Frith's eyes increased tenfold and now he did scream, the pain forcing its way up his throat and through his lips. His whole body recoiled, and he began to shake violently.

I'm going to have a seizure, he thought wildly. *This is how I'll die.*

Joah held him there for a few moments longer, and then dropped him to the floor. Frith hit the cold iron gratefully, curling up so that his knees were under his chin.

'You were supposed to be my brother!' Joah was shouting now, the strange distant tone vanishing from his voice. 'You were supposed to help me! How can you let me down like this?' He kicked Frith in the stomach once, viciously, and then turned away. 'AND WHAT IS THAT FUCKING NOISE?'

42

Sebastian drew his sword and stood at the ready.

'Are you sure this is wise?'

Wydrin was standing part way up the small hill, watching Mendrick at work. They had found a dent in the ground surrounded by unstable rock and under Wydrin's instruction Mendrick had set to work uncovering what lay beneath. A few hours later, and he'd stepped away, his stony face as expressionless as ever. By this time it was late afternoon and the shadows were growing long. Underneath the loose stones there was a wide panel of what looked like iron, engraved with sigils Sebastian didn't recognise, and now Mendrick was jumping up and down on it, causing a great reverberating clang that echoed flatly off the neighbouring hills.

'We can't get in there by ourselves,' said Wydrin firmly. 'So we're just going to have to draw the bastard out. He'll soon wonder who is knocking in his ceiling.'

'I can't believe it,' said Nuava. She was standing near the werken, Wydrin's dagger held uncertainly in one hand. 'I can't believe it's really here.'

'He has corrupted our very lands,' said Dallen. The prince stood next to Sebastian, an ice-spear held loosely under his arm. 'I can feel the Heart-Stone from here. It is very sick.'

'I still don't understand the plan,' said Nuava, a slight tremor in her voice. 'I mean, I understand that we're luring Joah out here.' She paused as the werken made another jump, stone feet clanging against the iron. 'But once he comes out, then what?'

'Ah, that's the interesting bit,' said Wydrin, coming a few steps down towards them all. She had Glassheart in one hand, and she waved it for emphasis, 'because I'm buggered if I know.'

Nuava opened her mouth, and then closed it again.

'What Wydrin means to say,' said Sebastian, 'is that we may be playing it by ear. We have very few advantages, save for surprise and a foolhardy disregard for our own safety. However, we hope that we can get some strikes in before Joah gets up to full power, and we hope that Frith is still in some condition to fight, somewhere in there.'

'Ah, hope,' said Nuava. She had gone slightly pale. 'We hope that we don't all die horribly?'

'That's the spirit!' said Wydrin. 'From what Mendrick can see, the weaknesses in the rock indicate that the hill will open down this seam here.' She pointed at a rough depression in the ground, a crack that ran down to the bottom of the hill. It was difficult to spot unless you knew where to look, half covered as it was in snow. 'So make sure you stay above and to the side of it. When Joah comes out, we don't want him to see us immediately. Sebastian and Dallen are our main force, whereas we are surprise back-up.'

'Always a pleasure,' said Sebastian. 'Wydrin, you'll have to move quickly if—'

The ground beneath began to shake. Wydrin scurried over to one side, waving them back hurriedly. The rocks and thin layer of earth covering the hill around the crack flexed and bucked, as though suffering an extremely localised earthquake. Nuava shouted in alarm, still holding the dagger awkwardly in both hands. As they watched, the hill itself cracked down the middle, revealing a dark crevasse and an iron door. Joah Demonsworn stepped from it, and immediately Sebastian felt his unease increase tenfold. The Joah they had seen before had been deadly but calm, cheerful almost. This man was in a black fury, and he looked as if he had been recently burnt; one half of his face was red and peeling, and parts of his robes were blackened.

'What is the meaning of this?' he demanded as he stalked out of the entrance. 'I cannot be disturbed at such a time—'

There was a shout from Wydrin, and Mendrick leapt from the

top of the broken hill down into the heart of the newly opened path, directly at Joah Demonsworn. The mage seemed to catch the rapidly approaching shadow out of the corner of his eye and he ran, but not quite fast enough. A ton of falling masonry caught him on the shoulder, throwing him face down onto the ground. Sebastian ran forward, sword held ready to his shoulder for a killing blow.

'Now!' called Wydrin. 'Let's bloody do it!'

Amazingly, Joah was crawling to his feet already, although he looked stunned and was holding his arm awkwardly. Sebastian kept coming, and saw an ice-spear go flying past him. It hit the rogue mage on the other shoulder and pushed him down again in a shower of jagged ice.

By Isu, thought Sebastian, *we might actually get a chance at this.*

Without pausing to think, he brought his sword down in a powerful arc, meaning to sever Joah's head from his body in one move and have done with it. But instead of the satisfying bite of steel into flesh, there was the strangest sense of drag – he saw the point of his sword enter Joah's neck, but it passed on through as though he were made of something insubstantial. Sebastian staggered with the momentum of the blow, thrown off balance, and Joah looked up, his eyes strangely blank.

'I do beg your pardon,' he said mildly. 'You believe I would not take precautions against mere steel blades?'

'Wydrin,' cried Sebastian, 'bloody get in there.'

He glanced up to see his partner, already climbing her way down to the iron door. *This is it, then,* he thought, *we've had the best possible start we could have had. We'll just have to hold out until Frith is back in the game.*

Sensing Dallen at his back now, armed with more ice-spears, Sebastian levelled his sword once more.

'I believe you took something of ours,' he said, 'and we would like it back.'

Something sharp was digging into Frith's chest. With some difficultly, he explored his cloak with his fingers until he found the source of the discomfort; it was Gwiddion, the griffin's small bird beak jabbing him in the rib. The body was cold now, his small black eyes dusty.

'Dead,' croaked Frith. 'Still dead.'

'As you will be, shadow-mage, if you do not get away from that abomination.'

Frith looked up from the floor to see Xinian looking down at him. She was no longer composed of shadows and half-seen things. Now she looked solid and real; he could see the deep warm brown of her skin, the sharp intelligence in her eyes. There was a scar on her left cheek, a horizontal slash, and she wore silver rings up both her arms.

'You see me now, little man? You see me clearly, yes? It is because you are dying. As you lie there, mewling on the floor, you move ever closer to the shade world.'

Frith shook his head. He felt as though every part of him had been beaten. His head was a hot ring of fire, and he could taste blood in his mouth.

'He will be back soon,' he said, and even those few words made his vision turn black at the edges. 'And he'll end it then, at least. He has to.'

Xinian the Battleborn scowled at him. The bruise-coloured light from the Rivener shone off her bald head.

'No, *you* must end *him*.' She paused, and looked behind her as though she had heard someone coming. 'I am going to give you a memory, shadow-mage. A memory that is a key. Let's see what you can do with it.'

She reached down and the touch of her hand on his forehead was blessedly cool.

'If you're a ghost, how can I . . . ?'

It was the same as when Joah had performed the 'crossing'. One moment he was lying on the floor of the Forge, the next he was in another place entirely. It looked like an abandoned city full of white marble buildings, lit with a strange, shifting blue light. The streets were empty. He saw Xinian there, looking much as she had done in the Forge, and she was running beside another woman, a mage in travelling leathers and a short cloak. She was carrying a long staff carved with mage words, and her pale blond hair was tied into a pair of winding braids that rested on her

284

head like a nest of snakes. Xinian carried a strange sword in her hand; the blade was a deep, shining blue and it curved to a wicked point. For some reason it felt familiar to Frith, although he couldn't place why.

'We have him now,' cried the blonde woman. They had stopped in front of a bulbous white marble building shaped like a fat teardrop. 'Where else would a bone conjuror like him hide, but in a crypt?'

'You wait here, Selsye,' said Xinian. 'And I shall go after him.'

The other woman's laugh echoed strangely in the silent street. 'Treasure of my life, but you do say some strange things. Of course we shall go together.'

'I have the god-blade.' Xinian's stern expression was familiar. 'Only I can kill him. You will be in danger.'

'I will be a distraction,' the blonde woman called Selsye smiled. 'I will keep his attention diverted while you move in for the kill. No one can wield that sword like you, my love, but we need all the help we can get at this point. We've already lost so many.'

Xinian pursed her lips, looking as though she might argue further, but in the end she nodded.

The two women entered the crypt, and Frith followed, a silent shadow. The memory faded before another came to take its place, and all at once Frith was in the middle of a pitched battle. He was in a low-ceilinged room, lit with magical fire. He saw the mage called Selsye, crouched behind a stone tomb, periodically firing shots of bright green flame from her staff towards a man in dark robes. It was Joah. He was standing against a rack of mouldering shelves filled with ancient skeletons, both hands held out in front of him, holding off the woman's magical attack with apparent ease. There were other shadows moving in the chaotic darkness: bony, skeletal shadows. Frith spotted Xinian herself, whirling and striking like a snake, dashing the skeletal assassins to pieces with her strange sword, but she was being pressed back into an alcove. As he watched, she held up her other arm, the one that ended in a stump, and a wave of freezing ice flew from it, trapping several of the walking corpses in a sudden snow drift.

'That's it, ladies,' bellowed Joah, 'come to your deaths!' He was grinning wildly, his hair hanging in his face. None of the gentle manners Frith had experienced from the rogue mage were in evidence here.

'It is your death that is coming for you, Demonsworn!' cried Selsye. She flicked an enormous fireball over the top of the tomb, and it crashed into Joah, blasting pieces of bone and rock across the small room, but when the flames had passed, Joah was still there. He laughed.

'They send you two to finish me? Have they learned nothing?'

He waved a hand, almost casually, and the lid of the tomb Selsye was hiding behind suddenly flew backwards, striking her full in the face. Frith heard the terrible noise the stone made as it crushed her skull to powder, saw the bright splash of blood against the dusty floor.

There was a howl of anguish. Xinian the Battleborn stormed across the chamber, her face wild with grief and fury. She elbowed past the reaching skeletons without even looking at them and threw herself at Joah.

To her credit, even Joah looked startled by the extent of her rage. He sent a bright pulse of red light shooting towards her that punched into her flesh just below the ribcage. Frith saw the burning hole left by the attack but it did not slow her down. In seconds she was on him, and Joah Demonsworn, genius and greatest of mages, was too surprised to do anything about it. She thrust the sword home with a scream of triumph and it burst out through his back.

For the briefest moment they stood together, two people joined by a sword. Joah glanced down at the hilt sticking out of his chest. He looked mildly surprised.

'But the demon,' he said, and blood ran over his lips. 'The demon told me . . . no steel can harm . . .'

'This is not steel,' spat Xinian through gritted teeth. 'Die now, and may my face be the last thing you see.'

Joah nodded, as if agreeing with her, and slid slowly to the ground. Xinian braced one foot against his chest and drew the sword out, before staggering away. She took four, maybe five steps, trying to reach Selsye, before collapsing onto the ground herself. The strange blue sword dropped from her fingers to land next to a grinning skull.

'And that is where it is still.'

Frith blinked rapidly. He was back in the Forge with Xinian the Battleborn standing over him, conspicuously missing the hole in her chest.

'The sword?'

She nodded once. 'The only thing capable of killing Joah Demonsworn is the god-blade. And it rests in the lost city of Temerayne, along with my remains, along with my beloved Selsye.'

Frith shook his head. There were too many questions. 'But his body was in a tomb in Skaldshollow! They said the mages gave him a full burial, because they honoured him.'

Xinian grinned at him without humour. 'It was not a mage that collected Joah's body, but agents of the demon. You are our last chance, shadow-mage, and you must stay alive.'

There was the clang of an iron door, and Frith could hear shouting. He tried to lift himself up onto one elbow, to ask Xinian more questions, but already she was fading from view.

287

43

Wydrin ran down the metal corridor, wincing at the sound her boots made on the strange floor. Glassheart was held ready in both hands.

'They'd better keep him busy out there,' she muttered to herself. 'I don't much fancy him popping up behind me.'

She emerged cautiously into a large round room full of stone benches and rusted instruments, lit with a strange purple light that gave her an instant headache. There was a still form sprawled on the floor.

'Frith?' Wydrin went over to him, sheathing her sword. It was Frith, but she barely recognised him. His warm brown skin was grey, and he'd lost weight, so that his already sharply angled face looked almost skeletal. His eyes fluttered open at the sound of her voice.

'Wydrin? Is that you?'

'Ye gods and little fishes, what has he done to you?' He was bleeding from his ears, and one of his arms was encrusted with blood. 'Can you get up, Frith? We need to get you out of here.'

'She gave me a memory,' he said. His eyes rolled up to the whites, before he coughed, blinking rapidly.

'That's it, keep talking to me,' she said. 'Even if it is nonsense, just keep talking. I need you awake.' She slipped an arm around his back and lifted him into a sitting position. He took hold of her arm and gripped it fiercely, as though they were walking into a howling gale and he might blow away otherwise.

'Wydrin, he broke into my mind, saw everything. He killed Gwiddion.'

'Come on.' Wydrin bit her lip, and pulled him inelegantly to his feet. They staggered together for a moment, until Wydrin convinced him to lean on her, one arm slung over her shoulders, her own arm wrapped around his waist. 'I'm sorry, Frith, I really am. Let's get you out of this shit hole.'

They lurched towards the far door. From outside they could hear the distant sounds of shouting and the occasional rumble as a magical attack hit the ground.

'When we get outside, we may have to make a run for it.' Wydrin shifted her grip on him, trying to ignore the boniness of his ribs. 'I don't think you're in any fit state to be taking on this Joah bastard.'

'I did burn him,' said Frith. Some strength seemed to be coming back to his voice. 'I burnt the bastard.'

Wydrin laughed. 'Glad to hear it.'

They'd reached the iron corridor. At the end of it they could see orange and blue light flashing. Frith squeezed her shoulder.

'I thought I'd never see you again.'

Wydrin glanced at him, but his head was hanging down and his face was hidden by his unruly white hair.

'Don't be ridiculous,' she said. 'You don't get rid of me that easily.'

Sebastian hit the ground, rolling so that his cloak flapped over him wetly. He looked up to see the wave of burning flame pass over him and hit the snow-covered outcrop behind him. A cloud of steam billowed like a ghost. *That was a close one.*

And they had been lucky so far. Joah seemed extremely distracted, throwing attacks without seeming to care where they fell, making strange mistakes, such as aiming a cone of freezing blizzard at Dallen, who only felt revitalised by such magic. Sebastian thought it could be the burns – perhaps the pain was making him careless – or the injury he'd taken to the shoulder when Mendrick had jumped at him, but, whatever it was, his lack of concentration had allowed them all to live this long. Dallen moved past him, throwing an ice-spear like a javelin, and beyond him, Nuava crouched behind Mendrick.

There was movement in the tunnel. Sebastian saw Wydrin come staggering out, supporting Frith, who was leaning on her heavily. They were moving as quickly as they were able to, trying to get to shelter, but Joah turned at their approach. All at once, his magical attacks died. The small hill grew very quiet. Sebastian could hear Dallen's ragged breathing, and the sound of the wind beginning to pick up.

'Aaron?' Joah's voice was quiet, but they all heard it clearly enough. 'What are you doing out here? You need to rest.'

Wydrin drew her sword, holding it awkwardly whilst still supporting Frith.

'Your big mage reunion is over now,' she said. 'So just back off.'

'This is the woman, isn't it?' Joah took a few steps towards them. 'Aaron, I thought we talked about this. We can have no distractions. These people, they will only keep you from greatness.'

Frith shook his head. 'There is no greatness, Joah. Only your madness. You have to let me go. You have to let all of this go.'

Joah reached up and touched his own face. Absently he began to peel away his burnt skin.

'Aaron, think about what you are saying. We could do great things! I am offering you a brotherhood you've never experienced.'

Sebastian shifted, getting ready to run. Joah was turned away from him now, apparently having completely forgotten about the rest of them.

'I want nothing from you,' Frith raised his voice. 'You are not my brother!'

For a few seconds there was silence again. In the dying light of the evening Joah looked like a raggedy scarecrow, some pretence of a man left on the hill to scare away the ghosts. He shook himself once, all over.

'Then I shall take from you everything you truly want.'

Sebastian moved immediately, running now towards the couple standing together at the mouth of the tunnel.

'Wydrin!' he shouted. 'Get down!'

But it was too late. Joah held up one hand and a bolt of silver lightning shot from the ends of his fingers, striking Wydrin square

290

in the chest and blowing her off her feet. Sebastian had time to see the horror on Frith's face as she was torn out of his arms, and then the young lord was a churning mass of light and heat. Somewhere within it all, Sebastian could hear Frith bellowing with fury.

'You see what you can be?' screamed Joah. 'Look at your true power!'

A bolt of fiery light shot from the boiling mass that was Frith but Joah caught it somehow, moulding it into a ball of flames in his hands.

Sebastian crouched low and ran towards Wydrin's prone body. She had hit a pile of rocks and was sprawled with her red hair covering her face. Sebastian pushed it away, trying to see some life there. He placed a hand against her chest and almost felt his own heart stop. *No, no,* he thought. *Not like this.*

'Frith!' he called, half hopeless against the deafening roar. Joah and Frith were exchanging fireballs now; Joah's were landing with accuracy, Frith's were wild and unfocussed. 'I need you over here, Frith!' *If he is lost to his rage now,* thought Sebastian, *then we've lost her too.* 'Now, Frith!'

Joah threw an enormous wave of flame that blotted out the sky, and for a few moments everything was chaos. Sebastian covered Wydrin's body with his own, remembering Y'Ruen's attack on the battlefield at Relios. When it was over, he looked up to see Joah running back down the tunnel into the hill.

'He's retreating!' cried Dallen, who threw an ice-spear after him to be sure. 'We have him now.'

'No,' said Frith. The light surrounding him winked out, and he staggered. His face was the colour of old milk. 'We have to get out of here. The Rivener is rising.'

As he spoke, the ground beneath their feet began to jump and shake. Sebastian gathered Wydrin's limp form into his arms and they all turned and ran down the hill, Frith staggering to keep up. The rock cracked and splintered. Sebastian found himself dodging huge chunks of stone as they thrust up through the ground, and it was all he could do to keep on his feet.

They reached the lower ground and turned just in time to see the hill tearing itself apart. An avalanche of stone and earth rumbled down towards them as something moved under the fabric of the ground. A great stone and metal arm, like a werken's but much, much bigger, burst through, reaching for the sky with a clawed hand.

'By all the gods, what is that?' cried Nuava.

The metal and stone creature dragged itself free of the hilltop, shaking off the earth and stone like a dog in a muddy puddle. Sebastian saw Edeian-rippled stone joined to huge pieces of iron, all covered in glowing runes and darkly shining words. He saw moving parts, held together by rivets and magic, and he saw two pairs of enormous glowing eyes, like violet-hued lamps against a stormy sky. Free of the hill, the Rivener looked like the offspring of a man and a beetle – a humanoid shape with six jointed limbs, covered in plates of black iron like chitinous armour. There was a glowing aperture in the thing's head, a slot filled with swirling purple light, and just beneath that there was what looked like a caged platform. Sebastian caught one glance of Joah there, standing with his hands wrapped around the iron railing, and then the Rivener took three or four faltering steps, turning away from them. It was silhouetted against the red evening sky, a monstrous shape straight out of a nightmare, and then it was sprinting away from them, skittering across the hills.

PART THREE
The Graces' Own

44

Truss took the flask from his belt and held it between his hands. Heated by his wife that morning, he could still feel some remnants of warmth through his gloves. He unscrewed the lid and took a large gulp, wincing slightly as the warm grut burnt its way down to his empty stomach, before pushing the flask back through his belt loop. He'd have to pace the stuff; he was likely to be up here for several hours yet, and with little chance of anyone covering his post.

From his vantage point on top of Skaldshollow's southern wall he could see soft snow-covered hills, the distant brown blur that was the riverlands, and the looming presence of the mountains to the west, seeming to smudge out half the noon-day sky.

To his left he saw Ninnev approaching on the back of her werken; it was her job to patrol the southern side, back and forth, back and forth, while he sat where he was, his own werken a quiet pile of rock beneath him.

'Anything to report, Truss?' she called as she grew nearer. She was a few years older than him, her black hair cut short above her ears, and she rode a werken shaped roughly like a giant bear. Its green eyes shone white in the brightness of the day.

'Nothing of interest, Ninnev,' he replied. 'Unless you wish me to report a thoroughly frozen arse and an increasingly irresistible desire to throw myself off this wall?'

Ninnev smirked. 'No one wishes to know the condition of your arse, Truss, believe me.' She drew up close to him, the werken stopping dead in its tracks. 'No movement out there?'

'Nothing at all, honestly. I am sitting here waiting for the snow to fall.'

'Well, it's probably a good idea for you to sit tight for a while.' She nodded at his werken. It had taken substantial damage during the attack, and now a goodly section of its back right leg was patched up with the substance they half jokingly referred to as 'witch's porridge'. It was a rough paste mixed by Tamlyn Nox herself, used to fill cracks and holes when a werken was damaged. After the attack a great number of Skaldshollow's werkens were sporting ugly grey patches of the stuff.

'Aye, I know. You're right,' said Truss, frowning slightly. 'It just seems like I'm wasting my time up here. He isn't coming back, or at least, if he is, he won't just walk up to our front door. I should be down there, helping to rebuild, or drilling with the troops.' Reaching down to his belt again, he passed the flask of grut across to Ninnev, who took a grateful sip. She passed it back with a nod. 'Sitting here, staring out at nothing all day. Just doesn't seem like the best use of me and my werken, if you see what I mean.'

Ninnev shrugged, as though she wasn't quite inclined to agree one way or another. Despite everything, it was still difficult for them to question the Mistress Crafter's orders.

'Out of interest, what makes you think he isn't coming back?' she asked eventually.

Truss glanced behind her, looking down into the city. He could see the grey forms of werkens moving slowly up and down the streets, looking like drowsy beetles from here.

'Why would he?' he said. 'We're prepared now. We're an entire city, with an army behind us and a force of war-werkens. He won't take us by surprise again, and he is just one man. I don't care how much magic he has, he is just one man.'

'One man, over three hundred dead,' pointed out Ninnev.

'We let him in –' He paused, swallowing the rest of that sentence. *She* let him in. 'Who could have predicted that?' He shook himself abruptly. 'Bloody hell, but it's cold up here.'

Ninnev smiled. 'Spoken like a native Skald. Do you have water in your veins like the Narhl?'

Truss laughed. 'I've grut in my veins, mostly.'

296

There was a scrabbling on the wooden trellis that led up to the lookout post and a small, dirty head appeared over the ladder. It was a girl of about twelve years old, her hair cut close to her scalp. Her face was smeared with dirt and she wore a miserable collection of rags and furs. There was a bulky-looking pack slung over her back.

'What's this, then?' asked Truss, bemused. 'Have you come to take over from me, little one? Got sharp eyes, have you?'

Ninnev rolled her eyes at him. 'It's just one of Sal's little brats,' she said, waving a hand dismissively. 'Here to sell you hot bread and questionable meat, if I'm any judge.'

Truss shook his head at her and turned to the girl. 'Is that it, little one? Have you brought something to save me from starving to death? Ninnev here would happily watch me fall off my werken with hunger.'

The girl just looked at him blankly, impervious to his light tone. She was probably simple, he reasoned. Sal often took in wastrels like that: orphans left behind by tragedy, or children that had simply been forgotten by everyone else.

Ninnev huffed with annoyance. 'Well, speak up or get back down that ladder, girl. The top of the wall is no place for a lost child.'

The girl seemed to react more to Ninnev's tone, and she stuttered into action. Coming over to them she shouldered off her pack and pulled out a package wrapped in brown cloth. Truss caught the faint but unmistakable aroma of freshly cooked bread. His stomach rumbled in response.

'Bread, is it? Do you not talk, girl?'

She looked at him, eyes wide, before looking down at the stones beneath her feet and shaking her head.

'Ah, well, I'll take it. Go nice with a bit of warmed grut, I suppose. How much?'

Glancing back up she held out her free hand with three fingers pointing up.

'Three bits?' grunted Truss, glancing at Ninnev. 'I see old Sal has been raising her prices. What, she got more brats to look after these days?'

Ninnev frowned at him.

297

'I expect she has,' she said pointedly. 'Over three hundred dead, remember.'

'Oh. Oh yes.' Truss rummaged in a pocket, bringing out a handful of small copper bits. 'Here, kid, take this.' He leaned down as far as he could from the saddle of the werken, and the girl reached up. When her thin white fingers touched his he shivered compulsively. It was a little like being glanced by an ice-spear. 'There's five bits there, and give my regards to Sal.'

The girl shoved the pennies into a hidden pocket, before passing up the package of bread.

'Go on now,' said Ninnev. 'I think you've made enough of a nuisance of yourself.'

The girl nodded rapidly, retreating so swiftly that she almost went backwards off the wall. Their last sight of her was her short brown hair being tousled by the wind as she made her way back down the ladder, and then she was gone.

'Old Sal must be raking it in now,' said Ninnev, 'with all these extra hands.'

Truss shifted in his seat. His arse was still frozen, but the warm package of bread in his hands had brightened him a little.

'Ah, you've a cold heart, Ninnev,' he said mildly. 'I hope she'll be all right. Poor little mouse looks like she's been through a lot.'

Ip scrambled down the ladder, holding the face of the woman in her mind as she did so. A small insult, perhaps, but Bezcavar was much in the mood lately to make note of small insults.

Once the girl was back on the icy ground she ran, weaving in and out of men and women slowly making their repairs to the city, around werkens trudging here and there with carts full of building supplies. It was important to keep moving. If you looked like you were on your way somewhere, people were less inclined to look closely. The watchers on the wall had been fooled easily enough; to these people she was just another orphan child, a victim of Joah Demonsworn's brutal attack.

Joah. At the thought of him Ip's face creased briefly into a scowl.

Where is he? What is he doing? Bezcavar could feel his mind every now and then, a slippery, dark-red faceted thing linked to its own consciousness, but he had always been so difficult to read – in a way, his mind was the opposite of Siano's. Where the young assassin had been all cold surfaces and chilly reflections, Joah was a bewildering honeycomb of thoughts, ideas, passions. The demon could never touch it for long without becoming lost.

He was greatly taken up with something, that was for certain, and it involved the pompous Lord Frith, but the demon could tell little more than that.

He needs to hurry up, whatever it is, Bezcavar thought. *I can't hide out here for ever.*

Leave, then. It was Ip's voice, her real voice, so rarely heard now. In truth, the demon was startled to hear it. *Why don't we just go?*

And travel across the frozen wastes by ourselves? Your child's body could not live through it, as well you know.

We are clever, together, replied Ip. *We could find supplies, a map. If you would just let me come forward a bit . . .*

Enough. Bezcavar let its true shape surface inside the child's mind, just for the barest moment – something monstrous and blind surfacing from the darkest part of the ocean – and felt Ip scuttle back to her hiding places. *It is not your place to question me.*

Ip fell silent then, and Bezcavar was glad.

Rounding another corner, they came to Sal's hovel, a low draughty building that the other children said had once been a butcher's shop. Certainly there were strange, dark stains on the stones and the place seemed to perpetually smell of blood and mouldering flesh. Sal herself was sitting on a stool by the front door, a basket full of wrapped loaves on her lap, her bony hands wrapped around the rim in a vice-like grip. She was a withered prune of a woman, half lost inside the dusty black robe she wore, but her skinny frame hid a particularly vicious kind of strength; she may have looked ready to drop dead at any moment, but old Sal could clip a child around the ear with deadly accuracy, and her well-placed pinches always left colourful bruises. Ip could testify to that herself.

'There you are, my newly minted pain in the arse.' Sal was well spoken, her voice sharp at the edges. Not for the first time

Bezcavar wondered who she really was, and where she'd fallen from. 'What have you got for old Sal?'

She reached out and grabbed hold of Ip's forearm, squeezing until it was painful.

'Here.' Hurriedly, Ip reached into her pocket and held out the copper bits she'd made that day. Sal snatched them up, offering her a brief, snaggle-toothed grin.

'No messing about from you, is there, my little earwig? That's what I like to see. Any talk from around the town? Anything we should know from up on the wall?'

'They're bored,' she said. 'Waiting to see what will happen. They're trying to be prepared.' *Not that that will help them, when Joah returns.*

'Well, Bestina,' Sal crooned the name as though she knew very well that it was false, 'you'd best get below before we're all murdered in our beds, hadn't you?'

Knowing that hesitating would earn Ip a bruise, she turned away and headed through the shadowed doorway. Inside were a few dirty rooms linked by a corridor, and scruffy children lurked in every doorway. Most of them eyed her with distrust, or plain boredom; most of them were too hungry to care about the latest addition to Sal's orphans. Ip headed past them to the steps that led to the cellar, and walked down into the gloom; something about the dark and the smell of old blood comforted Bezcavar. In the corner, three children whose names Ip did not know were playing a game with stone markers. As she watched, one of them obviously lost, skimming his stone off into a dusty corner, and the other children merrily punched him on the arm, hard enough for Ip to see tears start in his eyes. *That's the thing with children,* thought Bezcavar, watching as the older two found that the game of beating the loser was more fun than the game of stone markers, *they are so open to the idea of cruelty they barely even have to think about it.*

Standing apart from them in the shadows, Ip's face split into its first genuine smile since Joah had vanished.

Little demons, every one.

45

'Let me see her!'

Frith barged Sebastian aside, and he was still strong, despite how ill he looked. Sebastian drew away. Wydrin was lying on a pile of blankets they'd thrown down, her eyes shut, her hands open with the palms facing up. Always pale, now she was a sister to the snows that lay about them. Every freckle stood out on her face with alarming clarity.

'Fetch me my silks. Now.' Frith glared at them all, his grey eyes fierce. 'You must have some left?'

Sebastian, glad for his hands to be doing something, rummaged through one of their bags until he came up with a handful of long fabric strips, all inked with mages' words. Frith snatched them from him, dumping all but one on the ground. Mendrick stood facing them, his stone body utterly still. Prince Dallen cleared his throat.

'My friend, I am sorry, but surely—'

'Be quiet,' said Frith. He tied the remaining strip around his hand and immediately a warm orb of pink light grew from the centre of his palm. Laying his hands on her chest, the pink light grew, flowing around her body like thick honey.

'She's not breathing,' said Nuava in a low voice. 'I've checked. Her blood is still.'

Frith ignored them all. The light grew stronger, until the hill was bathed in rosy light. Wydrin did not move.

'Come on,' muttered Frith. He was shaking with the effort of

301

it now, the first droplets of sweat forming on his forehead. In the strange pink light his eyes were lost in hollows of shadow. 'Wydrin, please. Come on.'

Sebastian knelt back down and placed a hand on her forehead, pushing her hair back from her brow. Her eyelids did not so much as flicker.

'Frith,' he said, hating himself for speaking, hating himself for saying anything at all. 'Frith, I don't think—'

'*Shut up.*' The pink light blazed with sudden brilliance, a strange grapefruit sun in the middle of that cold place, before suddenly winking out and throwing them back into the gloom. Frith fell backwards, gasping and trembling.

Wydrin lay utterly still.

'Frith, I don't think there's anything we can do,' said Sebastian. 'I'm sorry.'

'No,' said Frith, and now his voice was a broken croak. 'I won't allow it, I won't.'

'Look at that.' Nuava came over and knelt on the blankets next to Wydrin. She took one of Wydrin's cold hands in her own and held it up to them. The chip of green Heart-Stone in the palm of her hand was glowing, on and off, like a heartbeat. 'I've never seen one do that before. What do you suppose it means?'

Sebastian looked over to Mendrick, who was still standing without moving, his green eyes apparently fixed on Wydrin's inert form.

'I think it means that there's nothing *we* can do.'

Wydrin opened her eyes. It was the hardest thing she'd ever done.

She found herself lying on her side, her limbs curled up as though she were trying to deflect a blow. Around her there was a grey darkness, and underneath, a shining web of green light, shifting and trembling. It was holding her up, she realised. Without it she'd be lost in the void.

'Mendrick? Are you there?'

'I am.' His voice was faint, but all around her.

'What's happening?'

'You are dying, I believe,' he said, in his utterly calm voice. 'But I caught you before you went. The thread between us wasn't completely severed.'

302

'Oh.' She tried to move, and the web shivered alarmingly. She felt very weak. 'Well, thanks for that. Now what?'

'You must decide if you wish to go back,' he said. 'You must decide if you have the will to go on living, or—'

'Of course I bloody do!' Wydrin tried to sit up again and the net of green lights swung and pulsed. 'What sort of bloody question is that?'

There was a moment's silence from Mendrick. Wydrin pressed her fingers against one of the strands of light, watching as it shone through her palm, revealing the bones inside. She tried not to think about the yawning darkness below the web.

'Humans are so concerned with moving about and living,' Mendrick said dryly. 'I am not sure I understand it. Everything comes to the same end, eventually.'

'Yes, but not right *now*. I have things to do.'

'In that case, I will push you back,' said Mendrick. 'Be ready.'

It was like being thrown into the ocean fully clothed. The shock of the cold air and the warmth of her own body hit her all at once and Wydrin jerked violently, gasping for air. The small group of people all gathered round her cried out as one, and then there was a lot of shouting from Sebastian.

'By Isu! Give her some space, get back!' Completely ignoring his own advice he knelt in the snow and grabbed her, squeezing her into a backbreaking bear hug. 'Wydrin, you're alive!'

She smacked him weakly on the back. Behind him Nuava and Dallen stood together, joint grins on their faces, while Frith knelt in the snow next to her, his eyes wide with shock.

'I'm alive all right, although you're squeezing it back out of me, you big idiot.'

Sebastian held her at arm's length. 'How do you feel? What hurts? Are you warm enough?'

'I feel quite good considering how dead I was a moment ago, and my head hurts like a bastard, and I'm freezing bloody cold. What happened to Joah?'

'The mage fled,' said Dallen, 'in some sort of infernal machine. He still has the Heart-Stone.'

'He struck you with a bolt of lightning,' said Frith. She turned

303

to him and was alarmed to see that he looked even worse than he had in Joah's Forge; his cheeks looked hollowed out and his hair was plastered to his forehead with sweat. He also appeared to be shaking slightly. 'It must have stopped your heart. I couldn't – I couldn't bring you back.'

Wydrin glanced over to where the werken stood.

'My link to Mendrick saved me. It stopped me from falling.'

There were a few moments of silence. Wydrin saw the confusion on every face and sighed inwardly; there was no easy way to explain such things.

'How is that possible?' asked Nuava. 'We've never noticed such a benefit before.'

'Wydrin's link to the mountain-spirit is very deep,' said Prince Dallen. He looked pointedly at Nuava. 'I strengthened the link myself, in order to prove that the being you call a werken was a thinking, feeling entity. It appears this link prevented Wydrin's soul from leaving her body.'

'Never mind all that now,' said Wydrin. She tried to sit up. 'We have to get after that bastard, before he does any more damage.'

Sebastian laid a heavy hand on her arm. 'There is a lot we have to talk about. We need to hear from Frith about what exactly Joah has been up to all this time, and you need to eat something and have a rest.' He glanced at the young lord. 'You *both* need some food and rest.'

Later, when all the talking was done and Frith could barely see through his headache, he excused himself from the campfire and walked some distance away, trying to ignore how the cold wind cut through him like a fine blade. He walked until he found a likely spot and then, using the word for Force, focussed down to a blunt shape, he dug a shallow grave before wrapping the body of Gwiddion in a piece of his own cloak. He held it for a moment; it felt so light, like it was made of air and feathers. It hardly seemed possible that the griffin had once carried them across oceans: ever fleet, never tiring.

Wydrin appeared out of the evening's darkness; she was as quiet as a cat when she wanted to be. He looked up at her.

'I cannot just keep him in my pocket.'

Wydrin nodded, and knelt beside him. They sat in silence for a few moments.

'He was a good griffin,' she said. 'I mean, not that I knew that many, obviously.' She cleared her throat. 'He always smelt . . . he always had this particular smell. Like flowers from far away, and the sea.'

Frith placed the pitifully small bundle into the hole, and covered it over with dirt.

'Here.' Wydrin reached behind her and plucked a jagged piece of rock out of the snow. She placed it carefully on top of Gwiddion's makeshift grave. 'At least we'll know he's here.'

'He was an important gift,' said Frith. 'A blessing I did not deserve. Because of me, he is dead. And as unlikely as it seems, O'rin is in danger now too.'

Wydrin placed her hands on her knees, staring at the grave. 'This Rivener contraption. You think Joah will use it?'

'I know he will,' said Frith. 'Human life is nothing to him. He sees us as inherently inferior.' He paused, frowning. 'It's almost as though he doesn't mean it maliciously. As though humans are so inconsequential that he doesn't even ponder it.' Explaining the Rivener and its workings had been difficult. He had struggled to convey his horror as the small scruffy man had screamed inside the tank, his sense of creeping despair at the sight of his bright eyes turned cloudy.

'Then it sounds as though we will have to stop him, then, doesn't it?' She smiled at him lopsidedly. 'If we keep up these heroics we shall start getting a reputation.'

Frith swallowed. He felt as though he barely had the strength to stand, let alone fight Joah Demonsworn.

'The city, and then the sword,' he said, hoping he sounded surer than he felt. 'Temerayne, and the god-blade. If what Xinian told me is true, then it is the only way to kill him.'

'Of course, I always make a point of trusting anything a ghost tells me,' said Wydrin. Frith looked at her sharply, but she reached out and adjusted the rock on Gwiddion's grave, turning it to some angle that pleased her. He found himself looking at the hollow of her neck, the way her unkempt hair curled against her cheek. 'We know where the city is at least, although it sounds as though we're going to have all sorts of fun getting there.' When Frith had named the city, Dallen and Nuava had both started talking at once, proclaiming it 'cursed' and 'lost', although, curiously, they both knew where to find it. 'Sebastian is glad to hear there is a sword that can actually kill the bastard. His was quite useless.'

'Yes,' said Frith, and then, 'Wydrin, I thought you were dead.'

'The Copper Cat has nine lives, and all that.' She shrugged. 'The Copper Cat is also really bloody lucky, it seems.'

'I am the lucky one,' said Frith. He squeezed his eyes shut briefly, wishing he didn't feel so unwell. It was difficult to concentrate on the words, and they needed to be the right ones. 'I have been an idiot. All the time, I have been thinking about the past, about what other people wanted, when they are gone and there is nothing I can do to bring them back.'

'Are you all right?' She reached out and placed a hand on his shoulder. 'You really should rest while we have a moment.'

Frith nodded hurriedly. 'I am fine. I was given a second chance, and I spent it fretting over old stones and past obligations, I –' His head was swimming. Why was it so difficult to say, even now? 'Joah said my heart was conflicted, but it is not. I am simply a coward.'

'You are the last person I would describe as such,' said Wydrin, her voice for once entirely serious.

'The pair of you should go back to your fire.' They both looked up at Dallen's voice. He stood over them with an ice-spear held loosely in one hand; in the other he held a freshly killed rabbit. 'There are Arichok around here, and they can rush out of the dark and overwhelm you.'

'Thank you, your princelyness,' said Wydrin. She took her hand away and stood up, not quite looking at Frith. 'We wouldn't want anything to overwhelm us, would we?'

46

It had been a cold night in Ynnsmouth. Sebastian paused in his trek back to the hidden temple to lay the heavy pack at his feet. He looked up at the mountain; freezing fog drifted down from its peak like a swarm of ghosts. The trees around him were wreathed in it, skeletal and black.

It was a longer walk back this time, but worth it; he had not found the will in his heart to return to Ragnaton, and Athallstown, the village two days' travel to the south, was larger and better stocked anyway. With so many people coming and going, he was quite certain his face would not be recognised, and there would be no chance of seeing that grey figure, the kerchief failing to hide the disappointment in her eyes.

'Ghosts,' muttered Sebastian. 'Ghosts everywhere.'

He picked up his pack and got moving again.

In a little while he would reach a certain stunted tree, and from there he would head directly west along a dried-up stream. The stream would turn into a ditch, which would eventually grow deep enough to be almost a tunnel, with only a narrow strip of sky overhead. At this time of night, it would be pitch-black, but in the last few months Sebastian had grown intimately familiar with its every muddy hole and jagged rock.

A figure appeared out of the mist, running at such a breakneck speed that it collided heavily with Sebastian and spun away, almost falling to the ground. Sebastian had his sword ready in seconds, but the face that turned up to his was green, the eyes round and

307

yellow and shocked. After a moment he recognised Havoc, a brood sister who had cut her white hair very short.

'Father, you must come.' Sebastian was alarmed to hear genuine panic in her voice. 'There is a man in the valley.'

'What?' Sebastian shoved his sword away. 'Where?'

'He approaches the training slopes now. He is some way ahead of you. He knew the secret way, Father.'

'And you didn't stop him?'

Havoc looked at him uncomprehendingly. 'How should we have stopped him, Father?'

Sebastian shook his head abruptly. 'Never mind. Has he seen any of you?'

'We are hiding. But the others, at the temple – we cannot reach them before he does.'

Sebastian reached for the link with Ephemeral, that silver thread that joined them – it was something they had been working on over the last few weeks: a way to send messages, warnings, perhaps, when they were apart. But he could feel nothing save for the anxiety of Havoc, standing so close to him.

'By Isu—' Sebastian dumped the heavy pack between a pair of trees, resolving to come back for it later. 'Let's run. We may be able to catch up with him.'

Havoc went first, moving down the stream and into the ditch with fluid ease while Sebastian crashed along behind her, finding that the dark and his own anxiety had turned the path back into something unknowable.

They emerged breathing heavily at the bottom of the training slopes. Ahead of them the grass was empty save for a single figure, walking slowly up the gentle hill. At the top of the slopes the temple sat, warm lights shining from every window, and Sebastian felt his stomach turn over. This had to be a knight, perhaps returning from some distant campaign, and what would he think upon seeing those lights? That the Order were still intact, that there would be a warm welcome for him through those doors? Instead he would find a horde of women who would look monstrous to him, a horde whose exploits he may have heard tell of, may even have witnessed for himself.

'Quickly, you head up around, keep out of sight as much as you can,' said Sebastian, his voice low.

Havoc nodded once before running off into the dark. Sebastian watched until she was at the edge of the slopes, where the trees began, and then called across to the figure ahead of him.

'Who goes there?'

The man turned round and stopped. Even in the dark Sebastian could see his hand straying to the dirk at his belt.

'No need to be alarmed.' Sebastian jogged up the slopes, waving in what he hoped was a friendly manner. 'We weren't expecting anyone.'

As he drew closer, he saw that the man was indeed a Ynnsmouth knight – he wore the colours of Ryn, green and yellow silk in tatters across his back, and an enamelled badge at his throat very similar to the one Sebastian wore. His hair was blond and cropped close to his head, and he had a blond beard, secured at the end with a silver cuff. His plate and leathers were burnished and covered in mud.

'By the peaks of Ryn, I thought I was the only one left.' The man looked very pale in the moonlight, and then he grinned. 'I hardly dared to hope I might find one of my brothers here –' He paused, looking Sebastian over. 'Forgive me, but you appear to have suffered some difficult times yourself.'

Sebastian nodded, smiling. The other knight would no doubt be wondering why he was so scruffily attired. Very soon he would be wondering many things.

'It has not been easy,' he said. 'Where have you come from? Who are you?'

The knight took a step backwards, obviously eager to reach the sanctuary of the old temple.

'Sir Michael, of the Order of Ryn,' he said, looking around. Sebastian could see him taking in the tended slopes, the weapons racks. 'I have travelled up through Relios. It has taken some time. Everywhere I go I hear that my brothers have suffered greatly.'

Sebastian nodded. 'You were not at the battle of Baneswatch, Sir Michael?'

Michael shook his head, his face creasing into bitter lines. 'Alas, no. I was on the border of Creos when the Citadel fell, delivering a message to an official there for the Lord Commander. I fought, when the lizard women came –' He paused, shaking his head.

'I was injured, and taken in by a kind woman and her husband. I have been asleep for months, healing, and eventually I was well enough to make this journey.' He shifted, half turning towards the temple and its warm lights. Out of the corner of his eye Sebastian could see that the door was open, and a figure was standing there. 'I had thought this place would still be abandoned. May I have your name, brother? And how you came to survive such times?'

'It's a long story.' Sebastian put an arm round the knight's shoulders, subtly trying to turn him away from the temple. 'It is my task this evening to walk the perimeter. Perhaps you will accompany me?'

Sir Michael shook him off. 'I would much prefer to take a moment's rest at the Temple of the God-Peak. I have been travelling for weeks.' Sir Michael was looking at him with open suspicion now. 'What member of the Order does not offer rest and food to his kin?'

His hand strayed back to the dirk at his belt again, and this time he drew it. Sebastian took a step forward, his hands held out in front of him in a gesture of peace, already knowing it was too late. There were figures streaking down the lawn towards them.

'What you will see now will seem very strange – alarming, in fact,' he said quickly, 'but you must not panic. Please. I can explain everything.'

Sir Michael, hearing the footsteps behind him, turned to see three brood sisters running down the slopes towards him. With a cry he drew his short sword in his free hand and the first brood sister fell to the ground, her guts open and steaming. The other two, whom Sebastian belatedly recognised as Umbellifer and Pelenor, stood dumbfounded. Neither of them were armed, and their golden armour had long since been discarded.

'Please, stop.' Sebastian grabbed hold of Sir Michael's arm but the knight pulled away with surprising strength. In the dark the green blood on his sword looked black.

'They have infected our most holy places!' Sir Michael brought down another blow, this time catching Pelenor across the throat. Next to her, Umbellifer stumbled away, her hands held up in front of her.

310

'We have sworn an oath,' she said, her eyes very wide. 'Never to take another human life.'

But Sir Michael wasn't listening. He barged past her, intending to head for the temple itself. Sebastian drew his own sword and went after him, not quite fast enough to catch hold of the smaller man.

'Ephemeral!' Sebastian bellowed, not knowing where she was but suddenly desperate to see her face. 'Get them out of there!'

It was too late. Sir Michael flew up the steps and into the temple's main room, where around twenty brood sisters waited, confusion evident on every face. Sebastian caught him up and stumbled in behind him.

'He has the blood of my sister on his sword!' The Second stepped forward, her brow furrowed. 'I can smell it. Who is this human?'

'Listen, we all need to calm down.' Sebastian tried to step around Sir Michael, trying to block his way into the room, but the young man brandished his sword.

'You are harbouring these monsters here? Do you have any idea what they've done?' His lips pulled back from his teeth in disgust. 'You have betrayed us and tainted the god-peak.'

'No, you must listen.' Sebastian spread his arms wide, leaving himself open to attack. 'You have to trust me. It is a long story, but you must hear it. Otherwise—'

'I will cut you down where you stand!'

He took a step forward, as though to drive his blade through Sebastian's midriff. In that moment, everyone seemed to move at once. Sebastian felt someone hit him bodily from behind, throwing him to the floor. His chin connected with the stones and for a few seconds his vision went dark. Rolling over onto his back, he saw Sir Michael still standing, his sword doing its bloody work as the brood sisters tried to subdue him. Not one of them drew a weapon against the man – *the oath, the bloody oath!* – and as he watched five, then six of the brood sisters fell, their green blood filling the air with its acrid stench.

'Stop!' Sebastian struggled to his feet, ignoring the pain in his head. Ephemeral was there, she and Havoc and Umbellifor trying to overwhelm Sir Michael with the press of their bodies, while the knight screamed at them, his face twisted into a rictus of horror. 'Enough!'

Sebastian elbowed them aside and, unmindful of the knight's blade, punched the smaller man across the jaw, taking some small satisfaction from the sound of tiny bones breaking. Sir Michael reeled on his feet, blood gushing from his nose in a red spurt, and then he went to his knees, eyes rolling up to the whites.

'Enough,' said Sebastian again. The temple smelt like a slaughterhouse. 'Please, that's enough.'

47

Tamlyn stood in the entrance to the werken chamber, utterly still, not breathing. It was dark, the only lights the glowing eyes of the werkens themselves and a pair of dirty oil lamps by the Heart-Stone chest. Two of her own werkens were in here, stored while she repaired them, and she could feel the solid presence of their stones.

All is quiet, she told herself. There is no disturbance in the Edeian.

Even so, she had found herself checking more and more often in the days after Joah Demonsworn's attack. That pulse of awareness, the sense of dismay she'd felt in the Edeian after Joah had been awoken haunted her. Why hadn't she acted then? If she'd been more vigilant, if she'd considered the Prophet with eyes unclouded by her own need to destroy the Narhl . . . And despite their best efforts, they had failed to find the girl. She had apparently vanished as completely as Joah Demonsworn had.

She shook herself and strode quickly into the chamber, walking past those werkens still needing repairs. Every other serviceable werken was up in the city now, helping to repair the buildings and the streets that had fallen into rubble. They had lost a great number of werkens in the attack, and those they had left were precious; that was why she was insisting on keeping them underground when not on active duty.

Her war-werken, the one shaped like a great cat, had been thrown against a stone wall, crumbling its right back leg into jagged pieces. She paused next to it, briefly inspecting her own handiwork; the witch's porridge, as her soldiers called it, would need another day to set at least. Turning from that she went to the Heart-Stone chest, and slipping a key from round her neck, she opened it. Inside there was the final piece, the very last sliver of Heart-Stone. Their last chance.

The sound of footsteps caused her to turn rapidly. 'Who's there? Who is it?' She shut the chest and locked it rapidly, her fingers fumbling slightly with the key.

Barlow came down the steps, her broad face creased into an expression of caution. The heavy-set woman had her fur hat in her hands again, and was turning it round and round.

'You called for me to come, Crafter Nox,' she said, glancing around at the damaged werkens. She was limping slightly – a slice of stone, blown from the side of a werken, had hit the woman in the leg. She had been lucky not to lose it. 'I've just come up from the pit.'

Tamlyn took a slow breath to calm her beating heart. She realised she did not like being down here in the dark, and that in itself made her angry.

'Yes. I wanted to ask you about our other project, Barlow. What progress have we made?'

Immediately Barlow looked as though she'd rather be somewhere else.

'Oh. Yes. Well, it's going well. As well as can be expected. I mean, we lost some of our best masons, and the new pit is not in the easiest location. And, frankly, we could do with more people.' She paused, biting her lip.

Tamlyn shook her head. 'Absolutely not. The fewer people know about this, the better.'

'No one here will betray you.'

Tamlyn raised her eyebrows at that, and Barlow nearly dropped her hat.

'I mean only, uh, Mistress Crafter, that we, that the masons and I, we are all dedicated to protecting Skaldshollow.' She took a breath, apparently deciding to lead the conversation down a different path. 'Your plans are extraordinary, as ever, and we follow them as best we can, but you are the Crafter.'

314

'Yes,' said Tamlyn, 'I am. And Nuava was to have been, after me . . .' She trailed off, turning back to look at the Heart-Stone chest. The Heart-Stone was gone, and now Nuava too. They hadn't found her body amongst the others, but Tamlyn felt in her bones that she was dead. As dead as her brother.

Barlow cleared her throat. 'Crafter Nox?'

Tamlyn turned back. The weight of the stone above their heads was oppressive, and she was tired of being in the dark.

'Continue the work,' she snapped, 'we must be ready for further attacks. Have them working at all hours, if necessary.'

'Crafter Nox.' Barlow looked as though she were trying to swallow something bitter. 'The thing is, wouldn't we be better off sharing around the last shard of Heart-Stone? Creating as many werkens as possible from what we have left?'

'They would be small,' said Tamlyn. 'Small things, powerless. Good only for hauling heavy loads.'

'That could be what we need at the moment,' said Barlow in a small voice. 'The better to advance the repairs to the city, to get people where they need to be.'

'No. Repairs will happen, people will heal, in their own time. We need to be armed. Come on, I want to go up to the pit now.' Tamlyn strode for the stairs, and Barlow scurried after her. 'I need some fresh air.'

They took a pair of werkens up through the northernmost gate. Tamlyn's was her smallest werken, a solid, plodding model too square and blocky to look like any particular four-legged animal. Barlow rode a similar, smaller version, the main bulk of it hidden under piles of furs and a huge, sturdy saddle. Nodded through by a pair of guards with their faces hidden within thick fur hoods, they entered a small patch of evergreen forest, quickly turning off the main path and heading straight into the trees. Here and there Barlow could see signs that other werkens had been this way: heavy prints in the hard earth, broken branches. She had been back and forth herself several times in the last few days, mainly ferrying messages to those masons Tamlyn considered trustworthy enough to work on her secret project, and they were few enough in number.

315

Eventually the trees began to thin out, and they came to a space where the world suddenly fell away, revealing a newly excavated quarry. A handful of men and women moved around on the few werkens they had been able to spare. The earth and stone they had torn through, with feverish impatience, was still raw, and looking at it made Barlow feel uneasy. Under Tamlyn's orders they had also erected a huge wooden screen, so that anyone randomly approaching the secret quarry from the city would not be able to see what they were working on.

Tamlyn, leaning forward over her mount, peered down into the hollow. She wore her hair tied back and Barlow was concerned to note how pale she looked. Her cheeks were gaunter than they had been, and her eyes glittered constantly with an emotion Barlow couldn't read.

'We found a rich vein of Edeian here,' said Barlow into the silence. 'There's that, at least. Kerryn thinks that it may be of better quality than the stone we've been taking from the main quarry, although I suspect it's a little early to know that.' Barlow paused, thinking of Yun. He had been a workshy man, mostly, but the timbre of the stone had been his passion. He would have been able to tell them about the rock, but he had died screaming in a cocoon of flames. Barlow squeezed her eyes shut briefly. 'We're getting the pieces we need, at least.'

'Large enough?' asked Tamlyn.

'Large enough, yes,' said Barlow. 'It's certainly that.'

'Come on.' Tamlyn led them down a wide path, hard dirt beaten flat by werken feet, until they were in the belly of the quarry. The men and women working there stopped when they saw them approaching, and Barlow saw a mixture of emotions on their faces; pride, at the sight of the Mistress Crafter, and fear, for losing both her nephew and niece had not improved Tamlyn's already unforgiving nature. Barlow was also fairly sure she spotted a few faces that looked angry, mistrustful. *They have families to keep safe and homes to rebuild,* thought Barlow, *and we have them hidden in the woods working on Tamlyn's latest crackpot idea.*

They reached the wooden screen and passed through the small gate built into it. As they emerged through to the other side,

Barlow took a slow breath; the sight of the thing always gave her a yawning feeling in her stomach.

'There it is,' said Tamlyn, and for the first time there was a hint of warmth in her voice. 'It will be the pride of Skaldshollow.'

Initially, it was difficult to see, if you didn't know what you were looking for, but if you stared at the raw rock long enough, it would suddenly emerge, like a face hidden in the bark of a tree. A straight line here, an arching curve there, grey rock riddled with veins of pale green Edeian. A huge lump of rock rested just in front of them, twice as tall as a man and three times as long. And that was just its hand.

'It's something, all right,' said Barlow, taking her hat off and turning it around in her hands. 'It's certainly something.'

48

'That's great, Yerry, a good find. Do you want to put it over there with the others?'

The child edged in through the door frame, eyeing Ip warily. No older than seven, and under a layer of dirt that must have taken months to accrue, Yerry was a ghostly scrap of a child. In that dirty face her eyes were very wide, already filled with a mixture of fear and agonised curiosity. Bezcavar remembered that look fondly, from so many followers.

Yerry took the cat's skull she clutched in her small hands and placed it carefully at the foot of the shrine. Already Ip's small band had amassed a reasonable collection of bones and skins, all placed neatly around an old wooden crate. Ip herself had saved up a few scrounged pennies for a single candle, which she liked to light when all the children were there, so that the warm light ran sickly over old, yellow bone.

It was almost too easy.

Too long sneaking from place to place, too long with no suffering committed in the demon's name, too long living in fear of discovery. Tiresome, human concepts like fear were damaging to a demon, sapping Bezcavar's vitality. It had been fine while Ip was a guest of Tamlyn Nox, able to order small atrocities to order – Ip's lips twitched into a faint smile at the memory of Nuava and her knife – but without that and without a shrine, Bezcavar's grip grew weaker and weaker. Eventually, Ip had been forced to take a chance, falling in with Sal and her scruffy band

318

of orphans and strays, but within that unlikely setting, Bezcavar had discovered something new: children were curious, and children could be cruel.

It had started with a few stories, whispered into the ears of the younger children. They were so starved of attention that they drank it up, listening raptly, and then asking questions. Bezcavar told a good story too: about a wandering spirit, a being of wild magic, who needed the attentions of children to survive. The spirit needed strange things, Ip would tell them, and sometimes asked that they do strange things, but it was all to the good. And perhaps there had been the occasional promise of unspecified power – what orphaned child did not dream of having the means to live their own life? And Bezcavar had let a little of its own power seep through, bending the right minds just enough.

In no time at all Ip had many of the younger children living at Sal's ramshackle hovel scurrying around at her whim, and gradually, gradually the power was starting to come back. Yesterday, Bezcavar had convinced three of them to carve small cuts into the palms of their hands – an initiation, Ip had called it.

'Very good.' Ip crossed the room and straightened the skull with one finger. She had claimed the cellar as her own and no one had objected; the spiders and the black mould meant that she had it largely to herself anyway. It was, the demon reflected, a particularly apt place for a shrine; when the building had been a butcher's shop animal corpses had been strung up in the dark to keep them cool. Bezcavar could still feel the echoes of their pain, distant but pleasing.

Yerry stared up at Ip, caught between terror and a seven-year-old's need to ask questions.

'It will be ready soon, and we can make offerings to the spirit. Won't that be fun?'

Yerry nodded rapidly.

'Playing in the muck again, Bestina? That seems about right to me.'

Ip turned to see the boy Mikas. He stood at the top of the stairs, regarding them both with a look of disgust tinged with amusement, before making his way casually down the steps.

319

Inwardly, Bezcavar cursed. Yerry was already hiding behind Ip, one small fist curled into her rags.

'Shows what you know, Mikas.' Ip stood up straight. She was still a few inches short of him, despite their similar ages. 'What I know would turn your hair white.'

Mikas laughed and shoved past her, deliberately barging her with his shoulder. Ip stumbled back.

'What are you building down here in the dark? A doll's house for all the little babies?'

He stepped up to the shrine, peering closely at the old bones the children had carefully arranged.

'It's for the wild spirit,' piped up Yerry. Ip looked at her in surprise. The child's face was set into grim lines of defiance. 'If we bring things for the spirit, it will give us power.'

Mikas snorted. 'It's a load of old shit, is what it is.' He reached out with one hand and tugged sharply on one of the toughened skins they had used to cover the crate. A number of old bones, a few still with scraps of sinew plastered to the ends, scattered onto the floor. Ip jumped forward to try and push the boy away, but he threw a fist at her, almost absentmindedly, and smacked her square on the ear. Ip cried out and staggered away, one hand pressed to her head.

'It's not healthy, playing down here with this stuff,' said Mikas. He lifted his boot and carefully stamped a few errant rat skulls into powder. 'I'm doing you a favour, really.'

'No!' cried Yerry, and amazingly she ran towards the shrine herself, trying to save the bones, but Mikas just pushed her away.

'You're all just stupid babies,' said Mikas again. He pushed at the broken bones with his foot, before walking back to the stone steps. 'If I catch you playing with this stuff again, I'll pull your tongues out.'

Ip watched him go. Inside her, the dark cloud that was Bezcavar boiled and seethed. This was all new, this world of children, this hierarchy of the strong and the wilful. There was too little power now, too few offerings, but that would change. Bezcavar was used to waiting.

'He broked it,' said Yerry tearfully. She was picking up the bigger pieces and gathering them into her lap. 'He's so mean, breaking our stuff.'

The cat's skull was still in place on top of the box, and Ip looked into its blank eye sockets thoughtfully.

'Don't worry, Yerry,' she said, 'soon we'll break him.'

49

'You have quite the problem here.'

Sebastian and Frith stood in the cellar of the mountain temple, some distance from the unmoving figure of Sir Michael. They had tied him to a chair, and now he slumped forward, letting his bonds hold him up. Sebastian wasn't sure if he was truly asleep, or feigning it.

'We cannot let him go,' said Sebastian, already tired of the words. He'd had the same discussion over and over in the last week. 'We'd have a screaming mob on our hands in a matter of days.'

'And I assume you will not kill him.'

Sebastian glanced up at Frith's face, but there was no anger or cruelty there, just a considering look.

'No. There has been enough death, on all sides. He killed eight of the sisters when he came here, because I hesitated, and because I made them swear not to take another human life.'

Frith raised his eyebrows. 'They kept that oath?'

'The sisters seem to take these things quite seriously. They do appear to be developing their own sense of honour, for what it's worth. Although that's not to say that some of them wouldn't like to see this man dead.'

Sir Michael grunted and shifted on his seat. The blood under his nose had dried to a hard brown crust.

'The Second,' said Frith. 'She is the one that wants him dead the most, yes?'

'You have noticed that?'

Frith nodded. 'She speaks of it often when you are not close enough to hear. I would keep an eye on that one, Sebastian.'

Frith had arrived the day before, swooping down out of the sky on his black griffin. He had greeted Sebastian with the half-smile that was as warm as he ever got, and then announced that he would stay for a few days before flying back to Litvania.

Sebastian shook his head. 'I do not blame her. Sometimes . . . half the time I think she's right. That the brood sisters' nature is not something that I can change. My influence will not be enough.'

'Are you sure you should even be trying?'

Sebastian opened his mouth to ask what he meant by that, but Sir Michael spoke into the brief silence.

'Abomination.' He leaned his head back, glaring at them both from under swollen eyelids. 'Consorting with demons. Devils. Bringing them here to violate our sacred spaces.'

'You are awake, then?' Sebastian frowned. 'I have some food here for you, if you'll take it.'

'I will not give you the satisfaction. Abomination.'

Sebastian sighed. 'I have heard that one before.' He turned to Lord Frith, who was watching the bound knight closely. 'Shall we go up for some air?'

Outside, the day was filled with bright sunshine and it was unseasonably warm. Frith's griffin was sitting on the grass with its great black paws crossed in front of it, like an enormous and deeply unlikely cat. Its wings were folded along its back, and the sun painted rainbows across its oily feathers.

'I have missed this old fellow,' said Sebastian. He held out his hand to the griffin, and it briefly pressed the curve of its beak into his palm. 'He gives me hope somehow.' He grinned uncertainly. 'Perhaps I am desperate for hope from any quarter at this point.'

'I think Gwiddion likes it here,' said Frith. He stood with his arms crossed, but Sebastian couldn't help noticing that Frith's robes now sported a small embroidered griffin next to his family's tree sigil. 'The air is so clean.'

'It is good to see you both.' Sebastian turned back to Frith. 'It truly is. Did Wydrin send you?'

323

Frith nodded once. 'She was worried about you, but has business herself at Crosshaven at the moment. Apparently, now I am an errand boy to fly around checking up on people.'

Sebastian smirked at this. 'She mentioned a job when she was here, somewhere out at the Horns. Is that still happening?'

'It has already happened,' said Frith. He uncrossed his arms and plucked an errant leaf from among the griffin's feathers. 'When it became clear that you weren't going to get away from here easily, we decided to do the job by ourselves.'

Despite himself Sebastian felt a stab of sadness at that. 'Oh. How did it go?'

Frith shrugged. 'A man living out on one of the smallest islands had come across some sort of enchanted amulet, and set himself up as a king of sorts. He was using the amulet to steal children – it could summon violent spirits, this amulet. There was a fight. I dealt with the spirits, and Wydrin killed him. It was fairly straightforward.'

Sebastian nodded. Across the training slopes the remaining brood sisters were going through their exercises. Was it his imagination, or did they seem more listless today? He saw one or two looking over to them, and he could not read the expressions on their faces.

'Is everything all right with you two?' The question was out before he even knew he was going to ask it. 'I mean, it's impossible to tell with Wydrin, but you know she is practically a sister to me.'

Immediately Frith scowled, looking much more like the tortured lord who had led them into the forbidden Citadel of Creos.

'As far as I know there is nothing wrong with Wydrin at all. She is . . . as she ever is.'

Sebastian nodded, pursing his lips, and the expression on Frith's face softened a touch.

'I have some responsibilities at Blackwood Keep. It is not easy to combine my responsibilities as Lord of the Blackwood with . . . everything else.'

Sebastian nodded. 'Well, I'm glad you had the time to come and see me, at least. It's good to see a friendly face.'

Frith smiled, although it was a small, cold thing. 'That is all to the good. Although I doubt that Wydrin will be pleased with what I have to tell her.'

'We must kill him. It is us, or them.'

The Second stood behind Sir Michael, one clawed hand held perilously close to his bared throat.

'I told you not to come down here,' said Sebastian. The man was stinking now, a sour smell of urine and old sweat. Whatever it was they were going to do, it would have to be soon.

'You cannot tell me what to do, human.'

Sebastian sighed heavily. 'That's true, I can't. I can only advise you, I suppose. But you followed me from the battlefield at Baneswatch, so you must think something of what I say.'

The Second faltered, her hand drawing away. 'I do not understand you,' she said eventually. 'The blood of the dragon runs in your veins too, but you resist it.'

'That's just not true.' Sebastian ran a hand over his face. 'There is a link between us, and I know that is difficult for you to understand, but—'

'I understand completely. I know you feel it,' said the Second. She came and stood in between Sebastian and the bound knight, her dirty hair hanging in her face. 'I know you feel the need to hunt, and to kill. I saw it in your face when we chased the wolf. I saw it in your eyes.'

Sebastian shook his head. 'You're mistaken. Besides which, it doesn't matter.'

'It does matter!' The Second stepped right up to him, close enough for him to smell the dried blood in her hair. She had been hunting again. 'How can you seek to command us, as *she* did, when you will not accept your own nature? You turn away from everything that we are, and do not even try to understand.'

'I am not like you.'

The Second's pupils contracted to thin black slices, and her nostrils flared. After a moment she grinned, revealing her pointed teeth.

'I can smell the lie on you,' she whispered. 'And because you continue to try to convince yourself of that, eight of my sisters died by this man's hand.' She gestured roughly over her shoulder.

'Because you convinced them to take your ridiculous oath. Because you asked them to deny their nature. Because you deny your own.'

Sebastian looked at her for a long moment. 'We are not killing this man,' he said. 'And I ask you not to come down here again.'

The Second hissed. 'Then you doom us all.'

She stalked away from him and up the cellar stairs.

Later, Ephemeral came and found him. He was sitting on the grass slopes, letting the blue crystal globe Crowleo had given him roll from one hand to the other. He had spent some time looking into its depths, filled with the memory of the voice of Isu, but had found little comfort there.

'Father. I would like to speak to you.'

He patted the grass next to him, and she sat down, crossing her legs gracefully. Her braid hung over her shoulder like a length of spun silver, and she carried a book in her hands.

'You know, Ephemeral, that I am not really your father, don't you?'

She nodded, her yellow eyes fixed on the sight of Frith and his griffin, further down the training slope. The young lord was busily brushing the great animal down, his solemn face oddly relaxed in its concentration. 'I know you are not my father,' she continued. 'Not in the sense that humans mean that word. But it is my choice to believe that you are.'

Sebastian sighed. 'Some father I have been. I fear I have led you from one disaster to another.'

'You have given us choices we would not have had,' she said, her voice soft. 'On the battlefield at Baneswatch we had no choice at all. Now we have choice, and the uncertainty that brings.' She turned the book around in her hands, running her fingers over the leather. 'The knight in the cellar still lives. The Second says you will not kill him.'

'He has done nothing wrong, Ephemeral,' said Sebastian, and then he winced, shaking his head. 'I mean, of course he has done wrong, but he came here thinking he would be safe.'

'He was safe,' Ephemeral pointed out. 'We had taken an oath not to take another human life.'

326

'There was no way he could have known that. He saw only the enemy, an enemy that nearly killed him in Creos.'

Ephemeral nodded, still watching Frith on the grass below.

'And that is how they will always see us, isn't it?' she said. 'They will never take an oath not to kill us, and we must spend our lives feared and hunted.'

'Ephemeral,' Sebastian took a slow breath. There was too much sadness in all of this. 'In time, perhaps . . .'

'I will never be able to simply walk into the libraries I dream of, will I?' She paused, blinking carefully. 'I burnt a library once. Or I helped it to burn. And perhaps those debts can never be paid.'

Sebastian opened his mouth, and closed it again. He had nothing of use to say.

'This is coming to an end now I think, Father,' said Ephemeral, gesturing around at the training slopes, the temple. And then, 'Do you know what we will do with the knight?'

'I have an idea,' said Sebastian. 'Although it's not a very good one.'

Frith frowned. 'This will not be a particularly pleasant journey.'

Sir Michael had been bound and wrapped in an old sheet, and now he was slung across the back of Gwiddion, who had squawked indignantly at the intrusion.

'We have washed him down as best we can,' said Sebastian. He was still tightening the bonds that held Sir Michael to the makeshift saddle. It would not do for the knight to fall off in mid-flight, although he found he did not care about that overmuch.

'Where will you take him?' said Ephemeral. The brood sisters were gathered around the griffin. Their faces were tense, concerned.

'He'll take him somewhere remote,' said Sebastian. 'Somewhere no one has heard of Y'Ruen or her daughters.' He looked to Frith, who shrugged.

'I will fly far to the east, and find a large stretch of nothing to leave him in.' Catching Sebastian's look, he continued. 'Do not worry, it will be somewhere he can survive, at least.'

'Then this place will always be at risk,' said Tidal quietly. 'One day, he could make it back here, or far enough to be able to warn someone.'

327

'That's true,' said Sebastian. Briefly he met the Second's eyes, and ignored the look of triumph there. 'And equally another knight could stumble across us, now, next week, a year from now. With choice comes risk, I'm afraid.'

When Frith was ready to go, saddled up on the griffin, Sebastian grasped his arm firmly.

'Thank you, my lord. I owe you for this.'

Frith nodded, smiling faintly. 'Sir Sebastian, I have long since lost track of our mutual debts.'

With that he was gone, flying up into an evening sky bleeding scarlet at the edges. Sebastian watched them go, until the young lord and his griffin were a shard of darkness against the sunset.

'I think we must talk now.'

He turned back to see the Second standing with a group of around fifteen brood sisters at her back. He saw Tidal and Becoming in that gathering, and they all wore guarded expressions. To his left, Ephemeral stood with a slightly larger group. No one looked happy.

'It is that time already?' Sebastian rubbed the back of his neck, feeling the tense muscles there. Would they kill him now? Is that how it would end?

'You acknowledge that we are no longer safe here,' continued the Second as if he hadn't spoken. 'That we may never have been safe here. I wish to leave, to take my chances out in the wider world. My sisters wish to come with me.'

'There will be death on that path,' said Sebastian. Behind him he could hear murmuring from Ephemeral's group.

'Yes,' agreed the Second. 'Death for us, death for the humans that cross us, perhaps. But I will not wait here for them to come and kill us.'

Sebastian nodded, and turned to Ephemeral. 'And what about you?'

'We wish to stay,' said Ephemeral immediately. 'We are still sworn to follow you, Father.'

'You are a traitor to your blood,' hissed the Second. 'You have forgotten who you are.'

'No,' said Ephemeral, firmly. 'I am just finding out who I am.'

* * *

328

In the end, seventeen brood sisters left following the Second. They took a portion of their joint supplies, sharpened their swords, and trooped quietly into the dark trees at the bottom of the slopes. They left at night, under a sky full of stars.

Sebastian watched them go with Ephemeral at his side, a cold worm of fear in his heart.

50

Prince Dallen had led them to the outer edge of the Narhl settlement he'd named as Turningspear when Frith collapsed for the second time. It was a bright, windy afternoon, snow flurries playing around their feet like ghostly children. The strange black shapes that were the Narhl dwellings crouched on the horizon, while empty arachnos nests dotted the snows around them. One moment Frith was walking steadily with his head down, his shoulders hunched against the wind, and the next he was falling to the ground as though his knees had been cut from under him.

Sebastian carried him to one of the empty nests while Wydrin tried to ignore the sense of superstitious dread at the sight of those icy structures. She glanced at Dallen, and saw grief on the prince's face – he, too, was thinking of the last time they had sheltered in such nests.

'Let him rest,' said Sebastian. He backed out of the round hole in the ice wall and stood next to Wydrin. 'He's passed out. Exhaustion, I think, although I doubt sleep will heal him.'

Nuava sat on top of Mendrick, her hood pulled low over her face, while Dallen wandered away some distance, gazing at Turningspear.

'Whatever it was that Joah did to him in that place, it looks like it was permanent.' Wydrin sighed. 'Or at least, if it is healable, we don't have a healer to do it.'

Sebastian peered at her closely. 'You're not looking too bright yourself.'

She raised an eyebrow at him. 'I'm absolutely fine, although I am suffering from a severe case of the curiosities.'

'Oh, really?' Sebastian adjusted the hood on his cloak, fiddling with the badge that held it in place. 'Because I've just come down with a sudden dose of none of your business.'

Wydrin snorted. 'I'm not blind, Seb,' she said, keeping her voice low. 'Our young Prince Dallen gets the sweats whenever he looks at you.'

Sebastian sighed heavily. 'I don't know, Wydrin. The number of times I've dragged you out of a card game because you've failed to notice the men chewing their knuckles and sharpening their knives.'

'Card games I was *winning*.'

'But someone gives me a funny look and you're all over it.' The big knight looked away from her. 'Dallen is a good man, and I think I – we – were lucky to have met him. And that's all I'm saying on the subject. More to the point, what are we going to do about Frith? He's looking worse by the day.'

'I've spoken to him about the healing magic, that pink light he used on Jarath, but it seems he can't do the spell on himself.' Wydrin touched the ends of her gloved fingers to the hilt of Frostling. Frith had been poisoned, that much was clear, and not by any simple potion or blade. 'We'll just have to hope he lasts until we reach Temerayne, and perhaps there will be something there.'

Dallen came over to them, his sharply angled face tense. 'How is he?'

'He is very ill,' said Wydrin simply.

'We may need him up and about sooner than he'd like,' he said, gesturing over his shoulder. 'Because we are about to have company.'

The leader of the settlement of Turningspear was an enormous Narhl woman with broad shoulders and golden hair. She was as tall as Sebastian, and Wydrin thought that if they ever came to blows, the betting would be evenly matched. There was a great, single spear slung over her back, glittering with white ice, and she wore dark grey leathers fringed with spotted fur. She did not look pleased to see them, and there were two men with her, lichen covered and armed to the teeth.

'You approach Turningspear. What do you want here?'

In the end they had roused Frith and met the contingent from Turningspear halfway – Sebastian had reasoned that willingly meeting them face to face would create a better impression. Now that the settlement was within sight, Wydrin found her gaze drawn to it again and again; to her eyes it was even more alien than the great ice structures of the Frozen Steps. Here the buildings were formed of barnacle-covered black rock and deep blue ice, and they looked warped and twisted by the wind. *Like seashells,* thought Wydrin, *giant seashells with a lot of grumpy people inside them.* Beyond the settlement was the edge of the northernmost sea: a steely grey band every bit as welcoming and warm as this Narhl woman's face.

'May I ask who I am speaking to?' asked Dallen, stepping forward. The woman scowled.

'I am Ceriel, First of the Turningspear Riders. Do not trouble to introduce yourself, disgraced son of King Aristees.'

Wydrin raised her eyebrows. 'How could you know about that already?'

'My father has sent messages, no doubt. A bird to every settlement, with news of my failure. Is that right?'

Ceriel nodded once.

'You have no place here,' spat one of her men. Wydrin noticed he took care to stand just behind his leader. 'You are a prince no longer.'

Sebastian took a step forward, one hand on the dirk at his belt, and the man was abruptly quiet. Dallen shook his head in exasperation.

'Whether I'm a prince or not doesn't matter, you must help us.'

'Help you?' Ceriel cocked her head slightly, as if listening to a strange noise she couldn't place. 'You, who are cast out by your own father? You, who travels with warmlings?' Her pale eyes narrowed. 'Is that a Skald skulking behind you, with its werken slave?'

Wydrin glanced over to Nuava, who pulled her hood up to cover her face. Mendrick did not move at all.

'All right, you're obviously not interested in courtly niceties, so how about you talk to me?' Wydrin stepped in front of Dallen, pushing her furred cloak back so that Ceriel could see the dagger and the short sword at her waist. 'A few words with me might teach you some manners.'

'Wydrin . . .' murmured Sebastian.

'The short warmling has some tiny blades.' Ceriel smiled, and it was like a glacier slicing through a valley: slow and cold. 'How sweet. We shall see how much good her blades do her when she is blue and frozen.' The tall woman reached behind her for her enormous ice-spear. Frith, who had been standing quietly to preserve his strength, held up his hands, now strung with strips of painted silk. He looked dead on his feet.

'Do so much as draw that, Ice Queen, and I will cook you in your clothes.'

'Enough!' There was a tone of command in Dallen's voice that made even Wydrin pause. 'We don't have time for this nonsense. Ceriel, First Rider of Turningspear, it is vitally important we get to Temerayne. Can you help us?'

'Temerayne?' The man who had yet to speak shook his head in wonder. 'It is cursed. Lost. Why would you want to go to such a place?'

'We need something that is hidden there,' said Dallen. 'You know where it is, don't you? Then you will show us.'

'Absolutely not,' said Ceriel, her lip curling. 'We have no interest in serving disgraced princes and warmlings and Skalds. I should put you to the sword instead.'

'This whole land is in terrible danger!' Nuava pushed her hood back again. Her skin was flushed. 'There is a mage on the loose, and it won't be just Skaldshollow that suffers for it. He is mad, and he *will* hurt your people. You have to help us.'

Ceriel and her men exchanged a look, and Wydrin saw something pass between them.

'You've seen him, haven't you?' she said, adjusting her stance. Perhaps there wouldn't need to be any fighting here today. 'Did he come this way?'

Ceriel cocked her head again, considering. The men behind her now looked unnerved rather than defiant.

'No,' she said eventually, then, 'I don't know. We saw something, two nights ago.' The tall woman looked down at her boots. 'I was patrolling with the hunters at sundown, and we saw a shape caught between the edge of a distant hill and the sky. It looked –' she faltered.

'It looked like one of the old gods,' put in one of her men, his voice trembling. 'A huge, monstrous thing, a monster fallen from the sky. It crawled over the hill, and then it was gone.'

'Thank the mountain it did not come our way,' said the other man. 'You could go mad, looking at such a thing.'

'The Rivener,' said Frith. 'It is the Rivener you saw.'

'There have been stories whispered in the hunting places,' said Ceriel, her face grim. 'Stories about a great monster that has wiped out entire settlements.'

'They said anyone who was touched by it went mad,' put in one of her men. 'It is one of the old monsters returned. Our world is ending.'

'Believe me, there is a man controlling it,' said Dallen. 'A man we can defeat, if we get to Temerayne.'

'He has killed many of my people,' added Nuava, swallowing against some internal grief. 'I know that will mean nothing to you – you may even be pleased, I don't know – but he cares nothing for the Narhl either, and if he finds you, he will kill you.'

'Please,' said Sebastian. 'We are fighting to protect your lands.'

Ceriel fell quiet, looking at them each in turn. Behind her the dwellings of Turningspear sprouted like the shining black carapaces of some strange sea creature.

'We will take you as far as The Judgement of Res'ni, and what you do from there is your own affair. I will take you myself, with our fastest sea-wyverns.'

'Great. You are too kind. The Judgement of Res'ni sounds interesting,' said Wydrin. 'Wait, did you say sea-wyverns?'

The sea-wyverns were tethered to the sides of an impressive long boat, carved of dark wood and painted with fanged, snarling faces. There were three wyverns on either side, each a good ten feet long. They strongly resembled their flying cousins, but they had no wings, and their skins were silver rather than blue, glittering wetly with diamond-shaped scales. Their long faces were fringed with stiff white whiskers, and their eyes were pale moons. Sebastian stood and looked over the side of the ship, remembering Prince Dallen looming out of the dark on the back of his flying wyvern. That had been quite a shock. The sea-wyverns moved in a similar way, but instead of cutting through the air they slid through the sea like silver knives, churning the waves into a white frenzy. There were Narhl men and women riding on their backs, apparently guiding them to their destination. He could feel the wyverns down there – a cold silver thread in his heart, as the snakes had been.

Nuava had retreated to the small hold below, her lips drawn into a thin, unhappy line, but Wydrin was as at home as she'd ever been, examining every inch of the ship and asking endless questions of Ceriel. Frith was standing apart from them, resting against the still form of Mendrick. The Narhl crew were less than pleased by the presence of the werken, which they seemed to regard with both sadness and anger.

'This Temerayne place,' Wydrin was asking now, 'you said it was cursed?'

'You have not heard the story?' Ceriel raised one lichen-covered eyebrow. 'These hot southern places, they forget everything so quickly. You know of the gods Res'ni and Res'na? The twin wolf gods of chaos and order?'

Sebastian remembered the eggs in the Rookery, and how two of them had been etched with the shape of identical wolves. That had been just after Gallo had died.

'We know of them,' he said shortly.

'Well, once Temerayne was the wonder of the North. A great and shining city, a place of great civilisation and learning. It was said that you could see the lights from the towers halfway across Ede, and that every child born there was blessed. They remembered the old gods there – although then, of course, they were not so old – and every street had a shrine: to Y'Gria, Y'Ruen, O'rin, Res'ni and Res'na. The years passed and a new king took the throne of Temerayne, a man who prized civilisation and order above everything else. To him, the gods looked unruly. Distasteful. All save for Res'na, god of order and balance. He commanded that all the shrines be destroyed, and a new, central shrine be built for Res'na alone. Temerayne would be a beacon for order and peace.'

'Ah yes, destroying shrines,' said Wydrin. 'That's always a clever move. Can't go wrong with that.'

The tiniest hint of a smile blossomed at the corner of Ceriel's mouth.

'For a time, the city prospered. But the gods are always watching, or at least they were then, and soon Res'ni came to hear of this place, this place that venerated her brother but disregarded the other gods. She became wrathful.'

'She was the god of chaos,' added Dallen. 'Always unpredictable, always wild.'

'Res'ni sank the city of Temerayne beneath the sea,' said Ceriel, 'but not before sealing it over. No one escaped, and they lived out what was left of their lives trapped in that deadly prison. Res'ni decreed that if they wanted order, and a world unchanged, then they would have it, for ever.'

'Never piss off a god,' said Wydrin. 'That's what I always say.'

Sebastian smiled faintly. 'Did you not once smack Y'Ruen about the ear with that very same blade you're wearing at your waist, Copper Cat of Crosshaven?'

Wydrin shrugged. 'Never piss off a god, unless it happens to be really funny at the time.'

Ceriel frowned at them both, apparently trying to decide if they were joking.

'The city of Temerayne has been down there ever since,' said Dallen. 'Cursed and haunted, no doubt.'

'So this place is under the sea?' Wydrin puffed out her cheeks. 'You know, I may just have spotted our first problem.'

Ceriel looked serious again. 'When it was over, Res'ni left a monument to her punishment, and it is said that there is a way through to the lost city below.'

'Joah made it down there somehow,' said Frith quietly. 'When he fled from the mages.'

'As far as I know, no one living has ever been foolish enough to try it,' said Ceriel. 'Warmlings, it seems, have no sense at all.'

Wydrin laughed and lightly punched the tall woman on the arm. 'Ha! You've just got no sense of adventure.'

The ship sped on as the sky above them turned from bright blue to washed-out white, the taste of salt on every breath when a flurry of shouts from the wyvern riders at the sides of the ship announced that they had reached their destination. Sebastian moved to the prow of the ship with Dallen and Wydrin. Frith appeared behind them, his face ashen.

'There you have it,' said Dallen. He sounded as though he barely believed it himself. 'The Judgement of Res'ni.'

Ahead of them a giant wolf's head rent the ocean in two, apparently snapping at the sky above. It was a monstrous thing constructed of black rock, twice as tall as the tower in Pinehold had been and lashed with frothing waves. Curving black fangs jutted from the open muzzle, and from the side Sebastian could see a single eye, yellow and shining and mad. It was gold, he realised; an enormous eye made of gold. *Truly, the people must be afraid of it,* he thought, *or they would have prised that off centuries ago.*

'That doesn't look like it's going to be very easy to get into,' said Wydrin.

As they drew closer, Sebastian could make out rough symbols carved into the rock just above the wolf's giant staring eye. They appeared to be mages' words.

'It says "Order for all time",' said Frith, confirming Sebastian's suspicions. 'It looks like the stories are true.'

'You will have to climb up to the corner of its mouth, do you see?' Ceriel pointed to where the jaws met. That close to the sea, the rock was pitted and covered in barnacles and other sea life. 'In its throat, you will find the way down.'

'Can your wyverns get us that close, do you think?' asked Wydrin. Ceriel smiled coldly.

'They might be persuaded to carry you for a short time,' she said. 'But not your spirit slave.'

Sebastian saw Wydrin look back towards Mendrick, and sensed some sort of communication between them. Eventually she shrugged.

'He will stay here with you. And the girl. Nuava's been through more than enough lately, without being asked to jump into a wolf's jaws. It'll be me, Sebastian and Dallen going down there.'

Ceriel opened her mouth to reply, but Frith spoke over her. 'Have you forgotten me already?'

Wydrin shook her head. 'You're not well enough, princeling. You need to rest up. You can leave this one to us – we're the professional adventurers, after all.'

'It was the Black Feather Three, last time I looked,' he said hotly. 'Or have you already forgotten how my magic has aided you?'

'Oh, but I thought you were leaving all that behind.' Wydrin crossed her arms over her chest. 'You have more important things to do, after all, like getting wed and producing more little princelings.'

'By all the gods,' Sebastian held up his hands, 'we don't have time for this. Frith, we are just concerned—'

'The demon will have left traps down there for us, don't you doubt it. Without my magic, you will be dead in moments.' He glared at them both, and despite his deathly pallor his grey eyes were bright again. 'Besides which, I know where the god-blade is. You need me down there.'

'Fine,' said Wydrin. She looked back towards The Judgement of Res'ni, her eyes narrowing. 'I think we're going to need all the help we can get.'

In the end the four of them travelled across to the statue of Res'ni on the back of two sea-wyverns, each guided by a Narhl warrior. Settling as best he could in the wet leather saddle, Sebastian turned to see Wydrin waving to Nuava, who was leaning out over the side-rail. Dallen and Frith sat on the other wyvern, the prince looking much more comfortable than the lord. Sebastian suspected that dipping his boots in ice-cold water was doing Frith no good at all, but he was much too stubborn to admit it. For the briefest moment Sebastian considered reaching out to the mind of the animal beneath him, but he remembered how the snakes had writhed and hissed. Some things were best left alone.

The wyverns brought them as close as they could get to the bottom of the wolf's head, and they set about climbing the pitted rock face while the Narhl riders looked on. Sebastian could see Wydrin above him, moving with confidence and shouting the occasional curse word, and below he could hear the steadier progress of Dallen. How Frith was faring, he could not tell, but he reminded himself that when they had explored the Citadel, Frith had needed a stick to walk with, and he had still managed to make that journey.

Eventually, Wydrin's slim shape disappeared over the corner of the wolf's jaw, and he followed her shortly after. They stood in a dark space carved from rock, with a wide hole in the centre containing a set of spiralling steps. The roar of the waves crashing against the rock was deafening, and they were both soaking wet. After a few moments, Dallen hauled himself over the edge, followed by Frith. The young lord looked as pale as Sebastian had ever seen him, and the hand he leaned against the rock was trembling. The four of them looked at each other.

'Well, it seems there is a way down after all,' said Wydrin. 'Do you want to place bets on how far we get before we get our feet wet again?'

'More to the point, even if we retrieve the god-blade and make it back up here, how do we know they'll still be here?' said Frith, pointing back to the gap in the stone. The teeth of the wolf cut the sky into jagged sections. 'Having the sword will do us no good at all if we're stuck in the middle of the ocean.'

'They said they'd wait until sunset,' said Wydrin, shrugging. 'I think they mean it, and Mendrick trusts them.'

'My people do not break their oaths, Lord Frith,' said Dallen.

'In that case, let's get a move on.' Wydrin pulled the light-globe from her pack and passed it to Frith, eyeing the dark staircase warily. 'And best keep our weapons drawn.'

339

51

The way down was dark and echoed with the fury of the sea. They had to walk single file, so Wydrin kept her dagger at waist height and a careful eye on where she was putting her feet. Dallen was at the very front, and as yet had reported that the steps were dry. That, she figured, was a good start.

'So, Frith, do you feel like telling us what you remember of this place from that ghost's memories?' Her voice echoed flatly off the walls. 'What can we expect to find down here?'

There were a few moments of quiet before Frith answered, the sound of boots on stone filling the narrow staircase.

'I saw very little,' he said eventually. 'It was a grand, silent place, filled with dust. The two mages pursued Joah to a great tomb, and that was where they made their final stand.' He paused to cough. 'It ended badly. For all of them.'

'Sounds like it ended badly for everyone in this city,' said Wydrin. 'Let's hope we have more luck.'

They walked on for some time before Dallen called out and they came to a stop. After a moment Frith put away the light-globe and Wydrin saw that there was another light source: a rippling silvery glow, like the moon on water. The stairs had come to an end and they were in another dark round room with a large hole in the floor; it was this hole that shimmered with silver light. It was like looking into a pool of bright water, except that beyond it . . .

'Am I seeing that right?' Wydrin took an involuntary step backwards. 'Because if I am, I might have to throw up.'

The city of Temerayne lay beneath them, filtered through the pool as though they hung in the sky above it. Wydrin could see buildings of white marble and streets of pale green brick, all perfectly empty. Nothing down there moved.

'The lost city of Temerayne,' said Dallen, his voice hushed. 'I can barely believe it. That it has been hidden down here, all these thousands of years.'

'More to the point, how do we get down there?' said Sebastian. 'And how do we get back up?'

He knelt by the pool of light and pushed the point of his dirk past its surface. When nothing happened, he did the same with his fingers.

'There is no resistance,' he added. 'I believe we could pass through it.'

'I can get us down there,' said Frith, stepping forward. He pushed back his sleeves so that his silk bandages were revealed. 'With the word for Hold I can lower each of you through the portal. It will not take much effort.'

Sebastian grimaced. 'And back up?'

'There is a tower close to this entrance, look.' Frith pointed to a delicate spire reaching up towards them. 'If we can climb that, then I should be able to lift us up, too. I am reasonably confident of this.'

'Reasonably confident?' Prince Dallen looked horrified. 'Your confidence, my friend, is all that stands between us and a slow, unpleasant death.'

Frith shook his head slightly, and Wydrin found she recognised the look of impatience that creased his brow.

'During my imprisonment I learned a great deal about the Edenier, and I now have a much greater mastery of the mages' powers. As insane and murderous as Joah was, I do believe he genuinely wanted me to be able to make full use of the magic. I can do this.'

'You can stay up here if you like, Dallen,' said Wydrin, smirking slightly. 'Reckless adventure isn't for everyone.'

Dallen snorted, a most unprincely gesture. 'Reckless adventure I can take,' he said. 'It's cheerful suicide I'm more concerned about.'

341

'Here, I'll go first.' Wydrin stood in front of Frith and met his grey eyes with her own. 'It makes sense that our most skilful blade is the first into unknown territory anyway.' And then, in a lower voice that only Frith could hear, she said, 'Strangely enough, I trust you, princeling.'

He raised an eyebrow at that, a hint of a smile at the corner of his mouth.

'Stand at the very edge,' he said. 'Just there, that's it.' He put one hand on her waist, positioning her at the lip of the silvery hole. When he was happy with where she was, he raised both hands, an expression of deepest concentration on his face.

I trust him, oh yes, thought Wydrin, *for some bloody reason I trust him. What Joah did to him nearly killed him, and he's weaker than he was, and I could end up splattered all over the cobbles of some lost city.*

The link between you is strong. Mendrick's voice was suddenly inside her head. *As much as you will both ignore it.*

Mendrick? You can hear me down here?

Your voice is always . . . loud.

'There,' said Frith. 'Can you feel that?'

Wydrin made to shake her head, but then a warm feeling seemed to sweep up from her toes, a faint sense of pressure against her skin. Once, when she had been very small, her mother had taken her to a lake that was so full of salt it was impossible to sink in it. They had paddled around, her mother uncharacteristically relaxed for once, and they had laughed at that feeling of buoyancy. This felt a little like that; a pressure beneath, keeping you afloat.

'I can,' she said, half laughing. 'Bloody hell.'

'Take a step back.'

Inwardly cursing her life choices, Wydrin did as he asked. Instead of stepping into nothing and plummeting to her death, she found herself floating over the surface of the silvery pool, her boots submerged in its strange light.

'Good,' said Frith. He was staring at her steadily, and if anything he looked brighter than he had for days. *The Edenier,* thought Wydrin, *it reinvigorates him.* 'I'm going to lower you now.'

Slowly, so slowly, she descended down through the pool,

closing her eyes as the band of light passed over her head, and then she was hanging above the city.

'By the Graces,' she gasped, 'it's beautiful.'

It was – a fabulous confection of white marble and olive-coloured brick, glass glinting like stars in flute-shaped towers – but it was difficult to concentrate on that when she could see nothing but empty air below her boots. Gradually she moved downwards, as smoothly as a ship under a steady wind. She risked a glance upwards and saw the circle above her as a shadow in a watery sky. There was Frith, his face rigid with concentration, and Sebastian, who looked like he was regretting their hurried breakfast. Above her and around them was a sky that was not a sky; it was, she realised, the sea – a shifting, swirling expanse of blue and black held back by some unknowable force. The will of a god, she thought, and then abruptly she was nearly on the ground. The sense of pressure holding her in the air vanished, and she dropped easily to land on her feet. She waved up to the others to let them know that she'd made it down safely, then looked around.

At ground level the lost city of Temerayne wasn't quite as beautiful.

The fluted towers arose on all sides, their tops spreading wide like some strange species of pale lily, but down on street level the cobbles were thick with skeletons. Wherever she looked she saw grinning skulls and shattered ribcages, yellowed bone and piles of dust. Hundreds of men, women and children had died in the streets, their bodies lying under the sea-sky with no one to tend them. She saw skeletons clasped together, as though they'd died fighting or embracing, and ragged shapes hung from windows, finger bones clutching at nothing. The dead were numerous, ancient and utterly silent.

Wydrin looked back up at the enchanted ceiling. What must it have been like, she wondered, to have known that you were trapped down here, and would never see the real sky again?

Sebastian was making his slow way down now, his arms held out stiffly in front of him as if he could stop himself from falling with sheer willpower. When he got to the ground he just looked at Wydrin and shook his head.

'And I thought the invisible bridge was bad.'

Dallen and Frith came down together, holding arms awkwardly. The prince had his eyes shut all the way down.

Once they were all back on the ground, Wydrin drew her dagger again. With no people and no wind, it was unnaturally quiet – even the sound of the sea was lost to them down here.

'The silence, and that sky,' said Sebastian. He drew his own sword, following Wydrin's lead. 'To die in such silence . . .'

'I doubt it was very quiet, towards the end,' said Wydrin, nodding at the skeletons. 'People would have been desperate.'

'Let us find the sword and get out of here,' said Dallen. 'This is a cursed place. We should not be here.'

'The tomb was this way,' said Frith, pointing down the street. 'Let's go.'

They walked quickly. Wydrin tried, at first, not to step on the skeletons, but there were so many, and the bones so old that they collapsed into powder at the slightest touch. The creeping sense of unease only increased the further they walked; the skin between her shoulder blades kept prickling as though they were being watched, and she looked up at the empty buildings frequently, expecting to see unfriendly faces peering back. She wasn't normally so easily spooked – exploring abandoned old places was hardly a new occupation for the Copper Cat of Crosshaven – but the misery of the people who had died here seemed to hang over the empty city like a dark cloud, a psychic extension of the sea-sky above them.

'Look.' Sebastian nodded just ahead of them, and Wydrin could make out three sets of footprints. They were smudged here and there in the inconstant dust, but clear enough. 'They lead down the street, and they don't come back this way.'

'At least we're going in the right direction,' said Dallen.

'Of course we are,' snapped Frith. 'I've been here before.' He sounded as angry as ever, but he looked haunted, his cheeks the colour of ash.

'And what do you suppose that is?'

Sebastian was pointing up at the great dark dome that hung over the city. There was a shadow moving up there, directly above them. At first Wydrin took it to be the Narhl ship, but after a

344

moment she realised it was much too large, and moving too quickly. It was long, thickening towards the middle and then thinning out again to a narrow tapering shape. As she watched, it was joined by another similar shadow, and they curled around each other in a slow dance.

'Are they wyverns?' she asked, holding Frostling a little tighter.

'No,' said Dallen. 'Wrong shape. And that thing looks bigger than any sea-wyvern I've seen.'

'Lots of monsters in the sea,' said Wydrin uneasily. She was thinking of when she'd impersonated a Graceful Lady; she had barely thought anything of it at the time, but casually insulting the Graces seemed a lot more significant with the ocean hanging over her head. 'Let's keep moving.'

'We have no food for Skalds here. None of your hot food vomit.'

Nuava bit her lip. The last thing she wanted to hear about at the moment was vomit. She had hoped that sitting quietly in the hold of the Narhl ship would quiet her stomach, but she could not get used to the lurching sensation of the wooden panels beneath her and everything smelled overpoweringly of salt.

'That's fine, thank you,' she said, forcing a polite smile onto her face. 'Anything you can spare is greatly appreciated.'

Ceriel frowned at her. Nuava rather got the impression that the woman would have been more impressed if she'd responded with an insult.

'Here, then,' Ceriel put a pouch down on the small table. 'We call it Slake. Fish guts, fish eggs.'

'That's lovely, thank you.'

Ceriel gave her one more disapproving look before stalking back up the warped wooden steps. Nuava let out a shaky sigh of relief, and poked the bag hopefully. It had been hours since she'd eaten and she must have emptied out her stomach several times over, so perhaps she could manage a few Narhl delicacies. If nothing else, she was alone now and no one else would have to witness her indignity should her insides decide they weren't quite done punishing her yet.

At that moment her eyes met the glowing green lamps of the werken's eyes.

Not quite alone, after all.

'Ah. Uh, yes. Um.' She picked up the bag and glanced inside, immediately regretting it. 'It's food, that's what I've got to remember. I need to eat, I need to keep my strength up.'

Gingerly she poked a finger into the bag and hooked out a trembling mass of pinkish flesh. The smell of fish was very strong, but then the entire ship smelt of fish, and she was starting to get used to that at least. Steeling herself, she stuffed it in her mouth and swallowed.

'*Hurgh*. Mmm.' She forced herself to chew. Ignoring the texture of it, she nodded her head briskly. 'You know, it's not so bad. Cold, obviously, but not awful.' Methodically she worked her way through the rest of the pouch, and when she was done her stomach did feel a little more settled. They had left her a bone flask full of water, and she sipped at that carefully, willing herself not to be sick again. She'd already pulled all the muscles in her stomach.

'That must have seemed very silly to you,' she said. The werken did not move. 'I mean, I don't suppose you eat.' She cleared her throat. 'Not that we would know.' Hesitantly, she stood up and took a few steps towards the werken. 'There must be so much we don't know about you. Because that's what you are – a real living being, with . . . with a soul. You are the soul of the mountain, that's what Prince Dallen said.'

Still the werken did not move. Having grown up in a city where the werkens were regarded as one step up from furniture, if that, she felt mildly foolish – as though she were talking to an old toy and an adult had caught her. It was cold and damp in the hold, and the unsettling motion of the boat now felt like a wave of constant dizziness. She took a deep breath, trying to control the instinctive reactions of her body. She was a scholar, after all, a crafter in training.

But what did that mean now?

'Why did you never reach out to us? There's been no attempt to make contact, no communication from you. It's like you've just let us use you.'

Still the werken did not move. Perhaps it was all a lie after all, some elaborate joke being made at her expense, except that she didn't truly believe that. The woman, Wydrin, was boisterous and undisciplined, but she was also earnest in her own way, and Nuava was quite sure that although the Copper Cat paved her life with falsehoods, she wasn't lying about this.

'I would like to speak to you,' said Nuava, looking directly into the werken's green eyes. 'I really would. I have spent my whole life studying you, after all, and none of the werkens I was joined to . . . none of the werkens I have known ever spoke to me.'

There was a smattering of dry laughter from the doorway. Nuava turned to find that Ceriel had returned, and was leaning on the doorframe. Although she was smiling, there was a brittle glint in her eyes, like early spring ice.

'Foolish Skald child. You may as well ask the sky to speak to you.'

Nuava cleared her throat. She was embarrassed, but at the same time she knew she was doing the right thing. She was doing, in short, what Bors would have done, if he'd suddenly discovered that the werkens were sentient.

'If they are thinking, knowing creatures with souls, then do they not feel the need to reach out to other thinking, knowing beings?' Nuava's stomach grumbled and the taste of fish flooded her mouth. She tried not to grimace too openly. 'If we have truly treated them so appallingly, then could they not have said no?'

Ceriel shook her head.

'You are thinking of them as people in the same way we are. You are trying to understand them on your own terms.' The tall woman held her hands up and dropped them, trying to find the right words. 'You are a tiny fish, trying to understand the entire ocean. The ocean does not look alive to the fish, but it is full of life.'

Nuava crossed her arms over her chest. 'That doesn't make any sense.'

'Perhaps not.' Ceriel shrugged. 'I lead the people of Turningspear, and I lead raids, and I captain the fishing boats. I do not spend my days talking of spirits. To the Narhl, it is different, you see. We know that the mountain spirits live, because they are a part of us.'

Nuava looked at the woman's muscled arms, uncovered despite the cold. She could see the marbled pattern of her skin, dabbed here and there with lichen.

'Because you are close to the land? Closer than us, anyway.' Nuava nodded, glancing at Mendrick before turning back to Ceriel. 'Can you imagine, then, what it is to not be part of the land? To have to work to understand it?'

Ceriel frowned. 'I suppose I cannot.'

'We have so much to learn still,' Nuava pressed the back of her hand to her mouth. 'Excuse me.' She reached for the bone cup full of water, but Ceriel shook her head.

'Here, child, drink this. It burns away the water sickness.' She passed Nuava a long curved horn from her belt, stoppered with a wedge of wax. Nuava pulled the stopper free and took a gulp; the liquor inside tasted faintly medicinal to her, and it swiftly warmed her throat and belly. Almost instantly she felt better.

'What was that?' she asked, passing the horn back. She found she was smiling slightly. 'It was really good.'

Ceriel grinned, and Nuava thought it was probably the first genuine smile they'd seen from the tall warrior woman.

'We call it Comet's Fire. It's brewed from berries and nuts. The best thing for seasickness.'

'Your people get seasick?' asked Nuava. Ceriel laughed.

'Of course. Although our bellies are not as delicate as a Skald's.'

Nuava took another sip of the drink, her eyes on Mendrick again.

'It seems there is much we don't understand about the Narhl. We may have been wrong about a number of things.'

348

52

By the time they reached the mausoleum, the sky-sea above them was teeming with dark shadows.

'I don't like this.'

Wydrin was peering up at the shapes, one hand held over her eyes to see better.

'I believe it would be prudent to retrieve the blade and leave as soon as possible,' said Frith. 'This is not a place to linger.'

In truth he was more unnerved by the mausoleum itself. It was unchanged from his vision; still shaped like a fat seed pod, the top tapering up to a point, while faces carved from white marble stared out of oval-shaped alcoves. The entrance was dusty and dark, the wooden doors long since rotted away. He could see Xinian's footprints there, and the footprints of her lover.

'Agreed,' said Sebastian. He gave Frith a considering look. 'Are you ready, Frith?'

'Of course.'

Pushing aside his weariness and fear, Frith produced a ball of light in his right hand, and together they walked over the threshold. The crypt sprang into uncertain light around them; inside, the walls lost their pristine sheen, with greenish mould leaving mucky smears everywhere. There were more figures carved here, and with a start Frith realised they were death masks, people frozen for ever at the moment of their passing.

'It's down these steps,' he told the others. Looking back at him in the Edenier light, their faces looked too akin to the death masks in the walls, and Frith felt a wave of dizziness pass through him. 'Follow me.'

Silence enveloped them. Frith glanced up at the ceiling, so close to the top of his head, and tried not to think of the weight of the ocean hanging just above.

'What a place to be trapped,' said Wydrin, apparently thinking along the same lines. 'The gods certainly are cruel.'

'Of all the gods to offend, Res'ni is not the best choice,' commented Dallen. 'She was not known for her mercy, or indeed sense.'

'I can think of worse,' said Wydrin. 'Actually, you know what, best to avoid all gods as much as possible. More trouble than they're worth.'

They reached the large chamber Frith remembered from his vision – the same stacked rows of skeletons in the walls, the same stone sarcophagus in the centre of the room. There were two skeletons on the floor – a staff lay next to one of them, and the other was missing a hand at the wrist. Frith frowned.

'Xinian the Battleborn and her lover Selsye. They were just left here, then. No one collected their bodies.'

'Would the mages not come for them?' asked Sebastian. 'Surely their own people . . .'

Frith shrugged. He bent down and picked up the staff. It felt silky under his fingers, as though covered in spider's webs, and it had words carved into it. He half expected to be able to feel an echo of the magic it had once channelled, but it remained quiet in his hands.

'Perhaps they were too afraid to come down here just to collect some bodies. Or perhaps they didn't care. There is so much we don't know.'

'This has been left here, at least.' Wydrin was standing by the wall. In an alcove filled with skulls there was a large, curved sword lying on its side. Its blade was a deep metallic blue, and it looked impossibly sharp.

'That is not where it was left,' said Frith. For some reason, this worried him more than the hundreds of corpses surrounding them. 'It should be on the floor.'

'Bezcavar moved it, then,' said Sebastian, frowning. 'Or got someone else to, more like.'

Frith met his eyes, and knew that the knight found this unsettling too.

'Either way, we need it now,' said Wydrin, and she reached out and picked up the sword in both hands. In the very same moment, there was a tremendous crash from somewhere above them, and a reverberating crack that Frith felt travel up through his feet.

'Ah,' said Wydrin, looking sheepish. 'A trap. You'd think I'd started raiding tombs just yesterday.'

'Quick, pass it to me,' Sebastian held out his hand for the sword and she gave it to him. As his fingers touched it Frith saw Sebastian shudder, and for a moment he stood unmoving, as though struck dumb by the sword. Frith was about to ask him if he'd lost all sense when the knight seemed to come back to himself. Unsheathing his own sword he pushed the god-blade awkwardly through the leather sword belts that circled his waist. 'I have the feeling we're going to have to move swiftly now.'

There was another crash from somewhere above them, and Wydrin drew her sword and dagger.

'To the tower we saw coming in, then,' she said, eyeing Frith. 'I hope that magic of yours is still as strong, Frith.'

He gripped the staff in his right hand. 'Don't worry about that.'

They fell out of the tomb all at once, looking everywhere for the threat. There was another enormous crash, and now that they were at street level it was easier to tell where it was coming from. As one they turned and looked up.

'Ye gods and little fishes,' said Wydrin. 'The Graces' own have come for us.'

The sky-sea above them was teeming with sea monsters of all shapes and sizes. Frith could see enormous lizard-like creatures with tapering, steamlined bodies, their narrow heads lined with teeth like knives, and great armoured fish with segmented bodies and fanged maws that fell open like trapdoors. There was even what looked like a giant squid, swirling limbs pitted with barnacles and one great eye like a bulging bubble of ink. They were crowding above them as though the water had recently been seeded with food, and Frith supposed that it had, in a sense. He swallowed hard.

'Look at that one!' cried Sebastian. 'What is it doing?'

One of the monsters was pressed right up against the invisible barrier, closer than the others. It was one of the biggest, a creature not unlike a wyvern with its long, dragon-like face, but it was ten times the size, and its body was covered in green, oily scales. It had long limbs too, fringed with pearlescent webbing, and a crown of glowing fronds sprouted just beyond its bony forehead. It opened its enormous jaws, revealing multiple rows of jagged fangs, and then crashed its head against the force field. The entire city shuddered with the violence of it, and the tiniest crack appeared far above them. The monster opened its mouth and roared – muffled as it was, they all heard it.

'Why is it *doing* that?' cried Dallen as the monster crashed its head into the invisible structure once more.

'I think we're going to be in a lot of trouble very shortly,' said Wydrin, already taking a few hurried steps backwards. 'Look at that!'

The monster smashed its bony head against the invisible wall again, its mouth opening slightly to let a thin stream of bubbles past its jagged teeth, and for a few seconds the force keeping the sea out flickered ominously.

'Is it going to . . .?'

Another crash, and suddenly there was a tear in the sky and the sea was pouring down towards them in a solid band of grey and white. It hit the buildings behind the mausoleum and they were instantly lost to view in a fury of white water.

'Run!' screamed Wydrin.

They scattered up the street, Frith glancing behind him only to see the great sea monster pushing its head through the hole it had made, briefly plugging it before more of the invisible shield gave way. Water poured in like a black nightmare, and already it was at their heels, chasing them in a surging tide.

'We'll never make it,' he called to the others. 'We'll drown in minutes!'

'That's the spirit,' Wydrin yelled back, but anything else she said was lost in the roar of the deluge. There was another crash behind them and somehow Frith knew that would be the sea monster, having worked its way through the force field and now, inexplicably, hunting them down. And the others would follow. *They can pick us off like breadcrumbs in a pond.*

The tower was in front of them, but still too far. Frith glanced down to see black water surging around his boots, and then Prince Dallen was skidding to a halt, turning back to face the approaching wave.

'What are you doing?' Frith saw Sebastian say the words although he couldn't hear him. Dallen raised his hands and there was a brittle crack as the temperature of the air around them abruptly plummeted. Frith turned in time to see the devastating wave of water that was chasing them freeze instantly, black water turning silvery white. *Of course.*

Frith brought the word for Cold to mind and threw everything he had at it, summoning the Edenier like he never had before. The ice moved across the approaching water like a disease, and the sea monster, now thrashing in the space behind the crypt, was briefly caught in its icy fingers, but they were fighting against the sea. As quickly as they froze it, the water was pouring in through the rent in the sky.

'Build a barrier around us,' Wydrin was shouting. 'Quickly, before the water overwhelms it.'

Frith turned in a circle, crafting a curling wall of ice even as his fingers began to tingle with the pressure of the Edenier. Soon, he knew, the bandage on which the word was written would disintegrate, and then they would have to rely only on Dallen's natural ability.

Just beyond the warped wall of ice he'd created, Frith could still see the monster – it was dragging itself towards them, its jaws opening and closing mindlessly. If it got there, of course, it would crash straight through the ice, and still the water was streaming in.

'We need to get out of here,' said Sebastian. 'They can't keep this up for ever.'

The curved wall of ice was now as tall as the closest buildings. Wydrin ran to it and slid her fingers over its surface – thanks to the uncertain, violent nature of the water it was warped and jagged.

'We have to climb it. Onto the top of these buildings, and to the tower. We'll have to be bloody fast.'

353

Sebastian looked less than pleased by the idea, but he took a pair of short daggers from his belt and began looking for a way up. The sea beyond the ice was rising rapidly, a black tide stinking of salt, and the monster seemed to be gaining strength from it.

'You go,' said Dallen. 'I can keep the water from completely flooding the city until you get back through the hole.'

Sebastian turned away from the wall. 'I'm not leaving you.'

'Oh, we definitely don't have time for this, boys.' Wydrin took Dallen's arm firmly and pulled him to where the wall was most climbable. 'Everyone, get up there, now.'

Frith slid Selsye's staff through his belt at the back, and began to scramble up the wall. It was freezing cold and slippery, and more than once he almost fell back down to the ground. Ahead of him Wydrin was making better progress, kicking her boots into the ice for purchase, whereas Sebastian was taking even longer than him. Dallen, who had obviously spent all his life around snow and ice, was climbing the wall with no trouble at all.

There was a wet, rippling roar from behind them. Frith risked a glance to see the sea monster now pressed against the ice they'd created, its confusion of teeth gnawing at it like a dog with a bone. Even more worryingly, the black water had reached the top of their self-made barrier and was pouring in, thundering like a waterfall. It wouldn't take long for it to fill up.

Wydrin was shouting something now, but he couldn't make it out. Frith redoubled his efforts, trying not to think about what it would be like to drown down here. At least, he reasoned, the temperature of the water would likely knock you out first.

Sooner than he'd expected he was at the top, and strong hands were pulling him over the edge. He turned round, and helped Wydrin pull Sebastian up too – the knight was incredibly heavy, carrying two great swords, and Frith had to wonder that he'd made it up the ice wall at all.

'Quickly now,' yelled Wydrin. 'Across these rooftops; we're nearly there.'

The water was all around them. Dallen used his cold-summons to freeze the rising water between buildings, so that they could scurry across. There was a sound like a thousand breaking mirrors behind them, and Frith didn't need to turn around to know that the monster had broken through their ice wall.

'Into the tower.' Wydrin stood aside to usher Sebastian and Dallen through a narrow window in the solid marble, and then caught hold of Frith's arm. 'Are you all right? Can you still get us up there?'

He raised his eyebrows at her. 'I suppose I shall have to.'

Inside the tower was a spiral staircase, littered with dust and bones. It looked like it had once been a family home – gilded picture frames still clung to the walls in places – but Frith had no time to examine further. They ran up the steps, scrambling to keep ahead of the rising black water. Dallen was still using the cold-summons to halt it as much as possible, but it surged up the stairs behind them in a boiling fury.

Coming out onto the roof, it was still possible to see the faintly glimmering silver portal in the sea-scape some twenty feet above them.

'Try not to move,' Frith said to Sebastian. 'I will try to lift you as quickly as I—'

The tower trembled and then rocked. An ear-splitting scream sounded from below. Frith peered over the very edge to see the sea monster curled around the base of the building, its body heaving against the stone.

'Shit,' cried Wydrin, 'we haven't got much time.' The city of Temerayne was now all but lost under the rising sea, finally coming to claim it after being kept out for thousands of years. The tower alone still stood, and from the vibrations it would not stand for much longer.

Frith took a deep breath, summoning his last reserves of strength. The Edenier churned in his chest and he pictured the words, trying to see them as clearly as he ever had. Sebastian and Dallen lifted off the ground together and began to float steadily upwards.

'I can do this,' he murmured. His head was throbbing, and a white-hot pain was growing behind his eyes. 'I am every bit the mage Joah is.'

Sebastian and Dallen reached the silvery portal and vanished through it. Frith let go of the words and stumbled, suddenly very close to fainting.

'I will send you up,' he told Wydrin. 'I don't think I can do us both. Just hold still.'

'Oh, don't you try any of that nonsense with me, princeling.' Wydrin slipped her arm around his waist and gripped him tightly. 'You either get us both out of here or I'm not going. I didn't pull your arse out of that shit hole for nothing.'

Frith bowed his head and summoned the words again. The Edenier was burning in his chest now, a dangerous fire that he feared would destroy him, but there was nothing left for it. Holding on to Wydrin tightly, he lifted them both off the roof of the tower just as it began to shake violently. Water coursed below them in a deafening whirlpool, and he caught a glimpse of green, oily skin and teeth like knives, rolling beneath the surface.

If that thing leaps for us . . .

He forced the thought from his mind and concentrated. They gained speed, Wydrin's arms wrapped around him tightly, the warmth of her body incredibly welcome. *In another time and place, I would be enjoying myself*, he thought, and he had to hold back a laugh. The pain in his head was blinding him now, but that didn't seem to matter very much.

'We're nearly there,' said Wydrin directly into his ear, her breath hot and tickly. 'Just a little further.'

There was another crash from below them as the tower fell, and they were briefly doused in a freezing shower of water. Frith felt a tearing sensation deep inside, the Edenier burning away the last of his strength, and he pulled Wydrin as close as he could.

'I love you, Wydrin,' he said absently. 'I should have said that, before.'

He felt her grow rigid in his arms, and he was dimly aware of a silvery sensation passing through his body before he was lost to the darkness.

53

Sebastian laid the unconscious form of Frith down on the makeshift bed. There were dark circles around his eyes, and he'd never seen the young lord so pale. His breathing was rapid and shallow.

'Well, he looks like a bag of shit warmed up,' said Wydrin, peering down at Frith anxiously. 'And they won't send any of their healers?'

Sebastian shook his head. The Narhl of Turningspear had led them to a shack on the very edge of their settlement and then left them there. Ceriel had informed them that they could build a small fire in this place if they wished, but nowhere else, and they were to be gone by morning.

Wydrin sighed and shook her head. 'Joah has poisoned him. That, and the strain of what he had to do in Temerayne. We need more than one day to rest.' She paused, and then added quietly, 'I think he was delirious back there.'

'Dallen has done what he can,' said Sebastian. Nuava was kneeling on the floor, attempting to make a fire out of their small supply of dry wood, part of which they had stripped from the walls themselves. 'Ceriel is afraid for her people. They saw some of the sea monsters we inadvertently summoned, and they want no part of it.'

'They can hardly blame us for that!' Wydrin paced back and forth at the end of the bed. 'How were we supposed to know we'd be visited by every ugly thing the sea could spit out?'

'I suspect that was Bezcavar's doing,' said Sebastian. 'Some sort of elaborate trap for anyone coming after the god-blade.'

Wydrin leaned over Frith and placed her hand against his brow. He didn't wake, but he stirred in his sleep, his lips forming some unsaid word. Wydrin frowned at that, and Sebastian was struck by the concern on his friend's face. He knew well that Wydrin carried the persona of the Copper Cat as both a banner and shield, but he also knew that underneath her feelings ran deep. It was unnerving to see her so exposed. He glanced over to the god-blade, which they had propped against the wall. Looking at it he felt unbalanced, as though the ground might drop away from his feet at any moment.

'He'll be all right, Wyd.' Out of the corner of his eye he saw Nuava glance up at the reassuring tone in his voice. *No doubt she thinks the Copper Cat is as tough as nails.* 'He's been through worse than this before.'

Wydrin pushed some loose strands of hair away from Frith's face, and then pulled back suddenly, as if annoyed with herself.

'Yes. And what if finally it's too much?' She shook her head brusquely.

'Wydrin,' Sebastian put a hand on her shoulder. 'Will you come outside for a moment?'

She frowned, but followed him out all the same. The twisted dwellings of Turningspear lurked off to one side, beneath a bank of darkening clouds.

'The sword.' Sebastian looked into her eyes, willing her to have spotted what he had. If she had seen it too, then perhaps he could step away from this madness. Unbidden, an image of Ephemeral rose in his memory, her delight at controlling the snakes written clearly on her face. 'Have you seen what it is?'

She raised an eyebrow.

'A bloody great sword, is what it is. A bit over the top for my tastes, but hopefully it will do its job.'

Sebastian closed his eyes and tugged at the short bristles of his beard. *Why couldn't she see it?*

'When Frith handed it to me, when I took it into my hands, I knew what it was immediately. It was like it *sang* to me, Wydrin. In my blood.'

'What are you talking about?'

'The blade of that sword, Wydrin. That strange, shining blue metal. It is part of Y'Ruen. It is made from her scales.'

Wydrin blinked rapidly, then looked back at the shack as if she could see the sword through its walls.

'A sword made from a scale of the dragon. I suppose it would have to be something quite special to defeat a power-crazed mage. But how could you possibly know that, Sebastian?'

'I don't know,' said Sebastian. 'I really don't know.'

But that was a lie.

54

Bezcavar stood on the chilly ledge, wriggling Ip's feet in the snow. The girl was still in there with the demon, and she was shouting something, but it had become easier and easier to push her to one side. Bezcavar twisted the girl's face into a grin as the freezing wind pushed at her back, easing her closer and closer to the edge.

'Bestina?' Yerry's voice was almost lost in the wind. 'I don't know if we should be doing this.'

Bezcavar looked down at the younger girl. Her dirty face was turned up to hers like a small uncertain moon. They were standing on the roof of Sal's hovel, having abandoned the cellar some days ago. Mikas had kept his word about keeping an eye on them, and Ip now carried several vivid purple bruises to show for it. The roof, though – no one came up here, no one would think to come up here. They had rebuilt their small shrine inside a make-shift shelter, and once more Bezcavar had felt the first stirrings of power. Reaching over with Ip's hand, the demon took hold of the smaller girl's fingers and squeezed them.

'The wild spirit will reward us for our bravery, Yerry. I told you that, didn't I? Stefen understands, don't you, Stefen?' The boy standing on her other side nodded rapidly. He was about the same age as Ip, but was much smaller and skinnier, still waiting for his body to catch up with him; he had an interesting liking for knives. 'Stefen believes, Yerry, and he will be rewarded.'

'I believe!' said Yerry, her voice squeaky with indignation. 'I believe in the wild spirit, I do.' The girl glanced behind her at the shrine as though expecting the 'spirit' to be there looking back. 'I just don't know if this will work.'

'It's easy,' said Bezcavar smoothly. 'The wild spirit values acts of bravery. When we jump off this roof, it will reward us and keep us safe. I've shown you before, haven't I?'

Indeed, Bezcavar had cut a few shallow wounds in Ip's arm, and had then simply healed them again. Yerry and Stefen had been suitably impressed.

'The wild spirit watches over you,' agreed Stefen. He was staring down over the ledge. 'Watches over all of us.'

Bezcavar nodded. It wasn't a huge drop by any means – Sal's hovel was a sad old shack, really – but it was high enough to cause either of the children some serious injuries. Some *painful* injuries. She supposed it might even kill them, and that would be an inconvenience, but Bezcavar thought it more likely that they would end up with a broken leg apiece. Again, there was that flurry of tension as Ip tried to bring herself forward, but Bezcavar held her back with ease. *I have to play these small games now, don't you see? Joah has gone, and I must take what suffering I can.*

'I will go first, then, if she's too scared,' said Stefen. 'I believe in the wild spirit.'

'I didn't say I didn't believe,' muttered Yerry, looking down at her feet now. 'Didn't say that at all.'

'I knew you could do it, Stefen.' Bezcavar grinned with Ip's mouth, placing one hand on the boy's shoulder, not quite pushing. Not yet. 'Say it's in the name of the wild spirit. Shall I tell you its name?'

The boy looked up at her, his eyes wide. 'It has a name?'

'It's only for true believers to know,' said Ip. She leaned down and put her lips close to Stefen's ear and whispered, 'Bezcavar. The wild spirit's name is Bezcavar.'

Stefen nodded rapidly. The wind picked up around them, as if reflecting the demon's mounting excitement.

'For Bezcavar,' said Stefen, and he took a step towards the edge. 'I do this in the name of Bezcavar—' Before he made it over he was yanked backwards, one arm flailing in the air. Ip turned to see Mikas there, gripping Stefen fiercely by the wrist.

361

'What are you doing up here?' snapped the older boy. Next to her, Yerry took a few rapid steps away from the edge of the roof. 'You're not allowed to play up here.'

'We're not playing!' Stefen tried to pull himself away, but Mikas shook him. 'We're worshipping the wild spirit.'

Mikas laughed: a snorting, unlovely sound. 'You're all stupid babies.' He dropped Stefen and came after Ip, his hands balled into fists. 'And I thought I'd told you about this before.'

'Shut up, mewling child,' spat Bezcavar. So close, they'd been so close. Suddenly it was difficult to disguise the voice, and he saw the other children look at Ip in surprise. The demon found it didn't really care any more. 'You are nothing to me. Nothing! A petty little bully, a whining child. I have had better than you splayed out on stakes so that I could watch their organs dry in the sun, and you expect me to cower away from you? I have tasted the blood of men and women from every part of Ede, I have torn the skin from—'

Mikas struck Ip across the face, a solid downwards punch that drove the girl to her knees. He followed that up with kick in the stomach that forced all the wind from her lungs and bent her in two.

'You're mad,' he said, still in a tone of mildly irritated dismissal. 'You've got a disease or something.'

Ip's nose was bleeding. The blood was hot against the girl's fingers.

'I'll have Sal throw you out,' said Mikas. 'Back onto the streets with the other mad people.'

Bezcavar tried to force Ip to her feet, tried to force her to tear this child's throat out, but her legs would not obey. There was a pain in her stomach like a jagged rock, and her throbbing nose was starting to block everything else out.

'Stupid, useless body,' muttered Bezcavar. Yerry and Stefen were looking at Ip with confusion now. 'To be trapped, in this place, with *this* . . .'

A distant fluting noise came from the south, and the other children all turned to look towards the city wall. Ip followed their gaze, still wiping blood from her nose.

'Those were the alarms,' said Stefen. He clasped his hands to

362

his chest, looking suddenly younger than he had a moment ago. 'On the walls. Something's coming.'

Bezcavar did push Ip to her feet now, ignoring the way the child's body wanted to lie curled up on the floor in a heap. They could just make out the dark grey line of the southern wall from where they stood, and the small plodding shapes of werkens and riders prowling its circumference. As they watched, the wall itself shuddered violently, sending up a plume of snow as something struck it from the other side. The alarms increased in volume.

Hardly daring to breathe, Bezcavar reached out with its mind, looking for that familiar presence – and there it was. There was no mistaking Joah's strange, fragmented mind, with its impossible honeycomb of ideas and tangents.

He came back for me.

Bezcavar turned on the other children, grinning with triumph. Mikas, who had lost both his parents to Joah's last exploits, had gone ashen.

'You'll pay for your insolence now,' she spat gleefully. 'Oh yes. I will have Joah make a special case of you, Mikas. I'll have him make something out of your bones, I think. Something pretty I can wear.'

'Bestina?' Stefen was staring, his eyes impossibly wide. There was another crash from the wall and they flickered briefly in that direction before returning to her again. 'What do you mean, Bestina?'

'Have we upset the wild spirit?' added Yerry. She looked like she was on the verge of tears.

'Oh no, dearest child,' Ip beamed happily at them both, 'you two have been an enormous help.' And she pushed Stefen over the edge.

Someone had put fresh flowers on their graves. Tamlyn Nox stood over them, wondering who that could have been. Barlow, perhaps? It seemed likely. They were the thick, fleshy blooms of the keening-wort, a hardy plant with solid blue leaves that were impervious to cold and actually quite pretty, if one found such things pretty. Tamlyn had seen them growing in the woods beyond the quarry, but had never thought to bring them back for her brother's grave. Barlow, though, Barlow might think to do that.

She bent and brushed some snow away from the black granite, the better to read the words they had carved there. Marlen and Trayla Nox, Crafters and Warriors, Together in the Stone. It wasn't a memory she allowed herself to dwell on, but it came to the surface unheeded now – her brother's warm, plain face, waving away her objections as he set out on the back of his werken, and his wife's long-suffering look that liked to pretend that she found him exasperating. Their faces on the day they'd walked into the mountain and not come back had been warm and happy. Their faces when she'd found them had been altogether different.

And then there were the faces of Bors and Nuava when she'd told them, small and round and full of sorrow.

'You shouldn't have left them with me,' she told the gravestones. 'I had no time for children, you knew that.' She shifted from foot to foot. Behind her, the lithe cat-shaped werken stood to attention, the only witness to her grief. 'You were reckless, and now . . .' She shook her head. 'Bors lies with you. Nuava, I don't know where she is. I will do the best I can, though, to bring her here to be with you. I'm sorry that in the end that's all I could do for them.'

The horns sounded, piercing the icy air like the wailing of ghosts.

Tamlyn snatched up her sword and scrambled onto the back of her werken, already urging it to the nearest stone stairwell. She could see people running – some towards the wall, some away from it.

She reached the top of the wide stone stairs at a pace and skidded out onto the flat top of the wall. There were other war-werkens approaching in both directions, she saw, heading towards a spot on the south-eastern apex. There was a thunderous crash, and she saw the wall shudder, throwing one unfortunate guard screaming off the side.

'No, no,' she murmured, urging her werken on. 'Not yet, he can't be back yet.'

She pelted down the path, moving faster than anyone else

would dare to on the thickly iced surface. Men and women who had been manning the guard stations hurriedly drew back to let her past.

'Bring all werkens to this wall,' she bellowed as she passed them. 'Ready all catapults! We are under attack.'

The wall under her werken's feet juddered and for a few moments they skidded perilously close to the edge. Tamlyn, utterly certain of her own ability to control the werken, leaned over the side and looked down. What she saw there threatened to unseat her, and she found herself thinking of the stifling heat in the Prophet's room, and how it had always smelled of madness.

There was a monster at their gates.

It looked like the largest werken she'd ever seen, but it was alien in aspect, twisted and beetle-like, and parts of it were made of darkly shining black metal. There was a cluster of violet eyes on the thing's deeply notched head, and it was using irregular serrated claws to tears chunks out of Skaldshollow's outer wall.

'Get a team out the southern gate,' she called to the soldiers who had followed her up the wide stairs. 'Surround it. We have to stop it before it pulls the entire wall down.'

The men and women scattered to carry out her orders, while small fires burst into life all along the wall as her soldiers brought up barrels from the guard houses. They were tipped over the side, splattering the monster beneath the wall with boiling oil and flame, but it carried on scraping its jagged claws against the stone; as Tamlyn watched, huge chunks of masonry fell away, and the surface under her feet trembled alarmingly. The fire, so effective in their clashes with the Narhl, had no effect on it at all.

The werkens clustered at the side of the wall were pushing great blocks of stone towards the edge. Enormous rocks the size of carts plummeted and smashed to pieces against the creature's stony hide. It paused briefly at this, before surging up the wall, thorned legs scrabbling for purchase.

Tamlyn cried out, horrified at the sight of those violet eyes lunging closer, and her team of war-werkens edged back. Glancing at them, she shook her head angrily.

'No retreat,' she called to them. 'You must hold it off for as long as possible. I will be back.'

Barely having to think about it, she turned her werken and sped back down the steps, scattering the men and women who had come in defence of the wall. She saw Barlow at the bottom, sitting atop a bear-shaped werken; the woman looked mildly stunned.

'Barlow!' she shouted. 'Get back to the hidden pit and get our project ready.'

Barlow was shaking her head before Tamlyn had finished speaking. Her furry hat was askew.

'Mistress Nox, there is no way it could be ready in time, I—' There was screaming coming from beyond the wall now – the team who had gone out the gate, no doubt. 'Most of the specifications are still only half complete, and we haven't even—'

'We have the basic structure, yes?'

'Yes, but—'

'Then get it ready, Barlow.'

Without waiting for an answer Tamlyn urged her werken on, flying down streets that were suddenly deserted – she caught sight of frightened faces staring from windows, and the occasional man and woman passed her, most still strapping on their armour. At one point she glanced back over her shoulder and was rewarded with a sight she suspected would be etched in her memory for the rest of her life, however long that might be: the monstrous insectile werken had breached the top of the wall, its misshapen head tossing back and forth as her soldiers rained down fire and rock. One of its grasping, clawed legs reached out, curled around a werken rider and held the soldier up as though examining him. After a moment, a wide aperture opened up in the thing's head, pulsing with violet light, and it dropped the soldier inside. What happened to him after that, she couldn't say.

Tamlyn turned her eyes from it, pushing her own werken fast enough for the frightened faces peering from windows to become blurs. Finally, arriving at the Tower of Waking she half jumped, half fell from her saddle and ran, heart beating frantically in her throat.

'The last piece,' she muttered through numb lips. The room

was dark, with every available werken already roused to the fight, but there was still a small oil lamp burning above the chest. Cursing her trembling fingers, Tamlyn took the key from around her neck and opened the lid; pale green light bathed her face, making it look sickly and old. 'The last piece, and our last chance.'

55

Inside the Rivener, Joah Demonsworn stared out through the new glass windows at the carnage going on around him. His arms were burning with spells, and his head swam with words – so many held in balance at once, changing and shifting and being brought together. It was dizzying, but the Rivener moved to his command, exactly as he had envisioned; the Edeian, the Edenier, the demon's artifices, and the Heart-Stone itself were working together in feverish unison. Distantly he was aware that the burns on his face were infected, but even that maddening itch was pushed aside by the complexities of the Rivener.

'Many people have told me I am mad,' he said to the empty room. Beyond the windows he could see the stone houses of the Skald, the people fleeing down the cobbled streets. Absently he instructed the Rivener to snatch up one of these struggling figures. 'Aaron was certainly not the first. He knows nothing of being a mage.'

There was a thud from behind him and he turned to see the woman he had plucked from the street land inside the glass chamber. He saw her roll over and look at him, her eyes wide and her nose bloody, and then the violet light surged in brilliance. The woman tried to climb to her feet, but the Rivener was already doing its work. Rather than standing up and throwing herself against the glass, as he had no doubt she intended, the woman slumped back down to her knees, her eyes becoming unfocussed. Above her there was a swirl of something almost invisible as the raw Edenier was siphoned away.

'It all works so well,' murmured Joah, his eyes still fixed on the woman. She was staring back at him with an expression of faint puzzlement. After a moment the floor below her dropped away and she fell down through the inner workings of the Rivener, to be dropped somewhere beneath it. If she was lucky, the fall would kill her.

Outside, the people of Skaldshollow were flinging fire and pitch, a flurry of stone and ice. None of it could harm the Rivener, although Joah kept himself aware of it, as he was aware of everything. It would not do to have to stop and make repairs before he had subdued this place. The Tower of Waking was in his field of vision now, thrusting up like a great flinty arrow head.

'The centre of Skaldshollow,' he said to himself. Inside, his mind repeated a mantra of mages' words: Hold, Lift, Force, Crush. 'From there I shall start. Even if Aaron—'

Something through the windows caught his eye. The Rivener was passing a series of taller buildings now, their roofs parallel with its wide abdomen, and a small figure stood atop one, waving its arms as though it wanted the Rivener to consume it. It took Joah some moments to recognise it – the demon girl's hair was short, and she was dressed in rags. The child Bezcavar had chosen to inhabit looked scrawnier than when he'd last seen her. With a start he realised it had been some time since he'd even thought about the fate of the demon.

He made the Rivener pause. The war-werkens hadn't stopped their barrage of missiles, and he heard them clanging and crashing against the Rivener's outer hide like giant hailstones. With slightly more care than he'd shown the people of Skaldshollow, he swept up the small form of Ip and delivered her to a narrow hidden door in the side of the Rivener's broad head, which he opened from his side.

Ip stood there, a slim and scruffy slip of a child, her brutally cut hair sticking up at all angles.

'Joah,' she said, and the voice was Bezcavar's, 'how good of you to drop in.' The girl's face twisted as the demon struggled to contain its emotions. 'You have a lot of explaining to do.'

He ushered her over the threshold and shut the door behind her. The complicated processes and spells that kept the Rivener moving were all suspended in his head, a hellishly complex web of cause and effect.

'I am quite busy at the moment.'

'Busy?' Ip surveyed the crowded central chamber of the Rivener, with its glowing violet heart. 'This is it, then, is it? This is what you've forsaken me for?'

Joah shook his head irritably. 'I have forsaken no one. Many things have come to my attention, and I had to deal with them.' He paused. 'You told me there were no mages left living on Ede. You lied.'

Ip snorted. 'Him? A poor excuse for a mage. A footnote in a long and glorious history, perhaps, but nothing in comparison to you. Speaking of which, I sent you to that place to kill Sebastian and his companions, did I not? When I last saw them they were all very much alive. Would you care to tell me why?'

Outside the barrage of missiles had increased, and one piece of rock landed a lucky shot, cracking one of the Rivener's great glass eyes. Frustrated, Joah reached out with the Rivener's limbs and smashed everything moving immediately around them.

'Bezcavar, this is not the time. I have important work to do, and I don't have the time for your petty revenges.'

'Petty revenge?' The voice went from withering sarcasm to thundering rage in a moment. Such a voice should not have been able to issue from a child's throat, and in spite of himself Joah took a step backwards. 'Need I remind you of what I have given you, Joah Demonsworn? The powers bestowed, the secrets shared?'

'You have taught me much, of course.' The girl's eyes had turned blood red from lid to lid, and her pale face was turned up to his, brow deeply furrowed. If not for her eyes, she would have looked like a child having a tantrum. He continued hurriedly. 'But you must understand, I have great works to perform.'

'I must understand?' The voice was softer now, and Joah recognised the danger inherent in that. 'Perhaps I need to remind you of our bond, so that *you* may understand.'

Ip reached up and took hold of his hand, her fingers cold, and with horror he felt his mind being peeled open.

'Do you remember the day, Joah, that I showed you my true face?'

370

'No, please, no.' The strength went from his legs and he bent suddenly at the knees, falling painfully to the metal lattice floor. 'Please, not that.'

'I took the memory from you because we have known each other a long time. As partners, as lovers. I knew that you could not live with such a memory, so I plucked it from your strange and glorious head.'

Her hand gripped his hard enough for him to feel the bite of her sharp fingernails. Inside his head he could feel himself slipping towards that great pit of darkness, the one he spent so much time ignoring, but he could not stop himself. He would be pulled in, and he would be lost in that memory.

'Do you remember yet, my love?' Bezcavar hissed, almost tenderly. 'Can you remember my face?'

He remembered a beautiful day full of sunlight, in the middle of a field of golden wheat. Bezcavar's human form then had been a woman of cold beauty, with hair the same colour as the gently rustling crops around them. That day they had found a small, isolated village, a collection of ramshackle buildings full of the hardworking poor, and they had killed them as they wished to – casually, without fear of retribution. Afterwards, they'd come to this field to rest, lounging amongst the stalks and the warm smell of the earth. The demon had been wearing the odd, spiky armour its host had favoured, and with a lurch Joah remembered how his heart had filled at the sight of her. He remembered brushing a strand of golden hair from her cheek and smiling fondly.

'You are an extraordinary creature,' he had said. There had been two spots of dried blood, one at the corner of her mouth, one on her full lower lip. 'I must know everything there is to know about you.'

The demon had smiled at him, raising one perfect eyebrow. She had slid her hand over his chest, pushing him back slightly. There had been blood on her hands too, dried in dark half-moon shapes under her fingernails.

'Everything, my sweet Joah? You could not wish to know everything. Your little human mind, as remarkable and strange as yours is, simply could not take it.'

371

Joah had snorted. 'Have I not proven myself more than mortal? Greater than any mage?'

'Greater than any mage, yes, but is that truly so great?' She was grinning at him, and he'd felt a stab of annoyance.

'We have done so much, and yet still you treat me like a child.' He had remembered the children in the village, running so fast that they couldn't even scream. 'Why must you continue to act like I am still the novice, scrabbling after every little scrap of knowledge you might throw my way?'

The pressure on his chest had increased, and the demon had turned her head slightly. It was an oddly predatory gesture, like a raven peering at the last juicy eyeball on a field of corpses.

'You believe yourself my equal, is that it?'

Joah had shaken his head, too late realising the dangers of this path. 'I only wish to know you. To know everything about you.'

The demon had leaned down as if to kiss him. 'Then know me,' she'd said, and her face changed.

Joah dropped to the metal floor, screaming and screaming. There was a bright slither of pain across his cheek as the burns there were torn open, and a hot flood as blood streamed from his nose, but it was nothing to the dark haemorrhaging in his mind. He was coming away from himself, cast out, floating into an empty night sky where nothing waited for him but *that*, the demon's face that waited for him in every shadow, in every mirror, in every breath, that tore away his skin and nested in his throat, that grew inside him and turned everything to worms, that . . .

A small cool hand settled on his brow and abruptly he was back, lying awkwardly on the floor of the central room of the Rivener. The demon knelt over him in its child form, its face blank and unconcerned. Joah was sweating and shivering all over, and his mouth and beard were covered in blood.

'There, there,' said Ip, absently. 'I think you will see things a little clearer now, yes?'

It took him a moment to find his voice.

'Yes,' he said eventually. He sat up. 'I . . . it is difficult for me, seeing you like this.' Joah paused, wondering if this sudden burst of honesty would cost him his life. 'You are not . . . as you were.'

The girl frowned. 'That is true enough. This vessel is not ideal, Joah, but it will change. Once we are done here we can journey back to Relios and seek out the last of my cults. There will be willing vessels there and I will be appealing to you once more. But you must listen to me. This new mage is not your friend. He is not your concern. And we have much to do.'

Joah got to his feet shakily. From outside the patter of missiles from the Skalds and their werkens continued, while the spells in his head hung in suspension, waiting for him to push the Edenier through them again. He wiped the back of his hand across his mouth, peering at the bloody streak that appeared there. His nose had stopped bleeding when Bezcavar had placed Ip's hand on his head.

'Much to do,' he agreed. 'And what are we to do first, Prince of Wounds?'

'Tamlyn Nox still lives.' The girl walked away from him and over to the glass windows. She traced one of the cracks with her finger. 'She has hounded me for the last two weeks, but she couldn't find me in the end. I would like to repay her attentiveness.'

'Then we shall go and find her.'

Joah immersed himself back into the web of spells, and the Rivener lumbered forward.

56

'Barlow! Barlow, where are you?'

There was no answer. The quarry was still hidden behind the trees. The last sliver of Heart-Stone was in a pouch resting against her chest. There would still be time. Tamlyn opened her mouth to shout again – no longer knowing why she shouted, really, just aware that she wanted to see another human being – when the forest around her began to tremble. Snow pattered down from the tops of trees and birds fled into the sky in a sudden cacophony. Tamlyn turned, already knowing what she would see.

The monstrous creature, the thing that was Joah Demonsworn returned, loomed over the tops of the trees, the clutch of violet eyes hanging in the air like alien moons.

Tamlyn threw everything into a single command – run! The werken sped off and immediately the creature was on her. She heard the explosive crash as tree after tree was ripped from its path, saw the debris of branches and earth flying past her. Any moment now, it could reach down and take her, any moment now, unless she got to the quarry.

In seconds she was out past the treeline and the secret pit gaped away in front of her. At first she could see no one, and then Barlow's portly form appeared at the door in the middle of the screen. Even from that distance, Tamlyn could see the look of terror on the woman's face.

'Is it ready?' she screamed.

Barlow opened her mouth, and then shut it again, before disappearing behind the screen.

'Damn you, Barlow!'

The werken scrambled forward, ignoring the paths now and heading directly down the side of the quarry, sending up dust and powdered rock. A shadow passed over them, and Tamlyn kept her eyes narrowed at the screen. It would be waiting for her there – her greatest project, the final werken. There was a low *crump* as Joah's monster put its weight on the area of the pit that had already been extensively mined, and then there was a roaring in Tamlyn's ears, a confused sensation of weightlessness, and sudden bright agony as the skin on the left side of her face was abruptly torn away by the gravelled floor of the pit. The creature had struck out at her, knocking her clean off her werken to land some distance away. Blood stung her eyes as she sat up.

'I . . . what . . .?'

Her werken, the one that she had designed to be shaped like a cat and faster than any other, was a pile of broken, scattered rubble. Tamlyn herself was twenty feet away, although closer to the screen than she had been. The monster, all rock and black iron and veins of Edeian, was watching her, its strangely insectile head turned in her direction.

'Barlow!' Tamlyn winced. She'd broken something deep inside. She had to hope it was only a rib or two. 'I'm coming, Barlow, and if it isn't ready I will skin you myself!'

Keeping half an eye on the monster she dragged herself to her feet, ignoring the sharp pain in her chest and the terrible stinging agony of her face – what was left of it – and half fell, half ran the rest of the way to the screen.

'Tamlyn?' Barlow was at the door again, her eyes wide and her face paper-white. At the sight of Tamlyn she took an involuntary step backwards. 'What are you . . .?'

'Run!'

But it was too late. Darkness passed over them and Tamlyn found she could feel the weight of the thing above her, like an impossible mountain hanging in the sky. In her desperation she tried to pull the pouch from its cord and pass it to Barlow – *our last chance* – but before her fingers found it the stone claw of

375

Joah's monster closed around her, lifting her off her feet and into the air. She saw Barlow's face turned up, slack with terror, and then the thing squeezed. The minor pain of her broken ribs was brushed aside in this new agony, and Tamlyn Nox screamed until she had no more air left in her lungs. There was blood in her mouth, hot and salty.

The pressure eased off slightly and she looked around as best she could. There were the thing's eyes, and now that she was this close she could see that they were just round glass windows, lit from within with sickly purple light. She thought she could see shapes beyond the glass, but her vision was growing dark around the edges.

'Fuck you,' she said, before spitting a mouthful of blood onto the creature's stone fist. 'Fuck you and the monster you rode in on.'

The claw tightened once more around her body, crushing bone against bone, and then the monster threw her out across the tops of the trees.

57

'Are you sure about this?'

Frith looked her steadily in the eye, and it took all of Wydrin's self-control not to wince. The magical outburst at Temerayne, the journey back across the icy wastes to Skaldshollow, the last spells to locate Joah Demonsworn; they had all taken a terrible toll on the young lord, and now he looked close to death, his skin thin and bruised, his hands trembling. But his eyes, still the colour of storm clouds, were unwavering.

'I can do this,' he said, and she tried not to notice the effort it cost him just to speak. 'It is not a spell I have been confident with in the past, but I have been thinking on it, on the words . . .' He paused to take a breath. 'As mad as he is, Joah showed me an awful lot during my time as his prisoner. I believe I can get us inside there. You, me and Sebastian. As I moved us before, at the Citadel.'

They were camped within a copse of trees at the top of the low sloping hill to the south-west of Skaldshollow. From their vantage point they could see the jagged hole the Rivener had torn in the southern wall, the deep grooves in the rock it had made as it scrabbled against the stones for purchase, and they could see the Rivener itself, curled awkwardly around the Tower of Waking like an attentive dog. It was full night now, and the city was almost completely dark, save for the violet eyes of the Rivener and the orange glow of a few fires still burning. When they had first come upon that view in the last smears of evening light, Nuava had dropped to her knees in the snow.

'Where are my people?' she had said eventually. 'Have they all run away?'

They could see no one, and no tracks. The city was eerily quiet.

'He is holding them there,' Frith had answered, with a certainty Wydrin didn't bother to question. 'Those that are still alive, at least.'

Now Nuava was sleeping fitfully, curled up under a blanket next to Mendrick. Prince Dallen had melted away into the woods, intending to scout out the immediate location. Sebastian, tending their small fire, shook his head.

'This will have to be entirely about surprise and misdirection,' he said. 'If he can stop us in our tracks with a single word, then we will have very little time to do this.' The god-blade lay on the ground next to him. The firelight sent strange ripples of colour across its curious metal. *Not metal,* Wydrin corrected herself. *Not if what Sebastian says is true.* 'We will have to hope that our sudden appearance will throw him off his guard.'

'Do not worry,' said Frith. 'I have no doubt Joah will be very surprised to see my face again.' He shifted his weight, wincing as he did so. 'He did seem to develop a certain fascination with me.'

'But you must let us do the work,' said Wydrin. 'You can't go in there all lit up with fireballs and who knows what else. You don't have the strength.'

Frith frowned at that. 'Indeed. Since I am apparently so frail now, you will not mind if I get some sleep?'

Wydrin sat back on her haunches. 'We make our move in the hour before dawn. Be ready.'

Frith turned his back on them, covering himself over with his ragged cloak. Wydrin waited for his breathing to even out, which didn't take long at all.

'He is exhausted,' she commented to Sebastian. 'Even just that small conversation wore him out. He doesn't remember much about our flight from Temerayne, or the journey from Turningspear.' She pulled a twig up from the ground and used it to push some shapes into the mud. 'I asked him, and he remembers the sea monster that came for us, but not much else.'

They fell silent for a few moments, the only sound the brittle crackle of the fire and the distant watery drip of snow melting somewhere beyond the trees.

'How did we get into this mess?' Sebastian said eventually. He caught Wydrin's eye and smiled faintly. 'Even for us, this seems like an especially doomed mission. If Joah is anywhere other than right in front of me, perhaps helpfully bearing his neck for the sword, then I can only see this going one way. Our own mage can offer very little help.'

Wydrin stared at the fire, letting herself become lost in the flames. The heat was a balm against her wind-chapped face.

'We have to try, Seb. What choice do we have?'

'I thought we always had a choice.'

She glanced up at him and saw that he was smiling at her, but his eyes were sad.

'Perhaps you missed the bit about the mad mage with a device that tears the souls from people?' Wydrin winked at him. 'Or maybe you thought that was a particularly strange dream you had.'

'Quite. But I seem to remember that there was a problem with a dragon before, and there was some question over what we would do about it, because we weren't getting paid, and there was this big army in the way, and you only had the one dagger.' Sebastian waved a hand airily, as if reciting a list of groceries. 'My point is, Wyd, that we seem to be racing after Joah Demonsworn by choice. Even if we retrieve the Heart-Stone intact it will do Skaldshollow no good at all now, and I'm getting the impression that the copper promise isn't what this is about.'

Wydrin returned to poking the earth with her twig. 'Well. You know. We're the ones who can sort this out. Who else is going to do it? People will die if we don't. We're the Black Feather Three.' Sebastian grinned at her. 'All right, shut up. All I know is, that bastard has to pay. For Bors, for Frith, and for the rest of Skaldshollow. I'm not letting it end this way.'

Dallen approached from the darkness, stepping up to the fire warily. Seeing the look that passed between him and Sebastian, Wydrin stood up and stretched her arms above her head until her shoulders clicked, and told them both that she needed to go for a piss. She glanced only briefly at Frith's sleeping form before she moved off into the dark, walking slowly to let her eyes adjust to the shadows.

When she was some distance from their camp, she heard Mendrick's voice in her head.

You intend to go through with this, then?

She stopped, keeping herself utterly still, before remembering that such evasive tactics would mean very little to the werken.

It's a plan, she told him. *I think it's worth a shot.*

And what do you suppose your companions would think of this plan?

Wydrin grinned to herself in the dark, glad that no one else could see the desperation of it.

Ah, they wouldn't know a decent plan if it bit them on the arse.

Dallen paced around the fire in a wide circle, his arms crossed over his chest. His movements were precise, controlled. *There is a man who has taught himself to conceal his emotions*, thought Sebastian. *A vital skill in King Aristees' court, no doubt.*

'You truly intend to go without me?'

Sebastian stood up. The sleeping forms of Nuava and Frith were still. He could hear a faint whistling snore coming from the girl.

'We need you here, Dallen.' Sebastian walked around the fire towards him. 'If this doesn't work, then you will have to go and speak to your father. I know how unpleasant that will be.'

'I doubt that you do,' said Dallen, with a raised eyebrow. His fingers brushed the bear's tooth that hung at his neck. 'To him I am no longer his son, Sebastian. He would likely kill me on sight.'

'Even your father wouldn't want a demon-worshipping murderer as a neighbour, I'm sure of it.' He smiled wryly. 'Particularly a warmling one.'

Dallen ignored his attempt to lighten the mood.

'I still think you would stand a better chance of succeeding if I were there. The more weapons the better, surely?'

Sebastian reached out and put his hand on Dallen's arm, the solid shape of his muscles clear through the thin cloth of his sleeves.

380

'I won't lie to you, Dallen. Whether this succeeds or not is largely down to luck. Another sword arm will not help us. And it would put you in danger.'

Dallen did smile at that, although his eyes were still cold.

'Is it the place of a warmling to tell Narhl royalty when they should or shouldn't risk their lives?'

'I – no. Dallen, I know we haven't known each other very long,' Sebastian felt his cheeks grow warm, and he glanced back to the fire to make sure the others were still sleeping, 'but I care about you. I want you. I . . .' He shook his head. 'It has been a long time for me, and in the past I have failed to protect those I loved. I won't fail that way again.'

Dallen stepped fully into the circle of his arms and kissed him, softly at first and then with a growing heat. Sebastian pulled the prince closer, wondering at the icy touch of his fingers as they pressed at his neck, remembering the night they had spent alone outside the cave. All at once it was very difficult to remain standing with any dignity, and he pulled away slightly.

Dallen glared up at him.

'Go, then,' he said eventually. 'Take this with you, though.' He pulled the cord from around his neck and passed it to Sebastian. Up close the bear tooth was carved with a series of interlocking wyverns. His fingers, when he touched Sebastian's, were icy cold, and with a shiver he recalled his skin in the darkness, smooth and unyielding as stone. 'It is the token of a prince, in our lands.' He tipped his head to one side, not quite a nod. 'If you show that to my people, they may listen to you.'

Sebastian took the cord and slipped it around his own neck, trying not to think of Crowleo and the blue glass globe he'd given him.

'I will come back,' he said.

'See that you do.' Dallen took a slow breath. There were beads of sweat on his forehead. 'I will hold you to your oath, Sir Sebastian.'

381

58

'And what should I do?'

It was still dark, with only the faintest band of indigo to the east promising an end to the night. They were as ready as they were going to be, but Nuava was taking some convincing.

'You look after Mendrick,' said Wydrin. She had already drawn her weapons, Frostling and Glassheart held loosely in either hand. Frith stood next to her, his hood drawn up to cast his face in shadow. They had all pretended not to notice how difficult it was for him to simply climb to his feet. 'And keep an eye on our good prince here too.'

Dallen, standing away from the embers of their fire, smiled faintly.

'This is our best plan, Nuava,' said Sebastian. He tried to sound more confident than he felt, but the girl just looked at him with wide eyes. She was standing with one arm looped around the werken's stone neck, as if she could gain strength from his solid shape. 'You and Dallen should move deeper into the forest, further away from the city, where you can't be seen. We don't know exactly what will happen, but if it can be done, we will kill Joah Demonsworn. And we must do it before he kills more of your people.'

'He will not stop,' agreed Frith. His voice was a whisper in the dark. 'He has no care for anything save the accumulation and control of power.'

'Wait, and watch,' said Wydrin. 'It'll be over soon, one way or another.'

Nuava nodded reluctantly.

'Let's do it,' said Frith, 'before I fall over.'

Sebastian stepped back and linked an arm through Frith's, while Wydrin took the other. He made sure to catch Dallen's eye again, although he found he had nothing to say.

'When you're ready, princeling,' said Wydrin. 'Let's go end this bastard.'

Frith tensed, and the darkness of the forest around them began to swirl and twist. There was a terrible wrenching sensation, and, next to him, Sebastian was sure that he would be dashed to the ground, and then the night sky was gone, replaced by a metal ceiling studded with baleful red lights. They were in a large circular room dominated by what looked like a glass tank in an iron wall, and all around them were scattered work tables and benches; just in front of one stood Joah Demonsworn, one side of his face red and glistening, while Ip, grubby faced and short of hair, sat on the table next to him.

There was a beat of silence, during which Sebastian caught Frith's agonised gasp as the magic exacted its toll, and then all hell broke loose.

Wydrin leapt forward, diving straight for Joah with her sword extended in a killing blow – it drew his eyes to her, and Sebastian took the chance to head to the other side of the mage, drawing the god-blade up and to one side.

A single blow, he thought, *and it's over.*

The demon was screaming, the face of Ip twisted into something inhuman, and with a blink Joah seemed to come back to himself. Immediately a wave of invisible force flew at them across the small room, flinging Wydrin back into one of the long tables, while Sebastian staggered back a few paces.

'Kill them!' screamed Bezcavar through Ip's throat. 'Do it now!'

A fireball surged across Sebastian's field of vision, exploding just next to where Ip crouched, and he glanced back to see Frith, leaning heavily against the wall with one hand held shakily out in front of him. Sebastian pushed himself forward again, bringing the god-blade around for a second attempt. It sang in his hands, and he could hear a faint whine as it cut through the air, but before he could even get close to Joah, he saw the indigo blade turn suddenly white, and his fingers were a frost-bitten agony. He cried out, trying to drop the sword, but it was frozen into his hands, a thick layer of ice dulling its wicked edge.

'Quickly,' cried the demon, 'kill the knight first! Crush his bones! In my name, Joah! In my name.'

Joah turned towards him, his brown eyes still faintly puzzled – one side of his face was a bloody ruin – and it was as if a huge hand wrapped around Sebastian's chest and began to squeeze. The sensation moved up his body, ethereal fingers closing around his throat.

'That's it!' Ip was crowing, actually dancing from foot to foot. 'I want to see the blood run from his eyes, my sweet, I want to—'

'Wait!'

Wydrin had climbed on top of one of the tables. She had sheathed both her weapons, and was holding out her empty hands, palms out. For a brief moment there was stillness in the room as everyone turned to look at her. Sebastian felt the last of his breath whistling in his throat.

'Wait,' she said again, 'Demon, I have a proposition for you. Stop throttling my friend, and I promise I will make it worth your while.'

'You think I could want anything more than to see Sebastian Carverson, oath breaker, die with his own blood on his lips?' answered Bezcavar, but the girl gestured to Joah and abruptly the crushing pain in Sebastian's chest and throat vanished. He gasped awkwardly and half collapsed onto the floor.

'I know exactly what you want, demon,' said Wydrin. 'And I'm going to give it to you.'

'Wydrin,' Frith's voice was barely there, and Sebastian could see that the young lord was now kneeling on the floor, his strength completely gone. 'Wydrin, what are you doing?'

'See, I know something about you, demon.' Wydrin walked along the table and idly pushed a bottle off the edge with her boot. It hit the metal floor with a tinkling crash. 'About this whole deal you have here. Your host has to be willing. Am I right?'

'No,' said Sebastian. His throat was an agony but he forced

the words out anyway, because he could see where this was going. 'Wydrin, listen to me.'

'Your host has to be willing, and young Ip was. What else did she have to live for? They were going to sacrifice her at that temple eventually anyway. But she's just a human child, and it will take years before she's the sort of host you can really have fun with.' Wydrin paused, and scratched her nose. 'I can see from the bruises on your face, Bezcavar, that you haven't been having much fun lately.'

'Get to the point, whore creature,' snapped Bezcavar.

Wydrin stopped, looking steadily at the girl and ignoring the rest of them.

'Let Sebastian go and heal Frith of his sickness. Restore him fully, and I will be your willing host.'

Sebastian shoved himself to his feet, still trying to pry his fingers away from the frozen sword.

'I'm older than Ip by quite a bit,' continued Wydrin, 'but I'm not so old. I'm young, and strong, and I have all the skills of a fighter raised in Crosshaven. And it's been said I don't scrub up so bad, given enough patience and soap.'

Ip turned to Joah.

'What do you think?'

Joah Demonsworn looked at Ip, and Sebastian saw so much in that look: desperation, loneliness. Hope. With a new host for the demon, and Frith restored, the mage would have everything he could want, however warped that might be. Joah nodded his head the tiniest fraction and Sebastian knew that it was already too late.

'Wydrin, no!' he bellowed. Frith was trying to get to his feet, trying to do something – the hood had fallen back and the look of horror on his ravaged face was stark.

Ip shrugged, one narrow shoulder rising and falling. 'It is done.'

Frith cried out as he was suddenly enveloped in a glowing, ruby red mist. Wydrin drew Frostling again.

'Demon, if you look to double-cross me—'

'Stop whining, human,' Bezcavar flapped one slim hand impatiently. 'I am doing as you asked.'

The red mist faded back into nothing, and Frith stood up,

looking mildly stunned. His skin was back to its more usual warm brown, and the dark circles were gone from his eyes. He was standing up straight again, and even the emaciated cast had vanished from his wiry form – he looked as well as Sebastian had ever seen him, even after the healing waters of the Mages' lake.

'How are you feeling, princeling?'

Frith shook his head as if to clear it. 'Wydrin, of all the ridiculous, foolish things you've ever done—'

'That sounds more like it.' Wydrin beckoned to the demon. 'Come on, then, shorty, a deal's a deal.'

It happened so quickly that later Sebastian would examine his memories over and over, sure he must have missed something. The child Ip dropped to the floor in an ungainly heap, and Wydrin rocked backwards, nearly falling off the table. Joah, who still looked somewhat lost, glanced between the two of them uncertainly.

'Wydrin?' Frith's voice was stronger now, and filled with dread. 'What have you done?'

There were a few beats of silence. Sebastian found that he could not take his eyes from Wydrin. She was shaking her head like a dog with a wasp in its mouth, and then abruptly she stopped and grinned. Her eyes were filled with blood.

'Now this is much better,' she said, and her voice wasn't her voice at all.

'Demon,' Sebastian edged forward, the god-blade held out in front of him. 'You will vacate that body at once.'

Frith stared at the woman on the table. Save for the eyes it still looked like Wydrin, but there was a subtle difference in the way she was standing, an uprightness that felt a million miles away from her usual poised swagger.

'What are you going to do, good sir knight?' said Bezcavar with Wydrin's mouth. 'Run your friend through? Cut off her head? I don't really see you doing that.'

'It was a mistake,' said Sebastian. He was speaking through gritted teeth. 'She didn't mean it. Take it back.'

'Oh, but she did. It's fascinating really, but she's rather fond of both of you.' Wydrin frowned ponderously, an expression Frith had never seen her pull before. 'I can tell, you know, when someone is truly willing. All part of being a demon. Now that I'm in here, in her head, it's darker than I was expecting. All the things she never said. Especially to you.' The demon turned Wydrin's head so that the blood-filled eyes were gazing directly at Frith. 'I'm sure I don't know what you've done to inspire such loyalty.'

'Wydrin.' There was a rushing sensation in Frith's chest. 'Wydrin, are you still in there?'

'Oh, she's still here, but I have her firmly under control. I know better than to let this one . . . to let this one . . . out . . . I . . .'

The demon shook its head again, frowning fiercely, and for the briefest second the eyes flickered back to their more usual green. Wydrin staggered as though she'd been struck in the stomach.

'Stop that,' came Bezcavar's voice again, although now there was a note of panic.

'Wydrin!' Frith tried to meet her eyes. 'Wydrin, I know you can hear me. You have to fight it!'

'Come back to us, Wyd,' Sebastian reached out a hand to her, 'you're stronger than it.'

'That's where you're wrong!' Wydrin grinned, her eyes bloody again. 'I am not some cloak to be shrugged back off again, and I—' She screamed suddenly, a howl of frustration and pain. She staggered back and half jumped, half fell off the table, landing at the bottom of the steps leading up to the Rivener aperture. She glanced up at them, and her eyes were green again.

'Get out of here, you idiots,' she said, before running up the rest of the steps and jumping down into the Rivening chamber. She hit the floor in there, writhing in the violet light as though she'd fallen into a pit of snakes.

'No!'

Frith ran, meaning to smash the glass open and drag her out, but the light of the Rivener shimmered, and he saw her eyes roll up to the whites as something wraith-like and barely visible streamed from her body. He had time to see her shiver convulsively, once, and then the floor below her opened, dropping her body out of sight.

For the briefest second, Frith found he could hardly breathe, and then he felt the Edenier blossom in his chest – a pure, white light, a power he'd never even guessed at before. It was as if he were the taper, and he was ready to burn the entire world.

Turning on Joah, he held out his arms.

59

There was a moment's shocked silence, and Sebastian just about had time to register Wydrin's limp body passing out of sight before Frith seemed to actually explode. In the resulting wave of force Sebastian was thrown bodily across the room, colliding painfully against the metal wall before collapsing on the floor, the god-blade torn from his grasp.

'Aaron!' Joah had thrown up a force field of some sort around himself, which was holding off Frith's numerous attacks. Even so, the mage was bent over with the effort of keeping it in place, his lips twisted into a grim line. 'Aaron, stop this!'

'I will destroy you!' The young lord was a beacon of light, the Edenier peeling off him in bright, shimmering streams. Sebastian could smell sulphur and burning hair. 'I will destroy all of you!'

The small figure of Ip lay on the floor, disregarded. Sebastian inched over to it, trying to see if there was any life in the girl's face.

'We can work together now,' Joah's face, twisted and burnt, was all the more terrible for the expression of hope that was trying to blossom there, 'don't you see? There's nothing to get in our way!'

Sebastian pressed his fingers to the girl's throat. There was a pulse, rapid and shallow. The floor beneath him shuddered suddenly, and he looked up to see that the ceiling above the bright shape that was Frith was beginning to glow a deep, ruby red. The magic was overpowering the Rivener.

'Frith!' he shouted, not expecting to be heard over the noise.

'The woman was a distraction,' said Joah, 'your feelings for her, a mistake. Now that she's dead . . .'

'We have to get out of here!' Sebastian tried again.

It was too late. There was a shattering explosion, so loud that Sebastian felt his ear drums cramp painfully, and a deafening screeching noise, which he belatedly recognised as metal being torn apart. The chamber was flooded with weak daylight. Risking a glance upwards he saw that Frith had blown the top of the room off; twisted fingers of blackened metal clutched at the dawn sky. A beacon of green light shot upwards, and Sebastian caught sight of Frith and Joah, their bodies lit from within so that he could see their bones.

As quickly as it had happened, it was over. Frith was swaying on his feet, his white hair standing on end. Joah was on his knees. His eyes looked too wide in the blasted ruin of his face.

'That was quite the display.'

They all looked towards that voice. That new voice.

Sebastian pulled himself up on his elbows, and his breath caught in his throat. Standing on the far side of the chamber, amongst the debris of the tables and equipment, was O'rin, god of lies and tricks. Sebastian himself had never seen him, but he'd heard both Wydrin and Frith's descriptions and it could hardly be anyone else; the figure stood nearly eight foot tall, his body covered with a thick cloak of black feathers, his giant bird's head cocked slightly to one side, as if amused. His yellow and black eyes glistened.

'I thought it was likely time to check up on you again, young Lord Frith, but I have to say –' he gestured with his leathery grey hands '– I did not expect this. Whatever this is.'

Joah stood with his mouth hanging open. Luckily, Frith recovered himself first.

'It's a trap.' He stepped forward, waving a warning. 'You must leave, O'rin, immediately. This man means you harm.'

'The one with the crispy face? Surely not, lad,' O'rin chuckled. 'There is little any of you can do to harm a god, you must know that.'

Sebastian scrambled for the god-blade, which had landed some feet away from him in the violence of the explosion, but Joah was faster. His arm twitched and the sword leapt into the air, turning in a deadly arc as the ice melted from it in a shimmer of steam. O'rin caught sight of the shining blue blade and he must have known it for what it was, or else recognised an artefact of his deadly sibling, for he collapsed into a whirling confusion of black birds. In seconds the chamber was full of them, flying in circles and squawking madly, but they didn't seem able to fly up past the roof, despite the empty sky that was waiting there for them.

Sebastian held an arm up over his face, trying to see what was going on.

'O'rin? You must leave, now!'

Joah was laughing, the god-blade clutched in both hands.

'I helped to make a trap for you once before, god of lies. You thought you could evade it for ever?'

The birds flew up still, crashing into whatever invisible force was keeping O'rin inside the Rivener. They fell, one by one, delicate bones broken or simply stunned, until abruptly O'rin was back, lying on the floor, his eyes rolling in his great bird head.

'Frith?' he croaked. 'Why do you trap me so? Did I not help you?'

'It's not me,' Frith cried. The young lord gestured at Joah as though to throw him back with another spell, but all but two of the silk strips from around his arms had disintegrated into ash. Instead he knelt by the god, trying to help him up. 'This was not my doing, you must believe me . . .'

Joah ran, staggering slightly under the weight of the sword, and brought the god-blade down in a sweeping blow. Sebastian managed to draw his own sword and get its blade in the way, but the god-blade sheared through it as though his broadsword were made of mist, and it continued its deadly journey. The blue sword struck O'rin just below his beak – coming within a hair's breadth of decapitating Frith too – and split the god's neck open in one blow. There was a dreadful screech, as of a thousand birds calling at once, and then something that wasn't blood burst from the terrible wound, black and shining like oil. Frith scrambled away, crying out in revulsion as the substance soaked into the

391

knees of his trousers, but Joah was already there, one hand delving into the torn flesh of O'rin's neck.

'Do not do this.' Sebastian stood with his broken sword useless in his hand. 'You can still step back from this. Your soul is not entirely damned. Believe me, I know.'

Joah laughed, and with a brief gesture summoned a flickering wall of white light between them. Sebastian touched his fingers to it and wasn't surprised to find that the wall burnt them, raising painful blisters. Turning away from the two of them, Joah held a handful of the black oily flesh up to his lips and shoved it in his mouth, smearing his beard and chin with the stuff. He chewed and swallowed, and then licked the palm of his hand, while O'rin's life's blood seeped through the metal grill underneath him.

'I can feel it,' he said.

Frith backed away, gesturing to Sebastian, who snatched up the god-blade from where Joah had discarded it.

'Oh no,' said Joah, absently. 'I don't think I want that little relic hanging about any longer, not now I have the power to destroy it.'

He lifted one hand, fingers flexing like the legs of a dying spider, and the brightly shining blade softened and then ran, melting like candle wax. Sebastian cried out and dropped it, and within moments it was little more than a stain on the floor. The elaborate silver hilt was untouched.

'Good, good,' muttered Joah, turning back to O'rin's corpse. He didn't appear to be taking much notice of them now. 'I can feel it changing me.' He took another handful of the flesh, pushing it down his own throat slowly. He swallowed hard. 'It's changing me inside, and outside, and it's . . . this must have been what it was like for those first mages, when they struck down Ede and ate her. It must –' The words dried up. His face had lost all its colour, leaving a gaunt, paper-white mask half ruined with burnt flesh. It seemed to be growing longer somehow, as though it were made of dough and someone were pulling it into a subtly different shape. His eyes wept black tears. 'I feel strange.'

Above them, the sky that had been clear and blue a moment ago was darkening, turning purple, and then red at the edges.

Sebastian could see a rippling, barely visible skein up there, as though a bloody caul had been pulled over the surface of the world.

Frith took his arm. 'Let's get out of here.'

The world twisted again, and the last thing Sebastian saw as Frith spirited them away were Joah's hands, now long and tapered, delving back into O'rin's corpse.

PART FOUR
In the City of the Dead

60

Ephemeral held her hands under the water, palms facing up. The boggy water was cloudy with silt and algae but she could still see the tiny amphibians swimming there; they were a darker green than her own skin, their perfectly formed limbs kicking wildly, tickling her fingers. She considered clenching her hands into fists, an act that would no doubt crush the creatures into sludge – something she would have done without a thought a year ago. Instead she let her hands fall away, and the swarm of tiny baby frogs vanished back into the tepid waters of the swamp. She thought of Sebastian, now in the city of Skaldshollow, somewhere beyond these swamps and forests. It was strange to be without him, and she found she had a hundred new questions every day, but there was nothing to be done about that; she would just have to wait. She stood up to see Crocus coming towards her, crashing through the water and mud and stirring up a hearty stench.

'There's a settlement half a day's walk from here,' she said. Ephemeral's sister was broader across the shoulders than she was, and when she spoke for any length of time her brow would furrow slightly. It still didn't come easily, to talk so much. 'Flute and Havoc mapped the place out on their way round it.' Crocus reached into a pocket and retrieved a slightly damp section of parchment, which she passed to Ephemeral. 'Here, look.'

Ephemeral turned it around in her hands, tracing a finger around the boundaries of the settlement. It was a very rough

397

drawing of the place, marked out in a dark red wax that Havoc had made for the purpose of drawing maps on the move. Looking at it, Ephemeral felt a twin jolt of jealousy and pride; Havoc was so clever at making things.

'It is good,' she said. 'I will put it with the others.'

Sliding the pack from her back she removed a thick leather tube. Inside were several such makeshift maps, contributed by many different brood sisters.

'We will go around the village, then?' asked Crocus. They were walking through the swamp water together, the muck coming up above their leather-clad knees.

'You know we must,' said Ephemeral. 'We must keep out of sight as much as possible. Until we are ready to move.' Havoc emerged from the trees, recently returned from making maps. Her short hair shimmered around her green face like a halo.

'There are people nearby,' she said, her face bright with excitement. 'A man, a woman and a child.'

'How close?'

'A short walk,' said Havoc, her face growing serious. 'I can show you.'

Ephemeral looked to Crocus, who shrugged. 'Quickly then,' she said. 'And let us be as quiet as possible.'

Havoc led Ephemeral and Crocus away from the relatively solid area where the sisters had made their camp into a wilder part of the swamp. Around them the last light of the day was a dirty orange, pooling in dribs and drabs on the brown water. The continual buzzing of the insects was growing louder, as though they sensed the coming of the night.

After a time, Havoc crouched low in the water, holding up one clawed hand in warning. Ephemeral narrowed her eyes and yes, there was movement ahead. Between the trees two adult humans were moving back and forth slowly, their eyes on the boggy water that came up to their shins. They both wore aprons that bulged at the bottom, and, as Ephemeral watched, the female one bent down and plucked something from the water, placing it carefully inside the wet apron.

'What are they doing?'

'They are collecting these,' Havoc retrieved something from within her own pack and passed it over to Ephemeral. It was a fat pale lump, hard to the touch. 'They grow in deep places in the swamp.'

'What do they do with them?' asked Crocus. Ahead of them a child had now come into view, obviously less interested in harvesting than its parents.

'They eat them,' said Havoc. When her sisters looked at her incredulously, she shrugged one shoulder. 'Try it.'

Ephemeral sniffed the lump cautiously, before nibbling one of its tumour-like protuberances. It tasted like water and dirt and mushrooms, and yet there was a deep, savoury undertone that made her want to keep on eating. She passed it over to Crocus, who took a large bite.

'We could probably move closer,' said Havoc. 'They could not smell us from where they are.'

Indeed, humans didn't seem to be able to smell anything much, but even so, Ephemeral felt her stomach tighten slightly. Too well, she remembered how the girl in the red cloak had screamed. She remembered the face of the knight who had come to them in the darkness and killed so many of her sisters.

'This is close enough.'

The child was jumping about now, taking big exaggerated steps to cause the biggest possible splashes. The male human raised his voice, and although they couldn't make out the words, Ephemeral sensed distinctly that the child had been admonished for her behaviour.

'Do you remember being small?' asked Crocus in a low voice. 'Do you remember being . . . not what we are now?'

Ephemeral looked at her sister. She was watching the child intently, her yellow eyes following her every movement.

'I remember the birthing pits. Although it is hazy,' said Ephemeral. This was not something she had thought about in a long time. 'I remember closeness, the sense of you all, pressed in around me. The heat of our mother's fires. The bare flesh of the rock.'

'I remember being half formed,' said Havoc. 'A sense of being incomplete.'

Ephemeral nodded, pleased that Havoc had found the words she could not.

'It is like the frogs before they are frogs,' she said, thinking of the tiny animals she had held in her hands. 'Before they are frogs they are strange things, with no arms or legs. They are unfinished.'

The two adult humans were starting to move away, their aprons heavy with collected tubers. The child was hanging back, apparently unsatisfied with the layer of mud she had already accumulated.

'We were finished when the blood awoke us,' said Crocus.

Ephemeral frowned. 'I don't know if that's true.'

'Humans start off small, and get slowly bigger,' said Crocus. 'How—'

'Hello.'

They turned as one to the small figure standing a few feet away from them. The child was older than the one they'd been watching, but the physical resemblance was such that Ephemeral knew at once that this was a relative; an older sister perhaps. She had an apron full of tubers. Her dark hair was pulled back from her face and she was watching them with open curiosity.

Ephemeral fought down the surge of fear that immediately threatened to close her throat. She glanced at her sisters. They were both utterly still, waiting for her orders.

'Hello,' she said. Talking suddenly felt like the hardest thing she'd ever done. 'Is this your swamp?'

The girl looked amused at that. 'This is everyone's swamp. Are you a green jenny?'

Ephemeral blinked rapidly. The child's parents were no longer in sight, and she couldn't see the other child either.

'A what?'

The girl took a few steps forward, trying to look at all three of them at once. 'A green jenny. They're spirits of the trees and water. They look after all the tiny animals here, and they don't really like humans so they hide away. Is that what you are?'

'We are green jenny's cousins,' said Havoc. 'We are just here for a visit.'

The child nodded seriously. 'If you come back here, don't hide. Say hello to me, at least.' She smiled. 'It is so boring, harvesting the eelwort. And I won't hurt you, I promise.'

Ephemeral smiled tightly. 'We will be sure to do that, then.'

400

There came a distant shout, and the girl gathered up her apron strings. 'I have to go now, green jennies. See you next time!'

She ran off, crashing through the mud and water much as her smaller sibling had done. Ephemeral and the brood sisters stayed where they were until she was gone, none of them daring to speak.

'We should move away from here,' said Crocus eventually. 'If she speaks to her parents . . .'

'Agreed,' said Ephemeral.

They walked back, being extra vigilant in case they should cross the family's path once more. Ephemeral found herself thinking of Sebastian – soon, he would call for them. She could feel it in her blood.

When they were back at the camp, she sought out his voice in her head, listening for that silver chord that was his presence in her mind; this was something they had worked on together, before they had been forced away from the training grounds. For a moment she could feel him – still incredibly distant but as familiar as her own blood, and she could tell that he was troubled. She frowned slightly, wondering what could have befallen their father in the city of Skaldshollow.

401

61

The first clue that they were no longer where they had been was the soft orange glow warming Sebastian's eyelids. He opened his eyes into blindingly bright sunshine, a heat on his face so intense that he could already feel sweat trickling between his shoulder blades.

'Where are we?'

He sat up, feeling grains of sand between his fingers. Golden dunes surrounded him, dotted here and there with pale rocks and not much else. A deep blue sky, entirely innocent of clouds, reached from horizon to horizon. Some distance away Frith was already climbing to the top of one dune, his thick bearskin cloak discarded.

'Frith, what are you doing?'

The young lord didn't turn around at the sound of his voice, and shortly he was lost to sight over the top of the dune. Sebastian got to his feet, stumbling slightly as his vision blurred and his head swam. Frith's transportation spell was not the most pleasant way to travel.

'Frith, wait!'

Clambering awkwardly in boots made for rock and snow, Sebastian followed Frith's shallow prints over the summit of the dune and looked down at a collection of ruins, half hidden amongst the sand. He could make out a rough shape of what might once have been a temple made of yellow rock, but either time or some sort of natural calamity had broken it all apart, caving in the roof and shattering the walls; with the sand swamping it like some sort of static sea it was difficult to tell which. Frith was already picking his way over the crumbling walls, apparently heading for a portion of the temple where two flat sections of the roof had fallen against each other, creating a dark, shadowy space. Sebastian called him again, but he still didn't respond.

'By all the gods, Frith,' Sebastian muttered, before stomping down after him. His legs were longer than the young lord's, and when he caught up he grabbed Frith by the shoulder, spinning him around to face him. 'Where have you brought us?'

Frith glared up at him, his grey eyes ablaze. The fury and the grief there hurt Sebastian's heart, and with a lurch he remembered Wydrin's limp form falling from sight, beyond their reach.

'Please, Frith,' he said, consciously softening his voice. 'Tell me what's going on.'

'I've brought us to where we need to be.' He gestured to the dark space behind them. 'There are tools here, things that will help me defeat Joah Demonsworn.'

Sebastian glanced from the dark space back to Frith's unwavering gaze. 'What about Wydrin, Frith? Can you not find her?'

Frith shook his head abruptly. 'I have already done the spell.' He raised both his hands, a strip of soiled silk hanging from each wrist. There was a flicker of dusty light between his fingers and a dull red glow appeared. There seemed to be shapes beyond the glow, dark figures and a shifting, tremulous web of shadows, but nothing that Sebastian recognised. 'If she were still alive . . . I don't know what this is showing us, but it is not Wydrin. I saw what happened to people who went through the Rivener.'

He dropped his hands and the eerie red glow vanished. With his right hand he produced Crowleo's light-globe, and turned to head into the ruins. After a moment Sebastian followed him, ducking awkwardly under the shattered roof.

'What is it you hope to find here?' From what Sebastian could see in the wavering light the ruins had long since been emptied of anything useful. Huge blocks of sandstone littered the floor, along with one stone column that had cracked down the middle. The air was thick with dust, and smelt of acrid desert nights and old blood.

'A head start,' replied Frith. He was moving off to the back of the temple, skirting the fallen column and climbing over the occasional low block. Wydrin's deal with the demon had certainly healed the young lord; any sign of his old limp had completely vanished. Thinking of that, Sebastian felt a surge of anger. How could she do such a thing? And after his own disastrous dealings with the same cursed creature. He bit down on the anger, knowing too well that it was a disguise for sorrow.

'It is below these stones.' Frith was crouching next to what looked like a random jumble of sandy bricks. 'After all these years.' He pushed the debris out of the way as best he could and, underneath, was a smooth grey stone, quite unlike all the others. 'This one is wedged in,' he said. 'I don't think I can drag it out without disturbing the objects beneath it. Can you help me?'

Sebastian crouched on the other side of the flat stone and together they pried it up and shifted it over, with Sebastian taking most of the weight. Underneath there was more sand.

'Are you going to tell me what this is about?'

Frith glanced up at him briefly, before running his fingers through the sand.

'When we first met,' he said, 'you would call me, "my lord". Do you remember that? Wydrin didn't, of course, and never did, but you always paid the proper respect. That seems to have lessened somewhat, these days.'

Sebastian stared at him. 'What are you talking about?'

Frith continued to run his fingers through the sand, sifting it and pushing soft piles of it out of the way.

'In the Blackwood they will be preparing the castle. There was still so much missing when I left, and I had to commission a carpenter to make all new furniture. There were some bits and pieces left, of course, some items that Fane and the Lady Bethan didn't burn or sell, but it all felt tainted. It was to have been a new age.'

'Frith, she could still be alive,' Sebastian cut in, hating the desperate hope in his own voice. 'Everything was chaotic. We can't know exactly what happened.'

'She jumped into the Rivener, and it tore her soul from her,' said Frith in the sort of patient tone used to instruct a particularly stupid child. 'Her body fell from the chamber into the streets, and

I saw what the Rivener did, Sebastian, and you do not want to see it, you do not want to *contemplate* what that would mean.' He stopped and took a breath. 'All that is left to me is vengeance. It seems that after everything that's happened, that is all I was meant for after all. And this will help me achieve it.'

He pulled something from the sand. It was made of rough black metal and was the size and shape of a large grapefruit. It looked like it had been constructed from strips of black metal, turned and bent to create a jagged ball. There were shapes welded into it, crude markings that Sebastian vaguely recognised from the interior of the Rivener itself.

'What is it?'

'I told you that when Joah held me prisoner we exchanged certain information. He took my memories, flicked through them like a book. It was most unpleasant. But the door opened both ways, and although there was plenty that Joah showed me deliberately, in order for me to progress as his pupil, I also saw a great deal that I do not believe he intended me to see, including some of his earliest memories of the demon.' Frith turned the rusted globe of metal over and over in his hands. 'When the other mages came for him, when they'd decided that they could no longer pay the price for his genius, he started to construct a weapon. This was it. He called it the Edenier trap. And this,' he gestured around the ruins of the temple, 'this is where he made it and there should be other parts buried here. This was a temple to Bezcavar, back in the age of the mages. We're in the largest desert in western Creos, known as the Desert of Bones.'

Sebastian eyed the object warily. 'And what does this thing do?'

'Well, it's actually a forerunner of the Rivener, in a sense, although instead of extracting the Edenier from a soul and storing it, it has a much simpler approach. The Edenier trap destroys magic. He intended to deploy it against his enemies, rendering them devoid of the Edenier and unable to pursue him.'

Sebastian looked at it. The thing looked unspeakably ancient, a rusted relic from another time.

'And this thing works?'

Frith shook his head. 'It never did. Joah could not quite get it right, and Bezcavar convinced him that it would be a waste, just to destroy all that magic. Wouldn't it be better, the demon suggested, if you could just take it and keep it for yourself?'

They sat for a few moments in silence. Sebastian thought he had never been in such an unnaturally silent place; even the mountains of Ynnsmouth had the wind for company, and the eternal sounds of ice melting.

'You think you can finish what Joah started.' It wasn't quite a question. Frith nodded.

'It will involve using what I know of the demon's tools, and I am fairly certain that doing that helped to push Joah towards his madness, but it is our best hope.'

'I can testify that having anything to do with that creature isn't a wise move,' said Sebastian. He felt uneasy just looking at the Edenier trap, and he didn't think that was entirely due to recent events. There was an aura of darkness to it that seemed to suck the light from the light-globe. It sat within its own shadows. 'Frith, this is too risky. We can find some other way.'

Frith laughed, and the bitterness in that small sound turned Sebastian's blood cold.

'Did you not see what he became, before we ran away? We are no longer dealing with Joah the mad mage.' He shook his head. 'With O'rin's blood on his lips, he is something else altogether. We need to destroy the Edenier inside him, or it will never be over. Whatever the cost.'

Sebastian sat back on his haunches. 'If you think you can do it, Frith, then I'm with you. I'm with you to the end.' He found himself remembering the night he had met Wydrin for the first time. He saw her standing in the middle of the cobbled street, waving her dagger at the retreating thugs who had been trying to kill him, laughing so hard she had doubled over, clutching her stomach with mirth. When she'd got the last of her giggles out, she had turned to him and grinned, offering him a hand. 'Come on, big man,' she'd said. 'That ale in your stomach will be getting lonely by now.' Wydrin, who had been reckless and stupid and loyal. He bent over the half-filled pit and began searching through the sand himself.

'Just tell me what you need.'

62

Nuava hit the ground rolling, snow in her mouth and gasping for air. Moments ago she had been dozing by their small fire, thinking about the stew that Bors would make for them sometimes – venison and mushrooms, steeped in grut and simmered for hours – when there had been an enormous crash, flinging her bodily into the snow. She glanced up to see Mendrick standing with his stony back to her, and beyond him, a group of men and women she didn't recognise. Narhl men and women. They had spears.

'Wait!' she spat watery snow onto the ground, tasting dirt. 'You have to help us, you have to—'

One of the men threw an ice-spear at her and she threw herself out of the way, landing awkwardly and gasping as the flash of cold caught the very edge of her coat, freezing it stiff instantly.

'Skald scum,' spat one of the women. 'You should not have left the walls of your city.'

Where was Prince Dallen? Nuava looked around wildly but she couldn't see him. He'd been off scouting, as he spent so much of his time doing.

'You don't understand.' She held her hands out to them, palms facing outwards. She could see nothing but hatred in their eyes. 'Skaldshollow is under attack, and we're all in terrible danger.'

'Oh, we know all about that.' A man at the front of the group stepped forward. He was tall, with long black hair that tumbled in braids down his back. He grinned at her, and she saw that there was lichen in his black beard. 'That is why we are here,

407

snivelling Skald warmling. While your paltry warriors are fighting this new threat, we will blast your walls down and drag you all out to die in the snow.'

Nuava had climbed to her feet while he was talking, her heart thudding sickly in her chest. Mendrick still stood, unmoving, just to the front of her. *I am a crafter of the Edeian,* she told herself firmly, *I will not let them see me afraid.*

It was easier said than done, though. When she spoke again her voice broke like thin ice. 'Joah Demonsworn will come for you next,' she said. She wished she still had Wydrin's dagger with her, for comfort if nothing else. 'He will not be satisfied with the souls of my people. He won't stop until the whole of the North is a wasteland, empty of people and tainted with evil.'

'Tainted with evil?' The man's grin dropped away abruptly, his pebble-coloured face a collection of sharp angles. 'Your people have been poisoning this land for generations, creating your abominations and enslaving the mountain.' He gestured to Mendrick with his spear. 'The loss of the Skalds will be a blessing to the land.'

Unconsciously, Nuava took a step towards Mendrick.

'Let her be the first to fall,' called one of the warriors. Another stepped up, and now three or four ice-spears were levelled at her. Nuava had a moment to catch a quick movement in the trees off to her right, and then the spears were falling. She screamed, scrambling out of the way, knowing she couldn't possibly make it to cover in time, and then a bulky shape moved abruptly in front of her. There was a shattering explosion, throwing her to the ground again, and her scalp stung in several places as a shower of small rocks pelted the back of her coat. Someone was shouting at her, telling her to run.

'Go, Nuava! Hide!'

She glanced over her shoulder and saw two things at once: Mendrick, who had apparently moved into the path of the ice-spears, was now a broken collection of rocks, a ruined chunk of stone where his head had been, and Prince Dallen was there, standing over the werken's body, a sword in one hand and a spear in the other.

The werken moved!

'What is this?' one of the Narhl warriors was jeering. 'Not our exiled prince, surely?'

'Dallen!' Already the soldiers not glaring at Dallen were circling around the icy ruins of Mendrick, coming for her with cold glee in their eyes. The prince didn't turn when he shouted this time.

'Just run, girl!' he said. 'Get away from here!'

Swallowing down a sob, Nuava turned and half ran, half fell out of the clearing and into the trees. She could hear pursuit close behind her, could even hear their laughter. *I won't make it ten feet*, she thought, trying not to think of Mendrick's body, dead because he had defended her, or Prince Dallen, who would likely be joining him soon. Instead, she tried to think what the sell-sword Wydrin would do.

For a start, she would put something between her and their bastard-spears.

Immediately she veered off to where the trees were thickest, crashing through undergrowth and the hardened snow as she did so, feeling branches tear at her clothes and scratch her face. There was a thunderous crack as an ice-spear hit a tree behind her, splitting the trunk, and then a series of thuds as they threw more. She felt the temperature drop, her fingers bright with agony and the air in her chest seemingly made of daggers, but she kept moving, and they didn't quite catch her.

She ran deeper into the trees, always heading to where the foliage was thickest. They were fast, and they were still laughing, but she was smaller than them, and she sensed that their passage through the trees was not so easy. The laughter turned to cursing, and even better than that, it grew quieter as she gradually gained a lead on them. Gasping for breath now, a sharp pain in her chest steadily growing, she kept on moving, grimly ignoring the thin trickle of blood from the scratches on her face and the biting cold in her hands. Soon, she was in a part of the forest so thick that the sky was a distant blue mosaic above her, cut into a thousand pieces by the black branches that reached across it. The sounds of pursuit faded, and then she couldn't hear them at all. Eventually, she paused by an enormous fir tree and leaned against its trunk, trying to get her breath back. *Listen*, she told herself. *You must be careful now.*

She listened. There was silence in the trees, with only the sounds of her own breathing and the creaking, wet sounds of the forest. She could not hear the Narhl, and she could hear no battle. Was it over already, Prince Dallen lying dead in the snow next to Mendrick? Or had she run so far that the noises were muffled?

She looked around, trying to get some sense of where she was in relation to Skaldshollow. She was somewhere in the east of the forest that blanketed the mountain next to her city; a wild place, with no paths or signs of human habitation. The forest was big, she knew that much, and she'd grown up with stories of children foolish enough to wander into it with no guide. It was their fate to be eaten by wolves, or taken by the Narhl, who would use their skins as blankets for Narhl children. Or, at least, that was what the grown-ups had told them. She tried to imagine Prince Dallen, with his proud, kind face, skinning a child and found she could not.

'Even if that story is a lie, I suspect there are still plenty of creatures in here that would happily eat me.' Her voice sounded tiny and unsure, but the simple human sound of it was reassuring. 'I could well be in trouble here.'

She decided to keep walking the way she'd been heading; it wouldn't do to double back and stumble across the Narhl patrol. Perhaps they had given up already, and gone back to their plan of attacking Skaldshollow while its people were distracted. She almost hoped they would. It would serve them right.

Everything she'd had – her bag of scavenged food, the flask of rum borrowed from Wydrin – had been back at their camp. Even her warmest hat had fallen off as she'd run from the Narhl, and although the walking kept her blood moving she could already feel the temperature dropping. How much time had passed? She looked up at the sky and was dismayed to see the clear blue starting to darken to an ominous indigo. Sooner than she wanted, she saw the bright glint of stars in the sky, and a deep, insidious sort of cold began to seep into her bones. Wrapping her arms around herself she stumbled onwards, trying not to think too closely about any of it, about how she was lost out here on her own, her brother dead, her newly made friends far away. And Mendrick dead, of course, the consciousness she'd only just realised existed blasted away in a moment of violence. He had moved by himself – Wydrin was much too far away to command the werken, and even if she had, how could she have known to move him just then? No, the werken had *chosen* to move, a concept that would have been unthinkable to any Skald. If the Narhl were right, perhaps Mendrick had returned to the mountain, one small part of the mind returning to the greater whole, but she couldn't help feeling that was of little comfort.

Some time later – she could not tell how long, save that the sky was black and the forest lit only by frosted moonlight – her legs gave way beneath her and she fell to the ground, rolling awkwardly into a thorn bush and coming to rest with her chest pressed against frozen mud. The shock of it knocked a sob from her, the first in hours. She would die out here, away from her home and her family, and she would be no great crafter of the Edeian – just a lost child in the woods, her corpse covered in snow and chewed on by animals. She let herself cry, harsh sobs at first, eventually dissolving into miserable sniffles. The tears warmed her face and seemed to wake her up. *I've been walking in a daze*, she thought. *Things are bad, but I'm no idiot.*

She sat up, rubbing a cold hand across her wet face. After a few moments she realised the thorn bush she'd fallen into was both large and old, and if she shoved herself far inside, it was reasonably dry, the thick twisted branches above keeping most of the snow off. She dug herself a small space, and after some trial and error, had the makings of a fire. By this time she was certain that the Narhl were no longer on her trail, but even so, as she coaxed it into life with the flint and a blunt cooking knife she'd been keeping in her pocket, she kept the flames small, just enough to warm her hands and bring some life back into her frozen feet.

Inside the thorn bush, the fire became her entire world, so bright it blotted out the cold and the black. Nuava stared into it, telling herself the same things over and over until her eyelids began to droop: *Things will look better in the daylight, and I will be able to find my way. Things will look better in the daylight, and I will be able to find my way. Things will look better in the daylight . . .*

* * *

411

She awoke at dawn with a gasp, certain that only a noise could have brought her out of sleep so suddenly. The small fire had long since died, and the forest was still largely dark; the steely grey light of dawn painted the bush and the trees in insomnia's colours, bleached and half-unreal.

There was a sharp crack, off to her left. The sound of a branch breaking on the ground, as if trodden on by a heavy boot. Slowly, Nuava came out of the bush, trying to look in every direction at once. Again, she thought of Wydrin's heavy dagger.

Another crunch, and a shifting of foliage. And after that, a sigh. Nuava heard it clearly, and it was close. She balled her fists at her side, torn between running and facing down whatever had followed her. All around her the forest was still draining away the night's shadows, and every darkened space seemed to hold a threatening figure. She remembered the horrors of the centipedes' lair, of being caught in their terrible, grasping pincers. She had survived. Compared to that, being out in the woods alone was nothing at all.

Nuava took a deep breath. 'Who's there? I can hear you.'

For a few seconds there was nothing save for the rustle of leaves and the drip of melting snow, and then another crunching footstep in the bracken, followed by a low groan. Nuava tensed, still primed to run. The noises seemed to be coming from just ahead, where a pair of tree trunks grew closely together, each wider than Nuava with her arms held out to either side. There was a patch of darkness between them, and in that space she could see movement. She was almost sure of it.

'Come out of there,' she said, willing her voice to remain steady. 'I can see you.' Something pale and dishevelled flopped out of the dark patch between the trees, falling heavily against a trunk and clinging there. Nuava could make out long dark hair hiding a downcast face, and torn clothing. The figure groaned again.

'Who are you? What do you want?'

'I've found you.' The figure shook its head, and a sense of eerie familiarity tickled at the back of Nuava's mind. She swallowed hard, barely daring to believe it. 'I told them I would do that at least, and I did.'

'Tamlyn?'

The figure raised its head, and Nuava felt her mouth drop open with shock. One side of her aunt's face was a bloody ruin, her right eye caked shut with blood, her lips purple and bruised. There was dirt in the wound too, and Tamlyn was holding herself awkwardly, as though just standing and talking were the hardest things she'd ever done. The side of her face that wasn't torn to pieces was smudged with dirt, one brown eye staring steadily out of the muck, and it was that cool, determined stare that Nuava recognised most of all.

She ran to her, pushing her shoulder into the older woman's armpit so that she was forced to rest her weight on her niece.

'Aunty, what happened?' Nuava felt a moment's embarrassment as that babyish word escaped her lips, but Tamlyn didn't seem to notice.

'I found you, girl.' Tamlyn squeezed her shoulders, despite the effort it obviously cost her. 'I lost your brother, but not you.'

'Please, Tamlyn, what is going on?' Nuava helped her to walk a few steps. The dawn light was growing brighter all the time, and there were birds singing in the trees. 'Mistress Crafter, you have to tell me what happened.'

At the use of her old title Tamlyn seemed to come together somehow, and when they stopped she stood a little straighter.

'Damn it, I feel like my head has come loose. Joah Demonsworn is what happened, of course.' She paused to cough. There were twigs and leaves stuck in her tangled hair. 'He came back, and the creature he brought with him –' she bared her teeth – 'it is a devil. A giant devil.'

'I've seen it,' said Nuava. She felt enormously relieved – both that she was no longer alone and that her aunt was alive – but it was tempered with a sense of terrifying responsibility. Tamlyn was very badly hurt, possibly even close to death, and Nuava was the only one around to help her. 'He called it the Rivener.'

'Bloody thing. Crushed me. Threw me from the pit. I landed in a tree, caught up in all the branches. Took me a whole day to get down.'

'It's all right, Tamlyn. I'm here to help you now.'

'Yes.' They had been shuffling forward, Nuava trying to guide her aunt to a nearby patch of clear snow, but now Tamlyn stopped.

413

She turned to look at Nuava, and the older woman was grinning, her lips gummy with blood. 'Yes, you'll help me. We have work to do, girl. Our finest work.'

Nuava simply nodded and looked away, concentrating on getting her aunt moving again. Her insides felt cold and her heart was beating too fast. For a few moments Tamlyn Nox had looked as mad as Joah Demonsworn.

63

When Wydrin came round she was on her hands and knees, her stomach clenching painfully. She gritted her teeth until the urge to vomit passed, and then slumped back down onto her side, shivering and clutching her head.

'Fuck me, that was a bad idea.'

It was like the worst hangover she'd ever had, multiplied a hundred, no, a thousand times. When she'd been very young, no older than thirteen or fourteen, she'd got into an argument with Jarath over who could stomach the most rum. All night they'd been drinking shots of an evil substance out of small tin cups, and the next morning she had gone down to the docks with the very real intention of throwing herself into the sea – anything to stop feeling so rotten. Luckily for her she hadn't even been capable of that short walk, and had instead fallen into an alley outside the nearest pie shop. Eventually the owner had taken pity on her and had brought her out a bacon and potato bake, wrapped in buttery pastry and still hot from the oven.

The memory was so vivid that she had to press her hand to her mouth, concentrating furiously on not being sick. She stayed where she was for a time, breathing hard and trying to see past the pounding behind her eyes.

It was the taint of the demon. It had been inside her, however briefly, and it felt like every part of her was filthy, lessened in some way. When she had touched minds with Mendrick, she had caught a sense of something huge and tranquil: a cold presence,

415

distant and clean. Bezcavar had been pain and fire and misery and madness, like being buried alive under a pile of corpses at a battle where everyone had died in pain and terror. She had felt the demon slip fiery tendrils around her mind, flowing into every place she kept hidden.

The relief when the Rivener had torn it from her had been immense.

Her stomach sour but quiet, Wydrin lifted her head and looked around. She was on the floor of someone's front room; it was furnished simply enough with table and chairs, thick woven rugs on the floor, some painted plates hanging from the walls. There was a door leading to a rough stone staircase, the steps cast into shadow, and another door that was still ajar. Wydrin could see the street beyond, but she had no memory of how she'd got there. She could hear nothing at all, not even the wind that habitually howled around Skaldshollow's walls. And there was something else as well; the light was all wrong. The sliver of daylight coming in through the crack of the door was a deep, murky red, as though they were experiencing some kind of doom-laden sunset, but something about it set her teeth on edge. The light just felt wrong, as though the entire place were trapped inside a red glass bottle.

She climbed shakily to her feet.

'I fell from the Rivener, then.' She patted herself down as she spoke. Nothing appeared to be broken, although she reckoned her backside would soon be sporting an exciting range of black and purple bruises. Her dagger and her sword still hung on her belt, thankfully. 'Fell back down into the city and managed to get a roof over my head while I was unconscious. That was bloody clever of me.'

'I dragged you here.'

Wydrin spun. Seconds ago she would have sworn she was alone in the bare room, but now there was a figure standing in the far corner. She was tall, with dark brown skin and a shaven head, and her left arm ended in a stump. The woman was watching Wydrin with cold amusement.

'And who might you be?' Frostling was already in her hand, red light spilling along its length like wine. 'And, thank you, I suppose.'

The woman raised an eyebrow, sending a flurry of creases across her smooth forehead. There was a mage's word tattooed on it, although Wydrin could not have said which one.

'I am Xinian the Battleborn.'

Wydrin nodded. 'The ghost who spoke to Frith. I guessed as much. I have to say, you look remarkably sprightly and solid for someone who has been dead a thousand years.'

'In this place, I am as real as you.' Xinian came forward, circling the room and moving with a careful grace. She did not appear to be armed, so Wydrin lowered her weapon. 'What have you and your friends done, sell-sword? This city has been torn out of its rightful place and cast half into the world of the dead.'

Wydrin shrugged. 'I have no idea. It's the sort of thing that seems to happen to us.'

'But you smell of the demon,' said Xinian. 'Its reek is all over you.'

'That I can agree with.' Wydrin wrinkled her nose. 'When I get out of here I'm having a week-long bath.' She shoved Frostling back into its scabbard. 'I hosted the demon briefly, and then it was torn out of me by Joah's contraption. What happened to it after that, I don't know. Hopefully it has been scattered to the winds.'

Xinian stared at her, appearing to weigh her words. 'You survived the Rivener?'

'I have a link to . . . someone else. I thought it likely that it would keep me from losing my soul to that thing.'

'That was a foolish thing to do.'

'Well, I am known for my staggeringly intelligent plans.' Wydrin rubbed her face. Keeping up all this bravado was exhausting, and her eyeballs felt like they were trying to push their way out of her skull. 'What are you doing here?'

'I go where Joah Demonsworn goes,' the woman replied. 'He has this place captive now, frozen in place. A short time ago it was as if the sky was blotted out by a terrible eclipse. I felt this city shift closer to me, and now I walk it as you do. And I am not the only dead thing here.'

'It sounds to me as though something went very wrong, in that case.' Wydrin shook her head. 'I left them up there, with him. I shouldn't have done that, but I was desperate. Frith was dying, and I . . .'

The woman was looking at her too closely now.

'I have to get out of here,' said Wydrin. 'I need to know what's going on.'

'You may not find that so easy.'

In the following silence, there was a scraping noise from upstairs, followed by the heavy thump thump thump of footsteps. Wydrin listened, and caught the sound of a faint moan, as though someone had been disturbed in their sleep.

'There are people in this house?'

Xinian the Battleborn looked up at the ceiling. 'Not people as such, no.'

It shuffled down the stairs towards them, dragging one heavy foot after the other, its head lolling to one side. Its mouth hung open, exposing a black, swollen tongue, and its skin was an unnatural blue, riddled with cracks that glowed softly. Wydrin was reminded of the Heart-Stone, how it had glowed in a similar way in Joah's lair, casting its poison out into the world, but this was a man, or at least it had been one once. Now its eyes were blind, and its blackened fingers clutched convulsively at its sides. The rags it wore were soiled and torn.

'The Rivened,' said Xinian. 'Joah took their souls and cast them out, and now this darkened city has given them some semblance of life again. The dead are walking.'

'Oh great.' Wydrin took a step back, unsheathing Glassheart. 'I don't suppose the Rivened are looking forward to a restful old age and a quiet pint by the fire?'

The man with livid-blue veins turned his blank eyes on them, an expression of faint puzzlement creasing his face. The light that was inside him pulsed.

'It can see your soul,' said Xinian, in a matter-of-fact tone. 'You are about the only thing here left with one. And that will make it hungry.'

As if waiting for that very word, the husk that had once been a man leapt forward, mouth agape and fingers grasping. Wydrin stumbled backwards, bringing Glassheart up in an awkward defensive motion. The blade scraped across the Rivened man's forearm, slicing through the flesh like butter and revealing a solid mess of rotten muscle and congealed blood. Appearing not to notice, it reached for Wydrin and she felt its cold fingers settle around her neck before she buried Frostling in the creature's chest. This slowed it down slightly, but didn't stop it from snapping its jaws at her face.

'I would do what you can to separate its head from its body,' said Xinian mildly, as though advising the best way to gut a chicken. 'It is being powered by something other than a beating heart now.'

Grunting with disgust, Wydrin brought her sword up and ran it across the husk's neck, ripping a hole so large that its head flopped back at an awkward angle, throat gaping open, and then it fell away from her into the hallway. Once on the floor it struggled for a time, arms and legs working in the dust, and then it was still.

Wydrin put her hand to her throat. More bruises tomorrow.

'That was unpleasant.' She turned back to Xinian the Battleborn, who was standing with her arms crossed over her chest. 'This has happened to everyone who went through the Rivener?'

The woman nodded. 'There are few left in this city who did not suffer that fate. Joah has been quite busy.'

Wydrin sheathed her sword, and keeping Frostling in her right hand she pushed the door open and went outside. The sky over Skaldshollow was that deep, unsettling red, like a storm in hell, and although she could see the sun it was a milky disc hidden behind a shifting skein of membranous black. The streets were cast in shadow, but she could see some people moving out there. Slowly. Shuffling as the Rivened man had shuffled, and with that faint blue glow.

'Shit.'

'They will all desire your soul, sell-sword,' said Xinian from behind her. 'Everything here is stopped, or dead, and you are the one bright piece of life.'

'And you don't count?'

Xinian shrugged. 'I am an echo of a soul, given solidity by this dark magic.'

'Right. Obviously.'

Wydrin stepped out onto the street, treading as quietly as she could. To her right was the looming form of the Tower of Waking, and curled around it like a jagged tumour was Joah's Rivener. The strange red storm light danced across them both, the violet light of the Rivener's eyes like windows onto a nightmare. She looked back to the south, and she could just make out the portion of the wall where Joah had smashed his way in; it was a line of broken rocks now, and it was possible to follow the path of destruction all the way there. Crushed roofs, flattened houses, even the faint wisps of black smoke from fires only recently extinguished.

'All right,' she said in a low voice, talking more to herself than the mage ghost. 'I just have to be fast and quiet. Run towards the wall, keep my head down, and I'll be out of here. No one knows where I am, and Joah will assume I am dead. I can do this. I –'

She paused. Just for a second, she had felt Mendrick's presence in her head again, but as soon as she reached out for him it was as if the connection were severed. *Mendrick? Are you there?* But there was nothing; only a deep sense of loss, an emptiness where his voice had been. What had just happened?

'It may not be as easy as you expect, sell-sword,' said Xinian from just behind her. 'Do you think these creatures see through their eyes? You will smell of life to them.'

'Look.' Wydrin turned back to the mage, still endeavouring to keep her voice down. She would worry about Mendrick later. 'If you like, you could help me, instead of dispensing reminders of how doomed I am. You killed Joah once, didn't you? Well, that's what I intend to do again, only I'll do a better job than you. And it's Wydrin Threefellows, by the way, also known as the Copper Cat, and leader of the Black Feather Three.' This last wasn't strictly true, but Wydrin kept going. 'I'm not just any common sell-sword.'

Xinian the Battleborn looked at her for a long moment, her dark brown eyes cool and unflustered. Eventually she shrugged. 'You have the ego of a mage.'

420

'*Pft*. You've met Frith, right?' Wydrin turned away. 'You can help me or you can go to hell. I'm not dying in this place.'

Up the street, men and women who were now empty vessels, their skins filled with a roaring hunger, turned to look towards them. Wydrin got ready to run.

64

Joah sat alone in the heart of the Rivener. His body appeared to have finished its changes now, and although part of him was curious to see what he had been left with, he found he did not yet have the energy to find a mirror to examine himself. Instead he sat and listened to the new, surging voices that existed within his head. It was similar to the roar of the Edenier, that sensation of waiting power that had lived curled within his chest, but now it inhabited every fibre of his being. He felt tremendously aware of everything: the hot tide of blood moving within his veins, the rough wooden grain of the arms of the chair under his fingers, the taste of magic in his mouth, brackish and bitter. He could hear the screaming coming from the Edenier chamber, as the demon Bezcavar thrashed and raged inside it. That had been unexpected. It seemed that he still understood very little about human beings, even after all these years. He had thought that Aaron would join him, that his mage-brother would not even question his plans – were they not mages together? The last two in all of Ede? Surely they were destined to do great things together. And he had not expected the red-headed woman to make a deal with the demon in exchange for Aaron's life.

Joah raised a hand to the burnt side of his face, touching the hard scabs forming there.

He had known that Aaron was dying. Had known that he was ill. But it had seemed like such a small thing, a problem that would eventually be swept aside. Why had he not asked Bezcavar to heal him? It was always within the demon's power to heal wounds.

Joah curled his hands around the ends of the armrests.

Because the demon was ever a jealous creature. Hadn't it encouraged him to turn away from the mages of a thousand years ago? Hadn't Bezcavar's hand also been on the hilt of the sword when he'd cut his first rivals down? The demon wanted Joah all to itself.

Instead, the woman had saved Aaron, and in doing so removed Bezcavar from the equation entirely. Humans were so unpredictable.

He looked up at the Edenier chamber, where all the collected magic swirled along with the incorporeal form of the demon. It was difficult to see, but you could just make it out: a darker shape amongst the shimmering white of the magic. And you could certainly hear it: an inhuman voice screaming in rage and frustration. Screaming to be let out, to be allowed the sanctuary of a human body again.

Thinking of that, Joah looked towards one of the doors that led away from the Rivener's central room. That was where the girl had fled, the one called Ip that Bezcavar had been hiding away inside for so long. Joah had considered stopping her, but the new forces that were changing his body had thrown him to the floor and she had slipped away. Presumably she was still inside the Rivener somewhere, unless she had found a way out.

Joah stood up and approached the Edenier chamber. Immediately the swirling clouds of magic inside grew in violence, and the screaming so loud that he winced faintly.

'It's easier if you stay there for now,' he said. The screaming changed in pitch, and he looked down at his hands. The fingers were unnaturally long and pale now, ending in strange needle-like points. 'Think of it as a rest, my friend. I think you have done enough.'

The Rivener had done its job well. Most of Skaldshollow's people had given up their souls, and now there was a storm of magic inside the chamber. All pointless now though, of course.

'It doesn't matter,' he murmured. 'I am a god, Bezcavar. I am a being of Edenier.' His long hands reached up to his face again,

423

and fluttered there for a moment, like uncertain spiders. The skin that hadn't been ruined in Aaron's blast of fire was smooth and cold, and he didn't recognise the shapes he could feel. It would be so easy to go and find a mirror.

Instead he dropped his hands and walked back over to the windows, preparing to move the Rivener again. He sensed that he hadn't seen the last of Aaron Frith, and he wanted to have a little surprise ready for him.

Frith sat with several strips of silk laid out on the carpet in front of him. He was painting the mage words onto them with the ink that Sebastian had bought from the nearby market, and he was a little startled at how easily they came to him now. Once, he had struggled with this, concentrating so hard on every dot and swirl that he'd given himself headaches, and always O'rin was on hand to mock him, or to hit him with his stick.

Thinking of his old tutor, Frith frowned slightly. He remembered the panicked birds flying up at an invisible ceiling, crashing into it with such violence that they fell down with their fragile bones broken. O'rin must have been afraid at the end, and although Frith had no reason to love the old liar, it was still more fuel for his vengeance.

'How's it going?' Sebastian ducked inside their small, sand-coloured tent. They were on the outskirts of a heat-packed town on the edge of the Desert of Bones, the closest place to get supplies. Sebastian had been out all morning, seeing what he could find. Frith knew that the tall knight was anxious to return to Skaldshollow, and he was trying to distract himself.

'Slowly,' replied Frith. He finished the word for Control, and started the next for Fire. He would need a combination of spells in order to force the Edenier trap into the right shape, and then he would need to use the demon's knowledge. That would not be pleasant. The knight stood there for a long moment, and Frith deliberately didn't look up. He also knew that Sebastian would want to discuss what had happened to them – and to Wydrin – and he was not going to be drawn into that conversation.

'I'll leave you to it, then,' said Sebastian eventually. There was a kindness in his voice that made Frith pause with his brush not yet touching the silk. 'I saw a few food stalls in the town square. I'll get us something to eat.'

With that he was gone.

Frith completed the words and tied the strips around his wrists. When this was done he used the Edenier to float the half-complete ball into the air, and slowly turned it round, examining the symbols once again. The shapes etched into the twisted metal were not the familiar swirls and dots of the mages' words, but the oddly unsettling angular pictograms that the demon had given Joah. New tools with which to shape the world; ones bought and paid for with the blood and suffering of others. Cautiously, he reached out with one finger and brushed the smooth surface of one of the icons. It was slick under his skin, a sensation that caused him to frown; once, when he had been eight or nine years old, his brother Leon had dared him to put his hand inside a sack of offal that had been left in the kitchens. Never able to resist a dare from Leon, Frith had thrust his hand inside, and the sense of that cold slippery wetness came back to him now. Along with the urgent desire to wash his hands.

'It has to be done,' he murmured to himself.

First of all, he worked at taking the object apart, reducing it down to its component pieces. He examined them all, quickly seeing how they fitted together and how the spell worked. Each time he came into contact with one of the demonic symbols he would suppress a shiver, but that feeling lessened too. Eventually, they became an unpleasant tool to be endured, although more than once he thought of Joah's memory of the demon in the field, smiling with a beautiful face whilst cutting the words into the mage's skin.

Eventually his eyes began to sting, and he forced himself to stand up and walk away from the device for a few moments. His eyes fell on the staff that they'd rescued from Temerayne along with the god-blade – the staff made by Xinian's lover, Selsye. With everything that had happened, he had barely given it a thought.

It was a beautiful piece of work, carved from a pale wood he could not identify, and riddled with interlocking mages' words. As soon as his fingers touched it he knew it to be the opposite of Joah's Edenier trap in every aspect – carved from an Edeian-enriched material and moulded with Edenier, but with peace and control at its heart. The staff seemed to thrum with concealed power, all of it benign; there was no darkness here. He ran his fingers over it, marvelling at the gossamer feel of the wood. Like the Edenier trap, he could almost see how it worked, how it was put together. There was, he realised, an idea forming at the back of his mind – a risky one, a chance so slim it made a mockery of hope – but perhaps this was the time for desperate chances.

That, however, was for later. He put the staff down and returned to his work on the trap, shuddering slightly as he touched its cold surface once more. He carried on for hours, until he was startled to see Sebastian's shadow in the tent entrance again. The sun was setting, and the shadows were casting long and dark. He was also sweating profusely, and he wiped a damp hand across his brow.

'Have you not moved from that spot?'

Frith cleared his throat. He felt strange, as though he'd been in a deep trance for a long time. Coming back to the here and now was painful. In the here and now, he could see his own grief reflected on Sebastian's face.

'This is very complex work.' He shifted the pieces of the contraption out of the way and Sebastian ducked into the tent. In his arms he was carrying something bulky wrapped in brown linen that was already soaked through with grease, and a dark green bottle.

'A couple of roasted pigeons, a bottle of some local wine,' he said as he sat down, unwrapping the package. 'Feels like ages since we had any decent hot food.'

They ate in silence, passing the bottle between them. Frith found that his eyes kept returning to the pieces of blackened metal.

'I need you to do the spell again,' said Sebastian eventually. Outside the ruddy light of sunset had vanished into the inky desert night. 'You know the one I mean.'

Frith felt his jaw tighten. When they had first come here, after they had located the remains of the Edenier trap, Sebastian had insisted that Frith perform the 'finding' spell again, this time for Nuava and Prince Dallen. He had done so, and seen only the same strange shifting red light he had found when looking for Wydrin.

'Sebastian—'

'There is nothing to stop you trying it again.'

Frith wiped his greasy fingers on the woven mat before lifting his hands and summoning the word for Seeing, muttering Nuava's name first of all. Again, there was the flickering scarlet storm light. He looked at Sebastian, and raised his eyebrows.

'It is likely they are all dead.'

'There is no way to know what that light means. Try Prince Dallen now, please.'

This time, the dusty cloud of light depicted a scene they hadn't witnessed before. They saw Prince Dallen on his knees, his arms tied awkwardly behind his back. His face was covered in dried blood, a black bruise circling his left eye. As they watched, he spoke to someone they couldn't see, his long brown hair plastered to his forehead and cheeks, and then a tall Narhl warrior stepped into view. Prince Dallen stopped talking, and the man struck him across the face, rocking him back on his knees. It was very difficult to make out where they were; Frith could see an overcast sky, a rocky backdrop. The image flickered and died.

'He is alive,' whispered Sebastian. Frith felt a moment of pure bitterness; why should Prince Dallen be alive, when Wydrin was not? 'We have to go back there.'

Sebastian stood up, nearly knocking the tent over in his urgency.

'You don't know where he is,' said Frith, not moving. 'If he has been captured by his own people, then he could be anywhere.'

'I will find him,' said Sebastian shortly. 'You must take us back there with the Edenier. Now.'

Frith looked back at the twisted pieces of metal, shining blackly under the lamps. 'I will not leave my work at this crucial stage.'

'Frith!' Sebastian took a step forward, frustration and disbelief evident on his face. 'I'm talking about another human life here.'

'Your lover, you mean?'

There was a flicker of anger from the big knight then, and Frith wondered briefly how long such a fight would last, should they come to blows. Sebastian was a fearsome warrior, but he would not get far against the Edenier. He could feel it building in his chest again. So much easier to be alone, to just carry on with his work.

'Wydrin would go back for him. You know that.'

Frith looked down at the brown bones of their dinner. 'What will you do?' he asked eventually. 'They will have him under guard.'

'I will summon the brood army,' said Sebastian immediately, before correcting himself. 'Ephemeral and her sisters.' He paused, looking down at his hands. 'I wanted to keep them away from all this, for as long as I could. There has been enough killing, on all sides.' He looked up again. 'They have been waiting for word from me, and they will be in the riverlands by now. They have their own special abilities,' he continued, fingering the carved tooth that hung around his neck. 'With them, I will be able to find Dallen.'

Frith nodded slowly. 'I will take you, then, to the edge of the riverlands,' he said, getting to his feet. 'But I will not dally there. And you will rescue your prince alone.'

428

65

The world screamed back into existence around them and Sebastian stumbled, finding his feet suddenly on hard black earth instead of soft golden sand. Frith had brought them back to the bleak foothills on the outskirts of the frozen northern lands, near the smallholding where they had rented their mountain ponies. It felt like that had happened a hundred years ago.

Here, there was still some light left in the sky, and when he turned back to Frith he saw the younger man's face clearly. He was well again – Wydrin's ill-advised bargaining had done that much at least – but there was a desolation in his eyes that looked as cold as the mountains. He cut a slim shape against the brittle, greying grass, and Sebastian had a moment to wonder how much the Edenier had changed him. What did it take to turn a man into a monster like Joah, after all?

'I will leave you here, then,' said Frith. There was a cold wind blowing, and his words were clipped, shouting against it. 'When the weapon is finished I will return to Skaldshollow, and kill Joah Demonsworn.'

'You will need me then,' said Sebastian. All at once he felt strongly that this was wrong, that to split up was to doom them both. 'Remember that, at the end. I will want to be there.'

Frith nodded once. 'I will keep an eye on you,' he said, and in a rush of air and a shimmer of light, he was gone.

Sebastian let out a long sigh. The wind was growing stronger, and in the smallholding across the way he could see a few lamps starting to glow against the evening's darkness. Somewhere beyond these hills, Dallen was being tortured and punished by his own people, but for now he turned his face to the riverlands beyond, and began to climb the nearest slope. The wind filled his cloak and tried to pull it from his shoulders, and he had to lean into his strides to make progress, but eventually he stood on the low summit, facing the flatter lands to the south. The last light of the day danced silvery across the traceries of rivers, and, far beyond that, a thin band of green that was the forest. That was where they would be.

Closing his eyes, he tried to empty his mind of everything; his worries about Dallen, his sorrow over Wydrin – even his unease about Frith and the metal contraption he was now obsessed with. He cleared his mind, and then slowly filled it with the image of Ephemeral.

This was something they had practised between them for hours, hidden up in the craggy reaches of the mountains of Ynnsmouth. The other sisters had all felt his mind too – his blood bonded them all together – but it was strongest with Ephemeral, who had been the first to put down her sword at the battle of Baneswatch. He brought her to mind as clearly as he could: her pale green skin, like an unripe apple, the silvery swatch of her hair, so often tied into a braid with a length of red fabric she had picked up some-where. He saw her yellow eyes, so alien at first and then, gradually, familiar, and her habit of lifting her chin slightly when she had an urgent question to ask. He thought about the shape of her mind, and how his blood ran with her own – the red and the green.

'Ephemeral,' he murmured, 'can you hear me?'

They had tried this trick over numerous distances; at first, standing facing each other, and then in separate rooms, and then on either side of the training slopes. They had moved further and further, always able to find that slim, red and green thread again, but this was the longest distance they had tried by a significant degree. Perhaps this would all be pointless after all.

'Ephemeral,' he said again, knowing that the wind whipped away his words as soon as they passed his lips. 'Are you there?'

At first, nothing. And then, the faintest of whispers inside his head.

Father! I am here.

He could sense the excitement in her voice, and the warm sense of achievement. Alone on the hill, Sebastian smiled. 'Can you find me, Ephemeral?'

There was a moment's silence then, and he could imagine her standing very still, her brow furrowed in concentration.

Yes, she answered eventually. *You are on a hill. It is windy there.*

'Come to me,' he said. 'All of you. And come as fast as you can.'

There was no reply. He sat down on the grass, pulling his cloak around him and watching the distant forest. The light faded until he could no longer distinguish the riverlands from the trees, and despite the cold and the howling wind he began to doze lightly. He could feel their minds, as quick and slippery as the snakes' had been, gradually drawing closer. Deep inside he was frightened by this, and the Second's words echoed in his heart, but he pushed it away.

An unknowable amount of time later he awoke with a start, sensing movement out in the darkness. A flicker of something, a suggestion of change in that bleak landscape, and then the points of light grew slightly larger. It was still impossible to make them out clearly, but as he watched he thought he could see the crystal glitter of starlight against their wings. The sisters were coming.

Sebastian took a slow breath, marvelling at the sight despite everything that had happened. Gradually, they came into focus: the dragon's daughters, flying on gossamer wings, like dragonflies. The moonlight shone on their silver hair, and here and there on the weapons they wore. Soon, he could make out individual faces, and he saw Ephemeral in the lead. Her bright hair was tied back into its habitual braid, and she was grinning as she came. Sebastian suppressed an uneasy smile; how many people had seen that grin and known it meant a painful and messy death? Now Ephemeral's face was full of a simple, bright enthusiasm.

These are strange times, mused Sebastian.

Eventually they landed, hovering to the ground and then gathering together, stretching out tired limbs. Ephemeral came over to Sebastian. She bent slightly at the waist, a nod that was almost a bow. Sebastian had no idea where she had picked that up from.

'You called, and we came, Father.' She had composed her face on landing, but couldn't help smiling again.

'You did. Thank you, Ephemeral.' He glanced around at the other sisters. There were twenty-three of them in all, the sisters who had decided not to follow the Second. 'It is good to see you all.' He turned back to Ephemeral. 'How was the journey?'

'Successful. We mapped a large section of the land to the south, and discovered new flora and fauna.'

'And did you bump into anyone?'

Ephemeral shook her head emphatically.

'We were very careful, Father, to remain hidden. Just as you said.'

'Good.' Sebastian paused. Once more he felt lost again. He kept expecting Wydrin to interrupt, with a complaint or an off-colour comment.

'Father, should we not make camp?' said Ephemeral. She gestured to their surroundings; the only light came from the nearby holding and the bright stars overhead.

Sebastian smiled wearily. He looked at them, this strange bunch of other-worldly women, all with more blood on their hands than any knight he'd ever known. They were cold murderers, every single one. They had killed women and children with their bare hands, had burnt down towns and villages and chased the survivors with smiles on their faces. And now they were his only friends.

'Let's do that, Ephemeral. I have a lot to tell you all.'

66

'So, you're haunting Joah Demonsworn, then?'

Wydrin spoke in a low voice, peering cautiously around the next street corner. They were making very slow progress; the Rivened were confused and their bodies were rotting, but they lit up with hunger if they happened to spot her, and they displayed a remarkably determined attitude once they got moving. Wydrin and Xinian were working their way towards the city wall, with frequent pauses to separate heads from necks or simply run in the other direction.

'Yes,' said Xinian. The woman was leaning against the wall next to her, weighing a sword she'd found in her hand. Her magic was still inert, just as it had been when she'd been a ghost. 'You could say that.'

'What do you do? Move things around when he's asleep? Mumble curses in his ear? Spoil the milk?'

'It is not as easy as all that,' Xinian said quietly. Up the street, three husks were standing around a fallen werken, staring at it as if they almost remembered what it was. 'My ability to manifest comes and goes. For the longest time, I haunted the grove where Bezcavar hid his tomb, and I was just a voice in the wind. A shadow of who I was. When the demon brought him back, gave him flesh and blood again, I seemed to become stronger too. When your friend was dying, I became clearer to him as he moved into the world of the dead. And now,' she gestured with her sword, 'this whole place inhabits the world of the dead.'

'Here, look,' said Wydrin, 'they're completely transfixed by that werken there. I reckon if we're quiet and stick to the other side of the street, we can get past them without any bother.'

Together they turned the corner and moved swiftly across the cobbled road, keeping an eye on the group gathered around the werken. Wydrin wondered if they'd been werken riders before the Rivener had torn their souls from them. It seemed quite likely.

As they passed, one of the husks stumbled back from the werken, shaking its head slightly as though it sensed movement somewhere outside of its field of vision. Xinian elbowed Wydrin in warning and together they moved as far as they could to the other side of the street, skirting along the edge of the stone buildings. *The problem is,* thought Wydrin as she moved as silently as possible, *we make it to the end of this street and we have no idea what's waiting for us. Could be none, could be two dozen of the bastards.*

Right next to her ear there was the brittle tinkle of broken glass, and a blackened arm shot out of the window she was passing, fingers closing around the top of her arm with surprising strength. Unable to stop herself she yelped in surprise, and the three husks so captivated by the werken turned at once.

'What are you doing?' snapped Xinian.

'Doing? What does it look like I'm doing?' Wydrin yanked her arm away from the window, half dragging the Rivened figure through it after her. She had a moment to notice the way the pieces of glass had opened up the creature's chest and stomach, the way its eyes rolled wetly in their sockets, before Xinian's sword sliced easily through the husk's neck. The head, still looking mildly surprised, hit the cobbles with a thud before rolling down the street, but they were already in trouble. The Rivened that had previously been unaware of their presence were shuffling quickly over, and when Wydrin glanced back the way they'd come, she saw more decayed figures limping round the corner, moaning hungrily. Wydrin brushed the creature's slackening grip off her arm in a compulsive gesture of disgust.

'I think we'd better get moving, ghostie.'

They ran the rest of the way, no longer troubling to be quiet, and the Rivened followed, making low noises of desperate hunger in the backs of their throats. Four more lurched out of the building ahead of them, and Xinian kept running, taking off another head with a high sweep of her short sword as she moved past. Wydrin came on behind, jumping hurriedly over the body. In the next street was another fallen werken; it was the size of a house, one of the biggest Wydrin had seen. It had apparently been struck by something even bigger, as a huge chunk of rock was missing from its shoulder, and it lay in the street like a ruined temple. Wydrin and Xinian hurried behind it, glad to be out of the husks' line of sight.

The pair crouched behind the rock, breathing hard. The milky disc of the sun had moved to the west, and was now disappearing behind the horizon. The red caul that hung over Skaldshollow was deepening, and Wydrin did not like to think of being in this place after dark. She had no magical globe of sunlight, and no mage to create one.

'I can see now why they called you Battleborn,' she whispered to Xinian. 'I didn't realise mages were trained in swordplay.'

The corner of Xinian's mouth crept up a touch. 'This is why they call me Battleborn.' She held out the arm that ended in a smooth stump.

'You lost your hand in a fight?'

'No. I was born without it.'

When Wydrin raised her eyebrows, Xinian continued.

'My people believe that we live different lives, in different worlds, one after the other, and we carry pieces of those lives with us, into the next. In my previous life, I was a great warrior, injured in battle.'

Wydrin nodded, taking this in. From down the street they could hear shuffling and moaning, and the light was draining swiftly from the sky.

'But if you move from life to life, what are you doing here still? You should be in your new life by now.'

Xinian scowled. 'A simplistic view.'

'Hey, I'm just saying, that by your own rules—' There was a chorus of groans, and much closer. 'What do you say we find somewhere to rest up for the night? I don't much fancy running into these things in the dark.'

435

Xinian nodded shortly.

It wasn't easy. The Rivened were all over the city, and even a sniff of Wydrin's presence was enough to bring them shuffling in droves. The first two buildings they tried were equally infested with them, and as Wydrin cut them down, one after another, she thought of how Skaldshollow had been before they arrived – crowded with people, warm and full of life, going about their business. Now every fire was out, and nothing moved save for the shambling empty shells of those who'd had their souls torn from them. And all by a man who should have been long since rotten in his tomb. There was a rage building inside her, and that was good. Rage was useful.

Eventually they found an empty tavern, the door thrown open and a drift of snow half covering the entrance. Wydrin went in first, moving swiftly through three large rooms joined by wide wooden doors, her dagger and sword held in readiness. Several of the tables and chairs had been turned over, and in one corner she found the corpse of a man who had apparently died of some sort of head injury, his face covered in blood. She stopped when she saw him. Did they panic when the monster climbed over their walls and the sky turned red? Of course they did. She thought of Y'Ruen, moving slowly across Relios, burning everything and bringing death. She thought of the lost city of Temerayne, trapped under the ocean by the god of chaos. And Joah, who no doubt thought himself a god by now, killing people and, worse, taking their souls from them. Like they were nothing. Humans always suffered when they came into contact with the godly, it seemed. She scowled, her grip on Frostling tightening until her knuckles turned white.

'Is it safe?' Xinian whispered from the entrance. 'They will spot us soon enough.'

Wydrin dragged her gaze from the corpse and glanced once more around the tavern. There were still some half-full tankards on the tables.

'It's fine,' she said. 'And I think I spy a few unbroken bottles.'

She helped Xinian wedge the front door shut, and they used some pieces of sacking from behind the bar to cover up the small windows that looked out onto the street. Once that was done,

Wydrin went to the fireplace, thick with soot, and set about making a small fire.

'Is that a good idea, sell-sword?' asked Xinian. She was standing by the door, her arms crossed over her chest. 'They could see the smoke from the chimney.'

'I don't think those poor bastards out there are very good at putting two and two together any more. Besides which, if I have to spend another night freezing my arse off, I shall be as mad as Joah myself.' She paused, having banked the fire into a respectable blaze. 'And for the love of the Graces, Xinian, sit down and rest for a minute. We're not going anywhere tonight.'

The mage stood by the door for a moment longer, as if convinced that they might have to leave at any second, before shaking her head slightly and coming over to the fire. Wydrin had dragged two of the unbroken chairs over and Xinian sat in one, looking a little to Wydrin as though she had forgotten how to do simple, everyday things like sitting in a chair.

'I'm so hungry my stomach thinks my throat's been cut,' said Wydrin conversationally. 'I don't suppose you have any food on you?'

Xinian leaned forward, resting her elbows on her knees, staring into the fire.

'I have not had any need for food for quite some time, sell-sword.'

'Ah, right. Silly me. Still, plenty to drink.' Wydrin uncorked the mead she'd found behind the counter and took a swig straight from the bottle. It tasted as though it had been steeped in spices, and it warmed her up straight away. When she offered it to Xinian, the mage shook her head.

They fell into a silence then. Outside there was no wind at all, and every now and then they could hear a groan or a stumbling footstep. Wydrin rubbed her fingers across her eyes; tired, but too strung out to sleep. She kept thinking of Frith and Sebastian, wondering where they were. They would probably think she was dead, and, at the moment, that felt too close to the truth, trapped as she was in this place with a ghost and an army of soulless corpses. And she thought of Mendrick, whose link had saved her life again, and whose presence had been so abruptly cut off. She had a terrible idea she knew what that meant, but it was too much sorrow to contemplate in this awful, death-filled place. She took another swig of mead.

'Tell me about it, then,' she said eventually. Xinian looked up from the fire, startled. From the look on her face, she had been having her own long thoughts. 'I doubt I'll ever get the chance to talk to someone who lived a thousand years ago again. What was it like? The gods, the mages, the power. It must have been quite a time.'

Xinian stared at her for a long moment, her dark eyes shining. 'It is a long-lost age,' she said. 'Ede was strange then, and full of magic. This place –' she gestured around the small tavern, taking in the world outside too '– this place is riddled with Edeian. The stones whisper and walk, and wyverns still thrive here, but once all of Ede was such, and gods walked among us. The green woman, Y'Gria, was still seen in the wilder places when I was a girl, and Res'ni and Res'na could be summoned, if you had the power. And we were so powerful then. All the secrets of the world were there for us to discover, when Ede was young and full of magic.'

Something outside knocked heavily against the door, and they both shifted imperceptibly, but then it moved on.

'Joah Demonsworn wanted it all,' she continued, staring at the fire once more. 'The secret language of the gods wasn't enough. He said that they were keeping knowledge from us, and we replied, of course they are, they are gods. But there were others that agreed with him, others who were more powerful than me. The elders gave him permissions, knowledge, and turned a blind eye, because he was the most remarkable mage of his age. Of any age, probably. A genius. When he started learning to craft the Edeian, some eyebrows were raised, because so few people possess that skill, but no one thought to stop him.' Xinian smiled, and it was as cold as a razor's edge. 'Rumours started to circulate that he was opening new avenues of research, ones that were potentially dangerous. Some began to whisper of demons, and no one really wanted to believe it. He grew so powerful in that time. That reluctance to believe fuelled so much. And of course, by then, the gods had turned on us, and Joah's genius helped us to construct the Citadel. It would hardly be seemly, the elders said, to question him now.'

438

This time when Wydrin offered the bottle, Xinian took it.

'When it came out – the things he had done, the extent of the evil, the number of people tortured to death in his pursuit of power – there were still plenty of people who refused to believe it. Not Joah Lightbringer, our shining golden example. But he'd been travelling a long time, away from our temples in Creos and Whittenfarne, and when he came back, the madness was in him like a fever. The elders could deny it no longer.'

'And you were sent to kill him?'

Xinian tipped her head to one side. 'I was their greatest warrior. I had led armies, won battles for them. I had faced demons before, too, terrible beings that boiled up from beneath the earth at places that were suffused with Edeian. Mostly they were stupid creatures, too ruled by their own appetites and easily defeated. By that point, even the Edenier of the elders couldn't touch Joah, and they knew it would have to be an assassination, an act of violence that would bring him to an end.'

'And you had the sword.'

Xinian nodded, and some of the cold slipped from her face. 'My lover made that sword,' she said. 'Selsye was a skilled Edeian crafter, unrivalled save for Joah Demonsworn himself. She took a scale from Y'Ruen and forged it into the only weapon capable of killing a creature such as Joah. And it worked, too. I cut him down.' Her hand tightened around the neck of the bottle convulsively. 'I killed him. But not in time to save Selsye.'

'I am sorry,' said Wydrin after a few moments. 'That must have been hard.'

'Hard?' Xinian shot her a fiery look. 'Selsye was my heart and soul. She was the very bones of me. When I saw her fall, it broke me into a thousand pieces. I was glad to die then, and if I took Joah Demonsworn with me, then that was all to the good.'

Wydrin swallowed, and looked into the fire. It was easier than looking at the pain on Xinian's face.

'Wouldn't it have been better,' she said hesitantly, 'not to have loved? To save yourself from that pain?'

To her surprise Xinian laughed, although there was still a great deal of sadness in the sound. She passed the bottle back.

'Foolish child. Without Selsye and her love, I never would have made it at all. To suffer the sweetest joy and the greatest agony is preferable to a life lived apart from love. Joah may be back again, but I saved Ede from at least a thousand years of his evil, and without Selsye I would have died years before, having achieved nothing. Our short time together was the glory of my life, and I do not regret it. I cannot.'

Wydrin said nothing. Xinian looked at her, her gaze shrewd and thoughtful.

'Love is the forge that transforms us into who we are,' she said. 'To avoid that is to hide from life, child. But you are very young, and I think we have had enough tales of ancient Ede for one night.'

'I think you're right,' said Wydrin, not quite looking at the mage. 'If it's remotely possible, I'm going to try and get some sleep.' She put the bottle down on the floor. It would not do to wake up with another hangover. 'Things will look better in the morning.'

67

'You certainly have a lucky sweetheart, sir. Or do you have more than one on the go? A dangerous life that, no doubt, but with its own rewards.'

Frith gave the merchant a sharp look, and the man quickly shut his mouth, taking his money and saying no more about it. The handful of cheap silver baubles were swept into a small hessian sack, and Frith took it from him, nodding once before heading off into the market. He paused at another stall to buy food, water and wine, and then he left, glancing up at the sky as he did so. It was midday, and it would be unpleasantly hot in the cramped room he was renting, but he had given the landlord enough coin for him to be left to his own devices for as long as he needed solitude, and there was still so much work to be done.

A sweetheart, indeed. Frith hefted the sack in his hand, briefly imagining another life where he had brought Wydrin trinkets and jewellery, a life where he had chosen to pursue what he truly wanted, instead of adhering to the traditions left to him by his dead family. Would it have made any difference?

Back inside the sweltering room, he opened the shutters on the windows and emptied the paltry pieces of silver jewellery into the smelting bowl he'd acquired, taking a moment to pry free the various gemstones set into the metal. All were glass save for one tiny chip of emerald, which he slipped into his own pocket, and then he summoned the word for Heat, focussing it down into a fine point. Within a few minutes the confusion of jewellery in the bowl had melted down into a slop of malleable silver, ready to be formed into whatever shape he wished.

He paused, taking a swig from the skin of wine he'd purchased. The Edenier trap sat on the single table in the room, still half finished and seeming to draw darkness around it. There were a great many parts missing, and those he would have to replace himself and as quickly as possible. Originally, he knew that Joah had not intended the device to have any parts made of silver, but it was easier to work with and faster to imprint with the magical symbols.

Using multiple words in tandem as Joah had taught him, Frith lifted the liquid metal from the bowl with his mind and turned it over, moulding it and stretching it until it met his needs. When he had the shape he wanted, he summoned the demon's symbols and sank them into the metal. There was a moment of pressure, as if the metal itself was resisting, and then with a hiss they appeared, stark and somehow unappealing. Frith moved the metal over to the table, gently dousing it with the word for Cold until it had hardened sufficiently, and then with a delicate touch he slid it into the waiting slot within the Edenier trap. He felt a flicker in the magic as the spells within the device adjusted for this new piece. It was getting closer.

Frith let out a breath he wasn't aware he'd been holding, and sat for a few moments staring at nothing. There was a purity to this that he could almost understand; just him and the creation of something new. No distractions, nothing between him and it. And after all, at this point, what else did he have? An empty castle populated by people who served him out of loyalty to his father. A potential bride who didn't know him, and was in truth only interested in the expansion of her own lands. A graveyard filled with his family, and a lot of regrets. The memory of flying on the back of a griffin, his arms around Wydrin's waist and her laughter in his ear.

Soon, he would leave this place with the Edenier trap, and he would take it to Joah. He thought that the mage might be pleased, on some level, that Frith had completed something he had not been able to; of all the things Joah was, he was a generous man. *He wanted me to be his brother*, thought Frith. *Would things have been different if I'd accepted that offer?* He would show him the trap, and then he would set it off, and that would be the end of that. Joah Demonsworn would lose the magic that had driven him since his birth, and perhaps Sebastian would be able to kill him. Perhaps he wouldn't. Frith found it difficult to care – he would likely be dead either way.

Methodically he unpacked the bread and cheese he'd bought from the market and began to eat it, still staring at the Edenier trap. It wouldn't be long now. Not long at all.

Sebastian stood in the small clearing, trying not to give in to despair. It hadn't taken them long to find the place, but it was obviously too long to be of any use; the rocky pieces of Mendrick's body lay in the mud, already partially covered in snow, and Nuava's meagre belongings had been trodden into the dirt. The fire was cold ashes, and everywhere there were signs of violence, which the brood sisters only confirmed for him with their keener senses.

'Someone fled this way,' said Ephemeral, pointing to where the trees were thickest. She held Prince Dallen's token, the carved bear tooth, in one clawed hand. It was how they'd found his scent. 'And they were pursued by men who carry a similar smell to the prince.'

'Nuava Nox,' said Sebastian. His mouth felt numb. 'She was a young woman who managed to escape the city when Joah arrived. The Narhl must have taken them by surprise, and they would have had larger numbers.' He paused. 'We should not have left them alone.'

'The other group went this way,' said Havoc. She was standing at the far side of the clearing, looking off into the trees with keen interest. 'They took the prince with them, and he was bleeding.'

'We will find them, Father,' said Ephemeral. 'The scent is clear from here.'

Sebastian swallowed hard, looking at the remains of Mendrick. 'Then we should move fast.' He remembered the shifting red light that had been all Frith could see with the Seeing spell. 'We'll have to assume they caught Nuava. The Narhl have no love for the Skalds, but there is a chance they may have been more lenient with one of their own.'

They set off through the woods, heading north-west and gradually upwards, until the trees grew scarcer and the air grew steadily chillier. Here and there Sebastian would spot signs of their passage himself – broken branches, footprints – and he knew they were on the right track.

The trees dropped away entirely, and soon they were in the rocky mountain country Sebastian recognised from their trek with Dallen and his soldiers. He pulled up the hood of his cloak as the sun set, and they kept marching steadily; it took a lot to tire the brood sisters, and Sebastian let his own anxiety keep his feet moving. Night fell like an icy blade, revealing a blanket of stars and a strange shifting emerald glow in the sky to the far north. Hours passed, and dawn was still a distant wish when Ephemeral dropped back from leading the group and gently took hold of Sebastian's arm.

'The scent is fresher here,' she said. 'I believe our prey have made camp ahead of us.'

'I wouldn't call them prey, Ephemeral,' said Sebastian, but he looked where she pointed. The land rose steeply here, bare rock starting to push through the earth, and on a plateau ahead of them was a circle of weathered stone statues, each as tall as a man. It was too dark to see what they depicted. There was movement beyond the stone, and a pale blue glow – cold-lights instead of camp fires – although he could make out very little else. 'Tell your sisters to wait for the moment, and let's see if we can get closer.'

Sebastian and Ephemeral broke off from the main group and, making use of the uneven ground, made their way towards the statues at an angle, always crouching low, moving swiftly. In the past the brood army had had very little use for stealth, but they had taken to the concept easily enough, and now Ephemeral moved nearly silently across the rocks and snow. When they were close enough to see the men and women camped within the circle of statues they stopped, crouching motionless in a dip in the ground.

'They will have posted sentries,' he murmured. 'We must be cautious.'

Now that they were closer he could see around fifty men and women, some lying on the rocky ground and sleeping, others sitting and standing, talking and passing around food and drink.

The statues were little more than grey ghosts in that light, and curled around the bottoms of them – Sebastian blinked rapidly. There were wyverns here, four that he could see, sinuous and sleek, and at rest now. He saw a woman come over to one of them and adjust one of the thick leather straps that was bound around its head, and the long lizard snout opened and closed briefly, revealing a long, purple tongue.

'What is that?' Ephemeral was so surprised she spoke out loud.

'They are like dragons, but not really,' Sebastian whispered. 'A distant relation, perhaps.' He remembered riding the sea-wyvern out to the Judgement of Res'ni, powerful muscles surging through the water. 'I'm not sure how much they have in common with your . . . mother.'

'I can feel them,' whispered Ephemeral back. 'So alive! Can you feel them, Father?'

Sebastian shook his head, although he *could* feel them – a silvery thread, a sharp lizard keenness. He pushed the thought away and tried to read the movements of the Narhl soldiers, looking for clues. A group of five were standing over on one side of the statues, and they looked like they were having an animated discussion of some sort. One of the women stood motionless, a spear held stiffly to one side, all her attention on the man doing most of the talking. He was broad across the chest and his white and grey beard was thick with lichen. King Aristees. His great double-headed axe sat at his feet.

Sebastian pursed his lips, considering. Dallen's father was here, so perhaps the danger to the prince wasn't quite as dire as he feared. Yes, he had been exiled and disowned, thrown out of his home, but surely his own father would stop short of spilling family blood? Then he remembered the curl of the old man's lip when he'd looked from Dallen to Sebastian, guessing a link between them that had yet to be forged. And guessing it accurately. There was a man who knew his son, and he had leapt at the chance to be rid of him. What would he do now he had him back?

There was a flurry of movement from the centre of the camp. A man was dragged to his feet, his bruised face lit in cold white light. Sebastian clenched his fists at his sides.

'That is him,' whispered Ephemeral.

The guards dragged Prince Dallen around the camp, forcing him to walk the circumference of the statues. His father watched, shouting encouragement. Prince Dallen stumbled once or twice, and the soldiers jostled him to his feet once more. They were keeping him from truly resting.

Well, I am here now. Absently, his hand slipped into his pocket and touched the blue glass globe Crowleo had given him. *I could walk up there and negotiate his release. There must be something I could trade, a deal I could propose. No one has to die here.*

But, instead, he took his hand away from the globe and grasped the hilt of his sword. There was a quickening in his blood, a silvery thread that demanded the satisfaction of the hunt.

'Your sisters,' he said to Ephemeral, his voice barely more than a whisper, while he kept his eyes on Prince Dallen, 'and you, Ephemeral. I will not order you to do this. I will not order you to help me.'

'We swore an oath,' she said, her face still. 'Not to kill again.'

'I release you from it.'

'To be a knight,' she said slowly, 'is also to protect the weak. To save those who need saving.'

Sebastian took a deep breath. 'Listen, you must make your own decisions. You mustn't mindlessly obey me just because I am your father.' His eyes flickered to King Aristees. 'But I will ask you to help me, as a friend, to rescue my friend.'

'We will help you, Father,' she looked at him, her yellow eyes steady and without mercy, 'gladly.'

'Then let's bring them a nightmare on the sunrise.'

68

Dallen lifted his head wearily to look at the first glimmers of violet light spilling across the snowy lands to the east. His father's soldiers had left him alone for the moment, and he sat in the middle of their camp, his arms tied behind his back and his knees in the dirt, while his captors gathered around a cold-light to share out that morning's breakfast of raw fish wrapped in leaves. King Aristees himself was standing at the edge of the ring of statues, talking to a few of the wyvern riders they had with them – the Diamond Tail squad, judging from the geometric patterns picked out in white leather on their harnesses. Dallen recognised Odissin, leader of the squad, standing next to his father, her face pinched and solemn. In better days, she and Dallen had raced against each other, good-naturedly calling out threats and jibes into the wind as their beasts belted across the sky. Now she was careful not to make eye contact with him, instead keeping as close to his father as she could. *She's unsettled by the situation,* thought Dallen, *so she's sticking to what she knows: obey the king.* The wyverns were rousing themselves, he noticed, pushing up their long snouts and sniffing at the brisk morning air.

Someone slapped him on the back, slightly too hard to be friendly, and Dallen pitched forward.

'Not falling asleep on us are you, Dallen? You've a busy day on the sunrise.'

Dallen looked up into the grinning face of Nestor, a distant

447

cousin. With Dallen removed from the hierarchy, Nestor's branch of the family looked to gain power.

'You could try not to look quite so pleased with yourself,' replied Dallen through swollen lips, ignoring the way they stung as he talked. 'It's hardly a princely attitude.'

Nestor's grin flickered and faded.

'And I suppose a proper prince disobeys orders, and gets his soldiers killed. Is that right?' Nestor leaned down close to Dallen so that when he spoke again, spitting the words like poison, he coated the prince in a fine rain of spittle. 'I suppose a proper prince likes warmling cock?'

Dallen gritted his teeth and summoned the Cold instinctively, but Nestor just leaned down lazily and struck him hard across the face. Dallen rocked backwards, his head ringing. 'Enough of that. Your tricks won't save you now.'

Nestor stalked off, leaving Dallen to probe at the fresh cut on his lip with his tongue. He thought again of Nuava, wondering what had happened to the Skald girl. The group who had gone after her had come back empty handed, he knew that much, but she had run directly into the darkest part of the forest, with no provisions and no weapons. No one would know where she was. And on the heels of this, he thought of Sebastian, who had gone into that cursed city with his friends and not come out. As much as he had longed for the world outside the Frozen Steps, it seemed that it was destined to break his heart.

The sky was the deep purple of early dawn now, the stars slowly fading out of view as the silvery light of the sun stole their luminance. The scrubby land that spread out below the statues was still deeply shadowed in places, and Dallen found that his eyes were drawn to it. For a few moments, he forgot the men and women around him as he stared down at the snow and rocks below them. Had he spotted movement then? Was someone down there?

He looked to the wyverns. Their sense of smell was powerful, enough for the Narhl to use them to hunt down deer or the fleet-footed goats of the far north, and if there was anything approaching they should have caught the scent. But the animals showed no sense of alarm. One of them was up already, stretching its long, pale blue tail behind it as its rider started the day by rubbing its shiny body down with handfuls of clean snow. The other three wyverns were stirring too, and as he watched, one of them lifted its head and looked back down the hill. Not alarmed, not yet, but there was something.

'Hoy,' he called to the nearest soldier, a thickset woman with green lichen in her eyebrows. 'How many do you have on watch? And where?'

The woman frowned at him, casually passing a spear from hand to hand. 'I'm not supposed to talk to you.'

'We are very exposed up here,' he said. He was thinking of Joah Demonsworn, who had appeared out of nowhere and slaughtered his troop. Of the terrible stone and metal monster that had torn its way out of the earth. 'This is a bad place to make camp.'

The woman lowered her eyes.

'I'm sorry, your highness, but the King has been very clear.' She looked uncomfortable, as Odissin did. 'You are to be treated as a prisoner.'

Dallen turned away from her, biting down a frustrated retort, and that was when he saw death coming for them, fast and silent. A woman was running up the hill towards the statues, a sword in each hand. Her skin was pale green and her long white hair streamed out behind her like a flag. She bellowed no war cry, and there was a look of serene concentration on her face. Her eyes were yellow and full of murder.

'Watch out!'

But they were so fast. All at once lots of women were streaking up the hill, and then they were over the summit and amongst them. The Narhl soldiers were taken completely by surprise, most of them without their weapons, many still eating their breakfast.

The women were unnaturally quick, whirling and diving and lunging without appearing to need to think about it. Their reactions were instantaneous; Dallen saw one Narhl soldier, faster than the rest, fling his ice-spear at one of the green women, but, rather than shying away, she leapt towards the spear, smacking it from its dangerous arc with one blow of her sword so that it clattered harmlessly against the nearest statue, and using the momentum of her leap she turned and brought her other sword down across the Narhl soldier's neck. Dallen saw his blood spray crimson in the dawn light, and then he was down.

'Kill them!' his father was bellowing, 'Kill them all!' The king had a hold of his axe and was charging in a frenzy, but the green women were too fast, simply dancing out of his way. All around him, Narhl soldiers were falling, screaming in the dirt, bleeding out. Dallen scrambled awkwardly to his feet, stumbling backwards as a man with his chest torn open collapsed in front of him.

'Someone untie my bonds!' he cried, but even if they had wanted to, the Narhl soldiers had no chance to free him; they were falling fast now, and the smell of blood was overpowering. The woman with the green lichen in her eyebrows staggered past him, one hand pressed to her neck, her eyes wide and glassy. The woman who had stabbed her pushed her easily onto the ground and glanced up at Dallen, and nodded once before heading back into the fray.

What is going on? 'Stop, please!'

He saw his father beset on all sides by three of the green warriors, and he had dropped his axe in favour of a pair of curved blades. King Aristees was famed throughout the Frozen Steps as a legendary fighter but Dallen could see that his father was struggling. Soon, they would put him down too.

'Wyverns, to me!'

The big lizards were confused, cowering back against the stones away from these newcomers, but each of them turned towards his call, long snouts snuffling the air.

'To your squad!' he cried. 'Protect the squad!'

The biggest wyvern, Odissin's own, curled like a snake, jaws yawning open to reveal rows of shining white teeth. It made to strike at a nearby attacker, but a man appeared from behind the nearest statue, a man with long black hair and broad shoulders. Dallen was so surprised to see Sebastian that for a few moments he didn't recognise him, and then the big knight placed a hand on the wyvern's flank and immediately it coiled back in on itself, hiding its long head under its own tail. The other wyverns followed suit, drawing together as though frightened or confused.

'Sebastian?'

One of the women approached him – her white hair was cut

very short – and in desperation he summoned the Cold. He saw her blink with surprise as the temperature around them plummeted, and her eyebrows and hair were suddenly rimmed with frost. Another second and her blade gained an icy coating.

'I will freeze your blood in its veins, monster.'

'Dallen, stop!'

Sebastian left the wyverns, who were still mewling like pups, and jogged over. He placed a hand on the woman's arm.

'They're on your side, Dallen.' He stepped over the bodies like they weren't there. 'Are you all right?'

'Am I all right?' said Dallen, weakly. It really was Sebastian; his long black hair was tied back in its customary braid, and his blue eyes were narrowed against the cold. Dallen could see how he was looking at him; making note of every bruise, every cut. When Dallen didn't elaborate, Sebastian turned to gesture at the female warriors. King Aristees was now on his knees in the dirt, a smear of blood on his dirty white beard.

'These are . . . my friends, I suppose. The brood sisters. It's a bit complicated to explain, actually; remind me to tell you the story some time.' He smiled wanly. 'This one here you just tried to freeze is Havoc, and this is Ephemeral, their leader.'

Another one of the women stepped forward. Her hair was tied back in a braid like Sebastian's, and she was watching Dallen closely.

'Why –' Dallen shook his head. 'Why have you done this?'

'Why?' Sebastian looked utterly confused for a moment. 'Because they had taken you prisoner. They were beating you, killing you slowly. Frith saw it with his seeing spell.' He nodded to the woman called Havoc, who circled Dallen and cut his bonds with a quick stroke of her knife. 'I couldn't just leave you here.'

'So instead you come here with these . . .' he gestured to the green-skinned soldiers, lost for words – 'with whatever these creatures are, and you kill my people?'

Sebastian said nothing at all for some time. He was breathing hard. Now that the fighting was over, the dawn light seemed to fill the space between the statues like liquid gold. Dallen could see it reflected on the shining white hair of the warrior women, and in the pools of blood already being absorbed into the dark

451

earth. The wyverns still cowered, the sunlight turning their shining skins to brittle crystal.

'*They* were killing *you*,' said Sebastian eventually. 'I could not just stand by and let them do that.'

'Why not?' Dallen raised his hands once, and dropped them. 'I had accepted it. It was the justice I deserved for getting my squad killed. My father was too merciful. And now it seems that I am responsible for even more deaths.'

Sebastian took a step towards him, then seemed to think the better of it.

'I could not leave you here,' he said again. 'Wydrin is dead, and I could not lose you too.'

Dallen frowned. Despite everything, he had liked the mouthy red-headed sell-sword.

'What will you do now, Sir Sebastian?' he said, noting how the big knight winced at the use of that particular honorific. 'Kill my father in front of me too?'

Sebastian shook his head tersely. While they had been talking, the brood sisters, as Sebastian called them, had gathered the last of the living Narhl together and made them kneel next to their king by the largest statue. There were six of them left.

'Let's see what King Aristees has to say for himself,' said Sebastian. 'And then I expect we'll work it out from there.'

The old man glared up at them as they approached. Had he ever been bested in battle before? Seen his soldiers torn to pieces around him? Dallen didn't believe so.

'King Aristees,' said Sebastian evenly. 'It seems you are my prisoner now.'

'Aye, well. Just goes to show that I should have killed you on the spot. My axe thirsted for your blood, and I denied it. Not a mistake I'll be making again, you can be sure of that.'

'Oh, I'm absolutely sure of it, your majesty.'

Aristees actually chuckled at this. 'Heh. Well. Shall we get down to business, warmling scum?'

'Business?' Sebastian tipped his head to one side. 'What business could we possibly have?'

'You came back for my son, didn't you? That's what you want, isn't it? Well, he has always been a wrong 'un, and you're welcome

452

to him. He won't live long in your own lands, of course, eating your poisoned food and sweltering around your fires. But you can have him. I require three of your snake women here, and then you can go.'

For a few moments, everyone was silent.

'I beg your pardon?' said Sebastian eventually.

'I don't know where you found them, but I would certainly like to know. I've never seen such ruthless fighters.' King Aristees grinned up at them, revealing yellowed teeth. 'I saw one of them, there, tear out Nestor's throat with her *teeth*.' He barked laughter. 'They are cold-blooded and merciless, like us. I shall make one my wife. Imagine the sons I shall have!'

'Father,' cut in Dallen, 'what in all the frozen wastes—'

'It will be our greatest legacy!' boomed Aristees. He seemed utterly unconcerned by the carnage around him, or how close he'd come to death. There was a strange light in his eyes. 'No more weak sons who crave the warmth of unnatural appetites, only worthy successors to my throne, with blood on their teeth and claws.'

'I do not understand, Father,' said the one Sebastian had named as Ephemeral. She was standing with her swords still drawn and was peering down at King Aristees in great confusion. 'Does he wish to make us his queen?'

Sebastian ran a hand over his face wearily. 'We're going to need to have a long talk.'

69

Frith sat cross-legged in his room, the Edenier trap nestled on a rug in front of him. It seemed to hum with its own dark energy, so close to being complete now. He reached up and absently wiped the sweat from his brow. It was mid-morning and the temperature inside the inn was stifling.

'One more step,' he muttered to himself. As he watched, a shiny black beetle scuttled across the rug, heading towards the device. Halfway there it stopped, its tiny antennae waving furiously, before turning back and heading the other way. 'One more step and it is done.'

It was a thing of evil. Black twisted metal shot through with sections of silver, and all covered with the demon's icons; it seemed to crouch on the rug like some hibernating spider, simply waiting for the right season to uncurl its legs and start hunting. Except, of course, Frith knew what it was really waiting for.

He had taken Joah's pieces and his memories, and he had finished the thing, twisting and welding the metal, soldering it with magic and seeding it with power. It was constructed with both Edenier and Edeian, but ultimately it was a demon's toy, and that came with a certain price, just as the Rivener did.

'I cannot,' he said. He felt lightheaded. The beetle had crawled back under the gap between the rugs and vanished. 'I have done many things I regret. But to do this would be the end of me.'

He could, he supposed, leave this place now. He could use the Edenier to take himself home to Blackwood Keep. There Eric and the rest of his servants would have been spending their time making the castle a home again, as he had instructed them to do. By now there would be furniture in all the rooms, fires in all the fireplaces, and perhaps they would even have managed to erase the smell of blood from the Great Hall. The graves they had made for his father and brothers – they had no bodies to bury, but they had had the gravestones engraved anyway – would be well tended and covered in flowers. The pear tree that grew in the small graveyard would be bearing fruit; his mother had been fond of pears, and in a rare fit of sentiment his father had planted a pear tree next to her grave when she died. Now all their souls rested underneath its spreading branches.

If he went back there now he could forget about Skaldshollow and the monster resting at its heart, and instead throw himself into the arranged marriage proposed by Lady Clareon and her estate. The Blackwood and the Stony Dale would combine their resources and prosper together. It was, after all, what his father would have wanted for him – a chance to see the Frith name continue, and for the castle to be filled with a family again. History and responsibility had ever been his father's favourite subjects after all. He could build this new life for himself, and when he was old and grey – he grunted laughter at this, his hair already as white as it would ever be – he would tell his grandchildren stories about how, for a little while, he had been an adventurer, how he had defeated a dragon and travelled Ede in the company of sell-swords. Perhaps all his stories would end abruptly, and he would certainly never speak the names of Skaldshollow or Joah Demonsworn, but that would be an easier price to pay than the one that was facing him now.

Could he forget it, though? Could he forget any of it? Would he spend the rest of his life haunted by the violet light of the corrupted Heart-Stone, or the terrible rooms hidden away inside the Rivener? It was all too easy to imagine spending the rest of his life dreaming of the moment that Wydrin's body spun away into the dark, lost to him for ever. Or even worse, would he wake in the night remembering exactly how her hair had smelt, or the sound of her laughter, or any number of a thousand things he would be incapable of forgetting?

He had already lost everything that was important. This rage was too big to hide from, and he had never been very good at that anyway.

After a few moments he stood up and covered the Edenier trap with the rug. It was a relief to have it out of sight. Once that was done he retrieved his money belt, pushed his hair out of his eyes, and left the room.

Moving through the crowded streets of Holcodine, Frith couldn't help but be reminded of Krete. There was the same stifling desert sun and the same fetid scent of too many people in one place, but now he was walking without a stick, and his back was straight and true. He wound around the men and women on the street easily, keeping his eyes on his destination: the Storm Gates.

The huge circular monstrosity rose from amongst the shabby one- and two-storey buildings like a great flat tooth pushing through the flesh of the city. Bone-white stones blazed under the midday sun, the biggest and brightest thing in Holcodine. The upper wall was topped with huge bronze spikes, and if Frith forced himself to squint in that direction he could just about make out the severed heads that had been impaled there. Ravens perched nearby, looking bored now that they had stripped the skulls of all the juicy bits, and there was a wavering, ever-present roar, the cacophony that gave the Storm Gates their name: a thousand blood-thirsty citizens, baying for their day's entertainment.

When he stood outside the walls, Frith paused. Part of him wanted to leave – to go back to the inn, buy several bottles of wine and get enormously drunk. Instead, he forced himself to look at the place; up close the huge bricks weren't as pristine as they appeared. Closer to ground level the walls were thick with graffiti, mostly detailing who the author wished to see punished next, or which of the convicts had won their respect. Curiously, there were lots of handprints, all clustered together in a line that seemed to run the circumference of the building, daubed in dark, ruddy mud.

'They make all the prisoners do it before they enter the Gates.'

Frith looked down to see a grubby child at his elbow with a

tray of something sticky slung round his neck. The boy grinned up at him. He had a tattoo of an octopus on one cheek.

'What?'

'The handprints. I can tell you're not from round here, see, and I could tell you were wondering what they were about.' The boy sniffed. 'Every man and woman that fights in the pit leaves their print out here. Once they've done that, they belong to the Gates. Can I interest you in a snack, milord? For the games?'

'I don't—'

'We're doing a special deal on these today, milord.' The boy plucked a long thin stick off the tray and held it up for Frith to look at. There were small objects skewered on the stick, brown glistening things with lots of tiny legs. 'It's appropriate, see, for today's games. My mum covers them in fat and boiling sugar. Very tasty. Just two coppers.'

Despite himself, Frith peered closer at the stick.

'What are those, exactly?'

'Grasshoppers and stinging ants,' said the boy. 'You don't have to worry about the stings none, 'cause my mum chops them all off, see. The grasshoppers I catch myself.'

Frith drew up straight. 'No – thank you. Do you sell any drinks? Without insects in them?'

The boy snorted at him. 'Who'd put insects in a drink? That'd be stupid.' He reached under the tray to retrieve a brown leather skin, which he held up to Frith. 'Spring water with a touch of lemon. Perfect for a hot day like this, milord.'

'And where exactly do you get spring water from around here?'

The boy decided to keep quiet this time and simply grinned up at Frith. Sighing, Frith fetched a coin from his belt and exchanged it with the boy for the skin.

'Thank you kindly, milord. Enjoy the games!'

The boy sped off towards some other stragglers and Frith took a cautious sip from the skin. Surprisingly, it did appear to be lemon-water, and it calmed his throat a little. Pushing aside his doubts, he walked through the arch and into the Storm Gates, where he bought a ticket and made his way towards a relatively quiet area. Inside, the place was circular, with an enormous sand-covered arena in the centre, surrounded by rings and rings of stone benches, reaching up almost to the tops of the walls. Outside in the city the sound was softened by the thick stone walls, but inside the roaring of the crowd was deafening. Frith moved down the rows, passing men and women and children with their eyes fixed on the pit below, impatiently peering round him as he squeezed past. Most of them were shouting at the distant figures, and quite a few of them were chewing on snacks very similar to those sold by the boy with the octopus tattoo. Frith saw tankards of beer and ale everywhere, as well as countless skins of wine, and he wondered exactly how much vomit was cleared up at the end of every day's entertainments.

He took his seat and peered down at the arena below. Distantly, he was aware that he was avoiding his true purpose, but it was easier to pass this off as research. *I need to know exactly what goes on here*, he told himself. *If I am to do this, I must do it right.*

In the arena below, three figures were moving about, circling the pit. One, a man with skin the colour of red clay and a series of pale, white scars across his back and chest, was walking around with confidence, shaking his fists at the crowd and bellowing something Frith couldn't make out over the roar. This, evidently, was one of the champions of the Storm Gates; a convict who had survived so many trials he had now become a hero. He had been rewarded with a pair of small knives which he wore at his belt. They were polished to a high shine, and were of reasonable quality. The other two were much less confident. An older, wiry-looking woman with long grey hair falling loose down her back edged around the pit, trying to see all around her at once, while the other, a young man with a patchy beard and only a stained loin-cloth to his name, was visibly shaking. The two newcomers had been given wooden clubs. Frith watched closely. Were they both to fight the big man with the scars? He supposed that they might have a chance, if they could stay out of range of his knives and get a few lucky blows to his head.

There was a flat clacking sound, and part of the arena wall folded away, revealing a long dark tunnel. Instantly, the roar of the crowd grew until it was a tide of relentless noise.

Something scuttled out of the tunnel, and Frith felt all the hairs on his body trying to stand on end. It was a huge scorpion, easily as big as a small horse. It was brown, the colour of old tea, with long flat plates running across its back that shone wetly. Its tail, with its lethal stinging barb, flexed over its back experimentally, while its front pincers opened and closed.

The young man and the woman immediately retreated, flinging themselves back to the furthest part of the arena, the young man openly sobbing. Frith wondered what they had done to end up in such a place. The man with the knives and the scars advanced, actually running at the scorpion and shouting, and to Frith's surprise the creature scuttled away from him, apparently taking fright at this sudden movement.

The crowd went crazy, cheering his bravado, but Frith soon saw that it was more than that. The scorpion's confusion took it closer to the other two prisoners, and it circled towards them instead, the barbed tail flexing. The woman with the long hair decided to make a run for it, even dropping her club in her desperation to get away, and the scorpion was on her in moments. Frith heard her scream quite clearly over the cacophony as she was lost under the creature's scrabbling legs. It trod her to the ground easily enough, and then the thing dragged her back up with its pincers. The serrated claws flexed once, twice, almost convulsively, and the woman fell back to the ground in ragged chunks.

'Where would they even find such a thing?' he muttered to himself. To his surprise, the woman sitting next to him leaned over, gesturing with a tankard of foamy ale.

'Shipped over special from Onwai,' she said. She had warm olive skin and her black hair had been braided into a looping crown on her head, which she'd then covered with some sort of bright red paste. It smelt strongly of ginger. 'They have farms for them, where they breed them bigger and bigger, and feed them until they're as big as that bastard down there. From what I heard, the Master of the Gates had ten of them shipped over in the last batch, and this one's the runt.'

Frith frowned, imagining sharing a long sea voyage with such things locked up in the cargo hold.

'It seems a very cruel way to execute someone,' he said.

'Well, yes,' said the woman. 'That's the point.'

'I suppose you are right.'

Below, the scorpion had turned its attention to the man in the loin cloth, and was stalking him steadily across the sand. The young man was moving backwards rapidly, shouting something to the man with the scars and the knives. Frith could well imagine what it was – *Let's work together, let's help each other.* But the big man was keeping back, staying out of the creature's line of sight.

'It's got the taste now,' said the woman. She slurped from her tankard. 'This one won't last much longer.'

She was right. The young man tried to circle away, and when the creature made a grab for him with its pincers he actually struck it, the wooden club bouncing off armoured plate like it was a drum. The left pincer caught him round the midriff, holding him in place – he gave a single, ululating scream – and then the tail shot down, the wickedly sharp stinger striking the man in the centre of his chest. From Frith's vantage point it was possible to see the shining point emerge from the other side, slick with blood.

'There you go,' said the woman. 'It's a waste, putting this lot up against a scorpion. It's over too quickly.'

The other man, the one with the knives and the scars, was approaching the scorpion rapidly from behind while the creature was occupied with the other prisoner. He ran low, both knives held up in front of him, and when he got round to the side of the creature he stabbed viciously at the thing's head, trying to put out its eyes. The scorpion leapt backwards, dropping the young man, and now it was moving oddly. It seemed he had managed to injure it after all.

'This is more like it,' said the woman next to Frith approvingly. 'Got someone here who knows what he's doing.'

Overconfident from his success, the scarred man jumped forward again, knives moving in a flashy dance, tearing through the scorpion's eyes and bursting them. The creature squealed, and Frith felt the entire audience recoil at the noise.

'Son of a bitch,' cried the woman. 'He's got more luck than sense.'

But it wasn't quite over. Confused and blinded, the scorpion struck out at random with its pincers and quite casually sliced the scarred man's arm off just above the elbow. A torrent of blood blasted forth in a gory arc, and the crowd groaned as one. It had been going so well.

The man fell to his knees, clutching at the mess that had once been his bicep, too surprised to scream yet. Frith got to his feet.

'They'll bring others out to finish it off,' said the woman. She was waving at him to sit back down. 'You'll miss the best bit.'

Frith glanced back down into the pit. The man was lying in the sand now, marooned in a rapidly growing island of his own blood. The scorpion was lashing out wildly, thick drops of poison oozing from the end of its sting.

'Thank you,' said Frith, 'but I think I've seen enough.'

70

'Tell me about the worst ones. The murderers, the rapists.'

The woman looked at him oddly, as well she might. Frith kept his gaze steady, reminding himself that he'd already paid the Overseer a decent purse of coin just to have this conversation with her.

'We have a good many of them,' she said. She was a short woman with broad shoulders and a thick layer of muscle on her arms and legs, and the red vest she wore was pierced all over with silver rings that jangled slightly as she walked. At her waist, these rings bristled with dozens of keys, and she carried a long horse-whip in one hand. 'Here, we like to keep all the beasts together. Let me show you.'

They were within the workings of the Storm Gates now, patrolling shadowy corridors lined with sand and lit with guttering lamps. She led him down one corridor and out through a narrow training ground, the sand stained brown with old blood, and on through what Frith guessed must count as the living quarters for the prisoners here. Dark cells with rusted-iron bars dotted the Storm Gates like honeycomb, men and women standing well back from the Overseer. He suspected they were more than familiar with her whip.

'Here you are, then. The ugliest bunch.'

They came to the end of the line. The cells here were small and cramped, and there was a stink of urine and rotten food coming from them all.

'Salazar Gwint, who broke into an orchard and killed the entire family living there, before getting stupidly drunk on cider.' The man in the nearest cell was skinny and pale, the tops of his bare shoulders pink with sunburn. He peered out at Frith with eyes as dull as pebbles, absently picking at his peeling skin.

'A drooling idiot, if you ask me, won't last five heartbeats in the arena. Here, we have Brightly Tripps, a much better prospect.' The man in the next cell was well over six feet tall and nearly as wide around the middle. He grinned as he saw them passing, and winked luridly at the Overseer. 'Made quite a name for himself, taking his knives across Relios and leaving a trail of blood behind him. Won't have his knives in the arena though.'

'It's good to see you, oh brightly shining star of my dreams.' The man's voice was smooth and cultured. 'I dream of you every night, maiden of the midden, you and your delicious skin.'

'I wish he'd shut up though,' she added, not looking at him. 'On the end here we have Kathy Redfingers, who had a predilection for corpses. You should have smelt her when she came in, half the guards had to go and have a sit down.'

'Do any of them have families?' asked Frith. 'Are they leaving anyone behind when they step out into the arena?'

The Overseer raised an eyebrow, and then shrugged.

'There is one that might fit that description. One who still thinks his family are worth thinking about, at least.' She led him across the way to a cell opposite the others. Inside, a man sat on the ground with his elbows resting on his knees, his head held so low that his long grey hair covered his face. He did not look up at their approach. 'Jerston Blake. Got into a fight over a card game in a tavern. When the owner threw him out, he went back there in the early hours and killed the entire family save for one small boy, who hid under his bed. Long history of violence, this one. Not sure how he avoided the Storm Gates for so long, but he's here now. Married to one long-suffering wife, with at least five children that we know about.'

'I was drunk,' muttered the man, still not looking up. 'My blood gets hot when I've been at the drink; I'm not myself.'

'Nonsense, Jerston,' said the Overseer mildly. 'You keep claiming you were stone-cold drunk, yet you had the wiles to pick that man's lock and sneak your way to the upper floor. And you took your time killing them too, don't forget that.'

Frith stared down at the man.

'I would like to talk to the prisoner,' he said eventually. 'And I have a proposal for you both.'

It was late when Frith returned to the Storm Gates. Deep orange lamps were alight all over the city, and with the punishing sun vanished once more beyond the horizon, the evening was cool. He carried the Edenier trap wrapped in cloth and held securely under one arm. A guard was on the gate, waiting for him.

'Evening, milord.' As he spoke, his top lip curled into a sneer. 'She has it all ready for you,' he said. There was a brief pause. 'You must have a lot of coin, milord, and strange tastes. Most people are content to see these poor bastards die in the dirt.'

Frith looked at him, saying nothing, until the guard cleared his throat.

'Follow me, then, milord.'

The guard took him through the archway and led him on a new route through the warren-like corridors until they reached a small grubby room with mud on the walls. The Overseer stood in the doorway and, beyond her, Frith could see the man Jerston sitting on the only chair, his arms bound. He was staring past them both at something only he could see.

'You've arranged it all, then?' said the Overseer. There was a bright new dislike for Frith in her eyes, although he noticed she wasn't backing out of their deal.

'I have the banker's note for you.' He handed her a piece of parchment, which she peered at closely. 'This man's family will want for nothing, and you already have the first part of your payment.'

She nodded at the parchment before folding it away into a pocket.

'Looks official enough to me. You don't look the sort, that's all.'

'What do you mean by that?' The question was out before he could stop it, his voice close to angry again. He just wanted this to be over.

'This man might be scum, but he's done nothing to you. Although

464

I imagine that's not what it's about, is it? Most folks are content with too many drinks and a scrap, or a night or three in a pillow house.'

'You would kill him eventually,' said Frith, measuring each word. He couldn't afford to lose his temper now. 'Except it would be a public humiliation, and you won't stoop to getting his blood on your hands.'

'That's different. That's justice,' said the Overseer.

Frith glanced behind her into the room. The convict had been tied to the chair and his long grey hair hung in his face. 'If you have changed your mind, then I will ask for my coin back.'

The Overseer shook her head abruptly, making the dozens of rings on her vest jangle discordantly.

'Get on with it, then. There's no accounting for some folks.'

She stepped past him and waved him into the room. As he stepped through the door she closed it behind him, so close on his heels that he felt the wind of it push against his back.

'It's all done, is it?' Jerston was looking at him now. His eyes were red and raw, his face gaunter than it had been earlier.

'It has been arranged.' Frith put the Edenier trap down on the floor, still covered over with the cloth. It was heavy, and he was relieved to put it down. 'Your wife will receive a pension yearly from me for the rest of her life. It will be enough to see that your children are fed and clothed, enough for medicines if they require them.' Frith cleared his throat. 'I keep my promises.'

Jerston snorted. 'It's some promise, this. A blood promise.'

'Your alternative is to remain a prisoner here,' said Frith, 'until the day they drag you up into the arena, to be torn apart by dogs, or run through by a scorpion, and your family will struggle on in poverty.' He paused, wondering who he was trying to convince. 'This way, your death will be fast. And your wife and children will want for nothing.'

The man grunted and shifted in his chair. His right leg jittered nervously.

'What's it for?' he said. 'Is it like the Overseer said? You just like killing?'

Frith clenched his fists at his side. Inside him, the Edenier was roiling and churning. He remembered the day he had claimed

465

back his castle, the brittle noises as he broke bones with his magic, the terrible wet sounds Fane had made as he struggled to breathe through what was left of his lungs.

'No, it is not like that. It is difficult to explain. But you should know that when you die you will be helping to end a great evil.'

Jerston looked up at him, his face creased with confusion and fear. 'Aye. Well. Let's just get this over with.'

Frith nodded and moved to uncover the Edenier trap. In the yellow light of the dirty room it looked strange and tumorous on the floor, and Jerston visibly recoiled from it.

'What is that?' he said, his voice breaking a little.

'It is a device. I will place it in your lap, and I will need you to look into it.'

The corners of Jerston's mouth turned down and he shook his head. 'I don't think I like that none. I don't want that touching me.'

'It will only be for a moment.' Frith lifted up the contraption, carrying it carefully over to where Jerston sat. The man drew back, as though Frith approached him carrying a handful of poisonous vipers, but he didn't object again. Frith settled it on top of the man's legs, and it crouched there like an obscene bubo. He had to admit, he didn't blame the man for not wanting it near him.

'I need you to look at that while I . . . while I work.'

Frith went around the back of the chair, while Jerston sat awkwardly, his arms still bound. His head was lowered slightly.

'What is this thing?' he said again. He sounded distracted now, as though he didn't quite understand where he was. 'It looks wrong.'

'Just keep your eyes on it,' said Frith, before adding, 'think of your family.'

He drew a long-bladed knife from his belt and turned it in the light. He had spent part of that afternoon making sure it was as sharp as possible.

'Do it then, milord,' said Jerston. 'I'm ready.'

But Frith found for a moment that he could not move at all. It was as though someone had thrown a bucket of water over him, and he had woken in a place he didn't recognise. *What am I doing here? How have I come to this?* He looked at the blade

466

in his hand and was appalled to see his grey eyes staring back at him in the reflection.

Do this and you are no better than any of them. He knew that was what Sebastian would say if he were here; if he had guessed at the nature of the device, he would never have helped him in the first place. If he had known it required a blood sacrifice to work . . . If he did this he would be a murderer, just like Fane and his grinning pets, the Children of the Fog; torturing and killing in the name of a demon.

But this was his chance to end it. With this weapon, Joah would be powerless, and he would pay for all the suffering he'd caused, now and a thousand years ago. He would pay for the souls lost in the Rivener's blood-stained rooms, and he would pay for Wydrin's lifeless body, twisting away into the dark.

'Are you doing it, then, or what?' Jerston's voice was wavering now. 'Only I don't think I can keep looking at this thing and—'

Without another word, Frith took hold of the man's head firmly with one arm and ran the blade across his throat, pressing down with all his strength. There was a ragged scream that quickly disintegrated into a thick gurgle. Jerston jerked in his chair, nearly dislodging the device. Frith held him as still as he could, forcing his head down even as the blood surged out of him. It took only seconds, and he felt the bigger man shudder in his grip as the last of his life's blood left him. Jerston said something then, garbled with blood and pain, and Frith couldn't make out what it was, but when he looked down he saw that the Edenier trap had opened up like a flower, and inside it a dark mouth awaited.

Frith staggered away, dropping the knife from fingers that were suddenly numb. He had done it. The trap was complete, and it was ready. He had done what Joah Demonsworn couldn't.

'That's it, then,' he said, and his voice sounded less than sane to his own ears. 'It's all done.'

He reached up to wipe away the tears running down his cheeks, but his hands were red with blood.

71

Joah had found a mirror.

He stood for some time in front of it, his long narrow fingers
playing lightly over his face and neck. The burns inflicted on
him by Aaron were quite severe, and without salves or any other
sort of attention they had festered, leaving one side of his face
a bloody, pus-filled ruin. Luckily, thanks to the effects of eating
the god-flesh, it was not that side that drew the eye. Oh no. Not
at all.

A small, strangled noise escaped his lips and he realised that
he was laughing. Was this what he had wanted? Was this what
he'd been striving for all these years?

'This is power, then,' he said, nodding at the mirror. 'This is
what power looks like.'

He turned away from that view and looked around the
Rivener's central room. It was squalid and filthy, and two of
the Rivener's glass eyes were completely smashed. The Edenier
chamber boiled with the Heart-Stone's nauseous violet light, and
distantly he could hear the screaming of Bezcavar, trapped inside
the glass with the tainted magic.

'I have lost track of time,' he said absently. 'Most of the souls
have been harvested from this city now, Bezcavar, but you know,
I'm not even sure I need them.' He held up his hands, and twin
balls of flame appeared above his palms. 'I am a creature of the
Edenier now, like the gods of old. I do not need their words to
form the magic. I do not need anything at all.'

The noise from the chamber increased, and Joah tipped his head to one side as though listening to something very far away.

'But I don't believe that's true, my old friend. Yes, we have done much together, achieved so many things. Perhaps it is time we parted ways.' There was a flicker on the edge of his mind as Bezcavar tried to force him to remember, to share with him those memories that had once broken him. He shook his head sadly. 'There is no sense in trying to frighten me, Bezcavar. Do you not see? I am beyond such concerns now.' He summoned the memory himself, of the day that the demon had shown him its true face. He saw it as if from a distance, as the sight tore his mind into tatters and left him weeping on the edge of sanity. 'Do you truly think you can scare me with that memory now?' He gestured at his own twisted visage. 'When I look like this?'

The demon grew silent.

'You have no more power over me, Bezcavar, and nothing left to offer me, either.' He paused, looking back at the chamber. 'I fear that Aaron was right about you, after all. I have been a fool. What would happen to you, thrown back out into the world with no willing host? Your girl child is long gone, and I suspect you would not be welcomed back. There are no shrines of yours in Skaldshollow, and no people left to help you build one.'

Still silence from the chamber.

'You are pretending now to be gone, in the hopes that I will forget you are here.' He smiled fondly, twisting his face into stranger shapes. 'Always so wily, Bezcavar. But you forget, I am a god now. And gods do not consort with demons.'

He reached out to the chamber and turned the lever with the Edenier, opening the front portal. There was a moment of silence, before something black and furious boiled out the aperture, a half-seen shifting mass of smoke and grasping, feathery tendrils. Joah felt it surge past him, knowing that at any other time the rasping touch of the demon's true form against his skin would have driven him instantly insane. Now he just watched as it attempted, briefly, to get inside his head, before streaming out of the broken windows in twin plumes of dark smoke.

* * *

469

'I have had more than enough of this place.'

Wydrin gasped air into her lungs, leaning heavily against the alley wall, but Xinian was already next to her.

'Keep moving, or they will be on us again. Quickly, up these steps.'

Casting a look down towards the street – nothing there yet, they were slower when she was out of sight – Wydrin turned and followed Xinian to the end of the narrow passage. There was a set of stone steps there, leading upwards and half hidden behind barrels and storage crates. They moved swiftly, emerging up on a roof shabbily tiled in black slate. Wydrin moved over to the edge and looked down. In the street below were hundreds of the Rivened, milling about and bumping into each other, their faces blank. Just now they had been filled with purpose and hunger, running after them both with their oddly shambling gait, but now they'd lost sight of her, and with it their temporary purpose.

'Will they come up to the roof, do you think?'

Next to her, Xinian shrugged. Above them the red storm light raged on.

'That one in the house managed to come down the stairs to you. I wouldn't be surprised if they figured it out.'

Getting out of Skaldshollow had turned out to be a lot more difficult than Wydrin had anticipated. The husks swarmed wherever they went, and twice now the Rivener had lumbered into life, detaching itself from the Tower of Waking, before lumbering off across the city. They had watched it from the window of an abandoned tower as it made its way, back and forth, picking off those Skalds who had yet to have their souls ripped from them, a monstrous silhouette against the bloodied sky. Sometimes it would pause, dragging a clawed arm across the cobbled streets to score a long, deep trench in the fabric of the city. Wydrin did not know what Joah thought he was doing, but it made her uneasy.

The ranks of the Rivened were growing, and each time they tried to navigate their way down a street, a crowd of the poor soulless creatures would meet them, their jaws wide and their fingers grasping – too many to run past, or push through, and they showed no fear of their blades. Frustrated, Wydrin had tried to cut her way through the middle of them, Frostling and Glassheart stabbing and slicing until her arms ached, but no matter how many she put down, more would appear in their place, and they would reach for her, fingers unnaturally strong. Once, she had forgotten herself, lost in anger and desperation, and she hadn't moved away from them fast enough. Too quickly they dragged her to the floor and she had felt the blunt pressure of their teeth against her leathers as they tried to bite her flesh away. Luckily, she had managed to put her boot in the face of one, and then Xinian was there, solid arms dragging her bodily out of that mess. Since then Wydrin had been more cautious, and their progress towards the wall was very slow.

'What is that?'

Wydrin looked to where Xinian was pointing. They could see the Rivener from the rooftop, slumped in its usual resting position against the Tower of Waking, and something dark was gathering at its head. For a moment Wydrin thought it was a flock of black birds, but then it started to move away from the tower and its form was diaphanous and uncertain.

'I have no idea,' she said, 'but I doubt it's good news.'

The dark cloud swirled down towards the ground and out of sight. Wydrin watched, but the Rivener didn't move. The city was still eerily silent, save for the shuffling of the bodies below.

'Come,' said Xinian. 'We should keep moving, before they work out how to get up the steps.'

Wydrin sighed. 'You are relentless, you know that? No wonder they picked you to go after the crazy mage.' She rubbed a hand across her forehead, noticing as she did so that her fingers were trembling. 'Shit. I could really do with eating something soon.'

Xinian pursed her lips. 'I am not hungry. You are weak.'

'You're dead! Of course you're not bloody hungry.' Wydrin shook her head wearily. 'Why do I always end up with the dead ones?'

At that moment a voice drifted up over the wall, and Wydrin found herself standing very still.

'Come down here and join us, Wydrin Threefellows, and you won't feel hungry any more.'

Wydrin and Xinian exchanged a look.

'I know that voice,' said Wydrin. Worse than that, she knew

how it felt in her head. Cautiously she peered over the edge of the roof again. The Rivened were all still there, crowded together in the street, but now around half of them were all looking back up at her. A hundred different ruined faces, the same expression of gleeful rage. Every pair of eyes looking up at her was filled with blood from rim to rim.

'Bezcavar,' she said. 'Personally, I found your last host a lot more attractive. Smelt a lot better, too.'

Xinian had joined her at the edge of the roof, her sword held so tightly in her one hand the knuckles had turned white.

'It was interesting to be inside your head.' This time the demon spoke through three throats at once, producing an odd, discordant harmony. Wydrin watched the lips of the husks move and shivered. 'Not a very great mind, no, but interesting,' the demon continued. 'Lots of places you don't show anyone, and so much bravado. I would have liked longer to explore.'

'I'm sorry to have disappointed you,' Wydrin called down. 'But you left a bad taste in my head. How are you doing this, by the way? I thought your hosts had to be willing.'

'Why are you talking to it?' asked Xinian, her voice low so that only Wydrin could hear. 'We should move. Now.'

'Oh, I'm curious,' said Wydrin, her lips pulled into a tight smile. 'Always my biggest weakness.'

'These things? They barely qualify.' The demon was speaking through eight of the husks now, their cracked lips moving in unison, each pair of blood-filled eyes fixed on the roof. 'There's nothing left inside them at all now, save for hunger. Certainly nothing left that can object to my presence.' Two more husks opened their mouths. 'Not the greatest vessels, by any means, but certainly good enough for me to watch you die, Wydrin Threefellows.'

Ten more husks lifted their faces to the roof and opened eyes filled with blood.

'And as you can see, in this form I can inhabit more than one. Won't this be fun?'

Wydrin swore under her breath and stepped away from the edge of the roof.

'This might be a good time to run.'

They turned, meaning to look for another way down, only to

find a slim shape watching them from the far side of the roof. The girl was ragged and covered in dirt, her short hair sticking up on all sides. Wydrin immediately drew both her sword and her dagger.

'Wait,' said Ip, 'I can show you a safe way across the city. And I can't do it with my guts hanging round my ankles, can I?'

72

'It is very fine. You do good work, Crowleo.'

The woman smiled at him through the tears that were threatening to fall. Crowleo took hold of the hand that wasn't holding the glass globe and squeezed it.

'Thank you, Madame Jeane, it really was my pleasure. I hope it brings you some peace.'

Madame Jeane nodded uncertainly. They stood on the grass outside the Secret Keeper's house – and so Crowleo would always think of it, even though she'd been gone for well over a year now – and a cool wind was blowing up, tugging at the woman's scarves and revealing the pink mass of scar tissue on her lower neck. Absently she pulled the fabric back into place.

'I keep seeing him how he was. After the fire.' She looked up at Crowleo again, and this time a few stray tears made an escape. 'I can't get that picture out of my mind. When I wake in the morning it's the first thing I think of, and when I try to think of happier times, that's what I see.' She held up the glass globe, which was a deep green. The sunlight caught it and sent a flicker of emerald light across the grass. Crowleo knew that when she looked into its depths she would see her husband as he had been when they had first married: young, handsome, full of life. 'Now I shall have this to look at, always.'

Crowleo smiled again, and bid her goodbye. He watched Madame Jeane walk back into the forest, her steps a little steadier than they had been when she had arrived. Just a memory captured in the glass, and perhaps that wasn't all that much, but he was getting better at it all the time. Soon he would be able to craft the Edeian into more complex designs, shapes that held secrets and altered the perception of time. Holley, he thought, would have been proud. Or at least, she would have been secretly proud, somewhere underneath her cranky demeanour.

He made to go back to the workshop, but something in the grass glittered and caught his eye. Crowleo bent and plucked a shard of orange crystal from the ground, turning it back and forth and watching as the sun danced along its edge. He was still finding pieces of Holley's work out here, even after all this time, and he suspected he would continue to do so as long as he stayed. Thinking of that he remembered the Children of the Fog and their strange girlish laughter as they walked on down the path, multiplying as they came.

Crowleo took a long, slow breath. That was all over now. The Blackwood was peaceful, and he had nothing to be afraid of, out here by himself.

When he turned back to go inside and saw a man standing by his front door, he was so startled that he dropped the shard of glass and gave a low cry.

'Good afternoon, Crowleo.'

At first he didn't recognise the slender man standing by the house. Frith's white hair was slightly longer than when Crowleo had last seen him, and there was a difference in the way he was standing – an easier confidence than had been evident before. The clothes he wore looked well-used, and he was holding a long staff of pale wood in one hand.

'Lord Frith? I – where did you come from?'

'I will only be here briefly, as I do not have much time.' He walked over briskly and clasped Crowleo's hand in his own. 'You look well.'

'So do you, my lord.' Crowleo peered closely at the other man's face. 'But you look troubled. What has happened? Is it Sebastian?'

Frith opened his mouth as if to reply, then simply shook his head.

'Sebastian is fine. I need to access my vault. I assume that won't be a problem?'

Crowleo shook his head. 'Of course not. It is good to see you, if a little surprising.' Crowleo took a deep breath, reminding himself that Lord Frith was a mage. He was bound to do things like turn up out of the blue. 'I have some bread and dried fish, some preserves a client left with me yesterday. Would you like to stop for some lunch?'

For the first time a hint of a smile touched the corner of Frith's mouth, although it only made him look sadder.

'Thank you for your kindness, but no.'

'Then I shall make a pack for you to take with you when you go. You do not look like you've been eating enough.' Crowleo paused, wincing slightly. He sounded so much like Holley some-times. 'It is no trouble.'

'Thank you, Crowleo.'

'Is there anything else, while you're here? I have been crafting the glass again, and starting to get my own commissions.' He paused. There was still that sense from Frith that he was missing something, yet he knew that to pry would be a mistake. 'For you I would charge a discounted rate, of course.'

Frith smiled again, although it was colder now.

'No, thank you, but I do have one more secret for you to keep, Crowleo.'

An hour or so later Crowleo watched Lord Frith walk back across the invisible bridge, appearing to hang mid-air over the treetops below, the viewing glass held out firmly in front of him. The wind blew his hair around like a flag, and he seemed a little more uncertain of his steps, stumbling here and there so that Crowleo found himself clenching and unclenching his fists. He was no longer carrying the staff.

When he got to the end of the bridge, Frith leaned forward for a moment, apparently needing to catch his breath.

'Are you all right, my lord?' asked Crowleo. 'You look shattered.'

'I am fine,' said Frith, although the hand that he used to wave Crowleo away trembled slightly. 'Have you news of Blackwood Keep?'

'I hear of it every now and then, my lord. The word in Pinehold

476

is that it has returned to how it was before Fane showed his evil face here, although I think . . .' He paused, suddenly worrying about how much he should say. 'I believe they would prefer for the throne to not sit empty for much longer.'

Frith grunted.

'Dreyda visits frequently,' Crowleo said hurriedly. 'She wants to keep an eye on everything, you know what she's like. Under her instruction the library is growing again, although she argues frequently with your man Eric about the best way to spend your coin.'

'Good.' Frith nodded. 'Between them they will figure it out.'

'Won't you go and see them yourself? I'm sure Dreyda would love—'

'I must go now, Crowleo.' Frith gathered himself up. 'There is still so much to do.'

'Wait,' Crowleo passed him the small canvas sack he'd filled with bread rolls and a well-wrapped packet of dried fish, 'at least take this before you go.'

Frith took it, and smiled again. It looked more genuine this time.

'Thank you, my friend. Goodbye.'

The afternoon filled with a brittle, crackling sound, pressing against Crowleo's eardrums, and then the air around Frith surged with light and noise. Crowleo stumbled backwards, and in a blink the light was gone, along with Lord Frith. He stood there for a long moment, staring out across the treetops to where the Frith family vault was hidden.

'Whatever's happening, Sebastian,' he murmured, 'I hope you are safe.'

Negotiations were continuing on into the night.

Sebastian watched them from just beyond the circle of statues; Ephemeral, Crocus and Havoc were sitting cross-legged opposite King Aristees and his two closest advisors, all six of them talking animatedly across the silvery glow of the cold-light. Sebastian wasn't sure what he was more surprised by: that King Aristees would sit and negotiate terms with the people who had just slaughtered his own men and women, or that the brood sisters

477

would even consider his offer, as greatly changed as it was already. He thought of how they'd been on the battlefield of Baneswatch – confused, conflicted and, above all, young. Now they were arguing shrewdly, pursuing their own goals with a determination even Frith would admire. Ephemeral held up her hand, one finger stabbing the air as she reiterated something the Narhl king wasn't paying enough attention to.

'I cannot say I ever thought I'd see the day when my father would sit down with another people,' said Dallen. He'd appeared out of the darkness next to Sebastian, limping slightly. In the pale glow of the cold-light his face was a painful jigsaw of bruises. 'He barely approves of trade with outsiders, and even then it must take place beyond Narhl borders.'

Sebastian shrugged. 'It is a most unexpected outcome. I have been training the brood sisters for combat, in how to keep themselves safe. I didn't realise they picked up diplomacy along the way.'

'They are . . . extraordinary women.' Dallen glanced down at the stony ground, and Sebastian knew he was thinking of the men and women they had killed that day. 'I wish you had told me of them sooner.'

'How do you even start to tell a tale like that?' He had told them, of course; after King Aristees' surprise proposal, Sebastian had spent some time telling the remaining Narhl the full story. How their ill-fated journey under the Citadel had led to their unleashing the god of destruction on the world, how Sebastian's blood had brought her army to life, and how they were still linked to him, through that same blood. It had not seemed to dissuade the Narhl king. 'It's not really something you can casually drop into everyday conversation.'

'If I had known, I might have been able to warn them,' said Dallen coldly.

'Would that have stopped them beating you?' Sebastian took a slow breath, trying to keep his temper under control. 'I did what I thought best. I am not sorry.'

Dallen didn't say anything for a moment. 'The wyverns. I've never seen them behave like that. It was as though you commanded them with a look.'

Sebastian looked down at his boots. The silver thread in his mind was still there. He could tell that the wyverns were frightened by the taste of Narhl blood on the air.

'That is more difficult to explain, I'm afraid. I'm not certain I understand it myself.'

Dallen narrowed his eyes at him but said nothing.

'And now we wait and see.' Sebastian turned back to the talks going on in the middle of the stone circle. King Aristees was laughing at something, smacking one broad hand with the flat of his axe with mirth. 'I must admit, I do not know what will be the outcome of this.'

'What do you hope for?'

'Peace, as ever.' Sebastian looked at Dallen, who shook his head, smiling without amusement.

'I find that difficult to believe.'

'Dallen—'

'When you told us all the story of the dragon and her daughters, you told us of the battle in Relios, when she came and killed all your fellow knights. They had cast you out because of what you were and refused your help, but still you felt sorrow over their deaths. Am I correct?'

Now it was Sebastian's turn to be silent. He remembered walking the smoking battlefield afterwards, looking for survivors and finding only twisted, blackened corpses, all their humanity burnt away. They had hated him, yes, they had exiled him from Ynnsmouth and stripped him of his title. He had also felt their loss keenly, like a wound in his heart.

'I did what I did for love,' he said eventually, his voice little more than a whisper. 'I tried to save them, and I tried to save you.'

Dallen looked at him sharply and opened his mouth, but King Aristees was bellowing at them from the centre of the circle.

'Get over here, warmling scum,' he shouted, cheerfully enough. 'It seems we have come to an agreement.'

'Humans are strange.'

In the immediate aftermath, while the few survivors of Aristees' men patched themselves up and the bodies were respectfully moved out of the camp, Sebastian had taken Ephemeral to one side.

479

'Never a truer word,' he muttered. They stood at the edge of the circle. The sun was a distant white disc in the sky, giving out no warmth at all. 'Ephemeral, you must understand what it is they are asking of you and your sisters.'

'I understand,' she had said, shrugging one shoulder. 'He wishes to mate with one of us, to bring the dragon blood within his own tribe. I have done a lot of reading of human histories, and there are many such instances, particularly within royal families. Often it is used to broker peace, to form alliances.'

'That is correct, I suppose,' said Sebastian. 'It is no simple thing he asks of you, Ephemeral. It's not like trading food for money, or land for titles, it's . . .' He lifted his hands, and dropped them again. 'You and your sisters are still learning so much. I fear we didn't quite get to this stage of your education.'

'We are learning all the time,' said Ephemeral. 'Even when you're not here to teach us, Father, we are always learning. And I think,' she glanced at him, 'there are some things you cannot teach us.'

'I've no doubt about that.' Sebastian shook his head. 'What do your sisters think of all this?'

Ephemeral tipped her head to one side as though listening to an interior voice.

'They are curious,' she said eventually. 'These Narhl people are unusual. Everywhere we have been we have needed to hide ourselves for fear of humans discovering what we are. We are, as you know, easy to spot.' She gestured to her own face, pale green, sharply angled, and beautiful. 'The Narhl are unafraid, even though we have killed so many of them. They do not fear our green skin and sharp teeth.'

'You know that's only half the story,' said Sebastian, as softly as he could. 'We hide from the people of Ynnsmouth and Relios because the stories of what you did – of what you and Y'Ruen did – are still fresh in their minds. Here, those stories are distant.'

'Then that is also in our favour.' Ephemeral looked at him, her yellow eyes wide. 'Some of my sisters wonder if we might find acceptance here.'

Sebastian looked out across the bleak landscape, filled now with rolling fog. He missed Wydrin with a sudden, unbearable keenness.

She would have had many choice words about King Aristees' offer, and would have put them plainly to Ephemeral.

'To be married, though.' Sebastian grimaced. 'And to *him*. I hoped that you would come to forge your own relationships, of course. But to see you traded off in one—'

'Oh, we do not intend to marry,' said Ephemeral. She smiled at Sebastian's surprised expression. 'King Aristees is overly hairy and smells disconcertingly of fish. But it occurs to me that we are in a position of power here, with a great need of assistance, and there may be a way to make sure that everyone is satisfied to a degree. What is the correct term?' She reached up a clawed hand as if to pluck the word from the air. 'Compromise.'

Now Ephemeral rose from her seat on the ground; if hours of sitting in one position had made her uncomfortable, she didn't show it. King Aristees got up with more difficulty, leaning heavily on the staff of his axe.

'We have come to an agreement, Father,' she said. 'Although we cannot accept King Aristees' gracious offer to become his queen.'

'More's the pity,' grunted Aristees.

'We have agreed to an exchange of information and resources. Those sisters of mine who wish to will stay with the Narhl in the Frozen Steps for a time, learning about them and how they live their lives. We will teach them what we know of combat, tracking, and so on, and it is hoped that in time relations between us will grow warmer. In exchange, they will lend us a number of troops in the conflict against Joah Demonsworn.'

'Father,' Dallen shook his head wonderingly, 'all these years of ignoring the outside world, and you lower our walls for these creatures? Monsters who murdered your own men and women?'

Sebastian opened his mouth to speak, but Aristees spoke over him. 'Did you see these lizard-women fight? I would take one of them over ten of you. With their blood on our side, the Narhl will be unbeatable.' He shrugged. 'Their influence will strengthen us – only the cold-blooded could be so brutal. And if they require assistance with beating one crazed mage? Then we shall demonstrate our war skills, Dallen, and they will know where their true home is.'

Sebastian rubbed a hand over his eyes. 'Then you agree to help us take back Skaldshollow?'

King Aristees laughed. 'We have had many years' experience of harrying those walls, warmling. You would not be able to do it. I shall send a wyvern and a messenger back to the Frozen Steps, and have a hundred of my best soldiers at your disposal. You will see how the frozen lands fight then.'

'Good.' This was a new voice, cutting across the icy dark like an axe blow. They all turned to see a slim figure step out of the darkness. It was Frith, dressed in a sleeveless jerkin, the sand of a distant desert still coating the bottoms of his loose trousers, his bare arms bound in silk strips. Over one shoulder he carried a hessian sack, and his face looked as though it were carved from stone. 'Gather your troops at the southernmost wall, King Aristees, and ready them to storm the defences. Sooner rather than later.' Frith came into the circle of light, putting the sack down carefully.

'Who is this, to command me so?' bellowed King Aristees. 'Another warmling who desires to feel the edge of my axe?'

'I command you *all*,' said Frith, glaring round at them. He didn't seem to feel the cold. 'And you will all do as I say immediately.'

'Frith, what's happened?' Sebastian glanced at the sack uneasily. 'Where have you been?'

One of King Aristees' advisors tore the spear from his side and with a cry flung it directly at the young mage's chest. Frith raised one hand and the man and his spear were frozen in place, unmoving.

'I do not have time for this.' He turned to the king and produced a fireball, suspending it in front of him like a small sun. 'You will do as I say or I will burn you and any other Narhl that mean to stand in my way.'

'We've brokered a peace,' said Sebastian, holding up both his hands. 'The Narhl have already agreed to help, Frith. There is no need for threats.'

Frith kept the fireball burning for a few seconds more. In its orange light his eyes looked wild.

482

'That is good. Then I shall expect no more delays. Your troops, Aristees, at the southern gate, along with the brood sisters. You shall be our distraction, while our main force comes from the north. I shall return again shortly.'

The Narhl soldier lurched forward, released from the spell, and dropped the spear awkwardly to the ground. He retrieved it and stepped back, his eyes wide with confusion.

'Frith, what are you talking about? Distractions? What is our main force?' Sebastian shook his head. 'Where are you going?'

'To Nuava,' Frith said shortly. 'I finally located her with the seeing spell, and it seems she has the last weapon we need.'

73

Nuava crawled on her hands and knees over the flat stone
surface, following the seams of Edeian where they flowed through
the rock. Here and there she would pause and make some small
adjustment with her hammer and chisel, listening to the flat
chink echo around the quarry. This was crafting on the highest
level, and she was using every inch of skill she'd been taught
over the years – at long last she was crafting the Edeian as she'd
always dreamed she would. So why did this feel so wrong?

She looked up, glancing across the impossibly wide expanse
that was this werken's chest, and saw her aunt hobbling towards
her over the stone. Tamlyn was pale, her face the colour of dust,
and she walked now with one hand pressed to her midriff at all
times, but she showed no signs of slowing down. Her mouth was
a pinched line, and there was a feverish look in her eyes that
Nuava was swiftly learning to grow wary of.

'How are those connections coming along?'

Nuava sat back on her haunches and rubbed some stone dust
from her fingers.

'Good, Tamlyn. This piece is riddled with Edeian, and it's
relatively easy to make the links we need. I would never have
thought it, with the size of it.' She gestured weakly at the monster
they were resting on. 'Barlow found us the right materials, that's
for certain.' She paused. 'Do you know what happened to Barlow?'

Tamlyn lifted one shoulder slightly and dropped it, grimacing
slightly; even this small movement caused her pain.

'She was here when Joah's creature caught me, and that was the last I saw of her. If she went back to Skaldshollow . . .' Tamlyn touched her fingers to the red-beaded necklace at her throat. 'If she is back there, then I do not know what her fate could be.'

On the long painful journey through the forest, they had circled around the city, Tamlyn leaning heavily on her niece; swearing between her teeth but never slowing down. When they got close enough to see the walls, they had stopped, staring up at the shifting red caul of light that covered their city. Nuava remembered feeling like they were children lost in the forest, clinging to each other as the monsters closed in. She had asked her aunt, in a voice that sounded appallingly young, what she thought the light was. Tamlyn had only shook her head and spat on the ground, and they had moved on.

'Do you think anyone in there is still alive?'

'We won't know until we take a look, will we? And we can't do that until my Destroyer is ready. I'm going to head back up.' She nodded to the far side of the werken's chest, where its blunt head emerged from its sloping shoulders like a giant gravestone. 'It's not long now, Nuava. Not long until we take it into battle and we have vengeance for your brother. For Barlow. For all of them.'

She turned to go and her foot slipped a little on the smooth rock, almost casting her to the floor. She caught herself, but the effort forced a shout of pain from her throat. In an instant Nuava was on her feet and at her aunt's side, but the older woman pushed her away. The last of the colour had drained from her face and for a frightening moment Nuava thought she was going to pass out.

'Aunt, you are badly hurt.' Nuava swallowed a hard lump in her throat; they had had this conversation before. 'If we do not get you help soon, you will not live to steer the Destroyer.'

'I should be dead already.' Tamlyn gasped down a mouthful of air. 'By rights I should be dead in the trees somewhere. But I didn't die there, Nuava, and I will not die before I tear Joah's head from his stinking neck.' The force of her anger seemed to give her some strength back. 'Even if I have to smash this werken to pieces on his monster's hideous hide.'

With that her aunt began to hobble rapidly away. Nuava picked up her chisel once more, watching her go.

Hours later, as the weak light of late afternoon darkened to a solid grey, Nuava half slid, half stumbled down the makeshift wooden ladder they'd rigged to the side of the Destroyer. The whole thing was covered in a complicated latticework of wooden scaffolding, and looking at it made Nuava wonder how long her aunt had been working on this secret project. How many men and women had known about this and kept their mouths shut? It was a demonstration of the respect commanded by the Mistress Crafter; respect that edged into awe. Nuava tugged her fingers through her dirty hair, frowning. The same awe and respect that had allowed her aunt to make several unwise decisions on behalf of the people of Skaldshollow. With a shiver she remembered the slim shape of the Prophet, always hidden behind the gauze of her bed curtains, and then later, the smiling, handsome face of Joah Demonsworn as he tore her brother's heart from his chest.

She half fell from the last step, her fingers numb from carving stone. There was a small fire down by the werken's head, so she walked towards it. They had managed to scavenge some food on their journey here – several handfuls of small hard berries, a few thick root vegetables Nuava had dug up, remembering them from a botany book she had once studied, and one surprised snow grouse, which Nuava suspected had already been injured. Her stomach was growling painfully.

'Tamlyn? Are you there?' The shadows were starting to grow long and the temperature was dropping fast. 'I need a break.'

Her aunt lurched out from behind the curve of the Destroyer's head. There was colour on her cheeks again, and a thin sheen of sweat on her forehead. Nuava's stomach turned over at the sight of it.

'Aunt, you are feverish. Quickly, come over to the fire and rest, I'll find us some more food—'

'That's Mistress Crafter to you!' snapped Tamlyn, stumbling towards her. She was covered from head to foot in a layer of stone dust, and both her hands were red with blisters from the hammer and chisel. 'Have you forgotten who I am? It is time, child, to wake this bastard up. I have the stone, the last piece – the last piece of Heart-Stone.' She sucked in a ragged breath, reeling on her feet. 'Our last chance to avenge Skaldshollow. It is time to wake the last werken.'

Nuava felt her throat go dry. Her aunt was delirious with pain and rage, and in no fit state to take control of any werken, let alone one the size of the Destroyer. And underneath that she found herself thinking of Mendrick, how it – he – had stepped in front of the ice-spear for her, and been shattered into pieces for his efforts.

'Tamlyn,' she took a slow, deep breath, readying herself. 'Mistress Crafter. I think the Narhl were right.'

For a second Tamlyn just stood there looking at her as if she hadn't understood a single word.

'What?'

'About the werkens. Aunt, you must listen to me, please. I know that to us they have always been instruments and tools, but I saw – I've seen enough to know that there is something in the flesh of the mountain that is alive, and we are using it against its will.'

Tamlyn shook her head. 'Nuava, I don't have time for your childish nonsense. I should have known better than to trust you with this.'

'Tamlyn, I have seen a werken move without a command from its rider.' She could hear the desperation in her own voice. 'All I'm saying is, I'm not sure what we're doing, what we've *been* doing, is right.'

'You are a coward,' spat Tamlyn. 'Worry not, frightened child. You do not have to steer the Destroyer. As if I would trust that job to you anyway. Save your whining and your excuses for when we've taken the city back, and then I will have time to consider the depth of my disappointment in you.'

'You're not listening to me!' Nuava held up her hands, feeling a wave of despair wash over her. Maybe she was wrong, and perhaps they would both be dead shortly anyway, but she needed to say it. 'All I'm saying is that we have to consider that they were right all along, and what that means for us—'

There was a sudden flash of light next to their open fire, briefly blinding Nuava. She cried out, her hand groping for the chisel wedged into her belt, and then a stern voice was speaking.

'Is your werken ready?'

It was the other mage, Lord Frith, wearing a loose shirt and a light cloak. Impossibly he looked as though he had caught the sun on the tops of his cheekbones, his warm brown skin a darker shade than when she'd last seen him, contrasting starkly with his bone-white hair. He was glaring at them both with an expression of extreme impatience.

'You!' Tamlyn staggered backwards. 'What are you doing here? Where did you come from?'

The young lord shook his head brusquely. 'I don't have time for these questions. Is your werken ready? When can it be ready?'

'You are a mage,' said Tamlyn slowly. The feverish light was back in her eyes and she was swaying on her feet. 'Like him. I should have killed you rather than let you in our gates.'

Frith scowled. 'It was you who made a deal with the demon, Crafter Nox. Your mistake has cost us a great deal.' He paused, the muscles in his jaw clenching briefly as he held something back. 'Indeed, if I did not need the werken you have been constructing, you would already be dead.' He turned to Nuava. 'Is it ready?'

'What's happened?' She didn't like the bleak look on his face. In the short time she'd known him he had never been a friendly man, but now there was a chilly blankness behind his eyes that frightened her badly. 'I mean, besides the obvious.'

Frith looked at her without speaking for a moment, his features carefully composed.

'What's happened is I have constructed a weapon that could destroy Joah Demonsworn permanently, and I need you and Crafter Nox to take this monstrosity', he gestured to the body of the prone werken that towered off to the right of them, 'down to the city walls, and I need you to use it to crush the Rivener. Can you do this?'

'My aunt was badly injured, I don't know if she's strong enough.'

'Can you do this? For your brother? For Wydrin?'

Nuava caught her breath. 'Yes. Yes, we can do it.'

74

Wydrin ran, trying to move as quickly and as silently as possible, whilst keeping Ip's slim form ahead of her. The girl was leading them through a labyrinth of back alleys, taking sudden turns and skittering down darkened paths that looked like dead ends until they skirted past piles of barrels and boxes. Her gut instinct was telling her that they were foolish to trust the child, but if nothing else they knew for certain that the demon no longer inhabited her; the demon was in a dozen bodies now, and searching for them even as they ran.

'The girl smells like the demon,' said Xinian in a low voice. The warrior mage was keeping pace with Wydrin easily enough. 'It is the same smell you carry, only stronger.'

'Yes, well, thanks for that,' muttered Wydrin. They turned another corner and suddenly they were out in a wide street. Ip immediately pressed herself to the wall, and the two older women followed suit. The cobbles were deserted, and half covered in a fine covering of snow. With no Skalds left to sweep it away or turn it to slush with their boots, it would gradually cover the entire city. Lost, like Temerayne was lost.

'We are nearly there,' said Ip, her voice quiet. 'The trench lies to the north of the city, and it points towards the Bone Pit gate. In the trench, we will be out of sight. They kept werkens down there, where the Narhl couldn't see them.'

'The gate will be shut, I expect,' said Wydrin. 'That's how my luck has gone lately. We'll deal with that when we get there. How

489

do you know so much about this place, anyway? I thought when you were the Prophet you were mainly hidden up in the Tower of Waking.'

Ip glared up at her. Her expression was not that of a centuries-old demon, but she did look like a child who had done a lot of growing up recently.

'When Joah vanished on us – when he vanished on Bezcavar, I mean, I had a lot of time to get to know this place. I know all its nooks and crannies now.'

After a moment, they carried on, shuffling swiftly across the street and back into the alleyways that Ip apparently knew so well. Their ability to move quickly and with accuracy was all that had saved them so far – Bezcavar's presence had given the husks a burst of lethal energy.

Eventually the regular buildings died out, and they moved into an open area that was clearly some sort of staging platform for the werkens. Wydrin could see several great warehouses with wide open doors, and she knew that inside them would be workbenches covered in tools that would by now be gathering dust.

'Here, down here, quickly,' said Ip, already moving towards a raised platform in the middle of the work area. At first it looked like little more than a long stone wall, slightly taller than a tall man, but when Wydrin got closer, she saw that it was the edge of an enormous trench cut directly into the rocky ground. The raised platform was the first of a set of wide steps that led down into it. 'Quickly,' said Ip again, 'before Bezcavar catches up.'

'You don't have to tell me twice.'

They hurried down the steps, dark stone walls rising to either side of them, the sky becoming a long strip of baleful red above their heads. There were a few alchemical lights burning in alcoves set along the walls, and in what little light they provided Wydrin could see the hulking shapes of werkens, standing utterly still in the dark. The green lights that had burnt so fiercely in Mendrick's wolf-shaped head were absent from these stony giants.

'Why are they not glowing?' asked Wydrin. Within the trench her voice echoed strangely, so she lowered it to a whisper. 'The light of the Edeian . . .?'

'Their riders are all dead,' said Ip shortly.

490

The three of them walked slowly, cautious of what might be waiting for them in the dark. Wydrin glanced up at the turbulent sky and realised she had no idea what time of day it was – the eerie red light distorted everything, although her stomach was insisting it was well past any meal time imaginable.

'I have a question,' said Xinian. She was bringing up the rear of their party, her stolen sword hanging loosely in her hand. They passed another inert werken, and Wydrin glanced up at it, trying to make out the features on its roughly chiselled face. It was too dark.

'Go ahead.'

'Up until quite recently this child was inhabited by the demon.'

'Up until it decided to dump her for someone with a better sense of style,' said Wydrin. Ip shot a poisonous look at the pair of them over her shoulder.

'And presumably this demon inhabited the child at the time when she was learning her way around these streets.'

Wydrin winced. 'Yes.'

'Then forgive me, for I am just a centuries-old mage and clearly not as wise as a tavern brawler and a child.' In the dark Xinian's bald head shone with reflected pinkish light. 'But would that not mean that whatever the child knows, the demon would also know?'

At that moment, there was a flat patter of awkward footsteps. Wydrin looked over her shoulder to see around twenty figures shuffling and stumbling down the steps towards them, their emaciated forms bleeding into the shadows.

'You!' Wydrin unsheathed Frostling in an instant and brandished it at Ip's throat. 'I told you if you betrayed us I would cut out your lungs. Didn't I tell you that?'

'I didn't know!' Underneath the dirt Ip's face was very pale. 'I didn't think—'

'Shit.' Wydrin turned back the way they had been heading, only to see similar stumbling shapes moving hurriedly towards them out of the dark. Already they were close enough for her to see the bloody stare of their eyes. To either side of them the walls of the trench rose, smooth and unclimbable.

'Shit.' She pulled Glassheart from its scabbard. 'So now we're

491

going to have to carve our way through, ladies. Head for the northern side and don't stop for nothing.'

'I can see you down there.' The voice came from several ragged throats at once, the note of glee quite clear. 'And is that Ip I see with you? I did wonder where you'd gone, child.'

Ip pitched to one side, grasping her head and grimacing.

'What is it?' Wydrin grabbed her by one stick-thin arm. 'What's it doing?'

'It's trying to get back inside my head. Not forcing, exactly, but I invited it in once and it knows all my secrets.'

'Come on,' Wydrin yanked her forward, already starting to run. 'Keep that bastard out of your head and I'll buy you a pony.'

They charged into the thick of the Rivened, Wydrin going first, her dagger and sword a silvery blur. The husks fell back, wounds opening like flowers on their rotten flesh, but the more she pushed forward the more bodies surged in to fill the gap. They grasped for her, purple fingers yanking at her leathers and scratching at her flesh. She felt one grab hold of a fistful of her hair, twisting it so that her head was suddenly a beacon of pain. She screamed and thrust her sword into the creature's throat with so much force that the blow severed the neck, and the husk's head fell to one side, hanging by a ropey piece of flesh. There was very little blood – most of that had long since turned thick and black – but the smell was atrocious, a thick scent that crawled at the back of Wydrin's throat. Quickly, too quickly, they were surrounded. She felt Xinian at her back, could hear the heavy chop of blade against flesh as she took down every husk foolish enough to get close to her. Ip was crouched down by Wydrin's legs, stabbing wildly with a small knife she'd produced from some hidden pocket.

'Stay next to me,' spat Wydrin, 'and we'll keep moving forward if we can.'

One of the Rivened reached for Ip and grabbed hold of her arms, its mouth twisted into an approximation of a grin. Wydrin brought her sword down, Glassheart's blue glass stone catching the red light and turning it purple, but although she cut clean through the husk's arm, another came out of the press and grabbed Ip by her frantically kicking leg. Suddenly the girl was being dragged rapidly into the press of rotten bodies.

'No!' Wydrin made to go after her only to be pushed roughly back by three or four of the Rivened. She saw Ip turn back to her briefly, the dirty moon of her face slack with terror before disappearing into the swarm of demon-possessed corpses. 'No, wait!'

But she was gone. Wydrin cast about desperately and saw Xinian nearly on her knees, the warrior mage's face creased into an expression of disgust as the grasping limbs carried her down. Above her loomed one of the inert werkens, a huge dark figure roughly in the shape of a giant bear standing on its back legs. Seeing it reminded her of the Blackwood bears they had faced in Frith's forest, and all at once she was furious.

You! She called out inside her own head, as she had once commanded Mendrick. She felt desperately for that connection, for any connection. *Listen to me! I need your help!* One of the husks flung its arms around her waist, leaning all its weight on her, and another was grabbing her hair again, pulling her head back to expose her neck. Wydrin kept her eyes on the werken.

I know you can hear me! One of you, any of you, listen to me!

There was nothing. The dark figure remained dark, and behind her Wydrin could hear Xinian making strangled choking noises.

I know you can hear me! Wake up!

There was a flicker inside her mind, a brief crackle of green light, and suddenly the huge werken opposite them lit up with a lightning strike of emerald energy. Its eyes bled into life, green moons in a savage face.

Wydrin Threefellows. It was Mendrick's voice, cold and serene inside her own head. *You will not let me sleep, it seems.*

'Where the bloody hell have you been?' Wydrin was staggering under the weight of three of the Rivened now. She threw an elbow into the face of the nearest one and felt a small blossom of satisfaction as the delicate bones in its nose shattered. 'I thought you were gone!'

I am everything. I am the mountain. I cannot just leave.

One by one, every werken in the trench began to flicker into life, eldritch-green light painting the slick walls. Inside her head, Wydrin felt the dizzying sense of being in several places at once wash over her.

'Right, then,' she said, 'I think it's time to demonstrate some brute force.'

It was easier than it had ever been, and when the werkens started to move she was no longer sure if it was her controlling them, or Mendrick himself. The giant bear-shaped werken came first, falling down onto its front legs and immediately crushing the bodies beneath it. Some of them fell back, and Wydrin could hear a mutter of surprise move through the crowd.

'Oh yes, here we go, Bezcavar, you bastard.' Wydrin shook off the nearest husks and ran for the side of the werken. There were deep steps carved into its side, and she scrambled halfway up before turning and shouting down to Xinian. 'Get up here, Lady Battleborn!'

Xinian's arm thrust out of the press of corpses, and Wydrin reached down and dragged her up. The warrior mage looked bemused, but she climbed into the seat next to Wydrin, pausing only to kick a husk in the face as it tried to crawl up after them.

'What is this thing?' she said, looking down the trench as five other werkens began to move of their own accord. Werkens shaped like great bulls, cats and wolves, their eyes an unshifting green glow, stomped through the press of the Rivened, crushing them to a bloody pulp.

'This is my friend, the mountain.' Wydrin gestured round at the werkens and the walls, and then shrugged. 'It will take some explaining.'

'You will not escape.' The voices floated up towards them from the crowd, a hundred pairs of blood-filled eyes, a hundred identical smiles. 'I have so many bodies now and you have just that one, all delicate and filled with things that can be broken.'

'Bezcavar, have you ever dropped something heavy on your foot? A brick perhaps?' Wydrin settled in the seat, reaching out for the connection in her head, following that bright web of green light. She could feel the weight of the stone at her disposal, solid and riddled with Edeian. 'Let me show you what that feels like.' The werken leapt forward at her urging, crushing five or six of the flailing Rivened under its wide stone paws. 'Multiplied several hundred times or so.'

A flicker of unease moved across the rotten faces.

'No, wait—'

The mage corrupted the flesh of the mountain. My flesh. It was Mendrick's voice in her head. *I will not let that stand.*

As one, all six werkens turned and charged, thundering up the centre of the trench. All around them the possessed husks were trampled or thrown back until the werkens were lined up behind them, waiting further instruction. Wydrin grinned, and saw Xinian give her an uncertain look.

'I think we just found our way out of the gate.'

75

'And you have made the adjustments I requested?'

Nuava nodded. To Frith's eyes, she looked a good decade older than when they'd first met; the skin around her eyes was bruised and her dark curly hair was tied back half-heartedly with a piece of twine.

'Tamlyn and I have the saddle, in the alcove in the front of its head. If Joah sees anyone when the Destroyer comes, it will be us.'

She paused, and for a moment they both stood and simply looked at it. The Destroyer drew the eye, that much was for certain.

It crouched now, kneeling in the quarry with its head bowed, like a penitent man at prayer. It was humanoid in shape, certainly the most human werken Frith had seen, with broad craggy shoulders and a head that still had moss on it – if they'd had more time, Nuava had explained, they would have carved all the excess away, but, as it was, the werken would have to remain unfinished, its surfaces pitted and jagged with raw rock. It looked to Frith as though a part of the mountain had torn itself free and was now sitting patiently in the forest. While it was kneeling, the top of its head came above the treeline. Beyond it, the sky was a pale, blameless blue that was almost white.

'I don't understand, though,' said Nuava. She was absently wiping her blistered hands on a cloth, still staring at the Destroyer. 'Why don't you use your magic to get to Joah, like you did before?'

Frith shook his head.

'I cannot use the Edenier too close to him now. He will simply sense it, as O'rin did, and any chance of using my weapon in time will be lost. I must catch a ride on this beast, and get as close as I can first.'

'Is it time yet?' Tamlyn Nox appeared from around the Destroyer's jutting knee. She was limping heavily, but her eyes were bright. They had already split the last remaining piece of Heart-Stone between her and the Destroyer; she carried it sunk into the palm of her left hand. Nuava had dug out the stone that was already there with the point of her knife, belonging as it now did to a long-since destroyed werken – and the giant beast had its piece secured between the round holes that were its eyes. The Edeian glowed there now, a soft green light under the bright sky.

'Aunt, you should be resting. We agreed that you would get some sleep before we went back to Skaldshollow.'

Tamlyn Nox scowled at her niece. 'Sleep? What is the point of sleep? I shall be dead soon anyway.' She turned her attention back to Frith. 'What say you, Lord Frith?' She couldn't quite keep the scorn from her voice. 'Is it time for my Destroyer to kill that faithless demon-worshipper or not?'

Frith looked up at the sky, seeking out the sun. It was a tiny pale disc, frail and impossibly distant. He thought of Sebastian and Prince Dallen, and the small disparate force that would now be massing at the southern gate. He did not know what they would meet on the walls of Skaldshollow, but he suspected many of the Narhl soldiers and the brood sisters themselves would not live to see the rising of another bloodless sun.

'Let us go,' he said, nodding to the Nox women. 'Get it ready.'

Tamlyn Nox grinned, although there was no humour in it.

'Good. I will show the world what a real crafter is capable of.'

She turned and hobbled away, heading for the frail wooden ladder that snaked its way up the side of the werken's body. Frith would never have believed her capable of climbing it, if he hadn't seen her do it several times already. Nuava lingered a moment longer.

'You have changed,' she said eventually. 'Since you've come

497

back, you have been different somehow. I don't think I ever liked you, but now . . .' She frowned at him. 'Now I feel that we should fear you.'

Frith looked at her for a moment. 'Perhaps you should. Go and get the werken ready. I don't know how long Sebastian's forces will last out there alone.'

She glared at him, opened her mouth as if to say something further, and then turned away. Running to the rickety ladder she began to climb, hand over hand, with no apparent fear of the drop below her.

Frith watched her all the way to the top, and then circled around to watch the Destroyer from the front, marvelling at the craggy expanse of its chest, still hung here and there with moss and vines. The intricate carvings that were the Edeian crafter's mark were all over it, clustered particularly at its joints, at the places where stone met stone. In the early morning light it made the werken look like a heavily tattooed man, kneeling after a night of too much to drink.

Tamlyn and Nuava seated themselves in the alcove where the werken's head met its shoulders and tied themselves in with leather straps; a tumble from the Destroyer would be particularly disastrous. There was a moment of silence – Frith could see Tamlyn and Nuava conferring with each other about something, although he couldn't hear the words – and then the Destroyer lumbered into life, green eyes flaring like marsh mist.

Frith stumbled backwards, not quite able to keep a small cry of alarm from escaping his lips. The werken stood slowly, rising from its knees in one movement. Trickles and plumes of stone dust erupted around its lower half as those joints were called into action, and Frith heard the distinct rumble of stone against stone. All around them, the trees exploded with birds suddenly frantic to get away from this unexpected giant. The sky turned briefly black with hurried wings, and when it cleared, the werken was standing, its head bathed in brilliant cold sunshine, its lower half shrouded in the dappled shadow of the forest.

'By all the gods,' murmured Frith.

After a moment, the Destroyer leaned forward and extended one great arm down towards Frith. Its hands weren't really hands at all – again, Nuava said, they did not have time – but rather huge slabs of shovel-shaped granite. With some trepidation, Frith picked up the sack that lay at his feet and climbed up onto the offered hand, and then crouched uncertainly as the werken brought him up and round, next to the wooden platform built around the Destroyer's waist, some fifty feet off the ground. Frith stepped off hurriedly, before making his way around to the creature's back, where there were more leather straps waiting for him. Here he would not be in plain sight. The sack containing the Edenier trap he secured just below his feet, taking care to check the straps twice. If the device rolled away from him and over the side, then all would be lost.

'Are you ready?' Nuava's voice floated down from somewhere above him. She sounded both excited and frightened.

'I am,' Frith called back. 'Let us take our vengeance to the Rivener.'

There was a deeper rumble of stone against stone, and the forest around Frith lurched from one side, and then to the other. He dug his fingers into the straps and braced his feet against the platform as the Destroyer took its first steps.

The great southern wall of Skaldshollow lay before them, shattered into pieces. Sebastian could see long gouge marks in the stone that was still intact: the mark of the Rivener as it had invaded the city. There were inert werkens dotted around everywhere – some in pieces, some simply half covered in snow, their riders long since dead – and they had found many frozen bodies on their approach to the wall. Even the Narhl soldiers, who had been making many contemptuous comments about the Skalds since their arrival, said nothing at the sight of those bodies. Many had been crushed, their blood a bright pink stain on the snow, while many others looked like they had been burnt to death by Joah's attacks. These last the Narhl did their best to ignore completely, given their near superstitious dread of fire.

'Are your people ready?'

Dallen looked up at the sound of his voice. They stood beyond a row of broken rocks that looked like they had been torn from the wall itself; the Narhl soldiers standing together in a loose mass, talking and joking with each other, and the brood sisters, unconsciously standing in neat rows, their swords held by their sides.

'They are not my people any longer, Sebastian, but yes, this is what they look like when they are about to go into battle.' Many of the soldiers were passing around horns of strong drink – Sebastian could smell it on the still air. At the back of their company were five wyverns with riders, padding carefully across the snow. On the ground they moved tentatively, like a cat walking across wet ground. 'They will fight ferociously, I can promise you that. How they will fight alongside their new allies, I could not tell you.'

'Hmm.' Sebastian tugged at his beard. 'I think they share a certain love of the fight. As long as they don't start fighting each other, we should be fine.'

'Do you have any idea what we will find in there?'

Sebastian looked back to the broken wall. He could see no movement, no sign of any guards left. The eerie red light still hung over the city, poisoning the sky like an infected wound.

'None whatsoever, but if there is anything waiting for us, it won't be in the spirit of welcome.'

Sebastian raised his voice, addressing the men and women behind him.

'Once we're over the wall, head as best you can towards the Tower of Waking. There may be forces opposing you, but I know you can all handle a good fight.'

There were a few cheers at this from the Narhl contingent.

'By then Lord Frith should have brought us some support, and we will know which way this day is heading.' He took a deep breath, looking round at them all. Ephemeral stood at the front of the rows of the brood sisters, her face solemn, while King Aristees leaned on the staff of his axe, looking unconcerned. 'There may yet be survivors in there. If you find some, try to direct them beyond the city walls and into the forest.' Sebastian paused, thinking of how the last citizens of Skaldshollow might react when faced with a rampaging group of Narhl, or the brood sisters

500

with their sharp teeth and snake's eyes. 'If we can save anyone, then we must at least try.'

King Aristees bellowed laughter at this. 'I will direct the mewling Skalds to the blade of my axe,' he shouted, lifting the weapon and brandishing it at his own soldiers, who roared their approval back. 'This is the only mercy they need!'

'King Aristees, we have an agreement.' Sebastian's voice cut across the merriment. 'If you would like to break the terms of that, this morning's battle can go a very different way indeed.'

Sebastian felt his own irritation reflected in the brood sisters, and enough of them turned to face the Narhl soldiers for King Aristees to put down his axe. Behind them, one of the wyverns opened its jaws and roared in the back of its throat.

'Aye, there's no need to get twitchy. We are here with you, aren't we? My soldiers and yours shall fight side by side.'

Sebastian nodded, then glanced up at the sky. The sun was at its edge, pale and ghostlike.

'Then it's time. We go fast and we go quiet, at least at first. Follow me.'

Sebastian ran, keeping low, his sword held ready in both hands. Prince Dallen came next, his ice-spear held at one side. Behind them he heard the sound of a hundred boots running across the snow and rocky ground. Once they were at the broken wall, they began to climb – the Narhl were untroubled by the icy surfaces, while the brood sisters moved slightly slower. Sebastian pulled himself up rock after rock, watching Prince Dallen overtake him easily. When he reached the top of the broken wall, he stood warily, waiting for attack. The gatehouse was ruined, the roof pitched in with a giant boulder, and the street beyond was deserted. In the distance the Tower of Waking rose from the centre of the city like a twisted black stalagmite, and the Rivener was crouched next to it, a cancer on the rock. The shifting red caul of the sky was at its darkest there, as though that were the source of the infection.

'Where is everyone?' said Dallen, appearing at his elbow. His voice was low. Beyond him, Narhl and brood sister alike were climbing down the shattered wall into the city.

Sebastian shook his head. He couldn't tell if it were simply an

501

effect of the sour light, but he felt deeply uneasy now that they were within the walls.

'I don't know, but I doubt this is the whole story. Come on, let's get down there. And remember what I said about survivors.'

76

'How much further?'

Wydrin reached down and placed her boot in the face of one husk who had managed to climb further than the others. She kicked it off and turned back to Xinian.

'You see the wall that rises above those buildings? That's our way out.'

The werkens had eased their journey significantly, but it was still slow going. The Rivened crowded around them as they moved down the streets, and Wydrin and Xinian had the near constant job of repelling those who tried to climb up to them – one or two had even jumped from the roofs of nearby buildings in their desperation to reach the still-living. Bezcavar taunted them from below, speaking through the throats of the dead, but Wydrin thought its voice was growing weaker. Losing his grip on the Rivened, or perhaps it had simply spread himself too thin.

They reached the end of one street, the small convoy of werkens following on behind, and the vast northern gate was abruptly in sight. Wydrin nodded towards it.

'It might take us some time to get through that, but I reckon we can do it. We're nearly there.'

At that moment, the swarming crowds of demon-possessed husks all stopped moving. Instead of pressing themselves towards the werkens they simply stood still, ragged arms lying loose at their sides. And then as one they all turned and ran away, heading south. Wydrin watched with bemusement as the creatures that had harried them since she had woken in the shadowed city streamed past, not even looking up. In a few moments they were all gone, and they were left alone in a deserted street.

'What do you suppose that was all about?'

Xinian shook her head. 'Nothing in this place makes sense.'

'At least we will be out of it soon.' Wydrin gave Xinian a sideways look. She reached out to Mendrick and the werkens began lumbering forward again. 'What will happen to you? When we pass out of the city?'

Xinian pursed her lips. 'I do not know. Perhaps I will keep this solid form, but I doubt it. I am only here because Skaldshollow exists under the shadow of death. When I move beyond it, I may become a ghost again, a spirit in the winds. Or perhaps I shall vanish altogether, and have peace.'

'Do you want to go?'

'If I move on to the next life, there is a chance I will find Selsye again, in one form or another. I do not think she will have forgotten me. Not yet.'

Wydrin nodded. 'Well, I would be sad to see you go, Xinian the Battleborn. I think I could learn a lot from you.' She grinned at the other woman. 'You are a terror with that blade.'

Xinian smiled. It lit up her entire face, and Wydrin thought that, once, she had probably smiled often, before she had lost her Selsye.

'You could learn a lot from me, child, because you are a fool.' She leaned in close. 'You are willing to die for love, but not to live for it. What are you afraid of?'

Wydrin felt her cheeks grow warm, and hated herself for it. 'Oh, you know. The usual. Love is complicated. Love cuts you open and leaves you exposed. Choosing to be vulnerable goes against my nature.'

'So better to be reckless? Better to throw away the chance?' Xinian reached over and squeezed her arm. 'If you learn nothing else from this ancient ghost, learn that love makes you *strong*, not weak. It is your glory and your armour.'

'If you're going to get all sentimental on me, Xinian, I shall have to boot you into the next life myself.'

But she put her hand on top of Xinian's and clasped it briefly. Above them the storm light raged on.

Sebastian walked slowly, his sword held at the ready. All around him their small force was spread out, moving quietly through the streets. So far they had found numerous bodies, most half hidden under snow, but no living people, and no obvious threat. He glanced behind him to see the wyverns coming along behind – the creatures were reluctant to fly up into that dark red sky, so they were keeping them on the ground as reinforcements. But reinforcements against what?

Ephemeral appeared at his elbow.

'Report.'

'Nothing so far, Father. There are lots of dead humans here, and a scent of something we do not know – a scent of something evil. We also found a place where the street appears to have been –' she paused, searching for the right word – 'gouged open. It has been done recently, and it stretches far across one street and then over several buildings into another.'

'The Rivener?'

'Undoubtedly. Nothing else could have done it. It is both arbitrary and precise, Father. Joah Demonsworn did not care that he destroyed buildings when he carved those lines, but he did care where the lines were.'

Sebastian frowned. Something about that tickled at the back of his mind, and his sense of unease increased, but he could not think what it could be.

'Anything else?'

'No, Father, although—'

There was a murmur from the troops ahead of them, and Sebastian raised his hand for quiet. After a moment, he could hear it too; the flat patter of many feet striking cobbles. He looked around, but could see nothing yet.

'What is that?' asked Dallen next to him. 'Are those the Skald survivors?'

'I really hope so,' said Sebastian, but he lifted his new sword, borrowed from the brood sisters.

They came out of the side street just ahead of them; around a hundred stumbling, shambling men and women, their skins riddled with corruption and lined here and there with a strange, bluish light. When they turned their faces towards Sebastian and his soldiers, they all smiled an identical smile. Their eyes were filled with blood, and Sebastian felt his heart grow cold in his chest.

'Oh there you are, Sir Sebastian. I thought I could feel you in this place, and I just had to come and see.'

The voice, that old, terrible voice, issued through a hundred different throats in an eerie, whispered shout. As Sebastian watched, more and more of the strange walking corpses poured into the street ahead of them.

'Leave these people, Bezcavar,' he said. His voice felt strangled by his own rage. 'I will not have you defile them.'

'But they are already dead, Sir Sebastian! Are you really so sentimental over a bunch of walking corpses?' As one, the bodies at the front of the crowd grinned, revealing blackened gums. 'But of course you are. You fretted over your ridiculous knights, after all, and they were nothing but walking corpses too.'

Sebastian hefted his sword. 'You must be truly desperate, demon, to seek refuge inside that which is already decomposing.' He nodded to Dallen and Ephemeral. 'Be ready.'

'Oh, but Sir Sebastian.' There was glee in Bezcavar's voice. 'Don't you want to know what it was like to be inside your friend's body? The Copper Cat of Crosshaven, notorious sell-sword and spawn of pirates, was full of concern for you when she died. How does that make you feel?'

'Your taunts mean nothing to me, demon.'

'I left her body to rot on the streets somewhere here. Do you think you will find it, Sir Sebastian, amongst the rest of the dead?'

'This is the end for you,' said Sebastian. 'And you are afraid. I know that much.'

'I have a few tricks left up my sleeve just yet.'

A figure at the front of the crowd, a stout woman with greasy curly hair hanging in her face, lowered her head, body rigid with tension. Her blood-filled eyes creased at the edges and she began to weep bloody tears. When Bezcavar spoke again it came from her throat alone.

'I am the Prince of Wounds, the master of suffering. I give these people my final gift. May they exalt in the twisting of their flesh!'

The men and women in the first row began to writhe and twitch, bodies twisting unnaturally as though they were dolls tormented by some invisible hand. Death-bruised flesh burst apart and long shards of bone pushed forth, from wrists, from elbows, from shoulders. One man staggered as the skin across the tops of his legs split open to reveal twin knives of yellowed bone. The woman next to him threw her head back as twisted bone horns erupted from the fleshless expanse of her chest.

'I gift them with this pain, Sebastian,' said Bezcavar, still speaking through the woman at the front. Behind her, the terrible transformation was sweeping back through the ranks of the dead like a fever. 'A farewell present. And they are so hungry.' She grinned, her face covered in blood, and the rest swept past her, screaming wordlessly.

Sebastian had time to fall back into a defensive stance and then they were on them. They had no swords, but the long bone shards protruding from their bodies were razor sharp, and they fell on the Narhl and the brood sisters with the mindless abandon of the starving. Sebastian chopped down several in front of him with his broadsword, moving in an awkward circle, but they were pressed in around him and his sword was too big for such close combat. A Narhl soldier next to him fell to the cobbles, dark blood bubbling at his throat. The husk that had killed him knelt over him, mouth hanging open. A brood sister – Umbellifer, he thought, as he struggled to reach her – stumbled past him, clinging to a decomposing woman who had sunk the bone shard protruding from her wrist deep into her stomach. Umbellifer's teeth were bared, her yellow eyes furious, but she was lost in the press of bodies.

Sebastian threw a gauntleted fist at the nearest demon-possessed corpse, feeling grim satisfaction as it fell to the ground in a heap. All around him was chaos, and running underneath it like a silver thread, the joy of the fight. The brood sisters were a comforting presence, their swords, their fury, their deaths. They would not die alone. Sebastian gripped his broadsword in both hands, and grinned without humour.

This time, there was no enchanted armour; there was only him, and the roar of dragon blood in his veins.

Nuava leaned forward, testing the limits of the leather harness. Beneath them the forest canopy rustled swiftly past like a choppy sea, and here and there birds flew, startled at this sudden intruder. The Destroyer stomped through the trees, pausing here and there to tear one up by its roots to clear a path. Next to her, Tamlyn Nox was leaning heavily in her own harness, a sheen of sweat on her dirty forehead. She was breathing in ragged gasps, but her eyes were fever bright.

'I can't believe this actually works,' said Nuava, more to herself than to her aunt. 'That this thing can move at all.'

'It is the Edeian,' croaked Tamlyn. 'The Edeian . . . so strong. It's almost as though the mountain itself . . . is listening.'

Nuava looked at her aunt. The older woman was avoiding her gaze, keeping her eyes on the path ahead.

'Do you mean—'

'I need you to watch for obstacles, child. Shut up and make yourself useful.'

Nuava turned back, needing no excuse to do so. As terrified as she was, as exhausted as she was, this was exhilarating; to be this high above the forest, and to know that her own work had helped put them there. *I am a crafter*, she told herself fiercely. *If I die today, at least I will know that.*

The unbroken expanse of green ahead of them began to thin out, and there was the outer wall of Skaldshollow, a thin grey line with the northernmost gate sitting in the middle. Beyond that she could just make out the spindly top of the Tower of Waking, clouded as it was with the strange red storm that haunted the city. And there would be Joah Demonsworn, skulking within his Rivener. For better or worse, they were taking the fight to him.

'Straight on,' she told her aunt, 'straight on and through the northern gate.'

'There it is, the northern gate,' said Wydrin, urging the werken on. 'Once we're through that, we'll be safe.'

They had seen no more husks since they had all run off, and

now the gate was in front of them. Xinian leaned forward, peering up at the great wooden doors. They were made of dark witch-wood, and reinforced with huge iron studs.

'They look to be locked up tight,' she said, indicating the thick wooden struts, each the length of a tall tree, slotted across the doors. 'How do you propose we get through?'

'There hasn't been a door invented that can keep me out, I'm sure I'll think of something.' Wydrin paused. Sounds were distorted under the red caul as much as the daylight was, and it was difficult to tell, but she thought she could feel a slight vibration working its way up the werken's body. It was rhythmic, almost like foot-steps. 'Hey, can you feel that?'

The enormous wooden doors in front of them exploded. Wydrin was briefly aware of a smattering of wooden splinters pattering with dangerous force against her leathers, and then she was more concerned with the fact that she appeared to be flying through the air. All at once it was impossible to tell what was up and what was down, and she had no sense at all of where Xinian was. She crashed heavily into something that broke into pieces under her, and she rolled over and over, finally coming to rest in something cold and wet, which she quickly realised was a snowdrift. Her head was full of thunder.

'Ye gods and little fishes.'

For a few moments her vision went dark around the edges, but she forced herself up into a sitting position just in time to see an enormous stone monster go stomping past. She saw its leg, as wide as four tree trunks lashed together, swinging past her like a battering ram, its huge slab-like hands at the end of arms riddled with veins of Edeian. Wydrin shook her head and blinked in disbelief. All around her were bits and pieces of shattered gate, and then stumbling across the street towards her was Xinian, looking equally shocked.

'See?' she called across to the mage. 'I told you I'd find a way through the gate, didn't I?'

The older woman opened her mouth, possibly to form several curse words, but Wydrin was already on her feet. She had caught sight of something on the back of the enormous werken that had looked strangely familiar.

'Oh you stupid princeling, what are you *doing*?'

'What was that?' Xinian ran over to her.

'I don't rightly know, but I think I have business with it.'

'What? But the gate—'

'Sod the gate.' Wydrin looked around desperately – the giant werken was already halfway down the street, making steady progress with its enormous strides. 'Quick. Did any of our werkens survive that?'

She was already reaching out with her mind, and Mendrick answered in the form of the one werken still standing – a lithe cat-shaped creature, its head a narrow triangle. It lumbered towards her, trampling over the wreckage of the gate.

'Wydrin, what are you doing? You have a chance to get out of the gate.' Xinian glanced towards the retreating giant's back. 'It's him, isn't it? The shadow-mage.'

Wydrin grinned at her, already scrambling up the side of the cat-shaped werken. 'Oh don't worry, I have no intention of getting killed for him this time, Xi. I intend to save both our arses. That's what I'm good at.' She settled into the riding seat, and waved at the mage. 'Come on, are you going to help me get up there or not?'

Xinian shook her head abruptly, and then climbed up after Wydrin. When she sat down the werken lurched off in pursuit of its much bigger cousin.

'How exactly do you plan to get up there?' said Xinian. 'He was quite some way up.'

'Hold on.' Wydrin urged the werken on and they sprang off down the street, skittering across cobbles and snow. The giant werken grew so that it filled their entire field of vision. Each footstep seemed to shake the city to its foundations. 'I saw a rope,' she said as they approached. 'Hanging from a ladder. I think it's nailed into the werken's side.'

They came alongside the giant, the werken running flat out. Carefully, Wydrin stood up, half crouching to keep her balance. Above them, a tattered end of rope swung back and forth, a good six feet above their heads. From there it would be a short climb to the wooden ladder, and then a longer climb to the platform where Frith was. That was, if she could get to the rope.

510

'You'll never make that,' cried Xinian, shouting against the noise of the werken's progress. 'It's too far to jump!'

'That's why you're going to help me.' The werken was running at a steady pace now, keeping as close to the giant as it could get. Wydrin reached out to Mendrick and found his cold presence reassuring, but if the giant veered off its current course within the next few moments, they could be in a lot of trouble. 'Here, give me a boost.'

Frowning, Xinian also stood on the back of the werken, her legs planted as far apart as she could for extra balance, and crossed her arms in front of her. Wydrin nodded to her, and winked.

'And assuming you aren't immediately smeared into paste, what should I do?'

'Find Sebastian if you can,' said Wydrin. 'If he's alive, he will need help. Tell him . . . oh, I don't know. Tell him something.'

Keeping one eye on the precariously dangling rope, she thrust her boot into Xinian's waiting hand and then she was up and in the air, her arms outstretched. There was a terrifying sensation of yawning space beneath her, and then her fingers caught hold of rough rope. She grasped it to her, already turning too much, her heart hammering in her chest. There was a split second of nothing, her ears ringing, and then she collided with the solid stone leg of the werken, smacking the air out of her in one blow. Gasping, Wydrin's grip slipped slightly and she fell, only to grab the rope again just in time. A bright burning sensation on the palms of her hands told her how close she had come to crashing back down to the cobbled streets.

The rope was spinning now, sending her bouncing off the stone again and again, and very quickly her head was swimming. Scrambling for purchase, she got her feet flat on the stone and pushed, sliding to one side as the werken took another ponderous step.

'Keep going!'

She risked a glance down to see Xinian waving at her, she and the cat-shaped werken already disappearing from sight as they lost speed. Ignoring the burning pain in her hands, she began to climb the rope, hand over hand. It was hard, especially with the constant back-and-forth movement of the werken's giant leg, but

Wydrin had spent much of her childhood on pirate ships, and climbing the rigging was second nature. Quickly, she was onto the rickety wooden ladder, and this she shot up, eager to reach the relative solidity of the platform, which was now a darker shadow above her head.

This close to the werken's stony flesh she could see each crafter's mark, a darker grey against the stone, linking everything together. It made her think of the web of light that had caught her when Joah had struck her with the lightning. She was sure that Nuava would be interested to hear that, if she ever saw the girl again.

In minutes the platform was in reach, but before she could drag herself over it the ladder lurched sickeningly to one side; the iron studs attaching it to the side of the werken had shaken themselves loose. The whole thing swung outwards, threatening to cast her back down to the stones. Wydrin clung on, still not quite able to reach the lip of the platform. She filled her lungs.

'Frith, you idiot, help me up!'

For a few moments, there was silence. Wydrin looked down; the lower half of the ladder had already broken away, and the rope was nowhere to be seen.

'Perhaps this wasn't such a great idea. Frith, if you don't get over here . . . !'

An arm reached down over the platform and grabbed her hand. Awkwardly, Frith yanked her up, with Wydrin pushing herself off the remains of the ladder. They fell together onto the platform, the whole thing reeling sickeningly like a ship at sea.

'I had to undo the straps,' said Frith, and then he shook his head. 'I thought you were dead!'

'Well, that's still up for debate.'

At the sight of his dear, confused face – filled with health now, his grey eyes bright – her chest felt oddly tight. She was lying half on top of him, the momentum of the werken holding her there for the time being, so she leaned down and kissed him firmly on the mouth, letting herself close her eyes for just a moment. He responded immediately, one hand buried in her hair, the other circled around her waist to pull her closer.

If nothing else, this, she thought, trying to sear every moment of the kiss into her memory.

The platform beneath them shuddered, throwing them both out of the embrace and nearly over the guardrail. They both scrambled to their feet, clinging to each other to keep from going over the side.

'Ye gods, who's driving this thing?'

'I thought you were dead,' said Frith again. He didn't seem to be able to take his eyes from her. 'Wydrin, I have done things, terrible things—'

'Let's worry about it later. When we're not travelling through a city of dead people on the belt of a giant stone monster.'

'You don't understand. I have done things I can't take back. To wreck vengeance on Joah, to stop him—'

She put a hand on his arm, and squeezed it. His eyes were full of confusion.

'Frith, do you have a way to kill the bastard?'

He nodded once. 'I can destroy his magic. I just need to get close enough. Wydrin, I need to tell you—'

'There's a lot we need to talk about, but for now, I need you to focus.'

As if listening to her words, the werken took one final step and shuddered to a halt. Wydrin and Frith looked at each other, and then ran around to the front of the platform, just beneath the werken's broad and craggy chest. The air filled with the sound of agonising screeching as two hundred tons of ruined metal and stone began to move.

They had reached the Tower of Waking, and the Rivener was uncurling from its resting place, violet eyes flashing.

77

Nuava saw the Rivener move, turning its baleful eyes on them, and she felt her breath stick in her throat. She felt hopelessly exposed. It was looking right at them.

Next to her, Tamlyn choked out a cry of triumph. She was leaning forward in her straps, her face twisted into a fierce grin.

'I will tear you apart,' she spat, and the Destroyer's enormous right arm drew back, its great shovel-shaped fist level with its shoulder, and then it flew forward.

Nuava had perhaps half a second to brace herself before the blow landed, crashing into the Rivener's rounded shoulder. The metal and stone monster was actually pushed backwards for a moment, so that it sprawled against the Tower of Waking, its strange claws grasping at the sky.

'That's right!' bellowed Tamlyn. 'How do you like that, you ugly demon-tainted bastard?'

The Destroyer's left arm drew back, but this time when the fist flew, the Rivener reacted; one of its serrated claws shot up and batted the blow away. Its twisted, insectile head swivelled in their direction – Nuava caught sight of the ragged hole in the top – and then it pushed itself away from the Tower towards them. Tamlyn was already bringing the right arm back for another shot, but the Rivener scrabbled up close, getting in under their guard. All at once the violet windows that were its eyes were terribly close – for a brief moment Nuava thought she could see a figure standing beyond the glass, staring out at them, but whatever it was, it couldn't be human.

'Push it away!' she screamed at her aunt. 'We need space!'

The Destroyer took a step back, both stone arms crossing over its chest and then pushing out. The noise as the stone squealed across the metal was deafening, and Nuava found she was pressing her hands to her ears without even being aware she was doing it. Gradually, the Rivener was edged away, and her aunt even snuck in another blow, bringing the right fist up and across the Rivener's head. There was a brittle ringing noise, and glass was falling in bright shards from the creature's eye. Next to her, Tamlyn hooted with triumph.

'We may actually do this,' gasped Nuava. 'We may actually bloody do it.'

Amazingly, they were losing the fight.

The knowledge settled over Sebastian's heart like a shroud of cold silk. It was a simple case of numbers; his brood sisters and King Aristees' Narhl soldiers, against what appeared to be an entire city of resurrected dead, each of them armed with the jagged bone-knives that Bezcavar had gifted them with – weapons that could not be knocked out of hands, weapons that did not move as swords did, weapons none of them had faced before.

Normal wounds would not take them down. Sebastian had torn the guts out of a tall man, scattering his intestines to the cobbles, only for the man to lunge for him with a handful of scythe-shaped bones sprouting from his wrists. Sebastian had instinctively fallen back, saving himself from being blinded, although the very last shard had torn open his cheek under his right eye.

The others weren't faring any better. The brood sisters were as fearsome as ever, but they were pressed in on all sides, constricted by the streets and alleys of the city. The Narhl were struggling, faced with an enemy that only stopped if you could sever its head from its body.

At that moment, the ground beneath them shook violently, rocks and debris scattering in all directions. Sebastian looked up to see an enormous werken, impossibly huge, trading blows with the Rivener itself.

'By Isu,' he muttered, 'the mountain itself has come to our aid!'

Dragging his eyes from the sight, Sebastian brought his sword around in a deadly arc, disembowelling two husks at once, before pushing them to the ground with his boot and making short work of chopping their heads off.

'We must do something,' came Ephemeral's voice. She was next to him now, her face smeared with blood and decomposing gore. Her silver hair was stained red.

He could feel them now, each of the brood sisters, their connection heightened in the fury of the fight. A silver thread that joined them all, and beyond it, another presence . . . confused, alien, but familiar. The wyverns. They were still at the back of the main force.

Taking a deep breath, Sebastian reached out for the animals, as he had once reached out to the snakes. The strange reptilian shape of their minds caused him to recoil at first, but he pushed that feeling aside and commanded them.

Fight for me, he told them. *Hunt for me. Tear these dead ones apart.*

He felt their minds turn towards his – they were frightened, confused by the light and the smell of death.

Kill for me, brothers, sisters. He put every sliver of strength he had left into that connection. *Join the hunt.*

There was a hissing roar from down the street and the wyverns leapt forward, long tails pushing them up into the red sky and then down, landing in the midst of Bezcavar's corpses, thrashing wildly. Long white teeth flashed under the scarlet light, snipping limb from limb, brushing aside Bezcavar's horde with their powerful tails. They screamed in triumph, and the brood sisters screamed back.

They cannot stand against the dragon! No one can.

It was Ephemeral's voice in his head, clear and joyous. Sebastian bared his teeth, letting the pleasure of the hunt fill his chest. For a time, he forgot everything – his sorrow over Wydrin, his love for Dallen, the desperate horrors that filled the city – lost in a tide of death.

When he came back to himself, it was almost over. The streets were thick with dead – Bezcavar's puppets, the Narhl, and more brood sisters than he cared to see – but the demon had lost. The sisters were chasing the final corpses down, tearing their heads from their bodies with a ferocity that no longer seemed out of place.

The wyverns curled at the heart of it all, calmly tearing the flesh from the corpses that no longer moved.

'It is done.'

Sebastian stopped. Abruptly his sword felt too heavy, and his body somehow unfamiliar. He looked up to see Ephemeral and Crocus approaching with one of the possessed held between them.

'This is the last,' said Crocus. She gave the body a little shake. 'The last refuge of the demon Bezcavar.'

'Is that right?' Sebastian reached down and grabbed the corpse by the rags still twisted round its chest. Once it had been a portly man with a beard, although the walking death had made its face gaunt and strange. Its eyes rolled redly in their sockets. 'No more bodies left for you, Bezcavar?'

When the demon didn't answer immediately, Sebastian gave the body a brisk shake.

'There's always somewhere, for a creature like me,' said Bezcavar, pushing the words through dead lips with some difficulty. 'You have no idea, good Sir Sebastian. No idea who I really am.'

'There are no shrines to you here, demon. And no one left to carry your poison.'

He let go of the rags and hefted his sword in both hands, resting its point on the corpse's neck.

'You will not do it,' said Bezcavar, the voice making an attempt at sly now, although Sebastian could hear the tremble of fear beneath it. 'You are too merciful. You are the good one, the honourable one. You would not—'

Sebastian plunged the sword down through the middle of the man's neck. There was no blood, only a sudden waft of rotten stench. Held between Ephemeral and Crocus, the body hung there for a moment, skewered by the blade. Sebastian watched the blood drain out of the accusing eyes until there was nothing there but the glazed, dust-covered eyeballs of a man long dead. With a grunt he pulled the sword free again, grimacing at the muck that now covered the blade.

'And you have no idea who *I* really am, demon.'

Ephemeral and Crocus dropped the body, and Sebastian leaned down, wiping his sword clean on the corpse's filthy rags. It would have to do for now.

'I have never seen them behave like that.' Dallen came over, stepping around the corpses. He was looking at the wyverns. Sebastian took a slow breath. In all the fighting, he had forgotten to be concerned for the prince, but he was here. Still alive. 'What did you do to them?' He turned to Sebastian, half accusing. 'Is it the influence of your dragon women?'

There was a thunderous crash from across the city, and every head turned back to the giant battle taking place by the Tower of Waking. As Sebastian watched, the Rivener slashed its claws across the werken's head, and they all saw the huge chunks of stone that went flying into the air. The giant werken staggered backwards, bringing up enormous spade-shaped fists to ward the other creature off. It was in trouble.

'We need to help them,' said Sebastian, already moving. 'Quickly, to the centre of the city. If we can get there in time, perhaps we can harry it from underneath, or use range weapons.'

'Father!'

Sebastian looked up to see Havoc climbing down from a nearby roof. She jumped the last few feet, landing as gracefully as a cat, and then sprinted over to him, her yellow eyes wide.

'What is it?'

'I saw something. On the great stone man. I don't – I'm not sure how. But you should know.'

Sebastian felt a spike of annoyance. 'Spit it out, Havoc, for Isu's sake.'

She nodded once, gathering herself. 'Wydrin, Father. She is there, on the giant. Along with the white-haired lord.'

'What?'

With hope threatening to squeeze his throat shut, Sebastian turned to look once more at the stone giant. It was still desperately fending off the Rivener with shuddering blows which he could feel through the soles of his feet as much as hear. He could see the stone shape of it, and what might be a wooden frame running around its midriff . . . were there people on there? He shook his head in frustration.

'I cannot see. Are you certain?'

Havoc nodded rapidly. 'They are alive, Father, both of them, but . . .'

But for how much longer? Even if he couldn't make them out, he knew that the brood sisters all had unnaturally sharp eyesight, and every one of them knew Wydrin – she was one of the few humans they had ever spent time with.

'Dallen, how many people can a wyvern carry?'

The prince looked affronted. 'They will not fly far in this place, not in this diseased sky. More than three bodies and they cannot fly at all.'

Sebastian hissed through gritted teeth. 'Quickly, saddle one up. I am taking a wyvern over there now.'

'You are?' One of the surviving wyvern riders, a short woman with dark grey lichen covering half her face, sneered at him. 'A warmling?'

'Dragon blood calls to dragon blood,' he said bitterly. 'No matter how diluted, no matter how changed. That's what they've been trying to tell me all along.' Sebastian bent a knee in front of the nearest wyvern, and when it lifted its snout to him, he placed a hand between its eyes. He could feel the smooth blue skin and the rush of its blood, calling like to like. The animal grunted, and pushed against his hand.

'This one,' he said, standing up. 'Have it saddled.'

Wydrin staggered forward, and for one alarming moment all she could see was the distant street, cobbles half covered in snow, and then Frith's arm was around her waist, yanking her backwards. He thrust a long piece of leather into her hand and yelled directly into her ear.

'Keep hold of that!'

She grabbed on to it just as the werken pitched violently to the right, taking another blow from the Rivener. Chunks of stone the size of boulders went flying past them to rain on the city below. Struggling to keep her feet under her, she pushed herself backwards against the stone directly behind them, where Frith pulled her closer.

'What's this brilliant plan of yours, then?' she said, trying to gather her breath. It was very hard to think when the ground underneath your feet – the impossibly frail wooden ground beneath your feet – was pitching crazily from one side to another. She was reminded powerfully of being on board her mother's ship in the midst of a raging storm – with exactly the same chance of survival if you should be thrown overboard.

'This.' Frith pointed with his boot to a bulky sack still strapped to the platform. 'It destroys the Edenier. I have to get it to Joah.'

'How, exactly?'

For a moment, Frith only shook his head. 'When the Destroyer defeats the Rivener, I will be able to climb inside. Somehow.'

'Ye gods. That's your plan?'

There was a shuddering crash twinned with a screaming of metal, and more rocky debris fell past them. A number of fist-sized rocks fell on the platform, a few heavy enough to punch through the wood.

'I hate to say this, Frith, but I don't think our fighter is winning this match.'

As if to prove her right, the Destroyer staggered backwards, struggling to stay upright. Wydrin and Frith were nearly thrown straight off the platform, and the ground yawned alarmingly close. They clung to one another, and for a brief moment Wydrin found her face pressed to his neck – he still smelt of salt and winter, and his skin was warm under her lips. All at once a number of inappropriate feelings surged to the surface.

'Wydrin . . .'

She looked up into his eyes, as storm grey as ever. *Hopeless,* she thought, *I am bloody hopeless.*

'Look, if we want to get that thing over there, we might have to make a run for it. Otherwise we're going to be tied to this werken when it goes down, and still tied to it when the Rivener stomps it into gravel.'

Frith pressed his lips into a thin line. 'Whatever we have to do, I'm with you.'

Nuava and Tamlyn screamed as one as the Rivener's claws scraped across the Destroyer's blunt head just above them. The werken rocked back on its legs, fighting to stay upright, while Nuava felt herself pelted with rocks. One of them tore open her scalp and she felt blood cover her face in a hot sheet, the taste salty in her mouth. Temporarily blind, she blinked furiously, trying to force it out of her eyes. She needed both hands just to hold on.

'Tamlyn? Tamlyn, are you all right?'

Her vision came back to her, watery and blurred, just in time to see the very end of the Rivener's black claw slide into their small, broken alcove and thrust through her aunt's chest, pinning her to the stone. Nuava opened her mouth to scream, but there was nothing left in her. Tamlyn looked down at the piece of metal and stone that had nearly cleaved her in two, an expression of mild annoyance on her face, and then the Rivener withdrew its claw and her aunt's body with it. In that moment Nuava felt the Destroyer shudder all around her as the presence that was commanding it to move suddenly left it.

'No!' Finally she found her voice. 'Tamlyn! That cannot be it!'

She struggled against her straps, half out of her mind, screaming again as the Rivener raked its claws over the Destroyer's chest. The werken swayed sickeningly, and Nuava knew that it would very soon fall and that would be the end of it; the end of her family, the end of her people.

'Mendrick!' she screamed through a throat thick with tears. 'Mountain spirit, whatever you truly are! Help me!' She paused, gasping in a breath over her sobs. 'You helped me once, and I *know* you're there somewhere. I know that now. Please. Please help me.'

Child of the Skald, the voice was cold and beautiful in her head, *what would you have of me?*

Nuava cried out, half in surprise and half in joy. How could she not have known how beautiful the mountain was? How could she not have felt it before?

'Join with me,' she said. 'Let us destroy Joah Demonsworn together. He poisoned you, used you for ill.' She swallowed hard. 'I know we did too, but there will be no more of that now. Let me stand with you, this last time. Let me do that much for you at least.'

When the mountain spoke again, there was a note of reluctance there. *I can join with you, Nuava Nox, crafter of Skaldshollow. I can give you the deeper joining you crave. But you may not survive it.*

Nuava glanced to the place where her aunt had sat, at the smeared bloodstain that was all that was left of her.

'Do it,' she whispered. 'And know that is what I truly want.'

There was light then, glorious green light that filled her head and her heart, and cold and pain, yes, but that felt very far away, as though it were happening to someone else. She looked down at her hands and saw that they were veined with Edeian just as the rock was. All around her she could feel the mountain, not as a separate thing but as an extension of herself. Everything was connected with that shining green light.

'Of course,' she murmured. 'Of course it is. What else does a crafter do but line up the connections?'

78

'What's happening now?'

Frith clasped the sack to his chest and looked around. For the moment the Destroyer had stopped moving entirely. Next to him, Wydrin was peering up into the sky, one hand held over her eyes against the red storm light. He could scarcely believe it. She was here – scruffy and dirty and looking as though she hadn't eaten in days, but it was her. And that changed so much.

'I don't know. Look, what is that? Can you see it?'

Wydrin pointed above them, and Frith could see something: a wriggling reptilian mass, coursing across the sky towards them. The animal's mouth was wide open, bearing all its teeth, and its eyes were wild. On its back . . .

'Is that Sebastian riding one of those bloody things?' Wydrin shook her head. 'By all the gods!'

Two things happened at once. The Destroyer shuddered violently as the Rivener struck it again, and Frith felt it begin to pitch backwards underneath them. And a bare second later, Sebastian and the wyvern collided with the platform, the huge sinuous body and tail of the dragonkin filling the frail wooden structure with hissing, spitting life.

'Get on!' yelled the big knight. 'This thing is really pissed off.'

Frith let go of the leather strap, keeping the sack pressed tightly under one arm, and he and Wydrin scurried across to the back of the waiting wyvern. Its tail whipped back and forth like that of an angry cat, flinging aside pieces of broken wood and shattered stone. As they settled into place, Wydrin behind Sebastian and Frith behind her, the animal opened its long snout and hissed a low warning.

'Right, hold on tight.'

With a convulsive shudder, the wyvern shot off the platform and up into the sky, curving round in a tight spiral shape to bring them up out of the reach of the Rivener. Frith found himself almost unseated immediately, clinging to the leather saddle for his life. In front of him Wydrin gave a yelp of combined horror and amusement.

'I'm probably going to be sick,' she yelled to no one in particular. 'So you'd best keep your mouths shut.'

They climbed up and up, the violence of their movement calming down somewhat, until Frith risked a look over the side. Below them the Destroyer still stood, amazingly, and the Rivener was now prowling round it. There was a circle of debris and destruction around them – buildings crushed flat, the pieces of the Destroyer the Rivener had knocked away – and then further out, something else.

Frith felt his stomach turn over. 'Sebastian,' he called ahead, raising his voice over the freezing wind. 'Can you take us higher?'

He heard Wydrin mutter several curse words at that, but Sebastian obliged, pulling the wyvern upwards in its slow spiral. The whole of Skaldshollow lay below them, bathed in the unnerving red light. Frith nodded to himself. *Of course.* He put a hand on Wydrin's shoulder.

'Look down and tell me what you see.'

'Didn't I just tell you I was going to throw up?'

She did as he asked though, and he felt her stiffen in the saddle in front of him.

'Oh that clever bastard.'

'What is it?' said Sebastian from the front. Wydrin nodded downwards.

The mage word for Summon had been gouged into the very streets of Skaldshollow. Written there by a man who had very recently gained the power and, apparently, the knowledge of a god. A god who knew even more about the Edenier and Edeian than Joah did, and who had once built a weapon into the very flesh of Ede itself, many years ago.

'Which word is it?' asked Wydrin. 'Do you know what it will do?'

Frith tightened his grip on the sack. He could feel the weight of the device there, waiting for its time.

'It is the word for Summon,' he said, raising his voice into the wind. 'What it could summon . . . I do not know.'

'Oh, that's just pissing marvellous.'

'It is imperative we use the weapon against Joah before he activates it,' said Frith, leaning forward in his seat. 'We must do it *now*.'

'Look!'

Now Sebastian was pointing downwards. Frith leaned over to see the Destroyer suddenly lurching back into life. It was riddled with green light now, tracing the complex carvings that covered its hide, and as he watched it drew back its arm and smashed its fist into the Rivener's unprotected side. Joah's machine crumpled where it was struck and staggered backwards into the Tower of Waking. There was a splintering sound that Frith felt in his bones, and the Tower itself fell, shattered into thousands of deadly black shards.

'Seb, get down there,' said Wydrin, a new urgency in her voice. 'We need to see what's happening.'

They dove, swerving down in a graceful curve so that they passed close by the Destroyer's upper half. There they all saw the slim form of Nuava standing with arms outstretched in the remains of the werken's head. She was also covered in the green light of the Edeian, her eyes two beacons of green fire. She was smiling.

'Nuava!' cried Wydrin, half rising out of the saddle. Frith pulled her back down.

'There is nothing we can do for her,' he said, speaking directly into her ear. 'The mountain has her now.'

As they swerved out of the way, the Destroyer reached forward with both its arms and struck the Rivener on either side of its black insectile head. There was a screaming of metal, and its twisted claws flailed at nothing. From their vantage point they could see the ragged opening at the top of the head, still filled with violet light.

'There,' shouted Frith, 'if we're going to do it, it has to be now! Take us down.'

The wyvern dropped, and they crashed rather than landed inside the Rivener's central room. For a few moments, everything was confusion – Frith jumped from the wyvern's back, his arms still cradling the trap, while Wydrin rolled with somewhat less grace into a table. Sebastian leapt away and the wyvern was gone, flicking back up into the sky with an air of relief.

Joah turned towards them. Frith heard Wydrin cry out in horror, and distantly he wondered if any of them would come out of this with their sanity intact.

One side of Joah Demonsworn's face was a throbbing swollen mass of infected flesh, red and shining. Frith fancied he could feel the heat coming off it. The other side was worse, though. Much worse.

'Frith,' Wydrin was at his side, shaking his arm, 'we have no time.'

Frith quickly shook the trap out of its sack; it was difficult to think, back in the violet light of the corrupted Heart-Stone. Joah nodded once, as though not remotely surprised to see the Edenier trap.

'I thought you might do that,' said Joah. His voice was still soft and warm, the voice of a kind man, although now it was slurred and distorted through the mask of his face. The strange, stretched angles caught the light as he spoke, the membranous tissues quivering. In the burnt side of his face his single remaining human eye watered. 'You would have gathered the knowledge of how to do it from my memories, and you may even have had the wit to solve the problems I could not.'

'I will use it. One word from me and it's all gone.' Frith held his hand over the top of the Edenier trap, balancing it on the palm of his other hand. 'I will end it all here, Joah.'

'Will you, though? I wonder.' Joah glanced away, looking out through the broken windows before turning back to them. 'To use it would be to destroy your own magic. And I know very well how much you suffered to take that power. Can you just throw it away?'

Out of the corner of his eye Frith saw Wydrin glance at him. 'I can,' said Frith. 'And I will.'

'A suicide mission I can understand,' said Joah, still speaking in that conversational tone of voice. 'When you thought that you'd lost everything, it would be very fine to leave the world like this, wouldn't it? Your life sacrificed in vengeance.' Joah dipped his

526

head towards Wydrin. 'But it turns out you did not lose everything, after all. Does she know what you've done, Aaron?'

'Shut up.' Frith swallowed hard. He could feel, distantly, something pressing on the borders of his own mind. Joah trying to force his way in, as he had done before.

'Just do it, Frith,' said Wydrin. 'End him.'

'But do you not see, Wydrin of Crosshaven?' Joah's tone changed, became more businesslike. 'You will have seen by now the spell I have carved into this place. If I speak a word, that spell will bring forth something very interesting indeed. If I speak a word in the instant before Aaron uses the Edenier trap, you will all be powerless to stop whatever it is. No magic, no defence against whatever I choose to pluck from that lost dimension. And I am a god now. Do you not think that my reflexes will be faster than Aaron's?'

'Anything you summon, you will be powerless against it too,' said Wydrin. 'It would destroy you too.'

'Having just got over releasing one monster on the world, are you quite willing to risk doing it again?'

'Stop,' said Sebastian. 'It's not too late to step away from this madness.'

Joah grinned, splitting the swollen part of his face wide open. Blood and pus oozed down his neck and soaked into the tattered remnants of his green robes.

'Look at my face and tell me that again.'

For a few seconds, there was silence. Frith felt the tension on the back of his neck like a vice. Was it all a desperate bluff? He watched Joah's ruined face for any sign of his next move, but there was nothing human left there. It was like looking up at a moon on an alien world: strange and completely unknowable.

If he was too slow, by even half a second, Joah would unleash a monster. And when the Edenier trap went off, they would be powerless to prevent it.

He would have to be faster. In his mind he formed the first of the words, trusting to luck . . .

A shape dropped down behind Joah, a long dagger in her hand. 'For Selsye!'

Xinian grabbed hold of the mage from behind, wrapping one

muscled arm around his neck. Joah gasped, his lips half forming a word. Next to Frith, Wydrin was already leaping forward, shouting and drawing her sword. Xinian vanished in a wreath of red flames, as though just to touch Joah was instant death and then . . .

. . . Frith spoke the last word, in his mind and in his heart, and the trap unfolded like a flower in spring.

Wydrin was aware of light and sound, and the smell of burning flesh. She was also aware that she was falling, bumping into and being thrown off various objects as they crashed around the central room of the Rivener. She forced her eyes open and saw, dizzyingly, the view of the rapidly swerving sky through the hole in the roof, and then there was a crash that threw her straight out of the opening and onto a hard cobbled street.

She sat up, and spat out a mouthful of blood. 'I have had more than enough of falling off of things.'

Her right arm was a bright agony, and she could feel from the warmth spreading there that she'd been cut by something, and deeply. Ignoring it she struggled to her feet, trying to make some sense of the scene around her. Directly across from her was the twisted metal remains of the Rivener, its violet light extinguished. Standing over it was the Destroyer, lit up like a stone beacon. The sky above them was blessedly blue.

Sebastian was kneeling on the ground some distance away, blood pouring from a head wound. She ran over to him, stumbling on wobbly legs.

'Seb, are you with me? Are you all right?'

Groggily he shook his head at her. 'Never better. Where's Frith? Did the trap work?'

She looked back. Frith was standing on his feet, swaying back and forth slightly. His slim figure was easy enough to pick out against the churning hole that had once been the Tower of Waking. A churning hole that was growing faster by the moment.

'What the hell is that?'

He turned to her. In comparison to Wydrin and Sebastian, he was remarkably untouched by their violent journey to the ground, although his eyes looked distant and glazed.

'I wasn't quick enough, Wydrin,' he said softly.

'So that is—'

'The summoning,' said Frith. 'Joah managed to say it, just before I could stop him.'

The hole in the world was centred exactly where the Tower of Waking had been, and it was difficult to look at. It was as big as a house now, filled with black, shifting light, and already she could see the shape of something trying to come through.

'Is there nothing you can do?'

Frith looked at her and smiled sadly. He held out his hands to her, empty and scarred.

'It's all gone, Wydrin. The Edenier has left me.'

Wydrin looked back at the swirling black hole. Now it was as big as four houses, and she could see light glinting off something scaled and enormous. She took a step backwards, and nearly walked into Sebastian who had come up behind her.

'Do you think perhaps we should leave, then?' she said, unable to take her eyes from the shimmering black light. There was a roar, a roar that was all too familiar, and she took another involuntary step backwards. The hole was growing bigger all the time.

'How far do you think we'd get?' said Sebastian, drawing his sword. 'I for one have no more running left to do.'

There was a strangled noise from behind them. Joah Demonsworn, or what had once been a mage known by that name, lay on the ground. Something in the fall had torn open his guts and strewn them across the cobbles, but he was still moving weakly. His mouth opened and closed, pushing forth small noises that Wydrin realised were barking attempts at laughter.

'I saw its face,' he was saying. 'The demon's face. Have I told you?'

Frith stumbled over to the prone form. Wydrin couldn't read the expression on his face.

'That's all over now, Joah,' he said, not taking his eyes from the mage's ravaged form. 'You can forget it. Leave it behind.'

'Can I?' Joah reached out to him, fingers like knives. There was a terrible sliver of hope in his voice, like a broken bottle in the snow. 'Can I really forget it?'

'Yes,' said Frith. 'Be at peace now, Joah Lightbringer.'

Joah shook all over. Behind them, the creature that was clawing its way up through the portal roared again, and Wydrin felt her hair stand on end.

'Could we have been brothers, Aaron?'

Joah's last question hung in the air. Frith looked at him a moment longer, and then turned away. Wydrin unsheathed Glassheart and thrust the point through Joah's neck, not stopping until she heard the brittle screech of metal on stone, and then she leaned back and forth on the sword until his head was severed. His blood was black and oily.

'If we're going out, then you're going first, you mad bastard,' she spat.

Thank you for that.

Wydrin turned round, startled, and saw that Frith and Sebastian had both heard the voice in their heads too.

'Nuava?'

It was good to see him go.

It was her voice, too, but with an echo of something else underneath it. A coldness that Wydrin recognised.

'Where are you?'

I am here, with the Edeian.

Behind them, there was an inhuman screech and a great reptilian head forced its way through the portal into the daylight. It was Y'Ruen, but it was a Y'Ruen changed. Her scales, once the beautiful shining blue of the finest sapphires, were now dull and flaking away, revealing great patches of raw grey flesh. Her eyes, once the yellow of dragon fire, were blind, one covered in a white film, the other pitted and eaten away by parasites that Wydrin could barely imagine. The dragon roared again, opening her great jaws to reveal rotten teeth and the stench of a slaughter-house, and she pulled herself forward, thrashing her head back and forth.

'She has returned!'

Wydrin turned to see Sebastian reeling on his feet, his arms held out to either side. There was a look of beatific terror on his face.

'Sebastian, we have to go!'

'I can feel her, singing in my blood,' he murmured. What he said next was lost in Y'Ruen's roar. Wydrin shoved him, hard in the chest, and he looked down at her as though he didn't know where he was.

'All right, magic or no magic, I am not sticking around to get eaten by that bitch. We have to run, do you understand?'

She turned to go, dragging Frith with her. Sebastian seemed to come back to himself, and he was catching them up when Nuava's voice spoke in their heads again.

Get to a safe distance. We have this one in hand.

The Destroyer rumbled into life, reaching down with its great shovel hands for the dragon's head. Y'Ruen surged out of the hole, pulling herself through with sudden alarming strength; the great winding length of her neck, the shoulders bunched with muscle. The Destroyer took hold of the dragon, great slab-like hands pushing at her throat. Wydrin, Sebastian and Frith threw themselves out of the way to avoid getting crushed.

'What is she bloody well doing?'

There was an ear-splitting roar – Wydrin felt one of her eardrums pop with the force of it – and Y'Ruen sent forth a blast of flame, curling around the Destroyer like a burning shroud. The werken stumbled onto its knees, its head lost in flames too bright to look at.

'Nuava!' Wydrin made to run back, but Frith had his arms around her again, holding her in place. 'No!'

But the werken dug its enormous flat feet into the ground and began to push, carving huge grooves into the rubble and then it heaved itself forward, pushing it and the dragon back through the churning hole. Y'Ruen fought it, belching flame and raking her crystalline claws across the werken's stony flesh, but the Destroyer was implacable, immovable.

Wydrin had one last glance of Y'Ruen's terrible blind eye, rolling madly in its socket, and then the Destroyer gave a final enormous push, and they were both gone, falling back into the darkness behind the universe.

Wydrin curled her hands into fists. 'Nuava!'

But the hole had already closed.

79

'Wydrin, are you sure about this?'

Sebastian showed her the dagger, as if that would help. She poured another shot of strong rum and gulped it back.

'Of course I am. I have more than enough reminders of that place.'

She laid her hand out on top of the table, palm facing up. On the table next to it were rolls of clean bandages and two tubs of healing salve. They were holed up in an inn in the riverlands; for a few coppers and a promise to purchase a great deal of food and hot water – which they certainly had done, Wydrin alone being on her third bath now – they had what they needed to deal with a varied list of injuries.

Sebastian took her hand in his, and after briefly squeezing her fingers, used the very tip of the dagger to cut round the piece of Heart-Stone wedged in her palm. It took no more than a handful of moments, but Wydrin had thought carefully about which curse words she would treat Sebastian to, so she made sure to use every single one.

When it was done and the wound had been washed clean, Sebastian applied the salve and bandaged it for her too. Wydrin flexed her hand carefully, wincing.

'Well, that was easier to get rid of than that stupid tattoo of yours,' said Sebastian.

Wydrin snorted and slapped her arm, ignoring the pain. It was much warmer in the riverlands, and she had gladly sold her furs and stripped back to her leather bodice. The black sinuous shapes of the Graces that sported around her elbow stood out in stark contrast to her pale skin.

'I'll have you know I don't regret this tattoo for a single second. I am a daughter of the Graces.'

Sebastian laughed.

'I'm not talking about *that* tattoo, as well you know.'

'Ah, well,' Wydrin poured another shot, 'the less said about that one the better.'

Silence fell between them for a time. Wydrin still felt unutterably tired, and Sebastian, to her eyes, looked older. He had a bandage himself, a thick wad of fabric tied over the right side of his forehead, and his beard was growing thick again. He looked very little like the fresh-faced knight she'd met so many years ago.

Wydrin sighed, staring absently at the swirl of rum in the bottom of her glass.

'We lost so many, this time,' she said quietly. 'Bors, Tamlyn. Nuava. Xinian. There are barely any Skalds left at all. We should never have come here.' When they had left Skaldshollow, the last survivors of the broken city had been doing their best to rebuild. It would take longer now that they were without their werkens – Mendrick, or the mountain spirit, was truly gone – but Wydrin hoped they could salvage something from the shattered settlement they'd been left with.

'Bezcavar meant for it to be a mess,' said Sebastian firmly. 'It was a trap, all along. It would only ever have ended badly.'

'To lost friends,' she said, and offered up her glass. After a moment, Sebastian picked up his own, clinked it against hers, and together they gulped down the rum.

'It would be good to go somewhere sunny for a while,' she said. 'Somewhere sandy, maybe. The rum is always better in places like that.'

There was a knock at the door, and Lord Frith stepped inside. His hood was thrown back, and he looked as tense as Wydrin had ever seen him.

Sebastian stood up. 'Speaking of things that are a mess,' he murmured to Wydrin as he passed her, and then to them both at

533

the door, 'I will be scouting out the harbour, looking for the fastest ships home. Don't expect me back until late.'

With that he left. Frith went and stood by the fire, staring down into its flames. Outside a strong wind was blowing, rattling the roof and the rafters. Wydrin took a slow, deep breath.

'So do you want to talk about it?'

He looked up at her. His shirt was loose, and his hair dishevelled. Since they had walked away from Skaldshollow he had been distracted, absent almost. *The loss of all that magic*, thought Wydrin. *All that power.*

'It was demon's work, the device that I constructed. Did you know that? It was a terrible thing.' He paused, his eyes searching the room for something she couldn't see. 'I had to do terrible things, to make it work.'

'You did what you had to do,' said Wydrin, knowing he wouldn't listen. 'Joah would have done much worse if he'd had his way. He'd already done much worse.'

'I did it because I thought I had lost all hope,' said Frith. 'When I saw you fall, part of me *knew* you were dead, and I accepted it as a way of avoiding a choice that was nearly impossible.'

He stopped. Wydrin saw that his hands were shaking.

'I felt relief, Wydrin.' His eyes were bright with anger and tears. 'Part of me was relieved that all my choices were gone. That there could be only one path for me now.'

'Frith—'

'I can never forgive myself for that, Wydrin. For the relief I felt. I am a coward.'

He said the last word with force. Wydrin stood up, ignoring the throbbing pain in the palm of her hand.

'You? A coward? Never.' She went to him and pressed her uninjured hand to his face. 'I would kill anyone who even suggested it.' She reached up and pressed her lips to his cheek, kissing away the tears that were falling there. 'Arrogant, reckless, obstinate, perhaps. But certainly not a coward.' She pushed his hair back from his face, and looked into his eyes. The sorrow there was dimming, quickly to be replaced with something else. She bit her lip. It was still difficult to say, even now. 'The Copper Cat does not love a coward.'

'Wydrin—'

She smiled lopsidedly. 'We've been playing this game long enough, don't you think?'

They fell together against the wall with the violence of the kiss, and Wydrin half laughed as they kicked over the pile of firewood, sending one log rolling to the furthest wall. Firth murmured against her neck, some small plea, and all humour was left behind in place of a hunger long since denied. Wydrin pulled at his shirt, dislodging several buttons, and slid one hand over the taut muscles of his chest, and then kissed the trail her fingers left. Frith groaned at this, and pulled her towards the far door, where a bed awaited them.

'Oho,' she said, pushing him instead towards the table. The bottle of rum was quickly overturned. 'You are optimistic indeed if you think we will even get that far.'

'Whatever my lady desires,' said Frith, his eyes as dark as an oncoming storm, and for some time after there was very little talking at all.

'You truly intend to stay?'

The riverlands port was busy, and men and women and children moved all around them – bidding farewell, loading goods onto boats, buying fish fresh from the river or herbs from the far swamp lands – but they stood in the dark mouth of an alley, and Ephemeral wore a deeply hooded cloak. No one paid them any mind. Sebastian could see a narrow slice of her face in the shadows, and her eyes were solemn.

'Not all of us. Some have decided to return to Ynnsmouth, and they are making their own way. But I think this is the end of our time together, Father.'

Sebastian looked down at his feet. He knew that he should feel relief, but instead he felt fear – not for them, but for himself.

'I know you will hold your own against the Narhl,' he said. He forced himself to smile. 'I think they are about to learn an awful lot in a very short amount of time.'

'You taught us so much.' Ephemeral reached out and took his hand. She wore gloves, despite the warmth of the riverlands.

'Not enough,' he said, and then shook his head. 'I didn't learn enough from you. I didn't pay enough attention. I have been a fool.'

She smiled, her golden eyes shining. 'We must make our own way now, Father. But we will never truly leave you.'

There was a shout, and Sebastian turned to see Frith and Wydrin approaching. When he turned back to the alleyway, Ephemeral had already gone, vanished back into the shadows.

'You ready to go?' Wydrin was carrying a crate full of bottles of mead. When she saw him looking at it, she shrugged. 'It's a long bloody journey back to Litvania.'

'That is where you're going?'

'That's where we're *all* going.' Wydrin gave Sebastian a withering look. 'You look peaky. I'm not letting you out of my sight for a while yet, Seb.'

'I need to retrieve something from my family's vault,' said Frith. 'It may make a difference to our future plans.'

Sebastian looked at the pair of them. Frith had been quiet since Skaldshollow, haunted by the fate of Joah – there was much he would not speak of, and Sebastian imagined that the loss of the Edenier had not been easy for the young lord to take. And yet there was a peace between the two of them now, an acceptance that only a fool could not spot. Or anyone who did not sleep in the room next to theirs, at least.

'Then let's get out of this place.' Sebastian took a slow, deep breath, trying not to think about what he was leaving behind. 'Let's go somewhere where the rocks stay on the ground like they're supposed to.'

They took the first longboat south, making themselves as comfortable as they could amongst the sacks of grain and barrels of beer. Sebastian looked back as the boat drew away, meaning to take one last look at the mountains, and instead found his eyes drawn to a lone figure on the jetty. He had long brown hair, and a face mottled grey and white and brown, like a pebble. After a moment the figure raised his hand in farewell, before turning away and walking back into the shadow of the mountain.

536

Acknowledgements

If *The Copper Promise* was an unexpected journey, then *The Iron Ghost* was a Quest of Great Significance, and as such a cast of mighty heroes were on hand to help me through it, often with Unfeasible Weapons of Great Size (or so they told me to say).

Thanks firstly to everyone who supported the first book: bought it, read it, said good things, sent me photos of it, allowed me to draw dragons inside. It has been the busiest and craziest year of my life, and I remain staggered by the loveliness of readers and the book community in general.

Enormous gratitude to my wonderful editor Claire Baldwin, whose enthusiasm and wisdom were invaluable at every stage, and to the marvellous Caitlin Raynor, who kept me calm and supplied with cake on launch day. Thanks also to the whole team at Headline, particularly the design team who have given me two stonking covers in a row.

Thanks as ever to my agent, Juliet Mushens, who remains not only the best agent in the known 'verse, but terrifyingly good at karaoke and an absolute joy to work with. Big love must also go to Team Mushens itself: a unique support group if ever there was one.

Adam Christopher was there at the beginning (before I even knew it was a beginning), and remains an irreplaceable source of advice, support, and withering cynicism. Dude, when are we having that ginger beer?

Thanks to Den Patrick, who has been my debut buddy, my agent bro, my SRFC partner in crime and even, gods help him, my cat sitter. Big love to Liz de Jager, whose caps-lock-littered emails kept me going through hard times, and to Andrew Reid: beta reader, conspirator, top bloke. Thank you once again to Roy Butlin for top notch beta reading duties, and to the lovely John Wordsworth, who set me off on this particular journey. Huge gratitude to everyone who has attended Super Relaxed Fantasy Club in the last year. You rock!

Big thanks and love to my mum and to Jenni, who have been keeping me sane longer than anyone else. And finally, the biggest thanks of all to Marty – for ten years of laughing at silly things and having the best time ever.